By the Green
of the Spring

By the Green of the Spring

a novel by

John Masters

McGRAW-HILL BOOK COMPANY

New York   St. Louis   San Francisco
Hamburg   Mexico   Toronto

This book is the third and final volume of a trilogy entitled
LOSS OF EDEN
It is complete in itself, as have been the first two (*Now, God Be Thanked* and *Heart of War*). Each volume is wholly a work of fiction, in which no reference is intended to any person living or dead, except that many historical characters are mentioned and some occasionally appear on the scene.

J.M.

1 2 3 4 5 6 7 8 9 D O D O 8 7 6 5 4 3 2 1

LIBRARY OF CONGRESS CATALOGING IN PUBLICATION DATA

Masters, John, 1914—
By the green of the spring.
(Loss of Eden)
1. World War, 1914–1918—Fiction.   I. Title.
II. Series: Masters, John, 1914– . Loss of Eden.
PS3525.A8314B9   813'.914   81-5981
ISBN 0-07-040783-5   AACR2

To the victims of the Great War,
among whom were
the survivors.

Aftermath

Have you forgotten yet? . . .
For the world's events have rumbled on since those gagged days,
Like traffic checked while at the crossing of city-ways:
And the haunted gap in your mind has filled with thoughts that flow
Like clouds in the lit heaven of life; and you're a man reprieved to
    go,
Taking your peaceful share of Time, with joy to spare.
But the past is just the same—and War's a bloody game . . .
Have you forgotten yet? . . .
Look down, and swear by the slain of the War that you'll never forget.

Do you remember the dark months you held the sector at Mametz—
The nights you watched and wired and dug and piled sandbags on
    parapets?
Do you remember the rats; and the stench
Of corpses rotting in front of the front-line trench—
And dawn coming, dirty-white, and chill with hopeless rain?
Do you ever stop and ask, "Is it all going to happen again?"

Do you remember that hour of din before the attack—
And the anger, the blind compassion that seized and shook you then
As you peered at the doomed and haggard faces of your men?
Do you remember the stretcher-cases lurching back
With dying eyes and lolling heads—those ashen-grey
Masks of the lads who once were keen and kind and gay?

Have you forgotten yet? . . .
Look up, and swear by the green of the spring that you'll never forget.

Siegfried Sassoon (March 1919)

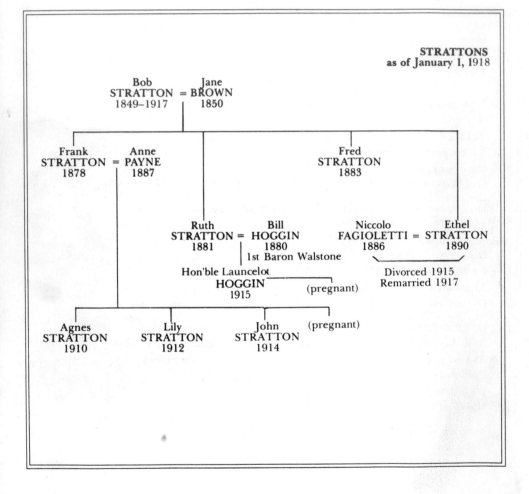

STRATTONS
as of January 1, 1918

Bob   Jane
STRATTON = BROWN
1849–1917   1850

Frank   Anne   Fred
STRATTON = PAYNE   STRATTON
1878   1887   1883

                    Ruth   Bill   Niccolo   Ethel
                STRATTON = HOGGIN   FAGIOLETTI = STRATTON
                    1881   1880   1886   1890
                              1st Baron Walstone
                    Hon'ble Launcelot   Divorced 1915
                        HOGGIN   Remarried 1917
                          1915   (pregnant)

Agnes   Lily   John   (pregnant)
STRATTON   STRATTON   STRATTON
1910   1912   1914

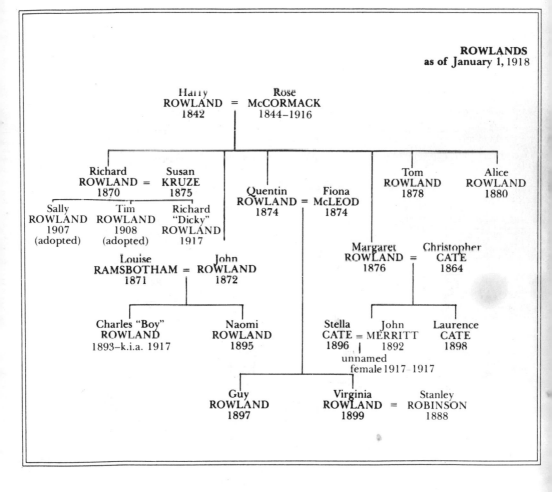

ROWLANDS
as of January 1, 1918

Harry
ROWLAND = Rose
McCORMACK
1842   1844–1916

Richard   Susan
ROWLAND = KRUZE   Quentin   Fiona   Tom   Alice
1870   1875   ROWLAND = McLEOD   ROWLAND   ROWLAND
1874   1874   1878   1880

Sally   Tim   Richard
ROWLAND   ROWLAND   "Dicky"
1907   1908   ROWLAND
(adopted)   (adopted)   1917   Margaret   Christopher
ROWLAND = CATE
1876   1864

Louise   John
RAMSBOTHAM = ROWLAND
1871   1872

Charles "Boy"   Naomi   Stella   John   Laurence
ROWLAND   ROWLAND   CATE = MERRITT   CATE
1893–k.i.a. 1917   1895   1896   1892   1898
unnamed
female 1917–1917

Guy   Virginia   Stanley
ROWLAND   ROWLAND = ROBINSON
1897   1899   1888

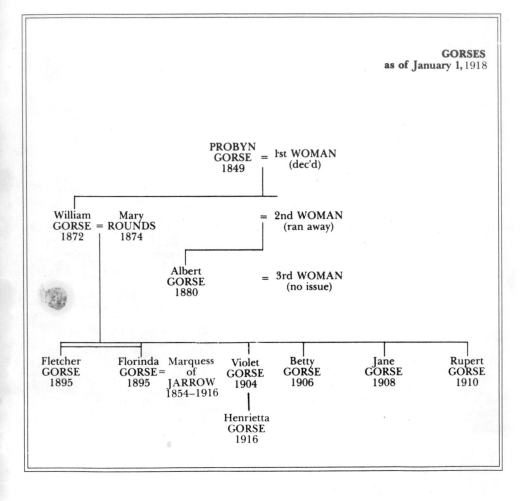

GORSES
as of January 1, 1918

PROBYN GORSE 1849 = 1st WOMAN (dec'd)

William GORSE 1872 = Mary ROUNDS 1874

= 2nd WOMAN (ran away)

Albert GORSE 1880 = 3rd WOMAN (no issue)

Fletcher GORSE 1895

Florinda GORSE 1895 = Marquess of JARROW 1854–1916

Violet GORSE 1904

Betty GORSE 1906

Jane GORSE 1908

Rupert GORSE 1910

Henrietta GORSE 1916

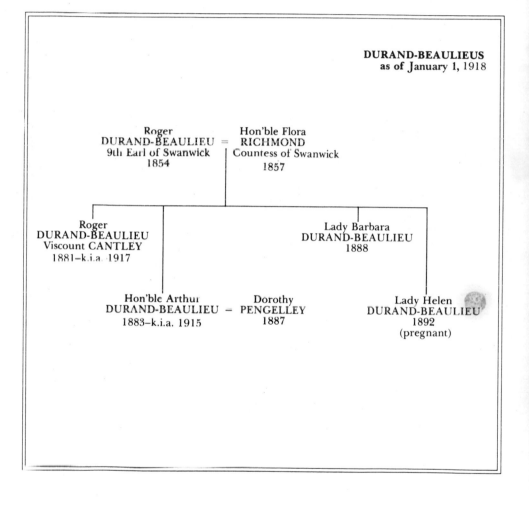

DURAND-BEAULIEUS
as of January 1, 1918

Roger
DURAND-BEAULIEU = Hon'ble Flora
9th Earl of Swanwick   RICHMOND
1854   Countess of Swanwick
                       1857

Roger   Lady Barbara
DURAND-BEAULIEU   DURAND-BEAULIEU
Viscount CANTLEY   1888
1881–k.i.a. 1917

Hon'ble Arthur   Dorothy   Lady Helen
DURAND-BEAULIEU = PENGELLEY   DURAND-BEAULIEU
1883–k.i.a. 1915   1887   1892
                                     (pregnant)

By the Green
of the Spring

January 1, 1918

1 As the arc of night passes westward over Europe, its veil of darkness is drawn across a continent in ruins. The war, that started with the assassination of an Austrian Archduke late in June of 1914, has engulfed most of the world. The United States is fighting now, alongside Great Britain, France, Italy, Portugal, and a host of lesser Allies. Russia, Holy no longer, has been knocked out, freeing more of Germany's still giant strength to be used against France and Britain on the Western Front. The ramshackle Austro-Hungarian Empire is struggling for its life among those savage peaks and high valleys which are its common border with Italy. France has suffered tremendous blows at Verdun in 1916, and all but collapsed in 1917; but has held. The British have bled themselves white attacking on the Somme in 1916 and at Ypres in 1917.

There are no more fleet actions at sea, only in the air. The war is waged over cities, under the earth, under the sea. Women die, rent by bombs. Children die, starved. On the battlefields men die by the millions, under machine-gun bullets and artillery shells.

The year of 1918 must be the year of decision, for the enormous strength of America is flowing to the battle at an ever-increasing pace. If Germany is to win on the field, it must be soon, for she is bleeding from manpower loss, from blockade. And the peoples of the world . . . can they stand another year?

BY THE GREEN OF THE SPRING

Walstone, Kent: Tuesday, January 15, 1918

John Merritt sat back in the first-class compartment, watching the familiar countryside slide by, now clear and green in the winter sun, now hidden by drifting puffs of brilliant white lambswool steam from the engine up ahead . . . familiar, in that he could recognize the places—there was the spire of Whitmore church pointing heavenward out of bare trees to the south; there was the Scarrow meandering down the shallow valley; there was the very place he had once walked with Stella, shortly after they were married, watching the moorhens in the reeds . . . yet all unfamiliar, too, because he was wearing the single gold bars of a 2nd Lieutenant of the United States Army, and the crossed cannons of the Field Artillery; because, having been gone barely nine months, England itself seemed strange, this carriage so small, the compartment so pokey, the grass out there so green even though it was mid-winter, the oast houses on the slope so like cowled monks. The brakes were moaning apologetically, the train slowing, the engine piping a short, high whistle . . . again, how strange!

He rose, smoothing down the long front of his greatcoat, took his peaked cap off the rack and set it square on his head, found his woollen gloves and slowly pulled them onto his big hands, lifted his rolled officer's valise off the rack, and put it on the opposite seat. The train eased to a stop opposite a long wooden signboard—WALSTONE.

John stepped down, a tall serious-looking young man with dark brown hair and grey eyes, a new maturity in him marked by tiny crows' feet at the corners, and lines sharp but as yet shallow in his cheeks. His father-in-law was there to meet him, even taller, nearly thirty years older, thin, sandy, the face thoughtful to the point of sadness—Christopher Cate: squire of Walstone, father of Stella. He stepped forward now, hand outstretched—"Johnny!"

John pulled off his right glove, took the other's hand, and shook it formally. He had grown very fond of his father-in-law, and admired him; but there was always a constraint. He would have liked to have hugged him, but in addition to the old English reserve there was now the unresolved problem between them: what had happened to Stella?

Christopher said, "Betty wanted to come, and your Aunt Isabel, but . . ."

"Is she here?" Johnny exclaimed. "How is she?"

"Three toes were slightly frostbitten when she was in the lifeboat, and the doctors in London think she might lose one of them sooner or later, but . . . she's here. That's what matters."

John nodded. Isabel Kramer was his aunt—his father's widowed sister; and he knew that for nearly two years she had been in love with

2

Christopher Cate and he with her; but Mrs Cate had vanished underground with the Sinn Fein in Ireland soon after the outbreak of war . . . so Christopher and Isabel could not marry. But this was the first time the man he called Father Cristopher in his letters had openly acknowledged their love.

A young woman in breeches, farmer's jacket, and felt hat came forward to take his valise and he exclaimed, "Oh now, miss . . ." But Cate said, smiling, "This is Bertha, head groom and stable staff, all in one. Norton joined the Garrison Artillery a week ago. He's past the age for conscription but he said he felt he had to do his bit, so . . ."

The girl had taken the valise and was leading the way off the platform into the station yard. They climbed into the trap, Bertha cracked the whip, and the pony set off at a steady trot toward the Manor. Neither Cate nor John spoke, for what they had to say was personal and painful.

At the Manor they at once went indoors, as Garrod the maid came forward to take John's valise. They turned into the drawing room and John paused. His sister Betty was running toward him with open arms; behind her he saw his Aunt Isabel in an armchair, a big walking stick leaning against the arm. Beside her stood a man he did not for a moment recognize—weather-beaten face, Royal Navy uniform, three straight gold stripes on his sleeve—a commander . . . then he remembered; it was Tom Rowland, Mrs Cate's brother, Stella's uncle.

Betty kissed her brother on both cheeks, hugging him tight; then John stooped to kiss his aunt, and felt her cheek wet with tears; then the commander came forward, "Hope you don't feel I'm intruding, Johnny . . . but I am very fond of Stella, too. Always have been. And I'm now stationed in Chatham, only a few miles away."

John said, "I'm glad you're here, sir." He spoke to them all—"My battery commander has given me a week's leave to try to find her. But first, what happened? How? Why?"

No one spoke for what seemed to John a long time, then his father-in-law said, "She had become a drug addict, John . . ." John noticed that now Father Christopher, like his friends at the School of Fire and in the battery, felt that he was no longer "Johnny," but "John": a man still young but aware of tragedy.

He said, "Is there any proof?"

"When she disappeared, and we started making inquiries, the midwife who delivered the baby in October confirmed that she had marks on her arms that could only have been made by repeated injections from a hypodermic needle."

John said, "What drug was she supposed to have been taking?"

"Heroin," Cate said. "The night she disappeared—Christmas Eve night—she was trying to get a prescription for heroin filled. The chemist she went to on Wilmot Street, down near the river in Hedlington, was closed, but he lives above his shop, and heard a fight in the street below. By the time he could get down and out there was no one visible except the figure of a woman walking toward the river. He thought there might have been some men running up the street, in the opposite direction . . . it was snowing, but not hard . . . He called after the woman, asking if she was all right. For a time she didn't seem to hear, then she turned and slowly came back up toward him. She said, 'Are you the chemist?' and he said 'Yes,' and she shouted . . . shrieked was his word—'I have a prescription! Fill it! It's urgent!' He took her inside and she gave him the prescription. It was for heroin. He thought it might be forged and started to ask her 'Whose signature is this?' when she grabbed the prescription and ran out . . . Her face was a bit bruised, one knuckle bleeding, and one arm hanging. He hurried out after her, but she was running away up the street, and in a few seconds disappeared in the snow . . ."

John said grimly, "Has the river been dragged?"

Isabel muttered, "Yes. She may have been thinking of that before the chemist came out . . . but not afterwards, I'm sure."

"What did she do, then?"

"Went to London," Tom Rowland said. "You can disappear in London. You can get anything you want there, if you know where to look."

"And can pay," John said. "But a woman can always pay, can't she?"

"Don't, don't!" Isabel cried.

John said, "We have to face it, Aunt Isabel . . . What has been done so far, Father Christopher?"

Cate said slowly, "I spoke privately to the Chief Constable . . . of Kent, that is. He has warned the Police in Canterbury and Hedlington—we don't have any other real towns—and he has spoken to the Commissioner of the Metropolitan Police, in London. The drug world is not very large, as yet, the Commissioner told him, and they think they have a good chance of finding her within a few weeks . . . My dear boy, I can't tell you how sad I am that this should have happened. I should have seen that something was wrong. I *did* see, but never guessed the truth. I thought she was lonely for you. I . . ."

"Don't blame yourself," John said briefly. "If anyone is to blame, other than Stella, it is I."

Cate said, "She took very little money with her." He looked full at his son-in-law—"You have suffered enough hurt through us. Leave us. Get an American divorce, and wash your hands of the whole beastly,

4

sordid mess. Stella is our responsibility. We will find her and look after her."

"It's the foul war!" Isabel cried.

John said nothing for a while, staring from one to the other of them. Yes, someone should have seen. But it was no use brooding on that. He said, "Thank you, Father Christopher, but I love Stella. Help me find her. And when we do, help me, this time, to understand her."

*   *   *   *

In Laburnum Lodge John felt that he was under water, the light filtering through depths of sea above. The curtains of the morning room were drawn back to reveal rain falling straight from a windless sky, an unshaped mass of unmoving, dark cloud above. There was no fire in the grate, for it was not a cold day . . . only damp, raw, and wet. Stella's grandfather, Harry Rowland, Member of Parliament for the Mid-Scarrow Division of Kent, was sitting in his usual big chair. He looked older . . . well, of course, he was, nine months older; but he looked more than old—he looked shrunken. Opposite Harry, in a straight chair, sat Alice Rowland, his daughter, Stella's aunt; and to the left, side by side on a big sofa, John and Louise Rowland—Harry's second son and his wife.

Alice said, "I blame myself, John": she, too, had noticed the change in him. ". . . I saw quite a bit of her, until—"she gestured toward where her left leg had been before it had been blown off last August in an explosion at the shell factory where she had been working.

Harry said, "I've spoken to the Commissioner, Johnny." The old eyes were sad, the beard thinner and whiter than John remembered—"They're doing all that can be done. They'll find her."

"It's the war!" Louise broke in fiercely. "It's taken Stella just as surely as it took our Boy."

"Stella hasn't gone for good," Alice broke in, looking at John.

"I don't mean that!" the little woman with Yorkshire strong in her accent cried. "I mean that she would not have done it . . . how could she? . . . if the war hadn't perverted everyone's values, destroying the good, the sane, the kind—elevating the cruel, the depraved?"

"Louise has joined the No Conscription Fellowship," Harry muttered, aside.

John Rowland sat silent beside Louise, hands resting on his lap, eyes staring dully at the carpet. John remembered him as a bluff gentleman farmer, proud of his farm, of his son Boy, his daughter Naomi, of England. Then he'd joined the anti-war movement, but now . . . he was no more than a husk; all the energy seemed to have passed into his wife, the dead Boy's mother. The German shell that killed Boy had killed him too, really.

Alice said, "How can we help, John? Just tell us."

John said, "When we find her . . . or she comes back . . . help her. Love her. I'll be over there. She'll be alone again."

"Oh God, the war!" Louise cried, her voice full of hatred.

*   *   *   *

The car in the ditch, the three bodies sprawled in and under it, blood congealing in a pool on the ground, Margaret Cate and her three companions hurried up the field, picked up hidden bicycles and, twenty minutes later in the dark of the January evening, slipped into the backyard of a house in a long row of such, in Cashel, Tipperary, hid the machines in the toolshed, hid the weapons under the floorboards of an upstairs bedroom, and repaired to the house's kitchen.

"We got him," Michael Collins said. "He was the one in the back. Yours, Lady."

One of the other men said, "The driver was Tim Fergusson. He was a friend of mine."

"Sorry," Michael Collins said. He made no other apology. There was a war on. One of the men stoked the stove and put on a kettle. Collins picked a copy of the *Irish Times* off the scrubbed deal table and said to Margaret, "Did you see this?"

"The notice? Yes."

She'd seen it that midday, when the paper arrived—a notice in the Agony column, reading *Stella Merritt, née Cate, 21, missing from her home in Hedlington, Kent, since Christmas Eve 1917; 5'6", full figure, brown hair, blue eyes, small mole right cheek, thought to be in London: a substantial reward will be paid for any information leading to her discovery; anonymity guaranteed. Write Box 8905.*

Margaret said slowly, "That's my daughter . . . she's run away."

"Same as you did?"

"I wish it was the same. But it isn't. I don't know what it's all about. I suppose they've put the notice in the *Irish Times* so that I can write and they'll tell me . . ."

"Why don't you? We can arrange it so they'll never trace the letter."

Margaret hesitated. She saw her daughter as she had been when she cut the ties that bound her to her children: young, lovely, virginal . . . a child just become a woman. She hardened her heart; it was too distracting from her real concern, which was the freedom of Ireland. If it had been Laurence now, the son of her womb, her only son . . .

She said shortly, "No . . . Thanks all the same."

*   *   *   *

John Merritt walked down Scarrow bank at Probyn Gorse's side in the late morning. The rain of the past two days had stopped, a cold east wind blew, hoarfrost rimmed the bare boughs and icicles made little chandeliers along the overhanging banks of the stream. This was the part of the river I saw from the train window, John thought, this was where I walked with Stella . . .

Probyn, old and stooped, sharp of eye and ear, his gait a fast shuffle, descended from eighty generations of poachers, said, "My Woman and I was sorry to hear about Miss Stella, Mr John. But she ha'nt done away with herself."

"I don't think so," John said.

"No more does my Woman," Probyn said. "She's in London, mark my words. And soon she'll get sick of it, the noise, and the people and the stink and the motor cars everywhere . . . she was brought up here, in Walstone . . . Would you like me to go up to London, look for her, like? I'd have to have some money."

John smiled down at the old man, "Thanks, Probyn, but I don't think London's the place for you . . . Do you need any money?"

"No, no, just if I was to go up to London and look for Miss Stella . . . We're doing right well. Eating like earls . . . better." He chuckled meaningly—"Lord Swanwick's got a little place in London, a flat, like, and soon they'll all be living up there and eating London food, which ain't like ours, stands to reason—because he's sold the Park to Hoggin, Lord Walstone that is . . . and when I said all, Lady Helen won't be with them. But she'll be in London. She is now, but don't ask me no questions about her. My lips are sealed."

"Lord Swanwick's sold the Park?" John said, wondering.

"'Course, you being in America and France the paper's didn't say what was important. He's sold it, and the furniture, or most of it. Any flat's going to be small after Walstone Park, no place for all them paintings and sofas and wardrobes and tables, stands to reason . . ."

"And Mr Hoggin's a lord?"

Probyn stopped and slapped his thigh, crying, "William Hoggin, 1st Baron Walstone in the County of Kent! For political services. You didn't see the Birthday Honours List?"

John shook his head and Probyn said, "No more did I. Why should I care who becomes Sir George Ballprick or Viscount Fartarse, begging your pardon, sir . . . but I heard, in the Arms, same day . . . Lord Walstone, Lady Walstone—that's Ruth Stratton that was—and the Honourable Launcelot Hoggin, them's who own Walstone Park now. And it's their pheasants my Woman and I eat whenever we want to, and right good eating they are too."

John said, "Still poaching then?"

Probyn said, " 'Course I am! What else is there for a man my age to do these days? Though, mind you, 'tis a shame poaching from the Park with the keepers His Lordship has . . . and I told him so to his face, Christmas Eve, not fifty yards from here, I did, His real Lordship, that is, not Bill Hoggin, His New Lordship."

"Well, be careful," John said. "I've had some dealings with Mr Hoggin, and maybe he doesn't have any blue blood, but he's a tough customer, and as sharp as a weasel."

They stopped at a gap in the untidy mass of bushes by the footpath and Probyn said, "My granddaughter's down, Mr John, visiting. She'd like to see you, I know. Told me so, when I told her, this morning, that you were at the Manor."

John hesitated. What did he have to say to Florinda Gorse? But there she was in the door of the thatched-roof cottage, walking out toward them, an open sable coat half-hiding her thin wool dress, her piled auburn hair glowing in the sunlight, one hand out—"Mr Merritt!" Her hand was warm and firm in his and he said, "Lady Jarrow . . ."

She looked straight at him, her green eyes fixed on his, "I feel I am to blame, Mr Merritt . . . I saw your wife in hospital one day last year. I was visiting Miss Alice, her aunt, after she had had her leg blown off. And I saw her one other time, in Hedlington when I came down to see Fletcher on a short leave . . . A good many theatre people take drugs, and I know the symptoms. I ought to have seen them. I did, I think, but dismissed the idea as impossible."

John said, "What could you have done?"

"Given her a hand," Florinda said simply. "No one understood her . . . perhaps I could have, a little."

"I didn't," John said. "It's been nice seeing you again, and—you are very kind. But I must go. I have to go up to London this afternoon, to see the Commissioner of Police."

"Wait . . ." Her hand was outstretched, holding his sleeve. "Did you see Guy Rowland out there—in France? He's in . . ."

"The R.F.C. . . . I know. No, I didn't have time. I'll be going back in a few days, and as we're still training, back in Brittany, there's a chance that I'll be able to get up to see him . . . or persuade him to fly down to visit us. What message shall I give him?"

Her eyes were large, her lips parted, colour coming and going in her cheeks. She whispered at last, "Tell him I . . . tell him that . . . tell him to come home quickly."

*　　*　　*　　*

8

John walked slowly along the graveled path leading from the workmen's bicycle racks to the Hedlington Aircraft Company's factory buildings, on the down east of Hedlington, Richard Rowland at one side of him and his sister Betty at the other. Richard was Harry Rowland's eldest son, and managing director of H.A.C. and the Jupiter Motor Company. In both firms the major financial interest was held by Fairfax, Gottlieb, a New York investment bank, of which John's father, Stephen Merritt, was currently chairman of the board. They had been talking about Stella and her disappearance; but no one had had anything new to say and after a few minutes John had changed the subject—to the present situation of the two companies. He had been managing Hedlington Aircraft until he left England to enlist, in April 1917, when America entered the war. For the last two years Betty had been, and still was, assistant to the firm's chief designer, Ginger Keble-Palmer.

Richard, answering John's question, said, "We have some difficulty, now and then, in getting materials . . . that's natural, considering that the U-boats are still a terrible menace. We have a permanent shortage of working capital because—like everything else—it's needed for the war . . ."

"Where it all gets blown into thin air," Betty murmured.

". . . but our real problem is labour. We are at last getting firm, big orders for the Hedlington Buffalo here, and for the new Mark II standard 3-ton lorry at J.M.C. We have just about reached the limit with the employment of women . . ."

"Until more tools and so on can be worked by power, electric or hydraulic," Betty said.

". . . so the men we do have are in a stronger position every day. And there are plenty of people ready to keep reminding them of it—people like Bert Gorse and those other swine down at H.E. 16— that's the local branch of the Union of Skilled Engineers. I tell you, as soon as the war's over, and the wartime rules are lifted, there'll be trouble here."

"Just here, or at J.M.C., too?"

"Both."

John said, "Might it not be better to come to terms with the U.S.E. now, when their hands are tied by wartime regulations? They'll be grateful . . . not many employers are trying to co-operate with them, I gather."

Richard said shortly, "No. And I'm not going to be one of them."

John did not hesitate this time, but said, "I think you're making a mistake, Richard. There's more than the contractual terms involved—there's the atmosphere of the factories, the temperature of the relationship between management and labour."

Richard stopped and faced him belligerently, "Are you hoping to come back to work here with us, John, when the war's over?"

John and Betty stopped, too. John said evenly, "I can't say yet. I can decide nothing till Stella's found—and the war's over."

Richard said, "Well, if you do, I'll be glad to have you back . . . *if* you don't take the union's side in disputes. That's not the way Americans are supposed to think. Mr Ford doesn't."

John said, "If I come back, I'll have to be free to give you my opinion, Richard. Times have changed. What's happening over there—" he gestured to the south, to France "—is changing everything."

"For the worse," Richard growled. "Look, I've got to go down to Hedlington to see Overfeld and Morgan about a modification the American army wants in the 3-tonners they've ordered. But we have a Buffalo going up on final pre-acceptance trials at three this afternoon . . . like to go up with her?"

"I'd love to," John said. "I'll come back at about a quarter of three, then."

Richard raised a hand in acknowledgment as he turned and walked briskly back toward the offices and his car. John turned to his sister, "How are Overfeld and Morgan doing?"

Overfeld was the American production expert who'd come over late in 1914 to help set up the Jupiter Motor Company; and Morgan was an American of Welsh lineage who'd been imported from Detroit as works foreman at J.M.C. when the plant was ready to operate.

Betty said, "Richard's becoming rabid about unions in general and the U.S.E. in particular . . . Overfeld's getting homesick. Richard offered to send him home for a month's leave last year, but his wife called that he wasn't to come—too dangerous on the seas, she said. Morgan's quite happy . . . but he agrees with Richard—there'll be trouble as soon as the war's over."

"There will be, if Richard doesn't bend."

Betty said, "I agree, but Richard won't hear of it. He's introducing more efficient methods, new machines, stiffer work rules, tighter schedules—all the time. To him the union, any union, is Satan."

"Sounds like a good Republican," John said. "Oh, I know we're Republicans—Dad certainly is—but that sort of politics seems a little, well, petty nowadays—when you look at the war."

"Oh, the war, the war!" Betty groaned. "But you're right . . . I just pray for it to end, but O, Lord, how long, how long? . . . I thought that Mr Wilson's Fourteen Points might bring everyone to reason—but not a hope."

John said nothing for a few moments, pacing slowly at her side; then they turned and started back, and he said, "How's Fletcher Whitman—who used to be Fletcher Gorse—Probyn's grandson?"

She said, "Alive . . . as of a week ago. He writes regularly, and he writes well. I'm keeping all his letters, of course. What he sees, notices, is amazing. He doesn't always have enough words to describe his insight fully, but when he does . . . he's a genius, John, a great, great poet."

"I know . . . What's going to happen—between you and him?"

It was Betty's turn to be silent, no sound now but the regular crunch of their shoes on the gravel. At last she said, "He must aim to be what he *is*—a poet. Poet Laureate of England, perhaps, unless he finds he must rebel against all that—old England, lords and ladies and pageantry and butts of Malmesey wine . . . If he is to reach the limits of his own potential, he must have more education. Not necessarily at school or university—but among people, books . . . talking with other poets, with statesmen, professors, turret lathe operators, herring fishermen . . ." Her voice trailed off.

John waited a moment then said, "And you? Where do you fit in?"

She said, "I think I want to be his wife, John."

"And give up your career?"

She said, "I'd like to continue my career, even after all the men come back, though I know there'll be plenty of pressure on Richard to fire me and put an ex-service man in my place. A lot of women are going to be forced back into the kitchen who don't want to go there at all . . . Look, unless Fletcher can make enough money for us both to live on, just by his poetry, it looks as though I'll have to work, too."

"Dad would settle a good income on you, if he approved of Fletcher."

"Probably," she said. "But I don't *know* whether we should marry, until he comes home for good. But he's going to become a great poet, whatever else happens."

*   *   *   *

A few moments later Betty walked into the crowded little office of the firm's accountant, three doors down the hutment passage from the managing director's. Alice Rowland, who had been the accountant since the first week of the year, looked up from a ledger where she was checking that the parts department was using the proper double-entry system of bookkeeping.

Betty said, "Mind if I sit down for a moment?" Her eye caught the crutches propped in a corner. Alice saw the glance and said, "They go on the bonfire February 11th. I get my artificial leg on the 10th . . . I

11

love this work but I shall really have to get a pair of glasses. My eyes aren't what they were. Whose are, at thirty-seven?"

Betty said, "John was here just now."

"I know. I saw you through the window. He looks so stern these days, especially in that uniform. We all met him at the Governor's the day before yesterday. I felt so helpless, and I know the others did, too."

"So do I. But it's when Stella's found that the real problems will arise. John will be back in France. We're the ones who must rescue her from what ever dreadful place she'll still be in."

Alice said, "It won't be easy." She added matter-of-factly—"I was a drug addict myself, for a time."

"You!" Betty gasped. Stella's Aunt Alice was such a cheery, unassuming, *nice* person, not pretty, but, well, *nice*-looking, that the words she had just spoken didn't make sense.

Alice said gently, "Yes, dear. And I have had a lover. The war has changed our women's world far more than this suffrage we've just been presented with . . . They gave me morphine for quite a time after I had my leg blown off. I became addicted, and suddenly found that I couldn't live without it. But of course I was in hospital, and the doctors could treat me, whether I liked it or not. And they did. They eased the withdrawal pains as much as they could, but it was still quite dreadful. We must remember that, when Stella comes back. Did you know that I am also a post office? An illegal and treasonable post office?"

"What?" Betty gasped. "What on earth do you mean?" Aunt Alice—someone's paramour; a dope fiend; and now . . . ?

Alice said, "I forward letters between Guy—my nephew, the air ace, and Werner von Rackow . . ."

"The German ace? But how?"

"They each write to me, as Dear Cousin. But the contents of the letters are actually meant for the other. The letters are sent to an address in Switzerland, where some crippled old lady lives who apparently really is a cousin of von Rackow's. She forwards them to von Rackow's fiancée, or to me, as the case may be. Von Rackow fixed it all up last November, then dropped private messages on Guy's aerodrome with all the details. Guy's commanding his squadron now, and he's a major."

"And he's what? Twenty?"

"Twenty-one next St George's Day."

"What do they write about?"

"Oh, nothing about the war. About the sort of problems there will be when it's over. How to help the children grow up without hatred.

Cure for the crippled. Retrain people who've only known war, and only have war skills . . . I see all the letters, of course, and I think that Maria Rittenhaus and whomever Guy marries are very lucky women."

Betty hesitated then said, "I hope . . . that the man you love . . . is all right."

"So far," Alice said briskly, "but it's over. He's married. I hurt his wife very much. Now, my dear, I must get back to work or my brother Giglamps will be here muttering that he knew he shouldn't have employed a woman in this job . . ."

* * * *

John Merritt and Fiona Rowland parted at the taxi rank outside Victoria Station, Chatham side. They had found each other on the same train to London from Hedlington earlier that morning, and had shared the same first-class compartment, otherwise empty. John was going up for his second visit to Scotland Yard—this time with the Chief Detective Inspector responsible for investigating drug traffic and drug-related crimes. He didn't know what Stella's Aunt Fiona was going up for—she hadn't said—but presumed it was for shopping. On the journey they had not spoken much; she had expressed her sympathy, and offered her help; and she had made some small talk—about her husband, Lieutenant Colonel Quentin Rowland, commanding the 1st Battalion of the Weald Light Infantry in France; about her daughter, Virginia, recently married to a war-crippled Battery Sergeant Major Robinson—a marriage of which she clearly did not approve; about her son Major Guy Rowland, D.S.O., M.C., the air ace, of whom she was, as clearly, very proud . . . yet all the time John felt that she was not really with him in the little padded box with the richly decorated plush cushions, the South Eastern & Chatham Railway's crest embroidered on them, rocking sedately toward London through the wintry Weald of Kent.

They found taxis, and drove away, John toward New Scotland Yard, Fiona toward the Charing Cross Hospital. There at the reception desk, she pushed up her veil and said, "I would like to visit Lieutenant Archie Campbell, Weald Light Infantry, please, sister. He has an abdominal wound, and had some additional surgery the day before yesterday."

"It is not visiting hours," the sister said severely. "Are you a relative?"

Fiona said, "When he was hit Mr Campbell was my husband's adjutant. My husband commands the 1st Battalion of the Weald Light Infantry." Her voice was cold. As a McLeod of Skye she did not intend to take any haughtiness from nursing sisters.

The sister relented. "Ah well, you may go up. 2nd Floor, Room 24. He is in with five others, all post-op cases. It makes it easier for the duty nurse to look after them."

Fiona nodded and headed for the stairs. She had visited Archie once before, as soon as she received Quentin's letter telling her where he was. He had told her that this last operation should make him fit again. Fit? The word made her shiver, for in it she heard the added unspoken words—"for general duty": fit for the trenches.

At the door of the ward she braced herself. If he could have been alone, it would have been so much easier, but . . . she walked in. He was in the far bed on her right, by a big window looking toward the back of Coutts Bank. He had been lying on his back, staring at the ceiling, but at the click of her heels on the tiled floor he looked round, his head moving slowly, as though much pain had taught him to move with care. She sat down in the chair beside his bed, feeling the tears well up in her eyes.

"Ah, Fiona, so ye've come again. Ye're a bad gairrl." She dabbed her eyes with a little handkerchief. He was speaking the broad Gorbals, which meant he would not be serious. He could speak perfectly good English when he chose.

She said, "How do you feel?"

"No ba' at a', lassie, considering hoo they've been poking arroun' in ma tripes."

"Oh Archie, do be serious . . . When will they let you out?"

"Two weeks," he said.

"And then what? Six weeks convalescence?"

"I'll make it four. Then . . ."

"Ask for a job at the Depot, darling." Her voice was low but urgent. Perhaps the man in the bed behind her could hear. She no longer cared. "I'm dying without you. Stay in Hedlington. They can't send you out again."

"They can, but they won't. Because I'll go, of my own accord."

"Oh Archie, I love you, I love you, and you're being so cruel . . ."

He said slowly, "I must go back to Quentin, Fiona. You don't know that man. He's stupid . . ."

"Yes, yes!"

"Narrow-minded . . ."

"Oh yes!"

"Obstinate, ignorant, insensitive . . ."

"Of course! That's why I . . ."

"But . . . he's a man to be loved. He's stupid, but he understands. He's narrow-minded, obstinate, ignorant, and insensitive only to what doesn't affect those he loves . . . the men of his battalion. And you."

She dried her eyes. She was a McLeod and must not disgrace herself before these wounded officers, perhaps one of them a clansman who would expect a sterner pride of her.

She said, "If he is killed, will you marry me?"

Archie searched for words for a long time, then said, "Fiona, I could not. You could come to my bed sometimes, with the models and the lady clients—though at this moment I feel so weak I can't believe I'll ever be able to pleasure a woman again . . . but you'll have but one husband. Quentin Rowland, of the Weald Light Infantry."

She got up to go, stooping to kiss Archie on the cheek. He was a painter, an artist, after all; and he would change his mind when he felt strong again, and could enjoy her body, and paint her flesh as he had so often in the glorious years before 1914. She had six or seven weeks. She could make him stay, secure in her flesh, in her love.

*　　*　　*　　*

Commander Tom Rowland, on the bridge of the old cruiser moored in the stream below Chatham, listened to the increasing drone of aircraft engines, and watched as the searching pencils of light from the shore-based searchlights leaped up into the sky, wheeled, circled, dipped, wavered. A silvery gleam appeared, caught like a metal moth. The guns barked in the night, and high up there little dark clouds blossomed under the full moon. It was light enough to see them now . . . four . . . seven, eight Gothas.

There was nothing more to be done. He had ordered "Action Stations" two minutes ago and the skeleton crew now manning the old ship were all closed up, guns manned . . . except that they could not be pointed high enough to hit an aeroplane. As aircraft became faster and their bombing methods more accurate it would be necessary to give all ships' guns a high-angle capacity . . . and some method of holding their aim on such fast-moving targets.

Giant spouts of water sprang up out of the river, bursts of orange flame sprouted like orange cabbages in the town to the south. The cruiser's own searchlights had one of the raiders caught and were holding it. A flurry of black smoke bursts almost hid it, then suddenly the silver streak became an incandescent glow, now diving down the sky, trailing a scarf of fire . . . to fall into the sea half a mile to the north. A ragged cheer swept the bridge and upper deck. The sound of engines receded, the searchlights went suddenly dark, the fires on land grew larger. He could probably pipe the hands to stand down from action stations, but he'd wait for five more minutes. It would be a pity, having volunteered for dangerous duty, to be sunk at anchor in the estuary.

The "dangerous duty," he had been advised in great secrecy, was a raid to block the channels by which German U-boats left their home ports on the Belgian coast, on their way to attack the British sea lanes. That meant sinking blockships at Ostend, and Zeebrugge, at least, under the noses of the German coastal artillery. No definite date had yet been set for the raids, but they would probably be in April. The part his ship, H.M.S. *Orestes,* would play had not yet been worked out, for detailed planning had only just started.

April . . . three months away; and after that, he'd be out of this uniform . . . or, if in it, dead. If he survived, he'd be back in his flat, living with Charlie Bennett, his friend, servant, and lover; and Arthur Gavilan would be teaching him the art and craft of fashion design; and . . . To his surprise, his acknowledgment of his homosexuality had made life easier for him on board ship. Half a dozen young sailors had joined his crew who, in earlier days, would have filled him with desire, and simultaneous shame, and self-despisal. Now, he was secure; he admired their graceful virility, their youthful beauty—but they were not for him.

Five minutes gone. He turned to the officer of the watch and said, "Stand the hands down from action stations."

"Aye, aye, sir!"

The boatswains' pipes twittered, while Tom took a turn along the bridge and back again. February 2nd . . . young Merritt had gone back to France, Stella not yet found. Poor devil . . . poor Stella, caught in the grasp of a demon she certainly did not understand, and perhaps no other human being did, either.

Daily Telegraph, Friday, February 8, 1918

TRANSPORT SUNK OFF THE COAST OF IRELAND
AMERICANS ON BOARD
2,187 SAVED—210 LOST

Yesterday afternoon the Secretary of the Admiralty issued the following:

The Anchor Liner *Tuscania,* Captain J.L. Henderson, was torpedoed at night on Feb. 5, off the Irish coast whilst carrying U.S. Troops. The following are the approximate number of saved:

U.S. Military		Crew	
Officers	78	Officers	18
Men	1935	Men	125
Passengers	3	Not specified	32
Total number on board			2397
Total number saved			2187

Late last night Reuter's Agency announced that, according to in- formation received in authoritative quarters, the *Tuscania* was tor- pedoed at 6.20 p.m. at a point ten miles from the coast. No other vessel of the convoy was hit. The details already to hand show that discipline was magnificent, and the character of the rescue work which was done by British vessels that rushed to the scene can be judged by the relatively small loss of life.

GRAPHIC STORIES

From Our Own Correspondent, *A North of Ireland Port*, Thursday. The *Tuscania* arrived off the North of Ireland coast on Tuesday afternoon. The voyage up to that had been without event, and the first sign of danger came at a quarter of six, when preparations were being made for supper. Two torpedoes were fired. The first missed the liner, passing a short distance from the stern. The second struck the ship full amidships, wrecking the engine-room and going near to No. 1 boiler. The dynamo . . .

Garrod, the old maid, came in and said, "Lord Walstone is here, sir. He asks if he may see you."

"A bit early," Cate grumbled, folding away the paper. "But show him in."

A few moments later Garrod returned and stood beside the door of the breakfast room, announcing formally, "Lord Walstone, sir."

Cate stood up as Walstone strode heavily in, "Sit down," he said. "Coffee, tea?"

"Tea please . . . There, thanks . . . An' lots of milk and sugar." Garrod left the room and Walstone said, "Sorry to disturb you this early but I 'ave to go to London, and, well, it's this . . . We've heard that your daughter's missing, Miss Stella that was . . . run away, like."

The beady little eyes were fixed on Cate's. Cate felt a surge of anger rise in him: what concern was Stella's tragedy to this jumped-up barrow boy with the boughten title? He said coldly, "That is true."

Bill Hoggin, Lord Walstone, said quickly, "I ain't just sticking my nose into your business, Cate. I want to help . . . Look, you've hof- fered a reward. Two thou? Make it five. I'll put up half . . . Get the boy's father to put up five and make it ten. He's a Yankee banker, ain't he? Advertise more. Let everyone know."

Cate said slowly, "You are very generous, Lord Walstone. We have been trying to keep the unhappy business to ourselves, but . . ."

"T'won't do," Walstone said forcefully. "Shout it from the house- tops. Later, they'll all forget . . . they forget everything."

"Perhaps you're right. And . . . I'm most grateful."

"Don't give it a second thought . . . One other thing—we moved into the Park yesterday and the Swanwicks moved out. Swanwick told

17

me that the gamekeepers are no more use than a woman to a eunuch. You know Probyn Gorse well? Known him all your life, eh?"

"That's true," Cate said cautiously. What had Probyn been up to now?

Walstone said, "He's poaching my pheasants. The keepers can no more stop him than they can fart a barn door down, but they swear it's him. So . . . d'ye think he'd take a job as gamekeeper, for me?"

Cate stared as Walstone slurped noisily from his tea cup. Probyn Gorse, gamekeeper? Set a thief to catch a thief, certainly, but . . . He shook his head. "It sounds a good idea, Lord Walstone, but I'm afraid Probyn is too set in his ways."

"All right, then. Is he superstitious, believes in witches and ghosts and all that hooha?"

"Very much so. He's a real countryman in that way—as in all others."

Lord Walstone finished his tea and stood up. "Good! D'ye have any old photographs of his father or mother? I hear they lived here too?"

"Oh yes, and his grandparents, though they died when I was very small . . . Yes, I have some groups at the village fete and a wedding or two, showing Probyn's mother, certainly."

"Could I see them?"

"Certainly." Cate got up and led the way to his library and music room. Why on earth did Walstone want to see photos of Probyn's mother—in her grave these thirty years? He found the heavy old album, thumbed through the stiff pages and the sepia photographs. "Here," he said. "That's Mrs Gorse. What was her name? . . . Lucy." He stared at the old photo over Walstone's shoulder, remembering Lucy Gorse as she had been in her fifties: quite tall, a long stern face, grey hair in a bun, often a shawl over her head, blue eyes, full bosom . . .

"Mind if I borrow this album for a day or two, Cate?" Lord Walstone asked.

Cate hesitated. Should he ask Walstone what he was proposing to do with it? But Walstone answered the question before it had been spoken—"I want Probyn Gorse as my gamekeeper at the Park. I'm going to show him it's a lot better life than poaching." He laid a finger alongside his nose and winked.

Five minutes later, his visitor departed in his chauffeured Rolls Royce, carrying the album; Cate returned to his library and stared a moment at the gilt-tooled rows of the philosophers. He pulled one down and opened it at the title page. The author's seal was inscribed:

Que scais-je?

Good old Montaigne! Even his motto expressed Cate's present feeling perfectly.

18

The Western Front:
Wednesday, February 13, 1918

2 Lieutenant Colonel Quentin Rowland, having refilled his pipe and got it drawing well, opened another letter. It was a cold day with a bitter wind from the north-east, but the men were in good billets, either in village houses or outlying barns well-stacked with straw. A few high cirrus clouds marked the sky's pale blue expanse from horizon to horizon over the rolling downland of the Somme. If one looked out of the upper back windows of the house that held his battalion headquarters you could see Amiens cathedral a few miles to the east . . . but the room he was now in, the battalion office and orderly room, was on the ground floor and faced west—toward the front line, six miles off.

He puffed contentedly. In the house next door someone was playing haunting Irish airs on a mouth organ. That must be Father Caffin, the battalion's padre. The battalion was going up the line tomorrow night. Meantime, nearly thirty-six hours more of peace, and calm. Time to read letters, and write them; time to give the men one more close order parade. Light Infantry drill demanded alertness, quick clean movements; the men were getting slovenly at it. If they didn't have pride in their drill, how could they hope to beat the Germans? He'd have to take the drill parade himself. Woodruff was a good adjutant, considering he was only a wartime officer, and not a gentleman either—his father ran the garage in Walstone; it had once been a livery stable, of course . . . but he couldn't be expected to take a drill parade, as a Regular adjutant would; he didn't have the standards. So, at eight o'clock tomorrow morning, it would really come down to himself, Kellaway, and Bolton, the new R.S.M., trying to beat six

19

hundred and thirty officers and men into shape in sixty minutes. It ought to be more than six hundred and thirty, but the battalion was chronically under strength. Bloody Staff! They allotted you a stretch of line to hold as though you were up to full War Establishment, when they knew perfectly well that you were two hundred men short . . .

This letter was from Virginia, his daughter; she thought she was pregnant . . . she was sure of it. So in eight months or so Battery Sergeant Major Robinson would be a father; and he himself, and the Leeds corporation dustman, would be grandfathers. It didn't seem to matter as much now as it would have before the war. But what about *after* the war? Then how would all these topsy-turvy situations and attitudes turn out?

The last letter, and he had deliberately kept it to last when he had seen the handwriting on the envelope, was from Archie Campbell. He opened it and read carefully: Archie had had a final operation in January, and had just been moved to a Convalescent Hospital in Dartford. Well, that wasn't far from Hedlington, so Fiona could go and see him often . . . Fiona had visited him three or four times while he had been in Charing Cross Hospital . . . Fiona had never mentioned that in her own letter to him—the only one in several weeks . . . Archie wrote that he just needed time and exercise to get his strength back, and was planning to come out again about the middle of March. The colonel would understand that when he did, he'd be put in a general pool of officers; therefore would he, the colonel, please pull every string possible to see that he was posted back to the 1st Wealds . . . if the colonel wanted him back, that is? Do I want him back, Quentin thought? By God, I do! He'd been miserably lonely without him. In the strains and crises of the front line, mutual trust had bridged the gap between Glasgow slum boy turned painter, and rich man's son become Regular officer of the old army, and between lieutenant and lieutenant-colonel. Most of all . . . Quentin winced, but it was true, and truth was all . . . they had shared Fiona; he as her husband, Archie as her lover. The discovery of that sharing, poured out by Archie in a dugout under bombardment, when it seemed that neither would live through the night, was the strongest memory in Quentin's life. Now Archie was with Fiona, or could be whenever he or she chose. He had sworn he would not return to the old love, but could he keep his promise? Would it not be best if he did? Fiona loved Archie, and despised him, her husband. But Archie was coming back to the battalion. So, let fate decide. He'd make Archie promise to marry her if he himself was killed and Archie wasn't. If it came the other way about, then he'd somehow find ways of making Fiona understand how much he loved her; and they'd share the memory of Archie, at least. And if they both went . . . poor Fiona.

There was a knock at the door and the adjutant, 2nd Lieutenant Woodruff, entered, saluting. "Orders for the move up, sir. We're relieving the 3rd Grenadiers in front of Albert."

"Guards?" Quentin said. "We'll have to see that all boots are thoroughly well polished, and clothing and equipment perfect. Let's hope it doesn't rain or snow."

Woodruff said cheerfully, "Perhaps it would be better if it did, sir, then they couldn't look down their noses at us if our turnout isn't quite perfect."

"That's a defeatist attitude," Quentin snapped. "Rain or snow, it'll fall on them too, and we're going to look as good as they do—*better!* Is that clear?"

"Yes, sir," Woodruff said. He didn't look very crestfallen, Quentin observed; these wartime officers didn't take dress and drill and Regimental custom seriously enough. But those things were the cement that held the battalion together in hard times. He said, "Archie Campbell hopes to rejoin us about the middle of March. If we can get him back, I'll reappoint him as adjutant. You will take over as Intelligence Officer."

"Very good, sir," Woodruff said. "I hope I've been satisfactory."

"Oh quite," Quentin said, "for a non-Regular, very good. But Archie, well . . ." He ended gruffly, "An adjutant is a personal staff officer and Archie suited me. I'm not easy to get on with, but he manages it . . . What news from your family?"

"All well, sir. My father's hired a new mechanic—Ben Hotchkiss, who lost a lung at Jutland. But he's a smart fellow. Dad has three cars for hire now, and he's put in an extra petrol pump . . . Sir, when Archie Campbell comes back, can I have a few days leave as soon as I've handed over to him? I want to get married."

"Married? Good heavens, I didn't know . . ."

"Well, I'm thirty-one, sir, and me and Addie Morris were walking out for two years before I joined up, and now she says it's about time we got spliced, and Dad and Mum say the same, so . . ."

"Of course, of course. Just as soon as Archie's back, off you go, and good luck to you."

"Thank you, sir."

*   *   *   *

At the lower end of the village a squad of men from C Company were marching out to fatigue duty, carrying picks and shovels and singing briskly to the tune of "The Church's One Foundation":

21

We are Fred Karno's Army
The ragtime infantry!
We can not fight, we can not shoot,
What bloody good are we?
And when we get to Berlin,
The Kaiser he will shout,
"Hoch, hoch, mein Gott,
What a bloody rotten lot
Are the ragtime infantry!"

As the sounds died away the three men sitting round a table in one of the village's four estaminets refilled their glasses with van blong and drank moodily.

Private Fletcher Whitman, Battalion sniper and, in another world, lover of Betty Merritt, said, "Don't know why this place isn't jam full, with us going up tonight."

"Everyone's spent their money," Private "Snaky" Lucas said.

"Or lost it at Crown & Anchor," young Private Jessop said morosely. "You must 'a won ten quid working that bleeding board, Snaky. You could stand us all another bottle, at least."

Lucas beckoned, and the young girl at the other end of the room came up with another bottle. "No sooner said than done," Lucas said magnanimously. "Next time, the luck'll change, eh?"

"Not bloody likely, with you running the board," Jessop said. He drank again. "Old Rowley and the Regimental were calling us everything bar darlings this morning, weren't they? What's the use of all that fucking drill? Presenting arms doesn't kill Jerries."

"Old Rowley was giving us 'ell because we *looked* like a ragtime army. And because we're taking over from some ruddy Guards tonight . . . D'you know what the sarn't major used to ask us blokes when I first got out to the Shiny? 'Wot's the rarest thing in India?' 'e shouts. We don't know, of course, and 'e says, 'Guardsman's shit . . . and what's the second rarest?' Still we don't know and 'e yells, 'Drafts from the Depot wot knows their arses from 'oles in the ground!' . . . This push ain't sigarno yet, but it's the 'ell of a lot better than when we come out of Passchendaele . . . and we need to be, 'cos the Jerries ain't near finished yet, you mark my words."

Fletcher drank, listening idly to the chatter round the table. They'd all drink as much as they could afford to buy this afternoon. But however much they drank they'd not get drunk—because they were going up the line. Tomorrow night, on the firestep, it would be easy . . . if you could win some rum.

Jessop was talking about his last visit to a red light house in

Amiens. It wasn't so long since the kid had had his first woman, arranged by the other blokes in B, when the battalion was up by Arras . . . There was a letter from Betty Merritt in his left breast pocket. It was a long letter, several pages, mostly about what they'd do after the war; but there was some local gossip—her brother's wife had disappeared; that was Miss Stella Cate, of course. They thought she was in London, hiding. Rum go, that. Couldn't imagine it happening before the war except maybe some young lady running off with a handsome coachman . . . Betty had heard that Anne Stratton was some months pregnant, which was very distressing news, as Frank had not been home for a long time and the baby could not possibly be his. The war was to blame, but would Frank understand that? He was such a straightforward, honest man, and so single-minded about love and duty, that it would be very hard for him to see that Anne had betrayed him not from lack of love, or love of other men, but from being overpowered by the misery that the war had brought upon her . . . The letter looked again to the future: he must learn, study, in the wider world, for he was to be a world-wide poet. He must learn more about educated people, especially women, about the very rich, the very poor. She would do anything to help him follow his star . . .

He pushed back his chair abruptly, "I've 'ad enough. Thanks for the van blong, Snaky." He went out. Snaky Lucas, now with twenty-two years service and so far unscratched from several scraps on the Indian frontier, and in action without a break from August 1914 to this date, said "Let 'im go. Poets and snipers is bad company. Another van blong, mademoiselle . . . and don't we all wish you was from Armenteers."

* * * *

2nd Lieutenant Laurence Cate lay on his stomach in the reeds by the north bank of the Somme a mile from the village where the battalion was billeted. His binoculars were to his eyes and his heart was pounding. Since settling in two hours ago he had observed much water life on the pleasant stream, here separated from the barge canal. After half an hour he had seen a pair of little grebes, in their winter garb of brown and buff. The sexes were indistinguishable and it was too early for them to have paired off for mating, yet he thought the two he had seen were male and female. Now across the river, swimming slowly into the focus of his glasses, in and out of the thick reed beds over there, was a much bigger bird . . . perhaps twenty inches along the water line . . . the lower body pale, the neck long and slender . . . he began to tremble with excitement: if his suspicion was right there ought to be a dark cap and obvious crest . . . but the crest was not so

23

obvious in winter, the books said. He had never seen one, so he didn't know, but it fitted. There should also be a rufous collar, again obvious in summer but barely visible in winter . . . yes, there it was . . . the big bird was diving now, bottom and webbed feet up . . . surfaced again, head shaking, nothing in its beak. It was barely fifty yards off now . . . if only it would come out of the reeds . . . In answer to his prayer, it did, swimming majestically into the open, now clear against the background of pale reeds and thin ice glittering on the surface of the river. "Great Crested Grebe!" he cried aloud, and again—"Great Crested Grebe!" What a lovely bird! It was still rare in England from the time, about 1860, when the plume trade for women's hats had reduced the numbers, the books said, to fifty pairs in all Britain. Then laws had been passed to protect the bird, and now there were supposed to be about six hundred pairs there. Here, in France, he did not know how many. Not many—French women had demanded plumes for their millinery just as voraciously as Englishwomen. This might be the best sighting in his life.

The grebe swam steadily away up stream, keeping close to the reeds on the south bank, and eventually disappeared. Half a dozen moorfowl were in view but Laurence rolled over on his back and stretched luxuriously. The air was cold, and the ground was hard frozen, but he noticed neither. He was wearing warm underclothes, a thick flannel shirt, and of course his barathea tunic and serge greatcoat . . . and he had seen a Great Crested Grebe. Movement caught his eye straight above him. He saw a flash of light, and then another, another, another. He put the binoculars back to his eyes and made out five small shapes . . . aeroplanes. They were high but he could see black crosses under the wings of three of them . . . so, three German against two British. Now he heard the faint chatter of machine guns, and shivered . . . machine guns, awful inhuman monsters. The five planes circled and swooped against banks of brilliant white cloud towering up to the zenith. The guns chattered, the water lapped in the Somme below him . . . a waterfowl quacked, two rose from the river with a whirr of wings . . . the aeroplanes dived, swooped, swung . . . one was suddenly a torch of flame, fire trailing far behind, now smoke. He turned over onto his stomach and searched the river. Where were the grebe, the moorfowl, the snipe . . . where were they?

*   *   *   *

Lieutenant Colonel Quentin Rowland sat at the makeshift table in the headquarters dugout of the 1st Battalion, the Weald Light Infantry. It was comparatively large, with a corrugated iron roof, two timber supports in the centre—and the floor was dry. Candles burned in empty bottles on the table, and on a row of ammunition boxes in the corner, where Quentin's batman slept when he was not following Quentin on his rounds. More empty ammunition boxes and a large case that had held nose fuzes for 4.5-inch howitzer shells contained papers in makeshift files. "Bloody bumf," Quentin muttered under his breath. The war would have been over a year ago if everyone didn't have to spend so much time filling out forms, answering damned silly questions from headquarters so that superstitious twenty-year-old brass hats could justify their existence. He looked at his watch in the wavering light. Ten to ten ack emma. Ten minutes before the fellows would arrive for the conference.

The gas blanket swung aside and a tall figure came down the three steps from the reserve trench outside. It was Captain Kellaway, his B Company commander, recently back from hospital, and now wearing a black patch over his left eye. Kellaway saluted, and Quentin said gruffly, "Morning, Kellaway. You're early."

Kellaway was a good officer—not a Regular, but an early volunteer, a millionaire dilettante, an expert on art, ballet, books, theatre, poetry, music . . . never seemed to have had anything to do with women. He'd been wounded twice—or was it three times now?—and had just got a Military Cross . . . but he made Quentin uneasy, so that he spoke more sharply than he intended.

Kellaway said, "Yes, sir . . . I wanted to ask you if you would consider sending a more senior officer than Laurence to command the raiding party. It'll amount to two platoons, at our present strength. I'd be happy to go myself."

Quentin started to fill his pipe, thinking. After a time he said, "He's been out some time now—eight months, isn't it? He's due for his second pip . . . I can't give it to him unless he's shown he can act independently. No, he'll command . . . give him confidence. That's all that's the matter with him . . . doesn't believe in himself."

"Yes, sir," Kellaway said. He was tall and thin, and in moments such as this, hesitant. In action he was quick and resourceful and brave. Now the one eye was troubled. He said, "What is the exact purpose of the raid, sir? I want to be quite sure that Laurence—and Sergeant Fagioletti and the men, understand," he added quickly, seeing a frown cross his commanding officer's forehead.

Quentin said, "The divisional commander wants one of the new German gas masks so that we can see if they've made any modifications to the old model—which could mean that they're proposing to introduce a new type of gas . . . The brigadier general—and I—and the gunners—want up-to-date German trench maps . . . We all, always, want prisoners, for identification purposes. And"—he looked up at Kellaway standing a little stooped across the table from him, his own eyes bulging, bright blue in the candle flame—"we want to arouse the offensive spirit in our men . . . keep them full of it, so that it's bubbling over all the time, and . . ." his voice rose—"*We want to kill Germans!*"

The gas blanket swung again and Regimental Sergeant Major Bolton stood in the entrance, the bowl of his steel helmet touching the beams overhead, but he did not seem to be stooped. "Officers and N.C.O.s for the conference, all present, *sir!*" he barked.

Quentin nodded and the men trooped in, saluting as they entered. Quentin said, "Sit down where you can . . ." He looked round; they were all here—Kellaway, the company commander who would do the detailed planning; 2nd Lieutenant Laurence Cate, his own nephew, who would command the raiding party; Sergeant Fagioletti, Laurence's platoon sergeant, who would be his second-in-command on the raid; Woodruff, the adjutant, to record what was ordered, and see to the co-ordination of the final plan with the troops holding the front line to right and left of the Wealds, and provide for the evacuation of casualties and the interrogation of prisoners brought back . . . The Regimental, his work done, saluted and went out. The gas curtain dropped into place behind him.

Quentin said, "We are going to carry out a trench raid. The objects of the raid are . . ."; he repeated, almost word for word, what he had just been telling Kellaway, ending, as before, with ". . . *kill Germans!*"

Then he gave his orders about the size and equipment of the raiding party, and after giving out some more details of its tactics and intercommunication, he said, "The raid will go out through A Company's front on the first night after the 16th when the wind is right— that is, from the south, or north, blowing down the German trench line—because we will be using gas shell mixed with HE in the preliminary bombardment, which will last fifteen minutes. You, Kellaway, arrange with the gunners for box barrages and SOS fire on success signals, emergency signals, and withdrawal signals."

"Yes, sir."

"The raiding party will cross the enemy wire by Brock's carpets— you will carry not less than two, so that you don't have to bunch up too much . . . No stretcher bearers. Once you've done your work, unwounded men can help carry any wounded back. Until then, no one turns back, for any reason whatsoever. Is that clear, Mr Cate?"

"Yes, sir."

"So . . . the raiding party will move up in the afternoon of the

16th into the reserve trenches behind A . . . and wait there till conditions are right."

"Yes, sir."

"Any questions?"

The circle of whitish-yellow faces, all staring at him, made him feel that he was the centre of some obscene performance. The gunner captain's hand was moving on his map board though his eyes were fixed on Quentin's. No one spoke.

Quentin said, "Very well, Mr Cate, you stay behind. The rest, dismiss, please. Thank you."

One by one they filed out, up the steps, through the gas curtain, and out. Laurence Cate too was on his feet, an army signal pad and a pencil clutched in his left hand, with a folded section of trench map. Quentin said, "This is your chance to prove yourself, Laurence." He spoke gently, for he had known his nephew since he was born. The boy took after his father Christopher Cate—never raised his voice, a gentle man, but of course a patriot, and a sturdy, dogged fighter. English gentlemen did not shout or yell or show anger; that could be left to lesser breeds without the law: Laurence's middle name was Hengist, after the Germanic king who had conquered Kent in the fifth century, from whom the Cates claimed descent. He would not fail.

The young man said, "Thank you, sir."

Quentin stood up. "You'll do all right, Laurence, but . . . *be there!* I mean, your mind as well as your body must go on that raid. When I've seen you in action before . . . at Nollehoek, for instance . . . I've felt that your mind was wandering. Commanding a platoon or a raiding party requires your whole attention, every moment . . . Sergeant Fagioletti is there to see to small details—that the men's pouches are full, rifles and Lewis guns in good order, Very lights to hand, that sort of thing. He is *not* there to tell you what to do. *You* are in command. So command."

"Yes, sir."

"That's all. Good luck."

*   *   *   *

The five soldiers squatted on their hunkers or sat on boxes of Mills bombs in the bottom of the trench, crowded into a side bay which had originally been dug out as a latrine bay, the site of a latrine bucket, but now disused for that purpose—though still redolent of it. It had been enlarged and was now used to store ammunition, wire, angle irons, and other paraphernalia of the trenches. Private Lucas, the old soldier, spouted the universal chatter of Crown & Anchor in a low continuous murmur, "Pick 'em up, lay 'em down . . . you comes on bicycles, you goes away in Rolls Royce motor cars . . . C'mon, Jessop, you're a man now, not a bleeding errand boy. I seen you stick your prick into a woman with me own eyes. Wot the 'ell good's a tanner?"

"You blokes shouldn't 'a been watching," Jessop, now seventeen years old—not quite sixteen when he had enlisted—grumbled. "That was private."

"We was only making sure she did right by you, seeing's we'd paid for it."

"Madame Fonsard wasn't that sort of woman," young Jessop said. He picked up the sixpence he had laid on the queen, and substituted a half crown.

Lucas whistled, and Private Brace said, "Cor stone the crows! Cyril wants to break the bank, Snaky."

Lucas restarted his patter. Sergeant Fagioletti and Corporal Leavey appeared round the trench traverse twenty feet away and Lucas made to sweep the box and the oilcloth marked with the game's symbols out of sight, for it was an illegal gambling game, though every Other Rank in the army had played plenty of it in his time—however short that time might have been.

Fagioletti raised his hand, "Me and Corporal Leavey know what you're doing, Private Lucas, so it's no use trying to 'ide it. And I'd march you all up before the captain, only Mr Cate said the blokes was to have it easy while we waited . . . so, I ain't seen nothing, see? But I'm not blind, see?"

"Right y'are, sarn't," Lucas said cheerfully.

Faglioletti said, "Just see you don't bet more'n you can afford, young Jessop, understand?"

"Yes, sarn't," Jessop mumbled mutinously. The Dago and Buckle-my-Shoe were good N.C.O.s, as N.C.O.s went, but no one was going to tell Cyril Jessop, any more, what he was going to do and what he wasn't going to do. He wasn't Mr Cate's stable boy now, nor yet a recruit what hadn't had his greens. He'd killed his man—many of them—and fucked his woman . . . ah, Madame Fonsard, what a woman . . .

"Wake up," Lucas said. "Shake 'em up . . . There she goes . . . Two Jam Tarts and the Mudhook . . . Pick 'em up, put 'em down. Nothing for you, Cyril, may I call you Cyril? . . . a bob for me old pal Jones 46 . . . Pick 'em up, lay 'em down . . ."

Jones 46, a farm labourer in the far-off times of peace, a twelve-month veteran of France and Flanders, muttered, "Wish the bleeding wind would change so's we can get going."

"Or stay the way it is for ever so we never have to go," Brace said.

"Just spend our lives here, playing the board and listening to Snaky's stories of Romance in the Shiny . . ."

"The Major, two Mudhooks, 'oo's in luck! Pick 'em up, lay 'em down . . ."

"Can't sleep a wink proper, waiting," Jessop said, ". . . never liked those bleeding Brock's carpets . . . catch your fucking boot nails in them just as much as if you was walking over the bleeding wire . . . 'sides, I feel like a monkey on a pole standing up there, every Jerry in a mile looking at me, his finger on the trigger . . ."

"One Rubadubdub, two Diamonds and the Jam Tart . . . and, me lucky lads, it's the 18th, and the wind is shifting to the south, the balmy south, it's four o'clock and getting dark, and I'll lay a Bradbury to a tanner that inside 'arf an 'our, we'll be served 'ot burgoo with strawberry jam, and a rum ration . . . Or p'raps it'll be bully and beef hearts."

"Christ, not the beans," Jessop said. "The Germans'd hear us a mile off, farting our way across No Man's Land . . ."

Corporal Leavey, a Jew or Buckle-my-Shoe, reappeared. "Roll it up, Lucas. Mr Cate's coming. We're going over at two-twenty ack emma, when the moon's down."

"Told you so," Lucas said nonchalantly, rolling up the oilcloth and stuffing the dice box into his pack. He put out his hand, "I saw you take that 'arf crown off the Mudhook, when the corporal came round the traverse, Jones . . . but I'd rolled, and you 'adn't won. So 'and over . . ."

*　　*　　*　　*

Laurence Cate stood on the firestep of the front-line trench, Captain Kellaway beside him and Sergeant Fagioletti immediately behind and below. The trench was jammed, for at the moment it contained its normal garrison of A Company men, plus the B Company raiders who would climb the ladders and start through the British wire in . . . Laurence peered at the luminous dial of his watch—two minutes.

Kellaway was muttering, "Sure you remember the signals? Red over green for withdrawal, and one minute after the green goes up the gunners are going to plaster the Boche front line, so . . ."

"I remember, sir," Laurence said. He thought, Captain Kellaway is more nervous than I am. Kellaway could imagine what it would be like, what would happen or might, what could go wrong, and the consequences. But he himself knew that if it got too bad he would withdraw into another, private world. It would not be by any act of volition—it would just happen, however much Uncle Quentin harangued him, and he'd be floating weightless over green fields and dense oak woods, hearing the songs of birds. It was a little like that now, in the real concrete world—the air almost still, not even a distant rifle shot or crump of artillery to mar the perfect silence, the sky clear, the air cold and frosty, a faint radiance where the half moon had just sunk below the horizon, the barbed wire dimly sensed against the crepuscular light, the ground iron hard underfoot . . . no owls or bats on the wing here, though, only the heavy breathing of the men along the trench.

British guns broke the silence with a concerted bellow. "Time!" Kellaway breathed, "Good luck." Laurence went fast up the short ladder and began to walk through the six-foot gap in the wire, marked on each side by small white squares of cloth impaled on the barbs of the wire. Sergeant Fagioletti was on his heels with the twenty men of Raiding Group A, and Sergeant Parker was leading twenty men of Raiding Group B through another gap in the wire thirty yards to the right. As they passed through onto No Man's Land proper, then hurried out to right and left to form an irregular line, the British artillery continued the prearranged concentrations of fire on the section of German front-line trench which was the target of the raid. Two Field Brigades of 18-pounder guns and 4.5-inch howitzers were firing the programme, some sixty guns in all.

The slight breeze was from the south-south-west, at about four miles an hour. The German trench was 160 yards away. Laurence increased his pace. The violent crashes of the high explosive and the softer phuts of the gas shells bursting in the German trench seemed quite isolated in the general vaster silence of the front. It would not last, but for now . . .

Laurence felt a sudden passing as of giant wings over his head, and cried "Down!" The men flung themselves down, Sergeant Parker's a second later than those closer to him . . . On the instant star shells burst high overhead, fired by the German artillery far to their rear, now casting a deathly whitish-green radiance over the frozen No Man's Land. A machine gun clattered . . . but to the left: on fixed night lines, Laurence thought. They can't see us . . . they still don't know we're here. The machine gun stuttered, stopped, began again, stopped, puzzled. The star shells sank toward the earth, their light spreading over smaller and smaller areas . . . darkness.

The wind was changing, not much but enough. "Gas!" Laurence called quietly, quickly pulled his own mask over his face, and jammed on the steel helmet over it. Now they could not hear him even if he were to shout. The bombardment would end in . . . fifty seconds . . . they were still firing gas and HE . . . twenty seconds . . . He leaped to his feet and ran forward, his revolver drawn. The two men carrying the Brock's carpet flung it over the first rows of German wire and Laurence ran over, stumbling, half-falling, ripping a deep gash in his left wrist. Fagioletti was beside him, and, there below, in the trench— dog faces, baboons with long curled snouts and huge plastic eyes. God, they were men, waving rifles, a pistol! Fagioletti's rifle cracked and two of the snout faces fell. Then they were down in the trench, man after man tumbling, crashing down. He heard the continuous rumble and crash of grenades as the men with the satchels of Mills bombs hurried left and right along the trench . . . snouted animals were crawling out of holes in the ground, from behind hung blankets, waterproof covers . . . who were they?

The British bombardment had stopped . . . no, it had moved on to the German reserve trenches, back, farther away He was in the German front-line trench and he had to see that they brought back a new model German respirator, prisoners, trench maps. He turned to Fagioletti and began to say something, but the sergeant was diving behind one of the gas blankets into the dugout below. He came out a moment later and put his mask close to Laurence's ear. Laurence heard the voice, muffled and distorted, as though from inside a distant cave. "Lucky the first time, sir. 'Ere." He held out one hand, showing a bundle of folded maps. "All 'and drawn, sir."

"Prisoners?" Laurence shouted.

"They're all dead in there, sir . . . our grenades, just now."

Two soldiers came along the trench, one with a first field dressing on his forehead, the other with a dangling wrist, a German Mauser automatic pistol in his other hand; and, between them, a bespectacled German officer.

"He speaks English, sir," the man with the Mauser said. "Lieutenant Podalski, 112th Saxons, he says."

"And very glad to be taken prisoner," the German said. "I'm a Pole, sir, and Germany means no good to my country . . ."

"Take him back," Laurence said, stuffing the trench maps into his tunic pocket. Trench maps—done. Prisoners—done. Respirator . . . ?

Fagioletti said, "The German officer's wearing one of their latest pattern gas masks, sir."

Laurence said, "Good." What else then? There was something else, that Uncle Quentin had shouted at him. Ah . . . *kill Germans*. Was he supposed to kill the wounded? There were half a dozen dead Germans in the trench or lying against the back wall, and Fagioletti had said the dugouts were full of more of them . . .

The silence, the sense of isolation, were wiped away, blasted into another continuum as a hundred German guns opened up with shrapnel, gas, and HE on the occupied section of their front-line trench. Laurence's head began to swim . . . there were machine guns mixed in there, too, the beastly foul machine guns. The noise was indescribable, a vast tearing of canvas as the machine-gun bullets swept low over the trench . . . the continuous shaking thunder of the artillery fire . . . It became quiet, green, everything moving very slowly, gracefully . . . calm—no death, no rage, no haste . . .

"Christ A'mighty, he's gone again," Sergeant Fagioletti thought, seeing the young officer's eyes glaze behind the eyepieces. It was no use shouting at him when this happened. It was like he had been taken away by someone . . . God perhaps. He'd saved their lives when he got them down just before the star shells went up . . . just *before!* How did he know they were coming? He'd got their masks on a few seconds before the wind changed . . . *before!* He'd led into the trench, like a ruddy maniac . . . but never fired his pistol, though that big Jerry feldwebel had his Mauser rifle aimed from no more than ten feet away. And now . . .

"You sit there, sir," he said, pushing Laurence down onto a German ammunition box. "Don't move, sir."

The Jerries were firing everything they'd got . . . machine guns on fixed night lines, of course, to cover the front of their own trenches; the guns the same, but actually onto the trenches. There must be eight machine guns going at it up there. If you stuck your hand up it'd look like a colander in half a second. But the Germans didn't waste ammunition. If they were giving the trench such a pasting, they were going to counterattack. And when they did, the machine guns would have to stop. The guns would lift, or stop, too . . .

He hurried along the trench, and found Sergeant Parker standing by a traverse, a Mills bomb in his hand, several of his men covering the traverse with rifles aimed. A Lewis gun was mounted on the parapet, but the gunner was down, keeping his head below the sandbags.

"What's up?" Fagioletti shouted.

"Jerries behind that traverse . . . don't know how many . . ."

"Listen . . . soon's this hate stops, we'll withdraw . . . warn your blokes . . . just up and run for it . . . we've got the prisoner, trench maps, respirator, everything."

"All right . . . Four of my blokes have caught packets . . . Two napoo, two wounded bad."

"Leave 'em all here . . . Soon as you see Very lights go up, run like 'ell. Got it?"

"Bob's your uncle, Dago."

Fagioletti hurried back. Mr Cate was in the same place, absolutely withdrawn. Fagioletti felt in his haversack and drew out the Very pistol and the two cartridges, checking by the light of the bursting shells that he had a red and a green.

Privates Brace and Jessop were beside him. He muttered through his respirator into Brace's ear—"You go with Mr Cate, see that he gets back. If he cops it, take the German maps out of his right tunic pocket. Got it?"

He struggled on along the short stretch of captured trench, warning the men to be ready to run for it. The Germans would come any moment now, probably from three sides at once—from each end of the trench, and from the reserve trenches, over the top or up the communication trenches . . . The shelling and machine gunning stopped, he raised the Very pistol, already loaded with the red cartridge and fired, reloading at once with the green, firing straight up. The red star burst, floated down, followed by the green. He scrambled up the front wall of the trench and out. The Germans had not fired star shell yet . . . because their own men were up in the open, attacking from the reserve trench. The British guns started firing, the shells bursting close. Mr Cate was there, Brace at his side. He broke into an ungainly run. They were on their way home! Oh God, dear Jesus, let us get back before they find out we've gone and open up with star shell and machine guns . . .

Laurence Cate suddenly tore off his mask and yelled at the top of his voice "Down!" The men hesitated, and Fagioletti shouted, "Sir . . ." But then they all hurled themselves into shell holes, or flattened their bodies against the hard ground among the scattered debris of war. Star shells soared and burst overhead, and again machine guns opened up . . . but now a dozen, not the solitary one that had fired during their advance. The bullets clacked and rattled against the flaring sky, but still on the fixed lines, for the gunners had seen no target. Two by two the guns stopped. The star shells fell to earth, fizzling. Again it was dark. Fagioletti began to push himself upright when Laurence Cate's sharp voice barked, "Wait!"

The raiders heard him and waited, frozen to the ground, halfway across No Man's Land. Forty seconds later five star shells soared up. No Man's Land was brilliant as under a full moon, more so, as though lit by searchlights . . . dead, empty, nothing but twisted tendrils of barbed wire, humps, broken boxes, wheels, all frozen, dead.

Slowly the stars fell, the darkness returned and Laurence Cate cried, "Now . . . run!"

The soldiers scrambled up and ran helter-skelter for the gaps in the British wire, marked by the white cloth patches, now moved to the outer side of the aprons. Fagioletti ran just in front of Cate. How in hell did he know? It gave you a creepy feeling. Where had he been, back there in the Jerry trenches? Where was he now?

"Go on, sir," he said. But Cate waited, crouched by a gap in the wire, counting the men as they hurried through and dropped into the British trench. Sergeant Parker appeared and Cate said, "All present, sergeant?"

" 'Cept four I lost, yes, sir."

"Sergeant Fagioletti?"

"Yes, sir . . . We lost two. Come on, sir . . . Jerry's going to start on us any moment."

He jumped down into the trench, stumbling against the back wall, then recovering himself, ready to give the officer a hand; but Laurence Cate was coming slowly down the trench ladder, which no one else had used in their hurry to get below ground level. In the trench he saluted, his hand to his steel helmet, facing the anxious Captain Kellaway. "Raiding party returned, sir. Four killed, two seriously wounded left in the German trenches. Prisoner . . ."

"I've seen him. He's talking like a gramophone . . . can't tell us enough. You've done brilliantly, Laurence, brilliantly! The C.O. will be very pleased. He told me to send you back to him as soon as you came in. He wants to hear your report in person. But see to your men first. The C.O. will wait for you."

*   *   *   *

His uncle was sitting on the edge of his makeshift bed, fully dressed except for his tie and puttees, the knee fastenings of the breeches undone, heavy grey wool socks on his feet, which were stuffed into rubber trench boots, a greatcoat thrown round his shoulders. A mug of cocoa stood on the shellcase in front of him, beside a lighted candle in a bottle.

As Laurence entered he said, "Sit down, boy . . . You seem to have done well. Here, have some cocoa . . . Wait a minute." He felt on the board stuck into the sandbagged wall behind him, found a silver flask and poured three fingers of whisky into the mug—"That'll make it taste better."

Laurence drank greedily. He had not felt thirsty until this moment but now his mouth was parched. His uncle said, "Tell me about it."

"It was the men, sir," Laurence said. "Sergeant Fagioletti pulled me through . . . and Sergeant Parker was very good, too."

"What do you mean, Fagioletti pulled you through?" his uncle growled. "You were in command, weren't you? If it had all gone wrong it wouldn't have done to tell me Fagioletti failed. *You* would have failed. Still, I like to hear an officer giving credit to his men."

Laurence hesitated. He must somehow make Uncle Quentin understand how useless he was when the terrible noise began, the earsplitting murderous violations of silence. But his uncle wouldn't understand, wouldn't accept if he did. Instead he said, "I would like to put Sergeant Fagioletti in for the D.C.M., sir."

Quentin Rowland said, "Was he wounded? Did he force on to his objective when others were hanging back? What did he *do*, that it was not his duty, as a sergeant of the Weald Light Infantry, to do?"

Laurence wanted to say, he helped me, he took command when I was no longer there; but Uncle Quentin would say, "You *were* there, man!" So he answered the C.O.'s question in a low voice—"Nothing, sir."

"Right," Quentin said. "And the same goes for you, Laurence. In a lot of battalions you'd be put in for an M.C. for tonight's work, but I'm not going to. You did your duty, well. No one in the Weald Light Infantry's going to get a decoration for that as long as I'm in command . . . But you have shown that you are fit for your second pip. You can put it up right away. Congratulations."

"Thank you, sir." Laurence finished the cocoa and rose to go. Quentin stood, too, saying, "Your prisoner's a real prize. Telling us all he knows . . . He swears the Huns are going to mount a major offensive next month."

"What front, sir?"

"Ours," Quentin said. "He says they're stockpiling artillery ammunition behind the front now, so that all they have to do is move the actual guns—and the extra infantry—from other fronts when they're ready, and that won't take long, with the rail network there is in northern France . . . Well, good night, Laurence."

Laurence saluted, "Good night, sir." He stepped up and out into the clean, cold air. The stars glittered frostily, the air was still . . . all just as it had been so few hours ago, before the raid.

Daily Telegraph, Tuesday, February 26, 1918

FIRST DAY OF RATIONED LONDON
THE VANISHED QUEUE

For the first time in its long history London was partially rationed as a war-time measure yesterday. The limit of supplies to the individual was placed on meat, butter, and margarine. The outstanding features of the actions of the authorities were:

Disappearance of food queues.

Little demand for meat at meals away from home.

Cheerful acceptance of the new state of affairs by the public, caterers, and tradesmen.

Satisfaction of the Ministry of Food that early reports proved the scheme to be sound, and successful.

From the public point of view, so far as the opinion of eight to ten million people can be estimated from general discussion in restaurants, clubs, and public conveyances, the scheme met with almost universal support and approval.

AT THE RESTAURANTS

FEW MEAT MEALS SERVED

Restaurant proprietors regarded yesterday more or less as an experiment, but so few meat meals were served that many of the establishments that continued meat courses will probably abandon them after this week. The lunching public, in business areas, particularly in the City, had decided by a large majority not to dispose of even a half-coupon on a Monday . . . "About 1 percent of my customers" said a manager "have asked for meat meals . . . I could have sold five times the quantity of fish I prepared originally, and when I saw how the public was steering I secured some more fish. If this continues I shall join the ranks of the meatless caterers next week."

Cate read on, interested in the mechanics of the business. How would they prevent people selling their meat coupons? How would they detect forgery? A thought struck him--how would Stella get any meat if she was hiding somewhere in the jungle of the city, a non-person as far as the rationing authorities were concerned?

There had been a brief letter from John Merritt in the morning's post; he was in a camp "somewhere in France," and it was raining all the time. That was Brittany, Cate thought. They expected to move up to the front soon. Nothing about Stella . . . but then he himself had promised to wire, telephone, and write any news of her, as soon as he had any. John was relying on him.

He left the table and walked into the hall, to the telephone, and made a trunk call to Scotland Yard. The Commissioner's assistant said, "Yes, Mr Cate, I know the case . . . No, I'm sorry, we still have no clues . . . Yes, we are making certain that any unidentified female bodies reported to us are not your daughter."

Cate hung up, and went slowly to his library. As some men can not face the world, in hard times, without a drink of whisky, so he felt the need for the support of a philosopher. One of them, through the centuries, would have found words to give him strength.

Rawalpindi, Punjab, India:
late February, 1918

3 Lieutenant Fred Stratton, M.C., stood at attention before the desk of the commanding officer, 8th Battalion Weald Light Infantry. Beside him stood the adjutant of the battalion, Lieutenant Claude Mitchell, who had marched him in to be presented to the C.O., Lieutenant Colonel R.D.Q. Pulliam. Salutes had been exchanged, introductions made. The colonel said, "Stand easy, Stratton . . . Well, you're here at last, and we need you. This is a territorial battalion, as you know—I'm a stockbroker, really—but we like to think we are as good as the Regular battalions—almost."

Fred said nothing. He was tempted to say, "I'm a mechanic"; and perhaps a couple of years ago he would have; but now it would be inappropriate. He was an officer, and a *sahib*, a *pukka sahib*.

The C.O. continued, "You have, what, three years' experience on the Western Front, and an M.C., while we don't have a single officer or man here, except one of the C.S.M.s, who's even seen it. So I'm giving you command of B Company right away, where there is a vacancy. And you'll be promoted captain at once . . . As soon as you've settled in, I will want you to run a course in trench warfare, for the officers and senior N.C.O.s . . . Take him to the regimental *darzi*, Claude, and have him properly outfitted, by the day after tomorrow, for the dress rehearsal . . . How are you on drill, Stratton?"

"A bit rusty, sir. Didn't have much time for drill in France, though Colonel Rowland made the battalion do a lot whenever we were out of the line."

"Ah, Colonel Rowland, a legend, a legend . . . Well, that's all." He nodded. The two junior officers saluted, wheeled, and marched out.

Outside, Stratton said, "Dress rehearsal for what?"

"Friday's ceremonial parade for the Governor. We and an Indian battalion and a battery of 18-pounders are going to parade on the Maidan, where His Excellency will inspect us in review order, then we will march past to impress our subject native populace . . . only none of them will be there to be impressed. Now, let's see, you've already been allotted a quarter, I think? So we'd best get to the *darzi*."

"Who's he?"

"Tailor. He'll measure you for some drill uniforms, rather more regimental than those things you picked up in Egypt."

"But this rehearsal is for the day after tomorrow."

The adjutant was a plumpish man of about thirty, with sensuous lips, slightly bulging brown eyes, and thinning fair hair. He nodded now, smiling, and said, "Your uniforms will be ready for you tomorrow. Your bearer—I will get you one within the hour—will see that they are washed, starched, and ironed before the parade. You will also need a sweeper and a dogboy."

"I don't have a dog!"

"Better get one. A bull terrier's the best sort of dog . . . they like to bite natives. You have to have a dogboy anyway, otherwise the local population would suffer from unemployment, and it would be our fault."

"How much do I pay him?"

"Six rupees a month to the dogboy, twenty-five to the bearer, and ten to the sweeper . . . Tomorrow, at this time I will give you an hour's drill instruction—with your permission, Captain Stratton." He smiled a cynical smile. Fred thought, I don't like the bastard; but he's interesting, and he knows a lot. I'd better learn. This is a strange place, this India, this Shiny India he'd heard so much about from the Old Sweats of the Wealds when he was at the Depot, and in the 1st Battalion, until they'd all been killed off, or sent back to Hedlington as instructors . . . or even survived in the trenches, living fossils, like that Private Snaky Lucas he'd once had in his platoon . . .

*   *   *   *

"Royal Salute . . . preseent . . . *arms!*" The rifles crashed up to the present, the officers' swords swept up to the lips, then down.

Fred stood rigidly at attention in front of the centre of B Company, his sword hilt at his right thigh, the blade, flat, pointed down and forward. The massed bands of the battalion and of the 108th

Punjabis played "God Save the King." His Excellency the Governor of the province, wearing a grey frock coat, flanked by Aides de Camp in scarlet and gold, with gold aiguillettes, held his grey top hat three inches off his head.

"Royal Salute, for the Governor," Fred had asked the adjutant— "Why?" "Because he is the King's representative" was the answer . . . He was a long way off, and Fred couldn't see him very clearly but he certainly didn't look very impressive. It was funny to think that that little man could order all these troops about . . . even now the field guns were barking out the fifteen-gun salute to which he was entitled.

"Slope . . . arms! Order arms!"

Now came the inspection. His Excellency was walking forward across the sere grass of the Maidan. The brigadier general, in command of the parade, was strutting out to meet him. They met, more salutes, then the little group moved to the right of the line to inspect the horses and guns of the 18-pounder battery . . . The Maidan, which Fred had learned meant Plain, or parade ground, was also used for polo. Today it was almost empty of spectators except for perhaps two hundred women and children and a scattering of men—all British—behind the saluting base where the Union Jack fluttered in a gusty dusty breeze on top of its tall flagpole. Those were the hangers-on of the garrison—wives, sisters, nannies of officers; but, as Claude Mitchell had foretold—no natives. Well, to hell with the black buggers, Fred thought. This country belongs to us, we won it fair and square, and if they don't like it, they can do the other thing. Some liked it all right—to his left, beyond the last man of the Wealds, were the tall turbanned soldiers of the Punjabis . . . whoever *they* were. He hadn't had time to find out; and what did it matter?

He straightened. The grey top hat was swimming into view at the extreme edge of his circle of vision . . . coming close. Both A.D.C.s had large woofly ginger mustaches, round faces, pale blue eyes. The brigadier general was short and fat with no mustache but the same pale blue eyes. The Governor's eyes were brown.

The colonel said, "Captain Stratton, sir . . . just joined us from our 1st Battalion in France."

"France, eh? How long were you there?"

Fred realized with a start that His Excellency was three feet in front of him, and that he was the one being asked the question. He said, "Two years, eight months, one day, sir."

His Excellency's teeth shone in a smile. "I see. Time passes there on leaden feet, eh? Well, you deserve a rest and I hope you'll have one here. This is a beautiful province, and the people are friendly and loyal. The Punjab provided more men for India's war effort than all the other provinces combined. And do you know what the word Punjab means?"

"No, sir," Fred said.

His Excellency realized that he was holding up the parade and said, "Well, you'll learn, you'll learn." He passed on. Fred relaxed, thinking, there's too many things to learn in this country and I don't have the time. Soon's the war's over I'll be going back to France, and . . . *France?* There'd be no France after the war. So what would he be doing? Finding a foreman's job in Hedlington or Birmingham? Not bloody likely! Hadn't he just decided he was an officer and a sahib?

"The brigade will march past in quick time!"

He waited, at ease now, as the Governor's party took their positions on the saluting base under the fluttering, jerking Union Jack. First the guns would march past the Governor, then Colonel Pulliam would form the Wealds into close column of companies, the Colours, as now, between B and C; then "Quick March! . . ." and round the Maidan they would go, the dust rising and blowing away on the Asian wind, the dresses of the watching women fluttering, like the Colours, which now must fly free. He prayed that his company would keep a good line. They were only Territorials, but this was all that they'd been doing for three years now. They ought to be good at it.

They were off. The band changed from its measured beat for the artillery to "Green Grow the Rushes O," played at the lightning fast step of Light Infantry . . . bum bum bum beat the bass drum . . . Christ, it must be 150 paces a minute. His legs were twinkling as fast as they could, his sword was wobbling in his hand, the Colour bearers must be having a godawful time marching straight into the wind with the heavy silk banners flapping and gold cords and acorns flying . . . He was almost up to the saluting flag. He remembered he had to give the order himself . . . "B Company . . . Eyes . . . *right!*" He jerked the sword hilt up to his lips, and then down once more into the salute. One day he'd dig the point into the ground and then . . . They were past, God knew how he'd done. The brigadier general and the C.O. were up there beside the Governor . . . "B Company . . . Eyes . . . *front!*"

He heard the bellowing of C Company commander behind him. The band was slowing to the pace of heavy infantry. The Punjabis must be coming up to the saluting base. The battalion was wheeling round and back to its original position in line. His Excellency would be leaving any minute now. What the *hell* did Punjab mean? Why were there no spectators at the review, if the Punjab was so patriotic?

The starched collar of his tunic was cutting into his neck, and his armpits were dark and wet with sweat. The cold weather was almost over, they said. He was hot and uncomfortable . . . but safe. If this was the price he'd have to pay for being a sahib—it wasn't too bad.

✦   *   *   *

That evening Fred was standing at the bar of the Rawalpindi Club with Claude Mitchell, drinking *chhota pegs*—small whisky and sodas. From the ballroom the sound of ragtime penetrated faintly to the bar, making a high-pitched counterpoint to the gruff voices of the men in there. The garrison was celebrating. His Excellency the Governor himself was present, somewhere, but Fred had not seen him.

Mitchell said, "Did you find what 'Punjab' means?" Fred shook his head—"It's a compression of Panchh Ab—five waters, in Persian. Five rivers flow through the province—Sutlej, Ravi, Beas, Jhelum, Chenab. It ls a beautiful province, as H.E. said . . . Himalayas to the north, fertile plains below, the rivers . . . this is the breadbasket of India, produces most of the wheat . . . Even the cantonment isn't too bad, though I never think I'm going to run into Ortheris, Learoyd, and Mulvaney here, as I do in Lahore."

"Who are—those men?"

Mitchell turned and stared at him in astonishment, eyebrows raised comically. "Not weaned on R.K.? But, of course, you are not a public schoolboy, are you?"

"Of course I'm not," Fred said curtly. "And I don't try to hide the fact. You can take me or . . ."

Mitchell raised a plump hand, "Please, Fred . . . may I call you Fred? Please don't take offence. Between you and me, nor am I. Grammar school. This accent and the rest are protective colouring. But *they* were all brought up on Rudyard Kipling. After all he is the poet of the Empire, their Empire, isn't he? Ortheris, Learoyd, and Mulvaney were privates—imaginary—in what was probably the Northumberland Fusiliers, serving in India, in several of Kipling's short stories. If you're going to stay in this country more than a month or two, you'd better read some of him . . . An Indian *babu* I know, a very intelligent man, says that Kipling understands India very well. He adds that he doesn't understand Indians . . . but that's none of our affair, is it? I'll lend you *Soldiers Three* and *Kim* tomorrow . . . no, not tomorrow, I'm going out duck shooting to a *jheel* about twenty-five miles from here, near Mandra. Hey, why don't you come with me?"

"I don't have a gun," Fred said.

"I'll lend you one . . . We take the Frontier Mail to Mandra Junction and then a tonga about five miles to the dak bungalow, which is right by the *jheel* . . . some snipe at this time of year, too, but mainly duck, on their way north. What say?"

Fred hesitated. He didn't want to make a fool of himself and he knew nothing about duck or snipe shooting . . . Still, it appeared to be a favorite sport here, so he'd better learn.

"All right," he said. "Thanks."

"Great! Now, we ought to show ourselves on the dance floor. The C.O. likes his officers to dance, not just sit in here boozing, still less lurk in the snake pit poodle-faking . . ."

Fred finished his drink, scribbled his name on the chit—he had already discovered that sahibs never paid cash for anything in India—and followed Mitchell out of the bar, straightening his tie and checking his bugle-horn lapel badges as he went.

Mitchell stopped in the wide arch that opened onto the ballroom, surveying the crowded scene. The women were a moving sea of colour . . . very few plain white, mostly pinks, blues, and greens, with a few yellows. The men were all wearing khaki drill slacks and tunics, with shirt, collar, and khaki tie. There were not many medal ribbons, except on the older men, and the white-purple-white of Fred's Military Cross was quite conspicuous.

"Ah," Mitchell said, "just the ticket for you. Come along."

"What . . . ?" Fred began, following.

Mitchell stopped in front of a woman sitting in a chair against one wall of the ballroom. She was alone, but a vacant chair and two empty glasses on the small table beside her indicated that she had not always been. Mitchell said, "Good evening, Daphne. May I introduce one of our new company commanders? Captain Fred Stratton . . . Miss Daphne Broadhurst-Smythe."

Miss Broadhurst-Smythe was about thirty, quite tall, with a long face, blue eyes, hair of a rich mouse colour, and a pale complexion, lips also pale, mouth wide, and the hint of a frown between her eyes, which were set rather close to her high-bridged nose. She was not beautiful and had a vaguely vacant air, as though not fully aware of who or where she was.

Fred thought, now what do I do? Mitchell made a small gesture with his head toward the dance floor and Fred started. Of course! He said, "Would you care to dance, Miss Broadhurst-Smythe?" God, what a mouthful!

She said, "Thanks. That would be lovely."

She had an exaggerated upper-class accent, he noted. They moved onto the dance floor, Fred leading cautiously. He had been quite a dancer as a young man, but that was before the war, and dances had changed a lot since 1914.

"Do you live here?" he said.

She said, "My father's a colonel in the Remounts . . . I keep house for him . . . My mother died three years ago."

"Sorry to hear that," Fred said.

She cut in, "Daddy was Skinner's Horse . . . 1st Bengal Lancers, you know."

"Oh good!" Fred exclaimed. Jesus, this wasn't easy. He said, "I only arrived Monday . . . from France . . . via Egypt." He trod on her toes and muttered, "Sorry . . . bit out of practise."

"It doesn't matter."

"I'm going duck shooting tomorrow with Mitchell—Claude."

"Jolly good," she said, but she didn't sound very excited. "Daddy loves shikar . . . He's back at the table. Let's go there and I'll introduce you. He always likes to know who I'm dancing with. Too many cads about in officers' uniforms, these days, he says."

"Quite right," Fred mumbled. He followed her to the table. The colonel was very tall, thin, grey-mustached, narrow-headed with close-cropped grey hair. Daphne introduced him and the colonel sighed, "Ha . . . M.C., I see. France?"

"Yes, sir . . . 1st Battalion of the regiment."

"Good regiment . . . though of course this is only a Terrier battalion. You weren't a Regular, were you?"

"No, sir." He can tell by my accent, Fred thought; and then, belligerently, what the hell's it got to do with him?

"Do you ride?"

"No, sir."

The colonel's expression became condescending—"Pity . . . Shoot?"

Fuck you, Fred thought. Aloud, he said, "No sir . . . but I'm going out after duck with Claude Mitchell over the weekend. I thought I'd better learn for when I get back to England. My brother-in-law has a big estate and preserves pheasants."

"Pheasants?" the colonel said suspiciously. "That's an expensive game. Where?"

"Walstone, in Kent." Fred paused a moment then said, "My sister is married to Lord Walstone, of Walstone Park."

"Lord Walstone," Daphne said with a religious sigh.

"Hoggin that was," her father said. "Saw it in the New Year's Honours."

"Yes, sir."

"Lord Walstone," Daphne repeated. "You must come to tea with us soon, Captain Stratton. How about next Thursday?"

*   *   *   *

The two men tramped along in the darkness before dawn, twelve-bore shot guns under their arms, Mitchell's blue roan cocker padding to heel, stars lighting them along the pale road, four inches deep in dust, between its unkempt borders of prickly pear. It was a mile from the dak bungalow to the *jheel,* and they had now covered nearly half of it. The night was warm, but not hot, with a slight wind from the north carrying the green smell of the fields, under the young wheat, and from beyond, a fainter breath of the Himalayas.

"Nearly there," Mitchell said. "Heel, Sligo!" The cocker, who had strayed sniffing, dropped back to his proper position. "You'll have all the fishing fleet after you now that they know you're related to a lord."

"Brother-in-law," Fred said flatly. "And he was only Bill Hoggin till January 1st."

"Good enough for the girls of Rawalpindi," Mitchell said. "Since the war began the best they've had is solicitors not yet articled, shoe salesmen, bank clerks, all dressed up as officers . . ."

He turned off the cart track, slipped through a gap in the prickly pear, and said, "There we are." In front, a hundred yards away, a body of water perhaps three hundred yards long by a hundred wide glistened ghostly pale in the starlight. Darkness woven into the shimmer at the edges showed reed beds ten to twenty feet thick. A distant quack broke the silence and Mitchell muttered, "They're beginning to wake up . . . Here." He led on fast along the right side of the *jheel* until they reached a low mud wall, semi-circular in shape—"The blind . . . we built it last November at the beginning of the season." He moved into the semi-circle and sat down, his eyes now level with the top of the wall. He whispered, "They always get up just before the sun rises, then make two or three circuits of the *jheel* before flying off to their grazing grounds. So don't hurry your first shots—they'll be back . . . There may not be many. It's late and a lot have already started for Tibet and Sinkiang—that's where they breed."

They waited, side by side, the shot guns broken and cartridges laid out on top of the mud wall—No. 4 for the hard-breasted mallard. Fred wondered what he would see when the light came, beyond the pond, or *jheel* as they called it here . . . houses, cottages, trees? Or just the reaching flat plain, broken up into so many small fields, here and there little hovels seemingly made of straw? . . . He wouldn't shoot at a female if he could help it. She might be carrying eggs already, if it was so late in the season. Mallard drakes were distinct enough with that brilliant colouring he remembered from England . . . but would they be the same here?

He turned to ask Mitchell, but Mitchell spoke first—"They're getting ready. Load!"

The light was spreading from the east, behind them, as they looked down the long axis of the *jheel*. A stunted, twisted thorn tree guarded the far end of the lake like an ancient gnarled sentinel. To the right there was a field, green beginning to show along the ground. A tendril of mist was creeping out from the water across the field, nearly two hundred yards away. The water shone more brightly every moment . . . small dark objects were floating on it . . . over his shoulder a dull orange fire was burning below the horizon, three palm trees silhouetted against it. A clattering and quacking suddenly erupted and Mitchell breathed—"There they go!"

Dark lumps separated from the water, rose into the air, broke up into individual elements and began to whizz round the *jheel*, twenty feet up. They were coming straight over . . . Fred had his gun ready, loaded, safety catch off, the barrel swinging ahead of the lead mallard. Both men fired together, and then again, the second barrels. One duck hurtled into the water, "Mine!" Mitchell cried. "Watch it, Sligo!"

They waited, tense, as the flight circled the *jheel* and came again. Again Fred aimed carefully at the leading mallard drake, its plumage now brilliant green and black in the glowing light of dawn . . . both barrels . . . both missed. Another bird crashed down, this time hitting the ground ten feet behind them with a hard thud. Once more the flight wheeled over the sun, and came back, now nearly a hundred feet up. Fred swung more easily, gave his chosen bird a bigger lead, and, slanting his finger across the triggers, fired both barrels at once. The mallard wavered, half-turned as feathers flew out of its breast, then slowly curved down to earth, the angle of its fall increasing as its wings folded in death. To the right, Mitchell had killed another, a female. They waited, but the sun was breaking the rim of the horizon, and the flight of mallards, now reduced to a dozen, were winging fast across the plain toward the south.

Mitchell broke his gun and took out the cartridges with which he had immediately reloaded as soon as he had fired. "They won't come back till the evening," he said—"The evening flight . . . Short but sharp, wasn't it? . . . Rather like going over the top, I suppose?"

"Not much," Fred said.

"Well, let's walk up the fields on the off chance of putting up some snipe. There are two or three small *jheels* along here and the ground between's apt to be marshy, which snipe like . . . roast snipe for breakfast, yum yum!"

"Then what? It's only half-past six and we can't spend more than a couple of hours after snipe, I suppose."

"We go back to the dak bungalow, and do some Chinese P.T.—that is, sleep . . . or drink a few bottles of Murree beer, of which I brought two cases, as you saw . . . eat tiffin, which will be curried chicken—it always is, in every dak bungalow and inspection bungalow in India."

"What about a girl?"

Mitchell stopped and looked at him in mock horror, his thick eyebrows raised, the curved full lips making a moue of shock. "A woman? Out here barely five miles from Mandra Junction? My dear Fred Stratton, there are a couple of brothels in 'Pindi, which officers patronise—one even has a white girl in it—Rumanian, I believe . . . but apart from that, unless you can get any of the fishing fleet to part their legs for less than a wedding ring, you will have to be a virtuous celibate while serving in the Brightest Jewel of the British Crown. You must set an example to the natives. You must show that you are impervious to the petty lusts which make them what they are . . . unreliable, idle, ignorant, subservient . . . and dark-skinned. This way. We'll begin on this line."

A thin Indian peasant appeared from a mud hut at the edge of the field, wearing nothing but a turban and a loin cloth, his hands clasped together in silent supplication or obeisance. Mitchell said, "No, we are not going to tread on your crops . . . *chale jao!*"

*　　*　　*　　*

It was near ten o'clock at night, and a fire burned in the grate in the dak bungalow's central room, used for dining, drinking, and reading the old copies of *Blackwood's.* They had taken the evening flight, killed one duck—the flight was only six birds, all very wild—and then a mist had settled on the *jheel,* and they had returned damp and chilly to the bungalow. Now, dinner eaten—roast duck from the morning's bag—and the bearers gone to their places in the servants' quarters, Sligo curled up on the dhurrie under the open window, the two men talked. Whiffs of charcoal smoke, mixed with the acrid tang of a *bidi,* drifted in from outside, to be instantly drowned by Mitchell's pipe.

"Not a bad day," Mitchell said. "Six duck, four snipe . . . and a peacock."

"Why were you so upset when I shot it?"

"They're sacred to some Indians. The natives become restive if you shoot them. They even forget who's master."

"I don't understand how we can rule India," Fred said. "It was forty-eight hours in the train coming up from Bombay. I didn't see a white face except some of the other passengers. I thought there'd be British troops on guard everywhere. Why, there are more Indian soldiers here than ours."

"There are . . . but no Indian artillery, except mountain guns. If anyone's going to dish out whiffs of grape, it'll be us . . . Look, there's always been an Indian intellectual class. And now a middle class is coming into existence. They want to take over, and now they can say—every Indian can say when this war's over—that they've earned the right. They've fought everywhere at our side, and they're all volunteers, every man jack . . . in France, Gallipoli, Egypt, Palestine, Mespot, Persia . . . everywhere. They've had heavy casualties— especially from here, the Punjab. They're saying, 'Look, I'm grown up. Give me the keys.' "

"What are we going to do," Fred said, "just walk out?" He felt indignant. Brown-skinned people were inferior to white-skinned. The Old Sweats in the regiment when he joined had told him the only way to treat niggers was to kick them in the arse . . . and India belonged to England.

Mitchell said, "I don't know. I only know there'll be trouble . . . which means work for British soldiers—Aid to the Civil Power, Fred. Out in the streets shooting rioters. And it's always in some stinking city, in the middle of the hot weather. It's worse than the Frontier, which is fine, as we've just been told we're due up there in November. Just as *it's* ready to blow up too, if you ask me."

"What's their grievance?"

"They—the tribesmen who live along the North-West Frontier, object to us telling them whom they can shoot and plunder and whom they can't. They're fanatical Muslims, and we are infidels, so fighting us becomes a little jehad, a Holy War. And at the moment, where is the army that used to give them a real fight?"

Fred frowned, then said, "Oh, you mean it's in France."

Mitchell nodded—"Or dead. You haven't seen much of the 8th Wealds yet, but what do you think of us, compared with the 1st Battallion?"

Fred said, "They aren't a patch on us—them. There's no snap . . . pride . . . toughness of body and mind, I suppose."

"Why should there be? What have we done to learn those things? Parade for Governors and Viceroys . . . shoot rioters armed with bricks . . . bash our charpoys from Calcutta to Rawalpindi . . . No, the tribesmen can see perfectly clearly what's happened—the old army, British and Indian, has been sent off to fight a war somewhere else. The second-rate, the dregs, are left to guard the Frontier, so . . . let's have a bash. We'd better tighten up before we go up there, to the Frontier"—he jerked his head to the west—"because now we aren't fit for it . . . Another *peg*?"

"Yes, please . . . make it a *bara* this time."

"Ah, you're catching on."

*　　*　　*　　*

Fred was having tea with Miss Broadhurst-Smythe, and her father. The colonel was able to join them as it was Thursday, which, Fred had discovered, was always a whole holiday in India. The bearer, in spotless white with the yellow achkan and black cummerbund of Skinner's Horse, and the regimental crest on his starched turban, had served tea, and left. Fred held his cup warily, his little finger extended, like Daphne's.

The colonel was eating fruit cake and speaking angrily through it, as he was not in a good temper—"The natives need teaching a lesson," he said. "Damned fellow didn't stand up when I went into his shop before tiffin . . . Karam Chand, the cloth merchant. When I first came out to this country Indians had to lower their umbrellas or parasols if they passed you on the pavement . . . never saw one in a first-class compartment in a train either . . . They'll start ogling our women next."

Daphne said, "The war's upset them. They've been to Europe and killed white men, even if they were Germans."

"You think we'll be all right?" Fred asked cautiously. "I mean, that we'll stay in India for a long time?"

"For ever," the colonel said vigorously. "These people can never govern themselves, quite incapable of it. Look at the native States— corruption, inefficiency, nepotism, debauchery . . . Why, in . . ." He cut himself short.

Daphne said eagerly, "What, Daddy?"

"I can't tell you. Not even if you were married. Things go on in the States that no decent Englishwoman should hear—or would understand. And that's what the whole of India would be like if they were ever given self-government here . . . And as for the Frontier, why, the tribes would be on them before you could say knife . . . and knife would be the right word. In a month there wouldn't be a rupee or a virgin between the Indus and Delhi . . . Have a piece of cake, Stratton."

"Thank you, sir." Fred took a slice off the proffered plate.

Daphne said, "What's Walstone Park like, Captain Stratton? May I call you Fred? I seem to have known you for so long."

"Please do, Miss Broadhurst-Smythe."

"Please call me Daphne."

"Thank you, Daphne . . . well, Walstone Park's a very big house, a mansion, and it's also the estate, the park . . . about a thousand acres, I think, and . . ."

Daily Telegraph, Thursday, March 7, 1918

ROUMANIA SIGNS PEACE

According to a Bucharest telegram received via Vienna at Amsterdam yesterday, and forwarded by Reuter's correspondent, the preliminary peace between Roumania and the enemy Powers was signed at Buftea on Tuesday evening. The text of this treaty is as follows:

Animated by a common wish to terminate the state of war and restore peace between Germany, Austria-Hungary, Bulgaria, and Turkey on the one part, and Roumania on the other part the signatories . . . after an examination of their full powers, have agreed . . . that . . . a fourteen-day truce is to run from midnight March 5, 1918, with a period of three days for its denunciation. Complete agreement exists between the signatories that a final peace is to be concluded within this period on the basis of the following agreement:

I. Roumania secedes to the Allied Powers the Dobrudja as far as the Danube.

II. The Powers of the Quadruple Alliance shall provide for the maintenance of a trade route for Roumania via Constanza to the Black Sea.

III. The frontier rectifications demanded by Austria-Hungary on the Austro-Hungarian-Roumanian frontier are accepted in principle by Roumania.

IV. The economic measures corresponding to the situation are likewise conceded in principle.

V. The Roumanian Government undertakes to demobilize immediately at least eight divisions of the Roumanian Army . . .

This treaty has, of course, been forced on Roumania by the course of events, over which she had no control . . . The terms propose to ignore the principles of nationality and do violence to Germany's own declarations against annexation . . .

Cate sat back, drinking his coffee. What all that boiled down to was that Roumania had been knocked out of the war: which would free the enemy to move more troops to the Western Front, and against Italy. It was another chill warning that when the expected German assault came, it would be no light matter. Whom would they attack? The British line seemed to be the favorite, in the rumors and speculations; but surely it would be better, from the German point of view, to attack the French? Everyone knew by now how close the French had been to collapse last spring and summer. Their morale could not be high . . . and it was such a short distance, in a straight line, from

Verdun to Paris . . . and so to the Atlantic ports where the Americans were pouring in.

Americans . . . John, Stella; he must not call the Commissioner again or they'd write him off as a damned nuisance . . .

Garrod came in with the mail, for the postman was late today . . . perhaps the train had been late; and there had been very heavy rains, flooding the Scarrow across some roads. His heart leaped when he saw the handwriting on the top envelope. He opened it with trembling hands:

London, March 6, 1918 . . . My dearest, darling Christopher—It has taken me for ever to get this letter started. It is to tell you that as soon as Stella is found, and I am sure it can not be long now, I will return home. Being in England, so close to you and yet so far, so impossibly separated, is tearing me apart—just as it did before I left last time. I don't want anyone else, only you . . . Isabel.

Cate's head drooped and a tear fell on the letter in his hand. He hardly heard Garrod's low murmur—"Mrs John Rowland, sir . . . She said it was urgent."

Then his sister-in-law was in the room, pulling up a chair, too intent on her own business to notice his state—"Christopher, you've *got* to come in with us now. Roumania out of the war . . . ghastly offensive coming, thousands of dead, wounded, maimed. We must stop the war *now*, by any and every means available to us . . . strikes, sabotage, lie on the railway lines, in front of lorries . . . You're not listening."

"I'm listening, Louise," Cate said wearily. "But there's nothing we can do . . . least of all when it's the Germans who are just about to mount an offensive."

"But we must!" she cried. "It'll hit our children, our families . . . Quentin, Laurence, Guy, even Naomi . . . And, Christopher, you must realize that Laurence simply isn't fit for the front line. Everyone knows that, but you."

"He's there," Cate said. "He'll have to do his duty, like the rest of us."

France: mid March, 1918

4 Lance Corporal Naomi Rowland, First Aid Nursing Yeomanry, stood by the front wheel of her ambulance, beating her gauntleted hands together to keep them warm against the bitter cold. The moon was high and full, a round pale yellow disc smiling—leering, surely—down on her, on the poplars lining the Somme canal and its placid waters, the dense reed beds at either side, and the line of motor ambulances, each marked with a big red cross on the canvas sides and roof, waiting at the barge station of St Sauveur. One barge had already been unloaded of its cargo of wounded men—men too severely wounded to be able to withstand the bumping on the pavé all the way from the Casualty Clearing Stations to the base hospitals or ambulance trains; but there was a delay in getting the next barge unloaded, and while the Royal Army Medical Corps orderlies and the convoy medical officer struggled, the F.A.N.Y. drivers waited.

Naomi lifted the steel helmet off her head and rolled up the balaclava cap she had been wearing over her ears. The convoy commander or lieutenant would be shouting orders any moment, and she couldn't hear very well with the balaclava down . . . but, oh how the cold bit into her unprotected ears now! She covered them with her gauntlets and walked up and down, stamping on the hard ground of the wharf, muttering to herself, "Hurry up, hurry up!"

"Cars seven, eight, nine, ten . . . move up!" the command was clear, in the lieutenant's high, clear voice. Naomi climbed up quickly into the driver's seat and waited for No. 8, ahead of her, to move. Her engine was turning over quietly, as they had not switched off. No. 8

began to move and Naomi engaged first gear and crawled along behind . . . so close to the edge of the wharf, just behind the squat wooden bollards where the barges tied up for the night in peacetime . . . wheels along the edge . . . brake carefully—the ground was hard now, but with half an inch of snow or black ice there, you could slide gently between the bollards and over . . . at the wharf the canal was eight feet deep.

An R.A.M.C. orderly came to the side of the ambulance, peering up at her, "Ah, it's Miss Rowland . . . congrats on the stripe, miss . . . saw it when we was coming down but didn't have time to say anything." He ran round the back of the vehicle to open the doors, as other orderlies walked carefully across the planks linking the next barge to the land, carrying stretchers. Naomi saw the first wounded man's face quite clearly as he passed—clammy white under the full moon, hollow, dark eyes staring up at the moon, a pale stubble on the chin, but young, so young, eighteen, nineteen . . . and below—there was no substance below his chest, the blanket lying almost flat on the stretcher. What had happened, how could a man live with nothing below the chest? The springs of the ambulance creaked as the orderlies loaded the stretcher into the back . . . here came the next, this one unable to stare at anything, because his whole head was swathed in bandages, an Egyptian mummy being transported from one four-thousand-year grave to another, for eternity . . . And another . . . A whistle shrilled, and Naomi grabbed the snap front flap of her gas mask, slung high on her chest, ready to rip it open and put on the mask. Damn, damn, her balaclava was down again and she couldn't hear. The orderly ran past, shouting up at her, "Air raid, miss! Gothas! Take cover!"

Naomi jumped down from her seat, jamming the helmet onto her hair and pulling the chinstrap under her chin. She began to run as she heard a long whistling sound and then a tremendous crash a hundred yards to her right, toward the village of St Sauveur up a gradual rise from the canal. The next bomb seemed to be coming straight at her and she flung herself flat on the ground. Waiting, she jammed her hand into her mouth, she must not, would not scream. The bomb struck in the reeds across the canal and burst with a heavy muffled explosion under water. A few seconds later a torrent of icy mud and water splashed down on her. She scrambled to her feet and began to run again . . .

She stopped. Where was she to go? Where was there cover on this flat wharf beside the canal, shining silver in the moonlight? Looking up she could see the bombers silhouetted against the moon . . . three, four, and now she heard the drone of their engines inextricably mingled with the whistling and intermittent thunder of their bombs. Dirty swine, deliberately aiming at ambulance barges, all clearly marked with red crosses . . . Those wounded men were alone, and *they* could not run for shelter.

She walked back to her ambulance, willing herself not to run, or crouch. She reached it and heard two voices calling, "What's happening? Miss, miss, where are you? . . . Don't leave us."

She stuck her head in through the open back flap and called "It's all right, fellows. I won't leave you. The Germans are dropping a few bombs . . . the red crosses make good aiming marks but they haven't hit one yet."

A man chuckled and said, "You're a good 'un, miss . . . Who are you?"

"We're the Fany," she said, sitting on the back floor of the ambulance, her legs dangling. In the moonlight she could see the three men—the one with no body, the mummy, and another—the one who had spoken just now. She began to talk in a low voice, but loud enough so that they could hear above the droning and the crashes—"I'm Naomi Rowland . . . my father's a farmer in Walstone, Kent . . . my grandfather used to make Rowland motor cars . . . I was in the Women's Volunteer Motor Drivers for a time, then I transferred to the F.A.N.Y. We . . ."

The sound of the engines was fading, and the explosions had ceased. Footsteps were coming along the wharf, running. The lieutenant was there, peering in—"Rowland? Well done . . . We're finishing loading now."

"Yes, madam." The lieutenant ran on. Naomi said to the men, "We'll be moving off soon. The road's pretty bumpy but I'll do my best to dodge the biggest potholes."

The wharf was alive with movement again in the moonlight. The fourth casualty for No. 9 was brought up and loaded in; Nos. 10, 11, 12, 13, 14 were loaded. The lieutenant hurried down the line—"Move off in order, following me in No. 1."

The R.A.M.C. orderly jumped in beside Naomi. Naomi moved slowly off in her turn, following No. 8 off the wharf onto the narrow road up to St Sauveur. The orderly said, "Wish I 'ad your nerve, miss. Feel proper ashamed of myself I do, lying under the 'edge while you was sitting on the back there . . . saw you plain as a pikestaff in the moonlight, and those bleeding, beg your pardon miss, those Jerries aiming at you."

Naomi said briefly, "I doubt if they could really see the red crosses from where they were. They were very high . . . And we'd be less likely to be bombed if the army didn't use barges to carry artillery ammunition up the canal . . . and put ammunition and ordnance depots right next to base hospitals and ambulance convoy quarters."

He said something more, but she did not answer, for she had not listened. This was no time for small talk . . . driving a heavy ambulance with four desperately wounded men in it, on a narrow French road, only dim blue headlights, following the faint red spot of the tail light of the car in front . . . with army lorries likely to be crashing along the same road in the opposite direction, loaded with petrol or high explosives, or guns moving up at a canter, or those ghastly monster tanks on their wide treads, clanking and growling through the night, taking up the whole road . . .

The convoy crawled through St Sauveur, turned west . . . five miles to go to Advanced Base Hospital Number 26 . . . change gear, touch the brake . . . swing carefully round something in the ditch, an A.S.C. lorry, boxes strewn all over the place, . . . slow still more . . . infantry marching up, steel helmets glinting in the moonlight, shoulders bowed, here and there a man looking up, but it was too dark in the cab for any of the soldiers to recognize that it was a woman driving . . .

Lights ahead . . . long lights, pointing lights, weaving back and forth. The orderly beside her whistled through his teeth—"Them Jerries is following us around." They were searchlights and now suddenly, directly over the dark hump of No. 8 ambulance in front of her, Naomi saw a Gotha caught in them, a silver moth, and at once dark blobs spouting all round. "The ack acks have got the bastard," the orderly shouted exultantly. Naomi looked down . . . the road, the road! The convoy was moving toward the searchlights. It must be another raid, different Gothas—the first lot had unloaded all they had on St Sauveur. An anti-aircraft battery was in action close beside the road, the long barrels jerking, the guns barking with sharp cracks. From the field beyond, a pair of searchlights sent up white needles to stab the sky. She heard again the crash of bombs and saw bursts of yellow and orange light, all from directly ahead.

"They're aiming at the hospital," the orderly muttered.

"Or the ammunition depot," she said.

The convoy was slowing, but moving on. Here was the hospital drive; it had once been a big château set in lovely parklike grounds, now occupied by huts and shacks of every kind. There in front was the graceful three-storied facade of the château itself. Flames seemed to be rising from the back of the great building, mixed with clouds of black smoke, that grew thicker as the convoy of ambulances approached, crawling up the curving, graveled drive. The car in front stopped and Naomi stopped, waiting. A voice from behind the canvas cried, "What's up now, miss?"

She called back, "The Gothas have been following us from the wharf. It's how they find their way home."

They chuckled behind the canvas. The ambulance shuddered to the crash of bombs, none now very close, but the earth was shaking under their irregular explosions. The cars inched forward, as their casualties were unloaded, three cars at a time. The orderly jumped down and hurried forward to take his share in the unloading. As soon as a car was empty it swung on round the drive, ready to return to the F.A.N.Y. convoy camp.

Naomi's turn came, and a gang of orderlies hurried up, opened the back, and began to carry out the stretchers. Searchlights were still wavering across the sky, but she could not hear engines. Or big bombs. There were a lot of smaller explosions, but they didn't sound like bombs, and they fell into similar patterns . . . two or three, then suddenly half a dozen, like a string of crackers, now and then one much bigger.

A man came hurrying down the château's main front steps and ran to Naomi's ambulance. He peered in and said, "I've got to get some armoured electrical cable from the Engineer Stores Park . . . no other transport . . . will you take me?"

Naomi said, "We're unloading casualties, sir."

He peered closer, "A woman! In this?"

"We're the F.A.N.Y., sir," she said, with some asperity.

"It's urgent, miss," he said. "They can't operate in there without light and their cables have been burned out. I've got to get them hooked back onto the town supply. It really is a matter of life and death."

Naomi hesitated then said, "There's our lieutenant, at the foot of the steps. Ask her. If she says yes, I'll take you."

The man said, "Right," and hurried off. Naomi saw him in the diffused glare from the fire at the back of the château, gesticulating a little, the lieutenant looking up at him—she was short and the man was taller even than Naomi, who was 5'10". Then they both came toward her, and the lieutenant leaned in, "You know what Lieutenant Gregory wants, corporal?"

"Yes, madam."

"Take him, get it, bring him and it back here, then return to camp on your own. I'm taking the rest of the convoy back as soon as we're all unloaded."

"Very good, madam."

"You're unloaded now . . . hurry up and get that back fastened, please, men . . . All right, Rowland. Good luck."

Lieutenant Gregory scrambled up beside her and she engaged gear and moved off, pulling out of line to pass the cars in front of her. She said, "You'll have to tell me where to go, sir."

"All right . . . left out of the château gate . . . sorry to let you in for this."

"It shouldn't take long."

"No . . . but all that crackling and flashing ahead is an ammunition dump going up—mostly 18-pounder and 4.5-inch howitzer shells, I believe. The Gothas dropped two smack in the middle . . . and we have to go past it to reach the Engineer Stores Park."

Naomi said nothing. The moon was still high but its light was not bright as it had been earlier. Perhaps the smoke from the hospital fire, and the exploding ammunition, or other fires, was obscuring it. And she had no car to follow, but must find her own way, on a strange road. It was impossible to go faster than ten miles an hour.

She swerved violently to avoid something humped black in the road . . . a dead horse . . . on, even slower for a time until she regained her confidence . . . "Right at the next cross roads," the lieutenant said. His voice was a little unsteady and Naomi felt better. She said, "Are you a sapper?"

"Yes. Temporary officer only, of course."

"Are you mad, married, or Methodist?"

"Eh? I'm sorry, I don't understand, miss."

She kept her eyes on the dim road, the faint blue glow from her headlights illuminating it, now often overridden by brilliant flashes from the fields to the left. Things whistled overhead, whining away into the distance, or crashing into the earth, the trees, the road . . . shells or parts of shells from the exploding depot.

She said, "My uncle's a Regular. Weald Light Infantry . . . I remember him saying that all Royal Engineer officers are mad, married, or Methodist."

He managed a laugh then and said, "Not guilty on any count, miss—corporal . . . This is like something out of *The Inferno* . . . straight ahead here . . . God, that one was close . . ."

It had been, indeed, since it had ripped a long gash in the canvas cover over Naomi's head, but it had not exploded, whatever it was. To their left an area of about a hundred acres was coruscating like a giant 5th of November firework display, yellow flashes bursting out of the ground, out of the scattered heaps of tarpaulin-covered shells, orange and red flares darting into the sky leaving trails of smoke.

They passed it and Gregory said, "Close now . . . left . . . there, that's the gate. The cable store's close." He jumped down and ran to the barbed wire kniferest pulled across the entrance to the Park. Then he ran to a small wooden hut close by, and banged on the door. It opened at once and a soldier appeared. He saluted, and came out. The two men hurried down between the huts beyond, and disappeared into one. Three minutes later they reappeared, each carrying two heavy coils of armoured electrical cable over his shoulders.

Naomi ran round and opened up the back flap of the ambulance. The men dumped the coils inside and the lieutenant helped her refasten the back. The soldier returned to his hut, and the lieutenant climbed back beside her. He said hesitantly, "There is another way round, to get back to the hospital . . . It'll take us fifteen minutes longer, but . . ."

She said, "I thought it was a matter of life and death, sir."

"It is . . . yours, too."

She said nothing, but headed back, retracing her course. Lieutenant Gregory was obviously a little nervous; and he really seemed to be worried for her safety, too. Because she was a woman . . . she'd not have any condescension from him, or any other man, ever again.

They were approaching the ammunition depot. It had lost none of its infernoesque qualities—if anything, they had increased. She felt herself crouching over the wheel, and forced herself to straighten up: she did not present any smaller target that way, and she could see the road much better. The lieutenant huddled beside her said, "Christ . . . well done, miss . . . pheeew!" Light glared in her eyes now, as a dozen shells from a dump close to the road went off together. A splinter clanged against her steel helmet, jerking it off her head. The lieutenant grabbed it before it fell over the side. Now there was a hole in the canvas beside her as well as over her head . . . two hours' work there, re sewing all that, and redoping the patches. lucky nothing mechanical had been hit . . . yet.

The maniacal fury of the explosions fell behind. The lieutenant lit a cigarette with shaking hands and offered it to her. She shook her head, saying, "Thanks, no, sir."

She had done it, forced the lieutenant to do what he really knew ought to be done—get back to the hospital by the fastest route. All her life till now she had relied on people, particularly men—her father, her brother Boy, Rodney Venable; but Boy was dead, her father a broken man, and Rodney Venable—a ripple in time past. They came to her for reliance now . . . the girls in the convoy; her father, when she was home on leave, she knew; this male lieutenant. She would stand on her own feet now; she wanted to, and she had no alternative . . . except grovel.

The lieutenant said, "I'm Ron Gregory, Miss Rowland. I'm really an electrical engineer—Manchester University. I don't think I've ever felt more humble . . . or admired anyone more . . . than this past half-hour, watching you."

"We're the F.A.N.Y., sir," she said.

He said, "I know, but you're even more, Miss Rowland. I'd . . . I'd very much like to meet you again. Do you get a few hours leave at any time . . . go into Amiens? Could I come and call on you?"

She turned into the driveway of the château. The fire at the back seemed to have been subdued, but black smoke still rose heavy and dark in the moonlight over the whole great building. She said, "We're No. 16 Convoy, F.A.N.Y., . . . based at Ailly at the moment. But I don't know when . . ."

He said, "I'll come over tomorrow . . . to thank your C.O. for letting you drive me to the Park depot . . . and to tell her what a great job you did. Then we'll fix something. Surely we can find some free time before the big German push starts? You've made me feel . . . well, a better man, Miss Rowland."

"Thank you," she said. "Here we are, sir."

*　　*　　*　　*

Major Guy Rowland, D.S.O., M.C., commanding officer of No. 333 Squadron, Royal Flying Corps, led his squadron round to the northwards in a gentle turn, maintaining his altitude at 12,000 feet. Ten other Sopwith Camels of the squadron followed round in tight formation of four Vs, each flanking aircraft stepped up slightly above its leader, each V slightly above the one ahead. The winter sun was climbing in the east, over his right shoulder, the rays now glistening on the thin layer of hard-packed snow covering the ground far below. The dark trench lines were to the left, for the squadron was ten miles the German side of the front.

Guy turned his head briefly to check the formation of his four flights . . . a plane short in A and C, one damaged on landing yesterday and one shot down the day before, no replacement arrived yet. The formation was good, just as he had ordered and practised it—flights and machines close enough to act in concert, far enough apart to give the individual pilots and flight leaders room to maneuver. They were well disciplined: his predecessor in command, "Sulphuric Sugden," had seen to that; but now they were more, they were almost of one mind, one spirit. When he led them into action, they opened fire simultaneously without any signal from him; if a pilot was about to be trapped by two or three Germans, suddenly four of the Three

Threes appeared, trapping the Germans. His own score of kills had almost ceased to climb; but his squadron's had doubled, in the two months since he took over. He felt now that he was a Master of Foxhounds, not himself killing foxes, but finding them, leading his pack to them, indicating the way to attack, then supervising the action to correct anything that went wrong, to whip them off onto more important scents if . . .

"Tally ho!" he shouted to himself, and waved his gloved hand, pointing downwards. Three dark specks were racing eastward over the white mantle of snow. He stared hard as he flipped the Sopwith's nose down . . . A.E.G. bombers, probably G.IVs—machine guns nose and tail, so attack from below: crew of two . . . on their way back from bombing the infantry in the trenches, probably. The flights were behind him, hurtling down at close to 150 miles an hour, guns cocked and ready. They'd intercept in a minute and a half, five or six miles farther east . . . have to watch the petrol, as the wind was 25 to 30, dead in their faces for the trip home. He looked at his watch . . . 8.24 . . . cut off the action at 8.34 unless by chance it led back to westward. He was diving straight under the leading A.E.G. now, about 400 yards away and at the same altitude. A short burst of tracer bullets flying over his head from behind made him frown in anger—the range was much too great yet . . . but he looked round quickly. It was B Flight leader who had fired, to attract his attention. He was pointing up now . . . specks glittering in the sun; probably Jasta 16's Triplanes. Guy pushed his right hand out toward the specks, palm flat. B Flight leader waggled his wings in acknowledgment, and turned his flight up into the sun, to protect the others as they closed in on the A.E.G.s.

More specks appearing in the north . . . more Triplanes. But he wasn't going to let those A.E.G.s get away. He looked round at D Flight leader, and pointed ahead at the A.E.G.s, the hand stabbing. D Flight continued on course to attack the lumbering bombers, as Guy led A and C up to join B against the Triplanes.

As the Camels climbed, engines roaring, Guy's peripheral vision caught smoke . . . tracer fire . . . an aeroplane falling. One of the A.E.Gs was down . . . another . . . Now for the Tripes . . . five of them . . . where was Werner? Must be sick, he'd never allow his planes to wander round the sky in penny packets like this . . . or on leave, getting married, as he'd said in his latest letter . . . the last A.E.G was down in flames, and D Flight hurrying back up to join him . . . Above, B Flight waited, circling wide round the Germans . . . he was up level with the Fokkers now, and half a mile to the west of them. D was 3,000 feet down still, a sitting target if the Fokkers dived now

. . . of course they'd pay the price, for Guy would then dive behind them with his other three flights. Suddenly the Germans turned and headed east, in long shallow dives. Guy looked at his watch . . . 8.31.

He wheeled the Three Threes back into formation, flying north, 12,000 feet. 8.34. He waved his hand slowly round his head in a wide circle, and swung on course for home. Down there were the front lines . . . two bumbling Harry Tates spotting for the artillery . . . four, five, six observation balloons . . . . the spire of Amiens cathedral . . . Mirvaux . . . stick forward, blip, on, blip, ease back, blip, on, . . . bump, bump, roll . . . switch off.

The adjutant of the squadron was waiting as he taxied into place. Sergeant Frank Stratton, his fitter, ran forward to help him down. The adjutant came forward, his wooden leg creaking in the immaculate King's Dragoon Guards' field boots. Guy took off his flying helmet and swung it free. Now that he wasn't personally killing so many Germans, it was a relief not to have to face the vomiting of the old days, which from the beginning had invariably stricken him when he landed after a kill. "What is it, Dandy?" he asked. "We got three A.E.G.s—G.IVs I think. We'll have to confirm it."

"The Wing Commander will be pleased, sir," the adjutant said. "He's here. In your office. With a Member of Parliament."

"An M.P.," Guy groaned. "More ruddy stupid questions, explanations they don't understand."

He saw that the adjutant was smiling, and stopped. "Oh. It's Grandfather—the Governor, my father calls him."

"Yes, sir. Visiting the front. He says he's only got a few hours, then this afternoon he's due in Amiens to visit the G.O.C., L. of C., and see some rear installations . . . He said he has a granddaughter somewhere round here with the F.A.N.Y.s."

Guy nodded—"My cousin Naomi. She's at Ailly . . . I drove down there last week, after the big Boche air raid. She was fine. Has a Sapper pursuiter after her, apparently."

He opened the door of the hut and stopped, seeing his grandfather in one of the hard chairs against the wall, the Wing Commander standing by the window. Guy saluted, and his grandfather rose unsteadily to his feet, holding out his arms. "Is it all right to hug a major?" he asked as he embraced his grandson. Guy saw tears in the old man's eyes; his hair was very white and he had shrunk inside his clothes, the heavy overcoat hanging loosely on him.

The Wing Commander said, "I'm off, Rowland . . . Call me as soon as you've spoken to your pilots."

"I'm pretty sure we got three A.E.G.s, sir."

"You personally?"

"None, sir."

The lieutenant colonel nodded and said, "Talk freely to your grandfather, Rowland."

"I'm not a front bencher," Harry Rowland said. "But some of the important ones seem to listen to me. Churchill does. Even the P.M. always has time for me."

"Because you're an honest man, sir," the colonel said. "A good politician has to know one when he sees one, however rare they are." He in his turn saluted, and went out.

The adjutant said, "Do you want me, sir?"

"No, Dandy. See that the I.O. gets on with the pilots' reports before they forget the details . . . You'll have lunch with us here, Grandfather?"

"Certainly, my boy."

Guy pulled out the swivel chair, with padded arms, that was his own and said, "Sit here, Grandfather . . . I'll take you round the squadron later—you must meet the riggers and fitters as well as the pilots—we would all be dead ducks without them, but they don't get any glory."

"They have votes," Harry said. He sat down. Guy offered him a cigarette and the old man waved it away with a grimace, "Never touch those things. I'd love a cigar but the doctor's said no . . . Well, tell me, Guy . . . we in Parliament only want one thing, to win the war, as quickly as possible, and at the least possible cost. What can we do, as far as the R.F.C is concerned, to achieve it?"

Guy walked slowly back and forth across the front of the table while his grandfather leaned back in the swivel chair, listening, sometimes making a careful note in the small leatherbound book he had produced from an inner pocket—"I fly Scouts, and they're the most glamorous—we have dogfights with von Rackow and Richthofen and the rest of them. We get the publicity, but really a Scout is a defensive machine . . . our job is to protect our air space from intrusion. Often we enforce this by going into German air space and attacking their machines there, in the air or on the ground, but it is all for the same purpose—to protect our air space. What the air force needs to do now is attack, occupy the German air space . . . not to protect ours, but to further our war aims. We should bomb German submarine bases . . . arms factories . . . railway junctions . . . important road and rail bridges . . . The force that does these things must not think of itself as a sort of army or navy in a different uniform—it must be an *air* force, thinking and fighting in terms of the air, which covers the trenches, the factories, the fleets, the submarines, the railway junctions—everything. We hear that a new combined air service is going to be formed—that's what General Trenchard's supposed to be working on . . . and we younger men think nothing must be allowed to stop it, not jealousy or narrow-mindedness on the part of the navy, or the army, not shortage of money—nothing. We must use the air, everywhere, for our war purposes, and so we must be fully airmen, solely airmen, as much as the navy were sailors in Nelson's time . . ."

Harry said, "I know that something of that kind is under study now. I believe that the chief opposition comes from the navy."

"They mustn't be allowed to scuttle the idea," Guy said energetically. "They hate aircraft the way they hate submarines, because they make their expensive battleships vulnerable . . . but there must be a Royal Air Force, and when it is really working, the navy will be as eager to have it used to help them as anyone . . . That's the main point, the creation of a separate, independent air arm. We can talk about other things while we're going round. Ready?"

Harry Rowland struggled to his feet, putting away the notebook. "I'm ready, Major Rowland," he said. He patted his grandson on the shoulder. "Major Rowland," he repeated. "Who'd ever have believed it, four years ago? But I'd still rather it was Guy Rowland, Esquire, Kent and England, 6 for 33 against the Australians at Lord's. Will that day ever come?"

"Heaven knows," Guy said, holding the door open for his grandfather to precede him out into the wintry air.

* * * *

2nd Lieutenant John Merritt, U.S. Field Artillery, stood behind the row of four 75-mm guns, his binoculars to his eyes, observing the fall of the shot on the practise target, a hedge line on the snow-covered hillside three miles ahead. The shells were not falling evenly along the line, but bunching, mostly toward the right end of the 200-yard-long target. He raised his right arm over his head, shouting "Cease firing!"

The sergeants in charge of each half-section bellowed "Cease firing!", slapping the gunner of each gun on the shoulder as they did so. The guns fell silent.

At John's side the battery commander, Captain Hodder, said, "Now, what is the problem with the sheaf? You have a minute to find out."

John bellowed, "Repeat range! Battery left at five-second intervals!"

The left-hand gun fired at once, and five seconds later No. 2 fired . . . John watched, absorbed, through his binoculars . . . No. 1 was too far right . . . No. 2, the same . . . No. 3, on target . . . No. 4, on target . . . The first section was off. He shouted, "No. 1, No. 2, left 4 mils . . . No. 1, repeat range!" No. 1 gun fired . . . on target . . . No. 2, on target. John had begun to order "fire for effect" when the captain said, "End of mission, Mr Merritt . . . Mr Anspach, your mission . . . We are required to lay a smoke screen fifty yards in front of the previous target. You have three minutes to work out the necessary orders . . . Mr Merritt, fall out."

John saluted and left his post. An automobile was coming up the rutted farm road behind the battery positions, flying a two-starred flag from its right fender staff. The captain had seen, and was walking toward the car, which had stopped. The driver sprang down and held the rear door open. Major General Gary F. Castine, U.S.A., commanding general of the division, climbed down, acknowledging Hodder's salute. He was followed by a white-haired old man in a heavy civilian overcoat and a black bowler hat. John started and cried out, "Mr Rowland!" He bit his lip. He was at attention, saluting the general, and he'd been in the army long enough to know to keep his mouth shut. But Harry Rowland had seen him and was coming forward, hand outstretched, "Johnny! What a pleasant surprise! . . . This is my grandson-in-law, general."

"John Merritt," the general said. "I know him. Colonel Powell tells me he's a very capable young officer. Eh, Hodder?"

"Very, sir."

"This is Mr Rowland, captain. A Member of the British Parliament. He's been visiting the British front and asked to see ours, too. I know your battery's only just come forward from Camp Coetquidan, but I want you to show Mr Rowland what we can do. I want the British to know we're here, and we're ready."

"Very good, sir."

"Keep him through lunch and then bring him back to my headquarters . . . Sure you'll be warm enough, Mr Rowland?"

"Quite. Thank you very much."

The general saluted his guest and returned to his car. As the artillery officers waited, hands to the rims of their steel helmets, the car drove away. Captain Hodder said, "We'll continue the practise. Mr Merritt, you are excused the rest of the exercise to act as guide to your grandfather . . . Sergeant Tanner!"

"Sir?"

"Give Mr Rowland some waste for his ears . . . Mr Anspach, are you ready with the problem I gave you?"

"Yes, sir."

"Carry on then."

Anspach began to bark fire orders giving the range, elevation, and deflection for the new task. To one flank, fifty yards away from the nearest gun, John explained what was going to happen, and gave his binoculars to the older man. The guns bounded on their wheels, the barrels recoiled, slid forward. First Sergeant Montoya bellowed, "Ride that gun, soldier!" Smoke began to rise from half a dozen sources on the distant hillside, and John said, "The wind's not good for the task. It's blowing straight away from us, so to mask that line of hedge the shells have to fall closer together than we have guns for. If the wind was from the flank, the battery could do it well. As it is, there are gaps in the smoke, see?"

"I see," Harry Rowland said. "The guns fire very fast, don't they?"

"That's the best thing about the 75," John said. "It's a wonderful gun for speed and reliability . . . the weight of shell's not really enough for trench warfare, though. When our infantry attack, the French artillery have to provide the heavy support for them. We don't like it, but we can't help it . . ."

"No more news of Stella, I'm afraid, Johnny."

"She could be anywhere," John said. It was hard to wrench your mind from the reality of the battery, the guns, the exploding shells, the soldiers, to this personal tragedy, so unimportant, and yet so central to his life. Once the wrench had been made, it was hard to believe that anything else but that personal tragedy mattered.

Harry said, "I spoke to the Commissioner again the day before we left for France. He says he has not given up hope."

"Nor have I," John said. "I can't." His mouth shut in a grim line. He said, "The captain is making each gunner explain how he works out the corrections for angle of site . . . that is, the correction needed to be put on the sights if the piece is above or below the target. If the piece is above the target it's called a negative site, if it's below it's called a positive site. The firing tables give the elements of the trajectory corresponding to the actual range, but . . ."

*   *   *   *

Harry Rowland sat in the spacious lounge of the Hotel de France in Amiens, facing his granddaughter Naomi Rowland, Lance Corporal of the First Aid Nursing Yeomanry. They were drinking coffee and eating little pastry bonbons that the hotel staff somehow managed to serve up at the British teatime for the officers who, on short leave or passing through Amiens on duty from the Somme front, dropped in at the hotel for some civilization.

Naomi was looking well, he thought—rather stern in that uniform, but then she'd always seemed rather stern, even as a child, and as she had grown to her full considerable height the sternness had settled, giving her young face—she was twenty-two—a mature handsomeness instead of prettiness. She was saying, "We need more women out here, Grandfather . . . many more. There are still far too many able-bodied men doing work that women could do and would do better . . . clerks, drivers, cooks, typists, telephone operators. There's no reason why we shouldn't work closer to the front, as far forward as Corps headquarters certainly."

"I'm afraid Parliament would never agree to that," Harry murmured.

"Because you're all men," Naomi said impatiently. "In the dark ages . . . in China, Japan, India . . . in prehistoric times, do you think that women were put aside and told to twiddle their thumbs while the men fought? No! The women fought too! They had to! We can fire machine guns just as well as men can. Look at the Bolshevik women!"

Harry changed the subject: what Naomi was saying was in many ways quite true, but it wasn't a political or practical possibility, yet. If England were actually invaded, then it would be different . . . He said, "There's a lot of talk that the Germans are going to make a big assault on this front soon."

"We hear it," Naomi said. "We're ready." She too changed the subject—"Is there any news of Stella, Grandfather?"

He shook his head, "I'm afraid not . . . I've learned a lot on this trip and have a great deal to tell the Prime Minister. But it's been tiring. I don't know whether I'll be strong enough to come out again. To tell you the truth . . ."

From the corner of her eye Naomi saw what she had been looking for and made a small beckoning gesture, then waited. The tall officer with the flaming grenade badges of the Royal Engineers on his lapels came forward, cap in hand. Harry looked round as the young man stopped by his chair.

Naomi looked up—"Why, it's Lieutenant Gregory. This is my grandfather, Mr Harry Rowland. He's an M.P."

"Please don't get up, sir," the officer said.

Harry said, "Sit down, young man. Join us for tea. These little cakes are excellent." He looked at his granddaughter, "I imagine this is not a total surprise to you?"

Naomi found herself blushing. She said, in a small voice, "No, Grandfather. I told Ron—Mr Gregory—that I would be having tea with you here. We met . . ."

Ron Gregory said, "Miss Rowland drove me on an important job in the big air raids, sir. She was . . . marvellous. She ought to have got an M.C. at least."

"Nonsense," Naomi said. "It was just a job. I'm a F.A.N.Y."

The young man looked about thirty, Harry thought. He was gazing at Naomi with adoring eyes; but not possessive. He was the one who was possessed, and would be, if the affair passed on to love or marriage.

He said, "Well, Mr Gregory, while we're enjoying our tea tell me what you do . . . and tell me what we in Parliament can do to help you do better . . ."

*   *   *   *

Guy Rowland stood to one side of the engine nacelle of his Camel, watching Sergeant Stratton working on the sparking plugs, removing them one by one, testing the gap, cleaning them, replacing. The sergeant talked as he worked, "She's ready to do over a hundred now, sir, easy . . . if I could just find a good enough stretch of road . . ." "She" in this case, Guy knew, was Victoria, the motor bicycle which Frank's father Bob Stratton had built to break the 1,000 cc and all comers world speed record; and which had been flown to France for Frank to continue the work after Bob was killed in a factory explosion.

Guy said, "You could take a few days' leave and use that track near Paris."

"Thanks, sir, but I have to have observers, official timers, all kinds of stuff to prove the record's pukka. Besides . . ." his voice trailed away.

"What's the matter, Frank," Guy said gently. "You've been looking sort of sick, as though your chest hurt . . . for a long time now."

Frank turned back to the Camel. Speaking into the engine block he said, his voice muffled and choked, "Anne's having a baby."

"Why . . ." Guy began. He stopped, waiting.

"It ain't mine," Frank said. "Can't be."

After a time Guy said, "Do you think this is what your mother meant, when she wrote that you had to come home?"

"I suppose so."

"Go home now. See her. She may be as miserable as you are."

"I'm not going to see her or have anything to do with her," Frank said. "I'm cutting off my allotment. She's made her bed. Let her lie on it."

Guy thought, unhappily, oh this bloody war, which was making him famous and adored; and destroying so many others' happiness. He said, "What about the children?"

Frank said, "She can look after them . . . all four of them, when this un's born. May, that'll be, Mother says."

Guy was silent another long space, then said, "You're going to have to face her sooner or later, because of the kids, your three. You can't wash your hands of *them* for ever. Any time you decide to go, tell me."

"Thank you, sir," Frank said formally, lifting his head out of the machinery and turning to look straight at Guy. "But I won't . . . I loved her. And she might as well have shit in my eye." He returned to his work. Guy walked off, head bent. He was supposed to be back in his office to go over some orders with Dandy Stuart, the adjutant, but he couldn't face it. He walked on down one side of the field, past the ranked Camels of 333. Across the way was a squadron of Airco D.H. 9s, single-engined bombers . . . not big enough, not powerful enough. That would be improved as Geoffrey de Havilland worked out modifications of the original design . . . and when the American Liberty engines were available in sufficient quantities . . .

Poor Frank. He was suffering spiritual agonies, and it was changing his personality. The old Frank would never have cut off his children like this. Perhaps he would change again when the war ended . . . When *would* the war end, so that he himself could meet Werner von Rackow in peace, and talk over the ideas they were now exchanging by letter? Then those ideas and plans would have to be converted into deeds . . . how could the monstrous, slow mechanisms of governments be made to act? Well, they acted fast enough if it was war they were waging, didn't they? They must be refashioned to wage peace . . . That reminded him, he must send an orderly into Amiens to pick up the damask tablecloth he had ordered as a wedding present for Werner and his bride, Maria Rittenhaus. When the tablecloth arrived Guy intended to fly over and drop it onto Werner's airfield. Good old Werner! But what on earth would he do, as a sedately married man, when the war was over? What would *he* do? It was impossible to imagine . . . not what Werner von Rackow or Guy Rowland would do or become, but that the war would ever be over.

*   *   *   *

John Merritt was reading by the light of a hurricane lantern set on the small camp table by the centre pole of the bell tent. Rudy Anspach, with whom he shared the tent, was on leave in Noyon till midnight. It was cold but quiet, with no wind, the thin snow lying on the bare hard ground, the same colour as the rows of tents of Battery D, 137th Field Artillery.

John was reading the *Field Artillery Manual.* A few days ago he had been explaining to Mr Harry Rowland about angle of site, but it had not been a clear explanation because the matter was not really clear in his own mind. He had the book open at the proper page now, and was reading the section for the third time.

> 63. *Rapid determination of the angle of site.* The following examples illustrate the procedure in the determination of the angle of site:
>   (a) Example 1. The distance from the observation post to the base piece is 400 yards (Fig. 60). The distance from the target to the observation post, as measured with the range finder, is 3,700 yards; as estimated, to the base piece, 4,000 yards. The site reading of the target on the B.C. telescope at the observation post is 295; the site reading to the base piece is . . .

A noise outside made him look up. It was a heavy retching, coughing sound. He hurried out into the open. Someone was kneeling a little to the right of the entrance to the tent, vomiting. He began, "By God, soldier, you . . ." when he recognized the man in the starlight—Private Chee Shush Benally, the Navajo Indian who had joined the 16th Infantry the same day as he in El Paso last May. When John transferred to the Field Artillery, Benally had sworn he'd join him, and he had, just a week ago, when the battery moved up to the front.

John looked quickly up and down. No one moving in the officers' row of tents, some lights glowing through the canvas. Benally had finished vomiting. John grabbed him by the collar, lifted him, and pulled him into the tent. "Sit down," he said. "Wait. I'll see if I can rustle up some coffee for you."

He didn't understand how Benally had got himself out of the 16th—Benally merely said he'd told the top kick that unless he fixed the transfer, he and the other Indians in the outfit, and there were several, would put a curse on them all. A top kick can fix anything, he knew, so they'd got rid of him quick, telling the Artillery that he was a natural driver, and a wizard with a horse, which was true; and he'd come to the 137th Regiment and, though officially a driver, was used most of the time as blacksmith and saddler and, unofficially, had appointed himself John's striker, demanding $7 a month from John for the privilege.

John said, "What have you been doing, Chee?"

"Gettin' drunk," the Indian said, "what else?"

"What *on,* man?"

"Cognac . . . A bottle, bottle and a half . . . Are you all right?"

"I'm O.K.," John said. He ought to have Chee thrown into the hoosegow for drunkenness, but . . . Chee had taught him so much, those months together in the infantry, that he could never regard him as just another private soldier. He was John's teacher in everything to do with the natural world, including mankind, men, and their natures; yet John felt that he was responsible for the Navajo, as he would be for a child, for in certain areas Chee was as helpless as one— particularly when faced with a bottle of liquor.

Benally said, "Germans going to attack soon, eh?"

"Latrine rumors . . . but it may be true. We're going into the line next week, that's all I do know."

"Everyone know that," Benally said, "but Germans won't attack us . . . attack British."

"How do you know?"

Benally grinned—"Stars . . . wind . . . dumb Indian know *something,* Johnny . . . Ah, you called John now, right?"

John nodded. Benally said, "You got any liquor here?"

John said, "No, and if I did I wouldn't give you any. Can't you ever stop until you're paralytic blind drunk, Chee? How many times have I had to cover for you . . . at Bliss, on the troop train, on the ship, in the trenches? Why do you do it?"

Benally's square brown face hardened. He said, "Because our land taken . . . our skies no belong us, our water flow for white man." He laughed suddenly, his face changing as rapidly, "After war, you come Sanostee, John. We hunt elk together . . . our squaws make posole for us . . ." He put out his hand and rested it on John's—"No news?"

John shook his head. Benally said, "Why you not get drunk with me, eh?" John shook his head again. Benally said, "I will write my uncle . . . big shaman . . . ask him to sing for her. Don't know whether the sing will reach her, across the sea . . . never tried that before . . . but I think it will. Our sings reach the dead, so . . ."

John said, "Thanks, Chee. Go ahead. It'll be good to know someone else is trying."

"And when she's back, after the war, bring her to Sanostee, eh?"

"I don't know, Chee . . . We have to finish the war first, and then . . . I just don't know."

"Come Sanostee," Benally said. "No bad things there. Only sky, rocks, grass, water . . . wind to clean inside head . . . Come Sanostee."

Daily Telegraph, Wednesday, March 13, 1918

THE AIR RAID ON PARIS

**100 KILLED, 79 INJURED
FOUR ENEMY PLANES DOWN**

As was stated in the later editions of yesterday's *Daily Telegraph*, the Germans carried out another air raid on Paris—the eleventh since the war began—on Monday night. Apparently this raid was on a larger scale than that of Friday last, as nearly sixty aeroplanes are said to have been engaged in it, though many of them failed to reach the city, being driven off by defending forces and by the anti-aircraft guns. It is satisfactory to learn that four of the raiders were accounted for. One of them, a Gotha, was brought down in flames near Château-Thierry on the river Marne, about thirty miles south-east of Soissons, and its occupants were captured.

Unfortunately, the casualties were very heavy, though the number of persons actually killed and injured in the raid by the bombs was smaller than in the raid of Jan. 30, when forty-five people were slain and 207 injured; but the death-roll was greatly increased by a panic at a refuge at one of the Metropolitan Railway stations, where sixty-six persons, mostly women and children, lost their lives. Reuter's correspondent states that they were "asphyxiated," i.e. suffocated by the pressure of the crowd . . . One of the . . . Gothas brought down was burnt to ashes and the pilot and other occupants were burnt alive. Most of the crews of the other machines brought down were wounded . . .

Ghastly, Cate thought. Women and children trampled to death in panic . . . men burnt alive . . . it wasn't only the war that was becoming more inhuman every day, but the people waging it.

He looked at the clock on the mantelpiece—five to ten. He wasn't feeling very bright this morning—pray to God it wasn't the flu—and had got up late. He would have stayed in bed all morning, probably, if the Governor wasn't coming down. He'd made a ten o'clock appointment . . . wonder what it was about?

He folded away the paper and went out, as he passed down the passage seeing a big Rowland Sapphire roll past the windows. The Governor had always been punctual. He went to the front door to greet him, waving Garrod aside with a smile.

He's looking much older all of a sudden, he thought, as Harry Rowland stepped down from the car, aided by the young woman who had at last taken Wright's place. He shook the old man's hand, led him to the library, and helped him into a comfortable chair. "A little something?" he asked, smiling.

"A drop of whisky and water," Harry said, rubbing his hands. "Never used to take it at this hour, but the doctor said . . . my heart, you know . . ."

Cate poured, and handed over the glass. Harry drank and put the glass down. "I'll get down to business," he said. "Have to see Richard and John . . . Alice too, of course . . . when I leave here. Can't get hold of Tom—the people at Chatham just say they can give me no information, when I call. They tell me to write, and it'll be forwarded . . . That last trip to France tired me out, Christopher. Felt rotten when I came home, weak as a kitten."

"You're not as young as you used to be, Governor."

Harry nodded, "Who is? . . . So I've decided to apply for the Chiltern Hundreds. The only question is, when?"

Cate was surprised, though he knew he should not be. Stewardship of the Chiltern Hundreds, which no longer existed, was still technically "an office of profit under the Crown," and could not be held by a Member of Parliament. Applying for this non-existent post therefore meant retirement from the House. He'd seen Harry getting older—more quickly since Rose's death; still more quickly now . . . he ought to have guessed. He said, "I suppose there's no possibility of a General Election soon?" Harry shook his head. "The end of the war?"

"If it doesn't go on too long."

"I think another winter going up and down to London would be hard on you," Cate said. "October, November?"

"That's what I think," Harry said. "I suppose the P.M. will try to dissuade me. He's worried about losing seats."

"This one's safe enough for a Unionist, I would have thought," Cate said. "Either Liberal or Conservative."

Harry said, "I'm not so sure. In the eyes of a lot of people—and the number climbs every day, in secret, as the slaughter continues—we're both tarred with the same brush: we're responsible for the war. A good Socialist could give whomever stands in my place a bad fright . . . at the least."

Cate whistled long and almost silently. A Socialist, for Mid Scarrow? It seemed impossible, against nature.

London and Kent:
Thursday, March 14, 1918

5   Roger Durand-Beaulieu, 9th Earl of Swanwick, stood in the big third-floor drawing room, looking out at the rain falling steadily on Cornwall Gardens. His hands were clasped behind the back of his broadcloth suit, his shoulders hunched and his head a little stuck forward. He was frowning, not at anything in particular, but at fate. It was a two-story flat, two reception rooms, five bedrooms, large kitchen and pantry, servants' quarters above . . . certainly it was big enough for the four of them, except there were only three . . . where *was* Helen, and what in blazes was she doing, that was so hush hush? . . . S.W. 7 wasn't so bad an address. But it was very different from Walstone Park, where that fat profiteer was now lording it—literally—over the old place and the fallow deer and the pheasants and the village . . . while the heir to his own title was a damned Canadian cowboy, who didn't want it and had no intention of coming back to England to accept it when . . . Roger and Arthur killed in action in this bloody war, most of his money gone the same way, taken in taxes, then blown up . . . The bloody Huns had to be taught a lesson they'd never forget, but . . . Louise Rowland had been in the flat half an hour, with Flora—hadn't seen her arrive, but Flora had sent up a message, and Louise would come up and see him before she left. She'd lost a son, too—Boy, killed at Nollehoek in the Passchendaele battle, not long after Cantley. That had turned her pacifist, according to what he'd heard before they left Walstone. Losing a son ought to make one all the more determined to win, to avenge him, not go round snivelling that the war must be stopped. Well, Louise was a woman. Even Flora hadn't been so certain about the war as she used to be, since Cantley went.

He heard the door open behind him, and turned slowly. Three women came into the room: Flora his wife, the countess; Louise Rowland; and another, taller, gaunt, severe-faced woman in dowdy black clothes with a remarkable felt hat. Flora said, "This is Mrs Gorse, Roger, Probyn's wife."

"Ah," the earl said. He recognized her now, though he had not seen her for three years or more. She seldom left the cottage. It was Probyn's Woman, not really his wife.

Flora said, "Sit down, Roger . . . here." She and Louise sat down side by side on a sofa; the earl sat in an armchair opposite them; the Woman remained standing, arms folded.

The countess said gently, "Roger, what we're going to tell you will be a shock to you, so prepare yourself."

"What now?" the earl growled. Arthur and Cantley gone, what else could there be?

The countess said, "Helen has written to Louise telling her where she's living, and confirming what Louise and I have been certain of from the time Helen left High Staining last December. She's going to have a baby. It's . . ."

"A baby?" the earl interrupted, frowning. "That's impossible . . . or has she sneaked off and got married? Is that what the secret job is?"

"The baby's due next month," the countess continued patiently. "Boy was the father. They were going to get married on his next leave."

"He was killed," the earl muttered. "Where is she?"

"She's living in Soho with Ethel Fagioletti—you remember, Ethel Stratton that was, who married the Italian waiter, only now he's a sergeant in the Wealds. Helen wrote to Louise asking her to come and tell us . . . and to bring up Mrs Gorse to examine her. She wants Mrs Gorse to deliver the baby."

"Helen, having a bastard," the earl said. "Christ!"

"It's only because Boy was a brave man, and did his duty, as Cantley and Arthur did. It's quite possible that they, too, left fatherless children somewhere   We're going to Soho now to see Helen. Do you want to come?"

The earl snapped, "No!" He got up and returned to the window, staring out at the rain. He threw over his shoulder, "What shall I tell Barbara when she comes back? She's teaching a children's ride in the Park."

"Nothing," the countess said. "I'll tell her this afternoon."

Louise, speaking to the earl's back said, "I'm sorry Boy couldn't marry Helen, Lord Swanwick . . . but John and I are very happy that Boy did know love before . . . he went . . . and we're very happy too that he has a son, and we a grandson, of his body."

The women left the room, the Woman first, the countess last. She looked back at her husband, a dark figure against the rain-spattered window, his hunched dejected back to her, then she gently closed the door.

Three quarters of an hour later, the countess knocked on the blue-painted door of a little two-story house on Dean Street in Soho. The street smelled of cooking spaghetti sauce, and a barrel organ was playing Italian tunes, the organ grinder's monkey prancing on top of the machine waving tiny British and Italian flags. The house next to the one where they waited was a restaurant called Bertinelli's and in the doorway of the house beyond that was a very painted young woman with high heels, net stockings visible to just below her knees, and a tiny umbrella, staring discontentedly at the rain.

A sharp-faced little woman with small hands and feet and an incongruously large bosom opened the door. Her big blue eyes opened wide and she exclaimed, "You've come . . . !"

"I'm Lady Swanwick," the countess said. "Helen's mother. This is . . ."

"Oh, I know Mrs Rowland, and Mrs Gorse . . . from when I was a little girl . . . Come in, m'lady, m'm . . ."

She held the door open saying, "On the left . . . Lady Helen's working upstairs . . . Lady Helen!" She called up the narrow flight of stairs. "They've come . . . Her ladyship your mother and all!"

The visitors waited in the crowded little parlor, filled with bric-a-brac. A large photograph of a swarthy sergeant in khaki, against a painted backdrop of a park, stood on the centre table which was covered with a beaded and fringed cloth.

Helen came in slowly, Ethel Fagioletti behind her. Helen was carrying the baby high, and it was big, for a first child. She was pale, with tears in her eyes, but her mouth wide in a smile. "Mummy," she said, her voice trembling. The countess found herself weeping as she opened her arms wide to receive her daughter into them. Then Helen was kissing Louise Rowland, and beginning to talk—no, she was in no pain, only the usual discomfort, he'd been kicking since the middle of November, it couldn't be long now, she was so happy, Ethel had been so good . . .

The Woman, who had been standing aside, her face inscrutable, said, "We'd best go upstairs so I can have a look at you now, milady."

"Of course," Helen said. "Oh, I'm so glad you could come."

"Most of the women who visit me want me to get rid of a baby," the

Woman said. "This is better. Come on now . . . slowly, there's no hurry."

They went out and the stairs creaked as they climbed up to the bedroom above. Lady Swanwick said, "Well . . . what has Helen been doing all this time?"

"Sewing . . . crocheting things we can sell . . . helping me. She's a good Italian cook now. I had to learn for Niccolo, and I've taught her. She could always get a job at the restuarant next door."

"Not at the house next to that, I hope," the countess said grimly.

"Oh milady, we know what that is, but it can't be helped here in Soho. They don't do us no harm . . . One of the girls is knitting a cap for the baby . . ."

Louise said, "What are you going to do when the baby's come? We'd love to have them back at High Staining. Helen can work on the farm, or not, as she chooses. I'll look after the baby, as much as I can. You can come, too, of course."

The countess said, "We have room in the flat for them. The servants will talk, but they'd do that at High Staining. It can't be helped."

Ethel said, "Milady, m'm, begging your pardon, I have to stay here. My Niccolo wants me to . . . Lady Helen's talked about it a lot, and she says we're going to start a boutique, she called it, in the West End. She'll do most of the buying and selling and I'll help, and do accounts. I always was good at arithmetic."

"Buying and selling, what?" her ladyship asked.

"Hats, I think, milady, gloves, scarves, blouses, perfume, hand-bags, umbrellas, parasols . . . fashionable things. We'll live here and take the baby to the shop with us. He can sleep in the back . . . and one of us will always be there to look after him."

"What will happen when your husband comes home?" Louise asked.

Ethel's face fell, and she said, "Well, if it's only for a leave, it won't make any difference, I mean Lady Helen won't want me to work while Niccolo's at home. If the war's over . . . we'll have to wait and see, won't we? Perhaps Lady Helen will marry . . . she calls herself Mrs Rowland, m'm."

"Of course."

"I mean she's had her name changed to that, m'm, officially like . . . so the baby will be called Rowland."

The Woman came back silently into the room. The stairs had not creaked under her. She said, "It feels like the second week of April . . . everything quite right, head down. She'll probably tear a bit, but that's all."

The countess said, "I really think there ought to be a doctor, too, Mrs Gorse, and . . ."

Helen came in, buttoning the top buttons of her thick blouse. She said, "I trust Mrs Gorse, Mummy. I really don't want a doctor . . . Well, now we're in touch again, I feel so much better . . . but I couldn't bring myself to let you all know until I was absolutely sure that I was really going to have the baby, and wouldn't lose it through a miscarriage."

"Too late for that now," the Woman said. "You won't lose it, less you jump off the roof."

Helen said, "I won't do that . . . Do give Barbara my love, Mummy, and ask her to come down and see us. We're in all the time. Does Daddy know?"

The countess said, "Yes. He can't face it, yet. He will."

"I wish it could have been otherwise," Helen said, "but . . . I'm not sorry. Better this by far than not having anything of Boy's to love, in his place. Tell me when Daddy's ready for me to go and see him . . . Now, let's go and have lunch next door. Signor Bertinelli's a very nice man, and his wife's a marvellous cook. And we might see Russell Wharton, the actor, there. He lives just across the street."

Ethel Fagioletti said quickly, "Give me five minutes, milady. I have a few things to finish in the kitchen." She turned to the Woman— "Perhaps you'd give me a hand, Mrs Gorse?"

The Woman followed her out of the room without a word. Ethel led to the back of the little house, and closed the kitchen door—"I don't really have anything to do," she said, "but I thought we'd best leave the ladies alone . . . And I wanted to ask you if you can help me get a baby, next time my husband comes home."

The Woman surveyed the little woman with a half-smile on her severe face, "You want one, and can't get it, and your sister-in-law's got one, and doesn't want it."

"Poor Anne," Ethel said, "Franks's written to mother saying he doesn't want to see her again, or even his own kids . . . And she's not getting any allotment, so I don't know what's going to happen to her."

"Lady Walstone's given her a job in the laundry room at the Park," the Woman said. "Did it yesterday. And given them two rooms in the top of the house to live in, so she won't have to pay rent for the house in Hedlington."

"That's good of Ruth," Ethel said. "She might have taken Frank's side and cut Anne off. We are Frank's sisters, after all. He'll be angry at Ruth when he knows she's helping Anne."

"P'raps," the Woman said. "Can't be helped, can it? These things will happen, if you send men off from their women, and blow them up

. . . Look, I've a lot of work to do these days, and it's not much use trying to help you have a baby till your husband comes home. So, when you think that won't be long, come down to our cottage. I'm always there."

"Oh thank you, thank you!"

"Don't thank me till you miss the curse . . . and then give some of the thanks to your husband."

*   *   *   *

Guy Rowland sat at a half-hidden table in the Savoy grill room, opposite a beautiful young woman with shining auburn hair piled high on her head and held with a large diamond and emerald pin. She was Florinda, Marchioness of Jarrow, née Florinda Gorse. The meal was nearly over and the waiter was bringing them another of the bottles of champagne which Florinda had insisted on ordering. It was the last day of his forty-eight-hour leave—most of which had been spent in conferences at the Air Ministry.

"Can't you stay another day?" Florinda asked.

"Not a chance, I'm afraid." The light gleamed on the long scar on his right cheekbone and the permanent slight droop to the right side of his mouth.

She made a moue. "Other men would disobey orders if I asked them to."

"I'm sure they would," he said, putting a hand over hers. "But Boom Trenchard isn't their boss. He told me this afternoon, when we'd finished our conference—it was about how to teach air tactics to pilots before they went out to France—he said, 'The Germans are going to attack very soon now. Make sure you don't hang around in London, *whatever the temptation,*' and he looked at me very hard from under those beetling eyebrows, as if he knew the temptation would be a gorgeous girl with red hair and green eyes . . . ."

She lifted up his hand and laid it momentarily against her cheek. Then she said, "You were talking about von Rackow, earlier. Do you think you'll get together with him, after the war?"

"We will," Guy said slowly. "Just what we'll do then isn't quite clear in either of our minds yet . . . it'll depend in part on what state the world's in, where the help is most needed. I think that's going to be the key—love, some way to *use* the power of love, as we've been using and creating the power of hate . . . Perhaps it'll be something practical . . . form a new political party . . . I don't know. I really can't get to grips with it till Werner and I meet. The first thing we'll do when the war's over is go on a walking tour together. His wife'll have to come too, I suppose, if she likes walking."

"And your wife, eh?"

"Ah."

"Here, let's have another bottle of fizz."

He said, "I've had enough . . . and so have you, my darling Florinda."

"You always was a bleeding schoolmaster," she said in cockney. "Ordering me abaht, tell me when to sit up, when to lie down, when to pee . . ."

"You don't seem happy," he said. Her beauty gripped him by the loins and he yearned for her, remembering the nights he had spent in her arms fifteen months ago. And how he loved her, too.

She said, "Who says I'm not happy? What are *you* doing to make me happy, anyway?"

He said simply, "You don't seem happy to me. I know you."

She muttered, "Too bloody well!"

After a time he removed his hand from hers, where he had been gently holding it, leaned back, and said, "Are you going to come back to the flat with me? Or may I come to yours?"

She snapped, "No . . . Oh God, I'd love to, Guy, but I promised another man I'd be his mistress as long as I wanted to, and I haven't told him different yet."

His heart sank, though he kept his face calm and, he hoped, unmoved. He said, "Is that why you are unhappy?"

"I don't know," she snapped. "I'm . . . He's Billy Bidford, the racing driver."

"Millionaire sportsman, polo player, flyer, etcetera etcetera . . . R.N.V.R., isn't he?"

"Yes. I told him I might be in love with someone else."

"Well, are you?" He looked full at her, the hard blue right eye and the soft brown left eye. At last her own green eyes fell. She said, "I don't know. If I did, what would I do? I'm frightened of you, Guy. You're not twenty-one yet . . ."

"Next month, the 23rd."

"But you've killed, how many men?"

"And liked it," he said in a low voice. "That's one of the things I have to talk to Werner about. To find out if he is the same . . . what are people like us going to do when the killing stops?"

"Would you kill me, if I seemed to be your enemy?"

"I don't know . . . I don't know."

"Nor do I . . . I'm only giving a bit of myself to Billy—my cunt. As a matter of fact I'm just lending it to him. But with you, I'd have to give everything, and never expect it back . . . and I don't know yet whether I am strong enough for that, so . . . forgive me, dear Guy.

Can I get another woman for you for tonight? I know half a dozen who'd be round in their nighties in a flash, for you, if I called."

He smiled then. "No thanks, darling. For the moment, you or no one . . ."

"Not even Poitrine?"

"Good heavens, no! . . . Billy Bidford's in C.M.B.s, I believe?"

She nodded, and said, "He was at Dover but he's been moved to Chatham for some hush-hush job."

"So's my uncle, the man whose flat I'm using. I wonder if they've met. Uncle Tom's a commander . . . and a pansy."

She looked up sharply, "Plenty of them in the theatre. They're not bad, mostly."

"Uncle Tom isn't in the theatre," Guy said grimly. "He's in the Royal Navy. Straight stripes."

"How do you know, about him?"

"He has a servant, who lives in the flat, an ex-sailor called Charlie Bennett. He's a young Geordie, very handsome, even pretty, except that he's strongly built. Uncle Tom has a picture of him, nude, in his bedroom, and I imagine, vice versa."

Florinda whistled, "So he doesn't care who knows?"

"Apparently not. I hope it comes out all right for Uncle Tom. He was always very nice to me, when I was a kid . . . but the navy doesn't look kindly on homosexuals, any more than the army does . . . or the Royal Air Force will. General Trenchard confirmed what we've all known for weeks, that the air services are going to be united in a single new force—the Royal Air Force—on April 1st . . . two weeks' time. I must get home and to bed, darling. Can I get a taxi for you?"

"No, let's walk as far as Piccadilly Circus at least. We can look at the devastated French village they've set up in Trafalgar Square, and the Strand will be dark and empty and I can hold your arm and tell myself it's just for protection . . . can't I?"

*   *   *   *

Fiona Rowland started as the door bell rang. He'd telephoned ten minutes ago, so she shouldn't have been surprised, but she was. Thank God the cook and the maid had the afternoon off. She ran down to the front door and opened it breathlessly, one hand to her throat. Archie was standing outside in a thin rain, wearing a trench coat over his uniform, a swagger stick in one hand with the crest of the regiment embossed on the silver knob. His chinstrap shone brilliant ox-blood red, but the cap badge of the prancing horse and bugle horn were in bronze, and gleamed only dully under the leaden sky. She held the door open without a word and he walked in. "Up the stairs?" he threw over his shoulder.

"Yes," she said, following him. "Right at the top."

Upstairs, she closed the living-room door behind her and opened her arms. He moved slowly to her, took her arms, and held them against her sides—"You're looking peaked," he said.

"What else do you expect? I called the convalescent depot on Monday and they told me you'd been released. Where have you been?"

"Suppose I tell you I've been poking some of my old models, in Chelsea? There was one with a bonny ginger bush who could never get enough."

"Where have you *been,* Archie?"

He sighed, "Visiting my mother in Glasgow." He sat down.

She sat opposite, close, and said, "Archie, you have just recovered from a very serious wound and you are not fit for service in the trenches. And you have so much to teach the recruit officers at the Depot here. Stay here, and let us be lovers, as we were before the war, for ten years . . . ten years, Archie!"

"Then everyone in Hedlington would know that Colonel Quentin Rowland was being cuckolded on his own doorstep."

"Go somewhere else—there are army jobs everywhere. I'll follow you. There's nothing to keep me here, with Guy in France and Virginia married."

"No," Archie said slowly. "There isn't I suppose." He looked round the room, unbuttoning his trench coat. "They look good"—he nodded at the pen and ink sketches and occasional oils on the walls, all of war scenes and all signed "Campbell." He had done them and given them to his commanding officer, Fiona's husband, some as gifts, some on loan until he could collect them after the war.

She stood by his side, looking at a head-and-shoulders portrait of her husband. She said, "You make him look more spiritual than he is."

"It's there, all right," Archie said. "He just doesn't have any way of expressing it. You have to know him very well to see it."

"I've known him for God knows how many years and I haven't seen it. He doesn't have any soul. It's in *you,* and you're just transfering it to Quentin."

Archie said, "No, lass, he has it." The trench coat was off now, and folded over the back of a chair. He said, "Quentin has made me a great artist, or near great, because there is something in him that brings out what greatness you have, of any sort . . . That's why the men love him, in their way—he brings out courage in them that they didn't know they possessed, endurance beyond their endurance, sacrifice beyond sacrifice . . . He loves you. He knows you don't love him, and asked me whether I proposed to marry you. I said that I didn't . . ." He held up a hand to suppress Fiona's moan of anguish ". . . and he said that's not the way to treat a woman whom you've seduced and betrayed . . . but inside he was glad, because he knows that if I take you back, he'll never have a chance. But Fiona, I could no more be your lover again now, after what Quentin has become to me, than I could fly to the moon."

"You've become like *him,"* she cried. *"You* don't understand me now, any more than he does."

"I think I do," Archie said. "And I've come to say goodbye. I'm going back to the battalion tomorrow. It's all been arranged—medical boards, orders to get me out of the reinforcement depot, everything. You *must* learn to love him, Fiona. He's your husband, and he's a good man."

She said, "I have only loved one man in my life, Archie."

"You said just now that I had grown like him, that you see him in me . . . But from now on you must see me in him. Goodbye."

* * * *

We Socialists have the noblest heads, Rachel Cowan thought, looking at the profile Ramsay MacDonald was offering her in the little North London house where the meeting was being held. Well, Snowden, beyond MacDonald, hardly had a noble profile, just sharp and determined, thin-lipped, hard-jawed. But MacDonald was as imposing as Bertrand Russell, though without Russell's electric sense of energy.

MacDonald, who had been leader of the Labour Party in the House of Commons until he was discredited by his pacifist attitude, was speaking to Wilfred Bentley, Rachel's husband—though they used their own names for all matters, as had been agreed before they married early in the year. Bentley, his long aristocratic face contrasting strongly with MacDonald's craggy outline and mane of greying hair, was listening attentively as MacDonald said, "We hear the same thing—that Harry Rowland will not contest the next election . . . even if he's not opposed."

Wilfred said, "I believe it's true. He's tired, I think."

MacDonald said, "He's an honest man, though no friend of Labour. The Prime Minister will miss him."

Rachel cut in, "But Mr Lloyd George may not be Prime Minister after the next election."

Snowden said, "He will, assuming he's won the war . . . And you want to start nursing the constituency? It may be months before

81

there's a general election . . . though I suppose it's possible that Harry Rowland will apply for the Chiltern Hundreds before then."

MacDonald said, "The question is, can you afford it? The chances of your winning Mid Scarrow for Labour are very small, and the central committee can't afford to spend a lot of money in a doubtful cause, so you'll have to find most of it yourselves. Can you do it?"

Rachel said, "I think so. The party's growing by leaps and bounds in Hedlington and the countryside, as the war shows no sign of ending and more and more men get sent off to the Western Front to be killed. We didn't have a hundred members when I joined, right after I left Girton. Now we have nearly two thousand. We can do a lot with their subscriptions."

"Aye," MacDonald said thoughtfully. "Lloyd George is going to win the war, but he'll lose the peace, in this country, sooner or later. Right now all that the people can see is the Gairrmans, and victory. Afterwards, they'll see what they've lost, what might have been, if we'd not got into the war, or had negotiated peace earlier . . . then they'll remember what *we* have been saying all along . . . All right, I approve, and I'm sure the central committee will do so, too. Start as soon as you can . . . concentrate on those who've suffered from the war. Whoever is responsible for it, it's certainly not us—that's our strongest point. All the factory workers, especially the union men . . . everyone who's lost sons or brothers or fathers . . . everyone who's been badly hit by taxes, at the bottom end of the scale . . . the House of Lords has been hard hit by taxes, but we aren't going to cry for them . . . Go after the women. They've got the vote, they also affect the way their men vote, and in her heart of hearts there isn't a woman in the country who doesn't think this is a useless, terrible slaughter . . . Make everyone understand that we're not Bolsheviks, with murder in our hearts, but decent hard-working men, educated too, even though we dinna talk with plums in our throats . . . Sorry, Mr Bentley, ah dinna mean to be pairrsonal."

Wilfred laughed, "It's quite all right, Mr MacDonald. Winchester, Balliol, and the 60th Rifles leave their mark on a man, and I'm afraid it's indelible."

"Ah!" MacDonald said. "I saw in the wee biography you sent up that you were gassed and invalided out. And you have the Military Cross?"

"That's correct."

"Stress all those things. Opposition to the war coming from an officer of a crack regiment, with that record, is taken very differently from the cries of such as I and Russell and the rest." He turned to Rachel, "You are a Jewess, Miss Cowan?"

She said, "Yes. My real name is Cohen. My father runs a stall in Whitechapel. I won a scholarship to Girton. My best friend there was Naomi Rowland, the M.P.'s granddaughter. I've stayed with them, and I know the whole family quite well, partly from being arrested trying to stop people going to work in their shell factory, and helping Bert Gorse to organize the union at Hedlington Aircraft and the Jupiter Motor Company—both of which are majority-owned by a New York bank. The son of the chairman of the board of that bank is John Merritt, who's married to another granddaughter of the M.P."

Snowden said, "Work hard on those factories that are American owned, Miss Cowan. The Americans despise unions and labour. They bring their troops out against strikers. Our government would like to do the same."

Wilfred said, "You suggest that we should imply to the workers in our constituency that troops will be brought out against them if they don't bring a Socialist government to power? I'm afraid I don't agree. I think that would be incitement, and demagoguery."

Snowden accentuated his Yorkshire accent, "Politics is a dirty business, Mr Bentley. Tha' can't keep the kid gloves on, tha' knows."

MacDonald interrupted, "It's their constituency and they must woo it their own way. There's only one question left, which hasn't been made clear yet. Which of you is going to be the candidate?"

Rachel said, "I would very much like to be the first woman Member of Parliament, but we have discussed this at great length and we have agreed that Wilfred should be the candidate and I the organizer."

"The *eminence grise*," Snowden said, the French words sounding very strange under their Yorkshire overlay.

MacDonald said, "I would prefer to say, right hand, left hand, and who is to say which is which? They are both indispensable in politics. Well, let us hope that your chance comes soon, but not too soon. You need at least four months to get the constituency thoroughly mapped out and prepared . . . softened up, the artillery people say . . . horrible idea, but apt . . ."

*   *   *   *

Christopher Cate, titular squire of Walstone in the County of Kent, walked on Beighton Down with a smaller, limping woman, both in tweeds and sensible caps, carrying blackthorn sticks to help their steps over the uneven turf. It was not raining and the pale sunshine and pastel shadows of an English spring chased each other across the chequerboard of the fields of the Weald below. The wind tugged at the short grass, the bare boughs of a distant copse waved above the skyline to the north, larks rose, soaring, pouring out their wild lyric song to the windy sky. It was two days before the spring equinox.

Isabel Kramer said, "I'm sorry about that letter, but I had to tell you . . . I'm miserable, and frustrated, and I don't know how much longer I can bear it."

Cate said nothing. As long as his wife Margaret remained underground in Ireland there was nothing he could do to get a divorce. He desperately wanted to marry Isabel; she knew that; but he understood, too, her need to let off steam, to scream against fate.

They walked another ten minutes, and she said, "I can't be torpedoed twice, can I?"

Cate still said nothing. The U-boats were being beaten, but they were still doing their ghastly work. Some merchant sailors had been torpedoed two and three times.

Ten minutes later again Isabel said, "Walter hasn't been sent overseas yet, but it's only a matter of time."

"Where is he now?" Cate asked. Walter was her son by her first, and only marriage, which had ended nine years ago in widowhood. He was now a private in the American National Army.

She said, "In Camp Davidson, California."

He said, the words wrung out of him, but, he hoped, showing none of that pain—"You must go to him, my dear. I hate to think of you risking your life at sea, but . . . you are right—you should see Walter before he goes to France."

He wished that she was a more fearful person, so that the prospect of the U-boats would deter her—after all, if you have nearly drowned, spent thirty-six hours in an open boat in a winter storm, suffered frostbite, lost a toe and nearly your life . . . you are entitled to some anxiety over the prospect of a repeat of those experiences. But the fact was that he could not face the continued misery of the hunt for Stella without her support. In this matter he was alone . . . Laurence was away in France; Richard absorbed with his businesses and Susan with the adopted children; Quentin in France and Fiona here but not here, withdrawn into some private world since Quentin went overseas; yet she and Quentin had not been close, he was sure; Alice . . . ah, Alice had been wonderful, a real tower of strength, but she had so little spare time . . . Betty Merritt had been a strength, too; but Cate could tell that she had preoccupations of her own. Isabel had told him that she was in love with Fletcher Gorse . . . a most unsuitable match, on the face of it, but with this war changing everything, who could tell? And you had to remember that she was American, raised away from England's ancient prejudices and class distinctions.

Isabel said, "I told you I'd stay till Stella was found, but now I think I must go. It's my duty to see Walter . . . and I want to."

"Of course," he said.

They turned south and walking now into the wind, Isabel's hair tugging at its restraining pins, tendrils escaping out from under the tweed cap, they came down to Beighton and walked through it, respectfully greeted by the many who knew the Squire of Walstone by sight; and so on down winding lanes, between pleached hedges, to Walstone Manor.

As they walked in through the front door Garrod came hurrying down the passage to them. She stopped, controlled her rapid breathing, and said, "The Commissioner of the Metropolitan Police has been on the telephone for you. About an hour ago, it was, sir. He asked that you call back as soon as you came in. The number is on the pad by the machine, sir."

Cate looked quickly at Isabel, then hurried down the hall to the telephone in its little niche under the stairs. He cranked quickly, trying, like Garrod, to control his breathing—"I wish to make a trunk call to London, please, operator," he said. "Whitehall 7000."

He waited, Isabel standing beside him, her hand on his shoulder as he sat at the little table on which the telephone rested. "Scotland Yard? This is Christopher Cate, calling from Walstone, Kent. The Commissioner left a message for me to call him back . . . Yes, of course." He looked up at Isabel and whispered, "I'm through to his secretary. She says it will be a minute, as he has someone with him . . ." He waited. Then started and gripped the earphone harder. "Yes, Sir Richard, Cate speaking . . ." He listened for three minutes, while Isabel stroked his shoulder and neck. Then he said, "Thank you, Sir Richard. I'll be up on the next train." He hung up, his head sank for a moment, then he looked up—"They've found her. She's alive. Heavily drug-addicted but otherwise . . . not sick. The Commissioner said I'd better get the rest of the story from the people at the hospital where she is . . . the Limehouse . . . and Inspector Turnbull, who found her. He'll come to the hospital as soon as we get there and phone the Yard."

"When's the next train?" Isabel said. "Or, wait a minute! I drove down this time. We'll go up in my car. We can leave right away . . . Garrod!" The maid answered at once; Isabel knew she would not have gone far—"Can you ask Mrs Abell to make up a few sandwiches for us, at once? I don't know whether Mr Cate will be spending the night in London but he may."

"Have they found Miss Stella?" Garrod asked.

"Oh, of course, I should have said so at once. Yes, that's all we know."

"The Lord be thanked," Garrod said fervently. "None of us below stairs have been able to sleep a wink all these weeks, thinking of poor Miss Stella out there . . . heaven knew where . . . We were all sure she was alive, though."

"Well, she is," Cate said. "I just don't know what to do . . . what to think . . . what to prepare myself for . . ."

"I'll be there," Isabel said. "Now, pour yourself a big, big whisky and pour a smaller one for me while you're at it. I shall be driving."

*   *   *   *

They were sitting in the large bright room of the Specialist in Venereology of the Limehouse Hospital, looking out over the Thames below Tower Bridge, near the Pool of London—Cate, Isabel, Inspector Turnbull of the Yard's Drug Investigation Unit, and Dr Aloysius Kettering, M.D., F.R.C.P., the specialist.

Turnbull was speaking, "We found her by asking the hospitals to report any patient who appears to have recently been on drugs, especially by injection."

The Inspector looked rather like Bill Hoggin, Lord Walstone, burly, rolls of fat on his neck . . . which was to say he also looked something like the Minister of War, the Earl of Derby; but the Inspector's accent was of London, like Hoggin's; the earl's was not.

Turnbull continued, "The Limehouse told us the day before yesterday they had a patient come in for treatment of V.D. . . . sorry, sir, but that's the facts . . . a young woman, obvious gonorrhoea, but they also suspected drugs. She'd got needle marks, though she'd done everything she could to avoid having to bare her arms. It took us a couple of days to check it out . . . we had hundreds of leads and tips to follow, sir . . . But this morning early we came here, and it was her, all right—Mrs Merritt, whom we were looking for. She's lost a lot of weight, pale, hair dirty, runny nose, sore throat, eyes puffy from lack of sleep . . . all the symptoms of heroin. And she had a recently broken left upper arm, badly healed, so slightly deformed . . . I phoned the Commissioner."

Dr Kettering said, "Mrs Merritt is also pregnant, Mr Cate. About two months gone. An abortion would be easy at this stage and fully justified by the circumstances."

Cate's mind reeled under the blows. Stella, his darling blonde girl, Johnny Merritt's beautiful bride, the English rose . . . a drug fiend, injecting herself with vile drugs . . . pregnant by God knows who . . .

riddled with gonorrhoea . . . He whispered, "How are we going to tell John?"

Isabel said, "I think I'll have to do it, Christopher."

"But they won't let you up to the front."

"I think they will. Newton Baker, our Secretary of War, is a close friend of Stephen's—John's father, my brother. Or I can fix it through the Embassy. Virgil's very well trusted by Mr Page, the ambassador."

Cate's mind still raced. Stella had been living as a whore, to earn money to buy heroin. Obviously the police had tracked her down through those two channels—checking on the whores in the districts where drug traffic was heavy, particularly Limehouse and the Docks, London's Chinatown . . . and on the drug patients in the hospitals.

Dr Kettering said, "She can be rehabilitated, sir. But she has to be cleaned first—that's the word we use for detoxified—and weaned of her addiction. Then she has to go to a place where her past is known, where she can be helped in every way, and where she has something worthwhile to do with herself and her time. I would like to keep her here for two weeks—we have an excellent drug rehabilitation programme, as we see a lot of it . . . Then she should be able to go home."

Cate said, "She mustn't go back to the Cottage, alone. She must come back to the Manor, and live with us until the war's over . . . We should never have left her in Beighton, alone, when John joined up . . ."

"I have to have the power to keep her here for those two weeks," the doctor said. "Otherwise she can just walk out. She's over twenty-one, I imagine?"

Cate nodded. The Inspector said, "I can have her held pending investigation of a prostitution charge, sir. She was picking up sailors outside the Old Bull and Bush near the East India Docks, when we found her."

The doctor said, "Good . . . though she's so exhausted, so depressed, that I don't think she'd try to escape. At this moment she couldn't face the life she's been living the last three months . . . There's one other question. The husband's permission must be obtained, for the abortion."

They all looked at Cate. Cate said slowly, "You must get to him, Isabel, and tell him . . . tell him everything . . . Ask him what he wants to do, what he proposes to do, what he wants us here to do. If he washes his hands of Stella, we'll understand. We'll take her back. Meantime, we have to get her on her feet again. Whatever John decides, she'll need her health."

The doctor rose. "Shall we go and see the patient now, then? Very well . . . I warn you, sir, and madam, that she does not at all resemble the young lady who disappeared from Hedlington on Christmas Eve last year. Prepare yourselves."

*   *   *   *

Extract from the diary of John Charteris, Field Marshal Haig's Chief of Intelligence:

March 15. *It seems reasonably certain that the attack will begin within a week or ten days against the Fifth Army—and possibly the Third as well. D.H. has gone to London to put the whole situation before the Cabinet.*

March 18. *Anyhow D.H. has now warned (the Prime Minister) definitely that there will be an attack upon a very large frontage of not less than 50 miles, and has also reminded him that we are short of men; he has been told we will not get many reinforcements.*

The Germans now have 185 divisions on the Western Front . . . so that they should have something like 60 divisions available for one great attack . . . We have only 57 British divisions available on the whole front, but there is an arrangement with the French that they will send early reinforcements if we are attacked, and they are not.

March 19. *It is certain that the attack will be launched either tomorrow or the day after. And my W.A.A.C. typist has decorated my office table with daffodils! The first of the new spring flowers and very beautiful, but such a grotesque prelude to the battle.*

Daily Telegraph, Wednesday, March 20, 1918

COMING OFFENSIVE

Copenhagen, **Tuesday.**
The heads of the German army have invited a number of neutral correspondents to be present at the German offensive on the Western Front. These correspondents will leave for the front on Wednesday—Exchange Telegraph Company.

Liverpool Labour leaders who have just returned from a tour of inspection of the Western Front, interviewed yesterday, spoke in terms of hopefulness regarding the coming campaign. They went out with some doubts, but came home with great cheerfulness as to the outlook.

Cate thought, either the German military are putting on the biggest bluff of the war, or they are so confident of victory that they don't care who knows the exact day, place, and scale of their offensive. It was like the French 1917 offensive under Nivelle . . . everyone knew all the details beforehand and the result was a disaster. This time, a disaster for the Germans? But, with the Germans, one could not be so sure. They were good soldiers.

He picked up the paper and went with it to the library, meaning to finish his reading there, then rest a while. The events of yesterday had destroyed his resilience. All he could think of was that he was tired . . . then of Stella's gaunt face in the bleak hospital ward . . . then that he wouldn't know what to do when she came home . . . then that Isabel was sailing for France tomorrow, and from France directly to America . . . then—a tapping disturbed him and he looked up. Probyn Gorse was at the french window, tapping on the glass. Cate got up, opened the window, and stepped out. The morning was gusty and damp and fresh, the trees thrashing. He should have gone out for a walk before breakfast, and . . .

Probyn said, "I want to talk to you, squire."

"Certainly," Cate said. "Let's walk up and down the lawn."

"Miss Stella's found, eh?"

"Yes, Probyn. Not in very good shape. She's . . . addicted to a dangerous drug."

"She'll get rid of all that soon's she has something to do," Probyn said. "Have a hard time for a year or two, maybe . . . depends how soon she, or Mr John, find the right work for her . . . work that's hard, mind, and dangerous maybe. Don't worry about her . . . You know there's ghosts, squire, eh?"

"Ghosts?" Cate said cautiously. "I haven't seen one myself, but . . ."

"There's ghosts," Gorse said flatly. "Now I seen my mother two, three times this month . . . She's in the bushes, when I come back from taking a pheasant or two from the Park. Recognize her anywhere, that old black dress she always wore, necklace of those big black beads—jet . . . false teeth not fitting right so they made her jaw look funny."

"What does she do, Probyn?"

"Wags a finger at me, looking real sad, and angry, and I'm shaking in my shoes, then she disappears . . . Do you reckon she's angry at me 'cos I haven't married my Woman in church?"

A thought struck Cate and he said, "That might be it—she was always very particular herself in that regard, I remember. But you say you were carrying poached pheasants at the time. It might be that."

"Aye," Probyn muttered. "Mother always said poaching was a sin. Though my dad was better at it nor me . . . I can't sleep proper, thinking. A ghost can stand behind your pillow, making the air round you so that you can't sleep, but when you look, you can't see nothing. That's what Mother's doing . . ."

Cate said nothing. Probyn said plaintively, "But if I don't poach, what'll I do with myself?"

Cate thought of saying, "You could be a gamekeeper, you know"; but left it unsaid; and soon Probyn went, touching his cap then shuffling away fast across the lawn, his ginger-dyed hair blowing.

The Somme: Thursday, March 21, 1918—
the Vernal Equinox

6 To Archie, tramping carefully along the duckboards in the trench bottom, it was so much the same, and so different. It had been a comparatively dry winter, and the chalky soil of the Somme uplands drained better than the waterlogged clay of the Ypres salient; also there was a better slope to the land for the water to run off into the streams and rivers. The trenches were in much better shape they looked almost like the illustrations of trenches in the training manuals, with carefully filled sandbags, right-angle-cornered traverses and bays, intact firesteps, parapets, parados, and berms; the wire—when you could see it— standing firm in three or four rows of double aprons on upright angle-irons or corkscrew metal posts. Some of the faces were the same—here was Kellaway walking in front of him, just behind the C.O., and the black patch over his left eye served rather to emphasize that it was still the old Kellaway . . . the R.S.M., Bolton, small and perky with a large waxed mustache . . . but the C.O. was just the same, gruff, peering pop-eyed into every nook and cranny, staring into men's eyes, glaring at the stubble on their chins, examining the condition of their entrenching tools, mess tins, housewifes; Lieutenant Colonel Quentin Rowland. Archie had arrived yesterday, at two in the afternoon, and the C.O. had looked up from the Corps Comic Cuts that he was reading and said, "Ah, Campbell, you're back. Take over as adjutant from Woodruff right away. He's going on leave to get married"—and returned to reading the intelligence summary. It was now two in the morning, twelve hours later; and they had not mentioned Fiona.

The C.O. stopped, barely seen in the darkness ahead, and Archie heard him say "Who's this?"

A voice answered, "2nd Lieutenant Cowell, sir." Archie caught the gleam of spectacles. He'd studied the roll; Cowell had been out two weeks; had been a schoolmaster in Hedlington, age—forty-four.

"Everything all right?" the C.O. asked.

"Yes, sir."

"Well, make sure the sentries keep a sharp lookout . . . very sharp . . . a ground fog's forming. If it gets worse, tell your company commander. In that case, Kellaway, double sentries."

"Yes, sir."

They moved on. Around two more traverses; another platoon area. Archie heard the C.O. say, "Laurence, is that you?"

"Yes, sir."

"Everything all right?"

"Yes, sir."

Then the same instructions he'd given Cowell. The C.O. turned to the bulky figure of the sergeant behind Laurence, and said, "How many men in the platoon now, sergeant?"

Archie recognized Fagioletti's distinctive Italian-cockney accent as he answered, "Twenty, sir . . . we're eight under strength."

"So's the whole battalion . . . the whole B.E.F.," the C.O. growled. "Make sure there's plenty of extra ammunition ready by all your Lewis guns, Laurence."

"Yes, sir . . . Do you think the Germans are going to attack today, sir?"

"Or tomorrow," the C.O. said. "But we'll get plenty of warning from their artillery preparation."

He darted sideways through a gas curtain and into a dugout. For a moment the warm glow of candlelight illumined the trench, then snapped back to darkness as the curtain fell. Kellaway muttered to Archie, "We'd better follow him, but make sure no light shows . . . ready?"

They slipped through the curtain and down the steps. The C.O. was standing in the middle of the dugout floor, arms akimbo, glaring at five soldiers standing stiffly to attention, all fully clothed except for their helmets. In the middle of the floor was an upturned ammunition box, and on it the unmistakable oilcloth square of a Crown & Anchor board, complete with dice box. Kellaway sighed under his breath and the C.O. wheeled on him, "These men are gambling when they're supposed to be sleeping . . . or on sentry. They can't fight the Germans if they're dead tired." He turned back and faced the oldest man, a leather-faced soldier of over forty. He snapped, "I suppose you're running the board, Lucas."

Private Lucas said, "We was only passing the time, sir. No money was changing 'ands."

"You got it put away too damn fast for me," the C.O. grumbled. "You've had enough practise, God knows . . . See that they're all properly punished," he said to Kellaway; and "Yes, sir," Kellaway answered; but Archie knew he was thinking, what punishment can I possibly give to men who are already spending four hours out of every eight either on sentry or on trench fatigues, and whose presence as fighting men may be needed at any moment to beat off the expected German attack? But then, the C.O. was certainly thinking the same thing.

They went up, the C.O. turning just as they were about to slip through the gas curtain. He spoke to the private soldiers—"Sleep, all of you. We're going to have to fight within a few hours . . . to fight as we've never fought before. I rely on you."

"Yes, sir," Private Lucas said evenly, his face expressionless; the other soldiers mumbled something, looking bashful. Then one large man stepped forward. Archie did not remember seeing him before; but God knew how many privates had passed through the mill since he'd been hit in Nollehoek nearly five months ago. The big man said, "We'll do it, Colonel Quentin, sir . . . the others are showing me how, and we'll do it."

The C.O. stared at the hulking figure, who must have been nearly fifty and said, "You're . . . Willum Gorse. How long have you been with the battalion?"

"Came yesterday, sir, with the last draft . . . Mr Bolton there sent us all off to companies straight away and . . ."

"I didn't have time to see all of you," the C.O. said. "Well, I'm glad you're here." He nodded and left the dugout. In the trench outside he said, "Laurence, were those your men gambling in there?"

"Oh. . ."

Sergeant Fagioletti broke in, "It's my fault, sir. Mr Cate told me to keep an eye on the dugouts, but I was so busy checking the sentries that . . ."

The C.O. said, "You see that it's done, Laurence. And, that new man in this platoon—William Gorse . . . I know him. He's simple. I don't know how they took him."

"He volunteered, sir. He told me," Fagioletti said.

"Well, you'll have to look after him a bit."

"I will, sir."

The C.O. moved on. Kellaway stood aside, saluting, for they had reached the end of B Company's sector. The C.O. turned down a communication trench and slowly returned with his own party to the battalion headquarters dugout in the reserve trench area. "That'll be all till stand-to, Mr Bolton," he said.

The R.S.M. disappeared to his own bunk a few yards down the trench; and Archie, who had been stifling yawns for the past half-hour, said, "Anything more for me, sir?"

"No . . . yes, come to my dugout."

Archie swallowed a sigh and followed the colonel to the dugout next door. The C.O.'s batman was inside, dozing on the floor. Quentin said, "You can go now, Slater . . . Sit down, Campbell." He reached up and pulled down a bottle of whisky from the makeshift plank shelf set in the sandbag wall behind him. In the candlelight he poured whisky into two mugs, splashed in some water and sat down heavily across the "table" from Archie. He said, "I don't like it out there, Campbell . . . it's too quiet. I don't like the fog that's building up."

Archie said, "The Germans can't have planned on the fog, sir."

"No, but it's working for them, if they are going to attack."

"We're ready for them, sir."

The C.O. shook his head. The protuberant blue eyes stared into Archie's. "The Germans aren't to be trusted. They'll have thought up something to take us by surprise. I tell you, you can't trust the Huns an inch . . . I keep racking my brains what they'll do, that's different . . . use tanks, or something worse? A new type of gas which our respirators won't protect us against? That's the most likely . . . This fog gives me the creeps . . ."

Archie said nothing. The Germans could not have somehow created the fog, but . . . the C.O. was very nervous; *he* wouldn't sleep, whatever he told the soldiers to do . . . pity he couldn't relax with a little Crown & Anchor himself . . . or finish the bottle . . . but that wouldn't do, either, if he was expecting a severe battle at any minute.

The C.O. said suddenly, "Did you see Fiona?" His head was down, looking into his glass.

Archie said, "Yes, sir."

"How is she?"

Archie hesitated. Fiona was not in truth in very good shape, because she was lovesick for him, Archie. He said cautiously, "She's fairly well, sir." He drew a deep breath, "I told her I could never see her again. I'm afraid she didn't take it very well . . . she's still infatuated, God knows why, me being what I am . . . but it'll fade away, sir. You'll see. When you can go back and she can realize . . . what you are."

"She'll never be happy with me," Quentin said miserably. "I don't understand her."

Archie said, "I think you do, more than you know. And it doesn't matter. She must understand *you,* is what I told her."

"You did?"

"Yes, sir."

After a time Quentin said, "Well . . . you really don't want to marry her?"

"No, sir," Archie said firmly; and now, it was true.

Quentin said, "Well . . . thank you for what you said . . . I can only hope, when this is over, that . . ." His voice trailed away.

Archie said, "It'll be all right, when you can get back home, sir, and she knows that I've gone for good. Now, if I may, I'll get a little sleep, sir."

Quentin nodded and Archie, having saluted, stooped low under the beams, his steel helmet touching them, went out and to his dugout nearby.

*   *   *   *

Quentin rose some inches vertically in bed as a tremendous explosion shook the earth surrounding the dugout, lifting it a few inches, as he had been lifted, and let it fall back. Grey chalk dust trickled onto his face. The hurricane lantern still burned, the wick as low as it could be set. The first crash was blending now with others, some lighter, some even heavier, up and down the reserve trench lines, behind, in front, on both flanks. He was out of bed now, peering at his watch . . . 4.40 a.m. He grabbed his steel helmet off the hook where it hung, put it on his head and began to struggle into his boots. His batman came in through the gas curtain, fully dressed, equipped, and armed—"Are you all right, sir?"

"Yes. What's it like out there?"

"Shells bursting everywhere, sir . . . Never 'eard such a row, not even before the Somme . . ."

Then Archie Campbell came down, pale in the dim light.

"They've started," Quentin said. "Come on." He led out of the dugout and along the trench to the battalion command post, with its field telephones, orderly clerk, and sentry. The telephone rang even as they entered and Archie picked it up. It was Captain Ryding, commanding C Company in the front line—"We're stood to, Archie . . . some 5.9s falling in the trench, but mostly either just in front or just behind . . . and the fog's dense."

Archie said, "Same here . . . I smell something . . . Gas!"

He ripped open the top of his respirator pack, pulled out the res-

95

pirator, put it on, adjusted the head straps, and put his steel helmet on again.

He stooped again to the telephone and put the snout of his mask as close as he could. Working the field telephone with the mask on was a bastard. "Gas," he shouted, distinctly. "Gas here . . . be ready . . . for gas . . ."

The voice at the other end was distant and hollow, but Archie made out, "All right."

He turned and saw that the C.O. and the R.S.M., who had just arrived, and everyone else in the command post were now wearing respirators. The C.O. shouted, "My eyes are smarting. It's . . ."

"Mine, too, sir," the R.S.M. said. He turned to the clerk who was tugging at the side of his mask, "Don't take it off, man! The gas is phosgene . . . but they've mixed something smarting in it so we'll pull the mask off to wipe them, then . . . die . . ."

Quentin began to cough and weep inside his mask. Perhaps this was the trick the filthy Huns were pulling . . . perhaps there was something else to come. It was five o'clock, raining shells . . . mortar bombs too, light and heavy . . . shells of every calibre, whizzbangs, lights, mediums, heavies, superheavies . . . that was one of the 280-mm shells that had burst close behind the trench to wake him up at the beginning of the bombardment . . . plenty of those mixed in now. He had thought the bombardment leading up to the Passchendaele offensive on July 31st last year was the loudest and strongest he'd ever heard. This was worse. Perhaps that was the German trick, just a more savage bombardment than anyone had counted on. But they couldn't keep this up for long; and though they'd do a lot of damage and cause a lot of casualties, this by itself wasn't enough to break the line . . . not very deep, at least.

He said, "I'm going up the line. Archie, come with me. Mr Bolton, stay here and take messages, please."

Archie, the two batmen at his heels, followed the C.O. out into the storm—a thin quarter moon, third quarter, glowing dim through the fog. The stink of ammonal was heavy, choking, even through the gas mask. The trenches that had looked so trim a few hours ago were now falling back into the primeval condition that had epitomized the end of the Passchendaele battle. Bodies were lying in the trench bottom, some moving, some still. Most of the men were up on the firestep, rifles rested, staring into the dark fog. He thought for a moment the Germans were firing star shell, but realized that it was only the bursting of the projectiles themselves.

"Stand fast, men . . . stick it out . . ." He heard the C.O.'s voice under the storm, like a soothing recitative in a church a thousand miles away, or from an underground cave . . . "Well done . . . stand fast, Wealds . . . How many belts do you have with the gun, corporal? . . . Good . . . Keep your head up, Private Penfold, you can't kill Germans you don't see."

But they can kill us, those bloody German guns, Archie thought. Some shells must be going the other way by now, as the British artillery replied to the bombardment, but they could not be heard down here in the catacombs of the trenches.

They moved on . . . "Pull a third of your men down from the parapet, Ryding, let them stay in the dugouts till the Germans come . . . Change them round frequently . . . Stand fast, Wealds, stand fast!"

*   *   *   *

Laurence Cate stood on the firestep beside one of his sentries, Sergeant Fagioletti on his other side. They were all sweating in their gas masks, like everyone else. It was six o'clock, daylight permeating the fog, the land still murkily opaque to the west. The Germans hadn't come yet. They liked to attack at dawn itself, in that first light when you could just see movement, and trace the beginnings of colour. It was past that by now, and they had not come. This was the good light to go down on the marsh by Sheppey and lie watching in the reeds, as the colour came into flat arms of the sea, and the birds awoke and stirred and called to each other. His father had let him go alone on his bicycle to Sheppey ever since his tenth birthday. Once a bull had charged him in a field he was crossing . . . twice he had found horses grazing, and jumped up on one and ridden it round in the dawn, by the marsh and the calm sea . . .

"The captain's coming round again, sir," Fagioletti shouted in his ear.

Laurence leaped down from the firestep as Kellaway appeared, followed by his batman. They conversed shouting at each other through the masks, under the bellow of the bombardment—"Are you all right here?"

"Yes, sir . . . quite . . ."

"It's a bloody noise."

"Is it, sir? Yes, I suppose so . . ."

"Mind your field telephone is kept in order . . . Tell the men, stand tight, stick it out."

Kellaway passed on. Fagioletti said, "I've got some cottonwool, sir . . . You'd better put some in your ears."

Laurence said, "Thanks . . . I don't need it. Is it so noisy?" He shook his head. Perhaps it was, but you could pretend it wasn't, the same as you could be on the Isle of Sheppey instead of here. There was a place, close to where the railway crossed over, where Aunt Alice told him she had once seen a Marsh Harrier . . . that was rare. He'd go back there one day soon . . . soon . . .

*   *   *   *

The ground fog was bad, too bad to take off in normal days; but today was not normal. Lieutenant Colonel Freeman, commanding the 9th (Day) wing, to which 333 belonged, had spoken to Guy on the telephone at half-past five in the morning. The first part of his message—that the German bombardment had begun—Guy knew already; he could hear it clearly. The earth was shuddering even back here in Mirvaux. The second part of the message was an order to take the Three Threes into the air as soon as he could, and sweep the front, strafing the German front line and all areas immediately behind it where attacking troops and artillery could be expected to be massed.

The forward visibility was fifty to eighty yards in the pale but dense fog. Upward visibility . . . who knew? Guy prayed that the fog would not extend more than a hundred feet or so upward; the river fogs generally did not; but Very lights fired from the ground could go that high, and if fired when the ground staff heard their engines overhead, could enable them to grope their way back to earth. The wing commander had left the takeoff to his discretion and timing. If he made a bad decision, it could be disastrous for a lot of them.

He set his jaw and turned his plane down the field, A Flight in echelon to right and left behind him. The Camel bounced and lurched ever faster over the grass . . . rose . . . he eased the stick back . . . up into the fog, dense droplets condensing on the rudimentary windshield and chasing each other across his goggles . . . the engine muffled though so close . . . out! The sun about to rise dead ahead; and Fokkers, waiting, low, in the eye of the sun. He raised his arm and pointed. Looking round, he saw that all four flights were in position: ten Fokkers, thirteen Camels. The fight would be very close to the ground, just above the fog ceiling. He couldn't tell yet whether Werner was among them. Another quick glance away, this time down . . . the fog extended far in all directions. It seemed to fade away perhaps twenty miles to the west. But the great ground battle would be fought out under that white blanket, stippled with the glowing, fading red and yellow flowers of explosions. The Royal Flying Corps could do nothing yet—no strafing, bombing, nothing—except weaken the enemy air force so that later, when the sun had dispersed the fog, it could not play an effective part. So, for now—"Tally ho!" he shouted into the shrieking wind of his upward passage.

*   *   *   *

The pattern of the bombardment changed and Quentin looked at his watch—9.35 a.m. There was much less of the distinctive hiss of gas shells. There was plenty of gas still in the air but the Huns were not now adding to it. The heavies had come forward from counter batterywork and were plastering the front line, where he stood close to Ryding, next to two Vickers machine guns of the Machine Gun Corps. Another pair of guns thirty yards on, sited to fire in enfilade across the front had been destroyed by a direct hit from a 5.9 half an hour ago. The fog was as dense as ever. He listened tensely; heavy and light mortars, which had not been in action for some time, were now firing again at full speed, raining their bombs onto the front line and just behind it . . . field guns were firing on the second line . . . beyond that he could not tell. It felt like Zero Hour, the moment of attack . . . 9.40 . . . nothing to be seen beyond the reeling posts of the wire, the wire itself, great gashes hacked in it by the heavy shells, lips of craters newly gouged out of the earth . . . The heavies were lifting . . . over the trench, farther back. The infantry must be coming . . . no use firing lights of any kind. A Vickers to the left began a long chatter, and like rooks rousing from their roosts, the whole front line caught fire . . . Lewis guns stammering, rifles barking by the hundred . . . the men were all up on the firestep . . . and there at last, at last, were the Huns, coming crouched over the dry earth, running, making no other sound, one group here, under the fire of a Lewis gun, another there, dimly seen in the fog, one man falling, the rest coming on. He picked up the field telephone and said, "Mr Bolton, call for the SOS fire."

The R.S.M.'s voice was tinny—"Line cut, sir, but I think the guns are firing anyway."

Quentin jumped down into the trench, grabbed a rifle from a fallen man, filled his pockets with ammunition, hung a cotton bandelier of it over one shoulder—"Come on, Campbell," he said. "Let's see how Kellaway's doing." He stumbled fast along the trench, shouting as he went to the men on the firestep above him, "Keep at it . . . Aim, Wealds, aim! . . . Kill!"

*   *   *   *

Laurence Cate stooped lower to peer into the hedge, between the interstices of the alder and hazel. Yes, there it was, the beginnings of a nest, probably a blackbird's. Yes, it was a blackbird, for here was the mother bird to be, brown and pert, scolding him from twenty feet farther along the edge of the wood. And on the other side, the male, glossy black, bright yellow beak. Better move on or he'd disturb them. He forced through the hedge and into the wood. The leaves were the

99

bright pale green of spring, the ground damp and smelling of wet earth, bright with primroses . . . more nests high overhead, swaying as the boughs on which they were built stooped to the west wind, making small arcs against the sky . . . the fog had dispersed about noon, and the day become clear and fine and fresh. He walked on, keeping a sharp eye open for birds . . . but the copse belonged to the colony of rooks high above there, and the blackbirds in the hedge. It was only a small copse. He was soon out of it, walking across a field showing the earliest spears of winter wheat, over a gate, into a lane. There were men beyond the lane, spread out, moving to the west across the fields. They would disturb the birds. He'd see no more until they had gone. Here was a little barn . . . clamp, really, of the sort they kept turnips or wurzels in at home—low roof, dug half into the earth. This one's door was broken, leaning open on one hinge. Inside, blankets, planks on the stone floor, equipment cast away, greatcoats, rifles, gas masks, everything. He sat down, leaning back against the cold wall, staring straight ahead. No birds would come in here. But what . . . where . . . why, here? Gradually his eyes closed and he slipped sideways until he was lying flat on one side, on top of the blankets and refuse left behind by the men who had fled from this place two miles in the rear, about an hour and a half earlier.

*   *   *   *

In the portion of the old front-line trench where Quentin Rowland stood, with his adjutant and half a dozen other men, it was quiet. To right and left the trench had been completely caved in by artillery fire, boxing in the thirty yards, including one bay and a traverse, where the little party stood, some on the remains of the firestep, facing east, some on the crumbling rear wall, facing west. A field telephone lay in the bottom of the trench, but all wires from it had been cut long ago, before dark. No one answered, however often or hard you cranked the bell. It was near midnight of March 21st.

Quentin said, "Haven't heard or seen any Huns for a long time."

"No one has, sir," Archie said. He was bone weary, too tired to be afraid. There had been plenty of fear during the endless day, but fear of a different kind from any he had known before in the war. From arrival with the battalion in June 1916 he had endured waves of anguished fear that he would be killed, or maimed. The fear was of the clattering bullets that he had often seen cut off a man's life, rip blood from his lungs and mouth, fill his steel helmet with his brains . . . fear of the shells that made the terrible noise, and shook the earth, and could tear young limbs to shreds in an instant, and spatter whole men, as red pulp, against a wall of chalk. Today it had been fear of the unknown. What in the name of Jesus Christ was happening? The Germans had come in the fog   many had died there under the wire, tendrils of fog caressing them, crawling over them, testing— is this alive or dead?—like snakes looking for a meal. Some had passed mysteriously on, jumping over trenches and disappearing into the west . . . the shelling kept stopping, starting. Gradually the battalion had become broken up into separate parts, each isolated. There was no link between them—no telephone, no signals by Very light or flag, no aircraft dropped messages, no runners came sliding under the wire. No one came—not even Germans. Archie knew attacks; he'd attacked, and been attacked. You reached the enemy's wire, and you broke through, or not. You took the trench, or you did not. You had so many dead, but you knew where they were . . . the corporal and three privates killed by the machine gun that had suddenly opened up from the Pope's Nose . . . two more men missing, but you really knew they'd been blown away by the 5.9 just as you were going over the top . . . Today, where were they? Had the Germans succeeded, or failed? Where were *they?*

The C.O. said, "Those buggers are just sweeping on, through whatever holes they make. They're not stopping to mop up pockets of resistance." He walked angrily three yards up the trench and Archie felt rather than saw him swing back in the dark—"Clever swine!" He stopped opposite Archie and his face loomed white and close. "I'm not commanding my battalion sitting here with ten men . . ."

"Eight, sir," Archie said, "including me."

"Well, I'm going to find some more of my men and get back at those swine. We can move about a bit in the dark, but we won't be able to tomorrow . . . not without artillery support or smoke . . . I think A Company was overrun."

"I think so, too, sir. I couldn't see clearly for the fog, but I'm almost positive I saw Germans pouring into their trenches."

"I think B fell back before they were surrounded."

"Some of them, sir . . ."

"Fell back west . . . How far, we don't know. They may be in the second line . . . the third . . . the support . . . God knows how far back they went. But somewhere, back there, there must be a firm line again . . . Do you realize this is the end of trench warfare, Campbell? It'll be like 1914 again. Open warfare! We'll be out of these bloody trenches for good! No more rats . . . Gather the men here . . . Listen, men—we're going to get out and find some of the rest of the battalion. Keep together, in arrowhead, but close. Don't lose touch with the men on your right and left whatever happens. All bayonets fixed. Follow me, then."

He lifted his own rifle to the proper position for an assault, of the high port, scrambled up the back slope of the trench wall and out, waiting on the top until the eight other men had joined him. Then, moving slowly but steadily across the torn soil, he headed west.

*   *   *   *

John Merritt awoke from deep sleep with a start. What had awakened him? Music . . . a bugle . . . blowing the "Stand-to." Someone was running past his tent, "Stand-to! Stand-to! . . . Officers to the regimental post of command!"

Rudy Anspach was up, lighting the lantern, pulling on his field boots. Three minutes later the two young men were hurrying between the rows of officers' tents, fully dressed for battle, with steel helmets, greatcoats, gas masks, and side arms.

In the big headquarters tent the colonel was standing at the end behind his office table. They waited. After five minutes he said, "Everybody here, Ewing?"

The regimental adjutant said, "Yes, sir. Except for an officer each from Batteries A and F, on overnight leave."

The colonel nodded, then raised his voice—"All hell's broken loose on the British front. The Germans have attacked on a front of about fifty miles on the Somme. Details are not clear and won't be for some time, but it's obvious there's been a big breakthrough in front of Amiens. General Pershing has been asked to have troops ready to help, and he's ordered our division to move north, at once, to La Fère, which is twenty-five kilometres from here—a little over sixteen miles. The infantry move in an hour. We follow. Further details to battalion commanders at 2 a.m. here. Meantime, see that the men get some food into their bellies. That's all, gentlemen. Dismissed!"

*   *   *   *

In the first faint light Quentin Rowland stopped and spread his men out a little farther apart. They had been moving off and on for nearly six hours now. He had no real idea how much ground they had covered, but guessed it was close to two miles, perhaps three. After the first ten minutes they had been fired on from a shell crater. It took half an hour to establish that the inhabitants of the crater were an officer and nine men of the Northumberland Fusiliers. Quentin had ordered them to join him and again moved on, now nineteen strong. An hour later, two lines of deserted trenches having been crossed, they were fired on again. This time lights went up, illuminating the field, and machine guns fired from close range, the bullets clacking low, mostly overhead as the men lay pressed to the ground, but two of his men had been killed, and one too badly wounded to continue. It took an hour to work round to the flank of that post, which he knew to be German because they had shouted to him in German and broken English to surrender . . . They'd killed some of the swine, and then he was past . . . Christ, there *must* be a line somewhere, a Red Cap to say "All stragglers gather there, sir" . . . But so far, they had not met any other formed body, only figures who ran away in the darkness . . . single bullets from nowhere, short, doubtful bursts, from distant light machine guns.

And now at last, the light. He said, "Keep tight formation . . . but not too close there . . . Mr Wolfe, keep your men thirty yards behind me. If we are fired on, get out to a flank and give me covering fire."

"Yes, sir."

"All right. Advance!"

He moved off. It was amazing how little the ground here, only two or three miles behind the front line, had been affected by the war. The front lines had been so stable for nearly four years now. The Somme offensive had moved them forward a little, but since then—nothing. The copse over to his right, with the rooks stirring against the early light, might have been on the hill behind High Staining . . . the fields were sprouting a pale green fuzz of winter wheat.

A soldier on the right of the arrowhead formation said, "Someone waving at us from the edge of the big wood over there, sir. He's wearing a British helmet."

"The Huns have plenty of those," Quentin said; but he raised his arm and changed the direction of movement toward the wood, which stretched along the hillside and over the brow of the gentle slope to his right front. As he came nearer he saw two men standing, both officers. To right and left of them the edge of the wood was lined with British soldiers, lying prone, rifles and Lewis guns thrust forward.

One of the officers was a major and one a lieutenant. They saluted, seeing the crown and star on Quentin's shoulder, and the major began to say, "I have . . .", when a machine gun opened fire from the south-west across the rolling fields, and cut leaves began to shower down from the trees overhead.

Quentin dropped to one knee and turned to his party, shouting, "Run! . . . Take position there with the others!"

The major and lieutenant knelt beside him. Field grey figures were spreading out in the fast strengthening light from a row of barns and farm buildings half a mile away. The British soldiers in the wood opened a steady, aimed fire.

"That'll bring on their guns," the major said. "We've dug a little during the night . . . not much, though."

Quentin said, "What have you got?"

"A hundred and fifteen men, sir . . . Mostly my regiment, Duke of Wellington's, but some from everywhere—Gordons, Cameronians, Wiltshires, Worcesters, London Rifle Brigade . . . nine Lewis guns, one Vickers . . . they've been coming in ever since I got here about dusk last night."

"Any Wealds?"

"I don't think so, sir."

The lieutenant said, "A Jock told me there was nearly a company of Wealds in another farm down there"—he pointed north—"but . . ."

"Might be Kellaway," Quentin muttered. "Take a couple of men and run and find out, Campbell. Whoever they are, unless they have a brigadier general with them, bring them up here. We'll make this place a redoubt, and call it . . ."

"I have already named it Duke's Wood, sir," the major said respectfully but firmly.

"All right," Quentin said. "Duke's Wood Redoubt it is . . . Hurry up, Campbell. I want those men here in fifteen minutes."

He realized, looking at his adjutant, that Campbell was nervous about breaking into the open, even though he would be leaving the wood on the side away from the Germans . . . well, there might be Germans that side, too. Friend and foe were inextricably mixed up by now. The real trouble was that Campbell had only known the trenches and trench warfare. He felt naked out in the open, not realizing that in this war of movement the Germans could not be using massed, fixed, concentrated machine guns—only what weapons and ammunition they could carry with them. Nor could they get instant, overwhelming artillery support, because they wouldn't have good communications with the gun positions. No time to explain all this now, so he repeated, impatiently, "Hurry up, Campbell!"

Then Archie, with his two men, rose to their feet and hurried off northward through the wood, and at the far edge, with only the briefest pause, ran out into the open, and raced across the young wheat to the distant row of red brick barns and sheds.

*   *   *   *

Private Willum Gorse, on watch near the corner of one of the barns, shouted excitedly, "Hey, three men a-coming, sergeant . . . three men a-running . . ."

"Ours?" Sergeant Fagioletti asked sharply.

"Oh yes, I can see 'em clear . . . Why, one's an officer. It's Mr Campbell."

Captain Kellaway, his face drawn with worry and fatigue, his good eye bloodshot and blinking with strain, said, "Who? By God, it is . . . !"

Fagioletti waited, rifle rested on the brickwork beside him. For a moment he had felt a great surge of relief, when Gorse had said that an officer was coming It would be Mr Cate, who had disappeared yesterday . . . just vanished, no trace of him, no blood, no bones, nothing. What had happened to him? He must have been killed, blown to pieces by one of those Hun shells the size of a house. But . . . but . . . could he have just wandered off? You'd think it would be impossible in the trenches, but that day, yesterday, anything was possible . . . the fog so thick you sometimes couldn't see five yards, with your mask on, because it was full of gas, and something else that made your eyes smart and itch, and then on top of that the fumes of the ammonal and the reck of cordite from your own bullets firing. You felt like going mad, not knowing what was happening, what had happened, what would happen . . . fire at a Hun running across your front, tear off your mask and rub frantically at your eyes, choke, vomit, shit . . . He was thirsty, his mouth dry.

It was Mr Campbell all right, now speaking quickly to the captain—"The C.O.'s up there, Stork . . . that wood, they've called it Duke's Wood Redoubt . . . and he has over a hundred and thirty men, with several Lewis guns. He wants you whatever you've got here—to join him there right away, at once. Some Germans are attacking from the other side of the wood, but I don't think they're enough to get very close—yet. What do you have here?"

"Forty men of my company and twenty from other battalions. Four officers, two of them gunners . . . but Laurence Cate has gone."

"Killed?"

"We don't know. He just vanished some time yesterday, his platoon sergeant tells me . . . All right. It'll take me a couple of minutes to tell everyone and organize an advance. We can't just move up like a football crowd." He hurried off, calling, "Officers, all officers to me!" He came back toward Archie beckoning, as the officers began to hurry across the farmyard, and muttered, "Archie, bring up the rear with your men. Deal with anyone who tries to sneak off. We've got a pretty jumpy lot here."

"All right, Stork," Campbell said grimly. He checked the rifle that he, like his C.O. , had taken off a corpse yesterday and made sure that he had a round in the breech. These men were going to realize that

105

when Lieutenant Colonel Quentin Rowland gave an order, even indirectly, it would be enforced.

The men were spread out in two groups, side by side, in a loose line. Sergeant Fagioletti and one of the gunner subalterns were with the group on the right. They moved steadily up toward the big wood on the slope above. British rifles and machine guns chattered in the wood and German overs smacked overhead, but no artillery shells were coming close, though guns were firing all round the horizon, and occasional shells raised brown mushrooms of earth in distant fields. Archie felt completely lost. The guns weren't firing east or west, but in every direction; and they weren't in gun pits two miles behind the line, they were here—there, two 18-pounders, standing at the corner of a small copse, abandoned . . . and here was a dead man, in the field, a German officer, a bullet through the middle of his forehead, very neat . . .

Just as Kellaway had feared, a couple of men from the left group were dropping back. In a minute they'd vanish into the copse. Archie raised his rifle and fired a bullet a yard in front of the men's noses, shouting, "Get back in line, there!" The men stopped, startled, then ran forward to rejoin the rest of their group.

On the right Sergeant Fagioletti jumped down into a sunken lane and moved along it with half a dozen men spread out behind. The soldier on the left, Private Lucas, said, "I'm going to take a look in the turnip clamp there, sarn't. Maybe some bloke left a drop of rum in there."

"All right, but look sharp."

The soldier disappeared through the broken door, his bayonet thrust forward. A moment later Fagioletti heard him call, "Sergeant, 'ere, quick!"

"What is it?" Fagioletti yelled, breaking into a run. He burst into the twilit gloom of the clamp, and stopped short. Lucas was standing facing Lieutenant Cate. Cate was standing, too, looking puzzled, his mouth a little open.

Fagioletti stammered, "Sir . . . it's you . . . you're all right?"

"Yes," Cate said. "Where's the rest of the platoon?"

"Some of 'em outside, sir . . . what's left." He realized suddenly that the young officer would have some explaining to do. He said, "Come along, sir. The colonel's ordered us up to the wood . . . this way, sir." He caught Laurence's sleeve and pulled him out into the open, Lucas following. Cate said, "You needn't pull me, sergeant . . . Lucas, Jessop, Brace . . . spread out more!"

Lucas shot Fagioletti a strange look and said, "Yes, sir."

Fagioletti dropped back and said in a low voice to Lucas, "What am I going to say? They'll shoot him."

Lucas said, "Can't say he was with us all the time. The captain knows he wasn't . . . It's shell shock."

"That's it. Shell shock! And now he's over it."

"Is he?" Lucas said grimly. "We'll see."

*　　*　　*　　*

It was noon of March 22nd. The Germans had been passing by Duke's Wood Redoubt all day, mostly in small numbers, advancing in skirmishing order, but occasionally in larger masses of up to a battalion at a time. The garrison had fought off one small and one large attack, the latter supported by a dozen field guns. The guns had inflicted some casualties, but by now the trenches were deeper, the men driven on to use their entrenching tools with desperate energy. But for every inch the trenches sank, Quentin's gloomy anger increased. Back to trench warfare . . . it had been a real thrill, just like old times on the North-West Frontier, or before and after Le Cateau, to move across the open, fighting man to man, not machine to monstrous machine. He'd have to court-martial Laurence if he didn't do something really valuable today. Perhaps there should be a Court of Inquiry first, as no one seemed to know what had happened. Laurence himself couldn't explain how he got back into the turnip clamp where they'd found him; all he could say was, "I must have run away, sir . . . but I don't know." Whatever the truth was, he couldn't afford to let the men think that an officer would get special treatment just because he was a relative of the C.O.'s . . . But today Laurence would have the opportunity to redeem himself.

He turned to Archie, sitting beside him on the edge of a small trench, about three feet deep, which was his command post. "I'm going to counterattack before they bring up heavier artillery, Campbell. I've made my plan. Our object will be to break clear, so that we can continue the withdrawal as a formed body until we find a definite line . . . And I must do it before our ammunition gets any lower. I'm going to clear the Germans out of that little spinney over there, where they have three machine guns. I'll attack that with B Company, and as soon as they have got it, we'll start withdrawing, first to the barns . . . from there, we'll cover B back . . . and so on. We called them laybacks, on the Frontier . . . Send for all officers here, please."

*　　*　　*　　*

Sergeant Fagioletti gathered himself. They only had a hundred yards of open ground to cross. The Germans were shelling Duke's Wood Redoubt steadily now, and everyone's head was down, their bodies crammed into the shallow trenches. The colonel had given the officers the orders half an hour ago. Somewhere to his right, facing the little wood which was the objective, across the bare field, were half a dozen men with rifle grenades and launchers. The colonel had no artillery, but plenty of Mills bombs, so that was to be the artillery support. Better pray that some of the grenades landed in those Jerry machine gunners' ears . . . the Jerries hadn't had time to dig in, that was sure: they'd only sneaked into the wood an hour or so ago . . . Mr Cate had explained the orders very clearly: the captain was leading the attack on the right, Mr Cate on the left . . . forty men of B Company, the 1st Battalion, the Weald Light Infantry. There were about fifteen Jerries in the wood, the officers seemed to think—machine gunners for the three guns, and a dozen riflemen covering them . . . Must be nearly time to go.

"Ahhhh! Aaah!" He heard a high screaming gasp from close to and raised his head. Willum Gorse, twenty yards away, was lying half out of his slit trench, his hands upflung. "They've got me," he gasped, "legs . . ." He turned his head and moaned, "Legs . . ."

Private Lucas was there, in the trench. He called across to Fagioletti, "Both legs smashed above the knee, sarn't."

"First field dressing . . ."

"No more use than farting agin thunder," Lucas said briefly.

A whistle shrilled and Fagioletti, Lucas, and the rest jumped to their feet. The rifle grenades were fired with the distinctive loud hollow bang of the propellant cartridges . . . the men of B Company were charging out of the wood. There was the captain, his revolver outthrust. Every Lewis gun in the Redoubt was firing at the objective, to keep the German machine gunners' heads down . . . but where was Mr Cate? He'd been ten feet away, just now, before the Germans increased their shelling, as though they'd guessed that the British were going to sally out of the wood. Fagioletti had asked him if he was all right . . . "Quite, thank you, sergeant," he'd said, and smiled . . . smiled as though he wasn't just about to lead a charge across open ground against German machine guns. Fagioletti looked desperately around . . . no sign of him. The grenades had completed their trajectories and were falling into the wood . . . bang! bang! bang! Men fell, here, there, something plucked at his sleeve, then he was in, his bayonet at the throat of a German gunner, the man's hands up. They had the wood! The captain was there, a Very light pistol firing red in the bright daylight. "Where's Mr Cate?" the captain gasped.

"Don't know, sir . . . perhaps he was hit, by the shelling, just before we started. P'raps . . ."

"Perhaps," Kellaway said. "Turn those guns round, man, quick. The others are going to leave the Redoubt in three minutes after we gave the success signal, and that's gone up. They want covering fire."

Fagioletti yelled, "Lucas, Jones, Jackman, give me a hand with these guns . . . here, you, show 'em how to feed the belt in." He raised his rifle threateningly at the nearest German. Christ, Mr Cate was for it this time; deserting his commanding officer when ordered for an attack . . . punishment: death.

*　　*　　*　　*

The adjutant popped his head round the door of Guy Rowland's office and said, "Wing Commander on the phone, sir." Guy went through to the outer office; Major Sugden had had the machine on his own desk, but Guy found it interrupted his thinking, so gave it to the adjutant.

He picked it up—"Rowland here, sir."

Colonel Freeman's voice was weary—"Morning, Guy. Your dawn patrol back yet?"

"No, sir."

"I told you not to take it yourself because I was expecting orders. They've come. We're to evacuate Mirvaux—both squadrons. Move to Vercors le Château. I want you to lay out the site, while Tim Fairchild moves the squadrons.'"

"Very well, sir," Guy said. Major Fairchild was the commanding officer of the Bristol Fighter squadron that shared Mirvaux with the Three Threes.

"Fix details with him. I'll be sending you some extra lorries as soon as I can get some. God knows how many. The army staff are in, well, chaos is too strong a word . . . but only just."

"What's happened, sir?" Guy asked. "Have the Germans made another big breakthrough?"

"As far as we know, no," the tinny voice at the other end said. "But the battle's been going on for five days now and there's still no real line, nothing fixed. No one can say yet that the Germans are here, our chaps there. So the brigadier general has ordered all wings to find new fields twenty miles back."

"The extra distance will be a bit of a handicap to us," Guy said.

"Can't be helped. We can't risk the airfields being overrun by Jerry ground troops, or suddenly shelled by their heavies . . . Good luck."

Guy hung up thoughtfully. On the second day of the great German offensive he had flown back, on orders, to look for airfield sites farther west; and had chosen Vercors le Château and two others as good possibilities. There had been no time for more then; now he had to fly back, land and actually decide where the runway would be, where the aircraft would be pegged out, what billets would be available, where tents and workshops would be placed, what access roads were available and in what state. He'd need the quartermaster. He turned to the adjutant, "Dandy, we're moving. I want to see Gorringe as soon as he lands. Send for the quartermaster. Have the squadron staff car ready to go in an hour. Also my Camel."

The adjutant began to speak, but stopped suddenly, listening— "They're coming back, sir—the dawn patrol."

Guy cocked an ear and snapped, "They're not ours . . . Fokkers!"

He ran out of the hut, drawing his revolver. Eight Fokker triplanes were screaming in low from the east, out of the sun, their guns clattering and blazing. Thank God the squadron's not on the ground, Guy thought—only my plane. The Fokkers swooped down in line ahead, breaking off right and left to machine-gun the huts, tents, buildings, and the three aircraft on the ground—two Bristol Fighters and Guy's Sopwith Camel. He stood outside his command headquarters, aiming carefully with his revolver, and firing as each machine roared over his head. From the corner of his eye he saw flames and turned as his Camel exploded in a single mushroom of flame, followed by a towering column of black smoke. Simultaneously, the sound of machine-gun fire and the snarling and whining of aircraft engines increased. Behind him the adjutant shouted, "Ours are back, sir!"

The air was thick with planes as the twelve machines of Three Threes, returning from patrol, attacked the eight Fokkers. One Fokker, taken by surprise from behind and above, streaked down in flames . . . and another . . . a third was making a pancake landing half a mile to the north . . . one Camel was down, limping, dragging a wing, cartwheeling across a field, pilot probably wounded or dead before he hit . . . It was all over. The Fokkers were dots receding low toward the east, smoke trailing from one of them. The Camels were circling, coming in on the last of their petrol—one of C Flight dead stick . . . they were down.

Guy turned to the adjutant, "Tell them at Wing that we need two more Camels. Send them to Vercors at once, please."

*   *   *   *

The 137th Regiment, U.S. Field Artillery, was in bivouac behind La Fère, most of the men sleeping in barns and sheds, a few billeted in the scattered houses of the little hamlet. The battle still raged to the north, but the line no longer ran straight toward St Quentin—it bulged out ominously toward the west—and it was no longer a line. The Americans waited, ready.

Some men of Battery A, billeted in a cow barn, were singing a song that had been a favorite on the ship coming over:

Goodbye, pa; goodbye, ma; goodbye, mule, with your old hee-haw:
I may not know what the War's about, but I bet, by gosh! I'll soon find out.
Goodbye, sweetheart, don't you care; I'll bring you a piece of the Kaiser's ear.
I'll bring you a Turk and a German, too, And that's about all one fellow can
   do.

In Battery D John Merritt was walking behind Captain Hodder as he inspected the battery's teams of draft horses. The four guns were lined up in a field a hundred yards away, breech mechanisms covered by tarpaulins. Distant artillery to the north mumbled and grumbled under the munching of the horses at their nosebags.

Hodder stopped opposite a sturdy bay gelding, examined it carefully from fetlock to croup, then turned to the soldier standing at attention by the horse's head, "This beast's got catarrh, soldier. What are you doing about it?"

The soldier, John Merritt's Navajo friend Chee Shush Benally, said, "Singing, sir."

Captain Hodder eased his weight back onto his heels—"Singing, eh? What sort of songs? *Over there . . . K-k-katie?*"

"Navajo sing," Benally said, expressionless.

John said, "Excuse me, captain, but . . . I served with this man in the 16th Infantry. He told me a lot about how the Navajo cure sickness in men and animals. They perform ceremonies, which they call 'sings.' Sometimes they make sand paintings. He's not a medicine man, a proper singer, but he knows how to perform the ceremony."

Hodder said, "I see . . . Well, soldier, if that horse isn't well from your singing, by this time tomorrow, it'll get regular veterinary treatment, like any other horse in this battery . . . and you can do some singing in the guard house."

The Indian remained motionless, staring straight ahead. John knew he wasn't angry, or put out. The horse would get well; the white man would attribute it to pure chance.

He followed the captain. Down the narrow lane beyond the guns French infantry surged westwards in dense column, with horsedrawn cookers rolling on heavy iron wheels among them, smoke pouring from the tall chimneys, men, guns . . . tramp tramp tramp . . . neighing of horses, sharp yells of sergeants.

A car was coming the other way, flying the Stars and Stripes from its fender. Hodder looked up and exclaimed, "Good God, is General Pershing coming? Well, he doesn't go for eyewash. Let's get on with what we were doing."

The car crawled on through the dense press of the French, who unwillingly made way for it. A hundred yards away it turned into the field where the guns were, and an officer in a long greatcoat jumped out of the back seat and hurried forward. He was a major and Hodder saluted as he came up. The major gasped, "I'm looking for Battery D, 137th Field Artillery . . ."

"This is it," Hodder said briefly. "What can I do for you, sir?"

"General Pershing told me to bring that lady to see an officer in your command."

John thought, heavens, the lady must have some pull to get General Pershing's permission to come this far forward . . . and be sent up in one of the commander-in-chief's own cars, too. Then he saw a shortish woman in a fur coat and warm hat climb down from the car, helped by the soldier driver. She raised her veil and came toward them, limping slightly on a stick. "Aunt Isabel!" he exclaimed.

"Mrs. Kramer," the major said. "She wants to speak to a 2nd Lieutenant Merritt."

Hodder said, "This is Merritt. He's a 1st Lieutenant now. Go ahead, lieutenant."

John hurried forward, remembered he was in uniform, halted six paces from his aunt and saluted her formally. Then he rushed forward and hugged her—"What are you doing here?" he exclaimed, standing back. "How did you get General Pershing's permission? How . . . ?" Then he saw the expression on her face and stopped.

His aunt said gently, "John, we've found Stella. In London, a week ago. With the German offensive it's taken me a long time to get up here."

"How is she?"

"She's not well."

They were walking away from everyone else, across the field, guns to the right, horses to the left, toward the endless columns of the French infantry and artillery.

Isabel said, "She has venereal disease. And she is pregnant . . . two months."

The words beat him nearly into the ground. He waited a minute, while his aunt held his hand. Then, his strength recovered enough to speak, he said, "Where is she now?"

"In hospital, the Limehouse. The doctors think they can cure her of her addiction in two or three weeks, the disease in the same. She has consented to an abortion, but your consent is needed, too. Do you give it?"

John walked away from her toward the row of 75s. She had lost one child already . . . he had heard that babies born of mothers with venereal disease were sometimes born blind . . . she would be clear of the disease long before then . . . What miserable hours, days, weeks, she must have spent . . . alone, gripped by the craving, no way of escape . . . And he as helpless in the grip of the war. She must have something to hold on to, to live for, to become strong for . . . He could not bear to think of the men to whom she had sold her body, a prostitute, bartering that once pure beauty to them, for money—no, for the drug . . . But this was no time to think of that. He loved her.

He turned back to his aunt. He said, "I think she needs the baby. Tell her . . . she can keep it, if she wants to. But if she doesn't, I'll consent to the abortion."

"You must put that down in writing," she said. "Are you sure you're doing the right thing, John? It would be so much easier, if the baby was not born."

"I don't think so. I'm not against abortion at all. I just think that Stella needs, will need, the baby . . . I love her . . . and for her, because it's hers, I'll love it."

Isabel dabbed her eyes with a handkerchief. "You're a . . . a man, John. I promised General Pershing I'd go straight back as soon as I'd spoken to you. Then I'm going home . . . to California, to see Walter."

John stared at her, thinking—she's leaving Father Christopher. She must be in misery, as great as mine. She leaned her head against him and sobbed on his shoulder, while he patted her back, wordlessly.

*　　　*　　　*　　　*

Quentin Rowland, digging in on a showery hillside above the Somme, with a hundred men, from ten regiments, but mostly the remnants of his own Weald Light Infantry, said angrily, "This time we're not going to move. I don't care how many Germans surround us. Here we are and here we'll bloody well stay. I've had enough of being pushed around by a pack of Huns."

"Yes, sir," Archie Campbell said. It was April 2nd, and the battle had been raging for twelve days. Four times in those twelve days the C.O.'s party had found rations. The men were hungry but not starving. Six times they had found ammunition points, and for the rest taken ammunition off the dead, or out of abandoned wagons and lorries. Half a dozen times the battle lines had coagulated into a front . . . almost. Then the ceaseless German infiltration, like water through a sand dyke, had trickled by, followed by more and heavier units, and the sand had crumbled . . . another retreat begun, disorganization spread.

A soldier ran in from the edge of the village, knelt, and saluted by tapping his rifle sling with his left hand—"Sir . . . Captain Kellaway says there's a lot of men coming up from the next village. He thinks they're ours."

Quentin turned on Archie, "Stand-to, Campbell. I'm going to Kellaway's position."

"Yes, sir."

Quentin hurried down the muddy lane and into the farmyard, inches deep in mud and cow dung, where Kellaway commanded all the Wealds in the motley force. He was standing by the bar gate, staring through binoculars when Quentin arrived.

"Who are they? Can you see yet?"

Kellaway did not turn his head, "French, sir—at last . . . a whole lot."

Ten minutes later Quentin was facing a French general of brigade. The general was cheerful, decisive, and informative. The German assault had been halted on the 28th, at least for the time being. Foch had been made Commander-in-Chief of all Allied forces. Pershing had offered all that he had. More immediately, Quentin and his men were under his, the French general's orders.

"*Oui, mon général,*" Quentin said; then, to Kellaway, "Tell him I'll accept any orders from him except to retreat."

Kellaway spoke fluently for a few moments; the general laughed and clapped Quentin on the shoulder—"*Non, non, mon gars. Nous restons ici. Les Boches ne passeront pas . . . Tout le monde à la bataille, hein?*"

He started giving orders for occupation of a defensive position in depth, while Kellaway made notes. Half an hour later he was gone, communications were set up, and a French artillery officer with a field telephone was at Quentin's headquarters ready to supply artillery support. Quentin took Archie aside, and said, "Any more news of Laurence?"

"No, sir . . . just that one soldier saw him walking back out of Duke's Wood Redoubt, five minutes before B Company's attack."

"Send a message back . . . through the French gunners . . . to our army headquarters, that he is wanted for desertion, when under orders for an attack. Describe him."

"Yes, sir."

"That's under Section 39 of the Army Act."

"Yes, sir."

"But I hope to God he's been killed."

Daily Telegraph, Wednesday, April 10, 1918

PREMIER'S APPEAL FOR MEN FOR THE ARMY

MILITARY AGE 50

CONSCRIPTION FOR IRELAND

"The fate of the Empire, the fate of Europe, the fate of human liberty throughout the world is at stake in the present battle." Those were almost the opening words of the Prime Minister yesterday, as, in a crowded House, he began a most momentous speech of two hours' duration. From time to time he kept striking the same note—that Germany is bent on forcing a military decision this year, whatever the consequences to herself, that the battle will rage from the North Sea to the Atlantic, and that there is a possibility of it lasting seven or eight months on end. Never was a graver speech delivered by the Chief Minister of the Crown . . .

A STRING OF NEW PROPOSALS

Mr Lloyd George said that we had to prepare for the advent of 550,000 additional young men into the struggle, as Germany is calling up another class, that of 1920. Briefly stated, the measures of preparation are these:

1. A very strict comb-out is now in progress . . .
2. The occupational exemptions are to be cancelled by age blocks . . .
3. It may be found necessary to curtail the existing rights of appeal on medical grounds . . .

Other proposals, however, are quite new:

1. The military age is to be raised to 50 and in some special cases—e.g., doctors—to 55
2. The whole range of exemptions is to be revised . . .
3. The areas and compositions of the tribunals are to be revised . . .
4. The clergy and ministers of religion will be pressed to undertake con-combatant services . . .
5. The extension of the Compulsory Service Acts to Ireland on exactly the same footing as they apply to the United Kingdom.

IRISH UPROAR

Mr Lloyd George's moral case for bringing Ireland under compulsion was overwhelming. He quoted from speeches of Mr Redmond and Mr Dillon to show how absolutely the Irish Nationalists had accepted this war as their own; indeed he read one passage in which Mr Dillon himself had said that he would not oppose conscription if it were needed to secure victory . . . Irishmen, said

115

the Prime Minister, were being conscripted for the war in the
United States, in Canada, and in New Zealand . . . How then could
he ask young Britons of 18½ and men of 50 to stand in the breach to
defend Irish liberties while young Irishmen of military age
slouched and sheltered themselves at home? . . .

At this the uproar broke out anew. "It's a declaration of war
against Ireland," shrieked Mr O'Brien. "Enrolment will never begin" yelled a score of voices, young Captain Redmond, prominent
in khaki, leaning forward in a great state of excitement. Then the
Prime Minister went on to speak of the report of the Irish Conven-
tion . . . and announced the intention of the Government to introduce without delay a measure of self-government for Ireland,
enacting what is just to both Irish parties, and what he hoped could
be carried without violent controversy. "Keep it!" shouted the ragged chorus. "Keep it!"

Cate flinched whenever he saw the word "Ireland" in the paper, because Margaret was there, and his happiness, any chance of a life with
Isabel depended on finding her. That seemed as impossible as finding
any common ground between the Southerners and the Ulstermen.

He forced himself to read on, finished the piece, and leaned back.
Enough of Ireland, world affairs, and the war, for the time being.
Stella was home, at this moment having her breakfast in bed, upstairs.
Isabel was in mid-Atlantic, and he prayed briefly for her safety. And
Lady Walstone would be honoured, she had written in a small formal
note, if she could call on him at eleven o'clock this morning; she
needed his advice in some personal matters.

Personal matters, he thought; perhaps to ask if he had any suggestion as to how to get Frank Stratton to forgive his wife, Anne, soon to
have a baby by another man; perhaps some questions about the Wom-
en's Institute and village charities—work which Margaret used to do,
as Lady of the Manor, more recently Lady Swanwick, and now fallen,
with the title and the great estate, to this little mousey woman, Ruth
Stratton, Baroness Walstone, daughter of his father-in-law's works
foreman.

Perhaps it was about the staff at the Park. Hoggin—sorry, he
apologized to himself—Walstone, was converting the great pile into
the headquarters of his Hoggin's Universal Stores Limited empire.
Workmen were all over the place, putting in new plumbing, partition-
ing off great halls into office space, fitting in canteens, mens' rooms,
heaven knew what else. Lady Walstone might want to ask him about
suitable local girls to hire as maids, canteen cooks, dishwashers, and
the like.

116

He glanced at the letter again. Below her signature she had written "P.S. If there's anything my husband or I can do, or pay for, with respect to Mrs Merritt, please ask us." Stella, she meant. Alienists were very expensive, he had heard. Is that what she meant—that they would pay for an alienist's services for Stella—or wasn't psychiatrist the new word? It was a touching offer; but he had been slowly reappraising Ruth Walstone. She wasn't a lady, but she was a very good woman, of the best. Perhaps she could help Stella, somehow, as she was trying to help Frank and Anne Stratton, and, he knew, many others in the village. *Noblesse oblige* was the old saying; how did you translate that in her case? *Bourgeoisie oblige? Humanité oblige.* That was better.

The West Swin, Thames Estuary:
Thursday, April 18, 1918

7   The ships dotted the oily sheen of the estuary, fifteen miles off the Essex coast, invisible from those flat marshes, nothing in sight over the shallow waters but the tower of the West Swin light, darkened for years now by the exigencies of war. A line of three old cruisers heaved rheumatically at their anchors in the slow, shallow swell. To one flank another more modern cruiser, but still not of very recent vintage, rode ahead of two tubby ferry boats, and an ancient battleship. A third row contained seven destroyers in line, but these were all fast, modern ships of war. A fourth row contained twenty miscellaneous craft—tugs, minesweepers, and two monitors—low, flat, distorted ships the size of cruisers, but mounting only two enormous guns, and obviously of shallow draft. The haze of the estuary hid the fleet from anywhere but close, and no ship lane passed close; also, a destroyer on guard far to the south patrolled slowly back and forth at the edge of the normal passage to seaward, to ensure that no ship did stray off course to where it could observe the ill-matched fleet.

On board one of the three old cruisers, H.M.S. *Orestes,* Commander Tom Rowland, the captain, was talking to the officers and ratings of his ship: "We've been disappointed twice, but we mustn't lose the edge of our training. We're dealing with sea and weather, and you all know how they can change, especially in these waters . . . Last time, we delayed the fleet forty seconds because we didn't get our anchor up fast enough."

The West Swin, Thames Estuary: Thursday, April 18, 1918

He looked at Lieutenant Hardwick R.N.—"You've got to do some more work with the cable party, Number One."

"Aye, aye, sir," the lieutenant said. There were only four officers on the ship—Tom, Hardwick, Sub-Lieutenant Sherwood, and Engineer Lieutenant Arrowsmith. The crew numbered eighty instead of the three hundred or so which would be normal for such a vessel. Another peculiarity of *Orestes* and the other old relics anchored ahead of her was that below decks they were filled with bags of cement, and they carried no guns.

Tom continued, "Since the beginning of the month we've lost nearly forty men to this damned influenza. Once something like that hits in a ship, it's going to spread . . . so half of you are replacements, and I want to make sure you understand what we are trying to do, and the reasons for the way we are going to do it. You are all highly trained seamen. I think we have a higher proportion of killicks to O.D.s in this ship than in any ship of the Grand Fleet . . . which isn't strange as half of you have volunteered to join us from up there . . ." A subdued chuckle from the men crowded together on the foredeck showed that they appreciated his reference to the hated Grand Fleet. He went on—"Well, there is a large force gathered here, in Dover, and at one or two other places, and its job is to block the routes by which U-boats get to sea from their main base at Bruges, in Belgium. That means blocking the harbors of Ostend and Zeebrugge, which are linked to Bruges by short canals. Both places are defended by heavy shore guns, and harbor defences of all kinds—mines, more guns, concrete pill boxes, barbed wire, machine guns, soldiers. Both harbors will be dealt with in much the same way, but this ship is in the Zeebrugge force, so I'll talk about that now . . . The heart of the force is these three old wrecks, this one and those two up there. We're going to be sunk across the harbor channel, blocking it. But we'll never get there unless the defence guns are silenced, so a force of marines and volunteer matelots in khaki is going to land on the Zeebrugge Mole itself, right on top of the German guns, and put them out of action so that we can reach our positions in the channel. The men who are going to make that attack will be carried to Zeebrugge in those two Liverpool ferry boats, *Daffodil* and *Iris II*. The cruiser *Vindictive* there will go alongside the Mole and engage the German batteries on it at point-blank range with armour-piercing shell . . . they should do some damage . . . Two submarines loaded with explosive are going to ram that section of the Mole which is actually a bridge, to allow the tide to flow back and forth, and blow themselves up, so that the Germans can not send reinforcements out to the pill boxes and batteries on the end of the Mole . . . Any questions, so far?"

After a moment of silence a small Scots voice said, "Please, sorr, if we're gan tae sink oorsels in the channel, hoo do we get oorsels hame?"

A titter spread through the sailors, and the two younger officers hid smiles.

Tom said, "We are being accompanied into the channel by C.M.B.s—Coastal Motor Boats. One is specially allotted to each of the block ships to take off the skeleton crews as soon as we've opened the sea cocks . . . Time is very important. In order not to be seen by shore observers on our way in . . . and to be out of range of the heavy coastal guns when light comes on our way out, we must arrive just outside their range at dark . . . and we have to be out of range by first light, which is changing from day to day, but is now close to 4.30 a.m. . . . . It'll take the ships an hour and fifty minutes to get out of range . . . which means we have to break off the action by 2.40 a.m. . . . . By the same reasoning we can't get there before midnight . . . so in that two hours and forty minutes we have to subdue the Mole defences, take the block ships in, sink them athwart the channel—not along it . . . and get everyone off again . . . the crews of the block ships and of the submarines that are to be blown up, plus the main storming party on the Mole . . . That's all for now. I want Petty Officers to run through the exact jobs of their detachments the rest of the day." He turned to the sub-lieutenant—"Sub, I want to see you. Dismiss the rest, Number One."

The ratings saluted and doubled aft. The 1st Lieutenant called, "Boatswain, pipe cable party muster on the fo'csle."

Tom said to the sub-lieutenant, "Our C.M.B.—the C.M.B. allotted to take us off—is coming to the port gangway at one o'clock. Bring its captain to my day cabin when he arrives, and we'll talk about how we actually get our people onto his tub while we're sinking . . . where will we put the scrambling nets, do we use Jacob's ladders as well, which side is he to come up on? And then tomorrow we'll have another practise . . . unless the balloon goes up, again, in the meantime."

The young man smiled, white teeth flashing in a smooth young face, the face of an Italian renaissance page—olive skin, dark hair, dark eyes, full curved lips, the body as lithe and graceful as the face was hedonistic. Tom searched for an excuse to keep the young man on deck, just talking, drinking in his beauty, untouched by any sense that there was a utilitarian purpose for it; as, looking at women, he would think, she is here to produce children; and that beauty is to attract men so that they will fertilize her and continue the race. This beauty, of Botticelli or Fra Lippo Lippi, had no purpose but itself, beauty for beauty . . .

120

He was being unfaithful to faithful Charlie Bennett, even to think of Sherwood in such a way. But there was nothing sexual about it . . . or was there?

"That's all," he said brusquely and turned his back.

*   *   *   *

Tom sat in the wardroom of the old battleship H.M.S. *Dominion,* moored with the rest of the force in the Swin; but *Dominion* was not to go to Zeebrugge with the others: she was the mother ship, hastily sent to the wastes of the Swin when the men jammed into *Daffodil* and *Iris II* and the block ships began to get verminous, and restive from lack of any place to eat or sleep in comfort, rest, bathe. Tom said, "Another pink gin?"

"Aye, aye, sir," Lieutenant Billy Bidford R.N.V.R. said with a grin. "Never refuse an invitation from a straight striper, especially one with honourable gold lace all over honourable cap."

Tom began to frown; lieutenants R.N. did not speak so flippantly to commanders, especially not to one who was also captain of a ship. But Bidford was not R.N., he was Royal Naval Volunteer Reserve; he was one of the young madmen who drove the C.M.B.s at thirty-five to forty knots up and down the Channel, chasing German boats and looking for destroyers to use their two torpedoes on . . . and Bidford was a multimillionaire, racing motorist, and aviator.

When the Maltese steward brought the drinks to them at their little table, Tom said, "I was expecting Settle. He was commanding the C.M.B. allotted to us, only the day before yesterday."

Bidford said easily, "Down with the flu. We're all supposed to be able to do the job . . . we've all practised, and now the Commander C.M.B.s swears he won't change it again . . . If I go down with the bug, my C.P.O. will take over, but you'll get the same boat, Number 148 . . . I call it Florinda, unofficially."

Tom looked at his companion and said, "Wait . . . didn't I see a picture of you in the papers with the Marchioness of Jarrow at the Savoy, at a benefit for wounded soldiers and sailors?"

"Yes, sir," Bidford said. "Florinda, Marchioness of Jarrow. A very wonderful lady . . . I suppose I shouldn't even mention her name in a wardroom, but I don't care. She is a great lady, though she's . . ."

"Daughter of a factory cleaner, and granddaughter of the best poacher in Kent," Tom said. "I know her . . . knew her when she was a little girl. My family comes from that part of the world."

It was Bidford's turn to stare. He said, "Of course . . . It never crossed my mind, but you must be a relation of the air ace, Guy Rowland—the Butcher."

"My nephew," Tom said.

"My rival . . . I think," Bidford said. "Florinda has never said so, but she has a big photograph of him on the mantelpiece in her flat."

"Another pink gin, please, Florio," Tom said. He was getting a little tight. The waiting was awful. Seeing young Sherwood and lusting after him was worse. If that were Russell Wharton sitting there opposite him, he could come out and say just what he was feeling, what was on his mind. Here, he couldn't. Damn the bloody navy. Bidford too ordered another pink gin, the navy's drink of drinks.

Tom said, to himself, to hell with it. Aloud, he said, "As soon as this is over, I'm resigning my commission."

Bidford kept his face neutral. Tom said, "The navy won't give me a sea command, because . . ." He couldn't bring himself to state the full reason—"I want to be a couturier . . . dress designer. When I was in the Admiralty—Anti-Submarine Division—I was studying with Arthur Gavilan in my spare time."

Bidford whistled—"High society, sir. He's about the best we have in England. It's his Spanish blood, I suppose."

Tom said, "Well, I don't have any Spanish blood, but I'm going to be as good as Arthur—when I've learned."

Bidford said, "If you know Arthur, perhaps you know Russell Wharton, Noel Coward, Ivor Novello. They're all friends of mine, and of Florinda's, come to that."

Tom said, "I know them all. Good fellows . . . good actors . . . good friends."

Bidford had taken him up, realizing that his mention of Gavilan was a hint that he was a homosexual; all the three prominent actors whom Bidford had named were well-known homosexuals. But Bidford himself wasn't, surely?

Bidford, seeming to sense Tom's thoughts, said, "I was brought up in London . . . indulgent guardian, more money than was good for me . . . I was taking out chorus girls when I was at Eton. I've been financing plays ever since . . . keeps one in close touch with pretty actresses . . . So I'm in the theatre but not of it, if you know what I mean."

I know, Tom thought; he's saying that he appreciates that I'm a pansy; that he knows and likes many others of the same hue; but that he's not one himself. Fair enough.

Tom looked at his watch. "Time to return to my ship."

Bidford said, "Me too, sir. Though mine's moored alongside while all hands take a shower. You can't believe what we smell like after two weeks in a C.M.B."

They were up on deck now, and both fell suddenly silent. The sky was covered with high clouds. The underside of the clouds was irregularly lit by dull flashes, glows . . . purple, red, yellow, orange. The surface of the sea shook to the shudder of artillery. Over there, by Arras and Bethune now, the British Army was still fighting for its life. They said nothing. Bidford saluted and went to the starboard side, while Tom ran down the port gangway to the whistle of the pipes, to return to *Orestes*.

* * * *

"Force R will sail at noon by Method G-4."

The sodden flags flapped heavily in the slow, wet wind. The answering pennant hung from *Orestes'* signal yard. *Vindictive's* signal came down, the acknowledgments whipped down in every ship. It was half-past ten in the morning of April 22nd. Tom, on the bridge, watched as the long-practised preparations for sailing were put into actual effect. Smoke drifted blacker from the funnels as the stokehold crew—they constituted nearly 90 percent of the total—brought the boilers up to full pressure. *Dominion's* motor launch passed rapidly down the line of ships, handing over packets at each gangway. As soon as it had passed, the gangways were raised and stowed away at action stations. The launch reached *Orestes'* side, paused a moment, hurried on, its propellers churning up a greeny-brown wake in the shallow estuary. On the bridge Tom was studying the chart for the hundredth time. He would be at his post here for the next forty-eight hours, more or less. He had no navigating officer or officer of the watch—he would do it all, to be replaced by Hardwick if he were wounded or killed.

The bridge messenger said, "Morning paper, sir."

"Any letters for me?"

"One, sir."

Tom saw that the letter was from his sister-in-law, Louise Rowland, and opened it quickly. Louise had somehow got an inkling of what he was doing, and wished him safe return, though she wished even more strongly that the war could be over, and such missions unnecessary. Laurence Cate was missing in action in this ghastly German offensive; Stella Merritt had been found, and was at home, though not well; Virginia's husband, the one-armed Battery Sergeant Major, had been accepted as Head Porter at Wokingham School, and would take over in September; and Lady Helen Durand-Beaulieu had had a baby boy, of which the father was her own son, Boy. She wanted Tom to know, because she and John were very happy about it. Boy had gone, but he would live on in this, their grandchild.

He put the letter down and scanned the newspaper headlines . . . GREAT BATTLE CONTINUES . . . ENEMY ATTACKING NEAR ARRAS . . .

GALLANT DEFENCE . . . Then the paper reprinted a part of Field Marshal Haig's Order of the Day of April 11:

> To all Ranks of the British Forces in France.
> There is no other course open but to fight it out! Every position must be held to the last man: there must be no retirement. With our backs to the wall, and believing in the justice of our cause, each one of us must resolve to fight on to the end. The safety of our homes and the freedom of mankind alike depend on the conduct of each one of us at this critical moment.
>
> D. Haig. F.M.

A moving message, Tom thought, but not the sort that politicians relished, for it acknowledged openly that things were going badly. "Backs to the wall" . . . well, that was the way British soldiers liked to fight, as at Agincourt. He looked at his watch. One minute to noon.

From the fo'csle the 1st Lieutenant called, "Cable straight up and down, sir."

"Weigh!" Tom said. "Half ahead both . . . port ten . . . revolutions for nine knots, Mr Arrowsmith. Secure the fo'csle." The cruiser slowly gathered way. "Follow the wake of *Vindictive*, quartermaster. We shall be at four cables."

"Aye, aye, sir."

Force R, the West Swin contingent of the 140 ships in the Ostend-Zeebrugge raids, headed east down the estuary at nine knots. Tom paced the bridge, keeping one eye on *Vindictive* ahead, the two Liverpool ferryboats waddling along on each of her flanks. Ahead the destroyers were spreading out into a screening line. C.M.B.s followed in their wakes, and others weaved across the stern of the block ships and monitors, guarding flanks and rear.

The rain ceased. The glass was steady, rising a little. This time, perhaps . . . Tom looked carefully round the sky. He had told the crew that the success of the operation depended on timing; but it also depended, and to a much greater extent, on luck. Secrecy was of the essence. If the Germans got a hint of what was coming, it would not take them more than a couple of hours to mine the approaches to the channels, send out three or four U-boats to lie in wait, and reinforce the Mole defences. And the attackers would be steaming for about five hours, in broad daylight, from the general rendezvous off the North Goodwin Light, straight toward their destinations; there was no time to spare to make any feints. So the hint could come from one U-boat, returning from or going out on routine patrol; one German aircraft passing over en route to anywhere; one Gotha or Zeppelin going to or returning from a raid; one hostile-minded neutral vessel equipped with wireless. The enterprise was already one of extreme hazard, as Admiral Keyes had personally made clear to every man and officer. If it was discovered, it would be a holocaust, and a total failure.

Tom said, "You're not following exactly in *Vindictive*'s wake, quartermaster. Port ten until you are on . . . then straighten back."

"Aye, aye, sir."

Tom lifted his binoculars off his chest and carefully scanned the horizon. Sea, calm. Wind, south-west, about three knots. Nothing. The force sailed on.

*　　*　　*　　*

Tom Rowland peered at his watch by the light of the binnacle. Ten o'clock. Time to transfer half his crew to the minesweepers that had been running on each beam since the meeting off the North Goodwin Light. "Stop engines," he commanded. Astern he saw the faint outlines of the other block ships hold position, as they too stopped. The allotted minesweeper—a converted trawler—loomed out of the darkness to port and surged alongside. The scrambling net was out on that side. Tom stood in the port wing of the bridge, looking aft. Sherwood was there . . . that was his job now, to get the men into the minesweeper. The seconds ticked by. The trawler skipper was holding his little vessel alongside with his engine and rudder . . . Tom thought, surely I'd see forty men sliding down the net, even in the darkness?

Four minutes gone. What in hell was happening? Sherwood came panting onto the bridge, and gasped, "Sir . . . mutiny! The men won't go! They're all lined up on deck but, they won't go!"

"They won't leave us?"

"No, sir."

Tom paced the bridge once. Should he go down and personally order them over the side? What if they ignored him? Was he to take a revolver and shoot some of them, for refusing to be left out of the really dangerous part of the operation? He turned on Sherwood and snapped, "Tell 'em to get back to the engine room . . . and wave the sweeper skipper off."

"Aye, aye, sir!" The sub-lieutenant dashed away and Tom said, "Full ahead both . . . port ten . . . we've swung off course . . . Steady on east by north a half north."

"Aye, aye, sir . . . Steady it is. East by north a half north!"

Tom peered astern. The other blockships were following, picking up speed as *Orestes* was. He wondered if in them too the skeleton crews had refused to leave. Probably. The ships had been together a long time in the West Swin, and British matelots always seemed to know what was going on, even with no apparent means of communication. At the Swin, there was *Dominion* to act as a gathering point to such a plot . . . Thank God for a navy that would hatch *such* a plot.

An hour and three quarters to go . . . C.M.B. 148 was in position on the starboard beam, a low shape sliding easily through the water, with little wake, at what was for it a crawl.

Eleven o'clock . . . eleven-fifteen . . . the monitors were due to start their bombardment of the German coastal batteries in five minutes . . . four, three, two . . . one . . . there they went, brilliant orange flashes in the night way off to the south, close in to the sandy coast between Zeebrugge and Ostend. *Orestes'* engines throbbed steadily. They had been a worry to Tom from the beginning, for on this mission only the engines really mattered. He could if necessary keep station without a compass or any other crew but himself at the wheel. There were no guns. But if the engines failed before the ship was in the Zeebrugge channel the mission would have failed.

A deeper drumming, dead ahead, filled the night, and suddenly the darkness was split by close, livid flashes, seeming like Guy Fawkes' Day rockets as the first covering wave of C.M.B.s accelerated to full speed in front of the force, heading straight for the Mole, firing smoke canisters and star shell. *Vindictive* followed suit, and Tom watched, spellbound, as the brilliant stars fell down through layers of cloud, burning, disappearing, their tails twisting and turning and winding as chance fires in their midst forced them sideways or even back upward for a short trajectory . . . Eleven forty-five: the block ships were five sea miles off the Mole now: *Vindictive, Daffodil,* and *Iris II* barely two miles; and the submarines C 1 and C 3 a mile and a half.

* * * *

In the wheelhouse of C.M.B. 148, standing beside the Leading Seaman at the wheel, Billy Bidford peered ahead at the appalling but wonderful spectacle exploding over Zeebrugge. The noise had become deafening, even at this range. He could distinguish mortar bomb bursts, machine-gun fire, and the whip cracks of *Vindictive*'s shells at almost point-blank range.

Behind him his Chief Petty Officer gasped, "Sir! Green four five! Is it . . . ?"

Bidford started . . . something, a metallic gleam in the glaring, fading, flickering lights from the star shells and explosions . . . a number! He grabbed the wheel, pushing the sailor off his stool and rammed the throttle lever all the way forward. "Prepare to ram!" he shouted, a towering excitement boiling in his veins. The bow of the big motor boat lifted . . . too close range for the torpedoes—it was a

U-boat, crawling in on the surface, right in the middle of the fleet. The U-boat's deck gun was manned. Orange fire flamed from the gun and the shell cracked low overhead with a deafening bang. Again, and a splintering crash from forward on the starboard side told Billy a part of his bow had been shot away. Then they were on the submarine, aiming direct for the conning tower. The C.M.B. hit it at twenty knots, smashing a huge hole in the thin steel plate. "Board!" Billy yelled. He cut the engine back and jumped up, shouting to his C.P.O., "Take over! Back her off as soon as we're on the sub. Then stand by."

He slipped out of the little side door and ran forward, followed by three seamen with revolvers, and jumped down onto the U-boat's deck forward of the conning tower. The crew of the gun had vanished, knocked overboard by the shock, or jumped for their lives. Billy scrambled fast up the steel rungs fixed to the outside of the conning tower, and looked over. Inside, the hatch was battened down . . . just. He heard the last screws being tightened under the hatch even as he jumped down onto it. Furiously he fired three shots at the hatch with his revolver, without effect. The U-boat's engine was running, but the C.M.B. had made a big hole below the conning tower: it could not submerge. But the C.M.B. was still stuck fast, and being dragged along sideways. What the hell to do?

He made up his mind and yelled, "Back aboard! Hurry, man!" They scrambled back onto the C.M.B. Billy shouted, "All hands to the stern, back, back!" When everyone else was as far back in the C.M.B. as they could go, Billy, alone in the wheelhouse, again opened the throttle wide. The weight of the crew pushed the stern down, the racing propellers dragged it farther down, and the gathering speed of the U-boat helped with a sideways pull. The C.M.B. backed clear in a boil of water, its stern momentarily going under. The C.P.O. came forward, gasping—"Shall we ram her again, sir, farther forward?"

Billy said, "No. We'll torpedo her."

A seaman said, "We're taking water at the bow, sir!"

Billy said, "Make twenty knots, that'll keep the bow up." He stood behind the Leading Seaman, who had returned to his post at the wheel. The boat's bow rose slowly, and Billy heard water sloshing aft below. "Port fifteen!" he said. "I've lost her . . ."

"Red twenty, sir . . . about half a mile . . . six hundred yards . . . five hundred."

"Got her! Stand by to fire starboard torpedo . . . Fire!"

The long cylinder leaped out of its tube with a powerful hiss, splashed into the water, and raced for the target. Billy counted the seconds: should be about fifteen seconds . . .

A tremendous explosion lit the night straight ahead, and the submarine became luridly visible, as the conning tower flew into the air, and two long shapes, the two halves, broken-backed, lifted skyward, then slid back in a white boil of water.

The C.M.B.'s crew raised a ragged cheer. "Back on station," Billy said briefly. "Starboard twenty . . . See if there's anything we can do to patch the bow, Chief."

"Aye, aye, sir."

*   *   *   *

The block ships moved steadily on, hidden from the Germans on the Mole, by now spitting fire in all directions, and almost from each other, by the dense clouds of drifting, acrid smoke. Tom Rowland, on the bridge of the leading block ship, steering by compass and by guesswork, knowing that he was close, but not just how close, stood a foot behind the quartermasters, one at the wheel and the other at the engine room telegraph, and barked his orders as loud as he could, but even so they could barely be heard above the din of the fight.

12.15 . . . *Vindictive* should have been alongside fifteen minutes ago. And there she was, for the tops of masts gleamed now and then above the drifting black smoke set by the first wave of C.M.B.s.

"Starboard fifteen," Tom snapped; his present course would take him too close to the end of the Mole, if *Vindictive* was in the right position. He must get farther out to avoid the sandbanks that invariably accumulated at the end of any such mole or sea wall as this at Zeebrugge.

The bow swung to port. "Steady as she goes!"

"Steady, sir, steady!"

12.20. Tom bent to the engine room navyphone and said, "Arrowsmith, give her everything we've got. We should round the Mole in five minutes."

"You'll get it, sir," the engineer lieutenant answered. The engines, already at official full speed, began to grind faster as the ship's ancient boilers and ill-balanced reciprocating gear shook and heaved in a last frantic effort.

12.25. A tremendous explosion to starboard, louder than anything before, battered Tom's eardrums and seemed to send *Orestes* reeling to port. Pieces of shining metal arched far up above the smoke covering the sea, and a huge ball of orange fire momentarily blinded him. For a few seconds, by the sheer power of the explosion, everything else seemed to have become silent.

Gradually the noise of the battle climbed back to its normal, frantic level. Tom said to himself, but aloud—"One of the submarines . . . or both, absolutely together."

128

Now the end of the Mole was certainly isolated from shore. He could see it, close, and the unlit beacon light on it. *Vindictive* was 400 yards down. One of the ferryboats appeared to be pushing at her flank, holding her against the Mole . . .

Orestes shuddered to a shell, hitting her amidships. It did not explode, range too close, perhaps. The attacking wave of C.M.B.s were still at work in the enclosed space between the West and East Moles—the West Mole was the one being attacked, the other was much shorter, not continuous, nor joined to land. Ahead, clear in the star shells now being fired by supporting destroyers behind him, he saw the line of buoys marking the anti-submarine nets which hung from them across the harbor entrance, to entrap any British submarine trying to get in from seaward. There was a boom, too, all as shown on the aerial photographs taken a month ago. The Germans could have made many changes in a month, but Admiral Keyes had decided not to risk arousing any suspicions about Zeebrugge by repeating the photographic mission. The harbor guns were hitting *Orestes* regularly now, smashing through the cruiser's tall thin sides . . . and these shells were bursting. A C.M.B. ahead was launching torpedoes at German destroyers moored on the Eastern Mole . . .

"Port thirty!" Tom cried, seeing a gap in the boom defence. A German submarine must have been coming in or out just as the attack began. *Orestes* heeled far over in the savage turn to starboard, and, at nearly twenty-five knots, smashed through the gap in the boom. Flames were rising aft, astern of the funnels . . . and the engines were faltering . . . must have been hit . . . have to . . . Before he could move to the navyphone, it buzzed and Arrowsmith's tinny voice said, "Bridge . . . two shells in the engine room. Twelve killed, twelve wounded . . . boilers leaking steam badly . . . Very hot . . ."

"Stick it two minutes more," Tom said. "Half ahead both!"

"Aye, aye, sir . . . half ahead both."

Tom tried to ignore the shuddering of his ship to the blows of the shells, the smell of burning, the orange and red flames, the groans and screams. There was the position where he was to sink *Orestes* across the channel. The water was dark, intermittently lit by star shells and livid explosions. The cloudy sky shimmered with reflected light from explosions, from star shells, and from searchlights. The night was full of the growl of C.M.B.s' powerful aircraft engines rising to a scream as they skidded round under full helm at thirty-five knots . . . there, one was hit fair and square, exploding, disappearing with its crew, totally vanishing . . .

Tide: two knots, ebbing. Dead slack low water was what the admiral had wanted for the raid, because a ship, sinking, seldom goes down on a level keel; either bow or stern goes down first. The tide or current then catches that part and swings it with it; so that when the ship is finally down, it is lying along the line of the current, not athwart it. Here the tide would flow straight up and down the passage to the sea; and the block ships were to be sunk across that passage . . . but it had been impossible to find a night when dead low water coincided with all the other factors of distance and darkness, so: two knots, ebbing, half-tide.

"Slow both," he called, watching the bow and the dark, firelit mole walls to either side. A hammer smashed into his left arm above the elbow and he gasped, falling to the steel deck of the bridge. He pulled himself up with one hand. The arm was numb. God knows whether he had it still, he dared not look. He held onto the bridge rail . . . "Stop engines . . . Evacuate engine room! . . . Stand by stern anchor!" *Orestes* was slowing fast against the current, but her head was still running true. She was passing the point where she should sink . . . now! "Let go stern anchor!" A livid explosion swept him off his feet, reeling, half-blinded, against the rear wall of the bridge. Again he pulled himself upright, one-handed . . . there was no one else standing . . . three, four crumpled figures, their faces bright scarlet, uniforms burned off them . . . his own was singed, charring. "Open sea cocks!" he croaked into the navyphone.

"Aye, aye, sir! Sea cocks open!" The ship jerked to a stop, her head falling slowly off across the channel. A sailor ran up onto the bridge and shouted, "C.M.B. alongside, sir! All ready for evacuation!"

"Start evacuation!" Tom gasped.

What else had to be done? The ship was falling slowly across the tide, and sinking at the same time, held by the stern . . . Mustn't let her go too far . . . "Let go starboard anchor!" From the bridge he heard the roar of the cable running out through the hawse hole . . . barely twenty feet of water here, the anchor should bite soon . . . "Secure the fo'csle! Abandon ship!" He staggered toward the bridge ladder and suddenly knew he would not make it . . . not this time. The deck was slippery with blood, but he could not see . . . He was falling, his knees giving way under him. The blood was his own . . . It was dark, in a gradually fading inferno of explosions, shrieking steel, shrieking humanity.

Billy Bidford took C.M.B. 148 round in a short, sharp turn to starboard under the wall of the East Mole. It was tempting to make long graceful patterns on the water, and the boat was really more efficient that way . . . but one's life expectancy would not be long. Short sharp turns, ugly jerks to and fro, never holding a course or speed for long . . . even so, the deck was continually being swept by splinters from shells bursting on the water, and the upper part of the bow, damaged by the U-boat, was now gone from a direct hit. He still had to keep the speed above twenty knots, otherwise the bow would sink, and the boat would start taking water . . . then, Billy thought, she'd float for perhaps five minutes . . .

The wheelhouse was riddled with machine-gun bullets, but he had one torpedo left, and wanted a good target for it . . . Where were the blockships, *Orestes, Thetis, Iphigenia,* and *Intrepid?* Only three here . . . Ah, out to sea, at the entrance to the channel, another was stuck . . . either aground or caught on the boom defences . . . looked like *Thetis.* He turned sharply, at the wheel himself now, and headed back up the harbor. Three German destroyers on the East Mole were trying to get up steam to go to sea. Damn, they were behind torpedo nets. It was their guns firing, but at him now, though in some cases they could not be depressed enough to bear, especially as he got closer. Six C.M.B.s were still operating in the harbor.

The machine guns on either side of the wheelhouse chattered as they raked the decks of the German destroyers. Twelve twenty-five . . . the lead block ship was going down perfectly, behind him, to seaward . . . there'd barely be room between the cruiser and the Mole for him to get out. All the shore batteries seemed to have concentrated on her—it was *Orestes,* Commander Tom Rowland, the old pansy he'd been drinking with in *Dominion* only three days ago. Well, he might be a pansy but by God he was a good sailor . . .

He spun the wheel over, pulled back the throttle so that the C.M.B. slowed violently in the water . . . a salvo of three shells burst twenty yards ahead . . . they'd have been napoo if that packet had hit . . . Hard aport . . . *Orestes* was nearly down . . . Time to stop tearing round the harbor and go to take her crew off. He thrust the throttle forward and headed for the narrow gap between *Orestes'* bow and the East Mole . . . A hundred yards to go . . . "Make smoke!" he yelled to his C.P.O.

"Can't, sir . . . Just used up the last canister."

Billy swore under his breath . . . Fifty yards . . . a shuddering jar astern . . . half the decking blown away, a fire, men down behind him, the C.P.O. kneeling over them . . . He was through, swung the wheel left, jammed the throttle back, then into reverse. Swinging, swaying, the shattered bow thrust deep in the water, the C.M.B. stopped under the scrambling nets draping *Orestes'* port side, which faced seaward and so was protected from most of the fire.

Thumps and thuds rained down on the wheelhouse and all along the C.M.B as the men from *Orestes* slid or jumped off the nets onto her . . . twenty, thirty, Christ, how many had they got? They were supposed to have transhipped half the crew two hours ago, but . . . and they must have had some killed, to judge by the ship's appearance . . . "Ready?" he yelled. "All off?" Two guns in a battery near the end of the West Mole were firing straight at *Orestes'* exposed side, only half-hidden by the drifting smoke.

A sub-lieutenant shouted, "The skipper's not off yet."

"Hurry, man. We're sinking!"

"Here he comes!"

Four sailors were scrambling down the net, a body slumped between them, half-draped over their shoulders, half hanging free. They lowered it to the tiny foredeck of the C.M.B., then slipped down themselves. "All off!" the sub-lieutenant yelled.

Billy opened the throttle, and C.M.B. 148 moved forward . . . sluggishly, for water had been pouring in through the bows while she was stopped. Gradually the bow lifted, gradually the speed increased. They were carrying the wounded skipper of *Orestes* into the wheelhouse . . . left arm broken above the elbow, forehead and hands burned and bleeding, jacket burned off, trousers smouldering, a wound in the left leg. His eyes opened, staring at Billy, then at the sub-lieutenant—a beautiful young fellow, Billy noted. "Jerry," the commander gasped, "thank God you're safe." A shell from the German battery smashed through the wheelhouse four feet behind the wheel, removing Sub-Lieutenant Jerome Sherwood's head as cleanly as any executioner's axe could have. Blood spouted a foot high from the severed stump. For a moment Commander Rowland's eyes widened, and Billy thought, they are a lens, a camera, and on the brain behind, this image is now for ever imprinted. The eyes closed.

They were passing *Thetis*, aground off the end of the West Mole. Her scrambling nets were down, her decks crowded, but Christ, no C.M.B. to take the men off . . . must have been sunk. Someone was trying to launch the only boat but the davits were smashed. The German fire concentrated on *Thetis*.

Billy swung the wheel hard and once again throttled back. "Get everyone to the stern," he shouted to the C.P.O. The bow again sank as speed fell. He was alongside, yelling "Jump! Hurry, hurry!" How many men were the C.M.B.s supposed to take off the block ships? Forty, wasn't it? He had sixty, eighty now . . . Shells were hitting *Thetis* regularly, wounded and dead men falling off the nets onto the C.M.B.'s deck or into the sea. The deck was awash with blood, Billy's own jacket soaked with it from Sub-Lieutenant Sherwood's neck. A three striper was coming down *Thetis*'s side, to land on the wheelhouse. The nets were clear behind him—"All off," he croaked.

Billy thrust the throttle forward. Slowly, heavily the bow tried to lift . . . water was pouring in . . . must have been holed again, lower down. Commander Rowland was on his feet, holding one-handed to the rail, "Back, men, back, into the stern!" The bow would not lift clear. "Can't do any more," Rowland said. "They're being pushed off the stern . . ." Billy's C.P.O. slowly knelt on the deck, coughing blood.

Billy kept the throttle jammed against the stop. The 500-horsepower engine roared and shuddered desperately to give the boat enough speed to lift the bow clear, but it could not do it. Gradually water poured in, and gradually the bow sank, and the speed fell. The engine stopped, flooded.

"She's going, sir," Billy said quietly, in the sudden eerie silence. They were half a mile clear of the Mole, no one was firing star shells, and they were awash under a pall of drifting smoke.

A tall bow loomed out of the night to starboard. Someone up there shouted, "Object green nine oh! . . . It's a C.M.B., sir!"

Billy clearly heard the orders from the bridge, "Stop engines . . . full astern . . . port twenty . . . scrambling nets out starboard side . . . Slow ahead both . . . Stop engines . . . Get 'em out, Number One!"

Then it was quiet, until Billy realized he was hearing a noise and seeing a sight that had continued all through the battle—and still were . . . the sound of the guns, and the flash of their shells on the Western Front, thirty miles to the south-west.

* * * *

Tom Rowland lay in a bed in a small room in St Thomas's Hospital, London. He could see the Thames outside his window, but he could not see it very well, for most of his head was swathed in bandages and his eyes were not yet recovered from the flash burns the irises had suffered at Zeebrugge. His left arm was in a cast, and his right leg heavily bandaged—it turned out he had had three machine-gun bullets and a shell splinter in it, but no bones broken. He smarted or ached or throbbed all over; but mostly he longed to be well. The action, in all its bloody glory, had somehow acted like a giant conflagration to burn the Royal Navy out of his thoughts. He no longer dreamed of it, or missed it, or cared what it did or thought. He wanted to be well, to get to Arthur Gavilan's salon, and start really learning his new profession.

The sister came in. "Visitors for you, sir . . . famous visitors—Mr Wharton, Mr Coward, Mr Novello, and Mr Gavilan."

The four men trooped in as the sister held the door open. The nineteen-year-old Coward raised his hand in reverent salute and intoned, "We, Noel Coward, Russell Wharton, Ivor Novello, and Arthur

Gavilan, salute the gallant dead . . . You're supposed to say, what did the bloody old fool call me?"

Tom laughed. Pain stabbed his chest and he gasped. But he risked it and laughed again. These were his friends. They made him feel good. His place was among them. He said, "I've heard the story . . ."

Wharton said, "Zeebrugge must have been appalling, while it lasted. The papers have been full of it. A whole lot of V.C.s are expected to be announced at any moment."

Gavilan said, "You did the job, as the navy always does . . . Noel and I are both frustrated admirals, you know."

Tom did know; both men were great admirers of the Royal Navy. Coward said, "I'd have given anything to be there . . ."

Wharton said, "And you'd have come back and we'd have asked you what it was like and you'd have said"—he drooped one hand in a limp, effeminate gesture and changed his voice to a homosexual's lisp—"My dears, the *noise* . . . and the *people!*"

Novello said, "We're only allowed ten minutes. We want to tell you we're all waiting for you."

"I have a table ready for you in the designing room," Gavilan said. "And my head cutter's ready to give you a special course in materials."

"And as soon as you say the word, we'll throw a party for you that London won't forget for a long time . . . our London, at least."

Coward said, "If he gets the V.C., we'll ram it down their throats . . . One of us, a V.C. Then they'll *have* to change their stereotypes."

"They won't," Wharton said, "but it'll make some of them think, a bit . . . in private, of course."

They talked then about the theatre, about their friends and Tom's; then the sister came and said, "Time, gentlemen, please."

"Were you ever a barmaid, darling?" Wharton said. "You've got the tone off to a T . . . Ta-ta Tom . . ." He blew Tom a kiss, and the others followed suit as they left, the sister smiling as they trooped out.

"Now," she said, "you have another . . . this one swears he won't take more than two minutes."

A captain R.N. came in. Tom stared a moment, thinking, who on earth? Then he recalled. It was Captain Buller, the 2nd Sea Lord's Naval Assistant. Buller waited for the sister to close the door behind her, then said, "I'm here in an unofficial capacity, Rowland . . . You did very well at Zeebrugge—better than very well—brilliantly, and showed extraordinary skill and courage. You were recommended for a V.C.—which you will not get. The admiral tore up the recommendation. Instead he gave me this . . ." He put some papers on Tom's bedside table. "That is your request to be allowed to resign your commission, already approved. Sign it, and you will be out of the Service, effective at once. These"—he tapped other papers—"are the proceedings of a medical board grading you 4F, unfit for further military service in any capacity. The admiral says you have done your bit . . . but he won't have you wearing a V.C. It's unfair, Rowland, but the navy often is. You know."

"I know," Tom said. He was smiling, as best he could. He didn't want a Victoria Cross, because he'd never again have a uniform to wear it on. He had wanted to be out, with his friends; and now he was. "Thank the admiral for me, sir," he said. "I appreciate it. If you'll give me a pen and hold the papers against this board . . ." He signed. "There."

Buller said, "Well, goodbye . . . And good luck, whatever you do . . . By the way, Bidford, the fellow who rescued you and your crew, has a V.C."

He went out, the papers in his hand. The sister came in. "Now there's another, but I told him I'd have to see you before I let him in. How do you feel?"

"A little tired. Very happy. Who is it?"

"A man called Bennett."

"Charlie . . . show him in. We won't be long."

Charlie Bennett came in. Tom saw for a second the beauty of Jerry Sherwood, one moment glowing in the excitement of the battle—the next, disappeared, only a tall spout of blood from the handsome column of his neck. Had he killed the young man, by desiring him?

He held his hands out and Charlie took them, whispering, "Oh Tom . . . are you all right?"

"I will be . . . got chewed up a bit . . . it won't take long . . . four, five weeks . . ."

There were tears in Charlie's eyes. "I've longed for you . . . prayed for you . . . everything's ready for you at home."

"I'll come as soon as I can . . . Don't say anything. Just hold my hand, till they make you go . . . hold my hand."

Daily Telegraph, Saturday, April 27, 1918

SPRING DELICACIES

COVENT-GARDEN'S STORE

Two things are necessary for the enjoyment of Covent-Garden's best spring fare. The first, good taste, is claimed by most people, but the second, a well-filled purse, is not nearly so prevalent. Notwithstanding wartime conditions France is sending some excellent asparagus, that of Lauris being very fine, whilst another variety, the Cavaullon, is good enough for all but the most exacting of epicures . . . Much fresher than the French is Devonshire asparagus, which is uncommonly toothsome . . . Those whose path of duty is in the avenues of Covent-Garden look with longing eyes at the beautiful English tomatoes displayed in small quantities. As yet the beautiful "love apples" are worth more money than can be paid by people in ordinary walks of life; but with the advent of warmer weather supplies will increase and prices will fall automatically, although the prospects of very cheap tomatoes are more than remote . . .

The ready sale of cucumbers is not understood even by the men who distribute them daily in large quantities. One firm disposed of full 4,000 cucumbers in a single day. That of itself is not a remarkable achievement, but the fact that the market remains firm at 8s to 10s a dozen wholesale is passing strange. By whom these expensive cucumbers are eaten it is difficult to say, but the principal consuming centres are Nottingham, Sheffield, and Derby. Were it not for the insatiable demands of those towns the price of cucumbers would be much lower . . .

Some delicious fruits have already appeared on the market. A few English peaches were warmly welcomed, principally as gifts for wounded soldiers, many of whom, alas! were destined to enjoy them for the last time. The same may be said of new black grapes, perhaps the most comforting of all fruits in the sick-room. It is noteworthy that nearly all choice fruits are bought by people who are not indulging in selfish enjoyment, but giving them to those who have fought for the noble cause . . .

It was hard to concentrate on such arcadian prose when your son was missing, lost on the field of battle, which was now so huge and formless, since the beginning of the German offensive over a month ago. Since the original curt War Office telegram, he had heard nothing. He had had an item inserted in the Agony columns of the *Irish Times—Lt. Laurence Cate, Weald Light Infantry, reported missing in action April 3:* but Margaret had not responded, though he was sure she would have seen it.

But why had Quentin not written, with some details? Was the poor boy nearby when some big shell burst, and so vanished, as had happened, apparently, to John Kipling? Had he simply been cut off, and was now perhaps in hiding behind the German lines, waiting for the tide of war to swing the other way?

Garrod came in with the mail, laid four letters silently beside his plate, and went out. One of them was from Quentin: at last he had been able to write.

Cate hesitated before opening the letter; then steeled himself and slit open the back of the envelope. The letter trembled in his hand as he began to read:

Dear Christopher—I am sorry to tell you that Laurence is to be court-martialled for desertion. He was found by the Military Police in a village sixty miles behind the front, apparently working as a labourer on a small isolated farm run by two women, who tried to hide him from the police. I do not need to tell you how serious this is, as he was under orders for an attack when he vanished. I will see that he gets the very best officer available for his defence when the time comes, which will be soon, as his trial will not be long delayed in the present circumstances. No one can understand why he did it, except that in battle I and others have noticed that he was often "not there," and so this was in a way merely taking his body where his mind already was. My adjutant thinks he may be able to prove shell shock. We can only hope for the best. He is not wounded or sick. Nor am I, except for a scratch or two in the recent fighting. Yrs. Affec.— Quentin.

The letter fell from Cate's hand, fluttering to the floor. Slowly he stooped to pick it up . . . court martial; with the death sentence an obvious possibility . . . It was he who should be facing a firing squad, not Laurence! It was he who had not seen that the boy was by nature totally unfit for killing, for the human degradation of war. Margaret must learn of this, at once: she had always loved Laurence more than any of the rest of them. And he must talk to the Governor in case it came to getting a pardon. He must . . . He jumped to his feet, spilling his coffee, and hurried out of the house, his brain racing.

Hedlington, Walstone: Wednesday, May 8, 1918

8   They were crowded into the managing director's office at the Jupiter Motor Company factory in North Hedlington, five men—three bare-headed, the other two wearing on their heads the ceremonial headgear of factory foremen—a bowler hat. An asthmatic goods engine wheezed up and down the railway siding outside, shunting wagons into a train which, in due course, it would take down the river to Chatham. Every now and then it whistled shrilly, when crossing one of the service roads that ran between the factory and the barge loading dock. The windows were open, and the English present—Richard Rowland, Ginger Keble-Palmer, and Tom Pratt, were not wearing their overcoats; the Americans—Henry Overfeld, and David Morgan—were; the May morning seemed chill to them, although both had now been in England for some years.

Richard said, "Well, we're all here, so let's not waste time . . . especially as that is what we are here to talk about—how not to waste time in our plants—or, of course, energy, and money. Fairfax, Gottlieb, who, as you know are the majority owners of both these businesses, want us to increase production. They feel that this year there is going to be a great demand for lorries—trucks—and for heavy, long-range aircraft. We make both. They want us to achieve greater production while lowering the unit cost . . ."

"That means more capital," Overfeld said, pulling on his cigar. He was an automobile production expert, hired away from General Motors in 1914 when Fairfax, Gottlieb decided to set up the Jupiter

Motor Company to assemble road freight vehicles in England. Originally he had worked under Richard as assistant managing director;
but when Fairfax, Gottlieb, early in 1916, formed the Hedlington
Aircraft Company, Richard moved up to an overall supervisory position and Overfeld became operational head of the Jupiter Motor
Company.

Richard said, "Fairfax, Gottlieb understand that. They're willing
to provide it. Mr Merritt—Mr Stephen—is coming over as soon as he
can to discuss with us how much is needed . . . and, most importantly,
what for. He—and the rest of the board over there in New York—are
convinced that after the war wages will increase rapidly, as wartime
restrictions are removed. In some businesses that wouldn't be so bad.
By increasing wages as much as he did Mr Ford produced an entirely
new class of consumers—his own and other workers. But our workers
will not directly buy more lorries, or aeroplanes, so our aim is to
replace men with machines as far as possible, because it will be
cheaper in the long run."

Pratt said, "Not if we get shut down every other week by strikes,
Mr Richard, it won't be."

Richard said grimly, "No one's going to strike while the war's on,
for fear of being dismissed and put into uniform."

"Except the women," Morgan said. "They'll not be conscripted."

Richard said, "I was coming to that . . . We will increase the wom-
en's pay to bring it closer to the men's . . . even if they can't set up and
do exactly the same as the men can, we'll wink at those little things to
keep them happy and make sure they have no grounds to believe that
they are being exploited . . . But the men, well, they are going to get
more pay, too, *if* they increase their output, and to the extent that they
increase it. That's the guiding principle behind everything that we are
going to do."

"It's not so easy, Mr Richard," Pratt, the Hedlington Aircraft
foreman, said. "Men don't work one by one, if you know what I mean,
do they? They're teams, like, and to produce more everyone in the
team has to do more."

"That's just what we're aiming at," Richard said. "The productivity
bonus is to be calculated for the factory as a whole, not by individual
men, or even small teams, such as those that work on lorries here, or
on aircraft at H.A.C. . . . First, we will have another look at the
efficiency study Frank Stratton did eighteen months ago. Things are
changing as fast in the factories as they are on the Western Front. So,
first, we decide what new machines we want to use—how many,
where, why. Be prepared to justify your suggestions in terms of number of jobs eliminated or amalgamated. When we have an idea of that,

then we will bring the efficiency people in to help us work out how best to use them."

"The men won't like it," Pratt and Morgan, the J.M.C. foremen, said in chorus.

"I know they won't, because damned agitators like Bert Gorse have been at them . . . but you've got to make plain that more efficiency equals more production equals more pay. It's very simple, really."

"Them as is going to get their slips won't see it that way," Pratt said.

Richard said, "We can't help that. There's a war on. If we can produce more and use less men, releasing those men for the army, it's our duty to do so . . . Ginger, you've been looking as though you don't know why you were invited to this conference. Well, you design aircraft for us. You must think, at every step, how will this *produce* . . . will it be easy and cheap to set up for volume manufacture? Of course, we want the best product possible, especially as our airmen's lives will depend on it, but we also have to think, will we be better off making a hundred machines that are 90 percent perfect or two hundred machines that are 80 percent perfect, in the same time . . . that 100 percent increase in productivity being achieved by designing every little part, as well as the whole, with production in mind. You understand?"

"Yes, Richard," Ginger said. He didn't like the idea; he didn't like a good many of Richard Rowland's ideas, while liking the man. Richard was the product of another generation. His father, old Mr Harry, thought in much the same way, and Richard had learned from him. Their attitude toward the working men who were their employees was very ambivalent. In one area they regarded them as ciphers to be hired, punished, dismissed, as though they were no different in kind from the machines they worked at; in other areas they regarded them as members of their own family, uneducated, of course, but nevertheless solid, trustworthy true Britons . . . He'd have to tell Betty to think more about production, and she'd hate it. The loving care she spent on every last little detail took up a lot of her time. She'd designed some great improvements because of that worrying, gnawing search for perfection. Now the goal must not be the perfect but the producible.

Overfeld said, "What are we thinking about, boss? How much do we want to increase production? Fifty percent? A hundred? We have to have some idea."

Richard said without hesitation, "Triple . . . 300 percent. With an increase of not more than 100 percent in manpower. That means a *productivity* increase of 50 percent. And it's got to come from everywhere . . . purchase, sales, design, transport, accounting, inventory—the lot. That's all."

*　　*　　*　　*

Probyn Gorse was poaching trout, poaching by tickling, late in the evening, under the bushes on Scarrow bank, near where the Taversham to Walstone road was 200 yards away, and shielded by its own high hedges. He was poaching Lord Walstone's trout, because he was fed up with a diet of rabbits, and half the rabbits that Queen Alexandra and Mrs Keppel, his ferrets, were killing in the warrens these days were heavily pregnant females. Probyn didn't mind eating pregnant rabbits, but it might be bad for next year, especially as more and more country folk were out to get extra meat—city folk coming down, too . . .

He lay on the bank, hidden from all sides except directly in front, across the river. Both banks were Walstone Park land here, so the keepers might come from either direction; but they wouldn't. It was a chilly evening, but Probyn wore his old deerstalker hat with the flaps up. He always left his ears free, to hear, if he could. The sun had sunk an hour ago, the light was still strong . . . east wind, that's what made it cold and blew the smoke of the village fires faint in his nostrils. He moved his slightly cupped hand gently back under the overhanging bank. No, the keepers wouldn't be down here this evening. If they were out of their cottages at all, they'd be watching over the pheasants . . . as if *they* knew anything about how to raise pheasant chicks, those old farts his new lordship had hired after sacking the other old farts his old lordship had hired when the original keepers went off to the war . . . or to better-paying jobs in the towns, like Skagg, the previous head keeper. Skagg was a regular bastard, like most keepers, but he knew something about pheasants and trout and rabbits and hare. He'd 'a known better than to sit up watching over pheasant chicks in case Probyn Gorse came to take them; Skagg would 'a known that Probyn Gorse would wait till they were grown up, they made more and better eating then. So Skagg would 'a thought, p'raps he's down by Scarrow, I'll go and take a look . . . But Skagg was long gone, working like a copper in a big factory somewhere up north, seeing that the workers didn't steal anything: just the job for a gamekeeper . . . Something touched the side of his hand and he moved it gently back, feeling. It was a trout . . . a good big 'un, about a pound and a half . . . half as big again as the one he'd already got, that was wrapped in grass in the back pocket of his old coat . . . tickle tickle along the belly line . . . gently, firmly behind the gills, and out, here we are . . . He banged the trout on the back of the head with a stone, wrapped it

141

carefully and slipped it in with the other . . . Plenty to eat tonight, even if Bert came down, as he'd said he might, last time they'd met . . . Bats were swooping along the river now, and an owl was hooting from the woods on the far bank. He could see the lights of the big house glimmering up the rise: time to go home.

He set off in the darkening twilight, shuffling fast along the path that was part a right of way, part rabbit runs, and part the runs of otters that came, like him, to poach his Lordship's trout. After five minutes the lurcher at his heels, the Duke of Clarence, stopped suddenly, whining, staring into the dark ahead. "What is it, Duke?" Probyn muttered. An unearthly shriek arose from the bushes, the cry of a woman in torture. The hairs on Probyn's neck stiffened and crawled. Light gleamed and a face appeared, a face chalk white, lit from below by a greeny glow, a woman's face, shrieking, mouth wide, black wide bonnet on her head, the ribbons tied under her chin . . . Oh Jesus, his mother, again! And closer, more terrifyingly real than ever! Black-clad arms began to wave, but Probyn was running as fast as he could, back along the path, stumbling in his panic, the lurcher whining in front of him, tripping him up.

At last he stopped, sat down, and waited for his heart to stop pounding. 'Twas another, last warning to him, that's what it was! Mother had always hated him poaching . . . told him he'd come to a bad end, why when she was young they'd sent poachers to the colonies for that, Australia or America or somewhere . . . He could see her face, then, so sad . . . and now, worse . . . she smelled of all the years she'd been in her grave, a cold smell of wet earth and dead leaves . . . Now he had to pass by the place again, to get back to his cottage. Perhaps he should stand up and swear he'd never poach again, and if he did, God could strike him dead. Safer to say, I'll never poach again if I can help it . . . but what were he and the Woman going to eat, if he didn't poach?

He stood up, raised one hand, and cried in a quavering voice, "Mother, I swear to stop poaching, if I can . . . can't say fairer than that, can I?"

The Duke of Clarence appeared from wherever he had fled to, and licked his hand. "You was as scairt as me," Probyn muttered. "Good cause, too . . . Come on."

They went back toward the cottage, side by side now. Probyn slowed at the place where his mother's ghost had appeared, his heart pounding so that he was sure it could be heard a hundred yards away . . . but there was nothing. The Duke skirted the bushes wide, and five minutes later they slipped through the gap in the brambles and hazels and opened the cottage door.

Probyn stood a moment, eyes lowered, until they became accustomed to the light. Then he looked up. His son Bert was here, standing by the fire. The Woman was poking a piece of wood and moving a pot. She glanced at him and, almost at once, away; but not absolutely at once; there had been a hesitation. She had seen something in his face. He had not told her about the two previous visitations by his mother and he would not tell her about this one. It was between him and his mother. He fished in his back pocket, brought out the trout, and laid them on the table. The Woman picked them up, took them to the sink, and began cleaning them.

Bert said, "Willum's a prisoner, Dad."

Probyn sat down at the table. Willum was his eldest son, by the first Woman he'd had. He was a good strong man, but weak in the head. The army had no business taking him, but he was bound and determined to go, after the Germans killed Colin Blyth, his cricketing hero. Then, near a month ago, Mary his wife had had a telegram from the War Office saying Willum was severely wounded and missing.

Bert said, "She's had another telegram. Willum's had both his legs took off, and is in hospital in Germany . . . So Mary and her brats will be nearer starving than they was before."

Probyn said, "She can get money from Florinda."

"So could I," Bert snapped, "if I wanted to, but Mary thinks Florinda's a whore, and so do I . . . and she's become a proper upper-class parasite, into the bargain."

Probyn said, "What's Mary going to do, then?"

"Make more baby clothes for rich bitches, till her eyes drop out . . . wash more sheets and towels, till her hands moulder away."

"If that's what she wants to do," Probyn said coldly, "that's what she'll do." He didn't like this Albert, his son by his second Woman. Bert wasn't a country man, but smelled of steel and oil, and talked of a future where there would be no fields or woods, only factories, belching smoke, and in the factories, men like himself, snapping and snarling at each other.

Bert got up—"I'm going back to Hedlington."

"Plenty of time before you start for the station."

"I'm walking. We need all the money we have to organize the union."

*   *   *   *

Rachel Cohen knocked on the last door in the narrow street of small houses in North Hedlington. The street sloped down to the blackened and soot-grimed Scarrow, here at the limit of barge traffic, almost opposite the Jupiter Motor Company's factory. The door opened and a man in shirt sleeves and carpet slippers stood there, the *News of the World* in his hand.

"What d'you want?" he said. "If it's selling something, 'op it. We've got no money."

"It's Mr Griffiths, isn't it?"

"What if it is?" the man said suspiciously. He looked like a labourer, burly, walrus-mustached, about forty-five.

Rachel said, "I'm Rachel Cohen, secretary of the Hedlington Socialist Party. My husband's going to stand for this seat in Parliament at the next election, whenever that may be. Our programme is to negotiate an immediate end to the war, end conscription, bring our boys back, end all wartime regulations that operate against the working man. May we send you our material . . . news letters, announcements of meetings and speeches? We need your help. The country needs your help."

"H'm," the man said, regarding her more carefully. "End the war immediate, eh? That's a tall order, with the 'Uns bombarding Paris and knocking 'ell out of 'Aig."

"It can be done," Rachel said. "The Germans may be winning a battle now but they must realize that they can not win the war. Nor can we. No one can win. If you elect Mr Bentley, we . . ."

"Thought you said your name was Cohen," the man said, his brows lowering.

"It is," she said. "Mr Bentley and I are married but we agreed it would be best if I kept my maiden name." "My real maiden name," she might have added; for until recently she had been using the anglicized form "Cowan."

"Oh," he said, "one of these independent women, eh?"

"I suppose so . . . Perhaps you have sons liable to be conscripted?" Rachel said.

"Yes," the man said, his face settling grimly. "Our Charlie's just eighteen. They'll be calling for him any moment. And after that, Billy . . . Yes, I'll sign up. Me and my missus both."

Rachel wrote rapidly in her big notebook and said, "Thank you, Mr Griffiths. You won't regret it . . . and you'll help save England as well as your sons."

The man nodded and turned back inside, closing the door. The last of the day, Rachel thought with a sigh of relief. Home now, to find out how Wilfred had got on with his talk to the Womens' Guild . . . and another to the Mothers' League . . . and one to the Methodist Church people . . . She tramped wearily south along High Street, turned off up the hill and entered the little semi-detached house Wilfred had bought a week before their marriage in January. If they had children, it would be too small . . . well, only if they had Nannies and housemaids and all the other bourgeois trappings; but there was no time to think of children now. There was a war on, not over there in France, but here in England. She began humming Blake's mighty lines—

> *And did those feet in ancient time*
> *Walk upon England's mountain green?*
> *And was the Holy Lamb of God*
> *On England's pleasant pastures seen?*

She was still humming as she turned the handle of the front door and walked in. She stopped, calling, "Wilfred . . . are you home?"

The door of the room beside her opened and Wilfred came out. "Yes . . . I couldn't answer if I wasn't, could I?" He stopped, laughing, to kiss her cheek—"Bert's here."

Rachel walked into the room. Bert, sitting in the armchair by the fireplace, did not stir, except to raise a hand. She had lived with him for two years before meeting and marrying Wilfred, but that period of intimacy seemed unreal, a time of the imagination, not of the memory. He was a labour organizer in the Union of Skilled Engineers—sour, capable, violent. They needed such as him in the Socialist movement; even if they didn't, they were stuck with him, for there was no other place for him to go in England's present political structure.

She sat back on the sofa, and turned to her husband—"How was the day?"

"Hard work . . . uphill most of the way, but the events in France are making even the most diehard conservatives listen. And you?"

"Got a hundred and forty more names . . ."

"Money?"

"Didn't ask for any . . . we've got to show them what we're doing for them, *then* we can ask for money . . . What brings you here, Bert?" she said. "Want a beer?"

"Just had one," Bert said. He sat up straighter—"I come to tell you we decided down at H.E. 16 to come out into the open. We're going to tell Rowland we mean to organize the J.M.C. and the H.A.C., and if he doesn't like it   it'll be too bad."

"I hear they're getting more capital from America, and are going to put in a lot more machinery . . ."

"Throwing men out of work," Bert said. "That's why we've decided to come out of the bushes and take 'em on, bare knuckles. Are you going to help?"

Wilfred, standing across the fireplace from him, resting one long arm on the mantel, stroked his chin with the other hand and said slowly, "You are going to take dues from anyone who joins?"

Bert nodded, "Two percent of his weekly wage."

Wilfred said, "We want some of that . . . say, a quarter of what you take."

Bert started up, "Hey, 'arf a mo', wot in 'ell . . . ?"

Wilfred said, "Bert, you are the industrial arm of the Socialist movement, working for justice, a decent living, and good, safe working conditions for the working man. We are the political arm of the same people, working toward the same ends. Some of what we both want can be achieved by strikes, negotiations, and other industrial action . . . but other objects can only be attained by new laws and regulations . . . laws that will change the whole way this country is structured, as Lloyd George's finance bills of 1910/11 are already doing. You need our help, we need yours. Cough up!" He smiled down at Bert. Ah, good, Rachel thought, he's losing his upper-class aloofness. He can get down in the pit and fight with such as Bert. Then Wilfred coughed, and coughed again, and took out his handkerchief and held it to his lips. It was the gas he'd breathed before Ypres, in March 1916—two years ago in this bloody war.

"All right," Bert said.

*   *   *   *

Probyn and his Woman walked through the open gate of Walstone Manor and round the short drive, the old building on their left, smoke curling from the chimneys at the kitchen end, for it was half-past eleven o'clock in the morning and Mrs Abell was beginning to prepare the midday meal. From somewhere inside they heard a violin, playing sad music.

"Haven't been up here for ten years," the Woman said. "Lawn's not so well cut . . . rough edges there . . . needs more gravel here . . . windows aren't as clean as they should be."

"What can squire do?" Probyn said defensively. "With all the men off to the war and only women left to do the work? And them running off to factories as soon as they can. And the taxes eating him out of house and home?"

Then they were at the front door and Probyn raised his hand to knock. Normally he would have gone round to the kitchen door, but today he was paying an official call, with his Lady; and he would enter by the front door.

He knocked; they waited; the door opened and Garrod the old maid stood there. "Good morning, Mr Gorse," she said formally.

"Good morning, madam. Please come in. Did you wish to see Mr Cate?"

"Aye," Probyn said, "and Miss Stella too. We've come to tell her welcome back to Walstone. And to ask after Mr Laurence."

Garrod closed the door behind them, saying, "Why, Miss Stella's been home more than a month now."

"That's the truth," Probyn said, "but she hasn't been to my cottage . . . or any other house in the village."

Garrod said, "Just wait here, please. I'll tell Mr Cate you're here." A minute later she returned—"He's in the library. Come along."

They followed the maid along the passage and into the long room with french windows, which was Cate's library and music room. He was standing by the windows in front of a music stand, a violin held loosely in his left hand, the bow in his right.

He said, "Ah, Probyn . . . madam . . . I've been practising."

"We heard," Probyn said. "We come to ask after Mr Laurence. There's rumors in the village."

Cate put down the violin and the bow and fumbled for the handkerchief in his sleeve. He dabbed his eyes, and said, "He is to be court-martialled for desertion. I should have told you."

Probyn nodded and said, "Aye. That boy's been like another grandson to me."

"I'm sure it was shell shock," Cate said. "I can not believe . . ."

Probyn interrupted, "He should never have gone to the war, squire, and that's a fact. Well, we'll just hope some of them officers out there understand."

"I didn't," Cate said miserably.

"Fathers and mothers never do," Probyn said. "No use blaming yourself, though. It's nature . . . We come to welcome Miss Stella home to Walstone, too. She hasn't been down to the village."

"You're very kind. She's had a hard time, but she's getting better now, much better. I hope she'll be well enough to call on her friends, soon . . . We keep seeing Florinda's name and picture in the papers. She's looking more beautiful than ever, if that's possible. You must be very proud of your granddaughter, Probyn."

"Don't read them papers," Probyn said, "all full of lies, they are."

Cate said, "The last pictures of her were with Billy Bidford, the Zeebrugge V.C. I kept them . . . here." He held out a page of a glossy magazine. It was a photograph, full page, of Florinda and a young man in naval uniform standing beside a low, long, shiny racing car, two-seater, with strapped-down bonnet, hand brake outside, and flimsy bicycle-type mudguards over the high, narrow wheels. Squire's right, Probyn thought, she is more beautiful than ever; and squire still hasn't forgotten the nights she spent with him in this house, in the worst days of his loneliness. But squire was also changing the subject, which was Miss Stella.

He was about to open his mouth when his Woman spoke—"I want to tell Miss Stella so to her face, that we're glad she's back."

Cate's face fell and the lines of anxiety in it deepened. "Well," he began, "I don't know . . ." Then he made up his mind; and said, "Of course. Wait here, please."

He left the room. They waited, looking out of the window. Lamblike clouds glided across a high, pale blue sky. The song of birds was loud and the scent of honeysuckle heavy from the far hedge. They waited, not moving. They were both accustomed to waiting.

The door reopened and Cate came in leading his daughter by the hand—"Stella . . . you remember Probyn Gorse and his lady?"

Stella had her head down. Now she raised it slowly. Her eyes met Probyn's for a moment, then the Woman's, then wandered away. "Of course," she said, her voice low and small. She was pale and thin, her left arm was bent above the elbow, her hands trembled, but most of all she seemed to have lost all realization of her own beauty, of her position in life, of the secure love of her father and husband, of these people of her father's village.

Probyn said, "We was hoping you'd come to the cottage, but . . . we come here."

"Thank you," Stella said, the voice small and distant.

The Woman turned to Cate, "Bring her down, sir. Any time. She can help me cook a stew for Probyn . . . clean the stove . . . Or go out with Probyn. It'll do her good."

Cate said, "As soon as she's feeling a little stronger . . ."

"She has to come out," the Woman said. "We can all help her."

Again Cate said, "As soon as she's feeling stronger."

Stella turned and walked out of the room. Cate hesitated, then said, "I'll be back in a minute."

"Don't worry," the Woman said, "we'll let ourselves out." They followed Cate out of the room, but then he hurried upstairs after the slowly climbing figure of his daughter, while Probyn and his Woman turned the other way and out of the front door.

As soon as they were ten yards down the drive, the Woman said, "She's pregnant. Near four months."

"How do you know?" Probyn said grumpily. "You didn't put your hand on her belly."

"I know," the Woman said briefly. "A woman's face changes, her eyes, her skin . . ."

After a while Probyn said, "Can't be her husband. He's been away since April last year, 'cept when he was here a few days in January."

"But she wasn't—then. She's been taking drugs, and they've got her off them, but she's not recovered. That's what's the matter with her—still wants them . . . needs them, maybe."

"Who is the baby's father then?"

The Woman said, "A man, of course. She was prossing before they found her. Must have been, to get money for the drugs."

"Then why didn't they get rid of it? Any doctor would do it."

The Woman said, "The husband must want her to have it, because it's her baby and he loves her . . . She's a lucky woman." Then they were out in the lane, and after a while the Woman said, "We need some meat."

"I'm not going out," Probyn said. "Too hot."

"Last night you said 'twas too cold, and since then it's got colder."

"Shut your mouth, Woman, or I'll shut it for you." Probyn waved his gnarled and bony fist under her nose. The Woman sniffed and was silent. Probyn had something on his mind. You could feel, as surely as when a woman had conceived. He didn't want to talk about it, not even to her; but she'd find out, soon.

*   *   *   *

It was dinner time at High Staining. The master, John Rowland, sat at one end of the big table, his wife Louise at the other. Down each side sat the farm girls who had taken the place of the male farm labourers—Carol Adams, little Frances Enright, Joan Pitman, and the new girl, Addie Fallon, obtained early in February to replace Lady Helen Durand-Beaulieu. They all sat silent, oppressed by the aura of misery emanating from the head of the table. Boy was dead, and so was his father, in all respects but that he breathed, his heart beat, and his digestion functioned. During March and April all meals had been torture, for then the window glass had shivered steadily, shaken by the guns in France 140 miles away; and everyone except John had wanted to talk, all the time, to shut out that inaudible thunder and the creaking of the glass; but they had not been able to; and when someone did force out a banal phrase, the ensuing shudder and tinkle were all the more insistent.

One by one the girls finished their puddings, muttered their excuses and left the table. John and Louise were alone again. Louise gathered herself—"John, this won't do. You sit there like a corpse at every meal."

"I can't help it," John said, his voice flat.

"Boy's gone," she said. "Why don't you rejoin the No Conscription Fellowship and save other fathers' sons from following him?"

He shook his head wordlessly. She said, "And there's Naomi. She's doing very well, her commanding officer says. She will need a father whom she can talk to when she comes home, not a . . . an *embalmed mummy!*" Her husband again shook his head without speaking. She continued, "Then if you don't care about the peace movement or your daughter, do you care about High Staining?"

John showed a faint sign of animation—"That's all I have to live for," he muttered.

"Well, you're going to lose it if you don't buck up, because you're going to lose all the girls. They are getting more and more depressed. I found Joan crying in her room yesterday, and she's such a sensible little thing. She wouldn't say what it was, but I know. It's this house . . . the aura of misery and death. It's you!"

After a while he said, "I'll try, Louise."

"Think of them as your daughters," she said. "Think of Boy's son, our grandson."

"If only Helen would bring him down, and come back to live here," John said. "I could teach him to be a farmer."

"He's her son as well as Boy's," Louise said more gently. "She has her own life to live . . . but we are the child's grandparents, and Helen will certainly let us see little Charles, and come down to visit occasionally."

"Boy!" John exclaimed. "Call him Boy, then he'll be Boy, over again."

Louise said slowly, "For us, he could be, eventually. But not for Helen. For her there's only one Boy . . . I'm going up to London tomorrow, John. You don't need me for anything?"

He shook his head. She said with some exasperation, "You don't even care what I'm going to London for?"

He said, then—"What for?"

"I'm going to see Miss Marshall at the Fellowship, and ask her what they're doing about strengthening the movement in the provinces. It seems to me that since Bertrand Russell left, things have slowed down a great deal. I never did like him—even though I've come to agree with him about the war—and now he's fluttered off to some other pacifist group . . . Do cheer up, John. Remember Boy, the new little one."

"Boy," John repeated, his voice tender, "I'll try. I really will."

*　　*　　*　　*

Tim and Sally, the Richard Rowlands' adopted children, were playing cowboys and Indians along the hedge that bordered the lane. Watching them through the drawing-room window Susan Rowland thought, Sally's eleven and advanced for her age. She had had her first period two months ago and breasts were budding under the coarse woolen jersey. But Sally did not want to leave childhood and become a woman; she hardly ever played with dolls and then apparently only to please Susan; she was a tomboy, and liked to rough-and-tumble with Tim, and go birds' nesting with him and other village boys from Beighton and Walstone. That would have to be stopped soon. Not that Sally couldn't look after herself, *if* she wanted to. She knew the facts of life in intimate detail, having many times seen her natural mother in the sexual act with the men she brought home in her trade as a prostitute before a German bomb killed her and left the two children motherless as well as, what they had always been, fatherless.

At one time Susan had hoped to get an American governess for Sally, and Richard had said scornfully that there was no such thing . . . unfortunately, in this time of war, he had turned out to be right, and she had decided she must bring the girl up herself, until she went to boarding school . . . *if* she did. Richard kept saying she must; Susan wasn't so sure.

She was going to lose Tim to prep school this fall. He would be ten—quite old, according to Richard's and the other Rowlands' ideas . . . but too young to leave home, according to her own American ideas.

Her husband Richard interrupted her train of thought— "Tomorrow we present the new work programmes to the men at both factories."

"They're quite, well, hard, aren't they?"

"They're not hard," Richard said patiently. "They're efficient. If they are observed—and they will be, we'll see to that—efficiency will increase 72 percent in the next six months. Our output of bombers and trucks will triple, and . . ."

"I hope the war will be over by then," she said, struck by a sudden dread that it might go on till Tim was old enough to be sent out to it . . . even Dicky, the flesh of her own body, now just a year old and being given his supper by Nanny in the day nursery upstairs.

Richard said, "So do I, of course, so do we all . . . though it will cause severe problems, with all that demand suddenly cut off, as though by the turn of a tap. But we're working on finding new markets . . . The J.M.C. may do all right, but H.A.C. . . ." he shook his head. "In spite of what Guy believes, I don't see how we can sell many aircraft in peace."

"Then you might have to close H.A.C. down?" Susan said.

He nodded—"Yes. You can't burke facts. Bomber aircraft are used up fast in war—not in peace. If we turn them into passenger aircraft, they still won't be used up fast—one hopes."

"So a lot of men will be out of work?"

"There's going to be a great deal of temporary unemployment, when you think of the shell factories, the shell-filling factories, the military equipment factories, the . . . well, I can't think of any industry that will not suffer, except perhaps the pleasure industries. People are going to spend a lot of money on enjoying themselves when this is over."

If they have any money left by then, Susan thought; but not aloud.

* * * *

Richard returned to his office in the J.M.C. rubbing his hands together, Morgan, the works foreman, at his heels. He sat down at his desk—"That went very well, I think, Morgan, don't you?"

"Too well, if you ask me," Morgan said. "I'd have liked to hear some grumbling, muttering in the ranks . . . but they didn't say a word, and after you'd finished they just went off to their jobs, still not talking to each other."

"They'll get used to the new procedures," Richard said. "Are the new machines going to be installed on schedule?"

"Yes. By the fourteenth of next month. Except for the second overhead traveling crane. Can't get that in till the end of July."

The secretary's buzzer buzzed and her small voice said, "Mr Albert Gorse to see you, sir."

"Bert!" Richard exclaimed. "Well, show him in."

A moment later Bert came in, escorted by the secretary. He eyed the two men as the secretary went out, carefully closing the door behind her—"Morning, Mr Morgan," he said. "Morning, Mr Richard."

"Good morning, Bert," Richard said. "What can we do for you? A job perhaps?" He laughed; he had employed Bert before, and sacked him for inciting a riot at the plant. He had no intention of re-employing him.

Bert said, "The Union of Skilled Engineers has decided that J.M.C. and H.A.C. must become union factories—closed shop, U.S.E. factories . . . We at H.E. 16, the local branch, want to know whether you're going to help us, or try to stop us."

Richard opened his mouth to speak but Bert held up an imperious hand and continued—"If you help us, we'll work out a good contract for our members—your employees . . . and we'll see that it's fair to you, too, as the employer. And then we'll see that the contract is lived up to. There'll be no unauthorized work stoppages . . . no wildcat strikes or walkouts, no go-slows or work-to-rule . . . If you try to stop us, threaten or punish the men who want to join—we'll organize your factories just the same, and then we'll break you."

Richard, pale with anger, said, "Break me, and you'll break the factories. Then how many men will be out of work? . . . But you won't break me, or the factories, and you won't organize them. I will not have a union, and that's final."

Bert said patiently, "Look, Mr Richard, you're an educated man, and I'm not. You ought to see what's coming in this country, because I can . . . We're going to be tied to the Yankees, dependent on them, especially for money. You already are, we all know that. But the Yankee bankers don't live here—they don't know what the British working man wants, what he's thinking—and they don't care. They want efficiency, higher profit on capital, more output per man. But our blokes want to be sure they aren't going to be thrown out on the street, after twenty years, p'raps, just because the Yankee bankers want to put in more machines. You think you won't be your own boss here if it becomes a union factory. But are you now? Mr Stephen Merritt and his board are the boss. That may be all right for you, but it's not for us—the men and women who work here and at H.A.C. They want a hold on their own lives. And that's why we'll have no difficulty organizing the two of them."

Richard shouted, "Go to hell! Get out!" Bert, who had been standing throughout the meeting, his cloth cap on his head, turned and left without another word.

"Swine," Richard muttered.

Morgan said, "They've been getting members secretly for some time. They have about forty. Now they'll work harder at it, and they'll get more men. Women, too. That's how they'll take it out on us, for the new methods and machines . . . especially the ones who think they'll be got rid of, when the new programme's in top gear."

Richard said, "We'll do what I think must be done, to increase productivity. If we go under, we'll go under fighting. But if we go, the rest of British industry won't be far behind."

Daily Telegraph, Friday, May 17, 1918

ITALIAN NAVAL FEAT
DREADNOUGHT TORPEDOED

Our Italian Allies have just performed a naval feat of extraordinary daring by torpedoing in the harbour of Pola an Austro-

Hungarian Dreadnought. Wiring from Rome on Wednesday, Reuter's correspondent says that the Chief of the Naval Staff has issued the following communiqué:

"In the early hours of May 14 Lieut-Commander Mario Pelligrini, of Vignola (Modena), Torpedo-Gunner Antonio Milani, of Lodi, Leading Seaman Francesco Auglini, of Syracuse, and Leading Stoker Giuseppe Corrias, of Cagliari, with rare courage, praiseworthy individual self-sacrifice, and the greatest military and naval skill, eluded the active observation of the scouts and searchlights, and penetrated into the very strongly fortified military port of Pola. There they repeatedly fired torpedoes into a large battleship of the Viribus Unitis type.

"At dawn our seaplane squadrons, arriving in succession over Pola, found enemy-chasing planes already up. Our pilots brought down two enemy machines and forced another to land. All our machines returned safely to their bases."

Extraordinary and daring, indeed, Cate thought; but what was happening on the Western Front? He turned to the headline— GREAT AIR FIGHT DURING RAID INTO GERMANY—and began to read.

Garrod came in silently, laid two letters beside his plate, and went out. Cate glanced at the letters. One was a brown envelope, addressed in Quentin's handwriting, with a Field Post Office postmark and censor's stamp. He put the newspaper aside, waited a moment to steady himself, then opened it.

Dear Christopher: Laurence was tried yesterday by a General Court Martial, on a charge of deserting his commanding officer when under orders for action against the enemy. He was found guilty and sentenced to death. The finding and sentence are subject to confirmation by the Army Commander. I attended the court and can assure you that the proceedings were strictly fair. Laurence was defended by a Royal Field Artillery captain who was a barrister before the war. He brought out every point in mitigation that could be thought of by any of us. The facts of his desertion are unfortunately not in doubt; and were confirmed by six witnesses of all ranks. The court was assisted by a Deputy Judge Advocate General—another barrister—who saw that all proper rules were kept. The Court consisted of a Major General as president, two brigadier generals, and two lieutenant colonels, all except one from front-line infantry units. Laurence tried to plead guilty, but the Deputy Judge Advocate General at once told the president that was not permissible in a case where the charge could carry the death sentence. So the proceedings were carried out just as though he had pleaded Not Guilty. I am sorry I have to write this letter but I must tell you the truth. We must now wait to learn whether the Army Commander will confirm the finding and sentence. I will write as soon as I hear, which will not be for a week or two, as it is considered a very important case from every point of view. Yours affec. Quentin.

Cate put the letter down. His eyes ached harshly, but there were no tears. After what Quentin had told him in an earlier letter, about Laurence's two separate disappearances in battle, it was not possible to believe that the Army Commander would do anything but confirm the sentence . . . Could there be a pardon, somehow? But how could they pardon an officer when private soldiers had been shot by firing squads for the same offence? Haig's "backs to the wall" message to the troops would be important, too, for Laurence had run away just when the Commander-in-Chief was most depending on him, on every officer and man . . .

Margaret, he thought. She must be told. She had not answered or acknowledged his earlier notice in the *Irish Times*. He would put in another, giving details . . . but would the censors pass it? It would not be easy to word . . . Isabel would help him, but . . . He buried his head in his hands. Isabel was in California.

He heard the slow footsteps and did not look up. Stella had come down to breakfast. She said nothing. Surely she had seen him, his head in his hands? Heard him sobbing, deep in his chest?

Slowly he looked up. She was helping herself to a kipper, and turned as he watched, to look dully at him, and say "Good morning, Daddy." Then she sat down and began to eat.

Walstone: Wednesday, May 22, 1918

9 PROP X. So long as we are not assailed by emotions contrary to our nature, we have the power of arranging and associating the modifications of our body according to the intellectual order.

Proof.—The emotions, which are contrary to our nature, that is (IV.xxx) which are bad, are bad in so far as . . .

Garrod came silently into the library and said, "Mrs John Rowland to see you, sir."

Cate put the book down unwillingly. The long dead Spinoza offered more comfort to him these days than Louise's fierce energy. He said, "I'll go to the drawing room."

"I'm in the middle of cleaning it," Garrod said.

"Oh. But why you?"

"Tillie's in bed with this flu, sir. I haven't had time to tell you—she only took bad after breakfast."

"Well, bring Mrs Rowland in here, then."

He put the leather-bound volume back in its place on the shelves and waited, looking out of the tall windows, his hands in his pockets.

Louise came in, walking fast. She embraced him quickly, then— "Any news?"

He shook his head. "Quentin said it would take time. Sit down . . . a glass of sherry?"

Louise was small and plump and birdlike, her thick untidy brown hair turning grey, the brown eyes not friendly as they used to be, but sharp, and rimmed by little lines of anger. She said, "I'm going to make the N.C.F. take up Laurence's case. It's barbaric that he should be shot. How could he know what this horrible war was like? And he should never have been sent out in the first . . ."

"I know. He actually asked me once if he could go into the church. I ignored it . . ."

Louise said bluntly, the accent of her native Yorkshire becoming stronger—"No use crying over spilled milk, Christopher. We've got to save him. I'm going to get them to organize demonstrations against any executions—any at all, arising out of the war. That way, we'll avoid people focussing on the fact that he is an officer . . . and we'll get sympathy from a lot of fathers and mothers who will think, my son might be in the same shoes."

Cate said, "It's not public knowledge. Nothing has been published about it."

"No," Louise said energetically. "They don't want to remind people that these things are happening. But we'll publish it, shout it from the housetops." She saw the pain in Cate's face at the idea of all the world knowing of Laurence's tragic failure, and added carefully, "It's the only way to save him."

Cate said, "I suppose so . . . I wish they'd let me change places with him. He has a useful life to live for England. I . . . it's finished, everything *I've* lived for—the village, the people, the land itself . . . swallowed up by the war."

Louise said, "It isn't as bad as that, Christopher. Walstone will never desert you, so don't desert them . . . us. I must go. The train leaves in an hour and I have to get some medicine for John."

"John? Is he sick?"

She nodded—"It looks like this influenza. He's feeling miserable."

"Shouldn't he have some nursing?"

Louise said, "Perhaps. But who's to give it? The girls are tied up on the farm, I've got to go to London for Laurence's sake, and yours. John will have to take his chances . . . I'll call you on the telephone tomorrow morning to tell you how I got on."

*   *   *   *

Cate was shaving by an open window in his bathroom, looking out over the mirror at Walstone spread out in the valley below in the May morning. But there was something unusual . . . smoke . . . the baker's chimney must be on fire . . . no, the smoke cloud was too far off to be the bakery. It was beyond the village, somewhere down Scarrowside . . . close to Probyn Gorse's cottage. He finished shaving quickly, dressed, and returned to the window. Now flames were visible, and the smoke was towering high. Closer at hand someone was pedalling up the drive as hard as he could, straining and rocking from side to side on the seat of his bicycle. It was Billy Haversham, the fourteen-year-old son of the publican of the Beaulieu Arms. He rode past and round to the kitchen door. Cate went downstairs. Garrod was there, waiting at the foot of them. "Sir," she said, "Probyn Gorse's cottage is on fire. Billy Haversham . . ."

"I saw. Is he here?"

"Yes, sir. Here, Billy." The boy, who had been lurking in the shadows farther down the hall, came forward, touching his forelock. Cate said, "Has anyone been hurt, Billy?"

"Don't rightly know, sir," Billy said, his tone jumping from treble to bass in the uncertain manner of boys whose voice is in the process of breaking. "I was running down to see when Mr Fulcher caught me and told me to get my bike and come up here and tell you."

"Thank you, Billy. You can go back now. I expect they'll need every hand they can get down there." To Garrod he said, "I don't know when I'll be back." He thought a minute. It would take longer to get Willow saddled than it was worth. He grabbed one of his walking sticks, and calling "Keep the dogs back," slipped out through the front door, and set off as fast as he could walk down the slope and then across some fields, heading straight for Probyn Gorse's cottage.

When he got there Probyn and his Woman were out on the nettle patch in front of the cottage, together with fifty men and women, led by P.C. Fulcher. They were all staring at the smouldering remains of the cottage's roof. The thatch was gone, and the beams which had supported it were charred and smouldering but not burned through. Some men were setting up a ladder against the front wall, and first one climbed it, then another, then another; and others passed them buckets of water from the Scarrow and the man on top of the ladder hurled the water of each successive bucket at the beams.

Cate pushed through the crowd to Probyn. "What happened?" he asked.

The old poacher turned, his face haggard, the black eyes no longer snapping, the dried-apple cheeks fallen in—" 'Tis a punishment on me," he croaked. "Mother warned me . . . she told me!"

The Woman, beside them, did not turn her head but stood silent, watching the efforts of the firefighters, her arms folded on her bosom.

Cate said, "What do you mean, Probyn?"

Probyn said, "My mother told me to give it up . . . poaching, she called it . . . and I swore I'd do it if I could. But I couldn't. I took two of Lord Walstone's cock birds only the day before yesterday." He turned away, his back to the cottage.

Cate said to the Woman, "Do you have any idea what caused it?"

She shook her head without speaking. Fulcher came up and said, "Sorry the water's going down inside, Probyn, but we must get those beams doused."

"Doesn't matter," Probyn said. "Nothing to spoil in there."

"I took a look inside," Fulcher said. "There's some scorching of bedclothes, blankets, and the like, but soon as you get a new roof on there, 'twon't be long afore you can go back."

"I'll never live there again," Probyn said sepulchrally. "My mother warned me."

Cate walked forward and peered in at the front door. Fulcher was right. Miraculously little damage had been done. The thatch had burned straight upwards, and very quickly. He turned to the constable—"Where's Joe . . . and Peter and young Vic? I thought they were supposed to be in your emergency fire brigade."

Fulcher said, "Down with the influenzie, sir, every last one of them . . . and plenty more."

A bulky figure burst through the back hedge and advanced on the crowd, chewing a big dead cigar. The constable said, "Good morning, my lord. 'Tain't as bad as it might have been."

Lord Walstone shifted his cigar from one side of his mouth to the other, and said, "They can't live in here till they get a new roof. That'll take time. And money." He strode forward to confront Probyn and his Woman—"Anyone hurt? What about your ferrets and that dog?"

"Got the ferrets out," Probyn said. "The Duke's free at night. He's here."

Lord Walstone said, " 'Appy to hear it. Get your clothes together. I'll send a car down for you at ten. You can spend a few nights in the Park, and maybe in one of my cottages afterwards."

Probyn looked thunderstruck. "In the Big House, my lord? Us?" He turned to his Woman, obviously needing her guidance, whether to accept or reject. She said nothing, did not even turn her head.

Walstone said, "Well, that's settled then. I must get home. Can I give you a ride back to the Manor, Cate?"

Cate said, "There's nothing more to be done, is there?"

Fulcher said, "No, sir. Nothing here anyone would want to nick."

Cate said, "All right, and well done." He followed Walstone through the hedge, through a spinney, and through another hedge to the road, where the Rolls Royce was waiting, liveried chauffeur at the wheel—a man, for a change; old, beyond military age, but a man. They settled back on the padded leather upholstery and Lord Walstone said, "Very sorry to hear about Laurence, we are, me and the missus. Her Ladyship, I'm s'posed to call her now but I can't get used to it . . . Is there anything I can do?"

Cate said, "Louise Rowland's going to arrange demonstrations against military executions . . . I suppose I could ask you to speak to the Prime Minister and see if there's any chance of getting a pardon, or at least a reduction of sentence. But . . ." He looked straight ahead, not trusting himself to meet Walstone's eyes—"I don't really believe in any of that. We—my family, and people like us—have made the laws in this country for a thousand years . . . made them and enforced them. It isn't right that we should cry to have a law changed when it hits us. And I'm not sure that Laurence wouldn't rather die than spend the rest of his life in gaol."

Walstone said, "There'll be a general pardon soon after the war ends. 'As to be. So the thing is to make sure he's still alive then, eh? Well, I'll see what I can do. I'll talk to Lord Swanwick. He knows the ropes around the Lords better than I do . . . and you'll speak to Mr Harry, of course."

The Rolls was sweeping majestically round the gravel to the front door of the Manor. It stopped, the chauffeur climbed down, somewhat rheumatically, and held open the rear door. Cate made to get out but Walstone caught his arm and said, "Ruthie's baby's due next month. We want to name it after you—Christopher."

Cate said, astonished—"Well, that's an honour, Lord Walstone. Thank you. But what if it's a girl?"

"Christine . . . One more thing. I 'ope you won't offer to get that roof of Probyn's fixed too soon."

Again Cate was astonished—"But . . ."

Walstone laid a finger alongside his nose in the cockney conspiratorial gesture—" 'Cos he's better off in the Park. An' if he doesn't have a cottage to go back to, he might stay . . . seeing as his mother doesn't want him to go on poaching my birds and rabbits and hares and fish." He laughed, deep in his thick throat. Cate got out, and looked, wondering, after the retreating back of the Rolls.

*　　*　　*　　*

Cate walked slowly to the breakfast room. There was something debasing in the human condition that one felt hungry, longed for bacon and eggs or a savory kipper, while your only son was under sentence of death, and your only daughter a . . .

He sat down and opened the paper, but looked up as unfamiliar footsteps crossed the parquet and then were silenced in the carpet. "Tillie," he said, "what are you doing here? You only got out of bed yesterday. You're supposed to be resting."

"Sorry, sir," the kitchen maid said, pouring him his coffee. "Garrod's took to her bed, with the flu. She says to tell you she's sure she'll be all right tomorrow, but meantime, if you don't mind, it'll have to be me, sir."

"Of course I don't mind, Tillie. You're pouring like an expert." He sipped the coffee, glanced at the headlines, then put the paper down and went to the sideboard to choose his breakfast. While he was helping himself to a fried egg, the door from the passage opened and Stella came in. She was wearing a white batiste nightdress with blue trimming, her feet bare. He said, "Good morning, Stella," put down his plate, and went to kiss her. She stood staring through him, her jaws working. "Shouldn't you have your slippers on, dear?" he said. "And a dressing gown?" The nightdress, besides being very thin for the fresh May morning, the windows open, was also transparent. Her pubic hair was obvious, also the bulge of pregnancy.

Stella cried, "I can't stand it, Daddy, do you hear, I can't stand it!" Her hair was dank and lank and she seemed to have been sweating heavily. "I've got to have some! Send me back to the hospital, anywhere where they'll give it to me!" Her voice rose—"I'll kill myself!"

Tillie was still in the room, standing aghast by the sideboard. She came forward now, and reached for Stella's arms—"There, Miss Stella, why don't you go back to bed, and I'll bring you up your breakfast. Eh?" Gently she tried to pull Stella toward the door. Stella shrieked, "I don't want any breakfast, I want heroin . . . now, now, now!" She glared at her father, "Would they give it to Laurence before they shoot him, if he asks for it? The condemned man's last request? Why don't I kill someone . . . and then . . . and then . . ." She burst into tears.

Cate took one arm, Tillie the other. Together they guided the sobbing young woman out of the room, along the passage and into her bedroom. "Help her to bed," Cate said. He went over to the wash-handstand, picked up a tube of pills and looked at the label— Seconal. That's what they said to give her as a sedative. He shook out two tablets and filled a glass with water from the carafe by the bed. "Here," he said, "take these." Stella took them obediently. They stood, watching her, as she sank slowly back into the bed and deeper under the bedclothes. After a time she said, "I'll be asleep soon, Daddy . . . but then I'll have to wake up, won't I? And it'll be worse again. Get me heroin. I need it. I know how to measure small doses, so I don't go mad again . . . mad! If you don't get it for me, I'll have to run away again and get it for myself . . . the same way."

"But, your baby!" Cate said. "The last one died because of the drug . . . didn't it? You know it did. You wouldn't have an abortion, but you'll kill this one too."

Stella said, her voice cold, "I can't help it, Daddy. I'm sorry."

She closed her eyes. They watched her for a minute more, then left together, walking silent one behind the other down the stairs—then Cate to his music room, to take down his violin, and Tillie to the kitchen, hardly able to see for tears.

*   *   *   *

The patrol was ten men of the Royal Irish Constabulary, under a sergeant. All eleven were armed with rifles and carried bandeliers of ammunition slung across their chests. They were walking down the narrow-gauge track of the Dingle and Tralee railway, the heather and gorse and bracken-covered slope of Beenoskee to their right, as they walked west, and the waters of Dingle Bay glittering in the morning light to their left. Across the bay, Macgillicuddy's Reeks rose in shadow, the low sun behind them.

A steam engine whistled shrilly from behind, and the sergeant looked over his shoulder. That would be the seven o'clock from Tralee, a mixed train, like all the trains on this sleepy little line on the shores of the Atlantic. But it wasn't in sight yet. The patrol plodded on along the narrow paths outside the stone ballast, two men in front, then a hundred yards back the sergeant and five more, not bunched but within easy talking distance, then a hundred yards back three more men. They were not searching the railway itself, but using it, as they had every morning for the past week, to get from their barracks in Dingle to hunt for I.R.A. outlaws reputed to be hiding out in, and operating from the corries and gullies of Slievanea and Beenoskee. The I.R.A. had raided both Dingle and Tralee, as well as Castlemaine, set fire to several shops and murdered one suspected British sympathizer; but they were also thought to be supplying German U-boats, which were known to use Dingle and Tralee Bays, with information on British sailings and ship movements.

The patrol trudged on. The engine of the Tralee train, now less than a quarter of a mile away, whistled again, loud and long . . . I'm coming, look out, look out! The sergeant waved his men to the side and they all stopped, moving to right or left of the single line, waiting, their rifles rested. The little engine approached, rocking over bog and rock on the crudely laid and barely maintained rails. Steam hissed from cylinders and steam chests, black smoke poured from the funnel. The sergeant looked to see who was driving. It was usually Paddy Hearne, from Tralee. Yes, it was Paddy, staring at them through the round glass window on the driver's side, his hand on the throttle, no, on the whistle cord it must be, for the engine was whistling again. The sergeant raised his hand in salute as the engine passed, then suddenly hurled his rifle up toward his shoulder, for he had seen something on the footplate between the legs of the driver and fireman . . . a body, a man, a gleam of metal. But the rifle never reached his shoulder, as a man inside the first of the two little passenger carriages, propped at a window, fired and shot him through the heart. The sergeant toppled over backward, as a storm of rifle fire broke out from the train. The two constables at the point of the patrol had hurled themselves flat in the heather and were firing at the train as it passed, rocking along now at what was for it the dangerous speed of 25 m.p.h. All five of the constables with the sergeant had been killed or badly wounded; also one of the three men at the rear. The train pounded on round a curve, the whistle now silent, smoke trailing across the face of Slievanea. The point men ran back toward their comrades, to be joined there by the two survivors from the rearguard.

One said briefly, " 'Twas the Lady's lot . . . A woman was in there, firing straight at me . . . but the carriage rocked and the bullet went over my head."

Another said, "See what you can do for these poor fellows, Tim. I'll run on down to Tralee and get the soldiers out."

"The buggers'll have vanished by then," a third said. "Bad cess to them!" He stared down the empty line, slowly shaking his head.

Two miles away, the man who had been lying concealed on the footplate, rose to his feet, and said, "Stop her here, Paddy."

"This is a bad day's work for Christian men," the old driver said gloomily. He pulled back the brake lever and closed the injector. The train ground to a standstill. The man in the cab said, "It can't be helped, and it's for you as well as us."

The driver shook his head, "I didn't ask for this."

"Well, you're going to get it . . . Tell 'em you would 'a been shot if you'd raised a finger . . . and that's the truth. The Lady's back there, and if it hadn't been you, it would have been me."

He jumped down to the ground, to be joined by a dozen other men and a woman, all piling out of the two carriages that, with five small goods wagons, formed the train. A sandy road ran nearby and as the train stopped a motor moving van appeared from the direction of Dingle. The men who had carried out the ambush ran to it and piled in the back. A moment later it rolled on eastward.

Paddy Hearne, the driver, walked down the line to the half dozen genuine passengers, who had been on the train before the Lady's gang had stopped and boarded it in the wild moors. "Everyone all right?" he asked.

"Yes . . . but no thanks to those murthering shiteheads. One of the constables was firing straight at me . . . how was he to know I wasn't one of them?"

Paddy shrugged and shook his head. These were hard times.

Meanwhile the van drove on fifteen miles toward Tralee, then stopped. The gang inside got out, and scattered. The van proceeded, to be searched twice by police; but nothing and no one was found.

The next day, in a back room of a comfortable old house in Killarney, the owner of the house, a feed merchant of the Sinn Fein persuasion, brought his guest the day's paper. He was chuckling as he handed it to her—"You've laid them by the ears this time, Lady—five dead, two seriously wounded. And not one of your people scratched. They know it was you. Look!"

He pointed to the headline—OUTRAGE IN KERRY BY MRS CATE'S GANG; and underneath—CONSTABULARY AMBUSHED AND MURDERED FROM TRAIN.

Margaret read without much interest. She knew what had happened better than the reporters from the *Irish Times* could possibly know. It was a pity, in a way, that they knew it had been her work: better that the English should feel that they were fighting not particular people but a great amorphous, nameless, all-pervasive hatred. She turned to the front page and at once the word "Margaret" caught her eye. She tensed, feeling cold; and read on: *Margaret—Laurence under sentence of death for desertion—CC.* She read it again; and again; then laid the paper down. Her host turned from the window—"Exciting, isn't it? . . . Are you all right?"

She sat, thinking hard. At length she said, "Send a telegram to the Viceroy . . . have someone unknown give it to a boy, with money. It should read—take this down—'Margaret Cate wants to know situation regarding her son Laurence Cate Lieutenant Weald Light Infantry under sentence of death in France. Reply in *Irish Times* tomorrow or next day.' No signature."

"But . . . they may not answer. They may take no notice."

Margaret said slowly, "Yes . . . Add to the telegram, at the end 'Negotiations on her surrender possible.' "

The man's mouth was open—"But, Lady . . . they'll hang you!"

She said, "Please be quiet. It is painful enough to find myself considering giving up our fight, without having my nose rubbed in it."

"But . . ."

"Please leave me alone. Do not return until you have the *Irish Times* with their reply. No, I do not want any food." She stalked out of the room.

*   *   *   *

Cate held the telephone close to his ear as the Prime Minister's private secretary read aloud to him the text of a telegram received by the

Viceroy of Ireland from his wife, Margaret Cate. The secretary ended—*"Negotiations on her surrender possible."*

Cate held his voice steady, "What is the Government going to do?"

"The Prime Minister has not decided yet, sir, but he thought you should be told of this development."

"Would you hang her, while sparing Laurence?" Cate asked, his voice now trembling with a mixture of fear and anger. "A life for a life?"

The secretary's young voice was anxious, patient—"We don't know yet, sir. It is a very difficult decision for the Prime Minister."

Cate said, "I understand. Thank you. Thank him." He replaced the receiver and walked slowly to his study. Margaret had always loved Laurence the most. Stella's disappearance had not produced a word from her, but this . . . for her only son, she would give her life. In his study, his eyes dimming with tears, he found his violin, and began to play.

*　　*　　*　　*

Harry Rowland arrived late at 10 Downing Street. He had been held up at a committee meeting in the House, and now, at the end of the cul de sac, he had to struggle through a mob of a hundred men and women waving placards and chanting endlessly, "No more firing squads . . . no more firing squads . . ." Among them he recognized Bertrand Russell at once from his flying mane of grey-brown hair and aquiline face; and, just beyond Russell, his own daughter-in-law Louise Rowland. He wished that the demonstrators, shouting and chanting outside the Prime Minister's house, would direct their appeal more closely to Laurence's situation: he, for one, could not support a general ban on capital punishment in the army. What would happen if soldiers shot their officers, for instance, and got away with no more than a few years in gaol? How would that be worse than what they were already facing in the trenches?

He reached the door, panting, and said to the police sergeant on duty—"Harry Rowland, M.P., sergeant. I have an appointment with the Prime Minister."

The sergeant saluted and waved him in. Harry went slowly up the stairs to the Middle Drawing Room. Lords Swanwick and Walstone were already there. The windows were open and the noise of the demonstrators seemed louder in here than outside. The Prime Minister, David Lloyd George, was standing by the window, but back from it, so that people outside would make out no more than a general shape. He turned and said, "You're late, Rowland. Don't explain . . .

Listen to those people. I can see Russell and that dragon, Miss Marshall. Where's Clifford Allen?"

"In prison," said Winston Churchill, standing the other side of the window, a big cigar in his hand.

Lloyd George said to Harry, "Are you responsible for this demonstration?"

Harry said stiffly, "No, Prime Minister, I am not . . . though I knew it was to take place."

Lloyd George said, "Shut the window, Winston, there's a good fellow. We can't hear ourselves think . . . Now, you three have to persuade me that Lieutenant Laurence Cate, who has been sentenced to death by a court martial for desertion in action, should be pardoned." He swung on Walstone—"Are you any relation of his?"

Lord Walstone said, "No, Hi'm not. But Hi've known the family for some years."

Lloyd George turned to Swanwick—"And you?"

Swanwick shook his head—"Family friends. I think he's . . . I hate to say this, lost two sons out there myself . . . but I don't think he should have been sent out at all. He loved birds . . . animals . . . never liked to kill anything . . . even hated fox hunting."

The Prime Minister's massive head turned toward Harry—"Do you agree?"

"Yes. I don't know whose fault it is . . . The country desperately needs officers in the trenches. Every fit man ought to go. But we don't send out men with only one leg, or who are stone deaf, or blind. We don't send out haemophiliacs. Laurence, we have been told by his uncle, who is also his commanding officer, is constitutionally unable to take the noise, the fury, of battle. He retreats from it, sometimes only into a dream world, but sometimes, apparently, by physically removing himself."

"Deserting his commanding officer, the Army Act calls it," Churchill said.

The Prime Minister said, "Do you agree with what Swanwick and Rowland have said, Walstone?"

"Yes, I do. I 'aven't known the Cates hintimately for as long as they have, but all I've heard about young Mr Cate is the same as what they've told you."

The Prime Minister said, "Very well. I'll think about it."

The deputation looked from one to another. Harry knew the Prime Minister's ways best and headed for the door. The Lords Swanwick and Walstone mumbled goodbyes and followed.

Alone in the Middle Drawing Room with Churchill, the P.M. said, "What do you think?"

Churchill said, "I would strongly recommend that we do not interfere with the normal course of military discipline. Haig and Rawlinson think that they must make an example of anyone who deserts, in case the Germans should renew their attacks of March and April. They think that it would be particularly improper and inadvisable to let an officer escape execution when private soldiers do not, for the same crime."

Lloyd George said, "Would it help me with the country to see that he is pardoned? *Magnanimous gesture by P.M. saves young life* . . . I can see the *Daily Mail* headline now."

"Except, Prime Minister, that Northcliffe would make sure that *that* was not the headline. It would be more like . . ." he pondered a moment, waving his cigar . . . *"Prime Minister surrenders to pressure, pardons officer deserter* . . . and there would be a leader, written by one of his lordship's trained seals, about politics, loss of the will to win, betrayal of the fighting man. No, no, my dear Prime Minister, I am deeply sorry for the Cate family but we must do the right thing, which is to let the soldiers do what they think best. Rawlinson is not a butcher."

"Haig is," Lloyd George growled. "Now, how does Margaret Cate's telegram, that I told you about, affect the situation? She's saying, in effect, that she'll give herself up if we pardon the son, or commute the sentence. Can we do it?"

Churchill said slowly, "We can do it . . . But we'd have to see that the death sentence on *her* was carried out. And there's enough bitterness in Ireland over the imposition of conscription without adding to it by hanging a woman."

"It might be worth it. The young Cate business will be forgotten in a week, but if we get rid of his mother, we strike a real blow at the brains of the rebel movement in Ireland."

"And the guts," Churchill said. "She's a fanatic . . . brave as a lion . . . quite impervious to suffering, whether it's her own or others', in the cause. Yes, getting rid of her would certainly inflict a most severe wound on the rebels, but . . ."

Lloyd George said, "Nothing's really altered, has it? We've decided we must let the army deal with Laurence Cate as it thinks best. What Margaret Cate offers is immaterial. It might be different if the boy was being held by Irish terrorists . . . at least, the direction of our thoughts would be different, though we might well come to the same conclusion. So . . ."

"I suggest, no answer. Ignore her. It will turn her into an even more bitter enemy, but that can't be helped. Besides, from what I hear, she couldn't be more anti-English than she already is."

167

Lloyd George nodded—"Very well. And now that we've spent an hour discussing the fate of one young man, let's get back to our job . . . How is the influenza epidemic affecting the munition factories?"

"Absenteeism up 24 percent," Churchill said. "I've spoken to my medical adviser about a possible inoculation against it, and he says that at the moment there isn't one. But . . ."

"I've got to get to the House," the Prime Minister said. "We can talk as we walk. What are you doing to make *sure* none of that absenteeism isn't deliberate?"

The two men's voices faded down the stairs. Outside, the demonstrators continued rocking to and fro, shoulder to shoulder, placards waving, chanting, "No more firing squads . . . No more firing squads . . ."

*   *   *   *

Louise Rowland reached High Staining at midnight, riding up in the station trap after catching the last train from Victoria and changing at Hedlington. It had been a busy and exciting day. First, there had been a meeting at the headquarters of the No Conscription Fellowship to discuss general strategy in the light of the extension of conscription to Ireland. After much discussion it was decided to found an Irish branch, based in Dublin. Then had followed the demonstration outside Number 10. She had been there for the whole four hours of it. Early on, she had seen her father-in-law arrive; and when he came out later with Lords Swanwick and Walstone, she had asked him what the Prime Minister had said. But his reply was non-committal. Later the Prime Minister had come out himself, with the Minister of Munitions, and although the demonstration was kept up for another two hours, they did not return. Then, something to eat . . . back to Fellowship headquarters . . . more discussion, exhausting and exhaustive— where and how to raise more funds; legal loopholes to get conscientious objectors out of gaol, or hinder their being brought to trial; problems of public relations and propaganda; money again . . . list of prominent people who could or might be persuaded to come out against conscription or in favor of a negotiated peace . . . the future course of the war . . . dinner . . . and now at last, homeward in the balmy May night behind the clopping hooves. Normally she would have taken one of Mr Woodruff's cars, but none were available, so, it was the old trap . . . how much longer would there be a trap, and the smells of harness and horse . . . or the quiet of the night, in Kent?

The trap drew up to the front door and at once the door opened. The light was burning over the doorway. Carol Adams and Joan

Pitman, two of the farm girls, were standing there. She paid off the driver and walked toward them—"Sorry I'm so late, but . . ."

Carol Adams said, "Mrs Rowland . . . Mrs Rowland . . ." She broke down, burying her face in her hands.

Joan Pitman said, "Mr Rowland's dead. He died at eight o'clock. Dr Kimball came when we called, at six, when Mr Rowland seemed to get worse . . . but he couldn't do anything."

Louise stood stiff, facing the two young women, one sobbing heavily, the other upright and stony-faced. John—dead? She started forward, her legs unsteady. He had died while she was in London, thinking of everything in the world except him. He had been dead in spirit for six months. Now the body joined the spirit. "Let me see him," she said.

*   *   *   *

Lieutenant Colonel Quentin Rowland, commanding officer of the 1st Battalion the Weald Light Infantry, glowered across the makeshift table at the sergeant standing stiffly at attention the other side of it. He said, "I've never had such an application before. Men are detailed for a firing squad, they don't apply for it . . . And it is never provided by the condemned man's own battalion, unless no other troops are available. I'd have to ask the Army Commander to appoint us to carry out the sentence."

Sergeant Fagioletti said, "Yes, sir. I know, sir. The Regimental told me . . . but, we want to see it's done right, sir. We don't want Mr Cate to suffer. We think Mr Cate would rather see us, his men, at the last, rather than strange blokes from some other push. If you'll appoint me, and Private Whitman . . . Fletcher Whitman, battalion sniper, sir . . . we'll see that there's no mistake. Mr Cate won't know nothing."

Quentin stared at the plump, blue-jowled figure . . . Italian, really . . . excellent man in a tough spot, Kellaway said: he'd seen that himself. "I'll think about it," he said. "That's all."

The Regimental Sergeant Major bellowed, "Salute! About turn! March out!"

Fagioletti stamped out, the R.S.M. on his heels. The clatter of hobnails receded, the door closed. Quentin turned to his adjutant— "What do you think?"

"I think it's a good idea, sir," Archie Campbell said. "May I command the squad, sir—assuming we're given the job?"

"We will be," Quentin said. "No one else wants it. I'll telephone Army Headquarters at once . . . All right. You command—six men, and Fagioletti. All to be loaded with ball . . none of that nonsense about half of them being loaded with blank. Find a place against a wall. Dawn, the day after tomorrow. Your final signal to fire is not given aloud, but with the hand or sword. Blindfold, of course. No tying of hands or ankles. Practise tomorrow. You have to read the sentence and the confirmation by the Army Commander at the very beginning. He wears no rank badges or regimental buttons, as he's been cashiered. Cut them off before."

"I know, sir. I've been looking up the Manual."

Quentin stared silently out of the shattered window of the dusty room in the ruined village. The guns were loud, since the brigade was in reserve close to the British field artillery positions. At last, as Archie Campbell waited, watching him, he exploded with a single word— "Christ!"

*   *   *   *

Father Caffin laughed in the flickering candlelight, and raised his tin mug, which was half full of wine. "Here's to you, Laurence. You're a good lad, and I'll remember what you've told me about the difference between Hen Harriers and Marsh Harriers . . . I'll be looking for a parish in Mayo or Galway, anywhere far from Dublin and close to the Atlantic Ocean, when this is over. I never was much of a one for birds before, but now . . ."

"Priests aren't supposed to be," Laurence Cate said, his eyes twinkling.

Father Caffin started and then said, "Well, be the Holy Father! . . . I've as good an eye for a pretty colleen as the next man, I'll have you know. Putting on the soutane doesn't alter what God put under it. It just means I have to control myself . . . more's the pity."

Laurence drank some wine, smiling across the table. It was about four in the morning, close to dawn, he didn't know just how close, for he had given his wristwatch to his sergeant, Fagioletti, yesterday. He was sitting back in an easy chair, the only one in the village, though the springs were protruding into his spine. His tunic hung open, for the buttons had been cut off, as also the two stars on each shoulder. Fagioletti, doing the cutting, had started to unfasten the split pins that held on the brass shoulder titles WEALD L.I., but the adjutant, watching, had said quietly, "Leave them on, sergeant. We're not ashamed of him." His uncle, the C.O., had come about midnight and spent an hour . . . then Captain Kellaway . . . Laurence wished he could say a proper goodbye to all the men of his platoon, but he would say it to some of them soon—five, Fagioletti, and Fletcher . . . good old Fletcher. He'd taught him almost as much as his grandfather, Probyn, had.

Caffin said softly, "They'll be coming soon, Laurence. Is there anything you want to say to me . . . I'm not asking for a confession, you understand."

"No, padre. You know, I deserve to be shot . . ." The priest made a gesture of denial but Laurence insisted quietly, "I do. I'm not afraid. What was it Nurse Cavell said before they shot her? 'I must have no bitterness in my heart toward anyone.' And she was talking about the Germans. I certainly don't have any toward my own people, my regiment, my platoon, the men I let down . . . I hope it's a nice dawn."

"It is," a third voice said. Archie Campbell, pale-faced, was standing in the door, his Sam Browne belt and revolver holster shining blood red, the steel helmet gleaming dull green, the respirator square and boxy high on his chest. "It's time," he said.

Laurence stood up. Campbell turned, went out, and crossed the street. Laurence followed, Father Caffin's hand on his shoulder. The priest was speaking in a low voice, "We'll meet again, Laurence, my boy . . . you and me and Sergeant Fagioletti . . . and Boy and . . . and your Uncle Quentin and . . ."

"Tell my father I wasn't afraid," Laurence interrupted.

"I will . . ."

Campbell turned round the end of a free-standing wall, the house that it had once supported long gone. A faint greenish light spread in the east. Ten yards away seven men stood in line, eyeballs gleaming white, brass of equipment dully sparkling. Behind them Captain Sholto, the regimental medical officer, waited, shivering uncontrollably. Campbell began to read by the light of a torch held in one hand a short document held in the other—"Lieutenant Laurence Cate, 1st Battalion the Weald Light Infantry . . . At a General Court Martial convened at Conte-Mesure on May 4th, 1918, under the authority of General Sir Henry Rawlinson, General Officer Commanding-in-Chief, Fourth Army, British Expeditionary Force . . ." He read on rapidly, while Father Caffin kept his grip on Laurence's shoulder. The light spread and grew and took colour. They could clearly see the faces of the waiting soldiers now, Fagioletti on the right.

"The sentence of the court will now be carried out."

Campbell put away the paper and produced a big khaki handkerchief. Captain Sholto hurried forward with a circle of white cardboard in his hand and quickly pinned it on Laurence's chest directly over the heart. Campbell was trying to knot the blindfold behind his head but Laurence said, "Don't bother, Archie . . . I'd rather see. I can hear birds singing . . . That's a blackbird!" Campbell stepped back and snapped, "Firing squad, aim!" The soldiers sprang to attention and directly up into the aim, in the Light Infantry drill . . . "a blackbird,"

Laurence repeated, "the most beautiful song in the world . . . better than a nightingale." He looked directly at the men of the squad— "Thank you," he said. Campbell jerked down his raised hand. Seven shots cracked and Laurence Cate was thrown back against the wall behind him. There, his legs collapsed and he fell sideways to the ground, smiling at the blackbird, which still sang in the remains of a hedge close by.

*   *   *   *

The light spread through the window and gave colour to the walls of the little room, the faded photograph on the mantelpiece, the red and white flower pattern on the jug in the wash-handstand. The woman in the bed was grey-haired, pale, exhausted, her eyes closed, one hand hidden under the bedclothes, the other arm extended above them, the hand held by the tall man sitting in the hard chair beside the bed.

She opened her eyes and Christopher Cate said anxiously, "How do you feel? You were tossing and turning all night, until an hour ago. Then you began to sweat . . ."

Garrod the housemaid said weakly, "I'm better, sir . . . not well . . . better than I was . . . I'll get better now . . . Is it night or morning?"

"About half-past four . . . a beautiful dawn, fresh, lovely. A blackbird's singing in the hedge outside the kitchen. Can you hear it?"

"I can hear it, sir . . . Will you get to bed now, sir, please. You shouldn't have stayed." The hand pressed lightly in his—"It's not right is it, for us to be alone in my room all night. What will they say in the village?"

Cate laughed, patted her hand, and stood up—"I'll leave you . . . Dr Kimball says he'll come when he can. He's being run off his feet with this epidemic. Rest now."

Daily Telegraph, Monday, July 22, 1918

EX-TSAR KILLED BY BOLSHEVIKS

PROPERTY CONFISCATED

Amsterdam, **Sunday.**

A Moscow telegram says that the *Bjedneta* reports the death of the Tsar, as follows: "By order of the Revolutionary Council of the People the bloody Tsar has happily deceased at Ekaterinburg. Vive the Red Terror."

A decree of July 17 declares the entire property of the ex-Tsar, the ex-Tsaritsa Alexandra, and the Dowager ex-Tsaritsa, and all members of the former Imperial house, to be the property of the Russian Republic, including the family deposits in Russian and foreign banks—Reuter.

"Happily deceased," Cate thought: what a nice phrase for murder . . . judicial murder; another version of what had happened to Laurence. He shivered and looked across the table at his brother-in-law, Tom Rowland, dressed in a lightweight blue-grey suit, very fashionably cut, with a loose-flowing collar and an intricately patterned tie. He was also wearing suede shoes and patterned socks of matching shades of blue and grey. Tom looked up from his bacon, sausage, and fried tomatoes, and said, "Looking at my suit, Christopher?"

"Well . . . it *is* a little different from the uniform pea jacket, or the blue suit and bowler hat that all N.O.s seem to wear to town if they're in mufti."

"Don't forget the tightly rolled umbrella," Tom said, laughing. "Yes, it's different. But then so am I. Arthur—Arthur Gavilan—the man I work for—took one look at my blue suit and bowler hat and said, 'My dear Tom, this is a high-fashion salon for expensive ladies, not the In & Out!' So he designed half a dozen suits for me."

"It's very nice," Cate said. "It's just different . . . as you look different . . . and, if I may say so, better."

"I'm a happy man," Tom said. "That's why. I loved the navy . . . still do, always will . . . but, it's over. I'm a couturier."

He returned to his food. Cate's eye caught the coloured portrait of Laurence newly hung on the wall behind the sideboard. It had been done recently, from a photograph of him in his 2nd Lieutenant's uniform; but Cate had asked the portraitist to make him a full lieutenant, as he had been at the end. The hurt of his son's death would never leave him, nor the sense of guilt; but he could live; he must live. He felt for his handkerchief; for though he must live, he could not yet think of Laurence without tears coming.

Garrod came in with the post, and Cate put away his handkerchief—"Excuse me," he murmured, taking the top letter off the silver tray. It bore an American stamp . . . postmarked Bakersfield, Cal. He opened it and read:

Virgil cabled me your sad news. Don't blame yourself. Blame the war, for which we must all bear responsibility, all the peoples engaged in it, men and women alike.

Walter is in a camp near here and I see him at weekends. It seems probable that he will be sent to France soon. He is in the infantry, as a buck private, having refused officers' training. When he leaves, I shall go back east and keep

173

house for Stephen in Nyack for a while. After that . . . quien sabe? All my love, always . . . Isabel.

He put the letter down. Tom said, "It's been good of you to have me, Christopher."

"It takes my mind off other things," Cate said.

"I know. If there's anything I can do to help, about Stella, any time, let me know. I'm taking the two o'clock train to Town, if that's all right."

"Certainly."

"Arthur's giving an evening cocktail party for a few of his friends, and some of his most important clients. I mustn't miss that."

"Of course not."

The Western Front:
Thursday, August 1, 1918

10 "Where's your rose?" Quentin Rowland barked, glaring at the young private soldier standing to attention in the reserve trenches which the battalion occupied in front of Contalmaison.

"C-c-couldn't find one, sir," the soldier stammered.

Quentin turned on the man's company commander, jammed into the narrow trench a pace behind him, "Weren't enough sent up to you last night?"

"Yes, sir . . . I think this man must have lost his since dawn stand-to. Everyone in my company was wearing one then."

Quentin said, "Put him on a charge, being improperly dressed."

"Yes, sir."

Quentin moved on, followed by Archie Campbell, his adjutant, and Captain "Stork" Kellaway, B Company commander. Every man of the battalion was wearing a rose, mostly red but some white or yellow, stuck through the top buttonhole of his tunic. Quentin didn't like to see them there: they were supposed to be worn on the right side of the headdress, stuck through the chinstrap of the Broderick cap or the chin chain of the full-dress helmet. But the only headdress the men could wear in the line was the steel helmet, and unless they were also wearing camouflage netting covers there was no place to stick a rose. Campbell had suggested, when the problem first arose, that the men might wear the rose behind their ear, or between their teeth. Damned tommyrot! Quentin had wondered for a moment whether his adjutant was pulling his leg . . . civilians didn't understand the importance of tradition, of doing the same things year after year, century after century, and doing them right.

He stopped in front of the portly Sergeant Fagioletti and said, "Sergeant, why are you wearing a rose in your tunic?"

Like the young private, Fatioletti looked alarmed and astonished. His eyes wandered about, searching for help. The C.O. barked, "Answer me, damn it!"

Fagioletti stammered, his Italian accent very strong—"Because-a we was-a ordered to, sir."

Quentin's face and neck grew red. "*Why* were you ordered to, man? Do you wear roses every day? What would happen to you if you wore a rose in your tunic any other day?"

Fagioletti knew the answer to that and snapped happily, "On a charge of improperly dressed, sir!"

"Then why is it all right . . . why is it compulsory . . . today?"

Fagioletti remembered what the captain had told them— "Minden," he said. "There was a battle, and the men marched through an orchard and picked roses and stuck them in their hats. It was before I joined the regiment, sir."

Campbell could not restrain an explosive chuckle, quickly stifled. The C.O. said icily, "It was. It was in 1759 . . . we smashed seventy squadrons of French cavalry, and four brigades of infantry, under the crossfire of sixty guns, then reformed and marched back through the remnants—we and five other regiments—the six Minden regiments, which all wear roses on this day . . . the one hundred and fifty-ninth anniversary."

He moved on, asking a question here, giving a sharp reprimand there. At the end of B Company's trenches Captain Tanner, commanding A Company, was waiting. Kellaway saluted and stepped back, but Quentin said, "Wait a minute, Kellaway. You, too, Tanner. Listen . . . since March 21st we've been fighting for our lives, trying to hold the Germans. A month ago we knew we'd done it. Any day now we'll start advancing . . . and this time we won't stop till we cross the German frontier. They've all but shot their bolt . . . But when we advance, we have got to fight with the same sort of determination that we did when we had our backs to the wall. Make sure the men understand that. It's easy to fight desperately when you're cornered—you have no alternative. It's not so easy when you're attacking . . . why not take it easy, you think, we're tired, we'll push tomorrow, not today . . . I won't have it! Attacks will be pressed to the hilt, regardless of fatigue, casualties, darkness, anything. You understand?"

"Yes, sir," the two company commanders said together.

"Good. One more thing. The Germans know we are getting ready to attack. They may try one last thrust to put us off balance. We don't know where it will come, but knowing the Germans, we can be pretty sure it *will* come. Be ready, mentally as well as practically."

"Yes, sir."

*   *   *   *

John Merritt urged the chestnut into a trot. Beside him Chee Shush Benally, riding bareback, kicked his heels into the flanks of the powerful bay draft horse, close-coupled, heavy-hocked, broad-chested, and the horse followed suit. The fields, barely a mile behind the battery position, were fallow; there were not enough men left to work them; also, they were in range of German heavy artillery. The 137th Regiment was supporting infantry in the line near La Fère, but there had been no heavy fighting for a month and the colonel was pulling the batteries out of their support role in succession for seventy-two hours of intensive work to bring all men, animals, and equipment up to proper condition and scale. Battery D alone had lost four horses, one gun, two caissons, fourteen men, and a considerable amount of baggage and other equipment to enemy shelling and the general wear and tear of the battlefield. John had worked all morning, with Captain Hodder, on the men's pay rolls and family allotment rolls. Now, since chow, he had been exercising horses, assisted by Private Benally.

The two young men rode side by side, John posting to the chestnut's rhythm, Chee sitting loose on the bay's broad back. John's skin was pale, his eyes grey, his hair dark brown under the steel helmet, its chinstrap tight on the point of his chin. Chee was dark-skinned, square and squat with powerful arms and more than a hint of a beer belly hanging out over the belt of his khaki breeches. He said now, "You had news, John."

"How do you know?" John asked. The Navajo always seemed to know what was happening to him, without having to be told.

"In your face . . . eyes," Chee said.

After a while John said, "Yes. She's back on heroin, a very small dose. But her father is afraid it soon won't be enough, as she builds up tolerance. He's afraid she'll run away again."

The Indian said nothing. The sweat ran down his face in the August afternoon, the high sun blazing down on the parched fields.

John burst out, "And if she does that, she might kill the baby. It's due in October . . . She's got to have something to live for . . . but what can it be? How can I help her, save her?"

He dug his spurs into the chestnut's side and leaned forward, getting a firm control of the reins. The hedge ahead was thin, about

177

four feet high. He didn't know whether the chestnut had ever jumped before, and didn't care. He was at full gallop now; he gathered the horse under him, then spurred powerfully. The chestnut leaped like a buck and cleared the hedge by a good foot. John looked round. Chee was coming . . . that old bay had certainly never jumped before. But it was going to now. Up . . . over. The chestnut was feeling its oats, tittuping sideways and bucking mildly. He headed it across the field, for the next hedge . . . up, over, the bay following. Dust rose, clods of hard earth flew, the chestnut whinnied loud in excitement . . . back over the two hedges, round the big field at a gallop . . .

John eased back. "Whoa . . . whoooa," he cried, patting the chestnut's neck. "Easy now . . . Easy!"

Chee drew up beside him, reining in—"Christ, John . . . Top will have my blood . . . horses sweating . . ."

Now it was John's turn to say nothing. Chee knew perfectly well why he had broken out just now: if he didn't he would have burst. The horses hadn't been harmed. They'd dry off in the ten-minute walk back to the battery, and then . . .

"You ask for leave," Chee said. "Nothing happening here. You ought to be there, with her."

After a time John said, "I'll see the captain tonight. I'll just say . . ."

Chee said, "Don't want tell captain everything? You must, John. Hodder O.K. man. Won't talk."

John said at last, "I suppose I'll have to."

Then they walked the horses into the lane and headed east for the battery's position. As they turned into the battered village where men and horses were billeted, the 1st Sergeant came out of a house at the side of the road, saluted, and said, "Preparing them for the Kentucky Derby, were you, lieutenant?" His eyes wandered expertly over the horses, from nose to croup. "No harm done, as far as I can see . . . I was watching from an upper window, with my binoculars. Better not do that again, sir, or the captain might be watching, instead of me." He saluted again and bustled off.

John and Chee dismounted. John looked up at his friend's dark, impassive face—"I forgot to ask you, thinking of my own troubles . . . what do you hear from home?"

Benally said, "Mother sick, sir . . . the sore that will not heal. Inside. My eldest brother dead . . ."

John felt the same angry helplessness that often overcame him when talking with Chee, from the first days of their friendship at Fort Bliss, Texas, fifteen months ago—"What happened to him?"

"Coming back from Gallup in the wagon. Drunk. Fell out of wagon. Wagon wheels rolled over his chest, belly. He knew he'd die, but might live hours, days."

"God! Did he last long?"

"No. He had a bottle of Everclear in his pocket . . . He drank it all. People came in five, ten minutes. He was near a hogan and they'd seen . . . But he was dead. Drunk dead."

*   *   *   *

They were singing in the horse lines, lugubriously but with a stern emphasis, to the tune of "The Battle Hymn of the Republic":

> *Fifteen dollars for allotment,*
> *Fifteen dollars for allotment,*
> *And we've only got fifteen dollars left.*
> *Seven dollars for allotment,*
> *Seven dollars for allotment,*
> *And we've only got eight dollars left.*
> *Five dollars for a Liberty Bond,*
> *Five dollars for a Liberty Bond,*
> *And we've only got three dollars left.*
> *Two dollars for a Liberty Bond,*
> *Two dollars for a Liberty Bond,*
> *And we've only got a dollar left.*

John eyed his canvas valise. It was packed and ready, for the captain had given him his leave—ninety-six hours. In two hours the ration truck would take him back to Noyon and then . . . Le Havre—Southampton—London.

> *All we do is sign the pay roll,*
> *All we do is sign the pay roll,*
> *But we never see a god-damned cent!*

Victoria Station . . . that little old railway through the green fields and hop poles to Hedlington. There he'd take a taxi, if he couldn't get Betty to lend him her car for the trip to Walstone. His heart was beating fast and he thought, I must control myself. Sure, he was going to see his wife, for the first time in—how long? God, sixteen months: but it was not the flushed, lovely bride of those days. He was going to meet a drug addict, a woman seven months pregnant with an unknown man's child; and he was going to rescue her, by his love. But how . . . ?

A bugle blew sharply, insistently from the captain's post of command, the half-ruined village schoolhouse. John listened: Officers! On the double! He picked up his steel helmet, jammed it on his head, and ran.

The other battery officers were already there when he arrived, panting. Captain Hodder said, "Your leave's canceled, Merritt . . . The Germans are attacking in strength against our forward divisions, and against the British on their left. Our division's moving up, including all the artillery. I'll have orders from battalion in an hour. Get the battery ready to move within ten minutes after that. That's all. Dismissed!"

The two lieutenants and two 2nd lieutenants who completed the battery's complement of officers saluted and hurried out, as the 1st Sergeant and Supply Sergeant went in. It began to rain, a long awaited, heavy, summer rain.

An hour and a half later Captain Hodder shouted, "Drivers mount! . . . cannoneers in rear of your pieces . . . Post! Forward—Ho!" Battery D plodded across the slippery field and onto the pavé. John rode at the head of the second section which contained the 3rd and 4th pieces of the battery. Behind the third piece, he knew, was marching Chee Shush Benally; and behind the 4th, at the rear of the battery, Lieutenant Walden, the 2nd-in-command. The rain slashed down, drumming on his steel helmet, and running down the back of his trench coat, its skirts spread out to keep the saddle as dry as possible. At first he had to force himself not to think of Stella and the canceled leave. As the hours wore on the here-and-now forced themselves into his consciousness, pushing everything else out. There'd been a failure in the ration supply and both men and horses were hungry. Horses threw shoes and went lame. The marching cannoneers grew tired, developed blisters, and fell by the roadside, to be dragged to their feet and shoved forward by Lieutenant Walden and the sergeant at the rear. In places, without warning, the pavé dissolved into glue, the guns got stuck, and the section chief would yell, "Cannoneers on the wheels!"; and the cannoneers, marching behind the pieces they would serve in action, struggled forward and put their shoulders to the wheels of gun and caisson to help the horses drag them clear. On again . . . men falling, staggering to and fro, the rain still warm, but driving intensely into their faces, the rumble of artillery fire growing closer ahead . . . Captain Hodder was standing beside the road in the midnight darkness, his bugler beside him. As each section chief passed the captain called, "Cannoneers, mount caissons!" The cannoneers cheered raggedly as they stumbled forward and took the metal seats on the limbers and the fronts of the gun shields. There had been room for them from the beginning, but cannoneers never rode except in such an emergency as this, to save the horseflesh; in the field artillery, the horses were at least as important as the men.

On into the darkness . . . hour after hour, by farms untouched, through silent, shattered villages, across empty fields . . . The light of dawn spread and the column stopped. John dismounted, to rest his horse, and waited. American infantry were trudging past, going forward. The guns were very loud now, some shells bursting in the fields to the right. A galloping messenger reached Captain Hodder and shouted a few words, and handed over a small piece of paper. The captain nodded, glanced at the paper, then turned in his saddle, and shouted, "Hip shoot! Action right! Line of metal, azimuth one eight zero! Center sector, azimuth nine zero!"

*   *   *   *

Quentin Rowland, standing in the front-line trench with Archie Campbell beside him, muttered, "I can't believe it . . . I can't believe it . . . It's uncanny."

It was, Archie thought; it was too like March 21st to be credible. Then, as now, the trench was full of men, waiting. There was Kellaway, down the trench. There was Sergeant Fagioletti. There was Private Whitman. Again, his bowels quaked with the expectation of imminent battle. Above all, there was the fog, creeping over them since midnight, gradually thickening, until now, at four-fifteen in the morning, it was a dense pale curtain in the night, its greyness replacing night's darkness with an equal but more valuable cloak of invisibility, for this would last well into the day. But, instead of the storm of the German bombardment of that spring day, now there was no gun fire, but, from close behind, the rumble of tank engines. And now it was not the Germans who were going to attack, but the British. And poor Laurence Cate was gone, with thousands of others, in the nearly five months since the German storm had broken.

"Four-nineteen," Quentin muttered. "Good luck, Kellaway. You'll make it. Nothing can stop us now."

4.20. From far to the rear the British artillery, 2,000 guns, opened fire in a rolling barrage, starting fifty yards in front of the front-line trench and moving slowly across No Man's Land toward the Germans. The assaulting infantry climbed up the trench ladders and out into the open, officers using their compasses to keep direction in the fog. The tanks crashed over the trenches and the infantry took their places between and behind them . . . For miles to right and left the Fourth Army, the same Army (though renumbered from Fifth to Fourth) which had been so rudely hurled into confusion in March, now advanced, Canadians, Australians, British, with 500 tanks.

The German wire loomed out of the fog, the tanks crawled into it, onto it, crushed it. Kellaway, in the centre of his company's front line, shouted "Charge" in a cracked voice. His men swept forward. Good God, Kellaway thought, there are no Germans on the firestep . . . only one machine gun firing . . . there, a sentry throwing up his hands in surrender . . . there two officers trying to rally their men, firing their Mausers at an advancing tank, the tank rolling over them, crushing them into the earth . . . The Germans had been taken by surprise, even more so than the British on March 21st . . .

He jumped down into the trench . . . his men were mopping up, throwing grenades into dugouts, sending Germans streaming back across No Man's Land, hands up. The C.O. arrived, panting, his face scarlet, his blue eyes bulging. "We've got the first objective," he shouted. "On, on, men . . . The barrage is still moving! Keep close to it . . . keep the tanks moving!" He scrambled up the back wall into the open, waving his revolver in the air, and yelling, "On, Wealds, on!" The tanks rumbled on, in clouds of blue exhaust smoke, their guns banging, machine guns crackling. The wild excitement of the morning caught Kellaway by the throat. It was broad daylight, and they were already on top of the German second line. He jumped up beside the Colonel, and ran forward, screaming, "On, Wealds . . . on, on!"

*　　*　　*　　*

In Battery D Walden was dead, hit by a shell burst half an hour ago, at eleven o'clock. The Top Sergeant was badly wounded, propped up against a caisson, only half-conscious. Hodder was forward with the infantry commander, designating targets by telephone to John at the battery position; and, when the telephone lines were cut, by flag semaphore from a point on the slope about a mile ahead. The barrels of the 75s were red hot from continuous firing, the crews dead weary. No one knew what outfit of doughboys they were fighting with, for the German attack of early morning seemed to have cut across two divisions moving up. From their accents, some seemed to come from the Deep South, some from New York, and some from the Middle West. Whoever they were, they were fighting well, and hard, as the Germans came on, not in lines or masses . . . how the gunners and machine gunners prayed they would do just that, for a change! . . . but in blobs and trickles, grey-clad figures slipping down a hedge line here, along the edge of a wood there, vanishing; but where they had vanished, soon came the hammer of their machine guns, enfilading some doughboy position, killing or wounding the defenders . . . a few minutes' calm, half an hour, then more grey figures slipping down the field, machine-gun fire clacking low overhead to keep your own heads down.

The German artillery had been very accurate whenever it had chosen to pick on Battery D as its target, raining shells on the guns, the caissons, and the horse lines in rear with deadly effect. There'd be no more six-horse teams when the battery moved again; they'd be lucky to have four to each gun, then . . . But for hours on end the German guns had not engaged Battery D. Perhaps their ammunition train had not been able to keep up with the rapid advance, John thought. Or perhaps they were engaging other batteries of the 137th . . . with which no one had had any contact since dawn. This was a soldiers' battle, a lieutenants' and sergeants' battle, fought out at close range, in confusion, each man almost alone to do his best, to seize what opportunities were offered, to work together without orders or plan . . . an American battle.

The Top Sergeant's voice was weak behind him as he snapped out another fire order—"Sir . . . lieutenant . . . you're going to be out of ammunition in another five minutes . . . Better hold off on some targets unless the captain says it's desperate."

"They're all desperate, Top," John said grimly. "The Jerries are only 200 yards away now, the captain says, and still coming . . . And that was fifteen minutes ago. He may have been overrun."

"Gotta get up some more ammo," the 1st Sergeant mumbled. "There was a park back there a mile, beside the road . . . a dump. 75 ammo."

John looked round. Every piece had had some men wounded or killed, so all were being served by half the full complement of cannoneers. Yet none was out of action or so badly damaged that it could not be fired; so he could not take crews from one piece to reinforce the others . . . The telephone was in operation again, and another call for fire coming through from the captain. Thank God he was all right, but . . . "Germans advancing! From previous target, left six mils, down four . . . shrapnel . . . and for God's sake hurry!"

Behind him the 1st Sergeant cried, "Look, sir . . . !"

John couldn't look for a moment as he barked the new fire orders. That done, he turned. A column of three caisson teams was coming up the pavé at a gallop, each pair pulled by four horses. The German artillery spotters saw too, and a new storm of high-explosive shells rained down on the road in front of and among the galloping caissons. "Chee!" John yelled, throwing up his arms. "Chee!"; for he had recognized the Indian on the near horse of the lead team. Behind him, one driver guided each of the other two teams . . . One was down, the two lead horses struck simultaneously by German shells, down, the driver pinned, the horses struggling, kicking, blood spouting from throat and belly. The other teams came on. Chee wheeled his horses round behind the guns, reined in, and jumped down. "Get the stuff out!" he shouted. "All caissons full!"

"Chee!" John shouted, but the Navajo was running back down the road, drawing a knife from his belt . . . reaching the fallen team among the bursting shells, stooping, dragging the pinned driver free, leaving him at the roadside . . . cutting the traces of the two wounded horses, taking the bridles of the remaining, fear-crazed two, pulling, breaking into a run, the two horses at last pulling with him, the caisson coming, slow at first, then faster, wheels rumbling on the pavé . . . they only had a hundred yards to go; and now the shelling ceased with no more warning than it had started. They reached the guns. The cannoneers were frantically unloading the caissons, stacking the shells close at hand, by the gun trails.

The sergeant of No. 1 piece, on the left, shouted, "Sir! . . . Left!"

John turned . . . German infantry, a hundred yards away . . . coming on at a shambling run . . . He yelled, "Battery left, open sights, muzzle burst, fire!" The cannoneers dragged the guns round, rammed in the shells, the gunners spun the elevating wheel down, pulled the lanyards, smoke and flame belched, shell splinters from the close bursts flew back, clanging against the guns' shields. "Fire!" Again, again, again. The German infantry was melting away . . . all except six men, scuttling into the remains of a brick shed . . . they had a light machine gun, and a small mortar. The gun position would be untenable in a few minutes. The machine gun began to fire, sweeping the guns.

"Chee, wait!" John yelled, breaking into a run. The Navajo had snatched up a rifle with fixed bayonet and was running with it straight at the Germans in the ruined shed, firing as he went. John ran after him, drawing his pistol, firing. Two other men were at his heels, also firing; but Chee was there now, vaulting over the top of the low broken wall, dropping down, bayonet outthrust. They heard his rifle crack twice, the German machine gun stopped firing. A moment later they came out over the wall, three German soldiers and a feldwebel, unarmed, hands on their heads, Chee behind them, jabbing them in the buttocks with his bayonet, all running . . .

"Jesus Christ," the 1st Sergeant said. "The Chief came through. The son of a bitch must have thought they had some cognac in there . . . Now I'll die happy."

*　　*　　*　　*

It was the next day, just after dawn. The fighting had gone on until 2 a.m., but now there were no Germans in sight; a ration convoy had come up; and Captain Hodder had returned to the gun position.

"We held them," he said. "And the British are advancing . . . cutting through them like a knife through butter, the reports say . . . eight miles the first day. The French are advancing. And we're going to advance. Make all preparations to march order, so that we only have to hitch up and go when I give the order. The doughboys up there are in touch with our division headquarters."

John walked back to his section and found Sergeant Curran talking to the two gunners of the pieces. The three enlisted men turned, saluting, as John came up. "See that the men eat at once," he said. "Then make ready to march order—forward. We've got the Heinies on the run."

"They won't run very far," the sergeant said. "Those sons of bitches have a sting like a scorpion in their tails . . . Sure you're O.K. to move with us, lieutenant? You don't look too good."

John shook his head impatiently. His left arm ached where a small shell splinter had passed through the fleshy part of the upper arm, about midnight. His head throbbed and swelled from utter weariness. But he could not drop out now. He still would not sleep, for he would think of Stella. "I'm O.K.," he said roughly. "Get on with it."

The sergeant said, "Yes, *sir!*" John turned away. Now what did he have to do? Get some chow, walk about, supervising. See that the soldiers were doing their jobs . . . which they knew as well or better than he did. Impress the captain . . . What could he do about Stella? How could she be saved, even if he were at her side, in Walstone . . . or somewhere else?

"Sir . . . lieutenant . . . ." He turned impatiently. It was Sergeant Curran. "Sir, we can't find Benally. I thought maybe you'd given him some special job."

John said, "No . . . I haven't seen him since he cleaned out that German machine-gun crew. He got wounded then, and I sent him back to the horse lines. They were in that hamlet back there, what's its name?"

"Can't pronounce it, sir. But I'll send a couple of men back to search for him. There's some medics set up an aid post in it, from a doughboy outfit. Benally may have checked in with them to get his wound dressed."

John nodded, the sergeant went off, and John, standing amid the bustle of the preparations to move, looked about . . . corpses of Germans; a burying party digging graves for six Americans; dead horses;

one upturned, smashed 75—a direct hit just before dark . . . the debris of battle. Smoke was rising from kitchen fires in the little hamlet back there, where Chee might be. But when Chee was unhappy, he didn't go into towns or villages. Even in El Paso, when they'd got out of Bliss on a pass, he seldom wanted to go into town or over the line into Juarez and booze it up in a bar, like the other soldiers. He'd buy a couple of bottles of tequila and head out into the desert, with John at his side: and find a mesquite or stunted piñon and sit down in the thin shade and start drinking; and go on till he could hardly walk; twice John had had to grab the bottle and break it on a stone to make sure Chee could get back to Bliss . . .

He had told Sergeant Curran to search the hamlet. His eyes wandered round the landscape. The wood over there . . . some trees shattered by shell fire, but still plenty of cover. Chee liked a view, liked to see a long way, so no one could sneak up on him, he used to say. He'd be at the edge of the wood if he was there at all, looking out . . . not this way: he didn't care what the battery was doing, if he was in that mood. He'd be looking the other way, west, over the hills and seas and mountains and rivers to Sanostee.

He walked quickly out of the gun area and up the slope to the wood, then round the outside edge, where a thin hedge contained it. Chee was there, his back against a tree where the hedge had been broken down, looking westward, a bottle clutched in one hand.

"Chee!" John said sharply. No answer. The head lolled sideways. "Chee!" Still no answer, but the hand raised the bottle to the lips, Chee drank, the arm and hand again fell.

"We're under orders to move. Wake up, man!" He knelt and tried to lift the Indian, but his wound had weakened him, nor did he have the use of his left arm. He could not budge the sticky, dead weight. He looked round in desperation . . . nothing. Turning, he stumbled back down the hill to the battery position. The guns were lined up, the teams ready to limber up for march order twenty paces in rear, and Captain Hodder was walking up the line of guns toward him.

Hodder stopped as John approached and said, "Where have you been? Is your section ready?"

"No, sir . . . Private Benally's up there in the wood, wounded."

The captain looked hard at him—"Wounded or drunk?"

John hesitated, then said, "Both, I think."

Hodder said, "And you . . . You have another wound you haven't told me about." He gestured at John's tunic. John looked down and saw a big brown stain on his side. He realized what had happened and said, "It's Benally's blood, sir! I was trying to lift him, but couldn't . . ."

186

The captain turned on Sergeant Curran—"Take a team, and two corpsmen. Bandage him and bring him down . . . Where in hell does he get the liquor, Merritt?"

"I don't know, sir . . . He's always been able to smell it out."

"And now he ought to be up for court martial and the stockade . . . but he won't be. I'm recommending him for the Medal of Honour, for his work yesterday. If the corpsmen say that he ought to be sent to the rear, see that he goes, even if he has to be tied down."

Twenty minutes later the team came down, Benally being held onto one of the caissons by a corpsman. The other corpsman jumped down in front of John and saluted. "The bullet went through the left side, sir, but doesn't seem to have done any serious damage. He's been bleeding a lot, but . . ." He shrugged—"We've stopped that now."

John looked at his friend and made up his mind—"He'll come on with us," he said.

Five minutes later the battery moved off in march order, Private Chee Shush Benally unconscious drunk, tied to one of the steel seats in front of the gun shield of Piece No. 3, his torso heavily bandaged. The battery, the regiment, and the armies moved eastward, toward Germany.

Daily Telegraph, Saturday, August 24, 1918

WOMEN IN INDUSTRY

AFTER WAR PROBLEMS

There has just been published the report of a conference between organizers of trade unions, Bristol employers, and others concerned with the industrial employment of women . . . on the position of women in industry after the war . . .

The underlying fact in relation to the status of woman in industry is that her position as an industrial worker is, and always must be, of secondary importance to her position in the home. To provide the conditions which render a strong and healthy family life possible to all is the first interest of the State, since the family is the foundation-stone of the social system. It is accordingly the duty of the State to ensure that women are only employed as factors in industrial efficiency in so far as the interests of family life and the healthy development of the race are not prejudiced . . .

Presumably it will be possible for 400,000 women to return to domestic service or small workshops, from which they have been withdrawn, either by the attraction of higher remuneration or the needs of the country. If, however, women are to be persuaded to enter those occupations in large numbers the wages, hours, and

> conditions of work will require very considerable amendment. In particular, the conditions of domestic service will have to be greatly improved . . .

Quite so, Cate thought, but it would not be as easy as it sounded. When they built these houses three or six centuries ago in this country, builders thought of permanence, grace, stateliness . . . in earlier times, of defence, too. They did not think so much of comfort for the owners, and not at all for the domestic staff. The kitchen here at the Manor was a long way from the dining and breakfast rooms, and food had to be covered and carried. There was no central heating, so each room needed a fireplace, so coal scuttles had to be filled and carried, fireplaces cleaned, fires laid. The houses were often needlessly large, especially when the children grew up and left home . . . again, to make for graciousness; but large houses needed large staffs to keep them clean, and in good repair.

The Manor needed another maid, at least; but it was doubtful if he would ever find one. He could not afford the wages that would be asked; and young girls would no longer come here. *Their* rooms were small, their hours long. So the house would slowly decay. Was that what the war had been fought for?

Isabel had told him that though they could still get domestic help in America, they generally employed many fewer than in England; and that for some years now, certainly since the turn of the century, architects had been designing houses that could be run with small staffs, or even none at all. "I could run this place with one helper," she had said, sweeping a small elegant hand at the Manor from the front lawn one summer day last year. "I can cook. I can use a vacuum cleaner—ever heard of those, Christopher? You would learn to wash and dry dishes. I can iron . . . Of course, I wouldn't have much time to be Lady Bountiful to the village—open fetes, preside at the Women's Institute, and so on . . . but I don't think that part of your position is going to be so important after the war, if it exists at all . . . Of course it would be easier if we tore the old place down and . . ."

"Isabel!" he had cried, shocked; for the site of the Manor had been occupied since Roman times; and there was a line of Roman tiles in the cellar wall to prove it.

She had laughed then, taking his arm—"I was only teasing, darling. If I ever live here with you, we shall live in the correct, time-honoured English discomfort . . . except that there will be those

188

wonderful heated towel rails, and the lovely big W.C. with a view of the Down and the little bookshelf beside you as you sit . . ."

"Isabel!" . . . He heard his own cry again, from the past, as Garrod came in, her colour returned, her step nearly as perky as ever; but not quite, for age was advancing upon her, too.

"More coffee, sir?"

The Western Front:
August, September, 1918

11 The air was bumpy over Picardy, for the summer sun had blazed down on it all day, and evening thunderstorms were building up in the south-west, advancing now, black-fronted, across the cratered land far below. Guy Rowland led his squadron eastward at 10,000 feet in his favorite fighting formation, a stepped-up V of Vs, his rear flights being nearly 500 feet higher than C Flight, in the lead, and his own machine at the point. It was four o'clock in the afternoon.

The Camel heaved and dropped forty feet . . . up now on an updraught . . . lurch sideways . . . from the corner of his eye he saw that C Flight was suffering just as he was . . . violently up . . . the propeller blades momentarily catching the sun, forming a whirling gold disc in front of him . . . down, the bottom dropped out of the bloody air . . . steady . . . Something made him turn his head and look back over his right shoulder. The pilot at the right rear of the squadron, the wing man of A Flight, was waggling his wings. His flight commander had seen and was peeling off in an upward climbing turn. As yet Guy could not see what they were turning toward, but he swept his arm round and at the same time gave a touch to pedal and stick to pull his Camel up and round. As soon as he was into the turn he saw them—specks at 15 or 16,000 feet, in the south-west, the eye of the sun, and coming down fast . . . And many of them . . . he couldn't count properly for the glare of the sun on his goggles, but there must be about twenty: triplanes. Then they were on them, the Fokkers diving down through the formation with guns chattering and long streaks of tracer whirling off and past, curving in strange-seeming arcs

190

from the trajectory of the bullet and the deflection imparted by the machines' bank and skid. Yellow wheels: Jasta 16 . . . Werner would be here somewhere . . . cunning old sod, taking up two squadrons of the Jagdgeschwader when he normally never went out with more than one . . . Someone was getting on his tail, he glanced round . . . not quite ready yet . . . must be new to the front because he was settling down to steady his aim. Couldn't do that against good pilots and every German out here knew that the Three Threes was good . . . He made ready to spin out, when what he had been waiting for happened. A stream of tracer from the Camel which had been above and behind him hit the attacking triplane in the engine and cockpit. It fell out of the sky . . . No time to wonder what had happened to it. He swung violently left and found himself on a Fokker's tail . . . pulled the stick back to steady himself and immediately rammed It forward . . . tracer arching past his head. Bloody fool, he'd come within half a second of doing what that German had done a few minutes ago . . . and he would have ended up the same way, down there, dead. He pulled up and turned, looking for a target in the milling three-dimensional game of tag . . . a Fokker crossed at full speed—full deflection, he pressed the trigger and the tracer curved away from his gun muzzle . . . in front of the Fokker . . . damn, side slip, give it more bank with the rudder pedal, fire again . . . this time the bullets were striking home just behind the engine. The pilot started up, half-raising a gauntleted hand. Dead? No, his head was down, but he was controlling the machine . . . and tracer was flying past his own machine from behind. He crabbed round but the bullets kept coming . . . not close . . . well off to one flank. Dive, turn, twist, he was managing to keep one jump ahead of the German, but only just. Where the hell were the rest of his fellows? Someone ought to be able to get on the German's tail and shoot him down, if he was so preoccupied in this man-to-man chase . . . The Fokker swung round in a wide circle and Guy muttered through gritted teeth, "Now I've got you, you . . ."; for the triplane was exposing its underbelly in a graceful curve ending in a loop. Then Guy saw the yellow wing ends outside the black crosses. It was Werner von Rackow, claiming victory. When the Fokker flattened out from its loop Guy was flying level with it and about a hundred yards away. Guy raised his fist and shook it at the German, shouting, "Try it again tomorrow, and . . ." He knew perfectly well that von Rackow couldn't hear, but was sure that he would nevertheless understand the message. Then the two young men waved and, each banking away, the distance between them rapidly grew until they could no longer see each other's machines. At once Guy flew into towering cumulo-nimbus. Rain slashed against his gog-

gles and stung his cheeks. His hands ached cold inside the big gloves
. . . altitude 12,500 . . . remote rendezvous after a dogfight was
10,000 over St Quentin . . . north-west from here . . . The air cur-
rents inside the cloud were hair-raising . . . He felt himself being
pushed upward as though by a giant's hand under the Camel. He put
the stick forward until the nose was pointing almost straight down
. . . the altimeter needle circled remorselessly round, climbing . . .
in spite of everything he was being hurled upward at 2,000 feet a
minute . . . out suddenly . . . thrown out of the top of that particular
cloud—there were others to be seen towering much higher into the
upper air . . . He was at 17,000 feet . . . Where was St Quentin?
Think, man! Set course, north-west . . . He headed once more into
the cloud, nose down, once more to be buffeted, thrown about . . .
Down at last to 10,000 feet . . . in dense swirling cloud and hissing
rain. No chance of making a RV here or now. Back to base. He headed
west and twenty minutes later groped his way down out of the cloud
base at 300 feet and flew home, hopping over the hedges, farmhouses,
and hamlets of Picardy, to land in driving rain, the field already a
morass.

The adjutant was on the field as soon as he landed, and creaked up
to him as he jumped to the ground while Stratton and the rigger held
the machine against the wind. Dandy shouted into the wind—
"Moving airfields again tomorrow, sir."

"What a bloody nuisance," Guy said.

"It means we've really got the Huns on the run . . . I've given all
the necessary orders, except who's to lead the advanced flight."

"Show me where we're going, and I'll lead it myself."

*　　*　　*　　*

"The attack will be without artillery support," Lieutenant Colonel
Quentin Rowland said. "We'll cross the start line at twelve minutes
past noon, with the tanks leading . . . We'll have artillery observation
officers with us for use against German counterattacks, if there are
any."

Archie Campbell listened, sitting in the far corner of the barn,
notebook spread on his knees. The company commanders of the battalion were gathered for orders. The barn was undamaged, as were
the farm buildings a hundred yards away across the midden, smoking
with cow dung in the sun, rich-smelling on the slow breeze. The days
of pure trench warfare were over. They had been succeeded by a war
of movement—mostly retreat—following the German offensive of
March 21st . . . then hard slogging over old battlefields—

Contalmaison, Thiepval, High Wood, everything reminiscent of 1916 . . . barbed wire rusting in coils; villages still no more than heaps of rubble, but no longer smoking; unexploded shells by the thousands in the earth, with the unburied dead, white bones, cracked skulls, withered hands, broken boots, rusty rifles . . . And then the Black Day of the German Army, August 8th, and the beginning of the surge forward . . . the relentless pursuit, tenacious but uneven resistance, and . . .

"The enemy is breaking," Quentin said. "He's not broken, but he's certainly not the man he was. Risks which would have been criminal three months ago, even a month ago, are now no more than your duty to take."

That's obvious, Archie thought; no artillery preparation, when it had been an article of faith since 1915 that a long bombardment was necessary to soften up the enemy front-line troops, to break down the trenches and above all, to cut the wire. But now there was no wire, or very little. Attack at midday . . . heresy! Attacks were put in at dawn, so that all necessary preparations could be made under the cloak of darkness; and then there would be twelve hours of daylight to consolidate the captured positions against the inevitable counterattacks . . . but now the Germans didn't counterattack; and if they did, it was feeble, as it had been yesterday, and the day before . . . More heresy, attacking every day, instead of making long preparations and taking a series of careful bites. It is not necessary to advance in long straight lines, they said now, having said just the opposite for three years. It is not necessary to conform if flanking formations meet opposition—sweep on and take the opposition from flank or rear.

"Remember, *we are winning*," Quentin grated. "And we are going to go on winning until we have beaten the German Army to a pulp. We are going to break it into little pieces, and smash Germany until it falls apart . . . until there is no German Army, no German General Staff, no organized Germany. And it won't be long."

"How long, do you think, sir?" Captain Tanner of A Company asked.

"I don't know," Quentin snapped. "And don't think about it. The men can't be expected to fight well on September 1st if they are given to believe that the war will be over on September 5th . . . That's all."

The company commanders rose, saluted, and filed out into the hot, humid air. The Regimental Sergeant Major and Quartermaster followed. Father Caffin was on his feet, but he did not leave. Quentin looked at him, frowning. Caffin was a good regimental padre . . . the best he'd ever come across, in spite of his being a black Papist; but he was a Sinn Feiner at heart, Quentin was sure; his brother had been shot for treason after the Easter Rising, and that made Quentin feel ill at ease with him. He said now, "You want to speak to me, padre?"

"Yes, sir . . . I'm thinking the war had better end sooner than later. It's not only the Germans who are breaking. Our boys are getting tired of it."

"What do you mean?" Quentin snapped. "They're obeying orders, aren't they?"

"Yes, colonel, but you must have seen yourself, it's not with the old snap . . . Look how many boys we've lost, one way or another—since the March retreat. It's a new battalion, really. The new boys have the belly for it, but not the will."

Quentin paused. He wanted to rebuke Caffin—but the padre was right; the battalion was not the same as it had been in February . . . or before Passchendaele . . . or before Le Cateau. But what could he do about it? Try to be at the critical spots himself, when encouragement was needed. Try to instil into every man pride in his cap badge and shoulder titles; and his rank, so that even a lance corporal understood what a privilege was his to command six private soldiers of the Weald Light Infantry; pride in England . . . but you couldn't talk about that to British troops. They'd call you . . . or think of you, as . . . what were Kipling's words? . . . a jelly-bellied flag flapper.

He said, "Thank you, padre. It won't last much longer, and I think we can stick it out . . . Campbell, I'm going to visit the tank commander who's going over with us. I want you to collect the tank escort commander—Jenks, and his N.C.O.s, and bring them here in an hour. We'll practise signals between tanks and infantry, how to point out targets, how they can inform us what help they need."

He strode out, heading down the pavé to the west. The Germans were shelling the area, but very lightly, and the soldiers were ignoring it. Quentin's batman-runner rose to his feet from where he had been snoozing against an outer wall of the barn and followed him down the pavé.

Caffin said, to Archie Campbell, "I hope the colonel didn't mind what I said, but the fact is that the British Army is wearing down. English, Scots, Irish, Welsh . . . city, county regiments, north, south, Fusiliers, Rifles—they're all the same, all worn out."

"Passchendaele did that," Archie said.

"I agree . . . Now the only troops who fight with the old fire are the colonials . . . Australians, Canadians, New Zealanders, South Africans . . . Perhaps Lloyd George should make one of them Commander-in-Chief."

Archie said, "Perhaps he will . . . Hey, play us an Irish tune, padre. Now that the C.O.'s not here, play us 'The Wearing of the Green.' It's one of my favorites."

*   *   *   *

Sergeant Frank Stratton, Royal Flying Corps, stood beside his squadron commander's Sopwith Camel, with its black-painted wheels, and the red stabilizer that had been Guy Rowland's personal mark since he became the scourge of German pilots. Stratton carried a dog-eared notebook in one hand, from which he was reading aloud, as Guy stood at his shoulder—"We've stripped her down to what she was like when they were first building her, sir," he said. "The lower main planes are attached, there . . . locked by split pins . . . The upper main planes are in position, securing rods in . . . flying and incidence wires are in position, but they're loose . . . Now we have to true up the main planes. Chester and Hallows dropped the plumb lines, four of them . . . there, there, there, and there . . . Now, I've been adjusting the wires . . , we have to get seven things right . . . let's see, first the plumb lines are in line, seen from the side . . . Come here, sir . . . See?"

Guy nodded as he peered down the line of the wings from the left "They're in line."

"Second, the leading edges of the upper main planes are in line both from in front, and from above . . . There's no dihedral on the upper planes . . . Right?"

"Right."

"Third, the leading edge of the lower wing is symmetrical about the centre line of the machine . . . I checked it by measuring from the bottom sockets of the forward outer struts to the rudder post and to the propeller boss . . . Like this."

Guy watched as Frank bustled about his work. Guy had had part of an aileron shot away the day before and had made such a heavy landing that Frank was sure the main planes had been jarred out of true; hence this practical reconstruction of the machine, here in the open field at the squadron's new airfield east of Arras.

If Frank thought the work was necessary, it probably was; but Guy would have told him to go ahead even if he didn't agree. Frank needed to have his mind taken off his private problems.

"Fourth, we get the correct dihedral of the lower planes by placing straight edges along the front and rear spars and reading the angle on the Abney level . . . so   five degrees. Correct, sir?"

"Correct."

"Fifth . . . the stagger is the same throughout, and we measure that . . ."

Guy thought, the German ground troops aren't fighting as well as they have all through the war; but the air forces are just as good. Better, in some ways. They're attacking more than they used to. Richthofen's death hadn't been all bad for them . . . the Red Baron had been something of a prima donna, using his pilots as a Yorkshire landowner might use his tenants to beat grouse toward him—thus enhancing his own score at the expense of his squadron's. Guy was proud that while his own score had barely increased since he took over command of the Three Threes, the squadron had now recorded a hundred and ten kills in the last six months.

"Seventh and last, we have to see there is no wash in or wash out . . . That's it. She's all right. I was wrong."

"You don't know that," Guy said. "You've been tightening wires and securing rods all the time, to get this result. They might not have been true before you took her down . . . I saw this morning that you still have Victoria."

The sergeant said, "Yes, sir. No damage to her yet, though she got shook up on the last trip, when that A.S.C. driver put the lorry in the ditch."

"Oh, she was in that one, was she . . . with the spare engines and machine guns?"

"I hope you don't mind, sir," Frank said anxiously. "There was room, and . . ."

"Of course," Guy said, waving a hand. He faced his fitter and friend directly—"It won't be long now, Frank, though it isn't over yet. What are you going to do after the war?"

Frank lowered his hands and stared, first at Guy, then slowly round the airfield, the tents, the parked lorries, the Camels. "I really don't know, sir. I'd never thought . . . the war, ending? It doesn't seem possible."

"But it is," Guy said. "It's more than possible. It's a certainty, and soon."

Frank said, "Are you going to stay on, sir?"

Now it was Guy's turn to pause, thinking. Was he? He had realized for a month that the war would end soon. Why then had he not thought what he proposed to do with his life after it?

He said at last, "I suppose so. I was planning to design aircraft before the war, but . . . I think I'm better at flying them. Yet if they formed a company to fly people, and goods, about Europe . . . all over the world, perhaps . . . I would be interested."

"So would I," Frank said enthusiastically. "Would you take me on?"

"If I were in a position to do so, I certainly would," Guy said. "Mechanics are just as important as pilots. And wireless experts. That's an area which badly needs development—aircraft communications . . . for weather reports, for course setting and plotting . . . landing, even." Once again he looked full at the sergeant—"Any news from home?"

Guy had himself heard, in July, from his Uncle Christopher, that Frank Stratton's wife had given birth to a baby boy—not Frank's—in May. Frank must know, but he had not mentioned it. The baby had been baptized James.

Frank said, "I don't have a family now, sir . . . My brother Fred's written to say he's engaged to a Miss Broadhurst-Smythe. A colonel's daughter, she is. That's out in India . . . Do you want to take her up and try her out, sir?"

"Good idea," Guy said. "In fifteen minutes." He walked off toward his quarters. No good talking to Frank about Anne and the baby and the other children. Time might change that . . . The problem now was to test out his Camel for wing and structural soundness; and, when he came down, work out some tactics to give the Germans in general and Jasta 16 in particular a nasty shock in the near future.

*   *   *   *

The Minister of Munitions was sitting in a straight-backed wooden chair opposite the large desk of the Chief of the Imperial General staff. Behind the desk, but turned sideways, sprawled that officer himself—General Sir Henry Wilson, his long legs in immaculate field boots stretched out on the carpet. Churchill was smoking a cigar; the general's hands were folded across his long, thin belly.

Churchill said, "Well, Henry, how did he take it?"

Wilson picked up a piece of paper beside him and said, "This is what I sent . . . *Personal: Just a word of warning in regard to incurring heavy losses in attacks on the Hindenburg Line as opposed to losses when driving the enemy back to that line. I do not mean to say that you have incurred such losses, but I know the War Cabinet would become anxious if we receive heavy punishment in attacking the Hindenburg Line without success . . . signed, Wilson.*" He picked up another piece of paper—"This is Haig's reply—*With reference to your wire re casualties in attacking the Hindenburg Line—what a wretched lot! And how well they meant to support me! What confidence! Please call their attention to my action two weeks ago when the French pressed me to attack the strong lines of defence east of the Royes-Chaulnes front. I wrote you at the time and instead of attacking south of the Somme I started Byng's attack. I assure you I watch the drafts most carefully* . . . Haig has a very low opinion of all of you politicians, I fear, Winston."

Churchill said, "It is not he who is responsible to the British people for victory . . . and for carnage—but we, their elected representatives. He must be stopped from butting his head against a brick wall and suffering more enormous casualties. This is *not* the year for a big attack. The Americans are nowhere near ready in mass on the Western Front. The air forces are building, but have fallen behind schedule, and we will not be ready to bomb Germany in force till 1919 . . . What are you going to reply, if anything?"

Wilson stretched and said with a little unease, "Well, he is in command. And he is convinced that the Germans are breaking."

"He . . . and Charteris . . . have said that before," Churchill said grimly.

"I propose to tell him that my telegram was intended to convey a sort of distant warning. It's all so easy to explain face to face, but in writing . . . it's damnably difficult . . . I'm just as much against casualties as you are, but there's a good chance that we'll suffer fewer by finishing the war this year . . . if we can." He changed the subject—"Are you still with us in thinking that the R.A.F. should be got rid of as soon as the war's over?"

Churchill said, "Yes. And so is Trenchard. He agrees on the Independent Striking Force . . . so he ought, as he's now commanding it, and it's doing good work . . . but not a separate air force. The navy's even more strongly on our side. I don't think we'll have any trouble abolishing it as soon as the war's over."

"Who's on the other side?"

"Sykes, Brancker, I think . . . Brooke-Popham, Henderson . . . but they've got rid of him." Churchill rose, still puffing his cigar, and said, "If you'll excuse me now, general, I must return to my own little niche. Good day."

Wilson showed his visitor to the door, then again sat down behind his desk. His personal assistant came in with a sheaf of Registered Files. Wilson said, "Put them down there, Jimmy . . . You've seen Haig's reply to my telegram?"

"Yes, sir."

"What do you think he wrote in his diary?"

The young officer smiled—"Something about politicians making ready to claim credit for any success but absolving themselves beforehand from any blame if things go wrong . . . leaving it to him to make the decision, with the axe if he fails."

"Something like that," the mercurial Wilson said gloomily. "And all I wanted to say in the telegram was that that was just what L.G. has in mind."

The P.A. said, "I imagine that Field Marshal Haig is well aware of that, sir."

*　　　*　　　*　　　*

"The battle for the Hindenburg Line is the battle for victory. The enemy is at his last gasp, including his air force. All risks must be taken to keep up a relentless attack against him, and drive him finally out of the sky . . ."

There was much more in General Brooke-Popham's order, but those were the only words that Guy Rowland remembered. "Drive him out of the sky" might have been etched into his windscreen, so clearly were they written into his mind, as a sort of impalpable curtain between him and the enemy, mysteriously making each target more, not less, clear in his sights.

The Three Threes was returning to its field after a successful sweep over the Hindenburg Line and the area immediately behind it, which, comprising gun areas and ammunition dumps, was an integral part of the Line. The photographic and artillery-spotting machines were still up, flying leisurely along the Line, recording each pill box and bunker, each machine-gun nest and trench revetment. The German Air Force was not to be seen and the cumbrous British machines plodded up and down unmolested. Two squadrons of scouts patrolled the sky 10,000 feet above them, guarding, waiting.

Guy's squadron landed by flights, blipping and roaring, taxied to the flight ramp, and switched off their engines. Guy hurried to the officers' mess, which was set up in the village school house beside the field, and took his place at the table. It had been a good patrol—three enemy kills certain, one of the Three Threes downed but on the British side of the lines, and probably able to land without serious damage; there had been no telephone call in yet. He ate fast, as did the other pilots; today was the day he hoped to spring the great trap he had been planning for the past ten days. In conjunction with other squadron commanders, and with the overall supervision of the Wing Commander, the five scout squadrons had been working in a quite regular fashion to protect the R.E. 8s of the Corps squadrons that were doing the photography, aerial reconnaissance, and artillery spotting; one squadron out at such and such a time, to be replaced by another just one hour later, at an obvious rendezvous over St Quentin or Cambrai or Soissons . . . and so on during the day. But at the next changing of the guard on the patrol line, it wasn't going to be one squadron going out, but four . . . two of Camels and two of the newer Snipes. With luck they'd catch the Hun trying to pounce with two squadrons on the one that they would expect to meet. He paused in his eating and looked round the table . . . Morton, Warner, Irwin, Duncan, Aldrich, Adams, Stuart, Beardsley, Greaves, Palmer-Reed, Scurlock, Gorringe, O'Grady, Hubbell . . . Gorringe, Duncan,

O'Grady, and Stuart the adjutant, were the only ones left from the time he had joined; so, although he was just twenty-one and a half, he was one of the old hands. But he hardly needed the extra experience to make him the senior here. Apart from those four, only Greaves and Scurlock were in fact older than he was, both recent transfers from the army—Greaves a gunner and Scurlock a Seaforth Highlander, who wore the kilt at all times, certainly when flying and according to some of the fellows, in bed . . .

He got up, tapping his knife handle on the table for silence—"I think we're all here but I don't want to give out orders in mess except in emergency. Dandy, will you bring them all to my office in fifteen minutes, ready for takeoff?"

"Yes, sir."

Guy walked out; the details of the plan had been worked out over the past few days; the pilots had not been told anything except that there would be special sorties this day at 1 p.m. Now he had to make them understand the strategic plan—how they hoped to lure the Germans into the trap; and then, the tactical plan—how they meant to destroy them. It should not be difficult as they were all fairly experienced by now, except Morton and Hubbell, who joined the squadron within the past month and both just nineteen. Hubbell particularly had to be strictly enjoined not to act like the British cavalry of Wellington's day . . . with great dash, but no control.

Punctually at one o'clock, tanks full, machine guns loaded, lightly oiled and wiped off, the squadron took off into the west wind, at once starting a slow spiral ascent, still over the town and airfield, that would carry them to 18,000 feet, just a thousand feet below their maximum operational altitude. The rendezvous was over Cambrai, at 1.30 in the afternoon. The sky was clear in the battle zone, but heavy cumulus and cumulo-nimbus had begun to form west of the Somme, behind them.

From above, the Snipes of the squadron on routine patrol, nearly 10,000 feet below, were barely visible against the chequered background of the earth; only now and then a glint of the sun on wings or engine nacelles betrayed their presence. The aircraft the Snipes were protecting, the R.E. 8s, could not be seen at all. Guy peered at his watch . . . time for the patrolling squadron to go home, at the end of their fuel. This had happened before, by chance, leaving the R.E. 8s and the ground troops unprotected for ten minutes . . . This time it was planned. Yes, they were forming up. He could just make out twelve of them, in four Vs, heading west . . . gone . . . exactly 1.35 . . . The ambush would have a better chance if there were some clouds here, but then the Germans might be able to slip in unseen.

The wing man from the leading flight, D, drew level and waggled his wings. Glancing over, Guy saw the pilot—it was Greaves—pointing downward. He stared down . . . nothing . . . looked farther west . . . nothing . . . looked east. Suddenly they sprang out of the background, black dots racing across the fields—five . . . ten . . . twenty . . . two squadrons at least. He licked his lips with glee, and eased the Camel over, waggling his wings—exactly what he had hoped for. The other squadrons, ordered to take their initial cue from 333, nosed over behind and to both flanks. The four squadrons of fighters, forty-eight aircraft, dived faster and faster toward the earth and the German machines low above it. Now they were to the east of them, between them and their bases. Now the Germans must stand and fight it out.

The British squadrons came out of the sky in the formation they had waited in over the rendezvous, two squadrons ahead, two behind. The two ahead, Guy's 333 on the left and 60 on the right, engaged the enemy—Fokker triplanes and . . . ah, shiny metal, Junkers C.L. 1s, the first aircraft of all metal construction, fast, maneuverable, very hard to knock down, heavily armed, two machine guns forward and one on a ring for the observer, firing backwards . . . The flights of 60 and 333 were engaging, two at a time. Guy held off, D following him, as he circled a thousand feet above the melee. This must be Jagdgeschwader 1, led by Hermann Goering, Richthofen's successor and according to Werner von Rackow, an absolute four-letter man, but a capable pilot and commander, though as self-centered as the Baron . . . Three Junkers were breaking away from the fight, using their tail gunners to keep the attacking Snipes at a distance. Guy waved a hand, and dived, followed by the three green-wheeled, green-spinnered Camels of D Flight. They came up under the Junkers as they headed east at full speed, and all four planes opened fire at 400 feet, and struck home . . . but the Junkers' metal skins seemed to absorb the bullets . . . the Junkers flew on . . . the Camels fired again . . . again . . . The Junkers seemed to be unaware that they were being attacked. Furiously, Guy closed to a hundred feet and fired a long burst directly into the engine area from behind and below . . . At last, a tongue of fire spread from the machine, trailing behind like flaming silk as for a moment the leaking petrol burned all along its length, then the machine itself caught fire . . . Guy banked sharply, and looked over his shoulder . . . no one . . . Another Junkers was down . . . He turned and began to climb. One by one the other pilots of D Flight joined him . . . The two upper squadrons had come down farther east, and were engaging the survivors of the dogfight, and some Triplanes near ground level, which were heading for home as fast as they could. Guy remembered seeing four trails of smoke going down, but didn't know whether all had been German. He could confirm the one Junkers he had got, for that had nosed over and was even now burning in a wood five miles behind and two miles below him . . . Reform over Cambrai . . . two o'clock. The squadrons were nearly all there; stragglers would have to make their own way home. He waggled his wings and the four squadrons, two up and two down, each squadron in stepped-up echelon of flights, headed west for their airfields.

But the cloud mass was there now, a wall of white across their path, and Guy knew that there would be no flying over the top of it. It must reach 30,000 feet, far above the ceiling of any of the scout planes fast approaching them. He signalled to spread out and the machines spread to a hundred yards apart, completing the maneuver just as they entered the cloud. At once the familiar lurching and heaving began, mostly upward as the column of rising air carried his Camel up with it in the heart of the cloud. Guy kept an easy hand on the control column, and gentle feet on the pedals, moving them by instinct rather than thought, as the instruments told him what was happening. If you lose confidence in your machine, the instructor at Upavon had said, that's bad; if you lose confidence in yourself, that's worse; but if you lose confidence in your instruments, you're lost . . . and you won't be found . . . It was hard to believe that the Camel was strongly nose down, but the artificial horizon said so, so it must be . . . Now it was hard to believe that he was falling at 500 feet a minute, but the instrument said so . . . now he was on his left ear, so correct accordingly with rudder pedals and ailerons . . . a fearful drop, the altimeter down to 8,000 . . . an even more fierce rise . . . eight, nine, ten, eleven, twelve, thirteen, fourteen, the air was getting thin in his lungs as it had been up there at 18,000, waiting to spring the ambush . . . Levelling off at thirteen, so ease the nose down . . . twelve . . . eleven . . . he burst out into murky light, between two cloud towers, so thick that they were obscuring the afternoon sun and sending trailers of dense vapor across the gap between them . . . Something flashed out of the far cloud five hundred feet below him, and he gasped—Fokker Triplane! Jasta 16, yellow marks, large number 12 under the cockpit, nothing outside the crosses, not Werner . . . he was already in an attacking dive. The Fokker was crossing his front, full deflection, now a hundred feet below, 300 feet range. He pressed the trigger as the German pilot saw him and raised an arm. Why did he do that? His tracer arched into the engine, the cockpit; the arm dropped. The Fokker turned suddenly nose down, burst into flames and dived toward the ground, faster and faster . . . just before it disappeared into the eastern cloud mass, its wings were torn off by its speed. It vanished, a flaming rocket. Guy resumed course and at once re-entered cloud. Twenty minutes later he landed at his airfield, where Frank Stratton was waiting, jubilant, with the bucket. He waved it away— "Don't need it today, Frank . . . don't know why."

"Didn't you get any, sir? Mr Greaves said you got a Junkers C.L. 1."

Guy nodded—"I did. And a Triplane of Jasta 16 . . . just now. Its number was 12. It's a certain, but . . . I feel all right."

He walked away. He didn't feel all right. He felt depressed and uneasy, but the vomit had not come up into his throat as it always had, from the beginning, when he landed after killing. What was the matter with him?

The adjutant met him at the door of his office, looking concerned. Guy said, "What's the matter, Dandy? Didn't we do well?"

"I haven't had all the reports in yet, sir, but apparently we did very well . . . it looks as though we have four certain and one possible, for the loss of one . . . Morton."

Guy swore under his breath; the youngest of all his pilots.

The adjutant continued—"But while you were all up, the Germans attacked Army Headquarters with twenty-four big bombers—they seem to have been Friedrichshafen G.IIIs—escorted by Jasta 16 . . . The Bristols managed to shoot down two of the Friedrichshafens on their way home . . . but we would have got most of them if your four scout squadrons hadn't been elsewhere . . . or so the army commander says, with some heat, I gather."

Guy said, "We seem to have come out about even then . . . Werner von Rackow and I. He had some nerve to bring the Friedrichshafens over in daylight. But he . . ."

The telephone bell on the adjutant's desk rang. Dandy Stuart raised an interrogative eyebrow. Guy nodded and Dandy picked up the machine—"Three Threes squadron—Adjutant speaking . . . It's for you, sir. General Brooke Popham."

Guy held the earphone to his ear. The general was saying, "Rowland? You've heard about Jasta 16 and the Friedrichshafens?"

"Yes, sir."

"Don't worry about it. Bombing Army Headquarters does less for them than destroying German aircraft does for us . . . I'll be expecting the report on your ambush within an hour or so, right? Good. Now—the King has awarded you the Victoria Cross . . ." Guy heard the words but they did not register. He had won Britain's highest award for gallantry—the V.C. The simple Maltese cross, made of bronze from melted-down Russian guns captured in the Crimean War, bore the simple inscription—FOR VALOUR. The ribbon was plain crimson, and in the middle of it the holder wore a tiny miniature of the cross itself. The general was still speaking—"I'd have liked to recommend you for it for your leadership, for your sixty-four kills."

"Sixty-six, now, sir," Guy said.

"But there has to be some special occasion . . . and the award is specifically for your actions on August 10th, when you led your squadron to attack thirty Fokkers who were chewing up that Bristol squadron. As I said in the citation, you were wounded again, but you led your pilots into the attack and pressed it home, shooting down two enemy yourself, so that the much superior force of Germans finally broke off and fled. I won't read the whole citation to you—you'll see it in the paper, when you get one . . . but, congratulations . . . and I'll see that your squadron is off the roster till 6 a.m. tomorrow."

"Thank you, sir." Guy hung up. Now, he'd have to get Dandy to call up airfields all around to see if anyone had got Morton.

"What did he say, sir?" Dandy asked.

"Oh, I have the V.C."

Dandy took his side cap and hurled it out of the open window, yelling "Hooray!" He rushed out at his distinctive limping run, his wooden leg creaking loudly, bellowing, "The C.O.'s got the V.C. . . . the C.O.'s got the V.C. . . . !"

*   *   *   *

They were still at it in the mess at two in the morning, singing raucously in chorus. They had raided the messes of the other squadrons sharing the field. They had torn off Scurlock's kilt and escorted Guy down the village street carried in a dusty armchair like an oriental potentate, flanked by all the other pilots waving flaming torches. The mess waiters' little cubbyhole at the back of the house was knee-deep in champagne bottles—several cases of which had been brought in by a Bristol fighter from Amiens, on a mission officially unauthorized; but official enough so that the Wing Commander had personally telephoned the wine merchant in Amiens to have the champagne out at the designated airfield before the Bristol arrived . . . Morton had been returned, concussed by an emergency landing on a pavé road, and unable to give any account of himself when he was finally found. The congratulations had been said a hundred times, and Guy was sitting near an open window, thinking. It had been like this when Sulphuric Sugden was C.O., and got his second bar to the D.S.O., and I got my first . . . tonight is wilder, because this was the Three Threes' first V.C. . . . yet, not so lightheartedly happy. Too many months had gone by, too many good men—boys—not come back; too many uncles and brothers "gone west" here, in other squadrons, or in the trenches.

In a day or so, as soon as the news had had time to percolate through to Germany . . . it would probably be in the London papers tomorrow and the German ones the next day . . . Werner would know of it. He already had his Knight's Cross of the Iron Cross, Swords, Diamonds, and Oak Leaves, and he already had the Pour le Mérite, which they nicknamed the Blue Max. Perhaps he'd come over and drop a present of some sort. It would be a shame if the machine gunners on airfield defence got him, after all he'd been through. Quite possible, though. The Australian infantry claimed that it was one of their ground machine guns that got Richthofen.

He felt old and weary. The side of his face where Werner's bullet had cut the tendon was drooping, and though he had been laughing and smiling all evening, he knew that he looked terrifying. The officers were scared of him. Twenty five year-old captains—afraid to meet his eye, terrified he would find fault with them. How did he do it? "The Butcher wants to see you in his office," they'd say to each other. "He's sharpening his knife now."

In the chair beside him Dandy Stuart said, "You look tired, sir. I think that if we give them another half hour I'll be able to shepherd them to bed and you can get some sleep . . . And tomorrow you can start out after Mannock and Bishop and McCudden."

"I'll never beat Mannock," Guy said. "The war'll be over too soon."

"You'd beat him if you let the other pilots herd the Huns onto you, instead of vice versa."

Guy made to answer but a private soldier was edging his way round the door, looking about him. He recognized one of the squadron clerks and at the same time the man saw him and came over, a message form in his hand. He saluted and said, "Hawthorne, duty clerk, sir. This just came in."

Stuart took the message and read while Guy leaned back, sipping his champagne and staring at the ceiling . . . sleep . . . but in that sleep what dreams might come . . . even though it was not a sleep of death . . . yet?

The adjutant's voice was strange—"Sir . . ."

"H'm?"

"It's from Air Headquarters. One of the Corps has reported that a burning Fokker triplane crashed in its rear areas this afternoon. The pilot was burned beyond recognition but there is definite identification that it was von Rackow."

Guy closed his eyes. Here was the dream, the dream of horror. He said softly, "A locket . . . inscribed To Boy from Naomi with love." He jumped up, his heart racing, his body suddenly cold—"It can't be . . . It didn't have yellow wingtips . . . It was No. 12 and Werner's is No. 1."

But he knew that it was. Werner von Rackow's own plane had been damaged in some earlier sortie and he had taken another. It was Werner's arm that had been raised, between the thunderheads, as he recognized the red spinner and stabilizer of the Butcher's Camel, and in the same instant saw the flames of the tracer coming out of the gun muzzles.

Daily Telegraph, Monday, September 16, 1918

AMERICA'S WAR EFFORT

PRESIDENT AND STRIKERS

From our own correspondent, *New York*, Sunday. Even a year ago the signs of a greatly aroused nation were not always in evidence, but today those who know their United States well can not for a moment doubt that America is as wholeheartedly for the war as France or Great Britain . . . One may cite heartily the popular endorsement of President Wilson's ultimatum to some munition workers here who deliberately broke the agreement which the unions had made with the Government, defied the national officers of their own organisation, and went on strike. Mr Wilson's ultimatum amounted to a command in the name of the American people that the strikers shall either go back to work or join the army . . . The strikers are not very numerous, truly, but their conduct is regarded as pernicious from the standpoint of the country, which for the period of the war—employers as well as employees agreeing—has consented to submit all grievances to the War Labour Board and abide by its verdict. "In time of war," to quote the *New York World*, the foremost organ of democracy, "the American Government is not a suppliant for favor. In the name of the American Government and people, it commands."

Strikes, strikes, strikes, Cate thought gloomily—at home, abroad, connected with the war, connected with nothing. Surely there must be some better way to manage the relations between employers and employed? Why not . . . ?

Stella, from across the table, interrupted his chain of thought— "When I have my baby, I want Probyn's Woman to help me."

The remark came out of the blue: she had been eating silently, head down, as had been her custom ever since she had again joined him at meals. Cate said, "Don't you think you'd better go to Hedlington Hospital, dear? There may be complications, like . . ."

"This one won't have apnea," she said. "I know it. It's strong . . . I want to have it here."

206

"All right, then," Cate said. "We can warn Dr Kimball when your labour starts, so that he can come at once if Probyn's Woman thinks he's needed. She has a lot of experience."

Stella said no more. Babies, Cate thought . . . what a lot of them there seemed to have been this year; and Ruth Walstone's girl, born in June, about the only one to be born in wedlock, at the proper time . . . The Honourable Christine Hoggin, no less; and a sweet chubby little thing she was now, at nearly three months; also Virginia Robinson's, Guy's sister—hers was due any moment.

Ruth had come to the Manor not long after the child was born, ostensibly to show her to him; but actually to ask his advice about her sister-in-law, Anne Stratton, whose baby boy had been born two weeks earlier. Frank, Anne's husband, was not the father, and had taken it very badly—you couldn't blame him, could you? He'd cut her off, or to be more exact, cut himself off, from all association with her and the three kids they'd had before. Ruth was now asking him if he thought it would be a good idea for her to adopt Anne's bastard. Would it help heal the breach, by removing the child from Anne's care? He had not known the right answer to that one—only to praise her for the generosity of her impulse; and to advise her to wait. There was no hurry; and Anne herself would have an opinion on the matter.

And then there was Lady Helen Durand-Beaulieu, known now as Mrs Charles Rowland . . . Boy's "widow"; her baby was astonishingly like his father; even at four months one could see Boy's eyes, and the set of his jaw. They ought to come down and live at High Staining where they belonged. The village knew, of course; and of course, they understood. A great many women had been left with their wombs in bud when their lovers had taken the sacrament of death instead of marriage.

And Stella, his daughter. Oh God, he prayed, let the war end soon. Let John come back to her, and, with love and understanding, lift her out of this pit, and guide her to a new light, a new life. Let his service in the war, for all the evil it has done, all the misery it has spread, at least give him the strength and determination to do that.

Hedlington and Walstone:
late September, 1918

12 "I'm making the announcement tomorrow—that I shall not contest the next election, whenever it may be. And if there is no election before the end of the year I shall apply for the Chiltern Hundreds on January 1st."

Alice Rowland let the words hang a while in the silence of the breakfast room, broken only by the rustle of her newspaper as she turned one of the big pages. Then she laid the paper down and said, "They'll miss you."

"Who will?" her father, Harry Rowland, said, "I don't fit in any more . . . The war seems to have brought out the worst in our politicians, as it has brought out the best in our young men—and women."

Alice said, "I meant that Mr Churchill and the Prime Minister and Lord Curzon trust you, because you tell them what the people really think."

Harry nodded, swallowing a piece of gammon—"Perhaps, but my mind is made up. I'm tired. I'm old . . . and I don't like the people I have to work with up there . . . I'm going away."

Alice said, "You're going to live abroad?" She was surprised, for she had always imagined her father living on in Laburnum Lodge after his retirement.

"Live abroad? Good heavens, no! Abroad is . . . beastly. Beastly food. Garlic. Stuffy rooms and guttural squawks. Men kissing each other on the cheek, waving their arms!" He paused for breath, as Alice concealed a smile by sipping her china tea—"No, I'm going back to Devon. King's Tracy, under the Moor . . ." His voice grew dreamy— "I'd like to buy the vicarage, where I grew up . . . wonder if the big

yew tree's still outside the front door—don't see why it shouldn't be
. . . but the present vicar will be living in it. So I'll find a little house,
and . . ."

"Live by yourself?" she said. "You can't do that, Father."

He said, "Oh, yes, I can! I've been relying on other people too
long—your mother, then you. You have your own life to live . . . and,
to tell the truth, so do I."

He was seventy-six, she thought; and escaping from what had
happened to his England, not by going to beastly "abroad," but to the
wonderful, perfect past. Well, why not? He would have to get a housekeeper; perhaps she would live in, perhaps not. A few years ago she
herself would have felt it was her duty to go with him, to look after
him; and the thought came now, only to be at once dismissed. As her
father had said, she had her own life to live.

She said, "I'll come and visit you as soon as you get settled in, with a
housekeeper and maid, at least."

"That'll be very nice," he said. "I'll look forward to it." He bent
again over his gammon. Two minutes later he said, "Do you want to
live here, or shall I put it on the market? I wouldn't do that until
you've found a place of your own, of course."

She paused, thinking. But, really, the die was cast. She said, "You
can do it at once, Father. I'm going to move in with the Cowells . . .
Daisy and I have been discussing it ever since you first mentioned the
possibility of retiring to me."

"I never thought I'd be leaving Laburnum Lodge, though," Harry
said suspiciously. "I only decided I must do that, last night . . .
couldn't sleep . . . thinking of your mother . . . the boys . . ." His
voice trailed away.

Alice said nothing. He would forget; and soon, he did. He sat back,
relaxed, his breakfast finished. He spoke dreamily, "King's Tracy . . .
Joe Wood at the bakery . . . Warren Church, the squire's son . . . he
and I used to get into some scrapes, I can tell you . . . Susan
Chenevix-Trench, she was the prettiest girl I ever saw . . . till I met
your mother, of course . . . used to climb trees like a boy, afraid of
nothing . . ."

*   *   *   *

"Major Guy telephoned the wing commander and said he needed
some leave. Colonel Freeman gave him ninety-six hours and he took
my bike, Victoria, and rode off . . . after telling me to take ninety-six
hours too . . . a Bristol flew me over this morning."

Frank Stratton was talking to his sister, Lady Walstone, in the great
drawing room of Walstone Park. The room felt more enormous than

it actually was, because of her. She didn't belong in rooms like this, under those life-sized oil paintings of men in wigs and swords and lace ruffles.

She said, "We were all so pleased to hear about his V.C., in the paper . . . Goodness, it was only yesterday! How time flies!"

Frank said, "He's not taking much joy in it now, I can tell you. He and that German von Rackow were real friends, in spite of being enemies."

"His poor wife . . . widow now . . . if he was married. Perhaps he was a gay bachelor."

"He was married," Frank said shortly. "Major Guy went and dropped a wedding present on his airfield, at the time . . . Poor Victoria, I'll bet the major's giving her a hard time. After the major's finished with it, the tuning'll be in a mess, and everything'll need cleaning, and . . . it's worth it. Never seen a man look worse than when I saw him last. He'd just heard, and made sure, in his own mind, that he was the one that killed von Rackow." He stood up abruptly— "I'll be off now, Ruth. It's been good seeing you again."

Ruth stood up with him. She laid a hand on his arm—"Frank, see your children while you're here . . . *please!* They're upstairs, waiting."

"You had no business telling them I was coming," Frank snapped.

Ruth began to cry. Frank said, "It's good of you to give them a roof over their heads . . . and food. But I don't want to see them. They're not mine, any more." He went out, closing the door quietly behind him.

Ruth stood alone in the centre of the vast, baroque splendor, dabbing her eyes. In her dad's little house at 85 Jervis Street, she would have had a good cry, and enjoyed it, but here . . . the place was making her act like those ladies up on the walls, the wives and daughters and mothers of Earls of Swanwick—standing straight-backed, head up, like them, though the tears were streaming down her plump cheeks.

She did not hear her husband come in, only his gruff voice, "Patience on a monument . . . I thought you was having a heart to heart with Frank." She turned and he saw her tears—"What's the matter? What're you crying for?"

She said, "Anne and Frank . . . It's so sad. She's so lonely, she feels awful, she doesn't love the man, the father . . ."

"Either of them," Bill Hoggin, Lord Walstone, said sarcastically. "There was two, I know, who was hopping in and out of her bed."

"It doesn't matter, Bill," she said. "It was the war. If Frank raised a finger she . . . she'd crawl back on her hands and knees. But he doesn't want her."

"He may, in time," Bill said, more gently. After a pause he said briskly, "We'll be having a new head gamekeeper here by this time tomorrow, or my name ain't Bill Hoggin—1st Baron Walstone in the County of Kent," he added, rolling the mighty title round his tongue. "You run along now, Ruthie. Probyn Gorse has been called to the presence and heven now hawaits my summons in the 'all."

"Probyn?" Ruth said. "You're going to offer him the job of head gamekeeper? He won't take it."

"I think he will," Hoggin said. "Set a thief to catch a thief, that's my motto. He's the best poacher in Kent, everyone knows that . . . So all I had to do was make him think he'd better give up poaching. Cate and Kirby and everyone's told him to, but he didn't listen till his mother told him the same."

"But . . ."

"Run along now." He gave his wife a smack on her behind as she hurried out of the room by the far door. Alone, Bill went to the fireplace and pulled the great knotted crimson bell-pull hanging to one side of it. The door opened and Chapman the butler came in. Hoggin said briefly, "Bring Gorse."

The butler bowed silently. He'd never thought he would be able to stomach service under Hoggin, but in truth it wasn't bad. He knew his mind, he gave clear orders, he saw that what he wanted done was done; and he paid very well. So why should his accent and humble beginnings bother him? Rank is but riches, long possessed; Hoggin hadn't possessed them for long, that was all.

In the hall Probyn waited, standing, deerstalker cap in hand, the grey prominent through the reddish dye in his thin hair. "This way, Probyn," Chapman said and held open the ornate white- and gold-painted door. Probyn went in, head up. He wasn't afraid of Hoggin, any more than he'd been afraid of Swanwick. He just wondered what the lord wanted him for.

Hoggin, standing in front of the fire, hands clasped behind his back, heavy gold chain looped imposingly across the bow window of his expensive blue suit, said, "I need a head gamekeeper, Probyn. You been living in one of my cottages for three months now, since the fire. As head gamekeeper you get a better one, the big one behind the stables. You and the missus can move in there . . . there's a little plot that goes with it—an acre, it is, so she can grow tomatoes, peas, strawberries, anything she wants. Screw—a quid a week more than Skagg was getting, that'll be seven quid a week . . . no rent, of course."

Probyn's mind seemed to be stuck in glue. It had been very comfortable living in the little cottage these past months . . . hot and cold water in the kitchen, a geyser in the bathroom, a place for the ferrets and his gear. And now Hoggin was offering him really the same job he'd been doing all his life, only in reverse. If he didn't take it, he'd start poaching again. He knew it. And then his mother would come again, and . . .

He said, "Very well, my lord. I'll move today and start tomorrow."

*　　*　　*　　*

In the Head Porter's Lodge at Wokingham School, the old man pointed with bent back to the tap in the kitchen sink. "It drips . . . has for years. And the W.C. gets blocked . . . has for years. Of course we didn't have a W.C. when I come here first, in 1875 that was, just an earth closet down the back there."

"Who do you see to get things like that fixed?" Battery Sergeant Major Stanley Robinson, husband of Virginia née Rowland, Guy's younger sister, said.

"Clerk of the Works. Sam Gillis. Likes to be called *Mister* Gillis, but 'cor, I remember when he come here to clean the boys' boots, that was long after I come, in 1893 that was . . . You got a wife, ain't you?"

Robinson said, "Yes, she's with her mother now, having a baby . . . our first."

The old man hunched and crabbed through to the little parlor— "Well, ain't much room in here for a family . . . but you'll be all right till you have three. After that . . . you'll have to ask them to make you Clerk of the Works." He cackled feebly. Stan thought, it was clear why the Wokingham School governors had decided they must have a younger Head Porter.

The old man lowered himself into a chair and indicated another, opposite, for Stan. He said, "The young gents are in class. No one'll come by till twelve . . . you'll see . . . You'll have to have the uniform made special, on account of your arm."

"Of course," Stan said shortly. He had lost his left arm and a piece of the shoulder to a German shell in 1915, but was still sensitive about it—"Where do I get it made?"

"Cowper's in Reading. Cap too. One, green, with badge. The badge is the same as the young gents in the Officers' Training Corps wear, so it don't cost. One green uniform overcoat. Four pairs of white cotton gloves. Them's for greeting the governors, royalty, and the like. If your hands get cold you got to buy your own wool gloves. Black shoes or boots at all times when in uniform. They'll buy you one pair a year. The headmaster, you call 'Headmaster' when you see him— 'Good morning, Headmaster'—see? The other masters you call by their names . . . There's Mr Lamb, I don't know what he teaches, I know what he looks like . . . Mr Thompson, Mr Hayes, see? The young gents you call 'sir,' or 'Mr,' *not* 'Master,' even if their voices ain't broken. They're hot on that, I can tell you . . . The young gents don't get out of them gates after four o'clock, five o'clock in summer, less they have a pass signed by their housemaster or . . ."

The telephone rang. Stan started and made to reach for it, but the old man said testily, "I'm the Head Porter still, Mr Robinson."

"Sorry, Mr Hurdle," Stan muttered.

But it wasn't for Mr Hurdle, and after quavering, "Eh? What?" a couple of times, he handed it over. Stan recognized the voice at once—the clear high upper-class tones of Virginia's mother, Mrs Fiona Rowland. She said, "Stanley? This is Virginia's mother."

"Yes," Stan said. Gor, what should he call her?

"Virginia's pains have begun. They're still half an hour apart but the doctor has come and says everything seems fine. He has some other patients to see but he'll come back to stay when the pains get down to ten minutes. He thinks that won't be for four hours, at least."

Stan said, "Thank you, m'm. Can I speak to her?"

"I'm afraid not, Stanley. The telephone is in the hall and she's in another room . . . Oh dear, here she is, she's got out of bed . . ." Suddenly another voice came on, his wife's, hoarse, deep, warm with the Yorkshire accent she had deliberately acquired with the W.A.A.C. in Aldershot, so that he would feel comfortable with her. "It's started, darling, it's started," she gasped. "It isn't bad . . . It's lovely . . . Oh darling I love you I love you . . . wish you could be here. I heard Mummy talking and . . . I must go back . . . I'll call again as soon . . . as I can . . ."

Slowly Stanley replaced the instrument. The birth process of his first child had started. It was her first, too, of course. Old Hurdle was saying, "Well, I'll finish packing . . . I'll be gone by three . . . going to live with my daughter at Weston Super Mare, I am . . . suppose I'll be spending my time standing by her front door, touching my cap to everyone that passes, saying 'Morning, Mr . . .' . . . but I won't know their names, will I?"

* * * *

Louise Rowland looked round expectantly. She had heard something, or someone . . . surely? Wasn't it the front door opening . . . so now she would hear John's heavy step . . . but there was nothing. She closed her eyes and bent her head. He was dead. She had loved him once, and now that he was dead, the love seemed to be returning. In the middle and later years, she had not felt it, only a tolerant affection . . . recently, less than that—exasperation, even.

213

Carol Adams came into the room and said, "Good night, Mrs Rowland. I'm going up to bed now."

Louise said, "Good night, Carol . . . Wait." The young woman looked worn, bone weary. Louise remembered seeing her spread-eagled under Fred Stratton, in 1914. Did Carol remember? She had been very susceptible. Had she had any other lovers since then? The young woman was waiting, wondering. Louise said, "I was going to ask you to take up some warm milk for Addie, but I'll do it. You've done enough today."

Carol said, "I could do it, but . . . it isn't here we need the help, Mrs Rowland, it's outside, on the farm. With Mr Rowland gone, we just can't handle it, even when none of us has the flu . . . and I think Frances is going to come down with it next, tomorrow perhaps."

Louise said, "I don't know what we can do. Girls don't want to work on the land. There's a feeling that the war's all but over and they want to be home when the men come back, to get one, to have fun, get married. It's been a long time."

Carol said, "It's natural, Mrs Rowland." She hesitated, then said, with eyes averted, "I've become engaged, to Horace Woodruff. But I won't be leaving until he can come home," she added hastily.

"Horace Woodruff," Louise repeated, thinking, the garage man's third child. What would Carol's father, the Vicar of Beighton, think? She said, "How nice . . . What's he in?"

"Corporal, Tank Corps," she said. "He was home on leave last month and we saw a lot of each other." She looked up defiantly, "I think I'm going to have his baby."

Louise opened her mouth to say something, but closed it again and instead put out both hands. After a moment of hesitation the young woman came to her, and began to weep on her shoulder.

Louise patted her—"Don't worry, dear. It'll all come out all right. He'll come back . . . the war's nearly over. We . . . I'll help you."

*   *   *   *

"Bear down," the doctor said. He was an old man, grey-haired. Every doctor left in England now seemed to be old, Virginia thought—the young ones gone to the war. Pain gripped her in the lower part of the belly, contracting the muscles in a strong, steady spasm. She gasped, gritted her teeth, and pulled hard on the knotted towel fastened to the foot of the bed. A cool sponge was wiped across her forehead and she whispered, "Thank you, Stella." Stella was a strange girl . . . hadn't been so strange when they were younger . . . but she'd insisted on coming up from Walstone to the flat in Hedlington as soon as she'd heard that Virginia's pains had started—and she was about eight and a half months pregnant herself. Perhaps that was why she wanted to come . . . To one side Probyn's Woman watched impassively. She had been with Virginia for twenty-four hours without a break now.

"Bear down," the doctor said again. The pains were at less than three-minute intervals now. Her mother was standing beside her, one hand on her shoulder. But Virginia hardly acknowledged her presence. None of these people were really here, in their spirits. The only spirits present were those of herself, her husband Stanley, and even now growing out of her like a flower, their child.

The doctor said, "Very close now." The pains became continuous and with a slow firm movement she felt herself delivered of the living weight that had been in her for nine months, the child. She fell back, her hair spread dank on the pillow. She let go of the towel, as Stella's sponge came down again, to wipe off the sweat streaming down her forehead onto the pillow.

"It's a girl," the doctor said.

"Kate Robinson," Virginia gasped feebly. "It was Stanley's grand-mother's name. He loved her."

They were all silent in the big bedroom. Suddenly the baby filled its lungs and yelled. Virginia smiled wider and wider—"Give her to me," she said.

"In a minute . . . she has to be cleaned up a little. You, too. More hot water, please, Mrs Gorse." They were wiping and cleaning and wrapping her up. Stella was whispering, from miles away, "She's beautiful, Virginia. Lots of hair. It seems dark now but perhaps it'll change . . . She looks just like you."

"Hope not," Virginia mumbled. She was very tired. The labour had lasted a long, long time, all hard work. She wanted to sleep . . . but not yet. The doctor was giving her the baby. "There," she said, "there, there." The baby yelled more loudly. "There, there . . . beautiful Katie."

Stella said, "I'll call your husband. I have the number."

She floated out of the room; or did it only seem like that to Virginia? To her everything was floating—her mother, by the window, the doctor, the baby floating in golden light in the crook of her arm—Stella, pale, thin, dark-eyed, huge-bellied, so tired too.

*   *   *   *

"Nice place you've got here," Lady Jarrow said to Probyn's Woman. They were in the large old-fashioned kitchen, the window looking across to South Spinney. "Two bedrooms and the parlor—one bath, isn't it?"

"And another room we can use as a bedroom, if we were to have

215

more than four children," the Woman said, "like plenty of them old head keepers did."

Florinda took a gold cigarette case out of her handbag, found a cigarette and lighted it. The aroma of Russian tobacco filled the kitchen, competing with the smell of frying onions. She said, "Why did Granddad take the job?"

"Because his mother told him to stop poaching," the Woman said shortly.

"His mother?"

"She haunted him . . . two, three times . . . near dark it was, every time."

Florinda said softly, "Wait a minute . . . her ghost appeared and told Probyn to become a gamekeeper?"

"Told him to give up poaching."

Florinda puffed slowly on her cigarette, staring first at the ceiling, then out of the window. She said, "Who would benefit from that?"

"All the landowners . . . Lord Walstone most, 'cos he's got the most land, the most pheasants, trout, hares, rabbits, everything."

"And the most money. And he likes his own way. And he's clever . . . and unscrupulous . . . Wasn't it lucky that the roof burned off your cottage, so he could show Probyn how kind he was . . . and how much more comfortably he could live?"

"Yes," the Woman said, her expression unaltered.

Florinda said, "You wanted him to give up poaching, too, didn't you?"

"It was time," she said. "He's getting on."

Florinda said at last, "Well, I think it's time, too. Hoggin will want him to do his job properly."

"Which he can," the Woman said. "At least for a few more years."

"And he'll get a pension?"

"I saw to that."

"So we can thank Lord Walstone all the way round, I reckon."

The Woman smiled, for almost the first time in Florinda's memory, and said, "I reckon so, Florinda . . . and one day I'd like to thank Probyn's mother, too, if I ever met her to recognize her, so to speak. Probyn might have had a gun ready, any time. She took a risk, doing that."

Florinda said, "I suppose she was some out-of-work old actress, happy to get the money. And I don't suppose Lord Walstone told her Probyn might have a gun . . . Any news of Fletcher?"

The Woman said, "A letter, a month ago. He was still killing Germans but said it wouldn't go on much longer. He's written enough

216

new poems so they're going to publish a second book of them. It's going to be called *The Blood of Poppies*."

"I'll tell Hatchard's to send me a copy as soon as it's out."

"Your Guy's got a V.C., we saw in the paper."

Florinda stubbed out her cigarette on the lid of the stove, lifted the lid with the little iron hook, and dropped the butt in. Still with her back to the Woman she said, "Yes. But he's not mine, particularly. I expect he has lots of girls after him, out there."

"You were lovers when you were little," the Woman said.

Florinda nodded—"We were . . . Guy and Florinda."

"But you have another man now." The Woman said it as a statement, not a question.

Florinda said, "Yes. Billy Bidford . . . also a V. C. You'd think they were competing for me by acts of heroism, wouldn't you? And I take the winner."

The Woman said, "Tain't as easy as that, is it?"

After a long time Florinda said in a small unhappy voice, "No, it isn't . . . I love Guy, but now I'm afraid of him, too. Billy . . ." She shrugged helplessly.

* * * *

Her true mother's face was dim in Sally Rowland's memory, but she remembered how Mum would sit on the sofa, after she had brought the men to the house, and take off her dress, usually pulling it over her head, then step out of her petticoat, then sit smoking a cigarette and drinking some port and lemon, or a gin and water, just in her slip and the little satin liners she wore, that showed hair peeping out round the sides. The men got bulges in their trousers then, and kept telling her they were in a hurry and wanted to get to the bedroom; but her mother didn't let them hurry her. So, though the four boys were muttering, take 'em off Sally, take 'em off, she remained standing, in the middle of Bittern's Copse at the edge of Farmer Handle's land, to the north of Beighton, her dress hung over a bough, her bloomers on and the liners under them, her top bare. Mummy used to do that sometimes, sit with the men with nothing on above the waist. Of course, she had great big titties, with big dark points, while Sally's were as yet not much more than half-lemons stuck on to her chest.

"Take off those bloomers," Freddie Collins said. His voice was trembling and he had his hand on his trousers. She pirouetted slowly, arms raised and fingers intertwined. All four of them were breathing like the railway engines did when they were getting away from Walstone up the little hill toward Taversham. One of the boys was eleven, her own age, the others twelve and thirteen, farmers' boys, the greengrocer's son. They had eyes for nothing but her. They would do anything she commanded; they were her slaves. "Undo your buttons," she said, turning more slowly.

"You take those bloomers off first," Willie Wheeler choked.

"No, you first . . . all of you."

One by one they undid their buttons with trembling fingers. Two pricks sprang out, hard erect, big . . . not as big as Mummy's men's were, but big. The other two flopped out, little pink slugs, soft . . . She looked into those two boys' eyes, her lips curled in an understanding smile, and they could not meet her eyes.

She stopped gyrating, slowly pulled down her heavy blue-flannel bloomers, and, moving with arms hieratically outstretched, like a priestess in a Druid grove, hung them over the bough with her dress.

"Please, Sally, now!" Their eyes were as big as saucers. She had a lot of hair down there now, that had come quickly and suddenly and plentifully, much more than her titties, and curls of it were escaping at the sides of the liner, just as Mum's used to.

"Sixpence each," she said, holding out one hand as she continued to gyrate.

Two of the boys felt in their pockets and handed over their sixpences at once. One muttered, "I only got a bob."

"That'll do," she said. "I'll pay you back tomorrow . . . or it'll do for next time."

The last boy, the youngest, one of the two with a limp prick, suddenly stuffed it back, did up his flies, and ran off. Poor little fellow, Sally thought, he's not excited, he's just frightened. There had been grown men like that with Mum, too, which was strange, when you came to think about it, them being grown and knowing what they'd come for, but it was true, she'd seen it herself, and not only what Mum used to call whisky cock.

Freddie Collins had begun to caress his swollen prick, muttering in an agonized groan, "Show us yer cunnie, Sally, or . . ."

A gruff man's voice said, "So this is what you're all doing in the wood! Do up your trousers, Willie Wheeler . . . you, too! You get dressed, Sally, and go home. You ought to be ashamed of yourself, leading on these boys."

It was Farmer Handle. He had never been a friend of Sally or Tim; and since they had set fire to his hayrick two years ago, he had detested them. Though Richard and Susan Rowland had adopted them, Handle was always on the lookout for proofs of their shameful heredity.

Now he said, "Your dad and mum will hear more of this."

218

Sally, alone in the wood, dressed quickly. Her dad and mum were going to be told? What about the boys? And how had she led them astray when they were always pestering her to show them her cunnie? It wasn't fair.

* * * *

"She's got to be sent away to school," Richard said firmly that evening, the lamps lit against the early autumn dark, the children in bed, the fire not yet lit in the grate. "She's very advanced for her age, and she's much too experienced. Heaven knows how much she saw before her mother was killed."

"She'll be homesick," Susan said unhappily.

"Tim isn't, and he's only just ten. Sally's eleven and a half."

Susan said, "I think Tim *is* homesick. He doesn't come right out and say so in his letters, but it's what he doesn't say that is important. They are not cheerful, happy letters."

Richard said, "Well, he'll have to get used to it. We all do. And you *do*. School becomes a second home, and by the time you're getting fed up with it, you go home for the vac. When you're bored with home back to school . . . I don't see what alternative there is to sending Sally off to school. She's getting beyond what an ordinary governess—even if we could find one—can teach her. She's very bright. She can't go to the local school . . ."

"Why not?" Susan asked, knowing the answer—because it's not done to send children of the upper class to the village school; they would pick up local accents and make undesirable friendships.

Richard said, "You know she can't."

Susan said, "Could we send her to America, to school in San Francisco? She could go from my parents' house. I know they'd be delighted to have her."

"Until she got into trouble," Richard said, ". . . and how would it help, if you don't want to send her away from her home—here—to send her 6,000 miles to another country?"

Susan said, "I suppose you're right."

Richard said slowly, "It would be different if we all went to America. I can tell you, I've been thinking of emigrating. I have a damned good mind to do it, if the unions get too strong here. I like everything I read and hear about American business. I could do well there . . . but for now I have to stay, to help win the war . . . so that the damned unions can then pull down everything that millions of men have died to preserve . . . That's beside the point, for the present. Sally must go to school. Preferably a school that she can go to now and stay in until she's seventeen or eighteen. I know—Cheltenham Ladies College."

"Virginia hated it," Susan said.

"Because Virginia was very plain, and very lazy. Getting married has done wonders for her, she looks quite beautiful . . . a little fat still . . . I'll write to the Headmistress of Cheltenham Ladies College and see if we can get Sally in, starting next January. Meanwhile, she's got to be much more closely supervised here."

"I'll tell Nanny," Susan said. Poor Sally, she thought. She swore she never let the boys touch her. It was probably no different from what Guy and Florinda Gorse had done together at this age. Now—off to prison with her—the juvenile prison system of the British upper class.

* * * *

Mr Overfeld pushed his bowler hat forward over his eyes, lifted his legs onto the table, and leaned back in the swivel chair. He rotated the stump of cigar in his mouth from the left side to the right and said, "What's the total?"

David Morgan, the foreman of the Jupiter Motor Company, said, "Thirty-seven . . . and going up every day. And this is worse than the spring one. Two of ours have died already, and we didn't lose anyone then."

"What are we going to do about it?"

"The government says quarantine . . . keep people separate so they don't infect each other with their germs . . . get 'em out of the factory and away home as soon as they show any symptoms. But that's a lot of codswallop, because, look you, they're *infectious* before they show any symptoms!" His voice rose in Welsh excitement.

Overfeld said, almost to himself, "Can't separate workers in a factory, least not inside each group . . . maybe we can keep groups from getting close to other groups. Let's look into that . . . When will we have to shut down altogether?"

"Never," Morgan said. "Not with this plant setup. If we had a full Ford assembly line, there'd be a critical point where it couldn't be kept going . . . but we aren't up to that stage yet. Never will be, if Bert Gorse and his U.S.E. have their way."

Overfeld said, "Is there any way we can use the epidemic to weaken the union?"

Morgan said, "I've been thinking about that. So's the boss, I know. But it'll probably work t'other way. The union'll pay sick benefits for fourteen days, we only pay seven days, and only then if a worker's been with us more than a year. The union pays 100 percent of what the man—or woman—was getting at work. We pay 60 percent."

Overfeld said, "They pay 100 percent—until their funds run out. They don't have much reserve cash down at Stalford Street."

"No, but the National does, and they'll back H.E. 16, to break us . . . Look you, Mister Overfeld, we should tell the boss we must raise the benefits to fourteen days, and 100 percent, same as the union. And guarantee them their jobs back."

"I'll talk to him," Overfeld said, "but between you and me, Mr Richard's got a bee in his bonnet over unions. I don't like 'em myself, understand, but . . . you can't damage a boxcar by hitting it with a crowbar . . . but you can derail it with the same crowbar, if you use it right."

*   *   *   *

"The train was late," Wilfred Bentley said wearily as he hung up his coat and hat in the hall "Because the driver assigned to it went down with flu. We were held up twice by signals, because about a third of the signalmen on the South Eastern are down with flu . . . The meeting was to be attended by forty county secretaries . . . twelve showed up—the rest had flu . . . so it was canceled . . . so my whole trip was for nothing . . . And now . . ."—he sank down in a chair—"I think I have it."

Rachel, who had been writing columns of figures in her big account book, only half-listening, dropped her pen and jumped to her feet—"Wilfred!"

"Don't come near me."

"Too late," she said, "Since we were in bed together last night, and kissed this morning before you went off. Come upstairs."

Slowly he followed her. His head ached, his eyes hurt, his stomach was unsettled, his flesh shivered and crawled. She pulled back the covers, helped him undress, and put him to bed. She sat beside the bed—"I'll bring some hot tea and aspirin. I'll try to get a doctor, but . . ."

He waved a feeble hand—"Don't bother. There are people really ill with it. I'm not."

"I have to go out for a bit," she said. "Will you be all right?"

"Of course," he mumbled, his eyes closing.

She went out and down the stairs. Whatever he said, she must try to get a doctor for him; and there was one who would come if he possibly could—Rob Glennie, the young Scotsman from the Greenock shipbuilding yards, who'd managed to put himself through medical training without losing his Gorbals accent, or his Clydeside socialism. He was a fiery young man . . . agin the war, agin the class system, agin the English—and a good doctor. She put on her coat and hat and went out.

Half an hour later she was back, with Glennie. She waited in the

221

parlor until he came down again, his little black bag in his hand. His small alert face was weary: on the way here, he had told her that he had seen a hundred and two influenza patients in the last three days, of which four had died. She said now, "A little whisky, Rob?"

He shook his head—"More cases, and they don't like it if Jones the Bones comes in reeking of booze . . . This seems to be the same virus as the spring flu epidemic, but we're getting a lot of pulmonary complications now, and that's leading to a high death rate. The worst is what's called haemorrhagic oedema—'wet lungs' or 'dripping lungs.' If Wilfred starts to wheeze . . . has difficulty in breathing . . . makes wet noises as though he had water in his lungs, send for me at once. I'll come. Except for the next twelve hours. I'm taking three sleeping pills and knocking myself out, as soon as I get home."

"What can you do, if Wilfred does get wet lungs?"

After a long pause he said, "Not a bluidy thing . . . Keep him warm, and quiet. Lots of warm liquids. No alcohol. No solid food until his temperature's been normal for twenty-four hours . . . I must go."

"The bill . . ." she began.

He waved her aside—"Make me National Health Officer when he's Prime Minister." He was gone. She closed the door, and sat down, staring straight ahead. The newspaper on the floor at her feet showed the headline INFLUENZA EPIDEMIC SPREADS, GROWS . . . It was eerie to think that the flu, which was now threatening Wilfred's life, and at any moment might seize her, too, *could* also kill the war. The troops in the trenches were being smitten harder than they had been by enemy machine guns. The only reason they could hold their positions was that their enemy was in an equally bad state. Industry was grinding to a standstill, commerce suffering, sports dying . . . And she and Wilfred ought to be out in the streets, electioneering; for now it was definite that Harry Rowland would not contest the next election. Lloyd George was the sort of cunning swine who would call an election as soon as the war was won, to make capital of his successful waging of it. It could happen any minute.

Wilfred's illness could not be helped, and the constituency was in good shape. The labour troubles at Hedlington Aircraft and J.M.C. had helped. The bloody continuation of the war had helped. Now it only needed victory for many pent-up frustrations to burst out, in victory at the polls. The Liberals and Conservatives thought they were secure, at every point. She knew, from working with the people, walking with them, talking to them, that it was not so.

The doorbell rang and she went to answer it. Wilfred had wanted to have at least one maid in the house but she had vetoed it; they were working Socialists and did not believe in personal service of that kind.

She opened the door. It was Mary Gorse, Willum's wife. She was carrying a heavy burden in her arms. Rachel hurried forward, arms out. Mary said, "It's my Jane, Rachel. She has the influenza. I can't get any doctor to come to us. Little Rupert's got it, too, but he's not so bad."

Rachel laid the girl down on the sofa. She was ten, immature, childish of shape, heavy brown hair hanging across a pale, sweating face, dark eyes staring up at her. The pulse was high—temperature, about 103, breathing heavy, wheezing, bubbles . . . dripping lungs. There was nothing to be done, but hope, pray . . . but she was an atheist. Mary was on her knees, praying beside the sofa. Warm drinks . . . but the girl wouldn't be able to hold them down. Aspirin—not that, either.

She said fiercely, "The doctors would have come if you'd told them Florinda would pay."

Mary looked up, "I couldn't say that, Rachel." She resumed her praying, "Our father, which art in heaven, hallowed be thy name . . ."

Rachel shouted, "What's the use of praying to a God who doesn't exist? Don't pray—remember! Remember your child's dying because they sent your husband to have his legs blown off . . . they wouldn't give you enough money to keep a fire in the grate . . . and when you needed the doctor, he wouldn't come because he was busy dealing with little Lord Fauntleroy, who's eaten too much caviare!"

"Thy kingdom come, thy will be done, on earth as it is in heaven. Forgive us our trespasses as we forgive them that trespass against us . . . For thine is the kingdom, the power and the glory, for ever and ever. Amen."

"Oh, God! . . . Amen."

Daily Telegraph, Saturday, October 12, 1918

FEARS IN GERMANY

FINANCIAL PANIC

From Our Financial Correspondent, *Paris,* **Friday Afternoon.** The financial panic in Germany, which came like a thunderbolt to Berlin on Oct. 3, is spreading in all parts of the Empire, according to the latest Swiss information. There was another severe shock on Oct. 8, a warning of the coming debacle in the financial situation of Germany, notwithstanding the urgent efforts of the Press to quiet panic-stricken holders of German and Austrian securities . . . Capitalists are striving to liquidate their positions, notwithstanding the intervention of the German banks and the creation of a banking trust to buy up the mass of securities thrown on the market. German discipline and bluff will hold the field to the last. A Geneva message . . .

"German discipline and bluff" Cate thought; they were holding the field in France, too, at great cost to themselves, and to everyone else. It would only make things worse for them when the end, now inevitable, came. Why not give in, the sensible thing to do? But who had been sensible in this war?

Garrod, pouring coffee for him, said, "Bertha's in bed with the flu, sir. And Mrs Abell's staying in bed, too, though she's not sure whether it's the flu or something else."

She went out. Stella, sitting opposite her father, said, "When's the war going to be over, Daddy?"

He said, "Soon . . . it must. Then John will come back, and . . ."

He wanted to say, everything will be all right; but could not say it, for it would not be true. Stella was still addicted to heroin, and still turned in on herself, uninterested in anything outside . . . except Virginia's baby, perhaps. She'd been to Hedlington every day to see that, until Virginia took the baby back to Wokingham. What she needed was her own baby, even now kicking in her womb; and her husband. But when . . . ?

Stella stood up suddenly, holding onto the edge of the table. Her face went pale, then red, again pale. Garrod came in, as though warned by telepathy. Stella said, "Daddy . . . the waters . . . they've broken!"

Cate leaped to his feet, scattering the newspaper all over the table. "The trap," he cried, "but Bertha's sick . . . I'll telephone Richard to drive us . . ."

Stella said, "I shall have it here, Daddy. Send for Probyn's Woman."

She turned, Garrod's arm supporting her as Cate hurried to help. The three of them went slowly upstairs, leaving the coffee bubbling, the fried eggs and bacon warm under the domed silver lid, the toast half-eaten on the plates.

Walstone, Kent: Sunday, October 13, 1918

13 Probyn Gorse walked carefully through Woolmer's Spinney, his gun on his shoulder, unloaded. There was no moon, and the stars were intermittently wiped from the sky by fast-moving clouds. It was one o'clock in the morning, windy, not cold, raw with the promise of rain by dawn. Stopping, he peered up at the branches above him, now almost bare of leaves. The silhouettes of the roosting pheasants were clear enough now, where a month earlier it had been hard to see them in the leaves . . . too hard to make it worthwhile for the city poachers to come with their little .22 rifles and knock them off, easy as hitting them down with a stick. And they were easier to see by day, too, feeding in the stubble outside the woods; but not many poachers came by day. The weather was the real key; if it was cold and raining, they stayed in bed or went to sleep in a barn and took the first train back to London or Chatham in the morning. If it was a clear evening, with a red sky and an east wind, they'd put on their old warm poaching clothes and come down, especially in the middle of the week, when the money was running low from last payday. Tonight, it could go either way.

Probyn walked on, careful to make no sound on the dead leaves He knew all these woods like the back of his hand. He'd been poaching them for over fifty years, in all seasons, all weathers. The strange thing was to be wearing this heather mixture tweed suit and deerstalker cap, the uniform of the Walstone Park keepers. He'd protested, but Lord Walstone said he had to wear it when he was on duty: otherwise, he might be mistaken for a poacher by one of the other keepers, and shot by mistake.

A faint flapping noise caught his ear and he stepped easily behind the thick bole of an oak, listening. Might be the wind stirring the high branches ahead . . . might be one bough touching another with its leaves . . . might be some boy quietly clapping his hands together . . . hands in gloves. Who'd be fool enough to do that, this time of night? Jerry Tharp, maybe, young feller that worked in Woodruff's garage, might be him. He liked to go out at night, get himself a bird or two from wherever he could find it. No harm in him, but not much skill yet, either . . .

He slipped cartridges into both barrels and stalked forward, the gun now carried in front of him, across his chest. The flapping noise grew louder. He stopped again, thinking, not now in general, of what it might be, but of Woolmer's Spinney in particular . . . forty acres, longer north to south than east to west, sloping down about thirty feet to the east, hedges all round, except a post and rail fence on the north, on Jim Harvey's land; oak, ash, elm in the middle, hazel round the outside . . . and a pole trap in the very centre. That was it. He was about fifty feet from it now. He stepped out and in a moment reached the trap, a pole ten feet high, with a steel-jawed trap set on top of it. There was a small platform inside the jaws, and on the platform a piece of high meat, securely anchored to a short wire, which actuated the jaws. It was designed to trap birds of prey, and so reduce the numbers of them that could attack the pheasants as they grew. The flapping sound came from the wings of a bird caught in the trap. It was hanging head down, held by its broken legs, beating its wings against the pole. Probyn caught it by the neck and peered in the starlight . . . big, round flat face, white, with the beak line down the middle, big dark eyes. Tawny Owl. He forced open the jaws of the trap and, holding the owl by its thighs, smashed its head against the pole twice, then threw it away into the dark wood. He hadn't been here for a couple of nights; the owl could have been there nearly all that time: they died hard . . . probably from last night, though. Master Laurence had tried to bring up one of them Tawnies he'd found deserted. It flew away when it was nine months old, and he never saw it again, but till then it used to bring him mice it caught . . .

Big shoot come Saturday. Plenty of birds for the gentlemen, in spite of the other keepers being no more use than a sick headache. He'd tell Lord Walstone to get rid of 'em soon, and look for younger men. With the war almost finished and men coming out of uniform and eager for any job they could get, it wouldn't be difficult . . . but how many of 'em would want to be walking round a dark wood, in the middle of the night, after four years in the trenches? They'd rather be in bed, holding their wives' titties and thanking God they didn't have to be up . . .

He reached the north edge of the wood and stopped, looking out over the stubble. It wasn't a hard job. As he'd felt, and as Lord Walstone had said, it was no different really from what he'd been doing all his life . . . He'd catch a few poachers, lose a few pheasants . . . someone would try to bash him on the head . . . but he knew them all, every one of them, who might come out moonlighting from Walstone and Taversham and Beighton . . . London? That was different. But they were Englishmen, too, weren't they? Spoke the same language? It was a good game, this poaching and keeping, like the cowboys and Indians that the kids played in the village.

He set off back through the wood. Have to remember to reset the pole trap. They were against the law, but landowners who preserved birds winked at it. Just don't get caught, they said, or hinted . . . Right strange thing that was, about Miss Stella's baby. No one in the village knew what to say, so they were saying nothing. Thinking, though . . .

$$*\quad*\quad*\quad*$$

Gesticulating and speaking energetically, Lord Walstone strode up and down in front of the fireplace in the Blue Drawing Room at the Park. Sitting in a chair nearby was Mr T.D. Eaves, a withered gentleman of about seventy, a retired banker who looked and dressed like an eighteenth-century coachman, complete to breeches, hunting boots, stock, and usually a top hat, frockcoat, and foxhead crop. Walstone said, "The upshot of it is that Hi propose to restart the North Weald Hounds, and the first thing I want to know is—will you return as secretary?"

"Willingly," the old man said at once. "You will not have any difficulty reassembling a good pack, either. Hunts all over the country are having to retrench or close down altogether, because of lack of food for the hounds. But . . ."

Walstone raised a hand, "I know, Eaves . . . where will I get huntsmen and whippers-in and kennel men? The answer is, from the army. The war'll be over any day soon, and then, why, everyone'll be looking for a job—and they won't be easy to come by, 'cos they'll stop making guns and shells and tanks and aeroplanes just like that"—he snapped two pudgy, powerful fingers together. "What I want is to get everything organized—the members, the kennels, the wire fund, all ready to go as soon as I can get the hunt servants."

"You'll be Master, I presume?"

Lord Walstone puffed out his chest, thus somewhat reducing his paunch—"Yes, Hi will . . . In due course we will find a suitable Joint Master, but for the time being it'll be me. I won't hunt the hounds, of course."

Eaves made a non-committal noise in his throat. Walstone had spunk, but he rode like a sack of potatoes, and knew nothing about the technique of foxhunting. He'd been out several days in Lord Swanwick's time and had been a member of the hunt . . . wore the pink coat from his second or third day, oblivious of others' amusement . . . oblivious, or careless. Why should he care? Eaves was a rich man himself, but Walstone was . . . rich-rich, as he'd heard some young blood put it.

"All right, then," Walstone said. "You get started. Get the notepaper printed . . . find out who has hounds for sale . . . find out where the old huntsmen and whippers-in and kennel men have gone, what regiments—they're mostly in the cavalry, probably . . . We could circulate the Commanding Officers of all the cavalry depots and ask them . . . they'll probably have been kept back from France to teach the recruits how to ride, and look after their horses . . . speak to all the farmers in the district about wire . . . Lord Swanwick was very hot against wire but he didn't pay 'em enough . . . a banquet and ball for farmers p'raps? Every Christmas . . . that'd help to get their daughters married off . . . see what you can think of." He looked at the ornate clock on the ornate marble mantel behind him—"Half past." He raised his voice—"Chapman, is Probyn Gorse waiting out there?" A distant voice answered, "Yes, milord."

"Send him in . . . That's all, Eaves."

Eaves got up carefully, and stalked out with a short but courtly bow to his lordship. Probyn Gorse came in, deerstalker in hand, his purple suit carefully brushed, his hair re-dyed a stronger ginger.

Walstone said, "Are you shooting foxes?"

Probyn paused, wondering what the purpose of the question was. Lord Walstone wasn't a country person, so perhaps he didn't know that all gamekeepers shot foxes, unless their employers were also Masters of Foxhounds or otherwise closely associated with the hunt.

Walstone continued, "Because I'm going to restart the hunt . . . And I don't want any more foxes shot. No excuses, eh? They're to be bleeding well preserved, just like the pheasants, so the hunt can have good sport."

"If you don't get rid of the foxes, you won't have good shooting," Probyn said.

"Ho yes, I will, and all my guests too. You do whatever's necessary,

Probyn. Trap the foxes and keep them in cages and let 'em out the morning of the meet . . ."

"That's called bagging, milord. Mr Skagg used to do it regular for Lord Swanwick. It's against the law."

Lord Walstone's beady little black eyes glistened—"Between you and me, Probyn, fuck the law. Can't you give the ruddy foxes something else to eat than pheasants? Why don't you tie out chicken for 'em now and then? Meat. Eggs. Anything they'll like."

"That'll cost money, milord. But it would help."

"You tell Granger down in the village that you want to buy any of his chickens that don't turn out right . . . p'raps a dozen a week would do . . . Send the bills to the hunt secretary, Mr Eaves . . . Everything ready for the shoot on Saturday?"

"Yes, milord. It is still to be nine guns, and yourself?"

Walstone nodded—"Lord Taggart, Admiral de Lorne, the Duke of Taunton, General Sir Roger Mainwaring, Lord Justice Arnold, Sir Henry Mimms, Sir George Clark-Kent, Mr Francis Saintsbury, and Mr Morton Cross . . . with their wives, except Lord Taggart, who's a bachelor, likes little boys, I hear . . . Know any of 'em?"

"The Duke of Taunton has shot here several times, with Lord Swanwick," Probyn said, "and so has Mr Cross. Sir Henry Mimms' father came frequently in my young days. They were all good shots. They get plenty of practise," he added, not as a social comment, but as a matter of fact.

"All right, I'm paying the beaters seven shillings each for the day, and that's final. How many loaders did you get in the end?"

"Seven, milord, not counting me."

"H'm. So two will have to load for themselves. Well, it can't be helped. That's all, Probyn . . . Chapman!"

Probyn cut in—"Excuse me, my lord, there's something I ought to tell you."

"What is it?" Walstone said impatiently. "I haven't got all day."

"Your guns, milord. They're not worthy of your position."

Walstone stared, "What the 'ell . . . ?"

"You should get two pairs of Purdeys specially made for you. Then the other gentlemen's loaders won't be laughing up their sleeves at what you have."

"How much?"

"Five hundred guineas the pair, milord."

Walstone stopped in his tracks—"*Five . . . hundred . . . guineas?*" His look became suspicious—"Do you get a rake-off?"

Probyn said stiffly, "I have nothing to do with the transaction, my lord. Only, I do not wish my employer to look cheap 'cos it makes me look cheap, too. Now, if I may go, milord . . ."

"Oh go to hell . . . I'll get the bleeding guns . . . Chapman! Where's Her Ladyship?"

"Here, milord, waiting to see you."

"Send her in." Ruth came in, carrying the Honourable Christine Hoggin in her arms, smiling, as though it were quite normal for a baroness to have to wait in the hall to see her husband. She faced him now, gently rocking the sleeping baby, and said, "Bill, Probyn Gorse and his Woman are not married."

"Of course not," Hoggin said. "Everyone knows that."

"They're living in the Head Gamekeeper's cottage as man and wife," she said. "What are the Duchess of Taunton and Lady Mainwaring going to think if they ever learn that we are, I don't know the word, helping them to live in sin?"

"Overlooking it, is the right word," Hoggin muttered, but not very loud. "Well, what do you want me to do?"

"Tell Probyn he's got to marry her. Tell him we will pay for the wedding, the reception, everything. And you'll give the bride away."

Hoggin, left speechless, could only shake his head and gasp like a just-caught fish. Ruth said, "Thank you, Bill . . . It's time Launcelot started riding lessons. Mr Cate told me that the sooner you start, the easier it is. He's going to have to ride a lot when he grows up."

"There's no one who can teach him properly," Walstone wailed. "Just the girls in the stables, and none of them can ride very well. I know 'cos I've asked them to teach me, and they can't."

"He must start as soon as possible. He's near three and a half," Ruth said ominously.

"All right, all right," Walstone said. "Just as soon's the war's over and I can get grooms who know a horse's arse from its ears . . . as soon as the war's over . . ."

"Thank you, Bill," Lady Walstone said, and left the room, cooing to the baby, now awake in her arms. When she had gone Lord Walstone sank into a Chippendale chair, gasping "Pheeew!", pulled out his handkerchief and wiped his forehead. After a time he recovered his strength enough to sit up and shout "Chapman, send in the accountant!"

*　　　*　　　*　　　*

The Countess of Swanwick climbed down slowly from the first-class compartment as a porter hurried to help her. She was only sixty-one, she thought, but she felt older; and lack of proper exercise in London was making her stiff. She looked closely at the porter; she'd never seen him before. He was older than she by a good ten years, or he'd have reached her in time to help her down the step. The station itself hadn't changed . . . well, she'd only been away seven or eight months; but most things were changing so fast these days that it was quite a surprise, a pleasant surprise. Ah, there was someone she knew, Mr Miller, the stationmaster. He'd lost a boy in France, and was looking grim, depressed, or determined—it was hard to tell which . . . not only with Mr Miller, with everyone in the country . . . and the truth was that most people were all three. He recognized her and raised his gold-braided peaked cap—"Why, milady . . . we weren't expecting you."

She said, "I've just come down to get a breath of fresh country air again." Miller fell in beside her as she walked toward the platform exit. "We're not far from Hyde Park but . . . it's not the same as Walstone Park," she added, smiling. "Lady Walstone asked me to give her some advice about new curtains—they've been badly needed for years—so I came down and am going to take the opportunity to meet some old friends."

"Can I get you a taxi, m'lady?" the stationmaster asked. "Mr Woodruff's garage is just across the road."

Lady Swanwick shook her head, "No, thank you, Mr Miller. I shall walk about, and to the Manor. Mr Cate can drive me to the Park and I expect Lord Walstone will be able to provide transport to bring me back here in time to catch the 4.43."

"4.41 it is now, m'lady," Miller said anxiously. "You don't want to miss it."

"I won't," she said, nodding goodbye. She settled her head deeper into the fur-lined collar of her dark grey overcoat and walked slowly up the lane toward the Saxon tower of the church and the houses clustered round it, mud splashing her pale grey spats, her furled umbrella swinging from one wrist.

Walstone: seat of the Earls of Swanwick for, how long? A long time. Now seat of the 1st Baron Walstone—butcher, grocer, entrepreneur. She realized how much she had missed it. But the world was turning. They all had to make new lives. She reached the main street and paused. Directly opposite was a big barn with a sign reading WOODRUFF'S GARAGE, and two petrol pumps outside; and inside, three motor cars, and a small van; and at one of the pumps another car. Woodruff had enlarged his place since they left. She walked over, recognizing Mr Woodruff himself working the lever of the petrol pump back and forth.

"Good morning, Mr Woodruff," she said.

He looked up, but continued his work. "Why, good morning, Lady

Swanwick." A bit free and easy, she thought. No touching of the forelock, but friendly enough.

"I hope you and your family are all well," she said.

"Can't complain," he said. He turned his head and spoke to the driver of the car—"That's all she'll take . . . Seven and threepence . . . As I was saying, we can't complain. Our Tom came home to be married in March, but had to go right back out again afterwards. Our Horace got engaged to Carol Adams in September. They'll all be home soon, it looks like."

"I hope so," Lady Swanwick said. She remembered now that the elder Woodruff boy, Tom, had got a commission in the Wealds. How would that affect him when he came back to work in the garage here, and had to work the pump, as his father was now starting to do with a beer lorry? She said, "I didn't recognize that man in the car you just filled up."

Woodruff said, "No, m'lady. He and his wife come to live here in June . . . sort of accountant, he is, works in Hedlington but lives here. There'll be more like him as soon as we can get more houses built . . . small, modern ones, with decent plumbing, central heating even."

She said, "Well, I must be getting on." She wandered on, looking, observing . . . new paint on the post office front window . . . bakery chimney in worse repair than ever; Mr Jevons was really rather lazy . . . two new faces, both youngish women, shopping, so they presumably lived here . . . Ah, Mr Fulcher, his back to her, his hands clasped behind him, doing the same as she—observing. "Good morning, Mr Fulcher," she said.

He turned with the slow majesty of the law, his face changed, and his hand went to the peak of his helmet in a military salute—"Why, your ladyship . . . your ladyship . . ."

"I'm just visiting. How's your family . . . and you?"

"I'm as well as can be expected, seeing as I'm not getting any younger, milady. The missus was took ill last month, though. She was right bad and Doctor Kimball did everything he could, but she was getting worse, when Her Ladyship came down . . . Her new Ladyship"—he apologized—"and took her hand and sat with her all night. She was better next morning, but Her Ladyship sent for her chauffeur and took the missus to Hedlington General where they found out she had a sort of pneumonia, from the flu . . . before everybody else was getting it, this was . . . but in a week she was right as rain."

Interesting, Lady Swanwick thought; the Big House and perhaps the title are having their effect. She had not known Ruth Stratton, but she was probably a kindly enough soul; now she was becoming the Lady of Walstone, and carrying out her responsibilities.

She moved on. There was Mr Kirby, talking to Miss Hightower outside her little cottage. The rector's neck was hunched deep into his clerical collar and he was looking thinner in the face. Miss Hightower saw her first and exclaimed, "Lady Swanwick—how nice to see you here!"

The rector turned—"Well, well . . . you're looking well, Lady Swanwick . . . wish I could say the same of myself . . . getting older." A drop of rheum formed on the end of his nose and fell off onto his striped wool scarf, emblem of athletic prowess at his Oxford college in 1861. "Can't get around the parish as much as I used to . . . keep getting colds . . . not the flu, thank heaven."

"You should retire," the countess said "Weren't you thinking about that three years ago?"

The rector shook his old head and his white whiskers fluttered in the wind. "Who's the bishop going to find to replace me? I was hoping
  well, he's dead and gone, poor boy. When the war ends, perhaps . . ."

The countess walked on, heading now up the hill toward the Manor. The field across the road was where the village cricket team played, after they had picked up the cow pats. There was a new building near the gate into it, a smart green wooden hut with a little verandah, where there used to be nothing but, in the corner, an out-house for the men. Lady spectators were not supposed to have to go during a match, and there were no facilities for them. She walked through the open gate—the field contained no cows—and looked at the building. A brass plate on the front wall, beside the door, read "This pavilion was presented to the Walstone Cricket Club by Lord & Lady Walstone, July 18, 1918. IN MEMORY OF WALSTONE'S GLORIOUS DEAD."

She walked back out into the road. The pavilion was a nice gesture, though there would have to be a proper war memorial, too, when the fighting and the dying ended . . .

A smartly dressed young woman, passing the other way, paused and stopped, saying hesitantly, "It's Lady Swanwick, isn't it?"

The countess stopped, resting the point of her umbrella in the thin mud. She said, "Yes, but I don't think . . ."

"Adelaide Junkin, m'lady," the young woman said. "My father was cowman for Mr Taylor, and . . ."

"You won a scholarship from school and went to London, oh, ten years ago. I remember. You were very clever."

The woman said, "Thank you. Yes, I studied what they call Home Economics, and was teaching it in London—sort of day school for housewives—when my mother died."

"I didn't know."

"It was April. There was no one to look after Dad, so I had to come back."

Poor girl, the countess thought; dragged back from an interesting job and an independent life in London to look after her father, a crippled farm labourer, in a tiny cottage, in deepest Kent. She said, "You must miss your work."

The woman said, "Oh, yes, m'lady, but when Lady Walstone heard about me being qualified to teach Home Economics, she arranged for me to run two classes a week here . . . when all the women aren't down with flu! We have them in the school mostly, but sometimes we need a kitchen and then we can meet at the Big House, though we have to be sure there's nothing important on that night."

"I hope you get paid properly."

"Oh yes, m'lady . . . Lady Walstone gives me a pound a week, and the women pay sixpence a time, if they can. I get fifteen or twenty women in the class, mostly housewives, of course, but some girls just growing up, thirteen and fourteen . . ."

She spoke well, the countess thought, a London accent having replaced her Kentish burr. The girl was rattling on—"Lady Walstone's looking for a qualified nurse now to teach the women first aid and elementary home health care and medicine. Nowadays a lot of women want to learn how to tend to their families, especially what to do if someone catches this flu . . ."

"Quite," the countess said. They said their goodbyes and parted. Quite, she thought. The Swanwicks were not altogether forgotten here, but soon would be. The King is dead. Long live the King.

Now, in a few minutes she'd be at the Manor, and she must think what to say and what not to say. She could express her regret about Laurence, the poor boy. She could ask if he'd had any news of Margaret. She could commiserate over taxes . . . Christopher had no land left except the home farm . . . but what on earth could she say about Stella and the baby?

*   *   *   *

Ethel Fagioletti had recognized Lady Swanwick on the platform at Victoria, and had quickly entered a third-class compartment and looked out of the window on the far side. She saw the countess quite often, as Lady Swanwick came to Soho once a week, at least, to look after Charles while Lady Helen went shopping or visited her sister over in South Kensington. Ethel did not want to intrude or force herself on such a great lady; and she did not want to have to tell her why she was going down to Walstone. In fact her purpose was to visit Probyn's Woman; but Probyn was now head gamekeeper at the Park. To visit their cottage, Ethel would have to enter the grounds. And the gatekeeper would report that Lady Walstone's sister had visited, apparently without telling Lady Walstone. She had thought of entering the grounds by stealth, but she was no athlete, and the thought of being discovered was too embarrassing. So, she had had to arrange a visit to Ruth. Ruth had been delighted, in her letter, to invite her down . . . but then, how and when was she to be alone with Probyn's Woman? It was Lady Helen who had solved her dilemma. "Take a present down for Probyn and his Woman, from me," she'd said, "and tell your sister I asked you to deliver some private messages, personally. She won't question you." So it had been arranged . . . first, the formal visit; then, soon after lunch, she'd request to see Probyn's Woman; then back to the Big House for tea; then home . . .

At Walstone station she waited, half-hidden behind the station name board, until Lady Swanwick had gone; then she came out, crossed the road, and when Lady S was out of sight, took one of Mr Woodruff's taxis up to the Big House. The war was nearly over. If Niccolo was spared, he would soon be home. So this visit to Probyn's Woman had been arranged. By teatime she would know how to get pregnant. Probyn's Woman knew all about such things, and Ethel was to pay her two guineas to be told the secret, so that when Niccolo came back—*Sergeant Niccolo*—they would make love and, soon, soon, she would bear his child.

*   *   *   *

Lady Swanwick talked easily with Christopher Cate in the second-hand Daimler he had recently been persuaded to buy. He was still learning how to drive it, and was as yet by no means proficient at starting, and changing gears; but she felt safe enough, for there was little traffic on the roads, the weather fine and clear. She knew Cate well enough to ask after Isabel Kramer, the American widow who had been so frequent a visitor. It appeared that Mrs Kramer was living with her brother, Stephen Merritt, John's father; and that her son was now in France with the American infantry. Cate had asked after her children—Barbara, working at a riding school; and Helen—whose boutique was doing well: and whose baby was now six months old. They did not talk about Stella, or her baby, though she felt that Cate desperately needed to, but could not bring himself to do so, even to her. Stella herself had not appeared, nor her baby.

235

They reached the great steps of Walstone Park and Cate hurried round to help her down—"It's been nice to see you, Flora," he said.

"You, too, Christopher."

"Give my best to Roger. And come again . . . soon. There's always a bed for you—unless you'd prefer to accept Lord and Lady Walstone's hospitality."

She shook her head, "No, thanks. I knew Roger had to sell the place, but I loved it. I don't want to come back as a ghost . . . this visit will be bad enough." She turned. Lady Walstone was coming down the steps. Cate waved, got into the Daimler, and jerkily drove off down the long curved drive. The countess accompanied the baroness up the wide, formal steps.

*   *   *   *

They had had lunch—much too much food, served as though royalty were present. To Lady Swanwick's surprise, Ethel Fagioletti had joined them at the meal. She was tongue-tied during it and soon afterwards had disappeared on some mission to Probyn Gorse's cottage, leaving Lady Swanwick alone with the Walstones. They chatted aimlessly for a time; but small talk was not Hoggin's forte—he'd not been trained for it, and was obviously becoming impatient. Lady Swanwick judged her moment; and when she thought he was on the point of excusing himself, turned to Ruth Walstone and said, "Would you mind if I talked shop with your husband for a few moments . . . in private?"

Ruth started up—"Of course not, Lady Swanwick . . . I have plenty of things to do. When you're finished, just call for Chapman by that . . ."

"I know," Lady Swanwick said, smiling. Ruth hurried out.

Lord Walstone eyed the countess warily. What shop could she be knowing about? "Mind if I smoke?" he asked.

"Of course not," she said. Hoggin produced a fat cigar and lit it. Lady Swanwick said, "Lord Walstone, I want you to consider me for the position of an area manager in your H.U.S.L. chain."

Hoggin rocked back and forth on his heels in front of the fireplace, and his eyes narrowed. "Well, I don't know about that, your ladyship . . . What might be your qualifications in the food business?"

She said, "You have ninety-two shops open, all over the country. You plan to have a hundred by the end of the year, and you'll succeed unless there are hitches at Luton, Galashiels, and Barmouth. The other five shops are ready to open now."

" 'Ow did you learn all this?" Hoggin asked suspiciously.

"By reading the *Financial Times*," the countess said coolly. "You have divided the British Isles into ten areas, some geographically large, some small. London is an area in itself, for instance. Seven of your area managers are efficient, one is not, one is probably a crook, and one is very ill."

"That wasn't in the *Financial Times*," Walstone said, frowning at her.

"No. But I have been thinking of this for over four months, and I have been learning all I can about the administration of such a chain."

"Who've you been talking to?"

"Store managers," she said. "A countess can talk to anyone."

"You're right," he said grudgingly. "They'll all be flattered, particularly the women. Four of those area managers are women."

"Make it five," she said. "Dismiss the thief."

"But his area is London."

"So much easier for me. I won't have to move to Glasgow or Birmingham."

"You'd do that?"

She nodded, her fingers carelessly intertwined in her lap, her eyes on him—"Yes. But it would be a bore. I like London—and I know it."

Walstone said, "I know you can boss a lot of people . . . had a lot here, when it was yours, didn't you? But the H.U.S.L. stores is not there to look beautiful . . . or sell the best food . . . they're there to make money. We buy cheap and sell nearly as cheap. It'll be good publicity for me to have the Countess of Swanwick as area manager, specially in London, but"—he stabbed the air in her direction with his cigar—"you've got to make money, keep the managers' noses to the grindstone, see that no one fiddles, keep everything clean and simple and *cheap.*"

"I can do it," she said. "*And* make the stores look a little less like the inside of warehouses . . . serviced by automata."

He thought a long time, staring at her. Haughty, brainy, honest . . . guts . . . must be damned near starving to come to this. She needed the job, and she'd do it right. What was it they said, that meant that? *Noblesse oblige.* He'd seen it written out, and pronounced it *Nobles oblige.*

"All right," he said. "Done." He stuck out his hand.

The countess took it. "Thank you, Lord Walstone. When can I begin?"

*   *   *   *

Probyn's Woman said, "First, you got to go to a doctor, what specializes in women . . ."

"Gynaecologist," Ethel said.

". . . and have him make sure there's nothing wrong . . . there's things called polyps, and fibroids. It'll cost money, but it's got to be done, and I can't do it . . . don't have the microscopes and such."

"I'll do it," Ethel said, vaguely disappointed; but it made sense.

The Woman continued, "Then, you've got to keep your weight right . . . not too thin, not too fat. Your husband won't like you if you are, so you won't get as much seed . . . and being too fat or thin makes it more difficult for the egg to get fertile, see?" Ethel nodded. "Then, don't work too hard . . . don't work your fingers to the bone. A woman that's too tired won't conceive easy, see?" Ethel nodded again. "Now, you can lie anyway you like when your husband wants you, on your back, on top of him, but . . . which way do you usually do it?"

"Lying on my back," Ethel said, blushing, "with Niccolo on top of me."

"That's usually all right, but seeing you haven't got pregnant in all these years, try kneeling, and him coming in from behind, like you were dogs . . . but, when he's finished, don't jump up. Stay there, kneeling, for half an hour at least, with your head down and your tail stuck up . . . so the seed won't run out, see? . . . Do you wash yourself down there, afterwards, or use one of them douches?"

"Sometimes," Ethel said.

"Well, don't, not till the next morning, and then just ordinary washing, nothing stuck up inside . . . Now, that's all common sense, really, but it's all to help your body, that wants to conceive. But there's more than your body in this . . . making a baby is God's work, creating, see? He watches, and there's things He likes, and there's things He don't like . . . Eat coconuts . . . Do you have any green nighties?" Ethel shook her head. "Well, get some, and always wear green when your husband's making love . . . Wear old shoes . . . Share nuts and almonds with your husband before you make love . . . Keep a rabbit . . ."

"I can't, in London," Ethel wailed.

"A cat then, a female, and make love when the cat's in heat . . . eat lots of eggs when your husband's at home . . . Remember the maypole dances there always was here on May Day?" Ethel nodded. "Did you ever notice women chipping pieces off the maypole after it was pulled down on May 2nd?" Ethel nodded again. "Well, they kept the chips under their pillows. If they was unmarried, they'd get husbands. If they was married, they'd get pregnant . . . Now, there's things you can take, besides eggs and coconuts. Here's one . . . write this down . . . Take one pint of port wine . . ."

Ethel wrote eagerly in her notebook. This was more like it. She'd heard of love potions—who hadn't? The other things sounded queer, dotty . . . but the Woman knew what she was talking about.

*   *   *   *

Ron Gregory walked at the great Shire gelding's head, for Naomi, leaning on the plough handles, did not have enough strength left to guide the horse properly. They were ploughing the Home Thirty, both arrived yesterday from France on a short leave. Ron had not been thinking of leave, still less of visiting Naomi's home—but she had swept him off his feet; he had managed to persuade his C.O. to give him the leave; and here he was, trying to control and guide this behemoth of an animal.

"Hup, Duke! . . . Well done!" he gasped, as he struggled out of the way of the horse's huge, feathered hooves. "Hup!" He tugged to the left and Duke nearly pulled him off his feet.

"Not too much!" Naomi yelled. "Easy!"

"I'm trying," he gasped. "But he's so damned big!"

"Don't swear," she said. Half-turning his head he saw that she was laughing. He looked back. You couldn't let your attention wander for a moment . . . slowly up the long field, turning over the wet brown earth in long, shining curves, like waves . . . not very straight, one line wandering into another . . . a bit of land left untouched there, the wheat stubble still standing on it . . . couldn't be helped . . . turn Duke slowly, carefully—"Whoa back . . . hup now! Steady . . . Pull, boy, pull!" . . . down the field, into the October rain . . . back-breaking work, worse for Naomi, but at least she knew how to do it, while he, a city boy, knew nothing.

Half an hour later they paused. "Wish Helen was here," Naomi said, wiping the rain off her forehead. "She could plough as well as Hillman . . . he was our ploughman—joined up when the war began."

"Who's Helen?" Ron asked.

"Lady Helen Durand-Beaulieu, that was. She worked as a labourer here for a long time. She has a boutique in London now. She's married and has a baby."

She thought she would marry Ron Gregory, but he was not yet a member of the family. He did not yet need to know about Stella; or that Helen's baby was her brother Boy's, killed near Passchendaele last winter . . . Winter was coming again. And this flu . . . everyone down with it, or had been, or would be. And Daddy—dead.

"Ready?" she said.

"When you are." He stood up. They had been resting under a tree by the gate, Duke standing with one hoof arched, just touching the ground, five yards from them, his coat wet and dark, water running in rivulets under the plough harness.

"You ought to get a tractor," Ron said.

"We women can do it till the men come back," she said.

"But I think the men'll want tractors. And in the long run it'll save money, because you'll be able to get more done with fewer labourers."

"Perhaps," she said. "Ready? Hup, Duke . . . hup, I say!" Duke arched his mighty neck and plunged one heavy leg forward, then the next . . . the plough moved slowly up the field, curving the earth behind it in the rain.

*　　*　　*　　*

They were sitting in the drawing room before dinner, the five of them—Naomi, her mother Louise Rowland, the two Women's Land Army girls Joan Pitman and Addie Fallon; and Ron Gregory, the lone man.

Louise eyed Ron surreptitiously. Naomi had telephoned from Southampton the day before yesterday that she had a short leave, and was bringing a young man with her, a lieutenant of Royal Engineers. This was the young man . . . Boy's clothes fitted him, after a fashion, and by now she had got over the frisson of shock at seeing this stranger in her son's Donegal tweed coat and knickers. He seemed inoffensive enough . . . obviously very admiring of Naomi . . . talked all dinner time, yesterday, about the time they first met, in a German bombing raid, and how wonderful she'd been. It wasn't so clear what Naomi felt about him; no overwhelming passion, certainly. There'd be no recurrence of what had happened between Boy and Lady Helen last year. Naomi wasn't the sort to be swept off her feet. Well, any woman could be, by the right man, at the right moment in her life . . .

"It's a shame that the house is like a hospital ward, on your leave," Addie Fallon said to Ron.

"It can't be helped," he said. "I only wish I could be more use, but I'm afraid they didn't teach me any nursing at Birmingham University—just electrical engineering."

Naomi said, "What are you going to do after the war's over, Ron?"

Ron said, "I don't know . . . Get a job with Lucas, or some other big electrical engineering firm. Though all engineering uses electricity now . . . even shipbuilding. There's a great deal of electrical work in a ship—and the amount is increasing every day."

"What about cars?" Naomi said. "They have electricity, too."

"Certainly," Ron said. "Ignition coils or sparking plugs, lighting systems, some of the gauges . . ."

Naomi was staring across the table at the young man with a half

240

frown. She wasn't thinking of him at all, really, her mother knew; but of some personal plan or project.

Naomi said, "I think the lighting system on our ambulances is very poor. It's no better on any other cars that I've driven, or know of. . . . and I've driven many different makes since I joined the Women's Volunteer Motor Drivers in 1915."

"I quite agree," Ron said eagerly. "I've even thought of designing a better system myself, but . . ."

"You have? And you could do it?"

Ron answered, a little uneasy at her intenseness, "Yes, I think so. I'd have to do some experimental work first . . . To make something really better, really more reliable, we might have to look at different metal for circuits, better switches, better batteries."

Naomi said, "There's a great future for sub-contractors in the motor car business. They make a lot of money, without locking up so much capital as the actual manufacturers. Suppose we founded a firm which made good lighting systems for cars and lorries—practically *all* cars and lorries . . . Who owns the Shell Filling Factory, Mummy?"

Louise was startled at the sudden question—"Why . . . why, I think your Uncle Richard does, still, though we all have some financial interest. The Government gave him a loan to convert to shell filling, I think, but I'm sure that's been paid back . . . Why do you ask?"

Naomi said, "The war will end soon—we all know that. The Government will cancel all orders for shells—they have millions and millions of them stocked here and in France. Uncle Richard can't restart the Rowland Motor Car Company and make cars—there are too many other new firms in the field. I want to buy the factory buildings and make electrical systems for cars and lorries in them."

"Good gracious!" Louise exclaimed, feeling a little dizzy. "You, by yourself? Why, it's . . ."

"Not by myself," she said. "With Ron. We are going to get married . . . as soon as he asks me."

Ron Gregory was staring at her in open-mouthed astonishment. This was the girl he'd met under the bombs—brave, bold, determined . . . Of course, he wanted to marry her. He had been in love with her since that night. But he had not so far brought himself to ask her . . . she was too much above him, she would marry a young colonel with a title and three D.S.O.s . . . He rose slowly to his feet and, the words coming out one by one, said, "Will . . . you . . . marry . . . me?"

"Yes," she said. "As soon as the war's over . . . Meantime, keep working on your electrical plans for cars . . . We'll spend the rest of our leaves seeing where we can get the money we'll need. I have quite a bit, but we'll need more, so . . ." She returned to her dinner, not realizing that the other four in the room were staring at her, silent, amazed.

*   *   *   *

The two figures were lost in the huge room, mannequins in miniature satin chairs against the twelve-foot velvet curtains, and, continuing their stately march round the walls, the tall portraits in the heavily gilt frames. Ruth always felt this sense of smallness when she was in here. Of course it was her own fault; Lady Swanwick would have had her daughters in here, and the boys when they were younger, and their friends, and perhaps a footman or two standing by the door ready to take orders . . . at any rate, enough people to fill the room and make it seem what it was, a large, luxuriously furnished living room for a large and rich family.

The bigness didn't bother Bill Hoggin at all. He hardly noticed it, except to note that it was cold away from the two fireplaces, one at each end; but what house in England wasn't cold, in winter? He was smoking a cigar, and slowly twirling a glass of port in his hand, idly admiring the ruby colour of the wine and savoring the perfume of the Havana tobacco. His wife, who was knitting a khaki wool scarf, said, "I wish you wouldn't smoke in here, Bill. The smoke stays in the curtains and the upholstery. You should use the smoking room."

"We never had no smoking room before we bought this place," Hoggin said. "And you was, were happy enough to have your hubby there in the parlor even if he was smoking a fag . . . fags was all I could afford then. Now you want to send me off to the other end of this bleeding pile, ha, ha, that's a good 'un!"

She said patiently, "We didn't have people like the Duke and Duchess of Taunton to the house before."

"Then, why don't we both sit in the smoking room when we're alone? Or in the library—that's where Swanwick and Lady S used to sit, I know 'cos Chapman told me . . . Or build a little room at the back just for us."

"That would be very expensive," she said. "And we really have plenty of rooms, even with the H.U.S.L. headquarters here, and all the space they take up."

He said, "We can afford it. We can afford *anythink*, Ruthie. This has been a good year for me . . . very good. I've made a mint, I can tell you. I can have anything I want. So can you. Five-hundred-quid guns for me . . . what about a five-thousand-quid diamond for you? That'd show 'em, eh?"

She put down her knitting and looked up at him. She said, "I've been thinking about that, Bill. I mean, you being so rich. When you were a little boy, you didn't get enough to eat."

"Stone the crows, I didn't even wiv what I stole from the barrows!"

"And you went barefoot and cold and wet. And you watched rich folk through hotel and restaurant windows, eating beef and drinking champagne, and you saw them riding about in big carriages with four horses and footmen on the box . . . Now you've got it all."

"That's the bleeding fact," Bill said with satisfaction.

"But what are you going to do—get—now? You can't eat more than three square meals a day. You can't buy more than one or two pairs of those expensive guns. You have two Rolls Royce motor cars and goodness knows how many suits from Mr Poole and boots from Mr Maxwell . . . So what are you going to do now?"

Bill was puzzled. He said, "Why, fucking enjoy it, that's what."

"Bill! I mean, this is what you were aiming at, what you wanted to be and to have, from the time you were little. Now you have it, and are it . . . *now* what is to be your purpose in life? You're not old, you know. You have many more years to live."

Bill scratched his head. Trust women to put you a poser. He'd never thought of it the way Ruthie put it; but now he did, and it was a puzzle. He might answer—just make more money . . . and more . . . and more . . . But to tell the truth, he was already a little bored with the money, and the making of it no longer interested him that much. That's why he'd hired Lady Swanwick; it still interested her—'cos she hadn't got any, like she used to.

At length he said, "I don't know, Ruthie."

She said, "Well, think about it. I know what I want—to help the people of Walstone in every way I can. I never thought I'd be in a position to do it, but now I am, and I will, as much as they'll let me. But you? Walstone's too small for you . . . You ought to do something for England."

"What the 'ell can *I* do?" Hoggin wailed. "All I've ever known is how to buy cheap and sell dear. And I can't teach anyone that what doesn't already have it in their bones. I don't know anything about music, painting, dancing . . . except those girls at the Gaiety, waving their petticoats in the air . . . Books! I never read one in my life, except in school."

"There's no great hurry," she said equably, picking up her knitting, "but think, dear. Keep thinking. Anything you hear about, think whether it might be for you, a place for you to use your talents, *and* your money, for the rest of your life."

Chapman came in, after knocking discreetly. "Mr Cate has called, my lord. He's in the Constable Room."

"Bring him up." Chapman went out and Hoggin looked at his wife. "At last he's going to tell us. But what the hell can we say?"

"We don't have to say anything, Bill," she said, "except that we understand . . . that we will support him and Stella, whatever they decide to do."

Daily Telegraph, Saturday, October 12, 1918

BEYOND THE MEUSE

AMERICANS ADVANCE

American Army (France), Thursday (Noon)

There is, at last, progress to report along the whole front, and our line now extends for some miles beyond the Meuse. The operations on that flank for pushing the Boche away from the river were designed with skill and daring, and have proved entirely successful, and the result of the attack has been to thrust back the battle-line to the position it occupied when the Germans launched their formidable offensive against Verdun in 1916. The heights of the Meuse narrow down to a mere bottle-neck where our front of yesterday joined it. And it was this narrowness that created the difficulties of attack, the southern front being so short and the western covered by the river . . .

The risk was run, and an American unit was sent across the Meuse to Remiville . . .

Cate read on. He was in his study, reading newspapers some days old, because now at last he could concentrate; for he had told his world what it had a right to know. This had swept out the murk which had occupied his mind these last ten days. Only one person remained who must be told: Stella's husband, John Merritt.

After a while he put the newspapers aside, and went upstairs. Stella was sitting up in bed feeding the baby, which was dark brown, with short straight silky black hair, greeny-grey eyes, and high cheek bones.

Cate sat down on the edge of the bed and scratched the baby's back, as it dug both tiny brown hands into Stella's white breast, gasping and gurgling in its hunger.

He said, "Yesterday, I told all our relatives about the baby's colour. How shall we tell John? Do you want to wait till he comes home?"

Stella did not look well, nor did he feel that she was really present. The small doses of the drug that were being administered to her seemed to keep her in this state; but the doctor had warned him that unless action was taken to cure her of her addiction, larger doses would soon be needed; and larger doses had other dangers, involving increased psychological and physical addiction.

She said, her voice small and hoarse—"I don't know . . . He should not be surprised . . . There were all sorts of men by the docks, where I was . . ."

Cate said, "I think I'll go to Virgil Kramer—he's still Secretary of Embassy—and see if he can somehow get a personal private message out to John by hand. If he can not, then I think it would be best to wait."

"All right," Stella said. She glanced down at the feeding baby with lacklustre eyes.

Cate steeled himself—"And, Stella, the doctor says that the baby must be weaned within a week. Otherwise it will start to get addicted, through your milk."

"All right," Stella said again.

London: October, 1918

14 "Sweete Themmes runne softly," Guy Rowland murmured, stretching back in his chair, cup of tea in hand. It was a lovely warm afternoon of autumn, the plane trees dropping crisp brown leaves along the Embankment, the river flowing softly, as Spenser had begged it, toward the sea; but the tide had only just turned and soon the current would be a swarming, rushing of waters, carrying out under the arches of Westminster Bridge the barrels and flotsam, and pulling the barges fast down toward the Pool and the lower reaches.

Guy, in the new blue uniform of a major of the Royal Air Force, was having tea on the terrace of the House of Commons with his grandfather, Harry Rowland M.P. He had been back in England a week, officially posted home to bring the Air Ministry up to date on the experience of the squadrons actually facing the enemy; but, he knew, in reality relieved of command of the Three Threes. He had been proposing to wear his old R.F.C. uniform, as officers of the Royal Air Force were entitled to do; but the Chief of the Air Staff, Sir Frederick Sykes, would not hear of it; and had ordered him to have a uniform made at once. It was important, the general said, that the public should come to recognize and accept the new uniform, and no better way to do that than to have it worn by a man entitled to put up the ribbons of the V.C., the D.S.O., and the M.C. It was a bright pale blue, somewhat Ruritanian, but that didn't bother Guy because he really didn't care what it, or he, looked like. The killing of von Rackow had numbed him. That was why the wing commander had sent him home, with his score at 66. It would not grow any bigger. Mick Mannock would remain the top British ace, as Richthofen would be the German, von Rackow close behind him—all three dead.

A heavyset man in a frock coat stopped by their table and held out his hand, "I'm Carson . . . This must be your nephew, Guy Rowland." Guy was on his feet, shaking the proffered hand. Carson was saying, "We're all proud of you. After the war, if you want to come to Ulster, Ulster's yours . . . member of our parliament, a good job with one of the shipbuilding firms, anything."

He moved on, nodding. Guy sat down again. His grandfather said, "He thinks you'd be a counter to your Aunt Margaret. He knows all about her . . . talked to me about her the other day."

Another man stopped beside the table—"Good afternoon, Rowland. May I be introduced to the young hero? No, no, please don't stand up, either of you."

Harry sank back—"Guy . . . Mr Winston Churchill, the Minister of Munitions . . . Major Guy Rowland."

Churchill said, "Congratulations on your magnificent achievements, young man. Thanks to you, and others like you, we're on the last lap . . . at last. What are you proposing to do with yourself after the war?"

Guy said, "I don't know, sir. I haven't thought."

"Well, think. How old are you . . . twenty-one, twenty-two? We need young men like you in the councils of this country, sir. Men of action as well as of intellect. Men to translate verbiage into deeds. Men to unify the diverse energies of the nation and harness them toward a future even greater than our glorious past. Anything you may want to do, or have, is within your reach. You may count on my full support to get it for you. And I am not without some small influence in industry as well as politics . . . some small influence." He chuckled, lifted his cigar and moved on.

Harry said, "I hope you don't mind being shown off a bit. We're all so numbed by the war that a real hero is as good a tonic as a beautiful young woman might have been in our younger days, eh, eh?" A waiter brought them a second plate of buttered crumpets. Harry took one, leaned back, and said, "Well, Guy, if you really have no idea what you want to do, consider this"—he waved his hand at the towering facade of the Houses of Parliament. "As you know, I am going to apply for the Chiltern Hundreds as soon as the next election is announced. Why do you not stand in my place?"

Guy said slowly, "I hadn't thought of it, Grandfather . . . I suppose I could do the job, if I were elected. It can't be too difficult, seeing . . ."

"Seeing what asses do become M.P.s," his grandfather finished for him. "Quite right!"

"But . . . just now, it's impossible for me to think of anything with enthusiasm."

"Stale," Harry said, nodding. "That's natural. You were out over two years, weren't you . . . heaven knows how many aerial combats . . . sixty-six kills, not counting balloons . . ."

"But including von Rackow," Guy said.

"But you couldn't help it," Harry said. "You've told me, it was an accident . . . a terrible accident, as you'd promised yourself not to attack him, but an accident just the same."

"Was it?" Guy said. "I keep thinking back. All night I lie awake, seeing that Triplane dart out of the cloud across my front . . . The pilot's hand came up in a wave almost at once . . . my thumb was on the trigger, but an idea was in my head, two ideas—Why is he waving? Can it be Werner? . . . Simultaneously, it's a German, fire or he'll get away into the other cloud mass . . . But which came first? Did I fire deliberately, because I need to kill, knowing in my heart of hearts that it was von Rackow?"

Harry put his hand over his grandson's and said, "You mustn't think about it, my boy. You mustn't . . ." A shadow fell across the table and both men rose. The Prime Minister was standing beside them, a sheaf of papers in his hand, his heavy mane of hair stirring in the soft breeze. "You're Rowland," he said. "Harry here's grandson . . . Do you think there should be a separate air force or not?"

Guy said, "Yes, sir. The air covers the land and the sea. Airmen think and see differently. The air force would not be thought of as just another arm, like artillery. If you've grown up in it, you are three-dimensional."

"H'm . . . See Smuts when you have time. Tell him I sent you to have your brains picked. Anything you want?"

Guy said nothing, not understanding. The Prime Minister said impatiently, "Job? Medal? Promotion? Travel? . . . I'll send you round America if you like . . . lots of pretty women eager to get into your bed, parties all the time, and it won't cost you a penny."

"No, thank you, sir," Guy said. "I'm just . . . tired."

The Prime Minister nodded and walked rapidly away along the terrace.

*　　*　　*　　*

A bachelor gay am I tho' I've suffered from
Cupid's dart

But never I vow will I say die, In spite of
   an aching heart
For a man always loves a girl or two, Tho'
   the fact must be confessed
He always swears the whole way thro' To
   every girl he tries to woo,
That he loves her far the best.

The singer flung out his arms and swung into the chorus, everyone in Daly's Theatre humming with him; for this song from Freddie Lonsdale's musical comedy *The Maid of the Mountains* was as well known as Tipperary:

At seventeen he falls in love quite madly
With eyes of a tender blue,
At twenty-four he gets it rather badly
With eyes of a different hue.
At thirty-five you'll find him flirting sadly
With two or three or more.
When he fancies he is past love,
It is then he meets his last love,
And he loves her as he's never loved before.

Guy's companion in the box was a tall young woman with a placid face and deep, dark blue eyes, Helen Rowland—née Lady Helen Durand-Beaulieu. She and Guy had known each other all their lives, though Helen was five years older. Guy knew that she had borne his cousin Boy's baby, and had gone to call on her on his second day in London. She was living in a poky little house in Soho, though large enough for Helen, the baby, and Ethel Fagioletti (née Stratton), who owned the house, and worked for Helen in her Mayfair boutique. He had persuaded Helen to come out to the theatre with him; and she had agreed. He was wearing uniform, unwillingly, but General Sykes had given him a flat order to wear it on all occasions . . . and so, on arrival to claim the stall seats the Keith Prowse people had got for him, the theatre manager took one look at the ribbons on his chest and escorted them instead to this box, over the stage on the prompt side.

Helen leaned across and whispered in his ear, "What colour are *your* love's eyes?"

Guy muttered back, "That's a secret."

"Do you still see Florinda? You used to spend all your time with her, when you were ten. I was fifteen and despised boys, and thought love was stupid . . . but I suspected you of being in love with her."

"I haven't seen her this time," Guy said. "I read all the time about her with Billy Bidford, so . . ."

"She couldn't have been seen with you while you were in France, could she? You ought to call on her. She's in the phone book . . . She's been to see us a couple of times. She's nice, really nice."

Then they were quiet for a time, and stayed in their box during the intervals as Guy could not face the mobbing he knew he would receive if they went to the bar. As the end of the show approached he began to fidget and glance over his shoulder . . . they could get away now, and no one would notice; but Helen was enjoying herself so much, her face rapt, her chin cupped in her hands. Too late . . . the cast was lining up. A spotlight was turned suddenly onto their box and the whole of the cast was facing them. The leading lady stepped forward, holding a single large chrysanthemum to her breast. She began to sing, directly at him, where he sat frozen, barely fifteen feet from her.

> At seventeen I fell in love quite madly
>   with eyes of a tender blue.
> At twenty-four I got it rather badly
>   with eyes of a different hue.
> At thirty-five you found me flirting madly
>   with two or three or more
> But when I fancied I am past love, It is
>   now I've met my last love
> And I'll love you as I've never loved before.

She threw the chrysanthemum gently up into the box, where Guy instinctively caught it, then sank slowly into a deep curtsy, one hand to her breast. Marian de Forges was the darling of the musical comedy theatre, a good actress with a great voice, who could dominate powerful dramatic roles as easily as such mild fluff as this. She was of medium height, with flashing dark eyes, and probably of gypsy blood; no one knew her real name. She had never been married, though her name had been linked with half a dozen men's, including King Edward VII in her youth, the Kaiser, King Alfonso III of Spain, and Toscanini.

The theatre was on its collective feet, clapping and cheering. The building shook and swayed to the thunderous applause. "Stand up," Helen shouted, in his ear. "Bow."

Slowly he rose, the chrysanthemum in his hand. He saw the mouths open wide, heard the sounds, the orchestra, Marian de Forges singing, her arm raised . . . von Rackow's arm raised, in salute, in death.

*   *   *   *

The office was a shabby little place off Aldgate, a small old house that looked as if it might have been one of the survivors of the Great Fire of 1666, with three steps up to the front door and a small brass plate beside it, reading in a flowing script, *Toledano's, Bankers.* Inside the door a narrow dusty passage led a long way toward the back of the house, which was surprisingly deep, with doors opening off to each side. Behind those doors, which were all shut, little old men sat on high stools, stooped over large ledgers, writing with quill pens dipped in pewter inkwells. An urchin of about fourteen, gawky in trousers and coat he had outgrown, sat on a chair in the passage reading *The Boys' Own Paper.* He was the office boy and messenger. No women were employed at Toledano's. At the very end of the passage, the door on the right looked no different from any of the others, but behind it was the private office of old Isaac Toledano, son of the founder of the bank, and its sole owner. He had a small table instead of a sloping desk like the clerks down the hall, and there was a telephone on the desk, which was otherwise all but empty. A seven-branched menorah decorated the mantelpiece; there was no fire in the grate below, the windows were grimy and in one place patched with brown paper. The room seemed barely large enough for the desk, the old man, and his visitor, a young man resplendent in Royal Air Force blue.

Isaac said, "It ith good of you to come and see me."

"Glad to come, sir," Guy Rowland said. The old man must go out of his way, he thought, to look like a caricature of a Jew—curls like Disraeli was always shown wearing, a big hooked nose, a black hat he had only just taken off, when Guy was shown in by the office boy, and a black skull cap under it, frayed old black clothes. It was a wonder he was not wearing a mediaeval robe.

"We have met before," Isaac said. "Speech Day at Wellington. 1911."

"Yes, sir." Guy was surprised the old man remembered. He himself remembered very well because it had been his first Speech Day and he had admired David Toledano for being, and showing himself, so obviously proud of the bizarre figure of his father. Most boys were acutely embarrassed by their parents, who, they thought, wore the wrong clothes, or greeted ushers in too friendly a manner, or walked on the sacred Turf; but if David cared, he didn't show it.

"Vell, David writes that you are a very bright young man and I would do well to employ you . . . Vot do you think vill happen to the world ven the war ith over? Vot vill people need?"

Guy said slowly, "Reconstruction, first, sir, I think . . . roads, railways, houses, ships . . . But if there's one thing the war has taught it is that man can't compete with machines. In France, it was the machine guns and artillery and tanks . . . but the artillery couldn't have been supplied without lorries. And people are going to ask for more for themselves. I think that machinery will take over and . . ."

"In what area of bithneth?"

"Everywhere, sir . . . manufacture, retailing as far as possible, accounting, road making, shoe making, the lot."

"Vot about chemicals? Vill they grow?"

"I suppose so . . . especially chemicals that are used in machine making . . . better chemicals. We use chemicals for practically everything, already, to make batteries, steel, porcelain for insulators, to dope the wings of aircraft . . ."

"Aircraft. I remember David telling me that he vos hoping to start a new aircraft-manufacturing company, with you as a test pilot, he called it, and some other boy as designer. Do you still think there vill be a great increase in the demand for aircraft, once the war ith over?"

Guy said, "I wish I could say so . . . but I don't see how it's possible. I think we must have a British commercial airline at once, to fly regularly to all the big cities of Europe. But I don't see how it can need many aircraft—yet."

Isaac nodded and stroked his pendulous lower lip—"The Americans are going to be very powerful when the war's over. They will take over our markets—they are doing it now . . . unless we form companies big enough to fight them . . . You know Mond and Isaacs?"

"Sir Alfred Mond and Sir Rufus Isaacs? I've heard of them, sir."

"We've been talking about forming a big British chemical group. I'd like Isaacs to manage it, but he ith too much of a politician . . . and a lawyer." He looked up—"You can work for me as soon as you get out of the air force. I will pay you 5,000 pounds a year for one year. After that, we shall see."

Guy said, "I'm afraid . . ."

Isaac held up his hand. "The war ithn't over yet, young man. David ith not back. Who is to say some German bomb may not drop on you here in London, even after all you have escaped in France? . . . Come, it ith teatime."

He stood up with some difficulty and led the way out of the door and up a flight of stairs. A door at the head of the stairs blocked access to the second story. The old man produced a key from his coat pocket, opened the door, and waved Guy through. As the door closed behind him Guy felt that he had been transported into some new Aladdin's Cave. The light was soft, and coloured. Persian and Turkish rugs covered the floor and hung on the walls. There was a faint smell of incense, and gold gleamed everywhere, in the decorations, the menorah, the candlesticks on the inlaid walnut table. The old man led through an opening barred by hanging silk curtains into a room of pure luxury, and as purely oriental . . . low divans, silk cushions, the same subdued coloured light, a small reflecting pool, curved gold pipes, gold statues, one, in a corner, five feet high, of a naked girl.

A dark-haired young woman rose from the cushions and came forward. She bowed deeply to the old man, and said, "Tea is ready, Father. Shall I bring it in?"

He gestured and she went out. "Sit down," he said, "anywhere . . . that chair has a hard back, I believe." He himself lay back carefully on the cushions. The young woman returned and served them tea. Isaac said, "This is my daughter, Rebecca. Rebecca, this is Major Rowland."

She was nineteen or twenty, resembling more the typically Semitic features of her father than the heavy bluffness of her elder brother David. She said, with eyes lowered, "I have seen pictures of you in the papers, sir. David talked of you when he was at Wellington, so I have been cutting out everything about you."

"There has been much," the old man said.

The girl remained standing as the two men ate and drank. She served sweet biscuits in a silver tray and thin spread sandwiches. Then the old man made some sign which Guy did not catch, and she picked up the tea tray and left the room.

After a while the smell of incense became stronger, and now someone was playing a zither in another room. The old man said, "We must wait till David comes back. The war's finished there, but . . . we must wait till he comes back. If he comes back, he will inherit the bank . . . not yet, but soon. But he will need a chief man he can trust at his side . . . a man with more brains than David has. He spent all his time playing your Rugby football . . . and that is good too, for a banker, in England. But he will lean on someone whose brain is faster and better than his. It is my responsibility to see that he does not choose the wrong man . . . by giving him the right man. So . . . this right man would never own the bank, but he would do well . . . as well as anyone else in England . . . And if David does not come back, I will not have a son . . . Do you like the theatre?"

"Very much, sir."

"Good. I will arrange for two seats for you to a good play for tonight. You will take Rebecca. She has never been out alone with a man before, but she knows the world. She will not disgrace you. My chauffeur will bring her to the Grosvenor Hotel at eight o'clock. You may take her to the Savoy Hotel for dinner afterwards—the bill will have been paid. After that, bring her back here. The chauffeur will then return you to the Grosvenor."

Guy started to say something, feeling that he ought; but what was there to say?

*   *   *   *

"More potatoes, sir? Another beer?" Ex-Battery Sergeant Major Robinson was half on his feet, ready to serve his brother-in-law, beside him at the little table, with more mashed potatoes.

"No, thanks," Guy said. "I've had enough . . . though they're very good." He smiled at his sister, across the table from him, the new baby cradled in her arms. "And Stan, please don't call me 'sir' in here. I'm only wearing uniform because the C.A.S. has ordered me to . . . and because I have to wear it when I go over to Wellington."

Stan sat down, shaking his head, "Can't help it, Guy. Being in the army so long, it just comes before I can think, when I know you're a major." He laughed and began collecting food in one corner of his plate with his fork, then expertly scooping it up and into his mouth; as he had no left arm his wife cut up the meat for him before setting his plate on the table. He said, "Well, I'm out of the army now and I s'pose if I had an ordinary job, I'd soon forget about saluting, but I can't get an ordinary job, can I? Ruddy lucky to get this one, that's the truth. And here it's 'sir,' 'sir,' 'sir' just as much as it was in the army—even to kids no more than thirteen, with their voices not yet broken." He looked directly at Guy—"It don't seem right to me, Guy, if you don't mind my saying so."

Guy finished his food and laid down his knife and fork on the side of his plate. Wellington had taught him to eat fast, and here Stan had the disadvantage of lacking an arm, while Virginia was holding baby Kate in her arm, so he was far ahead of them. He said, "Have you always felt like this? That the class system here was all wrong?"

Stan swallowed and continued masticating his forkful of food; then said, "A bit, perhaps, but I was in the Regular Army, see? We respected our officers because they risked their lives more than we did. When something dangerous had to be done, they were always there. But after 1914 there wasn't no Regular Army. The officers we got—that were coming in when I was wounded, that was doing the cushy jobs back here in Blighty, they were all sorts. But civvy street's not like the army. We knew what our officers did to get their pay and the pips on their shoulders. We *don't* know what the bosses do to get all their money and Rolls Royces, except perhaps that their dad made a pile. My dad's a working man. I'm a working man. The working man's done his bit in this war, over there and back here, and what we're going to be asking for is a fair chance . . . a fair chance our kids can be Prime Ministers, or *bara sahibs*, or major generals."

Virginia had been sitting quiet, her eyes, always full of warmth and proud love, moving constantly from her husband, to her brother, to her daughter. She said now, "Stan thinks . . . he realized that Kate wouldn't have as good a chance in life as your baby . . . he doesn't mean just yours, of course . . . because of her accent, which she'll learn from him."

"And from you too, now," Guy said. "You've been working hard at it so they won't think you're hoity-toity when you visit Stan's people in Leeds. Mummy's horrified at it."

Virginia said, "I haven't really tried hard, it's just changed naturally, as I suppose it would have if I'd married an American or a Scotsman . . . But it's true, isn't it, what Stan says?"

Guy said, "Yes. But leadership in commerce and industry isn't the same as military leadership. It involves getting to the front of progress . . . perhaps cutting down on labour . . . making bigger profits . . ."

Stan said, "More scholarships to the posh schools would help. The Government could give 'em the money."

"Which the schools wouldn't take," Guy said. "If they did, the Government would be able to control what and how they teach . . . I don't see why industries shouldn't be persuaded to subscribe to scholarship programmes like that . . . all such scholarship funds could be tax deductible . . . There are ways."

Stan said earnestly, "We've got to find a way, Guy. We've got to have the same sort of feeling between the employers and the workers that we had in the trenches. After all, they're in the same boat, in a factory, as they are over there, in the trenches."

Guy said, "I agree, but it's going to be very difficult without equality of sacrifice. And giving money's not the same as . . . giving an arm."

He stood up—"I've got to go soon. I have to be at the Master's Lodge at half-past two, and I'm speaking in Great School at three. The Master wants me to talk about air fighting . . . how I shot down Immelmann, Boelcke, and Richthofen in single combat . . . the chivalry of the air . . . *but* must also stress the beastliness of the Hun . . . I suppose I'll have to give the boys their money's worth. It's hard to believe that nearly half of them were there when I left, three years ago . . . but I think I'll have to say something about what ought to be done next, in England, and the world. The war's nearly over, and they have to think of that now, the same as the rest of us."

*   *   *   *

The telephone rang, and the hotel exchange operator said, "Call for you, sir. Do you wish to be disturbed?"

"Put it through." Marian de Forges was speaking, wearing a beige gown and a hat, lolling on a couch in a French drawing room—"It was a privilege to sing for you the other night. I have a present for you."

"All right. Come round." Guy sank back, lighting a cigarette. A detachment of Guards marched by the window on their way to Buckingham Palace. Funny, his room was on the fourth floor, the music loud and martial, setting his feet to tapping in their Grecian leather slippers. He adjusted his dressing gown and went to the door where someone had knocked. He opened it. It wasn't Marian de Forges but a taller, younger woman, blue eyes, wide set in a longish face, oval chin, a diamond ring and a wedding ring. A small parcel dangled by a string from one finger—"Philippa," she said, "Duchess of Kendal . . . I have come to give you this, on behalf of the women of England." It was a box, which she couldn't open, lots of boxes, one within the other. The carpet was disappearing under paper and string—"This!" She pressed the catch, the lid flew open. Resting on a bed of watered silk was the winged badge of a Royal Air Force pilot, created in enamel, diamonds, and rubies.

He looked up. Her sable coat was off, and she was slowly unbuttoning her dark blue dress. He felt an erection growing as the curve of her bosom began to appear. There was a knock on the door, it was opened from outside and Marian de Forges sailed in, head high, carrying a huge box. She was wearing dove-grey and theatre make-up. She stopped, staring at the duchess, and said, "It *is* hot in here," took off her astrakhan coat, and began to unbutton her dress, meanwhile saying, "Open the parcel, Guy."

The room was filling with spectators, men and women, in the stands. He was fumbling with the parcel, more boxes within boxes. At last, the smallest one—a wristwatch, the case solid gold, the band gold in stretch links. On the back it was inscribed *To Guy from all of us*. The spectators were cheering and a band playing. The duchess screamed, "Who's 'all of us'? All you stage whores?" They were both practically naked now. The door opened and Florinda walked in. The crowd cheered wildly and Maria von Rackow, at his elbow, said seriously, "Make up your mind, Guy."

Florinda said, "I came to suggest a walk in the Park, Guy, but I see you're going to take your exercise indoors." Her clothes came off in a whirl, as though she was the centre of a cyclone. The grass was ankle-deep in tissue paper, petticoats, and champagne glasses. He had his fly buttons undone and his prick out, stiff as a pole, aching for their cunts, all now on display. They were rotating slowly in the centre of the floor, arms raised and arched over their heads. They sang in chorus, "Anything you want, Butcher, except . . ." Then they were silent. The crowd had all left and it was raining. The duchess screamed, "I got here first! Get out, you bitches!" Marian de Forges said, "Put it in!" Florinda began to cry, and Guy took her bare shoulders, "Darling, Flo . . . don't cry . . . I love you. I love you." She sank into his arms, and he awoke, his pillow wet with sweat and tears.

It was six and he could not get back to sleep, but lay in bed, staring at the ceiling, as the light grew. At half-past eight the waiter came up with his breakfast and the morning papers . . . Armies sweeping across the Lys Canal . . . British troops approaching Mons, Guy read. Mons, that was the first British battle of the war. It was a Sunday, like today. He remembered leaning out of his window, looking across the Combermere Quad and wondering where his father was. In those days the guns could not be heard in Kent, and certainly had never reached Berkshire, or even London, they were so small and few. He yawned and poured himself another cup of coffee. Yesterday had been a tiring day. Stan Robinson had made him think and that was always more tiring than mere physical activity. The only thing more exacting was physical fear. You wouldn't think it took much out of one to fly an aeroplane in good weather for an hour and a half, and it didn't in peace. But send the same pilot in the same machine up into aerial combat, and he'd come back—if he did—sweat-soaked, trembling, and exhausted. Then there had been the drive over to Wellington, half an hour with the Master . . . Mr Vaughan hadn't changed, still like a slightly puzzled bear, still liked to pop into his library through a concealed swinging section of books; he had recalled how Guy had tried to save Dick Yeoman from being sacked, but he didn't mention Dick's offence; too delicate, rather shameful . . . And after the lecture, wandering about the school, meeting boys he'd known as squealers, now school prefects . . . talking to Sheddy Fenn . . . eating dinner in Hall, not with the School Prefects at the High Table but with his own Beresford, the squealers at the bottom of the table gazing so hard up at his wings and ribbons that they barely remembered to get their second helpings . . . Port in the Common Room afterwards. There were a lot of gaps, from pre-war, now; most of the younger ushers he'd known were in France, dead or alive . . . Finally a late train up from Wellington College Station (alight here for Crowthorne) . . . which meant a change at Guildford, and then doz-

257

ing in a corner of his carriage to Waterloo. There'd been another man in the compartment, but thank heaven the man had had enough tact not to disturb him, flatter him, or ask questions . . . At last to the hotel, and sleep, and that peculiar dream, half-sexy and half-frightening.

The telephone rang and the hotel exchange operator said, "There's a lady down here wishes to speak to you, sir. Says she's Lady Jarrow."

"Ask her to come up."

He got up and looked at himself in the mirror—he needed to shave, but there was no time now. There was a knock on the door and he went to open it; Florinda came in, and by God, wearing that same plain tweed suit and hat, as though for a country shoot! He said, "Come in . . . for the second time. I was dreaming about you not long ago. You came here, and took off your clothes . . . together with the Duchess of Kendal and Marian de Forges."

"The Three Graces," Florinda said. "Which one did you choose?"

Guy said, "I can't remember."

"More likely you had all of us, in turn . . . I thought it would do you good to have a walk in the Park. I know it would me."

"I'd love it. Give me ten minutes to get shaved and dressed. And I'm going to wear mufti. I don't care if the General draws and quarters me, I'm not going to be mobbed by small boys, ancient clubmen, and nannies. Then back here for lunch, right?"

"Right."

"And I'll tell you about how I've been offered part of a bank, and a rich Jewish virgin heiress to go with it . . . and a seat in Parliament . . . and a trip to America . . . and a directorship at Handley-Page . . ."

"They've been taking you up into a high place, have they, even in your dreams, and showing you all the kingdoms of the earth?" Florinda said in a low voice. "And we'll not be seeing you among us down here in the mud much longer, eh?"

"I don't know," he said. "I wish I did. Come on, Flo! Let's be ten again, just for today. Please!"

*　　*　　*　　*

But that night he could not sleep, and after tossing and turning, and sitting up in bed in the dark listening to the silence—for the last trains had long since chuffed out of Victoria on their way to Brighton and Eastbourne and Shoreham and Hedlington—he got up, dressed, and went out. There was no moon, and clouds obscured the stars. The street lamps were not lit—because of us, he thought, the airmen, the flyers who might slide through the high night up there . . . under the high clouds, moving fast across the scattered stars.

What was that poem, the Highwayman? *The wind was a torrent of darkness among the gusty trees.* Wind down here, too, enough to stir the London planes, and shake down more of the remaining leaves. His new gold watch, luminous-dialled, showed half-past three in the morning. He was walking down narrow streets, dark, a cat stirring, nothing else, now along the river. He stopped and leaned over, staring down into the oily dark, the dimly seen swirl of water. It smelled of the sea . . . tide must be coming in . . . there was a bridge close to his right . . . Battersea. Royal Albert. A voice beside him whined, "Spare a tanner for a poor muvver, sir."

He turned, staring. It was a woman, in rags, shivering in the autumn chill, hand out. His eyes were used to the starlight now and he saw that she was pretty, and young, sixteen perhaps. She said, "I'll give you a good time for 'arf a crown, sir. Only I ain't got nowhere to go. 'Ere, I'll bend over and you can backscuttle me."

"Christ!" Guy groaned. He found some money in his pocket and pressed it into the girl's hand. Was this what Stella had been doing? He was walking fast along the embankment now . . . past tall buildings, deserted. No, two tall, dark shapes, a bull's-eye flashlight in his face, " 'Ere, 'ere, not so fast, young feller, what . . . ?" The light moved down his body and the man's tone changed, "Crikey, it's an Air Force officer, Bob . . . Are you all right, sir?"

Guy realized he was wearing uniform. What on earth had persuaded him to put that on, to go out and walk off his insomnia? "Quite all right, officer," he said. "Just can't sleep."

"I seen your picture in the paper," the other policeman said. "Major Guy Rowland V.C., that's who you are?"

"Quite right." He waved a hand and hurried on, past the Houses of Parliament, Westminster Bridge, Boadicea on her chariot, on again . . . trees, shapes huddled along under the wall . . . past the Savoy, Waterloo Bridge . . . over the river now, peering down into the black water from the middle of Rennie's masterpiece . . on, to the south bank, a row of railway arches to one side, the glow of a fire under them. He paused, hanging back in the shadows, looking. Four men and a woman were gathered round the fire, sticks and bits of refuse burning, the fire well back in under the brick arch, the other end blocked up, piles of dirty straw, a bottle passing round.

One saw him and stumbled out, "Hey, spare a copper for a hardworking man . . . ex-service man wot done his bit at Mons . . . Wipers . . . Waterloo." The three men were round him now, fingering his blue tunic, so clean and bright and new. They smelled rank, of sweat and gin. " 'Ow much 'ave you got on yer, mite?" one cried. "Cough it up, or we'll bash you!"

Guy emptied his pockets, but there was nothing. One of the men grabbed his wrist and croaked, "Ah, look at this, mites . . . Gold, that is . . ." He raised a big threatening fist—"Tike it off, mite, or . . ." They were drunk, Guy knew; he could have taken them all on . . . but a strange frozen feeling gripped him; he was paralyzed, by their situation, and its contrast to his own. Had the men really served over there? It didn't matter. Was the woman another whore, fifteen or fifty, raddled and riddled with V.D.? It didn't matter. The woman said, "No good telling the narks where we took the watch, guv, 'cos we won't be there . . . we're not anywhere, see, we're everywhere . . ."

"Who are you?" Guy whispered.

"The moles," one of the men said, pocketing the watch. "The people wot live underneath . . . Wot's them fancy clothes you got on, never seen anything like that before? Look like a bleeding circus ringmaster, you do." He flicked Guy's tie out of his tunic and pulled the end—"Anything in them ribbons? No, just bits of coloured cloth, that's what they are. Run along now."

Guy turned and walked away, head bent. The unlit street lamps marched on in slow time beside him, like grenadiers at a funeral. The darkness paled, but no cocks crowed for he was still in the city, again crossing the river, a giant dome taking shape out of the sky ahead, above it a golden cross and ball, dawn, people, pale and haggard, appearing to take over the city from the moles of the night.

It was full light. A City policeman, six foot four if he was an inch, with the carriage of a corporal of Guards, and the curved crest up the spine of his helmet, was standing in front of a long building, staring at him.

"Where am I?" Guy asked him.

The constable stared, saluted, and said, "In front of the Bank of England, sir."

*　　*　　*　　*

Guy sat back, listening, while his Uncle Tom talked with his partner, Arthur Gavilan, in the private office at the back of the salon on Maddox Street. Gavilan was saying, "Chanel's trimming everything with fur . . . even satin evening dresses. It'll put the prices up, but I think we'll follow suit, in our next collection."

"She's using the oddest furs, too," Tom said. "Monkey, I know, and heaven knows what else. The names are like *Peruvienne* or *Jacquerette*, which tells you nothing."

"It's best not to inquire," Gavilan said. "Let's just get the furs, and see what we can do with them . . . They're showing very wide-brimmed hats, too, mostly with chiffon veils, but I don't think that's going the right way. We should go toward smaller hats, hats that won't get blown off the head in a motor car. Talk to Jeanne about it." Tom nodded and Gavilan turned to Guy, handing over a swatch of material, "What do you make of that?"

Guy felt the texture—"It's silk, isn't it?"

Gavilan nodded, "Grosgrain, very heavy, holds a cut beautifully. We're using it in sweaters. Tom's done some very imaginative designs for them." He raised his voice—"Glyn! Are you still looking at those sweaters?"

A female voice from the salon chirped, "Yes."

"Bring them in."

"In a minute."

Gavilan turned back—"Last year the basic shape was the tonneau, but this year it's a slimmer line. We're trying to achieve it without losing the feminine shape. One way is to use belted tunics, which makes for a double-tiered skirt effect, but is oddly slimming—I don't know why, but it is."

A short dark-haired woman in her forties marched in through the open door, followed by three immensely tall young women, with long faces made up dead white, except for glaring scarlet lips. Guy made to stand up but Gavilan waved him down saying, "Models, Guy . . . We're going to show our dresses on these girls, and three others. They're wearing some of Tom's sweater designs now."

The girls pirouetted slowly, arms raised, then pranced back and forth. Guy thought, they're skeletal, bony faces, look like nothing on earth . . . it was much more fun, in his dream, with the Duchess, Marian, and Florinda. *They* looked like women.

One girl winked as she passed close in front of him and said, "I'm Fifi"; the second said, "I'm George, and I think you're the cat's pyjamas"; the third, finishing a turn, sat on his lap, put her arms round his neck, and planted a big red lipstick kiss on his mouth. She jumped up and the three trooped out. Guy found his handkerchief and began wiping his lips.

Tom laughed, "More conquests . . . but they're good girls, really."

"They don't look like it," Guy said. "To tell the truth, they don't look much like girls at all. And you're going to have them show off your new dresses?"

Gavilan nodded, "I've heard that one or two of the Paris designers are going to use live mannequins, and so are we . . . It'll be quite a revolution . . . Would you like to take one of them to a show or dinner?"

"Thanks," Guy said. "They frighten the wits out of me. And I'm sort of off ladies, for the moment."

*   *   *   *

"Do you think you're recovered now?" General Sykes's tone was curt, and he did not look up from the paper he was scribbling on.

Guy, standing at attention in front of the big desk in the Air Ministry, said, "Yes, sir. As much as I ever shall be."

The General looked up sharply—"What do you mean?"

"I find it hard to care about anything, sir."

"That's not the best of recommendations to command a squadron."

"I know, sir."

The General put down his pen and surveyed Guy as though it was the first time he had ever seen him. He said, "Too many attacks against odds . . . too many pilots sent out with twenty, thirty hours, sitting ducks for the Huns . . . a sort of R.F.C. shell shock, eh?"

Guy said nothing. The General said, "I was going to hold you here until the Germans crumpled, then post you to command one of the squadrons we'll be sending in with the occupation forces, but . . ." He pursed his lip—"You were in scouts all the time?"

"Yes, sir. The Three Threes."

"One of Trenchard's darlings," the General muttered. "So they got butchered more than the others . . . Have you ever flown a big machine, a bomber?"

"Yes, sir. Several times."

"What do you think of their future?"

"They should be the heart of the Royal Air Force, sir. They can attack targets well inside the enemy's territory . . . factories, ship-building yards, railway junctions, anything that affects the enemy's ability to wage war."

The General's eyes were gleaming—"So you believe in an independent air force, striking on Government directives based on national priorities? Rather than on what the army or the navy ask for?"

"Yes, sir. Though both of them would have to have a say in the priorities."

The General said, "I thought you were a Trenchard man."

Guy said, "I admire General Trenchard very much, sir."

"He thinks we ought to be an arm of the army . . . Ah, you're too young to be drawn into these personal feuds. We have to, because they aren't feuds to us, they are vital decisions which will save or lose the country, next time round . . . Would you like to work on the problems of air force policy . . . what its role should be, and, depending on that, what sort of aircraft we need for it?"

"Yes, sir. I care about that. I suppose because it doesn't deal with actual live people."

"Not yet," the General said. He stood up—"I am sorry I have not seen more of you. As I said, I thought you were a Trenchard man sent to spy on me. He and I do not see eye to eye professionally, and we detest each other personally . . . Perhaps he will come round to my way of thinking, but I doubt it. He is an obstinate man . . . I will send you to Handley Page, or Hedlington Aircraft. Which would you prefer?"

"Hedlington," Guy said at once, "that's where I live."

"Oh, good. Well, go down and fly their Buffalo. Get to know it well. Drop some bombs with it—fix that with Upavon . . . work out defensive flying formations for it in daylight attacks . . . Come back here in about a month—before Christmas, anyway—and start on the big problem . . . national air policy. Read what's been written. Lanchester's important. So am I." He smiled warmly—"Talk to people other than airmen . . . politicians . . . what's possible, what's necessary. You remember the first big Gotha raids in June 1917?"

"We heard about them, sir."

"They were heavy and did a fair amount of damage, but the response that was forced on the Government by public opinion—public demand to be protected, if you like—was out of all proportion to what they cost the Germans. By June this year London was defended by 469 guns, 622 searchlights, 367 aeroplanes, and over 10,000 men. Think what a diversion the Germans would have had to make if we'd put that number of aircraft and manpower into attacking *them!* Well, as I say, get some practical experience with heavy bombers, then come back here, and think—and write. That's all."

Guy saluted—"Yes, sir."

"One more thing. I want men who believe in the independent air force to carry weight. You're promoted to Lieutenant Colonel, from today."

*   *   *   *

He was in Hedlington, living in the flat with his mother. The letter had come this morning, and his Aunt Alice had sent it to him by messenger. Guy received it and took it at once to his bedroom. Werner was dead, so who could be writing, as from his "cousin," through the Swiss friend? His hands trembled as he opened it, sitting on the edge of his bed.

Dear Cousin—As you know I lost the one I loved in an accident. He is gone and it is not proper to bewail that the accident happened. I know that you feel as sad as I do, dear cousin, for I know that you loved him as much as I. Please come to

263

see me as soon as you can. We have much to share. And next May I shall have his baby.

Your Cousin

It was Maria von Rackow, Werner's wife. She was telling him that she knew it must have been an accident—in spite of the announcements in the German press that the German ace had been shot down by the Butcher, Guy Rowland. *Please come to see me . . . as soon as you can.* How soon? As soon as the war was over. He'd fly a Buffalo over to Germany, get a car, and go to her.

"Guy! Guy! Your Uncle Richard's on the telephone, for you."

It was his mother. He put the letter away into his breast pocket, went out, and picked up the receiver. "Uncle Richard?"

"Guy? When can you come up to the airfield? I've had the Air Ministry's official letter, and General Sykes's note and we're delighted, absolutely delighted. While you're here, studying bombing, we can look into facts and figures concerning the Buffalo's use in civil aviation."

"I can be with you in half an hour. I have a motor cycle."

"Good. We'll give you lunch here, and I'll get the Chief Pilot to have a Buffalo ready for afterwards."

Guy hung up. His mother, coming out of the flat's big drawing room, said, "Are you off to the airfield, so soon?"

"Yes, Mummy. I am here on duty, after all."

"Virginia telephoned while you were asleep. Kate's three weeks old today and weighs nine pounds four ounces."

Guy followed her back into the room. The walls were covered with framed paintings and drawings from the Western Front, all done by Archie Campbell, his father's adjutant and, he was certain, his mother's ex-lover. She seemed dejected, drained; in a way rather as he himself felt. He had lost interest in flying scouts in battle; she, in being a wife and mother. It was the war. It was ending at long, long, bloody last, but the prospects before them all did not seem particularly rosy.

Daily Telegraph, Friday, November 1, 1918

BRITISH ATTACK AT AUDENARDE

1,000 PRISONERS TAKEN

At 9.50 p.m. the following was issued:

Headquarters (France), Thursday (8.15 p.m)

The British Second Army attacked this morning south-west of Au-denarde, capturing all its objectives and about 1,000 prisoners.

> **On the rest of the British front there is nothing of special interest to report . . .**

Cate glanced at the other headlines: AUSTRIAN ARMY IN FULL FLIGHT . . . IMMEDIATE ARMISTICE . . . AMERICAN SUCCESS . . . SURRENDER OF TURKEY . . . REVOLUTION IN VIENNA AND BUDAPEST . . . DEMONSTRATIONS IN PRAGUE . . . IMPERIAL EAGLE TORN DOWN . . .

At last, at long, long last! Even the Germans were cracking, though they had not yet broken. One last push perhaps. It could not be more than a matter of days, now.

The drone of aircraft engines intruded on Cate's thoughts and he looked up, cocking an ear. They'd been flying those big four-engined bombers a lot out of Hedlington Aircraft since Guy came down. But this sounded louder than usual. He left the newspaper beside his plate and went out of the room and through the front door onto the front lawn. Shading his eyes against the hazy November sun, he saw that five bombers were flying in close arrowhead formation about six thousand feet up, a couple of miles to the south; and three other machines, these much smaller single-engined ones, like miniature darts, were circling round them. Ah, that must be what Guy had told him he was going to do, when he came to dinner a few nights ago—test formations for the bombers under simulated attack by enemy scouts. No one was firing their guns, of course, for Guy had also told him they would use camera guns instead, and the photographs, when they were developed, would show what sort of targets the attackers and defenders had had.

Very interesting, he thought, returning into the house as the heavy drone of the many engines faded to the north; but, good heavens, were they even now thinking of war, in the councils of the nation, when all everyone longed for was peace?

He supposed so; and, he grudgingly admitted, they'd better. Defeating Germany was not going to clear the world of war—only plant the seeds somewhere else. All the same, he wished Guy would take his deadly chess game elsewhere; so that one could dwell on the other aspects of man's new conquest of the air: a couple of hours to Paris, for a new exhibition at the Louvre . . . half a day to Madrid and Rome . . . one to Cairo and Athens . . . in a few years, New York, Montreal, Buenos Aires. The horizon, limited for so many years by the war across the narrow Channel, was widening to enclose the whole world.

The Western Front: November, 1918

I've lost my rifle and bayonet,
I've lost my pull-through too,
I've lost my disc and my puttees,
I've lost my four-by-two,
I've lost my housewife and hold-all,
I've lost my button-stick, too,
I've lost my rations and greatcoat—
Sergeant, what shall I do?

15 They were shining their brass buttons, sitting along the inside wall of the church, in shirt sleeves. Their work belied at least some of the words of the song, for most had button-sticks, all had pull-throughs, and some were using a housewife to mend tears in shirts or holes in socks.

"Can't believe this whole ruddy church is standing, 'cept for one big 'ole," Corporal Leavey said. "Didn't fink there was any church towers or spires left in the whole of France."

"There was plenty round Mons and Le Cateau, in '14," Private "Snaky" Lucas said. "And now we're nearly back there."

Private Brace said, "Think there'll be any more pushes, corp? If there is, it's my turn to have the flu."

"There's plenty caught it, and turned up their toes just the same as if they'd caught a Jerry shell with their name on it. We're all the age to get it . . . except Snaky. He was never young, even before he put in twenty years in the Shiny."

Young Jessop said, "Well, are we going to attack again?"

" 'Ow the 'ell should I know? The Kaiser forget to write me last week. And don't ask them questions, either."

The men along the opposite wall changed their song:

> *Lousing, lousing, lousing,*
> *Always bloody well lousing.*
> *Lousing all the morning,*
> *And lousing all the night.*

A young soldier, a nineteen-year-old arrived two weeks ago, his chin smooth as a baby's behind, gazed up in awe at the huge hole in the wall over his head—"What made that, corporal?" he asked.

Before Leavey could answer, Lucas, the old soldier, said tersely, "Mice . . . Pass me that button-stick."

> *Marching, marching, marching,*
> *Always bloody well marching,*
> *When the war is over*
> *We'll bloody well march no more!*

Sergeant Fagioletti strode into the church and bellowed, "Shut yer traps! This is a bleeding church, so don't use no fucking profane language in it!"

"All right, sergeant," one of the singers said. "We was only keeping our spirits up . . . If the church is so holy, why are we allowed to bivvy in it? It's Roman, isn't it?"

Fagioletti said, "Yes. But Father Caffin spoke to the priest here. The captain spoke to him, actually, and the priest said of course we could use the church, only we ought to fumigate it first, 'cos the Jerries had been using it for four years . . . Company pay parade in half an hour."

A cheer went up and Fagioletti raised a hand—"No one'll get any pay if the captain can't see his face in his buttons and his boots. The C.O. says this war's nearly over and we've got to get back to real soldiering."

"Have the Jerries packed in?" a voice asked anxiously, to be instantly followed by others—"Is it really over? . . . No more attacks for us!"

Fagioletti bawled, "I didn't say it was over. I just told you what I heard the C.O. say to the captain." He turned on his heel and marched out.

"Pay!" Private Jessop said dreamily. "That girl with the dark hair, that lives in the little house across the road—she'd go out with me if I

could wave five francs under her nose . . . into a field . . . a wood
. . hand in hand . . ."

"Not fucking likely," Private Lucas said, "with the rain pissing
down. Take her behind the altar. We won't look—we've seen it before
. . . some of us 'ave."

"In 'ere?" the boy said aggrievedly. "In the fucking church? You
wouldn't mind, would you, corp?"

Corporal Leavey was a Whitechapel Jew. Before his promotion his
nickname had been Ikey Mo, as was most Jews'; but once a man
achieved his first magic stripe, nicknames and first names became
taboo in the Wealds; that would be familiarity with those in authority.
Leavey was still called Ikey Mo behind his back, or sometimes Buckle-
my-Shoe or Four-by-Two, from cockney rhyming slang. He now said
briefly, "You blokes don't fuck in the synagogue and I don't fuck in
the church, and vice versa . . . Anyone got a Colney Hatch?"

He leaned forward, cigarette in mouth, while a soldier produced a
match and lit the cigarette for him. Lucas said, "Crown and Anchor
half an hour after pay parade."

"Where, Snaky? We can't do *that* in here."

"Why the 'ell not? Behind the altar, and those not in the game can
kneel on the front side, so any officer coming in won't want to disturb
the soldiers at their meditation . . ."

Then a bugle blew and Lucas cocked an ear. The youngest soldier
jumped to his feet—"Pay parade!"

Leavey snapped, "Hold your noise . . . It's 'Officers.' There won't
be any pay parade. I'll tell you what it is. The leading troops have met
resistance five miles up. The gallant 305th Brigade—what brigade are
we in now?—will move forward and attack on the left flank . . . Who's
got any money left?"

"I've got five bob . . . a bob . . . three and a tanner . . . six francs
. . . a tanner . . . sweet fuck all . . ."

"All right, let's 'ave a quick game before we go up."

"But how do you know . . . ?"

"Come on, we ain't got no time to waste." Lucas rummaged in his
pack, and drew out the Crown and Anchor box, and cloth, and hurried up a side aisle of the church to the altar, now covered with the
green and gold of the Trinity season. Behind the altar he rapidly
spread out the cloth, set the box in place, and rolled the dice. "Roll up,
roll up!" he began to intone in a low urgent voice. "You comes on
bicycles and goes away in motor cars . . . 'oo's for the Mudhook? The
Major? The old Jam Tart? . . . lay 'em down, pick 'em up . . ."

He did not stop when the main door of the church at the far end of
the building was opened, letting in a gust of cold rainy wind, then

banged shut again with a heavy clang. This time it was Company Sergeant Major Parr, shouting "Attention, B Company! Pay parade's canceled . . . the leading troops have met resistance five miles up . . ."

"Christ!" the soldier next to Lucas cried. "We've got to attack . . . again!"

"Goes away in motor cars," Lucas muttered, sweeping the money off the cloth and into his trouser pocket, sweeping up the box and cloth and dice, and returning to his place on the wall before the others, standing and listening to the sergeant major, knew that he had gone.

*   *   *   *

The voice at the other end of the field telephone line was thin, faint, and overlaid with a scratchy static, but 1st Lieutenant John Merritt could just make out the words—"Right eight mils, down twelve!"

He raised his hand from the instrument and shouted at the top of his lungs, "Deflection, right eight, elevation—minus twelve— Battery—one round—" He waited, watching as the sighting adjustments were made on the four guns lined up behind the thin hedge. The half-section commanders' arms snapped up in the signal "ready," and John shouted "Fire!" Flame jetted from the four muzzles simultaneously, followed by long gouts of smoke, which quickly dissolved and blew away on the rainy wind. John waited, the telephone again to his ear. Nearby, Chee Shush Benally, by now appointed to him by Captain Hodder as his horse holder—the only way to keep him out of more trouble, the captain had said—was squatting on his hunkers in a way only the Indians could manage, chewing some mildly hallucinogenic leaves that his relatives sent to him from Sanostee.

The forward observer, today the captain himself, advancing with an infantry battalion headquarters two miles forward, spoke—"The doughboys are going to attack in five minutes, Merritt. Their major thinks the Jerries will pull back just before we attack . . . they've got another position 400 yards on, in a village . . . and he wants to be sure to catch them as they cross the open. Be ready to put rapid fire on them when I give the order. You're O.K. for line now, but the target will be plus seven mils elevation."

"Yes, sir . . . What am I to do if the telephone line's cut?"

"Watch for Very lights. I'll send up red over green."

"Yes, sir . . . Chee, get up, take my binoculars—here. Watch for Very lights—there."

The Indian ambled forward a few yards until he had a clear view over the hedge, then stood, the glasses to his eyes. He really doesn't need them, John thought—he can see as well without them as most men with . . . He waited, the rain dripping off the rim of his steel helmet. The guns waited, water running down the barrels and trickling onto the wet ground, soaking into the heavy earth under the wheels. The horses waited, 200 yards back, in the edge of a village, their coats dull with rain . . . *feel I must tell you that the boy is dark-skinned, but has Stella's mouth and nose:* the words of Father Christopher's letter, brought to him by hand through mysterious channels, were imprinted before his eyes: *Stella is well, and so's the baby, though a little fractious . . . dark-skinned:* Father Christopher was saying that the baby's father had been a Negro or perhaps an Indian, a Hindu; *Stella's mouth and nose*—which probably meant that he did not have thick lips or other Negroid traits.

"Line dead!" the telephone operator shouted.

"Line party forward," John cried.

"Red Very!" Chee called back sharply.

"Stand by!"

"Green Very!"

"Gun fire, rapid—fire!" The guns barked and bounced, barked and bounced. A storm of German shells whistled and burst all round as the German gunners opened counter battery fire to cover the rearward movement of their infantry.

The Huns were moving back—farther away from the guns. The line was cut and the captain couldn't tell him just how fast they were moving; but there were no trenches or barbed wire to negotiate, and they'd be all but running . . . say a hundred yards a minute— "Elevation, plus three mils," he shouted . . . he watched the seconds tick off—"Elevation, plus three mils! . . . Elevation, plus three mils!" The battery's fire should be marching forward with the Germans, staying right on top of them. One last change of elevation. Now he ought to be on the new German position, in a village. The 75s wouldn't do much damage there beyond knocking off a few bricks. "Cease firing!" he shouted. He listened. Thump of heavy guns firing from the rear . . . then the shriek of the shells passing over. The French heavy batteries in support were opening fire on the new German front line. Their telephone had obviously not been cut.

At the guns, some cannoneers sponged out the breeches, others hurried forward with more shells to stack at the gun positions. John waited. The line party he had sent forward and the other, which the captain would have sent back from his position as soon as the break was detected, should find and fix it soon . . . *dark-skinned* . . . he grated his teeth together. For God's sake, find another target. He wanted the guns to fire till the cannoneers dropped from exhaustion, till the barrels twisted and melted, just so the war could be finished and he could get to Stella . . . *dark-skinned*. But Chee was quite dark-skinned. If Chee had been in London when Stella was there, doing what she was doing, he might have become the boy's father. He was not an abstainer from sex, John knew, for he had been to one or two of the innumerable whorehouses in Juarez, across the border from Fort Bliss, during their days with the 16th Infantry. Would that have made Chee a bad man, or in some way deformed or disgraced his son? He could not bring himself to believe it, in spite of his agony. So what was the real shame, the real tragedy, the real horror? It was surely in Stella's condition, that she should have to . . . say the word . . . prostitute herself to get money for the drug. That was what must be held onto, not the fact of the prostitution, or that she had sold her body to a black man or a brown man. Neither they nor she were to blame: the drug was, and the human condition that allowed it to take over a human being's personality, destroying all learned and inherited traits and behavior.

The telephone bell rang and the operator called, "Line fixed, sir. It was broken by shell fire a thousand yards forward . . . Captain on the line for you."

John took the instrument—"Sir?"

"Send up Anspach as O.P. officer."

"Yes, sir."

"And stand by to move forward. We've taken the old German front line and are moving on again in half an hour. The British are sending eight tanks to help and as soon as they arrive, we'll attack . . . I can hear the tanks coming up the road behind us now. Battery F will take over our tasks while we're moving . . . Hold on . . ." John heard the captain's voice, very remote, as he was apparently speaking to someone else, but with his mouth still near the telephone. "Yes, sir, Right, sir." Loud again, the captain said, "Battery F's all set. Move up to behind Goudraincourt. Got it?" John looked quickly at his map as the captain said, "Map reference 6793."

"Got it, sir."

"Get off your tail, then!"

John jumped up, shouting, "March order!" He stayed studying the map as the new 1st Sergeant, Clay, gave further orders. The gun teams came trotting up from behind, the cannoneers stacked unused shells back into the caissons, then sweating, pulled them round so that the teams could sweep up and begin the abattage . . . Across that field and into the lane, John thought, looking at the ground, then back at the map . . . trot east 2,000 yards, and when the houses of Goudraincourt were close ahead, find the best place for the guns.

Clay, now mounted, cantered up and saluted—"Battery ready to move, sir."

Chee was mounted, holding John's horse by the head. John swung up into the saddle and faced the guns and men of the battery—"Forward—Ho! . . . Trot—Ho!" Falling into place ahead of the leading gun, he spurred his horse to a trot. The Germans were still shelling the area, but he did not notice.

*　　*　　*　　*

"This is like bloody Mons," Private Lucas growled, shifting his weight from one foot to another. B Company was in open order, standing on the western slope of a mountain of coal slag. The rolling chalk uplands of the Somme, the pretty villages nestled in the folds, the green grass and the orchards, were all gone, with Picardy and its rich farmland. They were back among the coal mines and tall pit towers and wheels, and smoke from the factory chimneys of Lille drifting downwind on the rain far ahead . . .

Smoke curled out of the slag, for it was hot, from subterranean fires burning in its heart, and that was why Lucas shifted his feet. "We 'ad to take our positions on stuff like this at Mons," he said. "Might as well have lain down in the kitchen fire at 'ome."

"Bet the Jerries didn't have forty fucking machine guns a battalion at Mons," Private Jessop said. His hands were trembling and his voice shook, even though he had tried hard to control himself, and spoken in a deliberately grating manner quite foreign to him. "And you was fucking well lying down, letting the Huns come to you . . . 'stead of walking out in the open, like a lot of fucking dummies at target practise, like what we got to do."

"Shet yer trap, Jessop," Corporal Leavey snapped. "It don't make nothing better to fucking bellyache about it."

2nd Lieutenant Cowell, the platoon commander, resting on his ash plant farther along, said, "Keep the language down, men. That doesn't make things better, either."

Private Jessop muttered, "It don't do no good to yell when you hit your finger with a fucking 'ammer, but you do it just the same."

The German artillery was firing, but not heavily, and most of the shells were whining over the village with its slag heaps, its rows of mean houses, and the mines, which had been its life, to fall among the British batteries to the rear. The men of the 1st Battalion the Weald Light Infantry were lined up among those slag heaps, which they had reached an hour ago after marching up from the west, their pay parade canceled. All four companies were ready, and knew what their objective was: the far end of the village, 300 yards on. Some Germans were occupying the village, but no one knew just how many, or with what support in the way of machine guns and artillery. Another battalion of the brigade was to attack on the right, through another mining area, at the same time as the Wealds went in.

Lieutenant Colonel Quentin Rowland came along the line, accompanied by his runner, Campbell the adjutant, and Father Caffin, the battalion's padre. Quentin stopped at B Company headquarters and spoke to Kellaway—"Are you all ready?"

Kellaway said, "Yes, sir." His good eye wandered from the C.O.'s face to Campbell's—"We were to have a platoon of the Machine Gun Corps with us, in case of German counterattack. It hasn't come yet."

Campbell said, "They're coming up now, Stork. We passed them a few minutes ago."

Kellaway nodded and the colonel lowered his voice—"Have a good sergeant and a couple of reliable men at the rear when you go forward, Kellaway. You know what I mean."

"Yes, sir," Kellaway said, his mouth turning down. Everyone knew what he meant. The British Army was nearing the end of its tether. Ever since the great March retreat there had been a steadily increasing number of cases of desertion, and much more shirking of duty. The work was still being done, but at an increasing cost, and the cost was all being paid by the best.

Quentin walked on. When he was out of Kellaway's earshot he said, "A few months ago, an attack like this, with the ground unreconnoitred, no artillery preparation, and no tanks, would have been unthinkable. It would have been criminal, and I would have been stellenbosched for putting it on. Now, I'd be stellenbosched if I didn't."

Father Caffin said, "Jerry's still a good fighting man, colonel."

The C.O. said, "Yes, but he's changing as much as we are . . . more. Look at the deserters we got the day before yesterday—deserters or surrenderers, it doesn't matter—most of a battalion of Württembergers, with all but five of their officers. Württembergers! And they told our people that they'd been met on their way up to the front by mobs going to the rear, who shouted at them, 'Go back, you bastards, we've pulled the plug, don't go putting it back in.'" He looked at his watch and turned to Campbell—"Everything ready?"

"Yes, sir. This is our headquarters position for the first phase . . . Here's our gunner O.P. officer, Captain Thomason. He has a line to the guns and can get through to brigade for us, if we need to."

"Good," Quentin said. He looked at his watch again. Five minutes to go. He got out his binoculars, and, standing at the corner of a brick cottage, the end one of a row, stared through the prisms at the wasteland of garbage dumps, coal piles, scattered mine buildings that his men would soon have to advance over, and occupy. Looked rather like Loos, he thought. He shivered involuntarily. That was not a good memory.

*   *   *   *

Sergeant Fagioletti walked at the rear of B Company as it moved slowly forward, a long line of men, three deep, three platoons up, the fourth platoon following behind the centre; and with that platoon four machine guns of the Corps, being carried forward by their struggling, swearing crews. Each gun weighed nearly ninety-five pounds, the tripod as much, beside the boxes and belts of ammunition, range finders, water tins, and other paraphernalia that had to be manhandled with it.

They'd covered a hundred yards from the starting point—all well so far. No one edging back, or off to the flank. He had privates Green and Coley with him, good men. He'd wanted Snaky Lucas but Lucas had said briefly, "I ain't shooting no Wealds . . . 'sides, they need me in the platoon. 'Arf of 'em ain't learned how to piss standing up yet."

All well . . . but the Jerries hadn't fired a shot yet. Where were these buggers that had held up the brigade in front, so that the Wealds had been rushed up from that village with the church back there? Must be hiding somewhere, waiting. He was as wet from sweat as from the continual rain; that, no one noticed now; they'd been wet for a fortnight, and only noticed when they got cold as well, which was every night, sleeping in their sodden clothes . . . A long burst of machine-gun fire rattled from the right. The line in front wavered. The captain was waving his revolver in the air . . . centre and left platoons moving on, right platoon down and in cover, disappeared before you could say Jack Robinson . . . but the centre platoon was down now, too. That was his platoon, two or three men hit, but he couldn't see who they were from here . . . Mr Cowell was getting them on their feet again, and they were running, bayonets up. The left platoon was blazing away at a couple of sheds to the flank. Mr Huxley had got them charging, firing from the hip. Fagioletti found himself cheering hoarsely, waving his rifle over his head in animal triumph.

"There's a bloke, sarn't," Private Coley said, pointing his rifle a little to the left. Fagioletti saw that it was a man, crouched against a pile of rubbish and slatey coal. Fagioletti prodded him with his bayonet—"Get up, you bugger." The man did not move, his hands over his face. Fagioletti reached down and yanked him up. The hands fell away, showing a face with a hole in it, just above the nose. Brains were oozing out of the back of the head. It was Private Jessop, on his nineteenth birthday.

Fagioletti dropped the shoulders and moved on, now furiously angry. One of his men, young Jessop, what he and Snaky and the others had got his first woman for . . . The German artillery had learned of the attack and were firing . . . whizzbangs only, Fagioletti noted; four or five guns—not much. Another machine gun, this time from the left . . . and another from straight ahead . . . a man running, stumbling. The captain and Mr Cowell were taking the centre and right platoons on at the double, sweeping through the houses up there like a dose of salts. Mr Huxley had wiped out that M.G. on the right. German soldiers were walking back, by themselves, hands raised, *guerre fini* for them, lucky sods . . .

"Here," Coley shouted. "Another, right, sarn't!"

Fagioletti saw a soldier, lying behind a broken wall, covered in coal dust. He was about to run forward when the man called over his shoulder—"It's me—Whitman, battalion sniper. Fuck off, sarn't."

Fagioletti turned back. No one interfered with Private Fletcher Whitman, even if it was in a battle. He was like a leopard on a chain, only you weren't sure whether the chain would hold. He didn't need no sergeant or officer to tell him what to do. He was killing . . . mostly officers, picking his targets with that rifle and telescopic sight. He could knock a Jerry's eye out at a thousand yards, the blokes believed.

The centre platoon was in trouble . . . heavy artillery fire, and a lot of Jerries in the houses in front of them. Mr Wylie it was, the old 2nd in command's son, waving them on . . . now he was bowled over, that was a Jerry sniper got him . . . Here, three, four men had turned, were running back. Fagioletti dropped to one knee. The running men came close. He shouted, "Stop! Get back to your platoon!" One stopped, three came on, one screaming, firing from the hip— "Get out of the way, you fucker!" Fagioletti fired, aiming at the heart. The man dropped. Private Coley fired; another man fell. The third dropped his rifle and threw up his hands.

"Pick up your rifle," Fagioletti yelled, "and get forward."

"I can't do it," the man wailed, "I can't!" Tears streamed down his face, his whole body shook. Fagioletti said, "It's them or me." He put his finger to the trigger. Slowly the man stooped, picked up the rifle and, with a quick movement, before anyone could stop him, hurled himself down, neck first, onto the fixed bayonet. It pierced his throat, sticking out at the back, blood spouting.

The suicide was down, gargling in agony, blood spouting from his mouth. Private Green looked at Fagioletti; Fagioletti nodded. Green put the point of his bayonet to the man's ear as he lay howling and bubbling on the ground, and pulled the trigger.

They hurried forward. The left platoon was holding. The centre and right were on their objectives. Fagioletti reached the centre platoon headquarters and found Sergeant Rhodes in command, since Lieutenant Wylie had been knocked out.

"How's it going, Dusty?" he gasped.

"We got ours . . . The captain's taking your platoon round behind the Jerries on that side. You'd best get to them."

Fagioletti ran forward again. Four soldiers of the battalion lay sprawled on the soiled earth, two moving, two not. He turned over one who was lying face down—Brace. They'd been caught by a machine gun—Privates Brace, Fallow, Felstead, and Hart. Fallow and Brace were dead. Felstead's arm was broken, and Hart had got two in the belly. Felstead gasped, "We done it, sarn't, we done it . . . Mr Cowell's hit, not bad . . . but you'd best get to the platoon . . ."

"Where?"

"In the hand . . . shell splinter."

"Where's the platoon, you stupid bugger?"

"Up in them houses . . . someone's waving out of a window . . . the Jerries is running! The buggers is running! . . . Give me my rifle, sarn't."

"You can't fire with that arm, Felstead."

But Fagioletti could, and he ran on toward his platoon, every few seconds stopping and firing an aimed round at the Germans running away across the wasteland to the east of the village. "Jessop," he muttered, pulling the trigger, "and Brace"—firing again—"and England . . . Barnes . . . Fletcher . . . Spenser . . . Cook . . . Jenner . . ."

It began to rain harder, the wind slowly backing into the southwest.

*   *   *   *

Near midnight it stopped raining. The Wealds, huddled in makeshift trenches, ditches, and piles of rubble, were too weary to try to bale out the accumulated water. They just stayed where they were, soaked, shivering to a cold night wind, their hands numb holding the rifles, their eyes blinking, scratchy, staring into the darkness. Artillery of both sides was firing but it seemed indiscriminate, shells bursting here, there, somewhere else, without particular purpose or plan; and it was not heavy fire. The infantry were firing in the same manner—a lone machine gunner briefly scourging a slag heap, a few rifle pops, then silence . . . broken by another sudden outburst of automatic fire—but from where? There was no moon, and no stars, for the clouds had not broken up, only a faint luminous glow close to ground level.

At four o'clock Quentin, shaking with ague in the cellar of a miner's half-ruined cottage, looked round at the other occupants in the candlelight . . . R.S.M. Bolton, Campbell, Caffin, two runners . . . all looking exhausted, even the R.S.M. He hoped no one would notice that he was shaking and shivering. They'd think it was funk, but it was malaria, he was sure . . . ought to go and see Sholto about it, but what could Sholto do? They didn't carry quinine in the trenches even when they'd had a fixed Regimental Aid Post. This was mobile warfare, they'd got the Huns on the run at last, but the doctor now had little more than what could be carried in his own and his sergeant's haversacks. Nearly all sick and wounded had to be sent back to the C.C.S. these days. No one ever knew where it was, for it kept moving, too. You just told the men or stretcher bearers to keep walking west until they met Red Caps . . . The men were nearing the end of their tether. Caffin had told him so, and two of the company commanders had hinted at it. The R.S.M. too, though it had been wrung out of him. He knew it himself. He wished he could get them all together for one last time, formed in hollow square, bayonets peacetime bright, steel flashing in the sun, uncased Colours crossed over piled drums, and say to them, "Weald Light Infantry! Remember Minden! . . . Remember what the Duke of Wellington said at Waterloo, in the heat of the battle, 'Hard pounding this, gentlemen. We shall see who can pound the longest!' . . . *Wealds, we shall pound the longest!*"

He stood up abruptly—"I'm going round the companies. Hold the fort, Campbell."

Archie stood up awkwardly, grimacing with the pain of a knee wrenched falling over a low wall in yesterday's attack. He said, "I'd better come with you, sir."

Quentin rasped, "I said, hold the fort here. Keep badgering Brigade about the tanks that didn't show up yesterday. We must have them by six o'clock this morning, if we are to continue the advance."

"Yes, sir . . . But I don't think you know where A Company is. They moved their position, you remember, and you told me to co-ordinate it."

Quentin hesitated. Father Caffin was already on his feet. Campbell was right. "Very well," he said grudgingly. "Mr Bolton, you take over here."

"Yes, sir. Shall I send a couple of runners back with a message about the tanks?"

"No," Quentin grunted. "They know about it. Just keep badgering them on the artillery line . . . unless the brigade line comes in, of course."

He moved out into the darkness, stepping cautiously. Half-right here, down what had been a lane behind a row of houses. Most of the houses were still standing, and not severely damaged; and B Company was at the end of the row, facing north-east. The pattern of the gun fire had not changed, but he paused and listened to it for a moment, ducking instinctively as a shell screeched over fairly low, to burst 200 yards behind the village . . . Now he heard the other men's heavy breathing close behind him. On—carefully, it would be the last piece of bloody foolishness to break his leg, as Campbell damned nearly had, at this stage of the game. A low voice from directly in front muttered, "Halt! Who goes there?"

"Commanding officer and party."

"Give the password."

"Kent."

"Road . . . Pass, sir."

Quentin moved forward. The two sentries were standing by a wall, and he peered into the face of the nearest—"Where's Captain Kellaway?"

"Straight on, sir . . . about a hundred yards. He's where two streets cross."

"Private Lucas, isn't it?"

"Yes, sir."

"Colder than Bareilly in the hot weather, eh?"

"Yes, sir. No char and wads, either."

Quentin suddenly paused, whispering, "Hush!" He listened intently. The artillery pattern was changing. The British was the same—ranging, some harassing fire on rear areas. But the Germans . . . a deafening roar filled the night and Quentin and the others hurled themselves flat as a heavy concentration of artillery fire fell on the village. About forty guns were in action, he thought, trying to organize his mind . . . whizzbangs and 5.9s certainly . . . anything heavier? . . . No. But what . . .?

Private Lucas, crouched beside him, said, "The Jerries are getting ready to attack, sir."

Bloody Germans, he thought, bloody good soldiers. These were Prussian Guards, he knew from prisoners taken just before dark: now they were coming back, teeth bared, fighting to the last gasp. In the morning, the advance would continue, nothing could stop it; but now, here, the Prussian Guard had to be stopped. He heard whistles blowing ahead and off to the left in the darkness. All three forward companies were standing to. They'd been at alert all night, so it wouldn't take thirty seconds to come to full readiness. The SOS tasks were ranged in, the supporting artillery ready to fire with communications good to them. Each company, each platoon, each individual soldier would now have to fight it out by himself.

The German artillery concentration lasted five minutes and stopped as suddenly as it had begun, but not before the other soldier in the sentry post had gasped and fallen back, dead, half the top of his head gone, half his steel helmet with it . . . The Germans would come from close to, sheltered by the darkness. Christ, he wished his men were dry, full of food, rested . . . and full of spirit. But the bloody Germans had been out under the same rain, and you could bet they hadn't had any food or rum, and, God damn it, who was winning this war? He took the dead soldier's rifle, its bayonet already fixed, slung a bandolier of ammunition over his shoulder, and stood ready by the wall, peering forward.

Lucas began to fire, fairly fast. "Half-right, sir," he shouted, "sneaking through the rubble." A white Very light rose from B Company's headquarters and Quentin fired six shots while it was in the air, hitting four Germans, for they were barely fifty yards away. Machine guns from C Company ahead raked the front in long traverses; but the beaten zone was behind the Germans now assaulting B Company. The German second wave would catch it. Under the Very lights and star shells, and the yellow-red bursts of the British SOS fire, Quentin dimly saw Germans advancing farther back, falling in windrows . . . These nearest ones were the ones who had to be stopped. Campbell's revolver was barking. Father Caffin was kneeling, watching the spectacle with a strange expression on his face—horror, exaltation, compassion all blended in it; but he was not praying, not at that moment.

Two Germans burst out of the darkness onto them, a huge feldwebel and a Guardsman. Campbell got the soldier and Lucas, swinging round and firing without aiming, shot the feldwebel through the chest. Father Caffin leaped onto the fallen body, grabbed the Mauser pistol he had been carrying, and began shooting. "You're not supposed to do that," Quentin gasped.

"Ach, colonel darling, how could I be sitting out a foight like this?" the priest yelled.

The Germans came on in one more desperate wave, still only the leading ranks of the assault; the supporting waves lay dead and wounded in the sodden coal dust, caught by the Vickers and Lewis guns of the battalion, and by the artillery SOS fire, now rising to a screaming crescendo, as more and more batteries received fire orders from divisional and corps artillery grids, and joined in.

Now came the Prussian Guard in another attack, as fierce as

wolves, wounded, decimated, cornered. Quentin realized that the sentry post he had walked into had become by chance the protective flank of B Company's right rear, and hence of the whole battalion, for B was on the right, and echeloned slightly back from C at the point, with A on the other flank and D in battalion reserve round headquarters.

The sky was wavering, intermittent bright, darkness chased away. The rifle was growing hot in Quentin's hands. Father Caffin's Mauser was empty but he was wresting spare magazines from the dead feldwebel's pouches, ramming them in, and continuing firing. Campbell had the other dead German's rifle, and was firing steadily, his revolver in its holster, the flap unfastened. Bullets from B Company swept over and among them, for the main body of the company could not know that in firing at the Germans trying to work round behind them they were also firing at the little party by the wall.

They came, like the first charge, black shadows racing on under the dissected light, steel helmets gleaming, the short ventilation stubs on each side, faces pale, contorted, orange fire rippling from the muzzles of the guns at their hips. "Wealds, Wealds!" Quentin yelled, knowing that none of the regiment could hear him, except the two men so close he could almost touch, and the Irish priest.

"Wealds, Wealds!" he heard Campbell's yell behind him; then a choked gasp. He dared not turn, for the Prussians were twenty feet away. He fired, aimed, fired. The rifle was sent flying from his hand by a savage upward thrust of a German's rifle with fixed bayonet. The German toppled forward, a bullet from Lucas through his stomach; then another German fell on top of him, killed by Caffin's Mauser; then another, killed by some chance shot from elsewhere, for none of the four at the wall could fire—Lucas's magazine empty, Father Caffin knocked unconscious by a rifle butt on the side of the head, Quentin buried under three German corpses, and Archie Campbell—dead, a single bullet through the heart, lying face up, arms outspread, his mouth wide in the word "Wealds!"

Lucas systematically and quickly reloaded his magazine, and stood ready. No Germans. He pulled the bodies off the C.O., and as Quentin tried to struggle to his feet said, without taking his eyes off his front—"They've gone, sir."

"Retreated?"

"To 'eaven, sir."

Father Caffin groaned, swimming back to consciousness. Quentin knelt by him—"Are you all right, padre?"

Caffin groaned again, then muttered, "Depends what you call all right . . . Me head's splitting . . ."

Quentin looked round—"Campbell? Campbell?"

Then he saw the spread-eagled shape in the dimmer light, for the star shells were fewer and farther; but there was no doubt it was Campbell, and there was no doubt, as he knelt over him, that he was dead.

Quentin began taking off Campbell's watch, identity disc, and paybook, and emptying his pockets. He stuffed what he found into his own pockets; there may have been a snapshot, but he didn't look, he wouldn't look, now or later. It may have been of Fiona. It didn't matter. Everything but the disc and paybook would go to her.

He said, "Lucas, are you keeping watch?"

"Yes, sir."

A figure approached out of the darkness forward and Lucas growled, "Halt! Who goes there?"

"Kent, Snaky. I'm taking a message to old Rowley from the captain."

"I'm here," Quentin said. "Let me have it."

"To say we've beat off the attack, sir, and the captain thinks A and C did, too, but he's sending contact patrols out to make sure."

Quentin said, "All right. Go back and tell Captain Kellaway to be ready to advance half an hour after first light, with tanks in close support . . . Everyone except the severely wounded will stay with their companies. Everyone. Do you understand?"

"Yes, sir."

"Off with you, then." He stood, the first of the dawn light beginning to spread, a heavy figure in his burberry and steel helmet, and the respirator high on his chest, the rifle still in his hand, looking east toward the rising day.

Lucas was swaying on his feet and Quentin snapped, "Are you all right, Lucas?"

"Me? All sigarno, sir . . . just a mite 'ungry. Or p'raps it's the flu."

"Don't you dare! Rejoin your company. You did very well." Lucas shambled off, still swaying slightly. Hungry, Quentin thought, also thirsty, and dead beat. But he was an old stiff, he wouldn't give in.

He turned to Caffin. "If you're feeling well enough, padre, I'd like you to say a few words over Campbell here."

The priest said, "My head's still splitting, sir, but . . . of course. It'll be in Latin, you know."

Quentin snapped, "I don't care if it's in Pushtu. Go on."

The priest made the sign of the cross over the silent body, it too forming a cross on the black earth, and began to intone:

Miserere mei Deus secundum magnam misericordiam tuam.
Et secundum multitudinem miserationum tuarum, dele iniquitatem meam.

Amplius lave me ab iniquitate mea: et a peccato meo munda me.
Quoniam iniquitatem meam ego cognosco: et peccatum meum contra me est
  semper.

Quentin listened, his helmet held across his chest in one hand. The dawn breeze was bringing with it the smell of cordite and lyddite, of coal dust and slag, of the sulphur fumes of the chimneys; and under and over them all a deep, continuous low rumble, growing steadily louder and closer.

Libera me, Domine, de morte aeterna, in die illa tremenda:
Quando caeli movendi sunt et terra! Dum veneris judicare saeculum per ignem
  . . .

The dead Germans lay as neatly piled in death as Archie Campbell, none in agony or even the contortion of dying. The sound grew louder and Quentin cried aloud—"The tanks . . . I can see them . . . ten . . . twenty . . . thirty tanks . . . Advance, advance!"

Kyrie eleison. Christe eleison. Kyrie eleison.
Amen.

*   *   *   *

Battery D was in action behind yet another village. They all looked the same to John Merritt now. Smoke was rising from low hills ahead, where houses burned—houses and other works of man, set afire by the retreating Germans or by American artillery fire; nothing natural was in a state to burn after so many days of rain, though it had stopped now. The ground was sodden but at last beginning to dry out. Six months ago it wouldn't have mattered; then, the guns were in position and would not move, except short distances, long pre-planned to upset the Germans' counter battery intelligence. Now, it was different; they moved two or three times a day. The last great German effort had been stopped, on the Argonne, at St Mihiel and Château-Thierry. The armies were advancing.

John stood grim and silent to the right of the right-hand gun of the battery, by the telephone. He could see the battlefield for himself, 5,000 yards ahead, and with the binoculars, or Chee's bare eyes, could see the exact moves of the Germans, of his own infantry, and the British tanks supporting them; normally he did not give the fire orders, but relayed those passed to him by Captain Hodnett, the O.P. officer.

"New target . . . right seventeen mils . . . elevation plus two . . . ranging rounds!"

John barked the new orders; then—"No. 2 gun—fire!" The binoculars to his eyes he waited for the telltale burst on the hillside. It wasn't as easy to see them now as it had been in summer, when a puff of dust rose even in a planted hayfield. Now there would be a spout of mud, but small, for the 75 was a very light gun. He saw nothing, but Chee Shush Benally, beside him, said, "In the middle of the dark field, shaped like this." He made a triangle with his fingers and thumbs. John took Chee's word for it and gave the correction order from his slide rule, then barked—"No. 2 gun—fire!" Four rounds later, they'd bracketed the target.

John stooped to the telephone—"Ranged in, sir."

"Record as Target Four Seven Emma. There's a German company in front of it and we think they're going to pull back across it any moment . . . Here—"

The telephone went dead. John waited a moment, then cranked urgently. The bell rang; so the line wasn't cut. He said, "Captain? . . . Captain?"

Another voice came on, "Captain's been wounded, sir . . . bad, in the chest."

"Are the enemy moving on Target Four Seven Emma?" John interrupted. He was sorry that Captain Hodnett was wounded; but his business, as a Field Artillery officer of the United States Army, and as John Merritt, was to get the war over.

"Yes, sir, they're just coming out, going back. But . . ."

John turned away, "Battery fire! Previous target, rapid—fire!" He turned back to the telephone—"I'm coming up . . . Top!"

"Sir?"

"Take over as Battery Exec till Lieutenant Potter gets back. The captain's been badly wounded. I'm taking over the battery until the colonel sends someone else."

"Right, sir."

"There's the Firing Chart . . . Chee, get our horses!"

The Indian ran back and returned in a minute, mounted, leading John's big stout rough-haired chestnut. He swung up and stuck spurs into the horse's flanks. Boughs rattled on his helmet as he galloped through a wood on the flank of the village, then out into the open . . . across country, like old prints of foxhunts. For a moment wild exhilaration swept the hard misery out of his system. Chee, riding neck and neck with him, yelled, "You gone crazy, Johnny? We'll kill the horses!"

John said nothing, but bent forward, hurled the horse over a hedge into a lane, turned right in a shower of mud, and galloped through a deserted hamlet of ten houses, and out again. The Germans were retreating up the hill a bare 500 yards away. Tanks' machine guns spat as the monsters growled and grunted forward. The doughboys were moving, in long straight lines. He heard ragged cheering.

"It's over," he shouted. "It's over. They're beaten!"

Chee slowed his horse to a walk, pulling a bottle out of the horse's wallet. He put the bottle to his lips and tilted it back, letting the liquor gurgle down his throat in a torrent.

"What in hell are you doing, Chee?" John shouted. "We've got a job to do still."

"Not me," Chee said. "It's over. You said so, Johnny." He hiccuped and slid slowly off his horse, falling head first onto the ground by its off hind leg.

Christ, John thought, he must have been drinking all day; didn't notice anything. He had a head like teak; but eventually even teak got sodden. He jumped down, grabbed the bottle and put it in his own horse's wallet. Five doughboys were working on a field telephone nearby and he called to them, "Soldiers . . . my striker's been wounded. Send him back to Battery D, 137th, as soon as you can, or when he can move."

The nearest soldier came over and peered down. The smell of brandy emanating from Chee's mouth and nostrils was overpowering. The soldier looked up—"Wouldn't mind getting some of that wound myself, lieutenant . . . snake oil, them Indians call it, don't they?"

"Try to hide him," John said urgently. "He's got the Medal of Honor."

"We'll see that he gets back safe and sound, sir. It's over, after all, ain't it?"

"Not quite," John said, and again spurred his horse forward.

Daily Telegraph, Friday, November 8, 1918

BERLIN'S ENVOYS TO ARMISTICE MEETING

TIME OF ARRIVAL

At 11.10 yesterday morning the subjoined message was circulated by the Press Bureau:

(Admiralty, per Wireless Press)

News transmitted through the wireless stations of the French Government.

To the German High Command from Marshal Foch.

If the German plenipotentiaries wish to meet Marshal Foch to ask him for an armistice they are to advance to the French outposts by the Chimay-Fourmies-La Capelle-Guise road.

> **Orders have been given that they are to be received and conducted to the place fixed for the interview.**
>
> ### SIGNIFICANT REQUEST.
>
> #### THAT FIGHTING CEASE AT ONCE

. . . that fighting cease at once, Cate thought: that was what mattered. For when the fighting stopped, the killing would stop; and Stella would have a hope of seeing her husband again. He knew that John had received his letter about the baby—nameless, as yet—but he did not know how he had taken it.

From the far end of the table Stella said, "It looks as though it's really ending now . . . Is John coming back?"

"Oh, I think the chances of his being badly hurt now are very small."

"I meant, is he going to come back here . . . or go straight home to America?"

Cate put down the paper. "My dear child . . . of course he's coming here. It was he who said that there must be no abortion, that you must bear the child. He wouldn't have done that unless . . . unless he means to continue to accept you as his wife, and, I am sure . . . the baby, as his."

Stella said, "*He* may. I don't know whether I can."

She bent again over her toast. Cate, aghast, watched her for a few moments; then returned to the newspaper.

> ### REVOLUTION IN GERMANY
>
> #### HAMBURG IN REBEL HANDS
> #### THE OUTBREAK AT KIEL
>
> #### REVOLT AT CUXHAVEN
>
> **The latest information available last night serves to confirm fully the serious nature of the outbreak at Kiel. The whole town and, it is now stated, the surrounding districts, are in the hands of the revolutionaries. The report that . . .**

He threw down the paper and stood up. "Come, Stella. Let's go to the church and pray. For the world. For England. For Germany. For you and me, and John and the baby. For all creation."

Armistice Day, Monday, November 11, 1918

16 Alice Rowland limped fast down the vociferous High Street, deafened by Klaxons, men standing on top of anything they could reach, yelling, waving flags, girls draped round soldiers' and sailors' necks, engines whistling on and on in the station.

She turned down Plumer Street to No. 79 . . . she went slowly up the steps, for steps were always difficult with the artificial leg. She took the door knocker and rapped twice, then again. It opened at once and Daisy Cowell faced her, tears streaming down her cheeks, a slip of pink paper in one hand. Alice stopped, her hand to her heart, "Oh Daisy . . ." she cried. She had recognized the slip, as anyone else would have, since 1915, as a telegraph form: the biggest sender of telegrams was the War Office.

"No, no, Miss Alice," Daisy gasped. "I mean, yes—it's Dave . . . He's wounded . . . left hand and wrist . . . he's all right."

"Then he'll be home soon! Oh, Daisy, he's safe . . . safe at last!" The two women fell into each other's arms, sobbing, laughing, and crying. At length Alice stood back—"I was coming to tell you that the Governor has accepted an offer for Laburnum Lodge, and we must move out by today week."

"I have everything ready for you," Daisy said. "Your room's been fresh painted, just like your bedroom at the Lodge. It's much smaller, but it's nice and cosy . . . and Dave'll come back to us soon."

"Any day," Alice said. "The wound might be a blessing in disguise, if it hasn't done any permanent damage. Otherwise he might not be demobilized for ages. Now we can start the accountancy firm we've been talking about, at once."

The two women smiled at each other. He'll be back, Alice thought, soon I'll be in his arms, his body in mine, his strength crushing me, my female to his male.

He doesn't love me, but he'll make love to me sometimes, Daisy thought, and he'll be happy and when he's happy, I am. And Alice Rowland is a lady, and my friend, whatever there is between her and Dave, and she and I will always have that.

* * * *

Winston Churchill was in the Prime Minister's room in the Palace of Westminster. Both men were flushed and exuberant, talking in short energetic phrases, moving about jerkily, stopping, gesticulating. "We did it!" Lloyd George said fiercely. "Did it . . . spite of everything . . . the Huns . . . even Asquith! . . . the U-boats! . . . Jellicoe . . . you know I had to *order* him to institute convoys . . . "

The window was a little open and the sounds of celebration filtered in, with the music of a brass band somewhere far off, and the bells of the Abbey ringing wildly across the road, and high, formless female shrieking.

"What now?"

"Election! I'm going to the Palace . . . must be seen with H.M. . . . and I'll tell him, we'll have an election as soon as the law allows."

"When's that? Twenty-one days . . . Good heavens, at the end of the month?"

"No," Lloyd George shook his heavy mane violently. "No, no! Can't fix it properly by then . . . in December." He darted to his desk and turned over the pages of a desk calendar—"What's wrong with the 14th—Saturday? Though it'll take a couple of weeks to count the soldiers' ballots."

"Is it wise, do you think, to force the election so soon?"

Lloyd George said, "Winston, think! I will have to go to a Peace Conference. Wilson will be there, and Clemenceau, and Cadorna from Italy, though what *they*'ve done . . . Well, I must go with a set of cards in my hand, and the first ace, which I must have, is a strong mandate, a big majority for *me*. Not for the Liberal Party Asquith's a member of that, and I'm going to crush Asquith, and anyone who goes with him." He looked out of the window—"Squeeze Germany for all she's worth . . . perhaps a thousand million pounds! Hang the Kaiser!"

Churchill removed his cigar from his mouth—"I very much doubt whether the Kaiser can be indicted under any international law."

"We'll find some greedy lawyer who says he can . . . and it doesn't matter a damn whether he is or not. What matters is that we go into the election with proposals that the voters can get their teeth into . . . peace! money! revenge! We'll be swept in by a landslide. You'll see . . . Now, before I go to the Palace, what are your proposing to do about the munition factories? I won't have them all shut down"—he snapped his fingers—"just like that. That'll throw two million people out of work, just before an election."

Churchill said, "I was thinking of making an arbitrary decision that all orders more than, say, 60 percent finished should be completed. Orders less than that, scrapped . . . I'm also proposing not to bring back anyone who's now out with the flu—give them wages for the next month, and . . ."

"Wages till after the election," Lloyd George cut in.

"Very well, Prime Minister."

"Talking about the damned flu, H.M. will ask me for the latest figures." He sat down behind his desk and reached for the telephone.

"They're going down, at last," Churchill said, "but they're still very high."

The Prime Minister said disgustedly, "Engaged!"

Churchill continued, "World-wide, it looks as though this epidemic may kill off more people than the war has."

"I don't believe it," Lloyd George gasped. "Why . . . why . . . Loos, Champagne, Verdun, Gallipoli, the Somme, Passchendaele, Tannenberg, Jutland, the Argonne . . . all that?"

"More than all that," Churchill said.

*　　*　　*　　*

The 9th Earl of Swanwick stood in the window of his big drawing room in Cornwall Gardens, looking out. It wasn't raining, the church bells were ringing, people seemed to have poured out of the houses all round the square and were congregating in the actual garden in the middle. The railings had long gone, melted down to make steel for shells, guns, tanks. Bloody children went in and picked flowers, urchins who didn't belong in the surrounding houses at all kicked soccer balls up and down, skivvies and soldiers copulated among the bushes . . . Everyone was kissing everyone else now, all yelling their heads off . . . What was there for him to celebrate?—both his sons dead, his younger daughter an unmarried mother, running a bloody little shop selling stockings, hats, gloves, scarves, feathers—trade!

He heard the countess's footsteps behind him but did not turn. She came up and put her hand on his shoulder . . . "So it's over at last," she said.

"Too late for us," he said.

"I'm making plenty of money now," she said. "And we're all better off in London than mouldering in that old pile in Walstone . . . I know it's hard for you, darling, but things really aren't too bad . . . except for losing Cantley and Arthur."

The door behind them burst open, and they turned, to face their eldest daughter, Lady Barbara Durand-Beaulieu, dressed in her usual clothes—men's riding breeches, Newmarket boots and spurs, a hacking jacket, and a hard, dark blue hunting cap, a crop under her arm. The countess grimaced, then controlled herself; Barbara had smelled of the stables since she was two years old, and it was no different now—just more noticeable, because more confined in an S.W.7 flat than in a Kentish country mansion. There was a man at Barbara's side. She recognized Ben Watkins, Barbara's employer, the owner of the livery stable where Barbara worked as groom and riding instructor to the many children who hired Watkins's horses.

Barbara rushed forward to hug both her parents, in turn. "It's over," she cried. "It's over!"

"Yes, it's over," the earl said. He was staring at Watkins, who was dressed the same as Barbara. Barbara noticed and cried, "Oh, of course you haven't met Ben . . . Mr Watkins, Daddy."

Her mother said, "I have, of course. How do you do, Mr Watkins?"

Barbara took Mr Watkins's hand, and her face turned a deeper shade than its normal healthy, rain-swept red. She said, "Mr Watkins . . . Ben . . . and I . . . are going to get married—" The last words tumbled out in a rush.

"Good God!" the earl exclaimed.

"Oh! How wonderful," the countess said. "You're a lucky girl, Barbara. I know how Mr Watkins has worked to make his stable a success . . . and I think you're lucky too, Mr Watkins, though I shouldn't say it."

"Oi'm lucky, oi know thaat," Watkins said, in his natural, broad Wiltshire. "But oi love her, yer ladyship, and that's what matters, bean't it?"

"It be—it is," the countess said.

Barbara said, "We must get back . . . ten children due in half an hour . . . don't know whether they'll turn up, because of the armistice, but . . ." She hurried out, dragging Watkins with her.

When the door had closed the earl exploded—"He's a roughrider sergeant, ex-3rd Carabiniers! That's what Barbara told me when she went to work there . . . joined the army off the tail of a plough from the depths of Devon or Dorset or . . ."

"Wiltshire," the countess said.

"Forty years old if he's a day!"

"Forty-three. Barbara's thirty."

"Bloody yokel, marrying my daughter! Can't rub two pennies together, and . . ."

"There you're wrong, Roger. Mr Watkins has made a lot of money with his stable. I've seen this coming for the past three months, so I've been making inquiries. Barbara needs to be married. When Lady Barbara Watkins is one of the owners the stable will get still more clients, and can charge more."

"Do you realize . . . can it be possible? . . . that we might have grandchildren called Watkins?" the earl said, suddenly deflated and hopeless.

"Yes," the countess said firmly. "And we must accept it. Times have changed . . . Now, I must be about my master's business. Lord Walstone will not regard Armistice Day as an occasion for celebration, but as a day to make more money."

* * * *

Christopher Cate stood in his library, his violin tucked under his chin, the bow sweeping across the strings in the main theme of the last movement of Beethoven's 9th Symphony. Today, overwhelming joy was not enough; there must be grand sorrow mixed with it, and compassion, something of the greatness of humanity, and the puniness of man. Only Beethoven would do . . . In the servants' hall they were playing the tunes from "The Maid of the Mountains" over and over again on their gramophone. The green baize door had been left open since the moment when Garrod and Tillie, shrieking, had rushed in to throw their arms round his neck, and yell—"It's over, it's over!"—adding "sir" much later, as an afterthought . . . the musical comedy baritone was off-key, but the tune was catchy, under Beethoven's immensity. They didn't clash. It was right, even. He was playing for them, and they were playing for him, each in his own way. He was playing, too, for his son, whom he should have protected from the war; and for himself, who had lost his son, and the woman he loved . . . and for Stella, upstairs, in her room, with them but not with them, smiling, with no joy behind the smile.

Outside the wind tugged at the bare branches, but it was not raining. The windows were open and he could hear, with the Beethoven, and the musical comedy, the jangling of the church bells. Tomorrow Mr Kirby would organize some great feat of change ringing to celebrate . . . five thousand changes of Kent Doubles, his favorite, perhaps, but for now the bell ringers were just pulling wildly, so that the bells jangled and tumbled and thumped and tolled and tinkled in mad abandon.

He reached the end of the movement and realized that someone had closed the green baize door to the servants' hall, for he could not hear the gramophone now. And Garrod was waiting in the door of the library, presenting a silver tray, with a telegram on it; and there was the telegraph boy bicycling away down the drive. He put down the violin and picked up the telegram as Garrod slipped out of the room.

Walter killed in action November 7 don't cable write please please—Isabel

Oh, God, now she had lost her only son, her only child. She wanted him to write . . . of what? To tell her that he loved her? She knew that. That he was sad for her? She knew that. That he wished they could be together? God, she must know that. But he would say it all, so that she would have something concrete of his love to hold to, if only the paper of his letter.

Why don't you smite Margaret dead, God, you swine? As she had smitten so many others in her passion for Ireland? "Kill her! Kill her!"; he was saying it aloud.

*   *   *   *

The factory whistle mounted above the boiler room was screeching full blast. It must be the same down in Hedlington, but up here on the Down, several miles out, one could hear nothing. Pratt, the works foreman, came into Richard Rowland's office and said, "We won't get any more work out of 'em today, Mr Richard. Better give 'em the day off."

Richard hesitated. It was a bad thing to shut down an aircraft factory so suddenly, as several things had to be done before the workers could leave. You couldn't leave a wing half-doped, for instance. But he said, "All right. We don't have an armistice every day."

"Thank 'eaven!" Pratt said. "That would mean we 'ad a war every other day." He went out, tipping his bowler hat to the back of his head as he went.

The telephone on the desk rang. It was Overfeld from Jupiter Motor Company "I've sent them all home for the day, boss. No use keeping them here. Full day's wages, of course."

"Of course," Richard said, though a part of him thought obstinately, why "of course"? The loss of this half-day's work would reduce *his* income, not much but some . . . Well, it couldn't be helped. That was the way workmen were, and he had difficulties enough with Bert Gorse's machinations and the unreasonable demands he spawned in the factories.

291

"I'm going home," he told the secretary. "I'll be back tomorrow. You go home, too, of course . . . all the clerical staff. Pass the word."

"Oh, thank you, sir! Isn't it wonderful! It's over! My brother will come back . . ." She burst into tears. Richard patted her awkwardly on the shoulder as he went out, murmuring, "There, there."

Outside he found his chauffeur, Kathleen Owings, a tall, plain girl, in her green uniform, complete with breeches, being recklessly hugged and kissed by a dozen men. A small aircraft was looping the loop over and over again high above the airfield, and a Buffalo heavy bomber was flying up the field at fifty feet, waggling its wings cumbrously from side to side like some drunken namesake, a buffalo with wings.

The men fell back and Kathleen took her place behind the wheel. One of the men wound the starting handle and they drove off. "Sorry, sir," Kathleen said over her shoulder, "we're all so happy."

"Quite all right," Richard said. "It's over at last."

"Yes," she said. "The men'll be coming back."

"Yes."

He said no more, wondering if she was thinking of some particular man, a brother or cousin—a lover even . . . or about her job. Would he keep her, now that he could get a man again? Was it fair to sack her? But was it fair to keep her when ex-service men would need the job far more than she did; and could do better? No, that wasn't right. She could do anything a good chauffeur could do, except the hardest physical things, like lifting up the front end of a car to put bricks under when there was no jack . . . but how many men could do that?

At Hill House his wife and daughter came running out, Sally shrieking, "We've got some rockets, daddy . . . fireworks! I'm lighting a bonfire . . . huge bonfire . . . come and see." Susan was in his arms, murmuring, "Thank God, at last, at last," and Sally tugging. The bonfire was struggling to get going, pouring out grey smoke. Where had they got the fireworks from? Left over from Guy Fawkes' Day? Anyway they had them, and Joan, the old maid, and Mrs Baker the cook were there, giggling fit to burst their stays, while Summers had his arm round both of them, and boys from the village were running in to stand round Sally—she had a following of them, could twist them round her finger, *not* now by taking off her clothes . . . Roman candles flared, crackers jumped and spat all over the grass, Mrs Baker shrieked louder and Summers surreptitiously pinched her ample behind. A rocket fizzed into the sky and a boy yelled, "Send up another, Sally!"

The boy put a hungry arm round Sally's waist, and she slapped him off. She struck another match and lit the rocket's fuze. The rocket soared up . . . and another . . . the rocket sticks rained down. Mrs Baker shrieked, her face by now mottled with excitement. Summers became bolder, with no reproof or reprimand. More rockets rose, the bonfire burst into flame, and they all began to dance round it, shouting. Only Nanny stood aloof outside the circle, with Dicky.

The telephone bell rang inside. The front door was open and Nanny heard it, and called, "Mrs Rowland—telephone. Shall I answer it?"

"No, I'll go," Susan panted. The English were supposed to be so phlegmatic, she thought; but, given the right stimulus, they went hogwild.

She hurried into the house and picked up the receiver—"Mrs Richard Rowland here."

"Is this Tim Rowland's mother to whom I am speaking?" a man's voice said severely.

"It is," she said.

"This is Mr Babcock, the headmaster of Greystone's. I regret to tell you that I must expel Tim from the school, Mrs Rowland."

"Oh, good!" she exclaimed. Now she'd get him back. Her heart sank quickly. Richard would find another school for Tim.

"What? Did I hear aright?" the headmaster's voice was at first astonished; then again severe.

"I meant, how awful . . . what has he done, Mr Babcock?"

"He exploded a grenade in one of the boys' W.C.s not an hour ago. The W.C. is destroyed, of course, and also the cubicle in which it was situated. The walls and ceiling are riddled with splinters. It is a miracle that half a dozen boys were not wounded or killed, Mrs Rowland. But it so happened that Tim was alone in the, ah, toilet area, when he did this this monstrous thing."

"It is bad," she said, thinking, Tim knew he was alone. He's a smart boy, not careless at all. Where on earth did he get a real military grenade?

The headmaster continued, "And only last week he emptied a tin of Eno's Fruit Salts into the Matron's chamber utensil. She hurt herself quite severely when she, ah, had occasion to, ah, use the utensil."

Susan had a hard time suppressing her laughter: it was a funny image, especially as Matron was a very proper spinster.

The headmaster said, "If you would be good enough to come and fetch Tim as early as possible tomorrow, we will see that his clothes are packed, his laundry recovered, and his jams and marmalades returned from the dining hall to his tuckbox."

"Very well, Mr Babcock."

"I must make it quite clear that no part of his school fees for the term can be returned, as expulsion is clearly covered by section 43 of the school's . . ."

"I quite understand, Mr Babcock," she said, suddenly cold. "I will be there by eleven o'clock tomorrow morning. Good day."

She hung up. Hooray! Tim the little rascal back . . . Sally will be pleased. The staff will be pleased. Mrs Baker will bake him a special cake. They all love him now that he's a little gentleman, a real, wild, reckless, young gent.

*   *   *   *

"Bannu will be very pleasant until March," Colonel Broadhurst-Smythe said, waving a long hand. "It used to be called Edwardesabad . . . great man, Edwardes, one of the founders of the Indian Empire. No one took liberties with Edwardes. Very different nowadays."

Daphne Broadhurst-Smythe, Fred Stratton's fiancée, poured another cup of tea. Outside in the garden the *mali* was watering the rows and rows of zinnias and the air was full of the distinctive smell of laid dust. The sun was sinking through the dust of the plains, giving it a golden glow that lent haloes to everyone in it—the old man shuffling past the open gate of the compound, the syce coming in on one of the colonel's horses, walking it back from exercising it on the Maidan.

"You cross the river at Mari Indus, and change to the narrow gauge, and the Heatstroke Express, ha ha! It takes about seven hours to Bannu . . . 138 miles, I remember that well. Had to take a hundred hairies up there once . . . three of them died . . . heatstroke."

"Will it really be so bad now?" Fred asked nervously.

"Good heavens, no," the colonel said. "You'll find December and January cold as charity up the Tochi Valley . . . Dardoni, Miranshah, those places."

Moving the battalion by an Indian troop train would be quite an experience, Fred thought. And then—the North-West Frontier, and the "tribes" they talked about so often . . .

> If you're wounded and left on Afghanistan's plains
> And the women come out to cut up what remains
> Just roll to your rifle and blow out your brains
> And go to your God like a soldier.

They'd recited that gleefully to him . . . Bloody cock! None of them knew a thing more about the North-West Frontier than he did.

"With any luck you'll see some real action," the colonel said, putting down his teacup and warming to his subject—"Great men, the Pathans! An eye for an eye, a tooth for a tooth, that's their motto . . .

and can take your eye out at a thousand yards with a good rifle . . . but they still mostly have jezails . . . Dashed sporting chaps . . . all keep falcons . . . But," he lowered his voice, "can't trust them with a young lad."

"Father!" Daphne's voice was a rasp.

"Sorry, m'dear. Well, can't talk about that in front of young ladies . . . *unmarried* young ladies . . . ha, but that'll change in two days' time, won't it? . . . Tell you what, Fred, the Pathans are the fellows we ought to be defending, not the fat Hindus in the bazaars. Can't stand 'em . . . bow and scrape, and jew you out of every penny you have, if you give 'em half a chance."

Fred looked at Daphne, smiling. The day after tomorrow they would be married in the garrison church. Then they'd have a week's honeymoon, in Delhi . . . then—she'd come back to living with her father until the battalion returned from the Frontier. Then . . . well, that wouldn't be until November 1919, though surely he'd get some leave during the year. Time enough to think about what next.

Daphne said dreamily, "When you get privilege leave, let's go to Bombay . . . there are some wonderful shops in Bombay."

"Good idea," Fred said. He'd better start really saving up, he thought; no more late nights with champagne in the mess. The Frontier would be just the ticket for that.

He got up to take his leave, and stopped, thunderstruck. By God! There was an armistice in France. The telegraph message had come through just before he set out for tea; but then he had forgotten. How could he forget a thing like that? The 1st Battalion, out of battle, at last! This 8th Battalion, Territorials, all its plans and schedules liable to be changed. But, coming here through cantonments and the edge of the bazaar he had forgotten—it had slipped away. The masses of Indians were shuffling about their business; no bells were ringing; no one singing. The English men and women he saw were doing the same things they'd been doing yesterday, and every day since he came out. He said, "We ought to celebrate, sir, Daphne! It's Armistice Day! The war's over!"

"I believe it is," the colonel said.

*   *   *   *

The revelers in Hedlington never seemed to tire. The celebration had no particular centre, but just was, everywhere—by the station, in front of the Town Hall, up the hill by Minden Barracks, outside—and inside—the gaol, even along the mean banks of the Scarrow in North Hedlington, where most of the town's industry was concentrated.

At the corner of a warehouse by the river Violet Gorse was waving a half-empty bottle of gin in the air, and yelling, as she had been for some hours, her voice now no more than a croak. Her dress was torn, as always, her cotton stockings full of holes, and her shoes down at heel. She had been wearing lipstick, but now it was smeared all over her prematurely aging face. Her hair was falling down under the battered black straw hat perched on top. Two soldiers approached, reeling from side to side, arm in arm, singing "We don't *want* to join the Army, we don't *want* to go to war . . . 'Ere, wot's this?" One reached out, grabbed the bottle from her hand, and took a swig, passing it on to his friend. "Give us a kiss," the first soldier cried thickly and Violet fell into his arms, mouth wide. She glued her lips to his and stuck her tongue deep into his mouth. The soldier slid his hand down to her crotch and felt her slit through the thin material of the dress. " 'Ere," he grunted. "Let's 'ave a bit of cunt . . . We won, we won!"

"Two bob," Violet said, pulling back and holding out her hand. "Or 'arf a crown'll do."

" 'Ere, the women's giving it free today," the second soldier said aggressively.

Violet looked at them keenly. She wasn't drunk, at all. They were, she saw, but not enough to do anything silly; and they wouldn't get whisky cock. "C'mon," she wheeled. "Right 'ere . . . on my back, backscuttle, between the pillars, anything you want . . ."

The first soldier fumbled in his pocket, while the other said, "What about me? I'm stiff as a pole."

Violet said, "My sister . . . just round the corner . . . c'mon!" She took a few steps, the men following. Behind the warehouse her sister Betty waited, a ludicrous imitation of Violet in dress and manner, and Violet herself as ludicrous, and tragic, an imitation of the adult whores of the town; Violet was fourteen and Betty twelve.

" 'And over," Violet said, "four bob . . . Show it to 'em, Bett." Betty lifted the hem of her dress in a slow, would-be lascivious movement, revealing the long slit of her vulva. "Christ!" the second soldier gasped. "It's bald! How old are you?"

"Old enough," Betty said, holding open the lips of her vulva with two fingers of one hand. The men began to undo their fly buttons with feverish fingers.

Three hundred yards away the girls' mother, Mary Gorse, stood outside the door of a public house, a two-year-old girl wrapped in shawls beside her. A hand-lettered cardboard sign hung round Mary's neck—*Husband wounded prisoner Work wanted Help please*. Mary stood against the wall, looking straight to her front, not facing the men and women as they went in and out. No one spoke to her, or gave her anything when they went in; several did as they came out. She had ten shillings and a few pennies in her purse by now. It wouldn't be the same tomorrow, but today was Armistice Day, and the people were out of their minds.

A man stopped beside her and said roughly, "What kind of work do you want? What can you do?"

She turned toward him—"Sew . . . mend . . . darn . . . knit . . . laundry . . . cook . . . wash dishes, scullery work . . . clean house."

"Keep 'ouse?"

"Until my husband comes home," she said, "I could. I have four children."

"I don't want no children in the house, even if there was room for them. But you could come . . . no pay, meals, maybe two bob a week pocket money . . . but housekeep, do anything I want you to do."

She met his eye fully, and said, "That wouldn't be right, sir."

The man spat on the pavement and went into the pub. Mary waited. She only had three of her own children in the house now, since God had taken Jane with the influenza; but little Henrietta here was her Violet's, and must be looked after, just the same as the others. "Here," a voice said; a small coin was thrust into her hand—a threepenny bit. "Thank you, sir," she said.

Another 300 hundred yards on the youngest of Mary Gorse's own children, Rupert, eight years of age, was hurrying along the row of tinned goods in the Hedlington H.U.S.L. shop, quickly filling the pockets of his ragged jacket and trousers with tins of food. As he slipped toward the door a hand shot out from behind a stack of condensed milk tins that reached nearly to the ceiling and grabbed him by the ear—"Got you, you little bastard!" It was a woman with a long hard face, beady dark eyes, and a strong arm. She twisted his ear savagely, "Empty your pockets!"

"I ain't done nothing," he whined. She was hurting him, but he made it sound as though he was dying. The woman twisted harder. Fucking Christ, she was a hard 'un. His pockets were nearly empty, still no chance yet. She was dragging him toward the cash desk, shouting, "May, call the police!"

She was pulling, he was dragging back . . . why not go t'other way? He suddenly drove his head forward against her, butting her in the side, and at the same time lashed out at her shins with his booted foot. She screeched in pain and he broke free, running for the door, snatching up a can here, another there, as he went. He was out, tearing down High Street . . . sharp left, slow down, look innocent, a kid playing . . . "Hooray, hooray!" he yelled. "We've won, it's over!" There were some sailors, had a bit too much. They'd give him a tanner or two, and if he showed them where Vi and Bet were on the pross, more. Sailors always had soft hearts, and stiff pricks . . . how long would it be afore he got one of them himself, properly? He danced up to the sailors in an energetic hornpipe, shouting in his high, clear treble, "We won! It's over . . . Let's have a tanner so's I can buy a packet of tiger nuts, mates . . . you want girls . . . ?"

*   *   *   *

It was not raining, but all the road surfaces were slippery with mud, and the convoy was collecting wounded from far places now, and driving greater distances each day as the war moved toward Germany. The R.A.M.C. orderly beside Naomi on the front seat of the ambulance said, "Well, miss, it's over, at last . . . Didn't seem to be doing much celebrating up front, did they?"

Naomi said, "It'll take them time to realize that it's really true."

The orderly said, "The farther back we get, the happier they are, seems . . . look at them girls rushing up! . . . Gawd, they want to give us a kiss and a hug!"

Naomi slowed and the seven following ambulances slowed behind her. Half a dozen young women were hurrying alongside, blowing kisses, holding out their arms. Naomi looked down at them, took off her steel helmet with one hand, and shook out her hair.

"*Une femme!*" the nearest girl shrieked.

"*Oui,*" Naomi called back. "*Mais la guerre finie, quand même!* . . . Poor dears," she said, pressing again on the accelerator, "they really thought they'd at least get some men to hug."

"Never seen the F.A.N.Y.s through 'ere, that's why," the orderly said. He was in a talkative mood, but Naomi barely listened. The wounded soldiers in the back were too drugged to make a sound and she drove on, concentrating on the road with her eyes and intuitions, and the skills she had learned . . . her mind moved into newly familiar channels: the factory in Hedlington. Ron. Finance . . . Grandfather would help there, though perhaps not much. She might go to Toledano's, if Uncle Richard would give her an introduction. But before she saw old Isaac she'd better have all her facts and figures right, and reasonable. She knew that from family gossip ever since the J.M.C. had been founded, part of the financing having been Toledano's.

A sign pointed left—NO. 27 ADVANCED BASE HOSPITAL—and she turned into a muddy field. Several huge marquees had been set up in it, and white flags put out to mark the "roads." A soldier of the R.A.M.C. with white gloves directed her to the second of the large tents, all of which had big red crosses painted on the brown canvas roofs. She drew up outside the entrance and at once several men came out with stretchers, followed by a man in a white coat. He was carrying a bottle of champagne in one hand, a full glass in the other. He walked up to the side of the ambulance and peered in—"Ha, Lance Corporal Rowland as I live and breathe."

"Yes, sir," she said. It was Captain Freeland, a surgeon of the hospital, where she had delivered wounded often enough in the past month. The hospital itself had moved three times in that month, but always on the axis that was being served by No. 16 Convoy of the F.A.N.Y.

Freeland tilted his head and emptied the glass, poured to refill it, and handed it up to her—"To peace, corporal."

"I can't drink on duty, sir . . . or at all, in France," she said.

"What if I give you an order, corporal? The bloody war is over, at bloody last. Soon I won't see any more young men, young lovers, torn to ribbons under my hands, chewed, mangled, as though a mad tiger had been at them . . .

> None saw their spirits' shadow shake the grass,
> Or stood aside for the half used life to pass
> Out of these doomed nostrils and the doomed mouth,
> When the swift iron burning bee
> Drained the wild honey of their youth.

Isaac Rosenberg. Here, drink, for God's sake."

Naomi took the glass, drank it in one gulp, gasped and coughed as the bubbles tickled her throat and palate, then said, "Thank you, sir. It's . . ."

He interrupted—"Or would you prefer Théophile Gautier?

> Des déesses et des mortelles,
> Quand ils font voir les charmes nus,
> Les sculpteurs grecs plument les ailes
> De la colombe de Venus.
> Sous leur ciseau s'envolent et tombe
> Le doux manteau qui revêt,
> Et sur . . ."

Naomi said, "Thank you, sir . . . that is not a proper poem to recite to an unmarried woman."

The F.A.N.Y. lieutenant had appeared and was signalling to her to move off. She engaged gear, looking straight ahead, as the R.A.M.C. orderly climbed back up beside her. It was hard to keep her face straight. That was another of the indecent poems about women's private parts which poor old Rodney Venable used to recite to her while they were . . . better not think of that; though it would help when she came to do the same with Ron Gregory, as his wife. But Ron wouldn't recite French poetry to her, certainly not at such moments.

"Well done, corporal," the F.A.N.Y lieutenant said. "You've made excellent time. One more trip today . . . same collecting point . . . I'll be following in fifteen minutes with six more ambulances."

"Very well, madam."

*　　*　　*　　*

The guns were aligned in a straight line, facing due east, exactly twenty yards apart. All harness and saddlery and steel work shone in the wintry sun, glittering through the pall of cordite smoke that hung round the guns in the still, damp air. Captain John Merritt, confirmed in command of Battery D of the 137th Field Artillery, stood at the right of the line of guns, his binoculars to his eyes, his mouth set in its now habitual grim line. He flung out one hand without lowering the binoculars, and shouted, "Cease firing! Elevation, plus six mils . . . resume firing!"

Sweat ran in streams down the necks of the cannoneers as they brought up shells from the piles behind each gun, rammed them into the gaping breeches, slammed them shut, pulled the lanyards, checked the quadrants to see that the guns were back at the same elevation after each recoil. Sweat ran down the necks of the drivers and darkened their tunics as they galloped the caissons up to the guns, emptied them of ammunition, and galloped them back for refilling from the reserves stacked in the rear.

"Six minutes to go, captain," 1st Sergeant Clay shouted in John's ear. "Those barrels will melt if we don't slow down a bit, sir."

John said nothing. There were the Germans, breaking and running in disorder across the fields two miles away, in plain view. They thought that because the war was nearly over they could relax, and recoup, and maybe pretend they hadn't been thrashed. And these huge stocks of ammunition had been piled up for a final push to break right through and stream on into Germany. He wasn't going to let it lie here. Who would want to reload it and take it back to the States? So, the guns showed red hot, the crews struggled and sweated and strained, their red faces becoming stained with yellow and black.

Another change of fire order . . . four minutes to go . . . another . . . this time seven mils left. The Huns were streaming into a transverse lane up there, and heading off left-handed. "Cease firing! Shrapnel! Time setting—five point zero!" One minute to go . . . the firing rate increased to a frantic desperate madness, but still the shells were falling on target . . . "Left, two mils!" Ten seconds . . . four three two one . . . eleven o'clock.

John's left hand shot out horizontal from his body and he barked, "Cease firing!"

There was a naval order, "Finished with engines." Could he say now, "Finished with guns"? But in the artillery there was no such order. He turned to the 1st Sergeant—"Have the men fall out behind the guns and relax, Top."

He walked away, his hands behind his back. Silence. Total silence. Not a bird singing, not a man talking, not a gun barking. No wind to whine in the boughs . . . silence, his boots silent in the heavy grass . . . he heard something rhythmic—soft and close. He swung round sharply, frowning. "What . . . ?" he began.

It was Private Chee Shush Benally. Chee said, "We got to get out, John."

John said, "I know. Just as soon as we can."

"Why we not just disappear? They never find us, won't bother . . . too many others . . ."

They stood facing each other, two young men, the squat dark Indian private and the tall white captain. John said, "What's *your* hurry?"

Chee said, "Mother dying . . . younger brother sick . . . sheep dying because no one look after them. I'm going to skip, tonight . . . soon's I can."

John said, "Don't do it, Chee. The M.P.s will be out in force looking for deserters, now they don't have any battlefield work to do. You've got to get on a ship, remember. You can't ride freights from here to Gallup."

Chee scratched his head, then resumed his position of attention, remembering that they were in full view of the battery. He said, "I got to go, Johnny."

John said, "You won't help your family or your sheep if you're spending six months in the stockade . . . I've got an idea. You're a hero. An Indian hero. You have the Medal of Honor."

Chee said, "That and a nickel, I can buy a beer. Here, not there. No Indians served."

"I'll cable my father, to have Newton Baker bring you back for a national tour, as . . . ."

"Show what good citizen red man is?" Chee said. "Don't want to go touring, just get to Sanostee."

"You won't go touring," John said impatiently. "Once you're in the States, you tell my father what the real situation is and he'll see that they release you, with all the money that's due to you."

"How you going to send this cable?" Chee said. "No one can't send cables like that."

John said, "I'm going to tell the colonel that I want to see the general on a personal matter. General Castine never comes by the artillery without asking after my father and the Secretary. If you ask me, he's fishing for a job in Dad's bank, after the war. He'll see that the cable gets sent, especially as it's about a man from his division . . . and that will be advertised, too . . ."

Chee said, "All right, Johnny." He brought his head up to the salute—"When I come tonight, to clean boots and gun . . . I'll bring a bottle . . . cognac. We get a little drunk . . . sir!"

John watched him go, shaking his head. Now, how was *he* to get out of this man's army? His need was just as great as Chee's, in every way except the sheer physical. No one was starving. They were just dying, in other, more subtle ways. General Castine was the key. He might not have authority to release him at once; but he might have, or be able to get, authority to send an officer to England for some military purpose. They'd be very strict about letting fellows jump the line for getting back Stateside, but to England . . . that would be easier.

*   *   *   *

Looking down and ahead from his place in the pilot's cockpit in the nose of the big bomber, Guy Rowland thought, I can see people. The land was dead, murdered, cut to ribbons by some gigantic Sweeny Todd, but the maggots were alive and crawling out of the depths where they had lived for so long. There was a battery of guns, out in the open, no gun pits, the men standing round, looking up as he flew over at 500 feet, well below cloud level. There was a battalion of infantry marching along a road, in column of fours . . . women in a village street . . . A man behind a house there, ploughing, not a mile from the front line . . . but the lines, as he had known them all these years, were far back now, the deep wriggling trenches, like agonized worms crawling across the land, through the shattered woods, across the flooded marshes . . . The Germans were fifteen miles farther east, marching on eastward in good formation. In a day or two they'd be crossing the Rhine. He wondered where his father and the 1st Battalion of the Wealds were . . . Down there perhaps, or over to the north, where the ruins of Ypres Cloth Hall made a bigger lump in the myriad lumps of the landscape . . .

He'd seen all that he needed to see . . . Out over the coast near Zeebrugge . . . the Germans had removed the block ships long since . . . west for Dover, the white cliffs coming up now, the four radials

humming steadily out between the wings. His co-pilot sat silent beside
him in the dual cockpit . . . the navigator, behind . . . a photog-
rapher lay in the belly of the Buffalo, taking pictures . . . Dover
Castle, the flag flying, smoke everywhere . . . ah, bonfires, rockets! It
was over.

Now soon he would see Maria von Rackow. General Sykes would
let him go over as long as it was part of his job: and that it would be
. . . An election would come soon, everyone said, and the R.A.F.
might be fighting for its existence . . . Hendon coming up ahead; the
Big Smoke underneath and to his right . . . the wind sock hanging
nearly limp on its staff atop the control tower. He gave her right
rudder and came straight in from the south-east. She glided down,
engines sputtering and banging. These monsters were a lot easier to
land than a Camel, as long as everything was working all right. They
were steady . . . had to be, to make a stable platform as a bomb
launcher . . . and that would also make them easier targets for enemy
scouts . . . Ease back on the stick . . . down . . . rolling . . . throttles
all the way back . . . turn, taxi, stop.

The station commander was a major, waiting for him on the turf as
he finally jumped down off a wheel. He said, "General Sykes called,
sir. He wants to have your report tomorrow. Ten o'clock at the Air
Ministry."

"Thanks . . . Is my car ready?"

"Yes, sir." The Crossley rolled up and Guy climbed in, immediately
struggling into his greatcoat. The streets had been full of tension on
his drive out this morning. Now, four hours later, they would be
exploding, as he had seen, from a height, at Dover. If they saw his
uniform and ribbons they'd drag him out of the car and then . . .
God knew. Tear him limb from limb, one way or another.

He settled back, huddled into the greatcoat, collar turned up. It
was over, at last it was over. Poor Frank would soon have to face
Hedlington, and his life without Anne, if he insisted on cutting her
out, and the three children which were certainly his . . .

The Buffalo ran like a bird. There was no limit to what could be
done with a machine like that . . . Cairo . . . Cape Town . . . Delhi
. . . Australia . . . even America. But what about bad weather, which
meant bad visibility? On a long leg the weather could change totally
between takeoff and landing. He must learn more about wireless . . .

They were entering the centre of London, crowds everywhere, a
madhouse, women kissing and hugging any man they could get hold
of . . . buses overflowing with soldiers, sailors, and men in the blue
uniform of the convalescent depots . . . everyone waving flags, shouting, singing, weeping . . . the car was slowing down and the driver

threw over his shoulder, "Sorry, can't get on any faster, sir. Look at 'em . . . Well, we've all got something to celebrate, thanks to you . . ."

"And a few million others," Guy said.

The crowds had begun to infect him. Why not get down and join in? He wouldn't be killing now, just loving. He said, "I'm not going to the Grosvenor now, driver. Take me to No. 14 Half Moon Street, please."

"Very good, sir."

Slowly the car advanced through the streets, till at last it reached Half Moon Street. Guy jumped down, crying, "Thanks!" He ran up the steps of No. 14 and rang the bell. Soon a maid came to the door and Guy said, "I'd like to see Lady Jarrow, please. Tell her it's Guy Rowland."

"Very good, sir." She left him in the drawing room to the right of the hall and disappeared. Five minutes later the door burst open and Florinda rushed in—"Guy, darling! Oh, darling darling darling!" She hung her arms about his neck and swung round, her legs in the air—"It's over! I can't believe it! I thought it was immortal . . . like God!" She pressed her lips to his and kissed him, as they had not kissed since they were making love in his Uncle Tom's flat, nearly two years ago.

He broke loose and cried, "Let's go out!"

"Just what I wanted to do . . . but I didn't want to go alone . . . We'll drink, kiss everyone . . . but only one kiss per girl, for you . . . Oh, Guy . . . you're looking tired . . . and sad, in spite of everything . . . Let's have a bottle of champagne, and then . . ."

"No," he said. "Let's go out."

The door opened and the maid came in—"Lieutenant Bidford to see you, m'lady."

"Good God!" Florinda cried. "Show him in."

Guy stood back and Florinda said, "Now, don't be jealous, love, not today." Billy Bidford walked in, wearing naval uniform with a long blue greatcoat, swinging a pair of goggles in one hand. He stopped on seeing Guy and saluted formally.

"This is Guy Rowland," Florinda said—"Billy Bidford—he's with the Dover Patrol."

The two men looked at each other; each knew that the other loved, and had been the lover of, Florinda. Guy said, "I was flying over Dover a couple of hours ago, in a Hedlington Buffalo."

"I saw you, sir," Bidford said. "I had just made up my mind that Admiral Keyes would not need my services for the rest of the day and was about a mile out of Dover proceeding to London, as the navy says, with all despatch."

Guy whistled. An hour and three quarters from Dover to here, with the crowds in Town. "What sort of car were you flying?"

"A Sunbeam, sir."

"Please don't call me 'sir' . . . not today. We were going out to celebrate. Come along."

"I'd love to . . . all day, and all night."

Florinda linked her arms between the two men's and said, "You're afraid you're going to get mobbed, with your V.C.s? But think what the women out there are going to do to me, with two of you, one on each arm!"

"We'll look after you, between us," Bidford said, laughing. "The navy and the R.A.F. always work together."

Just for today, Guy thought.

*   *   *   *

"He's not greedy," Helen said, looking down fondly on the seven-month-old baby kneading her bared breast with small hands and smaller fingers. "He's like his father, a perfect officer and gentleman . . . Aren't you, Boy?" She teased the back of the baby's neck with her finger and stooped to kiss him on the top of his head, which was covered with fair curls. The window was open wide, though the day was raw, because Helen wanted to let in the sounds of Soho celebrating—barrel organs, accordions, mouth organs, the lyric plunking of a mandolin from an upper story across the road, a piano thumping away in the prostitutes' house next door, and above all, singing—in Portuguese, French, English, Spanish, but mostly Italian.

"They're enjoying themselves, and no mistake," Ethel Fagioletti said, adjusting herself more comfortably in her chair, and moving the ball of wool round to the side so that it wouldn't catch on her knees . . . not much point in knitting more khaki socks and comforters and balaclavas, now that it was over, but she'd got so used to it by now, her hands wouldn't know what to do if she stopped. She looked with pride and love at Lady Helen's baby. It might have been her own . . . one would be, just as soon as Niccolo came home. She felt heavy already, as though she were five or six months gone . . . she longed for the moment when Niccolo would come to her. That was funny, because she used to dread it, though she loved him—or thought she did. Could a woman love a man and yet fear . . . that?

Betty Merritt, sitting the other side of Helen, said, "I hope you boarded up your boutique windows."

Helen said, "We didn't bother. Ethel was sure the crowds weren't in a mood to break things deliberately, so we just locked up and came

305

home. No good trying to sell anything today. I would have been ashamed to, anyway."

"If we'd stayed, Lady Helen would have been giving it all away, if you ask me," Ethel said.

The three women sat in silence for several minutes, the baby gurgling down its mother's milk, Ethel knitting socks for soldiers but thinking of her husband's sexual equipment and her own soon-to-be-gravid womb, Betty looking out of the window into the street but seeing only the trenches, and Fletcher, standing on a firestep, safe at last. Without warning Betty found tears flooding her eyes. The other women pretended not to notice until her stifled sobs became too loud to ignore.

"What is it, Betty?" Helen said quietly. "Are you afraid, still, that he might not come back?"

Betty shook her head and at last muttered, "It's just . . . that I'm so happy . . . and so afraid. He'll come back, but will he be the same?"

Helen said, "I don't know, Betty." She shifted the baby carefully to the other breast, and put a wad of cottonwool over the released nipple, which was still dripping milk. "You'll have to wait and see." Now it was she who found her eyes filling, and Ethel saw that, and began to cry with her; so the three women cried together, almost silently, while the room grew louder and louder with the triumphant roar of celebration from outside.

*   *   *   *

The soldiers stood in a row behind a brick wall at the edge of a nameless village in Flanders, rifles rested beside them, bayonets fixed. They were staring eastward across a field, where brown and white cows grazed in damp, green grass. Tall trees beyond the field bowered a château. They were on Belgian soil, and in the village beyond the château church bells were ringing.

"Why the 'ell doesn't the captain order us to stand down?" a soldier muttered to the man next to him on the wall. "It's over. What are we standing here for?"

Private Lucas, the soldier addressed, said, "Because we haven't 'ad no orders to move."

"But that's what I'm asking, why the fuck 'aven't we got orders? Why ain't we 'aving an extra rum ration . . . throwing our 'ats in the air . . . dancing with the mademoiselles . . . slap and tickle with the mothers?"

Lucas sucked his teeth, spat out a particle of bully beef he had dislodged, and said, "You ain't been out two weeks. You don't understand. Shut up and watch your front."

He remained motionless, staring across the field, watching his front, the forestock of the rifle in his right hand, so that he could pull it up and into the firing position with a single movement. Sergeant Fagioletti walked up the line behind the row and finally took position behind the centre of the platoon he now commanded, since Mr Cowell had been evacuated with the wounded wrist and hand. He'd keep the platoon, too, because they wouldn't bother to send out any more officers now that the war was over. How long would it be before he saw Ethel again? It would be nice to try to give her a baby, very nice . . . but what was really important was to see her . . . Funny, he'd never thought of her that way before. It used to be the other way round, cunt first and the rest, later—if ever. A movement on the right caught his eye and he said sharply, "Where are you off to, Private Blaker?"

"Got to have a shit, sarn't."

"You stand where you are. The captain's coming."

"But . . ."

"Stand still, I said. You're on stand-to, Blaker. You shit your pants if you have to, but don't leave your post, got it?"

"Yes, sarn't, but . . ."

Fagioletti marched smartly to the right of his platoon line, where Captain Kellaway was approaching with his batman-runner and the company sergeant major. "No. 7 Platoon, all correct, sir," Fagioletti reported, and fell in at the captain's side. It felt funny, still, inspecting Stand-to out in an open field, not in a trench or a shell hole, on grass instead of mud, and no rotting Jerries, or the stinking legs of a Gordon Highlander sticking out of the sandbags . . .

Kellaway said, "So the war's over at last, eh, sergeant?"

"Yes, sir."

"When we stand down tell the men the colonel's trying to get a rum ration for the battalion, but we've been moving so fast this past week we're well ahead of the supply train, so   we'll probably have to do with beer and wine, from the estaminets."

"Yes, sir."

"All right. Stand down and return to billets."

"Very good, sir."

The captain passed on as Fagioletti bellowed, "Number Seven Platoon, stand down . . . Close on me . . . In two ranks, fall in! Listen! The colonel's trying to get a rum ration. We'll know soon whether he's got it . . . In twos—Number! Move to the right in column of fours . . . form, fours! Right! By the left—quick march! . . . March at ease!"

The twenty men trudged back across the field behind them and into the outskirts of the hamlet beyond that. Private Lucas's eyes were full of tears, but no one noticed, or would have believed it if they had.

Battalion Headquarters of the 1st Battalion the Weald Light Infantry was in a cowshed at the near edge of that hamlet. The shed was redolent of cow dung, which was even now being broomed and shoveled out into the midden by a girl and a boy of the farm, the girl about sixteen, the boy fourteen, both wearing torn, ragged clothes and wooden clogs. Lieutenant Woodruff, who had resumed his old post as adjutant on Archie Campbell's death, was sitting on a milking stool looking through a small pile of message forms and official envelopes, the stool set up by the low door to the shed. The shed was at present empty of cows, except for one, at the far end, heavy with calf and from all appearances very soon to produce.

Father Caffin sat on another stool opposite Woodruff, writing a letter on his knee, with a pencil and an army message form. Their commanding officer, Quentin Rowland, strode up and down the length of the shed, behind the manger where the cows were milked twice a day, a ship's captain on a dark and very smelly quarterdeck.

"Sure we've had no other orders yet, Woodruff?" he barked, stopping opposite the adjutant.

"No, sir . . . but we've got some decorations . . . A bar to the M.C. for Captain Kellaway . . . three D.C.M.s, one for the R.S.M. . . . six M.M.s . . . Fagioletti's got one."

"He ought to have had the D.C.M. I put him in for," Quentin growled.

Father Caffin looked up from his letter—"And you ought to have had your D.S.O. long, long ago, colonel . . . except that the general would never think of putting you in for it. We never saw him, so he never saw you."

"That's enough of that, padre," Quentin said, and resumed his pacing.

Woodruff exclaimed, "What on earth! . . . From the Indian Ordnance Depot, Lucknow . . . claim for rupees sixty-four annas fourteen pies four . . . on account of lost *pakhals,* to be paid forthwith by Lieutenant C.J.C. Rowland . . . That's Boy."

The colonel was back and overheard—"Boy?" He took the message from Woodruff's hand, read it, and swore under his breath— "Boy paid, I know he did. They've lost the cheque." God, he thought, the Indian Ordnance people would hound a man into his grave, and beyond. He said, "Look, Woodruff, see that it's paid, from the Imprest Account. Tell me how much, and I'll pay the same amount back, when I have it. But get the payment to the I.O.D. countersigned by the Staff Captain."

"Yes, sir."

Quentin resumed his pacing.

"Bejasus, these letters are hard to write," Father Caffin muttered. "And I'm not blaspheming, Woodie boy. I'm telling the good Lord that without his help I wouldn't be able to write them, at all . . . This is to the mother of Private Brace, who was killed back there in that mining village."

The adjutant glanced down at one of the pieces of paper in his lap and said, "He'd got a M.M. in this latest list."

"He worked for my father, before he joined up," Quentin said.

The priest laid down his pencil—"Ah! What pride in the house that would have been . . . a month ago." He picked up his pencil and began to write again.

The C.O. stopped beside them once more—"Still nothing?"

"No, sir. I expect they're still celebrating."

"They're far enough back to be celebrating," Quentin said. "Our men aren't. They're silent as the grave."

"They're in shock, colonel," the priest said. "The change is too sudden, the ending too final. The war was part of them, like a leg or an arm."

"We ought to be getting orders," Quentin said. "To advance! Push through the Huns, and if they try to shoot or delay us, sweep them aside without mercy . . ."

Woodruff said, "But, sir, we're to let them get three days' march ahead so that we won't clash with them."

Quentin's face was purple with rage—"So that they can cross the Rhine and march back into Germany in formed formations!" he bellowed, "with their arms, and guns, and bands playing and colours flying . . . an unbeaten army! Two days ago they were a rabble . . . defeated, smashed! We've been pulverizing them since August 8th. They *are* a beaten army, a beaten people! But it won't look like it when they get home. They'll be able to say, *we* weren't beaten . . . and they will say it! And you know what that means?"

He glared at the priest, and Caffin said, "No, sir."

"It means war!" Quentin thundered. "They'll come at us again . . . And we'll have to beat them again. And it'll cost just as much as it did this time. When will the bloody politicians ever learn?"

"I think this was a military order, sir," Woodruff said cautiously. "I believe it came from the High Command, Marshal Foch and Field Marshal Haig."

Quentin shouted, "Well then, Marshal Foch and Field Marshal Haig are wrong! Wrong! Wrong!"

He turned his back and resumed his angry pacing of the cowshed. The cow at the end began to low and the French girl ran to her, calling to her brother in Flemish.

Woodruff turned over another message and exclaimed, "Good heavens! Sir . . . sir!"

Quentin swung back sharply, "A message? Orders to advance and catch up the Huns?"

"No, sir . . . You've been appointed to command a brigade in India and will assume the rank of Brigadier General as soon as you take command. You are to relinquish command of the battalion at once and return to Hedlington by the fastest means."

"A brigade?" Quentin said. "But I'm not p.s.c. . . . In India? What brigade?"

"The Hassanpore Brigade, sir."

Quentin said, "But . . . then I'll have to leave the battalion . . . just when we've won . . . I don't want a brigade!"

Father Caffin said, "It's an order, sir. And I was wrong about the higher command. Someone up there must know what a wonderful job you've done."

Quentin muttered, "Who'll take over the battalion? There's no one senior enough. They'll have to send someone out from England." He walked out suddenly, saying, "I'll be back soon."

A few hundred feet away the men of No. 7 Platoon, B Company, were cleaning their weapons and equipment in another farmyard, in the open air, for there was no room for them inside the farm buildings or barns. Snaky Lucas, looking round, said, "All new faces since . . ."

"Since Mons? 'Course we are. Not many 'ad your luck, Snaky."

"Since the Somme . . . mostly since Passchendaele. Well, when we played the board we was really just passing our money round and round among ourselves, like."

" 'Cept most of it was sticking to you as it passed."

". . . now we 'ave new blood, new enthusiasm." He looked round. "I'll set up the board in the corner, behind that old cart. Come along one by one, easy like."

The young soldier next to Lucas said, "Why not set it up here in the open? The fucking war's over! We don't have to obey anyone's orders any more. Who's going to stop a little Crown and Anchor game?"

"Sergeant Fagioletti is, for one," Lucas said. "This is a regular battalion of the Weald Light Infantry, young feller, and don't forget it. Wars and peaces don't make no difference to us, and the board ain't allowed, so our N.C.O.s and officers will put us on a charge if they see it, see? And it's our jobs as self-respecting soldiers of the best regiment in the army to see that they *don't* see it, see? An' here's someone else who'll tell you the same thing." He glanced round, confirmed that he was the senior soldier present, and jumped to his feet, shouting, "Section, 'shun!"

The others struggled up and stood rigid. Lieutenant Colonel Quentin Rowland came up, walking heavily. He saluted and muttered, "Stand easy." He stared at Lucas, and at last said, "Lucas . . . they're sending me away."

Lucas said, "Away, sir? From the battalion?"

"Yes. I'm being promoted."

"Well, congratulations, sir. You should have 'ad it years ago."

"But, Lucas . . . I don't want to go." He looked round at the others, new men all, only a month or two with the battalion. He thought he'd ask them, do you understand? But before he could speak Lucas said, "They won't understand, sir."

"I think I'll refuse the appointment."

Lucas said, "You can't do that, sir. It's an order . . . 'sides, they wouldn't leave you with us."

At length Quentin said, "No, they wouldn't. Well, goodbye Lucas . . . And thank you . . . thank you, all of you."

The men stood rigid, tongue-tied. One of them thought, crikey, the old man's crying . . . what's happened? Only Lucas said anything—"Good luck, sir. We'll remember you."

Daily Telegraph, Tuesday, November 12, 1918

LONDON WELCOMES THE GLAD TIDINGS

GREAT SCENES OF JOY

London has heard no such paean of exultant joy as that which, just on the stroke of eleven, upon the grey November morning, thrilled the hearts of the whole population. The effect was magical and indescribable. A minute or so before the amazing outburst there was nothing in the aspect of the streets or the demeanour of citizens to suggest that anything unusual was astir. Under leaden, threatening skies, people were going about their business in the ordinary way, just as though nothing in the least unusual was happening or about to happen.

Then, of a sudden, came the sounds of gunfire, and as the maroons, transformed from portents of danger into signals for rejoicing, thundered out their message of peace, there went up from end to end of the metropolis such tumultuous cheering as no mere words could even faintly describe. The thrill of it will live in the memory alike of the oldest and youngest of us. So, too, will the unforgettable scenes that followed . . .

> . . . of all the day's impressive scenes of heartfelt jubilation none, perhaps, was more unforgettable, more thrilling . . . than that witnessed in front of Buckingham Palace at the moment when, in response to the tumultuous cheers of the surging crowd—cheers that seemed ever to grow in volume and intensity—the King and Queen came out on the balcony overlooking the forecourt to be acclaimed with full-throated fervour by countless thousands of their loyal and loving subjects . . .

It must have been a wonderful occasion, Cate thought. It would have been nice to have been there. But it had been wonderful here in Walstone, too, and Walstone was his place. He'd gone down to the village soon after eleven, to the clanging of the bells, and had a cherry brandy in the Arms. Old Miss Parsley was already tiddly, and would become more so. There were people in there that morning who never went into pubs, but that day the Beaulieu Arms, the Goat and Compasses, and the Green Man had become the heart of the village's celebration . . . and of its dedication. There'd be services of thanksgiving in the church, of course; but it was in the pubs that the people had first shared the grandeurs and miseries of victory.

He glanced at his watch: a meeting of the Mid Scarrow War Problems Committee in Hedlington at three . . . but would it meet? And if it did, what would they discuss? Perhaps the all-party committee would never meet again. The war and the nation's single, driving purpose had held it together: now the members would pull their separate ways, they who had been partners in the common great enterprise become enemies and rivals. It was a pity, for the problems that Mid Scarrow—and England—now faced were no less than they had been twenty-four hours ago; in fact they were greater—much greater, much more diverse, much more intractable.

Well, unless he heard to the contrary within the next half hour, he'd go up to Hedlington, and tell the other members of the committee just that.

Garrod came in and said, "Colonel Rowland's on the telephone, sir."

Cate jumped to his feet—"Quentin? Good heavens, where can he be calling from?" He hurried out and picked up the receiver— "Quentin? Where are you?"

"Calais . . . I've been posted to India, to command a brigade, and they've sent me home in a hurry . . . and now I'll probably be kicking my heels for a month in the Depot before they can fit us into a troopship . . . Christopher, will you call Fiona and tell her I should be with her tonight? Don't know when, the trains are in a mess."

"Certainly," Cate said. "But wouldn't you like to speak to her yourself?"

"No, you do it. Warn her . . . And, Christopher, find out whether she knows that Archie Campbell was killed in action a week ago. I tried to make sure she would be informed, but you never know . . . Tell her I'm bringing back his things . . . personal things."

"Very well," Cate said, puzzled. Who was Archie Campbell, that he should matter so much to Quentin's wife?

To the "Khaki Election,"
December 14, 1918

_17_ The wind was gusty from the south-west, with scattered banks of cloud at 5,000 feet, but visibility good below them. It was raining lightly, and damp. The rain spattered Guy's goggles as he swung the Buffalo to port on its final upwind landing run. The airfield was clear ahead, with twelve Fokker triplanes lined up on one side, and three S.E. 5 As of the R.A.F. on the other. His co-pilot said, "Air speed fifty-two, sir."

That was only five knots above stalling speed. Guy repeated, "Air speed fifty-two," and eased the throttles slightly forward. The wind was about twenty knots in the gusts, ten otherwise, and he'd better have a little more margin.

"Air speed sixty-five, sir."

"Air speed sixty-five," Guy said. Half a mile to go, dropping steadily, the big radials thrumming like huge banjos, the big four-bladed propellers whirling lazily. It was strange to see those Fokkers lined up there, as though for inspection . . . one bigger plane behind them, too . . . a Junkers of some new model, big, all metal, shiny.

The Buffalo touched down, the tail skid gradually settled. They were down.

An R.A.F. captain came forward from a group of men, most of the others wearing German uniform. The captain saluted, "Good morning, sir. They're ready. But they'd like to give you lunch first."

"All right," Guy said. His official orders from General Sykes had been to fly a Buffalo to an agreed airfield in Germany and bring back some German pilots who had volunteered to give the British information about their new aircraft types, and an important German politician who wanted to impress upon the Prime Minister the urgency of getting a peace settlement so that order could be re-established in the conquered country.

The captain said, "The German major asked if he could speak to you privately, sir."

Guy looked at the men standing twenty yards back and started walking toward them. The captain said, "It's the one in the middle, sir—Major Traustein." The Major barked a command and all the Germans sprang to attention, clicking their heels, their hands stiff down the seams of their trousers.

"Major Traustein," Guy said. "You want to speak to me? My German's not very good."

"I speak English . . . a little . . . enough, Herr Oberst," the German said.

Guy said, "Well, let's walk over here a bit . . . The rest of them can look over the Buffalo." The R.A.F. captain said a word and the young German officers rushed forward like children let out of school toward the huge four-engined biplane standing there so close in the light rain.

Walking away with the major, Guy said, "Well?"

"Herr Oberst . . . we have Frau von Rackow here."

"Here? Good God! How on earth . . . ?"

"We heard two days ago that you were coming. I spoke to the lady on the telephone because Werner had told me before . . . before . . . that it was her great wish to meet you after the war. It was his, too—Werner's . . . So we flew a pilot back to the nearest airfield to her home—their home—and brought her here in that Junkers J.1 . . ."

"So that's what it is. Nice looking machine."

"The cockpit and tank are armored, sir . . . Germany is in chaos. We can do anything we want to. So we wait here, keeping our discipline and formation as a Jagdstaffel in case we are needed. I did not fight the French and British to have Germany taken over by the Bolsheviks . . . Herr Oberst, Frau von Rackow is in that hut. I have arranged for you to lunch there with her, alone. It is all laid out—cold pheasant, wild pig, champagne, everything."

"All right," Guy said. "Thank you." He looked suddenly at the German, who stood stiff before the cold blue and the warm brown eye. Guy said, "It was an accident . . . I hope . . . I don't know."

The major said stiffly, "All the German Air Force believes that, Herr Oberst." He clicked his heels and bowed from the waist. Guy walked to the hut, his greatcoat unbuttoned, the peaked cap in his hand, the rain speckling his fair hair.

She was of medium height, blue-eyed, with long, braided golden hair. Her expression was clear and frank, her young face and jaw rounded. In the photograph Werner had shown him the night they spent together in the barn, she had been smiling. Now she was not, and there were lines of weariness round her eyes. Her body was heavy, in this fourth month of her pregnancy.

She was standing in the middle of the room, a table covered by a big tablecloth hiding whatever was on it behind her, chairs drawn up to it, a fire burning in the grate. She was wearing black, with a dense black veil drawn up now to show her face, and the blue eyes. She said, "Guy . . . Wait . . . Don't move . . . Oh!" She burst into tears and stumbled toward him, her hands outstretched. He took her and fell naturally against her, the swell of her belly pressing into him. She sobbed against him, while he patted her back and shoulder. She stood away at last and he pulled out a chair from the table and said, "Sit down, gnädige Frau . . . that's right, isn't it?"

She smiled through the tears, saying, "Maria, please, Guy . . . I speak English good enough?"

"Very good," he said.

"He taught me. His mother's English, you know."

"Yes."

They remained as they were then for some time without speaking, but looking at each other, she seated by the table, he standing. She said at last, "You received the letters . . . mine, too, after he died?" Guy nodded. "What are you going to do, now that it's over?"

"I don't know. I keep wondering what he would have done. What *we* might have done, together. I think we could have done so much."

"I know, I know! He was the same. The last time I saw him he kept saying, I wonder what Guy will do after it's over. The world will be in such a mess, he said, and it's only young people like us who can do what needs to be done . . ."

"I wonder . . . Look, Maria, we must eat. I have to start back in an hour or my general will blow me up. Let's see what we have here." He eased off the tablecloth, revealing all the good things the German had mentioned. He began to open a bottle of champagne, saying, "Not supposed to drink when I have to fly . . . but there wouldn't have been many sorties flown by the R.F.C. if that rule had been strictly enforced. Anyway, to hell with the rules. I'm going to have as much as you do."

He poured for her, and for himself, and raised his own glass. He said, "The navy—our navy—has a toast: the Immortal Memory. They mean Nelson, but . . ."

She said, "Ah, to us, it will be . . . him."

"The Immortal Memory," Guy said, and Maria said it with him.

They began to eat, facing each other across the table. Guy noticed that she ate very lightly, and after a time, enjoying his second helping of the excellent cold smoked wild boar, said, "You must eat more, Maria. You are eating for two."

She looked up—"I will name him Guy. Will you be his godfather?"

"Of course. What if it's a girl?"

"It will be a boy," she said with finality. "You must come and visit us, so that you can be, a little, his father . . . We have a big house . . ."

"A schloss," Guy said. "An eighteenth-century schloss."

"Yes. Thousands of acres of heath and forest . . . two villages. Werner's family is noble, mine is rich. We meant to have many children, and bring them up both German and English . . . Werner's mother's family has a big estate in Wiltshire." She looked up and at him—"I wish it could still be. When I have had time to say goodbye to him, in myself . . ."

Guy was about to speak, but held his tongue in check. She was blushing. The tone of her voice just now had been very soft. He understood that she was saying, give me time to know you, then—she was hoping he would take Werner's place—offering him marriage, herself, her fortune, estates, and homes in both countries. He could not give her an answer now, even if she had demanded it. Perhaps, soon, if he could bring the fire of life back into himself, as it had burned when he was a killer, the Butcher of the Three Threes . . . But now, he did not have it.

He said slowly, "Let me come back, Maria, when I have recovered. I am not . . . what I ought to be. I have not been since—that day. Perhaps I never will be . . . We must wait."

"I shall wait," she said. "When you have loved the best, and been loved by the best, nothing else is desirable . . . except another best."

*   *   *   *

Four hours later Guy was facing General Sykes across the big table in the Chief of the Air Staff's office. "Well, that's done," the general said. "Herr Flass has been sent on to the Prime Minister and the pilots have been sent down to Farnborough to have their brains picked. Now"— he leaned back in the big swivel chair—"I have been told that the Prime Minister—and others—have offered you safe seats in Parliament. Is that true?"

"Yes, sir."

"What have you decided?"

"I haven't, sir . . . But I want to fly . . . develop heavy bombers, and commercial flight . . ."

"You could fly as much as you liked. I'd see that you could always

317

get back into the R.A.F., with your present rank, or something more appropriate."

Guy said unhappily, "I don't know whether I'm cut out for Parliament, sir . . . debating, compromising, lying sometimes."

"You could do a lot more for the preservation of the idea of a separate air arm for this country, in Parliament, than you can in uniform. You're a good organizer and administrator, a good tactician—one of the best in all those things. But there are others nearly as good, or better in some respects . . . Douglas, Portal, Dowding, Slessor. You are unique in being a top ace, with the V.C., two D.S.O.s, two M.C.s . . . Parliament is full of hero worshippers."

Guy said, "Do I have to make up my mind now, sir?"

The general said, "Yes. The election date has been fixed— December 14th. There's no time to lose."

Guy thought, this is like an air fight, with Jasta 16 coming at you out of the clouds and you have to weigh a dozen courses of action and simultaneously choose one, and act. He said, "I'm sorry, sir, but in that case it's best that I say no. The only wise decision for me now is to stay with what I know and think I can do well—service in the Royal Air Force. Saying yes could do a lot of damage, to England."

The general surveyed him for a long time without speaking and at last shook his head—"We *had* to take your youth, out there. But it's a shame. That's all."

*   *   *   *

Winston Churchill stood in the little room off the Hedlington Oddfellows Hall, talking to Richard Rowland, Lord Walstone, and the Mayor of Hedlington. Churchill was smoking a large cigar, whose fragrant fumes filled the chamber. The door was slightly ajar so that through it they could see the people filing into the big hall, and the row of empty seats on the platform, the speaker's dais in front, the reading lamp lit over it.

Churchill said, "The situation is this . . . The Prime Minister has decided that everyone who voted against the Government in the debate on General Maurice's allegations—that was in April this year— will be regarded as an enemy, and will be opposed by a supporter of the Coalition—either a Coalition Liberal or Coalition Conservative. Your father, Rowland, voted for the Government, and though he has applied for the Hundreds, we are willing to treat you as a supporter . . . You have given the central office an undertaking to that effect?" He cocked an eyebrow interrogatively.

Richard said, "Yes. I have. Though I thought that General

Maurice's charges were well founded, and hear the same from everyone who knew of the situation in France at that time."

Churchill waved the cigar—"The substance of the matter will be settled by history, my dear sir. The politics of it is that the Prime Minister had to find some arbitrary way, some sharp knife, to divide the sheep who would support him in a new government, from the goats, who might not. He chose that debate . . . We are now sure that the opposition Liberals—Asquith's Liberals—will not put up a candidate. Considering how closely you came to defeating your father here in 1915, they think it would be a waste of money to oppose you when you will be in the sun of the Prime Minister's enormous prestige . . ."

Lord Walstone said, "There's a Socialist standing, Mr Churchill . . . A fellow called Wilfred Bentley."

"We know about him," Churchill said. "War hero . . . gassed, won an M.C., then turned pacifist, or at any rate, wanted peace negotiated . . . rather like that poet, Sassoon . . . Don't underestimate him, though we don't think he has much of a chance." He turned to Richard—"Make it short, Rowland. The P.M. won the war. Support him by voting for you. Hang the Kaiser. Squeeze Germany till the pips squeak. Back to business as usual as soon as possible. Bring the men home at once."

"I have heard that it would be wiser to keep conscription, now that we have it," Richard said.

Churchill raised his hands in mock horror, ash falling off his cigar onto his coat as he did so—"Good heavens, man, don't mention such a thing," he said in a stage whisper—"It *would* be a wise idea, but"—he drew his hand across his throat—"political suicide . . . Patience, Rowland, patience. Wait and see. Dear me, I sound like Mr Asquith."

A man with a big blue flower in his buttonhole poked his head round the door—"Ready, sir."

Churchill continued—"And when you introduce me, don't call me the Minister of Munitions. No one wants to hear the word any more. Just say, the Right Honourable, etcetera."

He turned to walk out onto the platform. The man with the buttonhole said, "There's a rough crowd come in, sir. Socialists, like. Looks as though you may get a rotten egg or two thrown at you."

"I am wearing my electioneering suit," Churchill said. "Lead on, Rowland."

*   *   *   *

Quentin and Fiona were looking at a large oil painting propped against a wall of the drawing room in their Hedlington flat. It was of a tall blonde woman—grey-eyed, slender—gracefully holding up a pin flag labeled *'06*, in the centre of a putting green, a large hotel or castle vaguely outlined behind. The woman was half-smiling, with parted lips, and her pose was extraordinarily voluptuous, for she was fully naked; but a putter dangled negligently from her left hand. Fiona said, "He painted that in 1906—just after I'd reached the semi-final of the Women's Championship. It was played at Dalmellie that year. Archie's teasing me, really, in that picture. He kept it in his studio till 1912, then gave it to me . . . I put it in storage. When we get to Hassanpore we'll hang it in our bedroom."

Quentin thought, good heavens, what will the Indian servants think? And the rest of the British, especially the wives? But if that was what she wanted, and she didn't care, why should he? And perhaps she was right, to put up this permanent reminder of the link that had now come to bind them together again, where they had been separated—the life and death of Archie Campbell, who had loved her, and left this memorial to that love.

He said, "All right, my dear . . . And most of the others we'll put in the *gol kamra* . . . that means drawing room . . . the war scenes. They're so awfully good."

She was staring at the picture of herself, as though mesmerized by her own beauty. She whispered at last, "I could never have believed, then, that he would ever leave me . . . least of all, this way."

Quentin took her hand awkwardly. He noticed that she was wearing Archie's big wristwatch on her slender wrist. He said, "He hasn't left you, Fiona . . . or me. I can hear him chuckling, as he used to . . . hear him swapping jokes with Father Caffin, our padre, in the dugout . . . see him crouched against the front wall of the trench, making sketches, before we went over the top . . ."

She said, "Perhaps he made the sketches to take his mind off . . . what might happen next."

"Perhaps," Quentin said eagerly. "They were awful, those attacks—most of them, till the end . . . knowing so many good men were going to catch it . . . and always, I kept thinking, what if Archie's one of them. How can I tell Fiona? Because she loves him, and I am responsible for him . . . And, Fiona, I don't know how to say it . . . I loved him, too."

She leaned forward and kissed him on the cheek—"You're right, Quentin. Archie will never leave us now. And we'll never leave each other, inside ourselves, because of him . . . I'd better get on with the packing. Will you be O.C. Troops on board?"

"Don't know," Quentin grunted. "Hope not. More damned bumf to deal with, if I am . . . But I don't become brigadier general until I take over in Hassanpore, and I expect there'll be some full colonels and generals on board . . . I'll start writing out and sticking on the labels. You've marked the trunks that are Not Wanted on Voyage?"

*   *   *   *

The crowd outside the Beaulieu Arms was small, indeed only courtesy could call it a crowd, for it was really half a dozen men and women, who happened to be passing by on their various errands, and saw the decorated Rowland Ruby car with the big placards on the sides, front and back—VOTE FOR ROWLAND; and the two men standing beside it, Richard the candidate, and the Conservative agent for the constituency. Richard was making a speech, the same one he was making half a dozen times a day; it was the same speech he had given in the Oddfellows Hall in Hedlington the night he opened his campaign, introducing Winston Churchill—hang the Kaiser, squeeze Germany till the pips squeak, back to business as usual, away with all forms of controls or compulsion, bring the men home.

One of the women facing him, a shopping basket over one arm, said, "That's it, sir, when *are* they going to bring the men home?"

Richard had had the same question asked nearly every time he spoke. No one asked the questions he himself would have asked—on what legal grounds could one hang the Kaiser? How exactly did you squeeze money or goods out of Germany without damaging your own trade and industry? But it was always this one. He said, "The Government is determined to bring everyone back as soon as it can be done. There are limitations of shipping and of accommodation at the various barracks where men must pass through the demobilization process. A considerable force has to be maintained in Germany until we are sure that the Germans have really disarmed, and can not restart the war . . ."

A man said, "That's all right, mister, but I know three or four blokes what's back already, what only went off six months or a year ago, and others, what volunteered in August '14, are still out."

"That's right," a murmur arose. "I've seen 'em . . . how did they get home so quick?"

"The Government is doing its best," Richard repeated, more loudly, "and if I am elected you may count on me to see that the process is speeded up, and that demobilization proceeds fairly as well as speedily."

The agent muttered, "Better move on, Mr Rowland. You're supposed to be in Beighton in five minutes."

Rowland waved his bowler hat in the air and cried, "Vote for me on the 14th—Rowland, Coalition Conservative!"

Then he climbed into the car, the agent took the wheel, and the car drove slowly off, Richard waving to the few passersby, who either looked blankly after him, seeing the message VOTE FOR ROWLAND on the sign on the back of the car, or did not notice at all.

Among the dispersing "crowd" Probyn Gorse turned to his companion and said, "I'd best be getting back to work."

The companion was Skagg, ex-head gamekeeper at Walstone Park. He said, "I feel like a Guinness, Probyn. It's a right nasty morning, except it isn't raining."

"I don't mind if I do," Probyn said, and followed Skagg into the public bar. Parsley, the ancient barmaid, looked up from polishing the bar and said, "Why, Mr Skagg, you haven't changed a bit."

"Two pints of Guinness, Miss Parsley," Skagg said. "I've put on a bit of weight, as a matter of fact. Don't get as much exercise as I used to."

"That's right," Probyn said, lifting the tankard of stout and drinking deep.

Skagg drank, put down the tankard and said, "Can't get over seeing you in them clothes, and head gamekeeper. But, everything's changed." He shook his head and drank again.

Parsley said, "It'll be better when the men come home."

"They won't all come back," Probyn said. "Only them as can still breathe . . . Mr Richard'll lose the election if he ain't careful. That Bentley was down yesterday, and he came right out and said it was a disgrace that some blokes could swing their way out, while others had to stay in and do the dirty work."

"That's it," Skagg said. "It's the jobs. The war jobs is getting less and less, the civvie jobs haven't started up proper yet, so there are ten men trying to grab anything that turns up, and those fellows who wangled themselves home are getting them . . . How's Cate?"

"Mr Cate's all right," Probyn said shortly. He stood up and away from the bar, "I'd best be back to work. Thanks for the Guinness." He went out.

Skagg said, "Another of the same, please, Miss Parsley . . . Is that right what Probyn said about Mr Cate? I heard that the daughter, Stella, had run away and had a black baby, though her husband's white, and that Laurence had been . . ."

Parsley, polishing a glass, said, "I've heard nothing about that, Mr Skagg."

Skagg continued, leaning forward confidentially—"And that Probyn married his Woman at last, after thirty years. That's enough to make a cat laugh."

Parsley said, "Mr Gorse married Miss Hyde six weeks ago, in the church here. Lord Walstone gave the bride away, and Mr Cate was best man. It was a very pretty wedding." She moved up the bar to a new arrival, saying, "The usual, Mr B?"

*　　*　　*　　*

Richard Rowland, walking past the main assembly shed at Hedlington Aircraft, paused, seeing a crowd of men and women gathered at the far end; and to one side, more, in single line. Ah, of course, pay day. He was about to move on, heading for the place where his car and chauffeur would be waiting, when he noticed a man beyond the pay table where Pratt was handing out the pay envelopes, a man standing with a big placard, facing the workers as they left the table. Richard could not read the placard, so walked forward to see. When he got close enough, and in the right position, he read—PART OF UNION DUES WILL GO TO BENTLEY ELECTION CAMPAIGN. OTHER GIFTS WELCOME.

Richard felt the blood first draining from his face and neck, then rushing back. He hurried forward and confronted the works foreman across the desk, shouldering the foremost workers in the pay line out of the way—"What is the meaning of this, Mr Pratt?" he snapped.

Pratt stood up, "What, sir? Oh, that. The U.S.E. have been collecting their dues from their members at pay day for weeks now."

"Why wasn't I asked? They have no right to collect their damned dues on our property! They can wait outside the gates and collect them there."

Pratt said, "It makes it easier, sir, for . . ."

"Why should we make it easier? And what about this? They're advertising that the dues are going to be spent in a political campaign . . . against me! And the non-union workers are being asked to subscribe, too. It's outrageous!" He turned on the man with the placard—"You're Fuller, aren't you?"

"Yes," the man said shortly. "Wing Rigger."

"Have you had your pay?"

"Yes."

"Well, take that sign off this company's property. And don't come back to work on Monday. You're dismissed."

The man said nothing, but turned and walked out, the placard still hanging round his neck, his leather collection satchel over his shoulder.

Richard turned on the foreman—"Get on with paying out." He stalked out of the huge shed into the open air. Damned insolence! Illegal, too, certainly, to compel the union members to support one particular political party. He'd get the lawyers onto that. It might be possible to take the U.S.E. to court over it . . . it would certainly deprive Bentley of funds, and bring the voters' attention to what was going on. This bloody war was responsible. If all the men hadn't been conscripted, and there hadn't been so many damned government regulations, he'd never have allowed the union to get a foothold in his factories. One member was like a rotten apple in a barrel . . .

*   *   *   *

A wind was blowing off the sea up toward the Moor, shaking the bare boughs with its damp, rough energy, bending the lush grass in the meadows where the Shorthorn cows grazed, riffling the feathers of the robin perched on the edge of the birdbath outside the leaded panes of the cottage's living room. Harry Rowland, sitting in that room reading the *Times*, could hear Mrs Lowndes working upstairs in his bedroom, which was directly overhead. She would leave before noon, to go back to her own cottage at the other end of King's Tracy, and he'd be alone again. He had thought that he would feel lonely; but though he had only been here a few days, he was already used to it, and did not feel any unhappiness, or wish for other permanent company. He thought, it takes time to accept this state . . . one is lonely when young, when you first leave home and parents and go out into the world; then more and more relationships pile up . . . you acquire a wife . . . children one after the other, the years pass and the house is always full, of people, of noise, of bustle, energy, sound, movement; gradually it all drains away, the children grow up, leave, marry . . . you are alone with your wife . . . she goes . . . you are alone.

He readjusted his spectacles and returned to the paper. The election campaign was in full swing all over the country. Lloyd George would sweep the polls and return with a large majority, large enough for him to ram any legislation he wanted through the House; but he had no real power base, except his prestige. The Liberal Party, as such, was still controlled by Asquith. This present schism would split it. The Conservatives would never accept Lloyd George as their leader, after what he had done to them with his pre-war finance bills. The Conservatives and Socialists would survive; the Liberals would not. The war and that little Welsh cad had destroyed them.

He got up. Time to take a little exercise . . . walk down to the Post Office and send off his letters to Richard and Alice . . . Look inside the church, if it was open; go to the churchyard and say a prayer by the twin headstones where his father and mother lay. That was his father's own Bible on the table beside him now, inscribed by the man who had given it, his father's friend Edward White Benson, first Master of Wellington, sometime Archbishop of Canterbury.

He was struggling into his overcoat now, the woollen scarf wrapped round his neck, the tweed hat pulled well down on his thin white hairs, woollen gloves on his blue-veined hands . . . now the stick . . . Mrs Lowndes knew he'd be going out, no need to call up to her . . . make sure he had his key . . . strange not to have someone open the door for him when he rang . . . and out into the wind.

The first few days he'd expected to meet a boyhood friend at every step; but they'd all gone, with the years. Joe Wood at the bakery—long dead . . . Warren Church, the Squire's son, died soon after the Boer War . . . The vicar knew his name of course—"Ah, the son of the fourth vicar before me, sir!" Bit of a windbag, young, too . . . ought to have been in the trenches, or at least a padre out there . . . Tom Palmer had recognized him. Tom had been a farm labourer, year or two older than he, a strong boy, used to throw the ball a mile in the village cricket team. Now he was in a wheelchair, living with his granddaughter . . . And Jane Sheldon, who'd been a church cleaner then, blind as a bat now . . . New houses everywhere, new faces, motor cars stinking in the street, horses bolting, motor bikes going bang bang bang outside his window where he was trying to nap . . .

He climbed slowly up the four steps into the combined Post Office and sweet shop run by Mr and Mrs Tilley—new people since the war began, they'd told him—and bought penny stamps for his letters.

Mrs Tilley, working at the little Post Office counter, said, "Windy day, isn't it, Mr Rowland?"

"Very," he said. "It'll rain by dark."

"That it will." A nice Devon burr she had, at least. He turned to leave. A woman's voice said, "Mr Rowland? Mr Harry Rowland?"

He stopped, peering shortsightedly. It was a tall woman, about his age—seventy-seven, eighty perhaps—grey-haired, straight-backed, better preserved than he was, the skin of her face quite smooth, and plenty of brown in the hair . . . blue eyes, big blue eyes, wrinkles at the corners, of course, but no spectacles.

"Yes," he said. "Do I . . . ?"

"Susan Hammond-Chambers-Borgnis," she said. Her voice was light and educated; a lady. She was laughing.

He said stiffly, "I'm afraid . . ."

"Susan Chenevix-Trench, then. I was born with two surnames and married a man with three."

Harry's jaw dropped. Susan Chenevix-Trench! Why, this was the laughing girl who climbed trees like a boy, this was his first love. She was still beautiful, still laughing, still gay. You could believe that she still climbed trees. "Susan!" he gasped, "I never expected . . . How long have . . . ?"

The lady said, "It will take us a month of Sundays to say all we have to say to each other, Harry. I've been away visiting some of my children, and only came back yesterday." She saw the question in his eyes and said, "Harry—my Harry—died in 1910. The children were all gone, and I moved back here to a little house on . . . but we shall walk there now, so that you know where it is, and you shall call on me tomorrow. Today I have to spend the afternoon working for the Liberal candidate for this seat."

"The Liberal?" Harry cried. "Mr Asquith's candidate?"

"Of course! You don't think I would support that awful Welsh lecher, do you?"

Harry laughed aloud—"Come on, my dear. We do have a lot to talk about . . . and celebrate!"

*　　*　　*　　*

Margaret Cate said, "It looks as though we're going to get twenty-five or -six seats unopposed. It seems incredible that the Nationalists can only find candidates for two-thirds of the constituencies."

"It's true, though," Michael Collins said.

"Then we shall win, by a large majority. If they don't have the will to fight, the voters will see it, and not vote for them—even people who are Nationalist at heart."

Collins laughed, his usual short, bitter laugh—"Don't forget the full name of the party is the Nationalist Home Rule Party. The Home Rule part has been a farce for years but no one recognized it until we came along and started a real fight for real Home Rule . . . Have you seen De Valera's election manifesto? Issued from Lincoln Gaol?"

Margaret shook her head and Collins picked up a newspaper and began to read:

> Every true son and every true daughter of Ireland is mindful of what the honour of the Motherland demands . . . that individual opinions and individual interests, with a nobility befitting the occasion, will all be subordinated to the necessity of proclaiming unequivocally to an attending world that it is no slave status that Ireland's heroes have fought for, but the securing for their beloved country of her rightful place in the family of nations . . .

"He's always been a great orator," Margaret said, "but what does he really mean? What do we mean—you and I and the rest of Sinn Fein?"

"The majority of Irishmen would say that by voting for us they were voting for Dominion Home Rule," Collins said, keeping his eyes on Margaret.

"But are we? And does anyone expect the British to give us even that much without keeping Ulster out of it?"

Collins said softly, "No."

"Then?"

"We will appeal to the Peace Conference."

Margaret realized that he was drawing her out; and said, "You don't believe that. That's not the course you think we should follow. Is it?"

"No."

"Then what is?"

"Sovereign independence for a united Ireland. That is what *we* are aiming at—*not* Dominion Home Rule. But we know the British will give us neither the one nor the other, so . . ." he made the motions of pulling an imaginary trigger followed by the cutting of an imaginary throat.

"The people would never vote for that," Margaret said.

Collins said, "Voting is not going to get us independence. Only fighting is. Come, Lady, you've known that all along, haven't you?"

Margaret said at last, "Yes. I did hope, when I saw that Sinn Fein was going to win so large a majority, that the other wouldn't be necessary. Because, before it's over, Irishmen will have killed far more other Irishmen than they'll have killed English."

Collins said sharply, "That can't be helped. And it doesn't matter. All that matters is an independent, united Irish republic . . . Let's get back to business. We've got to make sure we *do* win the election, whatever happens afterwards, so that outsiders will recognize the legitimacy of Sinn Fein as the true government of Ireland. How many Volunteers do we have in Cork?"

"Seven hundred and twenty-three," Margaret said, without looking at the paper under her hand.

"That's ample. What about Ulster? We're not going to let that go by default . . ."

Their heads bent together, they worked on into the night, the curtain drawn tight, the gas mantle hissing on its wall bracket.

*   *   *   *

"I'm not saying Mr Rowland's a bad employer," Wilfred Bentley shouted, so that his voice would carry to the back of the crowd gathered in the little park—"I am saying that you have a right to join a union . . . that the union has a right to collect its dues in the place where the men work; and that it has the right to use those funds as it pleases, according to its own rules and procedures."

Behind him his wife Rachel muttered, "Don't use such long words, Wilfred."

Most of the crowd below him, where he spoke from the bandshell, were men, wearing mufflers and cloth caps; and most of them were men usually employed by the Hedlington Aircraft Company, now come out on strike, union men and non-union men alike, in response to Richard Rowland's outburst of a few days back. There were women, too, anxious-faced, most of them wives of strikers. They all knew that the Hedlington branch of the union did not have enough funds to pay out adequate strike pay.

Wilfred said, "We've appealed to the National headquarters of the U.S.E., and though they haven't promised anything, the secretary's coming down this afternoon. We'll get the money for you. Don't you worry. Just stick together. Stick it out. Stand up for your rights . . . for the rights of the men who'll be coming back from France, and . . ."

"When will they be coming?" a woman called. "The war's been over near a month now, and there's none back that I know . . . plenty of rich men's sons, though, from what I hear."

Wilfred steeled himself, and shouted, "It's a disgrace! It's sheer incompetence. They've seen the end of the war coming for months now, and they've done nothing . . . except leave the way open for men to bribe themselves out, weasel out . . ."

The crowd cheered. This was the most popular subject of any speech—jumping on the Government about demobilization. Wilfred hammered on the theme, because Rachel and the local party secretary had advised him that he must; but he disliked doing it, for he knew that no government could have got a million and a half men back to their homes in a week or two, with a powerful enemy not yet even disarmed.

He shouted, "There's only one way to protect your rights as working men and women . . . to bring the men home . . . to see that your children get a fair chance in life . . . Vote Labour! Vote for me, Bentley, on the 14th! Thank you."

He jumped down and helped Rachel to follow. The crowd was thinning as he walked up High Street toward the middle of the town. He was wearing a big red buttonhole in the lapel of his jacket, and a muffler and tweed cap. It was cold and he'd have preferred to wear his overcoat, but Rachel had said no: the working men did not own overcoats and he had better not flaunt the fact that he did. He would have preferred to go from one meeting to the next by car; it would save time, and enable him to make more speeches; but Rachel said they must walk.

She muttered, "Here . . . the man with the bowler hat and the big woman . . ."

Wilfred stopped, his hand out, "I'm Wilfred Bentley, sir, madam. I am the Labour candidate for this constituency. I hope you'll both vote for me."

The man had stopped, hands on hips, his wife beside him, stiffly upright, one arm looped through one of his. He said, "I'm a Conservative, young man. 'Ave been all my life."

The woman said suddenly to Rachel—"Aren't you Miss Cowan . . . the lady who was with the No Conscription lot?"

Rachel said, "Yes, madam. We were trying to save some young men's lives."

The woman began to cry. "'Wish you'd succeeded . . . We lost our Billy, just two months ago."

Wilfred said, "We think the war could have been ended sooner. And we intend to see that there is never another war."

The woman said, "I'll vote for you, Mr Bentley . . . Promise you'll vote for him, too, George."

"We'll talk about that later," the man said. "Good day."

He strode on. Rachel said, "We'll get him . . . Rowland's played into our hands. I really think you stand a chance now."

"We'll see," Wilfred said.

A couple approached, the woman limping, the man in uniform, one arm in a sling, the wrist and hand heavily bandaged. Wilfred made to pass on, for the woman was well-dressed and had an air of wealth and breeding, while the man was an officer of the Weald Light Infantry, a 2nd Lieutenant, though by no means young. But Rachel exclaimed, "Dave Cowell! And Miss Rowland!" She turned to Wilfred, "You remember Dave, he let us use his classroom for a pacifist meeting once . . ."

"And got sacked for it," Dave said, laughing. "We heard you were making speeches in town and have been looking for you. I want to help. I've always been a Socialist, and pro-Labour, so . . . what can I do?"

"Get us some money," Rachel said. "Help us persuade the National headquarters of the U.S.E. to give the H.E. 16 branch money so we can pay the H.A.C. strikers. This is a turning point . . ."

"I understand that," Cowell said. "But why didn't you—and the rest of the party—join the Coalition? You'd have got more concessions from Lloyd George, you'd certainly win more seats, and you wouldn't be having this sort of money problem."

Bentley said, "Bernard Shaw harangued the party bigwigs and candidates the other day and said on no account must we join the

Coalition. He impressed everyone, so we agreed to stand on our own merits, free to do what we think right after the election . . ."

Rachel, walking beside Alice, said, "Won't it make trouble for you with your brother, Miss Alice, if you work for us?"

Alice said, smiling, "I'm not going to do any electioneering in public, but I'll work behind the scenes to help Dave."

Bentley said, "But you're not a Socialist, are you, Miss Rowland?"

"Dear me, no," Alice said. "I am not a political animal, at all. But it is my place to help Dave in whatever he wants to do."

Rachel said, "Well, that is wonderful"—thinking, that is as public an admission of love as I've ever heard.

They all stopped while Wilfred shook more hands, this time two elderly women, walking together, with shopping bags. To the side, Alice said to Rachel—"The one thing I hear everywhere I go is that there will be trouble if we don't get the soldiers home soon, and by a fair priority system."

"There's trouble already," Rachel said, "and it's helping us, because everyone knows we're not responsible for it."

*   *   *   *

"'E said he'd call you at ten o'clock and he wanted me to make sure you'd be in your office then."

Richard Rowland looked at the clock on the wall facing him. It was a quarter to ten. He said, "I'll be here. What's it about?"

"I don't know, Richard," Lord Walstone said, "but if I was you I'd do what he says, toot sweet. He sounded shirty. Ta ta, and call me back when he's done with you. I want to know, seeing as I'm supplying a lot of the spondulicks for your campaign."

"Right ho," Richard said, and hung up. A Buffalo was warming up outside one of the hangars, and he went to the window to look out. A mechanic standing on the lower wing was tinkering with the port pusher engine; the other three engines were running quietly, propellers whirling slowly. The plane had squadron markings and a number 3 painted on it. That was the machine Guy had flown to Germany to bring back some big Hun politician. He'd reported that the engines ran sweetly enough, but that they used about 12 percent more fuel than the specifications allowed for. As he'd been at low altitude both ways, on orders, that might be the cause—the Buffalo's service ceiling was 18,000 feet and it was designed to cruise at 15,000 feet—but . . . The telephone rang.

He went back to his desk, sat down, and picked it up. The voice was a man's. "Rowland? This is Dimmock, the Prime Minister's political secretary. We have reports that you have locked a lot of workers out of your factory because of some union activity."

Richard said, "I haven't locked anyone out. I told the union that they could not collect union dues, or voluntary political contributions, inside the factory, or on our property. Over the next few days, most of the workers went on strike. We don't have any new orders on hand, so it's not important yet. And they'll all be back soon. The union can't give them any strike pay."

The voice was hard. "The Prime Minister does *not* want a candidate he is supporting to appear as a union breaker. We are sympathetic to the aspirations of the unions. Let the union men do what they want in your factory."

"But . . ."

The voice was even colder—"You don't appear to understand, Rowland, that your political and business lives can not now be separated. What you do as a businessman will affect what you do and are as a politician. There is a chance that you may be beaten by the Socialist candidate . . . a chance that will become greater the longer you hold out against the union. Your workers are going to get strike pay from the National headquarters, I happen to know . . . Get them back *before* that is announced. Do you understand?"

"But . . . I can't just give in, cave in!"

"That's just what you'll do. If you'd had any political or common sense, you wouldn't have got yourself into this position in the first place, just before an election."

"Oh!" Richard said, angry at last. "Then it'll be all right to fight the union again after I've been elected?"

"*If* you're elected."

Daily Telegraph, Monday, December 30, 1918

**BRITISH NATION'S ANSWER TO THE
PRIME MINISTER'S APPEAL**

SWEEPING TRIUMPH OF THE COALITION

ONE WOMAN MEMBER—A SINN FEINER

THE NEW HOUSE OF COMMONS

Coalition Unionists			333
Coalition Radicals			135
Coalition British Workers' League			9
Unionists (Independent)	51	**Sailors & Soldiers'**	
		Federation	1

Radicals (non-Coalition)	28	Co-operator	1
Labour	62	Socialist	1
Independents	3	Irish Nationalists	8
National Party	2	Sinn Fein	72

The tale of triumph and disaster continued: Asquith had lost his seat, so had McKenna, Money, Runciman, Samuel, Simon, Trevelyan, and a dozen other ex-Cabinet Ministers. Lloyd George was back, of course, with Bonar Law, Balfour, Churchill, Austen Chamberlain, and many other famous names. And Cate's brother-in-law, Richard Rowland, had been defeated for Mid Scarrow, narrowly but definitely, by Wilfred Bentley. The Labour Party, with 62 members, would pull quite a bit of weight in the new House, especially as the Sinn Feiners had sworn not to take their seats, so reducing the total House from 776 to 704 members.

Practically all the pacifists had been swept away; Bentley had been saved from that debacle by his M.C., his war record, and by the fact that he had mostly fought on the issues of the future peace, not of the past war. Cate himself was a classical liberal, and was sorry to see Asquith go; but Bentley was a good man, a Wykehamist, like himself . . . strange to think of Winchester spawning Socialists and Labourites—what *was* the difference between those two, anyway?

Stella was giving the baby its bottle at the far end of the table. The child's skin was dark brown, but, as he'd written to John, one could see Stella's features in the face . . . the shape of the nose and mouth, the width of the forehead, the setting of the eyes—greenish eyes, strangely piercing for a baby—when he glanced up from the bottle, momentarily catching his grandfather's eye.

When would John come back?

He said, "Why don't we take baby for a walk in the pram? I'll help push it. It's a lovely day."

Stella said, "Not today, Daddy. Tomorrow, perhaps."

Cate picked up the paper again, hiding behind it. What were they going to call the child? John would have to give it a name, when he came.

London and Kent: January, 1919

18 Captain John Merritt, Field Artillery, United States Army, stood outside the door, smoothing down his hair, adjusting his overseas cap at the correct angle on the right side of his head, and patting down the front of his long double-breasted greatcoat. There was some mud on the back of it, from the fields near Issay le Conte where the battery had been billeted since the armistice. He would be able to get it off when the coat dried but he had been wet, off and on, ever since leaving Issay in response to the curt order, relayed to him by General Castine in person—*Report to Secretary of Embassy, London, England, by fastest means. Marshall.* Colonel Marshall was on the staff of the First Army.

He knocked on the door and a voice from inside called "Come in." He stepped in, halted, and saluted. His uncle Virgil Kramer was sitting behind the big desk, rising to his feet now, hand out—"Johnny!" John brought his hand down, extending it to grasp his uncle's. There was someone else in the room, standing against the window, silhouetted, a tall man, he too now stepping forward. The man said, "Johnny . . . John, don't you recognize me?"

John stared against the light, screwing up his eyes. "Why . . . Dad!" he muttered. "I didn't expect . . ." Then he stumbled forward and they were in each other's arms, and tears were filling his eyes. He laid his head a moment on his father's shoulder; then stood up and away, waiting.

"Why don't we all sit down?" Virgil Kramer said. They sat, in the comfortable leather-backed padded chairs. John felt that his father was surveying him, trying to see what the war had done to him. Virgil said, "I have your discharge papers here, John. You are needed outside the army."

"Did you fix this?" John said, turning to his father.

Stephen Merritt nodded—"Yes. And it's true—you are needed. I didn't tell the Secretary about Stella or anything personal . . . just about how much I needed you, in the bank."

"Did she know I was coming?" John broke in.

His father said, "No. I thought we'd let you tell her . . . The board has sent me over to make decisions about the future of the Jupiter Motor Company and the Hedlington Aircraft Company. Running both of them is too much for Richard Rowland . . . There's going to be a difficult period—it's started already. We're not going to get any new orders for the Buffalo aeroplane until we find a new use for it. Meanwhile, though the workers at H.A.C. went back to work, we've now had to lay most of them off . . . At J.M.C. we're going to have to face competition soon enough . . . from Germany, among others . . . and we must beat it. I want you to come back to New York with me. I've been talking with Richard for the last week and he thinks Ginger Keble-Palmer can take over the H.A.C., though he'll need a better-educated man than Pratt to assist him. We must do whatever is necessary to get Frank Stratton back, Richard said . . . We want *you* to start in where you were in August, 1914—at the headquarters of Fairfax, Gottlieb. The United States is on the threshhold of the biggest explosion in its history—explosion of industrial growth, financial expansion, commercial dominance . . . and it is people like you who must seize control of it, and guide it . . . Fairfax, Gottlieb will play a big role, and its chairman of the board will be one of the most important people in the nation, and hence, in the world. We don't have hereditary titles in the U.S.A., but the directors want to put you on the track. But you must come over now, and start in. Study our business. Visit all the firms we own or control. Weigh the men who run them. Analyze why they are succeeding . . . or failing. Investment banking isn't really to do with money, John, but with men."

"I've learned something about that, in the Field Artillery," John said.

His father sat back, lighting a cigar—"That's what we thought. You won't be young in ten years' time, John, when you take over. God help us, you're not young now."

John shrugged—"The war had to be won." After a pause, he said, "I must stay here. Stella will be miserable if I drag her away from Walstone . . . Beighton."

Virgil said, "She'd get the best and most modern treatment in the world, John, in New York."

John said, "Perhaps, but . . ."

Stephen cut in—"And we—the board—think that it would be better if the H.A.C. had a British managing director. We foresee a period of labour instability, and we think that the mere fact of your being American might make matters more difficult. We are not popular over here, in spite of having won the war for them."

"That's not the way they look at it, Dad . . . Dad, I can not and will not leave Stella. I think that if I take her away from her home she will be even more lost and unhappy, so she'll take even more of that beastly stuff. If you don't want me to manage H.A.C., I'll find some other job in Kent."

Stephen sighed, looked across at his brother-in-law, and said, "I surrender . . . We really think it would be best for you and for Stella if you'd come home, but . . . of course, you can go back to the H.A.C. I don't think the workers there will resent you—they know you. Now, do you want to telephone Stella?"

John paused, thinking. At length he said slowly, "No, thank you, Dad. I'd like to speak to Father Christopher, face to face, before I go to Stella."

His father said, "Let's call him, then. You could arrange to meet him at Richard's place in Beighton, Hill House."

*　　*　　*　　*

Christopher Cate had aged since John last saw him. The lines on his face were deeper, and seemed to show sadness rather than experience and concern. His troubles are worse than mine, John thought; and they surely shared an overwhelming sense of guilt—John because he had somehow failed to hold Stella's interest, her involvement, deeply enough to save her from the drug; and Christopher because he had not understood Laurence's unfitness for war; or Stella's . . . what? Was she naturally unstable? Dependent?

They were sitting in the drawing room of Hill House, alone in the house, rain falling outside the windows, a robin sheltering from it, searching for crumbs. A decanter of Amontillado stood on the small table between them, and each held a tulip glass of the wine in his hand.

Cate said, "She's getting a small dose regularly . . . every day. She administers it herself. Doctor Irwin, at Hedlington General, prescribed it when he was sure that she was an addict. For a cure she would have to be confined to an institution . . . but he is certain she would return to her addiction as soon as she was released, unless . . ."

"Unless what?" John asked at last.

"Unless she finds in herself . . . or there is created in her . . . a real *desire* to be free of the addiction. And that will never come—the Limehouse Hospital doctor told me this—from a negative force. That is, it will not come because she hates the drug and its effect on her, but only because she loves, and wants, something else even more . . . to attain which she must be free of addiction."

John drank deep. He knew that. He had felt it in his bones ever since he had learned that Stella was a drug addict. But what could the great positive force be? Could it be himself . . . the mere knowledge that he was her husband, that he loved her, that she could not be a good wife, mother, or lover in this state? He would now have a chance to try, at least.

Christopher Cate said, "I think . . . I hate to say this, I shall miss her so much, but I think you should consider taking her to America. Let her start again. A new world. New challenges . . ."

There's the rub, John thought. What challenges? To become the best-dressed woman in New York? To have her name in the society columns every other day? To give the most daring parties on upper Fifth Avenue?

He said, "That's what my father and Uncle Virgil think I ought to do. But she won't come. I know it." He stood up and Cate followed suit. There were tears in Cate's eyes and John felt his own welling up. He put out his hand—"Thank you . . . and . . . and . . . I'm so sorry about Aunt Isabel and you . . . and Laurence. He was a wonderful kid." There, it was said. Now perhaps they could share the burden of their sorrows.

Cate said, "Let's go over to Walstone now, and you can meet Stella, and see the baby."

*   *   *   *

She looked better than he had expected, though of course not as fresh and peachlike as when they were married; there were lines under her eyes, the lids were a little puffy, and the eyes themselves were shining bright, luminous. She was floating, he thought, smiling a little, present but not present. The baby was in her arms, staring at him with those strange green eyes.

He said, "Let's sit down, darling." She sat obediently. They were in the music room of Walstone Manor, rain beating against the french windows.

John said, "Father Christopher says it'll only take a few hours to get our cottage ready for us to move back into. We could go the day after tomorrow."

"All right, darling," she said.

He said, "But my father—and yours—both think we should go to America . . . to New York. What do you think?"

She said, "I can't leave this—" She gestured with one hand, indicating not the room or the Manor, but Kent, England, her bedroom with the little packets, and the needle. "I must stay here. This is my home. Everything'll be all right here."

He said, "Very well. Then we'll move back to the Cottage and I will take over again as managing director of Hedlington Aircraft." He looked at the baby—"What do you want to call him?"

She said, "I don't know . . . I haven't thought . . ."

He said, "I have been thinking, a lot. He is our son. Let us name him John Peace Merritt."

"All right," she said, "that's a nice name."

He got up, his legs feeling suddenly weak, and stumbled over to her, and knelt at her feet, one arm round her, one caressing the dark baby. "Oh Stella, I love you," he whispered. She bent her head, sighing. God, where was she? What was it like, where she went once a day, for how many hours? What was it like, coming back? How could he love her, so that she would not want to go, and one day would not go, again, ever?

*   *   *   *

John's sister Betty lifted the half-pint of beer, drank, set down the tankard beside her plate and said, "Dad wants me to go home. He told me to pack!"

"What did you tell him?" John asked. They were in the saloon bar of the Lord Nelson in Hedlington, where Betty was having her lunch, as she often did since Fletcher Gorse had introduced her to the cosy comfort of English pubs, and the simple delights of a good pub lunch—in her case today, a big bread and butter sandwich of Cheddar cheese, Dutch greenhouse tomato, and pickle.

She said, "I told him I was not going to leave until Fletcher came back from the army, and perhaps not then."

"Did he know about Fletcher?"

"A bit. I suppose Aunt Isabel told him . . . I said that Fletcher had asked me to marry him, and I had decided to wait till the end of the war to give him an answer."

"What's it going to be?"

She drank again, and looked at him carefully—"I don't know, John. I honestly don't. I love him . . . I am totally, blindingly in love with him . . . as far as I know. I was when we last met. I still am, I think . . . but there was the war . . . death . . . he in the middle of it

. . . I waiting, waiting. Would I ever see him again? He is so beautiful, would he come back with his face smashed, his eyes torn out, a leg and arm ripped off? What about his mind, his soul—the person behind the skin? Would he have become a killer, a rapist, perverted to violence for its own sake? I don't know."

John said, "He's not an educated man, is he?"

She said sharply, "No, and we don't believe in the class system, do we?" She stopped, and put a hand over one of his, "Sorry, John . . . No, he's not educated, and I have to think, what will we do, talk about . . . what things we can share, apart from lovemaking." She glanced up, daring her brother to comment—"Though that's important."

"Of course," John murmured.

"So . . . I must wait."

"How long?"

She shrugged—"Heaven knows. The Government here's got some cockamamy scheme to do with 'key men'—men they think are needed in industry at home, who will be released from the army first. As some of them will only have been out a month, while others, who are not considered 'key men,' have been out since 1915, they're asking for trouble . . . Anyway, I *have* to stay, to try to modify the Buffalo for civil air service. We'll get help from the Air Ministry. Guy was down here, flying Buffaloes on all sorts of tests, until just before Christmas, and he told us the Air Ministry will do whatever they can to help, if they get the money. They want a British civil air industry just as much as we do, otherwise the French and Americans will have a monopoly."

"Are you going to get Frank Stratton back?"

"Probably, soon. He's been classified as a 'key man,' which is fine from our point of view, if there are to be such people. But he may refuse to accept it, he's such a stickler for fair play."

"But he *has* been in the army since 1914 . . . Stella won't leave England . . . the Weald, really."

"I thought she wouldn't. What are you going to do?"

"Come back to H.A.C. The day after tomorrow."

"Good! We've all missed you. And Ginger didn't relish the thought of taking over, at all. Dad has asked him and he said he would if he had to . . . but he'd rather stick to designing. And he's right. It's a big job to alter the Buffalo. It's so *large* . . . money and fuel didn't matter when it was a bomber, but for a commercial passenger and goods service, they would. And we have to build in some more safety devices, in case we have to land in fog or bad weather. Crashes may have to be accepted in war, but not for peacetime fare-paying passengers." She stood up—"I have to get back to work." She reached up and kissed him on the cheek—"Be patient with Stella. And think . . . find something that will really challenge her. She is at her best, she is most her real self, in danger, hardship, emergency."

He nodded—"I know."

* * * *

Stephen Merritt faced Virgil Kramer across the table in the small, very expensive West End restaurant. The waiter had just served them their first course—real turtle soup; in spite of the war, and rationing, and shortages, you could still eat well in London, if you paid for it.

Stephen said, "John can't get Stella to move. So he's definitely staying."

Virgil said, "What can be done about her? Is John to be saddled for the rest of his life with a wife who is a drug fiend and with that black baby?"

"Drug fiend," Stephen muttered. "It conjures up such a picture . . . Chinamen lolling on bunks in underground dens of iniquity . . . a person crazy for the drug, whatever it is . . . I suppose Stella *was* like that, when she ran away. At least now they realize that she is sick, not evil, and that the only way to treat her, at the moment, is to give her regulated doses of the drug, under some sort of supervision."

"They don't allow that at home," Virgil said. "Heroin has been classified as a dangerous drug and it's totally forbidden—and that's that."

"So people who crave it will kill for it, rob . . . prostitute themselves. My God, Virgil, I can't bear to see my son, my only son, in this ghastly trap . . . And Betty apparently determined to marry this Fletcher Gorse fellow."

"He's a poet, Stephen, and a good one. I have his first book of poems, *At the lip.*"

"Poets don't make any money," Stephen growled. "She will have plenty of her own, of course . . . and he'll batten on her."

"I doubt that . . . Look, we'll all do what we can to help John and Stella, but the fact is that no one else can really help them. They can only get out of the trap, by themselves, their own efforts, guts—and love. I think John has them all. The way he has accepted that baby is extraordinary, and very, very brave. Peace Merritt . . . a good name . . . When are you going back Stateside?"

"Soon. Isabel shouldn't be left alone too long, after losing Walter."

"And pining for Christopher Cate."

"Yes." Stephen leaned back, "To change the subject, have you seen anything of Richard Rowland?"

"A little," Kramer said. "He's been up here two or three times

about shipping space for your Jones & Gatewood radial engines . . .
And Armbruster engine blocks from Columbus for his trucks. Why?"

"Our British plants have been having labour trouble, and I get the
impression from Overfeld that Richard is partly responsible."

"What are you going to do about it?"

"Go down and see for myself . . . talk . . . listen. But everyone
over here's been under such an incredible strain, for so long, that it
would be a miracle if there wasn't any such trouble. Before I do
anything drastic I'm going to tell Richard to take a long vacation . . .
In fact, I shall send him to the States, so that he can look at Henry
Ford's operation at first hand . . . meet the other members of our
board . . . but above all, have a rest and a change. His wife's American, from California, so she'll be pleased."

"I got the impression that he thought he was indispensable."

"He's not," Stephen said grimly. "And he *shall* take a holiday."

*   *   *   *

John Merritt walked up and down the edge of the airfield, between
that part actually used for landing and the buildings of the Hedlington Aircraft Company. At his side walked the Chief Designer of
the company, Ginger Keble-Palmer. The two young men walked with
heads bent, John with his hands clasped behind his back, Ginger with
his habitual stoop and ungainly stride, like a disjointed rag doll. "I've
been working on the problems ever since August, really," Ginger said.
"After we won that great victory . . . I've cut down petrol consump-
tion 4 percent by altering the design of the carburetor. But that isn't
enough. The Buffalo's just so big."

"We can't go back to the Lion," John said. "And I don't think that
size is the problem. We shall fill the aircraft if we can make the flights
regular, dependable, safe, and punctual." He broke off, looking at his
wristwatch—"Guy's late."

Ginger said, "He must have been held up." They resumed their
pacing. Ginger broke the silence—"Betty's been very helpful to me all
along. Especially since we started looking to peace."

He said, "That's natural."

Ginger said, "She's in love with Fletcher Gorse—Whitman, he's
been calling himself—you know?"

"Yes. She told me."

Ginger said in a low voice, "I prayed that he would be killed . . .
then perhaps I'd have a chance. That's what love did to me. Because
you know, of course, that I love her, too?"

John said, "Yes."

340

"Do you think she will marry him?"

"I don't know. Nor does she." They both heard the distant throb of aircraft engines and stopped, looking toward the west. The sound grew and the machine came in sight, huge, dark, four-engined, a thousand feet up.

"Handley Page V/1500," Ginger said. "Our competitor . . . look, four engines, mounted back to back in pairs, just like ours, only theirs are liquid-cooled and ours are radial . . ."

John said, "Ours is a little squatter, I think, and two or three feet shorter, perhaps."

"Three feet one inch," Ginger said. The machine was circling at the downwind end of the field, banking gently, now on its landing run, south-west into the damp, strong wind. Three minutes later it was down and Guy Rowland was waving to them from the cockpit, a lieutenant beside him and a sergeant in the rear cockpit. John ran up close as Guy cupped his hand and shouted down, "Want to see how the competition flies?"

"I've flown one," Ginger said. "You go up."

John clambered up a step ladder onto the wing and thence into the cockpit, squeezing into the co-pilot's place as the co-pilot joined the sergeant behind them. Guy pushed the throttles open, and taxied the machine downwind to the far end of the field, turned again, opened the throttles wide, and took off, climbing gently toward the west. The wind blew the roar of the four Rolls Royce Eagle VIII engines to the rear, and Guy, leaning close to John, shouted, "She's pretty good . . . six hours radius of action, without extra tanks."

"Cruising speed?"

"Ninety, at 6,000 feet. She weighs 29,937 pounds, fully loaded for takeoff."

"The Buffalo's nearly forty pounds lighter," John said.

"And carries the same payload. There's nothing in it between them there . . ."

Guy swung the Handley Page southward—"Haven't had time to say welcome home," he shouted after a time. "You're staying now?"

John nodded, and Guy said, "Good . . . I'll come down and visit when I can. I have things on my mind these days." He did not elaborate.

So do I, have things on my mind, John thought; and Guy is acknowledging their kinship. He would not have to hide anything from Guy. And some day Guy would tell him what his own problems were . . . perhaps to do with finding out who he was, now that the killing was over. It was a pity that he had to drink so much champagne in the search: his breath reeked of it.

*   *   *   *

John stood in the door of the little house, and listened to the sounds of a grinding mangle, through the slightly open window. He had knocked half a minute ago and now someone was coming. The door opened, and a girl of about twelve stood there, eyeing him up and down. Her clothes and shoes were torn, but clean.

John said, "Can I see your mother?"

"Mum's washing clothes, working the mangle. You can 'ear it."

John said, "I'll go through. I don't want to interrupt her."

The girl stood aside and John walked through the crowded little parlor to the kitchen behind. The table was piled high with dirty laundry, more filled the sink, and Mary Gorse was working the mangle. She was thin, gaunt almost, her dark-rimmed eyes shining as she turned to look at him, never stopping her work. John started: there, in a battered old armchair in the corner was Willum. He was sitting in the chair, but his legs did not reach the floor: he had no legs, only six-inch stumps, the trousers cut off and tied neatly round them.

Mary said, "Sorry I can't stop, Mr John . . . We heard you were back."

Willum said, "I can't get up, Mr Johnny . . . see what happened to me!" He laughed, without bitterness. "Look what the Germans did! Still, they didn't kill me, like they killed Colin Blythe, did they?"

John said, "When did you get home? My sister wrote and told me what had happened to you."

Willum said, "Why, them Jerries took me and put me in an ambulance and next time I woke up I was in a hospital with nurses and clean sheets . . . the nurses was Jerries, too, fancy that! Women speaking that funny! And I didn't have no legs, but I didn't know that for three weeks, 'cos my legs kept aching, like, so I knew they was there . . . but they wasn't!"

The mangle kept grinding. The girl and a smaller boy lifted the squeezed sheets and pillow cases and took them out into the tiny yard behind, hanging them up on the jammed rows of laundry lines. Each time they went in and out a wave of raw, damp air filled the room.

John said, "Can you move about at all?"

Willum said, "They made me a little trolley, dolly, like, I can sit on, and pull myself along by my hands."

"Do you get a pension from the Government? Your army pay still?"

"Ten shillings a week," Mary cut in.

"Why, that's . . ." John bit his lip. He had come, first to confirm that Willum was back from Germany, and to see if he could offer him a job. But it was impossible. He could not raise himself high enough to put sweepings into the bins, if he were to be given back his old job as floor sweeper and cleaner. He couldn't be a night watchman. He simply did not have enough mobility to do any job in a factory, except a clerical one—and he was all but illiterate. He'd see old Mr Harry: but Mr Harry had retired and was living in Devonshire. Someone called Wilfred Bentley was the new Member of Parliament, a Socialist . . . he should have some special feeling for the working man; but perhaps he was one of the pacifist-anti-war people, who would feel that what Willum had got was entirely his own fault, for taking part in a capitalists' war . . .

The mangle ground on. He turned to Mary—"Is there anything I can do, Mrs Gorse? Are you short of money?"

"Yes," she said, "always. But I don't want none of yours, Mr John." She smiled wearily, "We're not starving . . . the girls bring in a little . . . run errands, you know. We're not ready for the Workhouse yet. And Willum'll get a job one day . . . you'll see." She plunged her chapped and reddened hands once more into the sink, pulled out a sheet, and expertly fed it into the mangle—"You'll see."

Daily Telegraph, Saturday, January 18, 1919

FATE OF LIEBKNECHT AND ROSA LUXEMBURG

THE FORMER SHOT, FEMALE ANARCHIST LYNCHED
HORROR IN BERLIN

From Leonard Pray, *Rotterdam*, Friday. News and comment from Berlin makes the fact startlingly clear today that the announcement of the deaths of Liebknecht and Rosa Luxemburg, though heard with satisfaction by a few of their bitterest opponents, was received by the public generally with emotions in which fear and horror predominated—horror at the circumstances, fear of possible consequences. The city is described today as being in the same state of nervous tension as it was on the eve of the Bolshevik rising, when everyone felt that civil war was in the atmosphere . . . The whole liberal press condemning the deed and even the *Vossische Zeitung* declares:

Nothing can justify this exercise of lynch law, even against the author of the recent regrettable events. In the name of humanity we protest against it. It should have been left to a court of justice to make them harmless for the future . . .

Garrod came in and said, "Mr John is in the hall, sir."

"Bring him in, of course," Cate said; and a moment later John walked in, still wearing his overcoat. "Good morning, Father Christopher," he said, "I thought I'd drop by on my way to work to tell you that we've spent our first week back in the Cottage very peacefully. Stella seems very happy there. And Peace slept like a log, all night, every night. He's quite over the drug intoxication he got in the womb."

"Good, good . . . but Walstone isn't on your way to the H.A.C."

"Not really," John said, "but—to tell the truth—I wanted to be sure you don't mind my taking Stella away from here, the Manor, which was her home for so long and which she loves so much."

"Of course not, my boy! You must. It is you she must learn to depend on, and look to, not me . . . Have you breakfasted? Seen the paper? Miserable business in Berlin, isn't it?"

John said, "It is. Though our fire eaters will say they deserve whatever they get." He leaned over Christopher's shoulder and turned the page—"Look!" Cate read:

PARIS–LONDON BY AIR
A REGULAR SERVICE

L'Auto states that the official trial trip of a "Giant" Farman aeroplane, intended for service between Paris and London, will take place tomorrow, Jan 18, from the aerodrome at Toussu-le-Noble, near Versailles . . .

"Look below," John said; and Cate read:

AEROPLANES DE LUXE

The London News Agency announces that a regular air passenger and post service between Paris and London in connection with the Peace Conference at Versailles is to start shortly . . . These D.H. 4 peace machines will be of a specially luxurious as well as speedy type . . .

"See?" John said. "We have no time to waste . . . even though our sights are set a long way farther off than Paris."

Flanders: January, 1919

19 The 1st Battalion, the Weald Light Infantry, was on ceremonial parade, in the battered main square of Roulers. The steel helmets gleamed under new green paint, in the light rain. The web belts and buckles were uniformly green-grey, of the same shade, as also the webbing rifle slings; the trousers knife-creased to six inches below the knee where they were turned in and up one inch, below that hidden by eight exactly spaced folds of khaki puttee. The boots shone black with heelball and boot polish, the brass tabs shone, the fixed bayonets glittered with their peacetime silvery fire, for the sandblasting had been done away with. The new commanding officer, Lieutenant Colonel the Honourable Thomas Wylie, was inspecting, each company springing to attention at its own commander's order, as the colonel, his adjutant, and the Regimental Sergeant Major reached the right end of its front rank.

"Dirty buttons," the C.O. said. "Take his name."

"Gottim, sir."

"Mud on the puttee. Why didn't you see that, Captain Kellaway?"

"I . . . did, sir," Kellaway stammered, "but he had no time to get it off before we had to march on . . ."

"No excuse!"

The little procession crawled slowly on. In the rear rank of B Company Private Snaky Lucas muttered, "He don't see as much as Old Rowley did. Smith '46 up there's forgot his ruddy bayonet!"

From behind him Sergeant Fagioletti hissed, "Quiet in the rear rank!"

Lucas shut his mouth. The Dago was a good sergeant—not as good in peacetime as he was when it came to a scrap, perhaps, but all right. He was finding it hard to understand what all this square bashing was about, and why it was important. A lot of the new blokes felt the same, blokes that had come in since the retreat . . . over forty, half of them, didn't know anything about the army and didn't want to. Some of them would be going back to Blighty now, because they were "key" men. Other blokes thought it was a bleeding swindle, but the way he looked at it, it was good riddance. The Wealds didn't need blokes with their minds on their ruddy mortgages and grown-up children. It wasn't that sort that went in with the bayonet at the Kaiwan Pass in '99, or burned the nigger town down in Kurramabad in '06 . . . what the hell was that all about anyway? Something to do with a bloke in C Company being robbed in a *bibikhana*. Those were the days . . .

"General salute—present . . . arms!"

He sprang automatically to attention, and jerked his rifle to the present.

"Order arms!" Down, at ease.

"Unfix!" To attention . . . right marker stamping out . . . "Bayonets!" Rifle between the knees, bayonet off, searching for the mouth of the scabbard with the point, his left thumb over it . . . someone to his right couldn't find the hole, Fagioletti hissing "You'd be in quick enough if it had 'air round it!" Oldest joke in the army . . . Right marker's hand flashing up, straighten, at ease.

He waited. "B Company, move to the right in column of fours . . . right! By the left, quick march" . . . snap to attention, step out with the left foot, at the same instant jerk the rifle up into the trail . . . the band was playing, the bugles were screaming, the drums bang bang banging at 140 paces a minute.

"B Company . . . eyes . . . right!" Snap eyes right. There was the colonel, saluting, and behind him the adjutant, Mr Woodruff, and the Regimental, Bolton . . . a row of shop fronts at the back, and some watching Belgians, mostly women. The women here liked British soldiers: they spent more money than their own men did.

"Halt . . . Dismiss!"

He walked back toward his billet. The madame was there, arms folded. She was about fifty and her husband had come back a month ago from prisoner-of-war camp in Germany. She spoke now in a broken English she had learned during the war, together with a similar brand of German, to go with her French and her native Flemish— " 'Ave you 'ear . . . when you go on?" She pointed to the east, toward Germany.

"Not a thing, mother," Lucas said. The woman's two sons were coming home from the Belgian Army any day, and she'd need the room which Lucas now shared with three other privates of the Wealds. He went on upstairs. Payday yesterday and his pockets were still full, as he'd held off, mostly getting drinks off other blokes, particularly the young ones who'd stand him a beer and a fag to hear him talk about Mons and India . . . India, mostly. That's what they liked to hear, nigger servants bringing you tea in the barrack room, the *nappi-walla* shaving you while you were still asleep on your charpoy.

The other fellows were clumping up the steep stairs, crowding into the little room, hanging up their equipment, and helmets, taking off their wet greatcoats . . . no room to hang them all, but they'd got to be creased and pressed by tomorrow.

"I'm going to the estaminet," he said. "No more parades today. Let's have a booze up."

"You stand treat, Snaky?" Private Halton asked. "Wonders will never cease!"

"What I want is about eight pints of pig's ear," Smith '87 said, "but what we'll get . . . is van bloody blong!"

"Are you coming or not?"

"All right, all right, wait a mo . . ."

The estaminet was full of soldiers, and cigarette smoke, and the loud sound of voices. The four soldiers ordered a bottle of white wine and sat down at a scrubbed table. Nearby another group of four were gloomily singing one of the battalion's favorite billet-area songs:

> *Dan, Dan, the sanitary man,*
> *Working underground all day*
> *Sweeping up urinals,*
> *Picking out the finals,*
> *Whiling the happy hours away—*
> > *Gor blimey!*

The B Company men drank, half-emptying the bottle. "I'm bloody fed up with this bloody Art Karney," Smith '87 said. "Why the 'ell aren't we on our way 'ome? Or back in Blighty already—sitting in armchairs, wiv our wives and girls taking off our boots, and just waiting for us to say 'Up them stairs!' Aaah!"

Halton said, "Bloody square bashing in bloody Belgium while blokes in Ally Fucking Slopers Fucking Cavalry, wot 'aven't 'eard a shot fired in anger, go 'ome and take all the jobs that's going . . . I've 'alf a mind to start a fucking mutiny, and that's the truth."

347

At the next table they moved to the second verse:

> *Doing his little bit,*
> *Shoveling up the shit,*
> *He is so blithe and gay.*
> *And the only music that he hears*
> *Is poo-poo-poo-poo-poo all day.*

"Go and get another bottle of van blong," Lucas said. "You'd do wonders, you would . . . in your trousers. 'Ow long 'ave you been out? Four months?"

"Five," Halton said defensively. "And wounded once, Snaky. But they've demobbed a dozen blokes that didn't come out till a week before the fucking armistice! Is that fair, I ask you?"

"Don't ask me," Lucas said, pouring more wine. "Ask the Chief of the Imperial General Staff. Or what about forming up to Field Marshal Sir Douglas 'Aig? . . . 'Spose we set up the board?"

" 'Ere? We'll be for the Glasshouse, for sure. The Red Caps is always popping in and out of here."

"Not here, man, in the barn behind the church. Where we went last week. No one found out about that."

" 'Ave you got everything with you?"

Lucas nodded, saying, "Let's get four more blokes." He looked round the crowded room, searching for eager young soldiers who were likely to have money in their pockets and the innocence to lose it to him at Crown and Anchor.

"There," he began, "you go and whisper to . . ."

The outer door burst open and the Regimental stood in the opening. "Silence!" he bellowed in a voice that could have been heard a mile away. The men fell silent. "The battalion is to move at once . . . field service marching order. Fall in by companies! The bugles are calling now, but you blokes couldn't hear, you were making so much row on your own. Everyone back to his own billet to kit up!"

He turned to go, as a voice called, "Are we going on to Germany now, Mr Bolton?"

"I 'ope so. The Jerries has good beer, not this 'orse piss," another cried.

The R.S.M. said, "We're not going forward. We're going back, the whole division, marching on in lorries, as soon as they can find some for us. There's trouble in Calais and Ee-taps . . ."

"The ruddy Bullring!" someone said. "Wot the 'ell . . . ?"

"Shut up and get out now!" the R.S.M. bellowed. "At the double!"

*   *   *   *

Lieutenant Ron Gregory, Royal Engineers, stood by the window of the hut at the Reinforcement and Transit Camp, near Calais, watching the crowd of soldiers milling about outside. Another officer stood beside him; the third occupant of the hut was lying on his bed, reading a book; the fourth inhabitant was not present. The officer beside Gregory said, "What are they doing now?"

"Talking," Gregory said shortly. "Perhaps they're deciding to bash all officers' heads in."

The man beside him said, "They won't do that to us . . . to some of the M.P.s, and the sergeants on the camp staff, perhaps. They know we're just passing through on our way to demob."

Gregory cocked his head and tried to hear. A soldier in a greatcoat, standing on a box, surrounded by two or three hundred others, was waving his arms and shouting—"Comrades, we've done our bit, right? They're holding us here because a lot of us are trade union men. They're making sure the blacklegs get the jobs . . . *our* jobs. Who do you think is a 'key man'?"—he yelled the last words with great scorn "A 'key man' is a man that doesn't belong to no union and swears he never will, either!"

He stopped to draw breath, and a clear, harsh voice from the crowd shouted, "So what are we going to *do?*"

The speaker shouted back, pointing his finger, "Stay where we are. Refuse to obey any orders. They'll cave in and send us all back to Blighty, you'll see."

"Send a telegram to *John Bull*," another voice cried. "Tell 'em we want Horatio Bottomley over 'ere . . . He'll 'elp us."

"Shoot all the officers!" a voice cried.

Gregory thought, here it comes; but at once a deep murmur arose, and he made out men shouting, "No . . . no . . . what have they done?"

"Wot about Sergeant Byfield, then?" another voice cried. " 'E deserves shooting!"

"Sergeant Byfield, Sergeant Byfield, Bloody Byfield, Bloody Byfield . . ." A hundred took up the chant; suddenly the crowd broke up, most men streaming off in search of Sergeant Byfield, some dispersing. Gregory had never heard of Byfield; but he had only arrived yesterday, and expected to be on a ship within the week.

The orator was left almost alone on his box. He glared after the retreating soldiers and raised both arms to heaven; then jumped down and walked off, with three or four companions, their heads close. Gregory closed the window, went to his bed and lay back on it, his hands clasped behind his head, staring at the ceiling. God knew when he'd get home now. The camp staff were having no success in getting the men to return to their duty. So far no one had been hurt . . . except now, probably Sergeant Byfield; but there was no progress, either. Naomi was home already, he believed: the last he had heard, her convoy was to be disbanded the first week of the month and all the women sent back to England, their service with the F.A.N.Y. terminated. She'd be waiting for him in the house with the nice name—High Staining. He was rather apprehensive about the prospect. Was her mother as strong as she? Would they look down their noses, now that the war was over, because he was just an ordinary middle-class Londoner . . . his father was a dentist and his mother's father a haberdasher. He saw Naomi's face before him, her wide clear eyes looking into his. He wished she were here now. She'd know what to do, and honestly, he didn't. What could you do with five thousand angry men, who felt they'd been badly treated? And with whom you agreed?

The door opened and the fourth officer came in, closing the door quickly behind him and drawing the bolt. He was a lieutenant of the Royal Field Artillery, his name was Haddon, and that was all Gregory knew about him. Haddon said, "Listen, you fellows . . . I saw the camp adjutant, and they're going to make another effort first thing tomorrow, seven ack emma. The bugles will blow for parade, and an officer is to be at each barrack room and hut, calling on all men to get on parade. He's to read this, aloud, in the barrack room. It's a message from the Commander-in-Chief, Field Marshal Haig, that they are hindering the peaceful progress of demobilization, and endangering our victory over the Germans . . ."

"Does he say what'll happen if they don't get on parade?" Gregory asked.

Haddon shook his head, "No. I have no idea what can be done. These men are mostly Army Service Corps, motor transport drivers, ordnance corps . . . a lot of them were trade unionists before they were conscripted. They don't have the esprit de corps of the regiments."

"There are R.A.F. and Royal Engineers out there," Gregory said. "They have plenty of esprit de corps."

Haddon shrugged—"Well, here's the allotment. You're to Hut 45, East Camp. Here's your copy of Haig's message. Be outside the barrack by five to seven, the adjutant said."

"Armed?"

"Unarmed. No weapons of any sort."

One of the other officers said, "But *they're* all armed."

"Do you want to start a fight, five hundred against five thousand?"

*   *   *   *

Waiting outside Hut No. 45 in the East Camp, shivering in the raw early morning wind, the light just strong enough to see the puddles in his path, Gregory found himself shivering, too, from apprehension. He was not a professional soldier, nor an officer by caste, but an electrical engineer. He had not been closer than half a mile to the front line in his two and a half years out here, for there was nothing electrical to be found further forward than that. He had been under shell fire half a dozen times, and he had not liked it at all, for it had seemed inhuman, impersonal, mindlessly violent. What would he do if the men told him to fuck off? Or, worse, came at him yelling, grabbing him by the collar to throw him out? The pips on his shoulders had seemed like talismans for so long; now they might as well not exist . . . or even be a danger, marking him as an enemy.

He waited, peering at the luminous dial of his watch. A minute to go. He walked closer and stopped, listening. They were awake in the hut, and talking. The electric lights were on . . . the camp had its own petrol-driven generator, 220 volts A.C., 60 cycle, operated by his own corps, he'd found that out within an hour of his arrival . . . A bugle blew, the call taken up at once by another, and another. They were blowing the reveille all round the camp. He found the piece of paper in his pocket, opened the door of the hut, and walked in.

All the occupants of the hut—twenty-five or so soldiers—were gathered round a couple of beds at the far end. Someone was speaking, low-voiced, urgent—"We got to do something . . . more than tear Bloody Byfield's clothes off and whip him into town. We got to burn the records."

Gregory cleared his throat and cried, "Men!" It came out as a croak and he tried again—"Men! The bugles have sounded reveille. First parade is in forty-five minutes." They were silent, all turned, staring at him. He held up the paper to the light and cried, "This is a message to all of you from Field Marshal Sir Douglas Haig, Commander-in-Chief of the British Expeditionary Force."

The man who had been speaking shouted, "Shut up! We aren't listening to anything Haig has to say to us."

Gregory raised his voice and continued, "Your action in refusing to obey orders . . ."

The soldier shouted, "Sing, mates! Sing! The Red Flag!" He waved a hand in time.

"The victory won by our sacrifices over the past four years . . .."

They were yelling at the tops of their voices, Gregory yelling back at them. A soldier who had broken away from the group muttered in his ear, "Better go, sir. You've done your best." Gregory saw that the man was from his own corps, and said, "What are *you* doing with these scum? You're a sapper!"

"No use arguing now, sir. The bolshies are in charge, and no one's going to fight 'em because we're all fed up . . . me, too."

Gregory waited a minute, glaring at the singers. Some glared back, some would not meet his eye. He turned and left the hut.

The camp was in turmoil, men tumbling out of huts everywhere, forming groups, those coagulating into larger groups, all eddying hither and thither. After a time, as Gregory stood watching, a general movement began toward the central parade ground, outside the huts of the headquarters offices. He followed: might as well learn all he could, and the men didn't seem to have any animus against officers, unless perhaps they tried to take charge of . . . whatever was going on. A man in civilian clothes fell in beside him, and said, "Can you tell me what's happening?" He held out his hand—"I'm Wilfred Bentley, M.P. for Mid Scarrow."

"Oh, Hedlington," he said—"I'm Ron Gregory."

"A sapper, I see," the M.P. said. "I was 60th before I swallowed too much chlorine, early in '16. I came over on a night boat to see if I could help restore order. They're in a great tizzy about this in Whitehall, I can tell you."

"It looks bad," Gregory said. "They've got reasonable complaints—the demobilization system's very unfair, and it's working terribly slowly. There are very few men from the fighting arms here . . .."

"So I've been told," Bentley said. "Mostly ex-trade unionists from the technical services. Well, I'm a Labour M.P. so I don't think that's bad, and perhaps they'll listen to me."

"I don't know, sir," Gregory said. "There are a lot of agitators among them, egging them on to burn the records . . . perhaps burn the whole camp down."

They had come up behind the crowd now, which was gathered round a table dragged out from an office. A soldier was standing on the table—the same man Gregory had been watching and listening to yesterday. Perhaps six hundred men were gathered round him, and more hurrying up all the time. The man on the table raised both arms—"Comrades! . . . we're running around like chickens with their heads cut off. We've got to act together and toward a common end . . . We've got to form a Soldiers' Council."

Bentley's face was grave as he listened. Someone cried, "How are we going to elect the members? By corps and regiments?"

The speaker shouted back, "What do our bloody corps or regiments matter now? Elect by huts first, one per hut, then those meet in the main mess hall, and elect committees . . . We've got no time to waste. So, let's sing the Red Flag, then everyone back to his hut and get on with the election. Hut representatives to the mess hall at nine ack emma!" He raised his voice—

> *The People's flag is deepest red,*
> *It shrouded oft our martyred dead.*
> *And ere their limbs grew stiff and cold,*
> *Their life-blood dyed its every fold.*

Bentley shouted in Ron's ear—"I think I'll go to the mess hall, and talk to the hut representatives when they turn up."

"Good luck, sir," Gregory said. "You'll need it."

*　　*　　*　　*

"March all bloody day, march all bloody night, then ride in bloody lorries half the next day . . . what are those bloody A.S.C. blokes doing? Murdering all the Frogs in Calais? More power to 'em, I say." Smith '87's voice was aggrieved, as he set up the ground sheet that was to be half his bivouac with Private Halton.

"They might be shooting their officers," Halton said.

"The bloody A.S.C. don't have officers," Smith said. "Not like ours. Just foremen, really, and who'd mind putting a bullet in a foreman?"

A couple of yards away in the field Snaky Lucas was making a bivouac with Sergeant Fagioletti—" 'Ow far are we from Calais now, sarn't?"

"Don't know, Lucas. All I know is I want to get some kip and I don't want no rain. 'Ad enough of that to last me the rest of my life . . . Look, they're going to blow Cookhouse any minute now. Take my mess tin, I got to check all these bivvies before the captain comes round."

Lucas nodded without speaking. In a few moments the bivouac was up, two ground sheets making a little tent. The ground below was sodden . . . couldn't help that. The whole battalion was in the field, close-packed as ruddy sardines . . . looked daft, after so many years when you couldn't do it, because a couple of Jerry shells would have napooed two or three hundred blokes. There was the Cookhouse call—*Oh officers' wives have pudding and pies, But soldiers' wives have skilly.*

The buglers were getting better, not as good as they'd been in '14 of course, but better than the Boy's Brigade they'd sounded like ever since. Old Wylie would have 'em all the way up soon. A bit of a tartar, he was, in spite of being the Honourable . . . because of it, perhaps . . .

He took the sergeant's mess tin and his own, and wandered over to the cookhouse, without hurrying. It was set up in a lorry now, and that was different, too. Back in the company bivouac area, he sat down on the ground, and half a dozen soldiers gathered round, all eating the beef and potato stew out of their mess tins.

"I'd still be sleeping in a big bed in Roulers," Smith '87 said moodily, "if it wasn't for them bloody A.S.C. blokes."

"We oughter to be sleeping in our own bloody beds, back 'ome," another private said. "They'd be up shit creek if *we* all went on strike too, like those blokes in Calais and Ee-taps."

"Shut your mouth," Lucas said.

Sergeant Fagioletti came and stood over them. He said, "The captain's going to speak to the company as soon as you've all eaten. Ten minutes from now. Fall in by that tree at the edge of the field, there." He took his mess tin and moved a little aside, turning his back.

Smith '87 said, "Well, at bloody last we'll find out something . . . per-haps!"

Fifteen minutes later, when the men were gathered round the tree, silent in the late twilight, Captain Kellaway said, stammering now and then, as he always did—"Tomorrow morning we've got a v-v-very unpleasant job to do . . . We . . . two divisions . . . have been ordered to break up the s-s-strike at the camp outside Calais . . . There are f-f-f-five thousand men there, all in a s-s-s-state of mutiny, and all armed. The c-c-c-camp is f-f-five miles due west from here. We will advance at s-s-seven ack emma, in column of route. About half a mile from the c-camp we will open up into attack formation. At two hundred yards from the camp, we will halt, on orders, and officers to be detailed will advance, unarmed, calling on the mutineers to return to their duty, and parade immediately, without arms, on their parade ground. Two battalion snipers will be allotted to each company—we will have Privates Whitman and Hurling. If it becomes necessary, they will fire, on my orders, at ringleaders, to kill. These t-targets will be specifically pointed out to them by me. No one else will open fire unless the action becomes general. We are being supported by the whole artillery—a hundred guns—but they will not fire at all unless the situation becomes critical . . . That is v-very unlikely. We will be twenty-five thousand trained infantry, they are five thousand service corps and motor drivers . . . Keep calm. Keep your heads. These fellows are not Germans, they're Englishmen. But the mutiny must be put down. That's all. Get to sleep now."

The company sergeant major bellowed, "Company . . . shun!" The men stiffened to attention. Kellaway touched the rim of his steel helmet and moved away—"Company, stand at-ease! Break off."

The soldiers crawled into their bivouacs. Lucas said dreamily, "Just like aid to the civil power, in the Shiny. Only we won't 'ave no magistrate out in front reading the Riot Act."

"And these blokes ain't niggers," Halton said. "They're Englishmen, like the captain said . . . I don't like this. Buggered if I'll pull the trigger tomorrow."

Lucas said, "You'll do what you're ordered to. Who said you had to like everything you did, in the army?"

*   *   *   *

The battalion advanced across the downland east of the Transit Camp. Other battalions stretched to right and left in a huge semicircle. The 18-pounder guns and 4.5-inch howitzers were in position on the slope of the hill two miles behind, guarded by a battalion from a reserve brigade. The Transit Camp stood in ordered rows of huts under a hazy winter sun, smoke belching from one tall chimney . . . the camp incinerator, Captain Kellaway thought, marching in the middle of his company's line and a few paces in front, with his batman and Privates Whitman and Hurling, the snipers, close at his heels. Colonel Wylie was a hundred yards to the right, with Lieutenant Woodruff and the R.S.M. There was a barbed-wire fence round the Camp, and wire-cutting teams now ran forward from each company. The C.O. raised his hand and the mass stopped. The wire cutters worked for five minutes, cutting and pulling, until they had made a series of large gaps. Inside the Camp, the mutineers appeared suddenly to realize what was happening. They gathered, shouted, pointed, ran back into the huts, to reappear carrying rifles. Kellaway's heart sank. What a way to die . . . to be shot by people you really sympathized with, though . . . well, mutiny was mutiny. There'd be a bloodbath . . . the guns would open fire . . . and they'd wait here preventing any escape, till the massacre was over. There must be plenty of innocent men among them . . .

The wire-cutting teams ran back. All along the crescent bugles blew. The battalions advanced to the wire, and halted. Inside, the mutineers were massing, but without a real focus. Colonel Wylie called, "Detailed officers! Ready!"

Kellaway took his revolver out of its holster and handed it to his batman. Half a dozen officers of the regiment were doing the same, including the colonel. Inside the Camp a score of mutineers had taken up position at the corners of huts, rifles in hand. Farther off, toward the centre of the Camp in an open space, a group stood close round two flags, a Union Jack and a home-made red flag.

A man in civilian clothes came running out of the Camp, through a gap in the wire, toward Kellaway. He stopped, panting for breath— "For God's sake don't use the artillery," he gasped—"They've got real grievances . . . this can be settled without bloodshed . . . I'm Bentley, Member of Parliament . . ."

Kellaway said, "It's too late to change anything now, sir. We have our orders. You'd better stick by me."

The C.O. called, "Detailed officers—advance!" At his side the 2nd-in-command shouted, "By companies—load!"

The colonel, Kellaway, and the half dozen other officers, now all unarmed, who had been detailed to persuade the mutineers to return to their duty, walked forward—Wilfred Bentley at Kellaway's side.

Kellaway walked through a gap in the wire. A nineteen-year-old subaltern, Barton, just out, walked through the next gap to his right, the colonel through the one beyond that. Kellaway began to call out, "On p-parade, men! On your m-m-main p-parade ground . . . leave your arms in your h-h-huts!"

He was passing through a scattered crowd of them, some calling "Don't give in," but most silent.

He walked on, exhorting, "N-no one's going to get hurt if you get on p-parade. We c-c-can f-find out what the t-trouble is afterwards . . ."

He was twenty paces from the two flags. A man standing by the red flag was holding a revolver, fingering it nervously, licking his lips. Beside him another man, carrying a rifle, snarled, "This is loaded. Stop where you are, or . . ." He raised the rifle, aiming at Kellaway's heart.

"L-l-look b-b-behind me, m-man!" Kellaway cried.

Just outside the wire the khaki ranks remained steady, standing at ease, the skirts of their greatcoats stirring in the chill raw wind off the Channel. The 2nd-in-command held his binoculars to his eyes; beside him the Regimental stood motionless, his waxed mustache twitching, the steel helmet set squarely on top of his shaven head. In the middle of B Company's front rank, and four paces forward, Fletcher Whitman held his rifle in the aim, the cross hairs of the telescopic sight centred over the heart of the mutineer threatening Captain Kellaway. He couldn't save the captain's life if the mutineer fired; he'd been told not to shoot unless they fired first. So, if they were going to start something, the captain would be a goner. So would the mutineer, a second later, but that wouldn't help the captain.

At the flags, the man with the rifle, still threatening Kellaway, screamed, "Comrades . . . break ranks!" Kellaway realized that he was calling on the soldiers outside the wire—"Join us! We're fighting for you as well as ourselves . . . for all working men . . . comrades . . . !"

For a moment the scene froze. By the flags, everyone was silent, and motionless, mutineers' fingers ready on triggers. Outside, the battalions, veterans of Loos, Ypres, the Somme, Cambrai, Arras, Passchendaele, waited. Farther back the gunners waited by the massed guns.

Kellaway said, "On p-p-parade, m-man! M-m-my feet are g-getting c-cold!"

The mutineer with the revolver said, "Oh, fuck!," threw his weapon on the ground, and headed for the central parade ground. The man with the rifle yelled after him, "Bloody coward!"

Another man said, "What's the use, Jim? . . . The officer's feet's cold!" He laughed grimly and walked off, dropping his rifle. Now they were coming out of huts in twos and threes, drifting away from their defiant positions, streaming toward the central parade ground.

Colonel Wylie came up and faced the ringleader. He said, "A Court of Inquiry will meet to investigate this disturbance at nine ack emma tomorrow morning. Meantime, you're under arrest. Go back there and report yourself to my R.S.M."

The man glared, ground his teeth, and at last dropped his rifle. Colonel Wylie said, "Acknowledge my order, and salute."

The man said, "Yes"—grated his teeth again, and at last got it out, "Yes, sir. I understand, sir." His hand rose to the peak of his forage cap, then he marched off, head low.

Wilfred Bentley let out his breath in a long sigh, and said, "Well done all . . . Now what?"

The C.O. said, "The battalion will reform and march into Calais, and, this afternoon, entrain for Cologne. We are joining the Army of the Rhine at once."

*   *   *   *

They were marching up from Cologne Hauptbahnhof to their barracks on the outskirts of town, guided by an officer and a sergeant from the brigade staff. They were marching at attention, for Germans were watching. The band of another battalion was playing them in, but it was heavy infantry, and played too slow a beat until Colonel

Wylie sent the R.S.M. forward with the message to play at 140 paces a minute. Then the big drum beat faster and the Weald Light Infantry stepped out in their own light, fast pace.

Private Lucas marched easily from long practise, keeping his eyes fixed straight ahead but seeing a great deal peripherally from under the rim of his steel helmet . . . So these were the Jerries at home . . . big headlines in funny letters on posters . . . the captain said Germany was really in a state of civil war, outside the areas occupied by the British, French, and American armies of occupation . . . very shabby everything was, specially the clothes . . . kids thin, clothes in rags . . . and it was bloody cold, colder than Strensall Barracks in February . . . The shops empty, that he could see . . . but they must have something that a British pound note could buy . . . which reminded him . . . he was getting short of the ready and would have to set up the board as soon as he could . . . it was a hell of a long way to barracks . . . The colonel had thought so too, and they were changing arms, by companies. Smith '87, next to him, was grumbling under his breath, "Why in 'ell don't we march at ease?"

Lucas said nothing. If Smith '87 had served in the Shiny in the old days, he'd know you never let the wogs and niggers know you ever got tired, or scared. His father had told him once, "Dover is where niggers begin, my boy," and by God he'd been right. France was all niggers really, and Germany too, though they were better soldiers than any other niggers he'd ever come across or heard of . . .

*   *   *   *

Lucas was strolling down a narrow street in central Cologne, flanked by Privates Halton and Smith '87. Every now and then they stopped and peered in the shop windows, which, as Lucas had guessed, contained something, but not much. Money jingled in all their pockets, especially in Lucas's as he had set up his Crown & Anchor board the first afternoon, in a secluded part of the rambling ex-German infantry barracks; and, in the ensuing week, had won over eight pounds. Winston Churchill, now Secretary for War, had doubled the soldiers' pay, as one response to the Calais mutinies, and to bring their pay closer to civilian levels, thus partly defusing the demobilization and job issues; and the men had been expansive in their gambling, though in fact they had not yet received their first pay under the new rates.

Two children of about seven, a boy and a girl, held out their hands silently. They were in rags, the snow-bladed wind cutting through to the visible, dirty skin below. The girl had sores round her mouth, the boy round his eyes. Their feet were bare, and some of the boy's toes dead white. Lucas stopped—"You're going to get frostbite," he said. The boy stared, hand still out. Bloody foreigners, couldn't understand a word you said. Lucas raised his voice—"You're going to get bloody frostbite!" he shouted. "Lose your bloody toes! Look!" He pointed down. The boy looked down, saw nothing unusual, and looked up again. Lucas glanced round. The next shop up the street displayed three pairs of shoes in its window. He caught the boy by the ear and dragged him into the shop, calling over his shoulder, "Bring the girl, too."

"Hey, Snaky, we're not supposed to fraternize. Old Wylie was very hot about it."

"Fuck that!" Lucas said. He turned to the shopman, who was waiting apprehensively in the middle of his floor—" 'Ere, you, shoes for the kids . . . strong shoes . . . *dekko, joothi*, damn you!" He raised his foot and pointed.

"Ah, *schuhe*," the man said.

" 'Urry up, I ain't got all day."

The three soldiers stood, their forage caps agleam with the bugle horn and prancing horse badge of the regiment, their greatcoat buttons glittering, belt buckles gleaming, boots shining like anthracite coals, until both children had been fitted.

"*Danke schön*," the kids said in chorus; then they held out their hands.

"Jesus Christ!" Lucas exploded. "Well, let's 'ave a dekko."

He lifted the boy's shirt and stared; his belly was nothing but a hollowed-out cage. The girl lifted her own shirt; she, in contrast, was bloated and pot-bellied.

"Got any chocolate?" Lucas asked.

Halton said, "I have, but . . ."

" 'And it over . . . there . . . there . . . Now cut along or I'll *maro* your arses. *Jao!*"

The soldiers left the shop and continued their stroll. A woman's voice called softly, "Tommy! Want good time?" Two women were standing in an alley, shawls wrapped round their shoulders. They were both young, and one was carrying a baby of about a year old.

Lucas went over—" 'Ow much?"

"A shilling . . ."

Lucas said, "A whole shilling?"

The woman said desperately, "Nothing, then . . . *nur* chocolate, food . . . bully beef . . ."

Lucas said, "You ain't no whore, are you?"

The woman drew herself up and said, "Whore? What . . . ? Oh . . . No!" She sagged again—"I am wife's Hauptmann, captain . . . she, wife's Fregattenkapitan, navy . . . not wife's, widow's."

Lucas whistled through his tobacco-stained teeth. Officers' wives, going for a tin of bully. A tin of *Hoggin's* bully!

359

Halton said, "I got some bully . . . Fuller told me there'd be lots of women, and what they'd want."

"And I've got a bob . . . and one for you, Smithy, for your chocolate." He turned to the women—"All right, lead on."

"What about fraternizing?" Halton said anxiously. "I don't want to go to the Glasshouse."

Lucas said, "Fucking ain't fraternizing. I've fucked a lot of niggers in my time, but I never fraternized with one . . . Look, you—we follow behind . . . keep an eye out for Red Caps . . . got it? *Sumjow?*"

The women nodded and Lucas said, "Money when we get there . . . money *and* bully."

*   *   *   *

"If I 'ave another drill parade this week," Smith '87 said, "I'll . . . I'll . . . and don't tell me I'll do wonders in my trousers, Snaky. I'm proper browned off, and that's the truth. Drill, drill, drill . . ."

"And you're still not fit to mount a Viceroy's Guard," Lucas said. "This is a fucking Regular battalion. That's why they picked us out of the division and sent us to this 'ole."

"Cologne's not so bad," Halton said.

"I been out in the country," Fletcher Whitman said. "It's flatter than the Weald, and not so many hedges. The woods are all neat as new pins. Their gamekeepers must pick up every twig, just as though it was the lawn of a big house." He shook his head wonderingly. They were sitting in the Wet Canteen, playing dominoes. Outside sleet fell in long diagonals across the parade ground. The battalion had been parading inside the covered drill hall all afternoon, and now parades were over for the day.

"The Germans isn't so bad," Halton said, "considering they're foreigners . . . better'n Frogs, that's a fact."

Lucas said, to Whitman, "'Ow much did the captain tell you your first book of poetry has sold for you?"

"Two thousand, two hundred and forty-six quid," Fletcher said. "And the bloke what published it says there'll be more in six months, and God knows how much from the second book."

"And you 'aven't honoured that posh whorehouse by the cathedral with a visit? Or ordered champagne with your burgoo? Or stood all of us, your pals, pints of the best?"

Fletcher laughed, "I'll stand you all a pint, why not? But champagne . . . women . . ." He shrugged—"I'd rather be back in Walstone, out in one of his lordship's copses after a fine fat pheasant, with my granddad . . . only my granddad's his lordship's ruddy head gamekeeper now." He laughed again, good-humouredly.

Sergeant Fagioletti entered the Canteen, glanced round, and

headed for them. Lucas said, "Hey, sarn't, you come to have a pig's ear with us common soldiers? Or have they run out of wallop in the Sergeants' Mess?"

Fagioletti said, "Whitman, report to the company office right away. You're being demobbed. You'll be leaving on the 8.27 demob train tomorrow morning."

"Hooray!" Fletcher cried. "Home by midnight!"

"In Minden Barracks, Hedlington, by midnight, if you're lucky," the sergeant said. "The captain's going, too. Orders just in. Captain Fry from the 2nd Battalion is coming to take over the company . . . And the Regimental wants to see you at nine o'clock ack emma in his office, Lucas."

"Me?" Lucas said. "What have I done?"

Fagioletti said, "How much service have you got?"

Lucas said, at once, "Twenty-two years and ten months."

"The Regimental wants to know how much longer do you expect to serve?"

Lucas's jaw dropped. The sergeant had gone. Lucas looked at the other three. Whitman was murmuring "Betty!", his eyes closed, a slow beatific smile spreading across his face; Smith '87 was saying, "Lucky bugger, that's what you are, Whitman"; Halton was drinking deep from his tankard.

Lucas stared from one to the other of them. The Regimental was going to tell him his time was up. But where could he go? "Where can I go?" he said in a sudden panic. "What can I do? I'm a soldier . . . Everyone's dead . . . mum, dad, sisters, brothers, cousins . . . dead or never 'eard of me, 'cos I'm a soldier . . ."

Whitman opened his eyes and said softly, "They're dead, but the Regiment lives. That's what they taught us when we joined, wasn't it? . . . The Regiment lives for ever. And you want to live for ever in it, eh?"

Daily Telegraph, Monday, January 27, 1919

OFFICIAL REPORT OF THE PEACE CONFERENCE

LEAGUE OF NATIONS

DELEGATES' SPEECHES

PRESIDENT WILSON

President Wilson: **Mr Chairman—I consider it a distinguished privilege to open the discussion in this Conference on the League of Nations. We have assembled for two purposes—to make the present settlements which have been made necessary by this war, and also to secure the peace of the world, not only by the present settlements**

> but by the arrangements we shall make in this Conference for its maintenance. The League of Nations seems to me to be necessary for both of these purposes . . . You can imagine, gentlemen, I dare say, the sentiments and the purpose with which representatives of the United States support this great project for a League of Nations. We regard it as the keystone of the whole programme, which expressed our purposes and ideals in this war, and which the associated nations accepted as the basis of the settlement . . . I hope, Mr Chairman, that when it is known, as I feel confident it will be known, that we have adopted the principle of the League of Nations and mean to work out that principle in effective action, we shall by that single thing have lifted a great part of the load of anxiety from the hearts of men everywhere . . . I have only tried in what I have said to give you the fountain of enthusiasm which is within us for this thing, for these fountains spring, it seems to me, from all the ancient wrongs and sympathies of mankind, and the very pulse of the world seems to beat to the surface of this enterprise . . .

Cate looked up at his guest, Captain Kellaway—"What do you think of this League of Nations idea? Or haven't you had time to think about it?"

Kellaway, spreading marmalade on a piece of toast, said, "I think it's a good idea, sir . . . anything's a good idea, that might prevent us having another war like that. But whether it will work, I don't know. It'll take a long time, and perhaps another war or two, even worse than this one, to make the big countries let any League tell them what they can and can not do. We can only hope for the best . . . but I think it's a bad omen that Russia isn't in it, nor Germany—they'll have to be, sooner or later . . . and I suspect that America might not join, in the end, in spite of Mr Wilson."

Cate was silent. Kellaway had arrived from Germany the night before last, and telephoned him yesterday morning, asking if he could see him. He had been Laurence's company commander throughout Laurence's time in France. He had come to the Manor and Cate had asked him to stay the night. They had talked late, about Laurence, and the war, recognizing in each other a common view of civilization, a common sense of tragedy.

Now Kellaway said, "I have to go back to barracks soon, sir. They're supposed to complete my demob procedures this afternoon . . . they want to get us in and out as fast as possible. They don't have the accommodation to hold anyone for long . . . The regiment had twenty-one battalions in the field at the armistice . . ."

Cate said, "I would not like to lose touch with you. Where can I reach you?"

"91 Albemarle Street," Kellaway said. "My telephone is Mayfair 7744. Call, any time."

Cate said cautiously, "How will it feel, being a civilian again? Pretty good, I suppose."

Kellaway didn't answer for a long time. Glancing up, Cate was astonished, and moved, to see his good eye filling with tears. Kellaway adjusted the eyepatch on the other eye, and said, "Lost, sir. Orphaned . . . I have been incredibly lucky to survive . . . losing no more than one eye and bits of unimportant flesh here and there. But my real luck, my real privilege, is to have served with the men—and women—of this country, in the war. The war itself was unbelievably horrible. They—the men—were unbelievably magnificent . . . from our C.O., Quentin Rowland, and Boy, to such as Private Lucas, Private Whitman, Sergeant Fagioletti . . . and the uncountable dead . . . Laurence knew that, too, sir, before he died. His last words were 'Thank you'—to the firing squad."

London: February, 1919

20 Panting, Guy Rowland ran back to his place in the line-out. The cold wind slashed through his thin jersey in the parti-colours of the Harlequins' Rugby Football club. His body ached from the many times he had been tackled; his calves and thighs were stiff from running, jinking, and kicking; and he had been at it since practise began an hour ago. He would be twenty-two in a couple of months, but he felt a hundred. Still, covered in mud, bleeding from grazes on cheek and hand, he realized that for a long time he had not thought of Werner von Rackow or any other of his victims: he was not the Butcher, but an out-of-practise stand-off half. The cockpits of Sopwith Camels didn't prepare you for thirty minutes each way of top-class rugger.

The wing lobbed the ball down the line-out, a Colour got it, and slung it back at once to Guy. Before it reached him a White was on him, burly, blond-headed, coming like an express train. The ball and W.W. Wakefield arrived simultaneously, and Guy went crashing to the ground, holding tight to the ball. Then the heels were over him, and he rolled up, letting the ball loose from him to the Colours' side. A big boot got it out, kicking him in the stomach in the process . . . the scrum was gone, the pack dribbling loose, David Toledano in the lead. Guy ran to his position . . . perhaps it would bounce right, and they could start a passing movement . . . the White fullback tried to fall on the ball and failed . . . There, it bounced up into David's hands, and he'd swung round and thrown a beautiful pass back to the scrum half, who was running, jinking, about to be tackled . . . passed to Guy, just in time . . . the White fullback was on his feet, the Colours' forwards pounding up . . . no way to sell a dummy to his opposite number . . . thirty-five yards out . . . Guy pivoted, swung, and sent a drop kick arching up between the tall white-painted goal posts.

David was slapping him on the back—"Well done, Guy"; and the ref was blowing No Side. Wakefield, coming up beside him, said, "Good kick, colonel . . . Little out of training, aren't you, though?"

Guy nodded, still gasping—"I'll try to get fit again . . . but the general keeps sending me to Paris and Cologne."

Wakefield said, "Think you can play regularly, Toledano?"

David said dubiously, "I hope so. But my father's not very well, and wants me to start taking over the bank. If I could just turn out on Saturdays . . ."

"But you can't," Wakefield said, "not for the Club side. If you could train and play regularly you could get an England cap next year."

David said, "I don't know . . ."

They walked on, toward the changing rooms. There, as David and Guy sat side by side on a narrow bench, after their showers, slowly pulling on their clothes, David said, "What are your plans, Guy? Long-term plans?"

Guy stood up in front of the mirror, tying his Old Wellingtonian tie. He said, "I want to do something for civil aviation. I'm thinking of flying a British aircraft to Buenos Aires."

David whistled long and low—"That would make a sensation. What's the length of the sea crossing?"

"Eighteen hundred fifty miles from Bathurst to Natal."

"Would you use a Buffalo?"

"I'd like to, if we can work out a way to carry extra fuel . . . and feed it into the tanks in flight. Our present maximum range is not much more than 1,100 miles, with 800 gallons of fuel."

It was David's turn to stand up before the mirror, adjusting his tie. Guy watched him, admiring the placid honesty in the big, broken-nosed face, the thoughtfulness in the deep brown eyes. David spoke without looking round, but now watching Guy in the mirror—"When you've done that, would you consider coming into the bank with me? My father may have mentioned it to you . . . may have told you he would like you to. But now *I'm* telling you—*I* want you to."

After a time Guy said, "It's a great honour . . . and compliment . . . for you to invite me into something that you've made on your own . . . like being asked to become a member of your family. I just don't know, David . . . Ever since the war ended . . . no, before that . . . I've been drifting. Oh, I can do individual tasks that are set to me, or that I set myself, such as this flight, but the general direction of my life . . . its purpose . . . that's unknown to me. I keep searching, in a sort of haphazard way. I don't find."

David turned and Guy saw that he was blushing. He said hesitantly, "About being part of the family . . . you are . . . you would be, if you joined us . . . even without marrying Rebecca, though I'd be very happy if you did. She really admires you . . ."

"But no one can make her love me," Guy murmured.

"I think she does," David said, "but she can't show it, even to me, unless . . . well, unless you do, too. It would make her and Father so happy, too. We all love Rebecca."

"David," Guy said, "I've been in love with one girl nearly all my life. I still am. Now, there's another . . . I don't love her, but I owe her more than love. I owe her a life . . . Maria von Rackow. What the hell am I to do?"

*   *   *   *

They were walking down the narrow street together—Guy, David Toledano, and Helen Rowland. David was pushing a pram, containing a ten-month-old boy, with curly fair hair and blue eyes. Anyone who had known Boy Rowland would know that it was his son. Those two—David and Helen—were talking animatedly. Guy, walking a little behind and to one side, listened and watched. Most mornings he motor-cycled up to the Park from the little flat he'd found in South Kensington, and rode an hour on horses from Watkins' livery stable; and sometimes David Toledano rode with him. Yesterday Lady Barbara Watkins—Helen Rowland's sister—had mentioned that Helen would very much like to see him. Guy had determined to visit her—they had been friends all their lives—and David, overhearing, had wanted to come; for he had known her slightly . . . and now, the old contact re-established, a new direction came into Guy's thoughts. If old Isaac Toledano, and David, could try to produce suitable women for him, he could do as much for David. It might work. There were obstacles, of course, and they were both too sensible to be pushed into anything they didn't really want, but . . . it had great possibilities.

"I'm afraid the boutique's not doing so well since the war ended," Helen was saying. "Women don't seem to need to spend so much on themselves, now that their men are home. You'd have thought it would be the other way round, but it isn't . . ."

Guy cut in, "Isn't Ethel Stratton, that was, helping you?"

"Yes," she said. "She's very good, too. But I don't know how long she'll stay with me. She's desperate to have children, and Sergeant Fagioletti—her husband—is staying on in the army, and he will be allotted a married quarter in Germany in June. Then, of course, she'll go over to him."

"Won't get any babies unless she does," Guy murmured. Helen smiled at him and turned back to David.

David said, "I don't know much about boutiques, exactly, but I know something about business in general. Could I come and have a look at your place? See how you manage things . . . what your buying procedures are, accounting, stock records, and so on?"

"You are very kind," Helen said.

"And afterwards, please let me give you lunch."

"I don't really have time for a good lunch," she said. "And at the normal lunch hours I have to be in the boutique because that's when a lot of women come in to buy something."

"Dinner then?"

Guy sighed silently, kept his face impassive, and made cooing noises at the baby; who was called Charles Durand-Beaulieu Rowland, but was always addressed as "Boy."

*   *   *   *

The main banqueting room upstairs at the Café Royal was full to overflowing, of men and women in every variation of attire, from morning coats to velveteen jackets, from long silk gowns and sweeping hats to defiant trousers and bare, bobbed hair. The time was half-past noon; and the level of the noise in the big, red-hung room with the golden N's embroidered on everything in sight, had been rising steadily since the reception in honour of Mr Fletcher Gorse and his new book *The Blood of Poppies* had begun at noon. Champagne and white wine were being served by waiters; many of the newfangled American cocktails were also available. The noise increased as the invited guests increased their intake of alcohol; and the eclecticism of the dress reflected the variety of the worlds where Fletcher's poetry had struck the heart . . . Bloomsbury, Chelsea, Mayfair, the City, Westminster; politics, fashion, art, literature, commerce; the army, navy, air force, society . . .

Fletcher had a glass of champagne in one hand, the other hand stuck into the pocket of his khaki trousers, for he was wearing uniform. He had been demobbed a week before, but his publisher, Mr Edgar Kajayan, had specially asked him to appear as a private soldier. He supposed that he ought to be saluting all these officers—there was Mr Guy, now a lieutenant colonel; and there was a general, or p'raps a ruddy Field Marshal . . . and that must be an admiral, with gold braid halfway to his shoulder; but he didn't have his cap on, so he couldn't salute: just stand to attention, and the hell with that. Old

Rowley would have given him what for, but old Rowley was in India, a ruddy Brigadier General at last.

"Their faces are getting red as beets, with the booze," he muttered in an aside to Betty Merritt.

A tall, imperious, youngish blonde swept up, glancing at Betty as though she were something the cat had just brought in. "Mr Gorse," she said, "how can I tell you what your poetry has meant to me? I had two brothers out there in the Grenadiers, my husband, too—the Duke of Kendal . . . I'm the Duchess of Kendal . . . Philippa . . . You made me *feel* what it was really like. But . . ." again she glanced at Betty, close at Fletcher's side, as though to ask, who *is* this woman? She continued—"One thing I can not understand . . . you are a poet, so sensitive, so *spiritual* . . . how could you tolerate the filth, the brutality?"

Fletcher said, "Oh, you can live through anything if you think of what's coming later . . . a few bottles of van blong, and a fat French whore."

"Really!" the duchess gasped. Her eyes gleamed—"Ah, Mr Gorse, I don't believe for a moment that *you* ever have to pay for *l'amour*."

"Never a penny," Fletcher said. "Oh, Duchess, this is my fiancée, Betty Merritt."

The duchess turned, and recognizing defeat, said, "How nice! Well, I hope you are both very happy." She drifted away. Betty hissed, "We're not engaged! I never promised!"

"You better had, now," Fletcher said, "otherwise women like that'll eat me up, starting with my cock."

"Shhh! I . . ."

The voice was a man's, lisping slightly, "My dear Gorse . . . Mr Gorse . . . Private Gorse, would you prefer? . . . Allow me to congratulate you . . . a masterpiece of observation guided and informed by a vast human sympathy. And this . . ." the little blue eyes were sharp; it was the Secretary of State for War and Air, The Right Honourable Winston Churchill—"this is your fiancée?"

"Yes, sir," Fletcher said.

"Well, all good fortune to you. Marry him soon, young lady. This man is a national treasure, which needs protecting." He nodded and walked away.

"We must have time to . . ." Betty began.

"Excuse me . . . I'm Siegfried Sassoon. A poet myself, in my way—"

"Ah!" Fletcher said. "If I were fierce and bald and short of breath, I'd live with scarlet majors at the Base, and speed glum heroes up the line to death . . ."

368

Sassoon, tall, thin, and gentle-looking, flushed with pleasure—"It's rather bad-tempered, like *Blighters*—but that's how I felt. Poetry has to be about feeling, in the end, not facts . . . Do you know Isaac Rosenberg's stuff?"

"Yes. Is he here?"

"I'm afraid not. Killed in action last year . . . absolutely uneducated, but brilliant, brilliant . . . What sort of education have you had, if you don't mind my asking?"

"Nothing," Fletcher said, grinning. "Just school till I was twelve . . ."

Another man had come up. Sassoon stood back. The new arrival was small, with jutting grey eyebrows and thick pebble glasses. He thrust his hand out—"You are a great poet, sir. Thank you! I wish I had half of your"—he waved a hand, pulling a word out of the air— "your grace. Never flag. Never compromise."

He walked away through the crowd. Mr Kajayan was at Fletcher's side, crowing, "Do you know who that was? Rudyard Kipling! . . . and there's Bridges, and Masefield . . . There's Q . . . and Lord Curzon, Wilfred Bentley—he's a Socialist M.P. . . ."

"I know him," Fletcher said, unexpectedly. "Nearly put a bullet in him a few weeks ago."

"Admiral Jellicoe, Admiral Beatty, Augustus John, Thomas Hardy . . . first time anyone has persuaded *him* to come up from Dorchester . . . and Rosa Lewis, she hates *writers* . . . heaven knows what's made her come, except that most of the people who'd stay at the Cavendish are here . . . You're a success, young man. London is at your feet. What do you want to do with it?"

Betty spoke up—"We're going to get married, Mr Kajayan. As soon as possible."

*   *   *   *

Florinda Lady Jarrow crouched lower in the bucket seat of the big Sunbeam, an airman's leather helmet and goggles hiding her auburn hair, her body wrapped in a short fleece-lined greatcoat, like a British warm, heavy gauntlets on her hands. The driver, beside her, was Billy Bidford, recently released from active service with the Royal Naval Volunteer Reserve. They were driving from London to Walstone, Kent, where the Lord Walstone had invited a party to celebrate the end of the shooting season. Billy had not done much shooting before the war, but since the armistice he had taken it up as a restful change from his main avocation of racing motor cars.

Florinda shifted her weight in the narrow seat. This was built for men, with narrow hips, she thought disgustedly. They weren't expecting girls to travel in her—bloody fools, a car like this wouldn't look right without a girl in the passenger seat, unless it was actually racing.

Billy said, shouting against the wind of their passage and the throb of the engine under the long bonnet—"I'm planning a special race, to publicize British cars. London to Constantinople."

"Constantinople!" she cried. "Good God, Billy, that's . . ."

"Two thousand miles," he said. "Terrible roads . . . very few garages. It'll be a real test for the cars. We'll have it in June."

"That'll be interesting," she said. "I spoke to Guy Rowland on the telephone yesterday. He's planning to fly an aeroplane from London to Buenos Aires, in June."

"Is he, by Jove!" Billy exclaimed lightly. "Well, we'll see who wins the races . . . and gets the girl, eh?"

She said nothing; but thought, I love Guy Rowland. He's drifting, and drinking. Why the *hell* doesn't he come to me, so that I can give him everything I have, and am?

*　　*　　*　　*

Dr Charles Deerfield (né Hirschfeld) surveyed the calling card with apprehension. *Mr John de Lisle Merritt*, it read; and in the lower left corner, *The Cottage, Beighton, Kent;* in another corner, a telephone number . . . John Merritt, Stella's husband. They had not met. Years ago, in Hedlington, he had invited both Merritts to lunch, but John had not been able to come, due to an emergency at the factory—and after that, Stella had not wanted John to come. But now . . . had he found out? Was he coming with a revolver in his pocket? The war had made violence, and killing, so commonplace, so much accepted, that it was possible. But why send in a card? Why not shoot him in the street? Perhaps Merritt didn't even know about his relations with Stella. They always said husbands were the last to know.

He said to his nurse, "Show him in, please, Mrs Greene."

As John came in Deerfield stood up behind his desk, his heart palpitating. The young man was big, stern, severe-looking, his hair still military short, his jaw set, the grey eyes fixed on his own.

"Dr Deerfield?" John said.

"I'm Dr Deerfield."

"You lived and practised in Hedlington?"

"I did."

"You once asked Stella and me to lunch with you, but I couldn't come." Deerfield nodded, unable to speak. John continued—"I asked my uncle, who is Secretary of the American Embassy, to find me a good alienist. He made inquiries and recommended you, and two others. But you have at least met Stella, so I decided to come to you."

Deerfield breathed a touch more easily. The way the conversation was going, it seemed probable that he did not know. His trembling began to subside.

John said, "My wife has become a heroin addict, doctor. I need help . . . she needs help, to break her of her addiction, so that she can lead a normal life."

"Ah!" the doctor sighed. He sat down slowly behind his desk, his knees shaking anew with the relief. He surveyed the young man opposite. Put him on the sofa, to talk? That would make him seem like the patient whereas, of course, Stella should be. A momentary remembrance of her body, sprawled back in his Hedlington office, skirts up, knickers off, thighs widespread, made him shiver; he regained control of himself. Those days were over; he had other women here in London, but he had made sure that none of them were his patients. That game was not worth the candle.

He said, "I think you had better lie down on the couch there, Mr Merritt. It's more comfortable, and it gives you a sense, which you must have, that there's no hurry. Start from the beginning. Tell me what has happened . . . to Stella . . . when it happened . . . what you have observed of her actions . . . of her thoughts . . ." He took position at the end of the couch, notebook in hand; but he did not have to make many notes. He knew all this, up to the end of 1917, at least.

He listened, trying to keep his face calm, even though he knew that John could not see it. This was a terrible tale, of desperation, despair, prostitution, a dead baby, then an illegitimate baby . . . and now, regulated despair, under treatment to control her addiction rather than do away with it. He could say, it was all his fault. But he would not. It was Stella's nature . . . if it had not been he, it would have been another; if it had not been heroin, it would have been something else—brandy—men—gambling. She was destined to come to this point, as Christ to come to Gethsemane; but none could say whether Stella would or could be resurrected.

An hour later, he slowly closed the notebook and said, "Sit up, Mr Merritt. Take the chair there, opposite . . . Heroin is addictive both physically and psychologically. That is to say that the body comes to need it physically, and the psyche needs the states of mind it creates. Stella—Mrs Merritt—apparently is so addicted, in both ways. The addiction could again be removed in a hospital in a fairly short time, as it was when she was found, but she would again return to heroin as soon as released. She has to be made to want to be cured. And the first step is to rescue her from her past—her whole past, everything that has made her . . . Take her to America, Mr Merritt. Face her with a

371

challenge. I came to know her a little, before she fell into this, this sad situation . . . and I think that is the key word—challenge. Once she decides that she must fight and overcome the challenge, the cure will not take long."

"I understand," John said in a low voice. "Everyone who knows about it has said much the same thing . . . But how did she get addicted?"

Deerfield said, "That does not matter now, only *why?* Was it boredom? *Lack* of challenge, lack of danger? I don't know . . . I would not tell her you have sought my advice, if I were you. The decision to move must seem to have come solely from you."

*　　*　　*　　*

Arthur Gavilan leaned back in the swivel chair in the large drawing room that was his "office." The chair, built as a standard fixture for some board director's office, had been rebuilt and re-upholstered in Louis XV style; which ought to have looked dreadful, but did not. The rest of the room bore similar marks of Gavilan's impish eye and bold decisions. A gramophone on a large walnut table, with a stack of records beside it, managed to look both modern and eighteenth-century. The curtains, long and damask and gold-embroidered, framed an urban view down Maddox Street and yet seemed as cosy as French provincial.

Tom Rowland, sitting in a high-backed chair, also Louis XV, with his legs stretched out, crossed at the ankle, was studying a sheaf of patterns lent to him by Gavilan's head cutter, Gertrude O'Keefe. He glanced up—"Arthur, look at this—your sketches showed you wanted this dress made of Lyons silk, and cut on the bias from the waist down. Gertrude's got the cutting marked so that it would hang straight. I wonder why?"

Gavilan lowered his book and glanced over—"H'm . . . Oh, yes, that one . . . she talked to me about it, and we agreed to change it. That material is too light to hang well on the cross—I wasn't thinking. We'll go and look at it in a moment, when I've finished this chapter." He looked at an ornate desk calendar beside him on the table— "Damn, we have a would-be client to see first—Mrs Cullman."

"Gwilyn Cullman?"

Gavilan nodded, "He's soap . . . she's a niece of Lord Rameley . . . has aspirations of running a political salon to rival the Astors at Cliveden."

A young man in faultless morning coat and striped trousers stood in the doorway. "Mr G," he said, "Mrs Cullman's here."

Gavilan glanced at the Buhl clock on the red-marbled mantelpiece, frowning. "She's fifteen minutes early," he said.

"I know. She says her dentist put forward her next appointment without warning, so she hoped . . ."

Gavilan said, looking at Tom, "Shall we make her wait? Does she think her wretched dentist is more important to her than I am?"

Tom said, "Well . . . The poor woman couldn't help it, obviously. But she might have been wiser to ask Jeremy to give her another appointment."

Gavilan said, "Well, we can make her understand her place later, can't we? If we want to dress her at all. Bring her in, Jeremy."

"Gertrude, too?"

Gavilan nodded, and Tom composed his face into the look of polite indifference which Gavilan had demanded of him. Gertrude came in, a short square woman in her fifties, a large sketch pad and pencil in one hand—"Who is it, Mr G?" she asked.

"Mrs Cullman."

"Oi've seen her picture," Gertrude said, the Irish accent strong.

Jeremy the secretary appeared at the door—"Mrs Cullman, sir."

She came in, making an entrance—five foot six, about thirty, piled blond hair, expensively dressed, a fur swishing round her graceful neck, two diamonds on her fingers . . . a waft of expensive perfume, not too sweet, not too heavy for the time of day. Jeremy went out, closing the door silently behind him. The men rose, Gertrude standing behind them. Gavilan put his hand out—"I'm Arthur Gavilan . . . This is Commander Tom Rowland, my partner . . . What a pretty dress."

"Oh, thank you. It's . . ."

"Where did you get it? Harrod's?"

The woman started slightly, recovered herself, and waved a coquettish finger, "Ah, Mr Gavilan, it's we ladies who are supposed to be catty. This is a Worth design."

Gavilan pursed his lips and said, "Dear me . . . Do sit down." He made to move forward, but she had sunk into a chair facing them before he reached it. She arranged her dress and fur and smiled confidently at him.

"You would like me to dress you?"

She nodded. "Yes, please. I think you are so original . . . so daring. I don't want to look like all the other women, in their Chanels, Fratellis, Worths . . . as you say, there is something Harrodish about them, isn't there?"

Gavilan said, "I only dress from head to toe. Inside and out. Day and night. Summer and winter."

373

"Can I wear my own sports clothes?" the woman said anxiously. "I'm really rather good at golf and shooting, and . . . if I'm not absolutely comfortable, I . . ."

Gavilan said coldly, "If you're not absolutely comfortable, and absolutely confident, in my clothes at *any* time, we will both have failed. I can't have it known that I dress you, and then you appear in Yorkshire in some dreadful outfit that was bequeathed to you by your great-aunt. It is perfectly possible to be both fashionable and practical."

"Oh, of course. I understand. Certainly."

"It'll cost you ten to fifteen thousand a year, depending on how many dresses you need."

"That's all right, Mr Gavilan. Perfectly all right."

Gavilan nodded—"Stand up, then."

Hesitatingly, she rose, sweeping the fur round her neck. Staring at him, she realized that he wanted her to model herself and turned slowly, as she had seen a few live models do at modern fashion shows.

She turned, quite gracefully, but without the exaggerated movements of a professional, to display the swing and cling of the garment.

She faced him again—"Is that all right?"

"Take off your clothes. All of them."

"But . . ." She was blushing pink now, the firm line of her jaw dissolving.

"I can not decide whether it's worth dressing your body until I see it . . . My time is really quite valuable, Mrs Cullman, at least to me."

She undressed slowly, the colour coming and going in her face and neck. At last she stood naked before them, her face finally drained of colour. Gavilan began to speak, while Gertrude took notes and Mrs Cullman's teeth chattered—"Bust too big for today . . . might come back into fashion in a few years . . . bony hips . . . right shoulder an inch lower than the left . . . knock-knees, a little more than most women . . . face triangular, hair thick—best feature . . . neck long, very good for five, six more years . . . Turn round . . . buttocks big, should be tighter . . . need exercise there . . . Stand on that machine, there, please . . ." Gertrude went over as Mrs Cullman, still dead white, stood on the platform.

"Five foot five and seven eighths," Gertrude said. "Eight stone one."

"She needs to take off four pounds," Gavilan said, "mostly in the buttocks. You may dress again, Mrs Cullman."

She struggled awkwardly back into her clothes. This was the worst part, Tom thought. Arthur was deliberately cruel.

At last the woman was nearly dressed. Gavilan said, "You have some problems, Mrs Cullman, but no more than most women." She turned, reaching for her fur. The colour was coming back into her face. He said, "I'll dress you, on the terms we discussed."

She cried, "Oh thank you, Mr Gavilan . . . thank you! . . . When can I come for my first fitting? I need half a dozen spring dresses desperately, and . . . and . . ."

"Today week, 10 a.m. . . . punctually," Arthur said, unsmiling. He was on his feet, his crimson velvet suit glowing under the chandeliers. He took her hand and bent perfunctorily over it—"Good day." The door opened and Jeremy appeared. Mrs Cullman muttered, stammering, "Oh, thank you, thank you . . ."

She backed out. Gavilan sank into a chair. Tom said, "Really, Arthur! That was one of the worst yet."

Gavilan said lazily, "Do you fear women, Tom . . . or do you hate them?"

Tom said, "Fear, I suppose."

"Well, you'll never be a great couturier unless you learn to hate them as well, or at least despise them . . . And what's the best way of overcoming fear?"

"Attack," Tom said. "Conquer it . . . Oh, I suppose you're right. Heaven knows I'm here to learn, and you've had years of experience with them, while I . . . nothing. But . . ." he shrugged, saying no more.

Gavilan said, "When you strike out on your own, Tom, you'll develop your own way of managing things . . . but believe me, with women, especially women of fashion, either they dominate you, or you dominate them. Be warned! . . . Now, tell me why Admiral Beatty, at Jutland, didn't . . ."

*　　*　　*　　*

The Countess of Swanwick was sitting behind the desk in the back office of the Hoggins Universal Store in the Edgware Road, London W.2. The manager of the store, a woman, was standing across the littered desk from her, a harried look on her long face, tendrils of her greying hair escaping from the hairpins that should have held them in place. Whenever she came here, Lady Swanwick's eye always caught a few hairpins gleaming on the linoleum of the floor—no carpets in managers' offices, of course. Lord Walstone wouldn't have that any more than he would have carpets on the floors of the stores themselves.

Lady Swanwick said, "These accounts are simply not clear, Miss Bewsher."

"They're not quite ready, Lady Swanwick," the other woman said.

They never are, Flora Swanwick thought; all store managers had to send in weekly general accounts, monthly detailed statements, and an annual stock-taking record. The dates of the stock taking were arranged by area managers, and staggered so that all H.U.S.L. shops weren't closed at the same time. That allowed some leeway for cheating, in that goods could theoretically be moved from store to store in time to be counted several times; but Milner, Lord Walstone's private spy, was up to that trick, and any other that managers might think of. Lady Swanwick cordially despised Milner, but he earned his salary—whatever it was; there was no denying that. If she were suddenly to become head of the H.U.S.L. chain, she'd keep him; whereas, this poor woman . . . The trouble was that she had never held responsibility. She was the daughter of a provincial schoolmaster; she'd spent the war as accountant at a factory in the Midlands; but she wasn't up to managing a store by herself. The previous area manager should have found that out months ago.

Lady Swanwick said gently, "Your accounts are always late, Miss Bewsher. And the reason is clear. Look at this desk. It's a mess, Miss Bewsher. You can't find your own papers—the indents, the receipts, the cash records. Everything's higgledy-piggledy."

"There's so much to do . . . it all comes at once . . ." the woman muttered unhappily.

Lady Swanwick looked at her a long time. At last she said, "I'm going to tell Lord Walstone that you're not fit to manage a H.U.S.L. store."

"Oh, oh!" the woman wailed, searching for a handkerchief. Lady Swanwick continued—"But I think you may be suited for the accounts department in the head office." She rose. "I don't know whether he will agree to transfer you. You'll lose salary, of course . . . and you'll lose your participation in the store's profits, but at least you will not be out of work . . . *if* he agrees."

"Oh, thank you, thank you," Miss Bewsher sobbed.

Lady Swanwick said, "I'll return on Friday, to check these accounts. They must be ready in all particulars by then."

She went out, walked through the busy shop, and stood a moment on the kerb outside, thinking. Five o'clock. No time to look at the Oxford Street shop, as she had intended. The Edgware Road shop always took more time than she had planned . . . Barbara was pregnant; might visit her on her way home, and find out if she was all right . . . she shouldn't ride so much . . . but, being Barbara, the baby might well be born on horseback . . . She might drop in on Helen's boutique and buy herself a new hat. She'd earned it . . . She hailed a taxi.

When she walked into La Boutique Amicale, as it was called, she found herself looking at a man's broad back, which hid Helen. Ethel Fagioletti was there, at the side of the store, and hurried forward—"M'lady . . ." she called over her shoulder—"It's your mother."

The man turned . . . burly, swarthy, nose broken a couple of times, one cauliflower ear, a friendly, comfortable face, incongruous liquid brown eyes. Helen came round the little glass-topped counter, her arms out—"Mother! I wasn't expecting you. Why didn't you call?"

"Just thought I'd buy myself a little chapeau," the countess said. She looked inquiringly at the young man. Helen said, "Oh, this is David Toledano, Mother."

Ah, the countess thought, that's why he seemed familiar. She'd seen him before, at the Cates', or at some wedding, she thought. He was a Jew . . . very, very rich, but a Jew. Helen was looking at him with a sort of obvious ease, and affection. They must be seeing a lot of each other. Roger would have a fit, but Roger need not know until some decision had been made . . . not by him, or by her, but by these two young people.

*   *   *   *

The Turkish lanterns glowed red, the carpet imprisoned the glow, with the shimmer of silk, and the sheen of dulled silver in the menorah, in the curved ancient urns and flagons and the dark red carpets hanging on the walls. The naked girl's bronze breasts swelled in the shadows. A little bowed man in ragged clothes stood with hands clasped across his thin stomach before the old man sitting cross-legged on the cushions.

"He is seeing a woman who calls herself Mrs Rowland. She owns a small shop for women's clothes—not a dress shop, notions and such—in Great Marlborough Street, called La Boutique Amicale."

"Ah," Isaac Toledano said, sipping sweet, thick Turkish coffee. "What is her real name?"

"She was born Lady Helen Durand-Beaulieu, the younger daughter of the Earl and Countess of Swanwick. They used to live . . ."

"I know," Isaac said, "Walstone Park. Great wealth once, but not now. They are almost penniless. Anything more?"

"Mrs Rowland had a baby boy last April. I haven't found out yet who the father was, but I suppose it was someone called Rowland."

"A family of Walstone and Hedlington," the old man said. "I have holdings in two businesses managed by one of them, Mr Richard Rowland." He did not add, "and I intend that another, Guy Rowland, shall become a partner in my bank, and marry my daughter." There was no need for this petty hawker he hired occasionally as a spy to know that, even though he was a Cohen.

The man said, "He has seen her several times. Once was at her house, with another man. Also at her shop. Once he took her out to dinner, to Claridge's Hotel."

Isaac nodded, "See Levy on your way out."

The other bowed and backed out. Isaac sipped his coffee reflectively. David, getting involved with a Gentile. That would never do, even though she was a peer's daughter. He didn't mind David acting like one of them—that Rugby football he loved so much; riding with the foxhounds; drinking and singing songs in public houses with other young men; but, the blood, the race, must be preserved.

He clapped his hands, and in a few moments his daughter appeared, gliding in like some young girl summoned to her sultan's bed, head bent, eyes downcast.

"You called for me, Father?"

The old man said, "David is seeing a Gentile woman . . . It is not serious yet, but it could become so. Who is the most beautiful young woman of your friends? Not more than twenty-five. And, of course, a Jewess."

Rebecca said, "Oh, Rachel Sebag Montefiore, Father, without a doubt. But she is not very intelligent."

Isaac waved a hand—"That does not matter, with David." Guy Rowland will provide all the intelligence they need for the bank, he thought; and at home, who wanted an intelligent woman? A fertile one, yes. A devout one, yes. One who could run a household, yes. But intelligent? No.

He said, "David must marry among his people."

Rebecca said nothing; but she was thinking . . . David was devout, but he had seen much of the world. He had seen Jerusalem! He would respect his father, but—obey him in all things? She thought not. The times had changed, with all that blood on the sun, all those young men gone, gone. Gentile and Jew alike—gone.

Daily Telegraph, Saturday, March 29, 1919

THE TURF

GRAND NATIONAL DAY

For many reasons the first Grand National Steeplechase to be held with war a thing of the past will long be memorable. It will pass into history for the epoch-making occasion which it undoubtedly is, for the gigantic crowd which gathered on and about the

racecourse, and for the triumph of a grand horse in Mrs Hugh
Peel's Poethlyn with the top weight of 12 st. 7 . . . Admiral Sir
David Beatty, whose flagship, the *Queen Elizabeth*, is in the Mersey,
and who is to receive the freedom of the city tomorrow, was present.
He was in plain clothes, and just before the big steeplechase he
joined Lord Derby on the roof of his private stand . . . The public
were fortunate in the weather, for though the boisterous wind still
raged, it remained fine until the horses for the Grand National were
actually parading and forming at the start. Then snow began to fall
heavily, appearing like a blanket which was going to overwhelm
everything . . . it was then that Lord Lonsdale, acting most sensibly
and promptly, hurried on to the course and ordered the whole field
back to the paddock. A few minutes later the sun peeped through
again and at once a transformation had been effected, giving place to
perfect conditions for seeing the race . . .

Cate read the long report of the race with interest. Horse racing in
general was not one of his passions; but the Grand National was different, in a class and category by itself. Piggott had obviously had the
best horse in the field, but he had also ridden a good race. Poethlyn
was by Rydal Head out of Fine Champagne, and the name apparently
meant "liquor" in Welsh. He'd started the hot favorite at 11 to 4
against . . .

Across the table his weekend guest Guy Rowland said, "Did you
have anything on the race, Uncle?"

Cate laughed—"Not a penny. The National's too chancey for me
. . . but I always put a pound each way on something for the Derby."

"Have you ever won anything?"

"Yes," Cate said, laughing again—"I won thirty-six shillings in
1891." He put the paper aside and sat back, "Tell me, Guy, how is the
change in the Air Ministry going to affect you?"

Guy said, "You mean General Trenchard coming back as Chief of
the Air Staff, and General Sykes going to Chief Controller of Civil
Aviation? . . . Not much. General Trenchard has always been very
good to me, and still is. I thought he'd throw me out or send me to the
farthest place he could find, as I believe in an independent air force,
and when he left, he didn't. But now he has changed his mind, thank
heavens, and does . . . And General Sykes has told me that he'll find
something suitable for me in Civil Aviation any time I want to leave
the R.A.F. I think that he, too, was sure Trenchard would get rid of
me."

"And you're still planning to fly to Buenos Aires?"

Guy nodded—"That's coming along very well. We'll have to put in
extra fuel tanks to raise our total to 1,600 gallons of petrol—that's

exactly double what a Buffalo carries now. She does 1.41 miles per gallon in still air, all four engines running. We can put the tanks in the fuselage over the main spar . . . and move the entry ports forward about three feet on both sides. The petrol will have to be lifted seven feet up and seven feet out . . . that's too far to rely on engine suction through the carbureter, but I find that we can use little wind-driven propeller pumps, fixed on struts in the airstream to pump it out and up. I'm going to try to get Frank Stratton as my co-pilot . . . as mechanic and engineer, really, but he'll have to learn to fly well enough to take over in good weather while I have a snooze. It's a long way."

"Under whose auspices is the flight to be conducted—the R.A.F. or the Civil Aviation people?"

"Civil Aviation, though the R.A.F. will help. We're getting a lot of co-operation and promises of supplies, facilities, and money, from the big aircraft and oil companies . . . How's Stella, Uncle?"

Cate said slowly, "Not well, Guy . . . The baby's strong and growing, though."

"Will it be all right if I go over there tomorrow? I thought I'd try to get John to walk on the Down with me, and then perhaps I'd take them all to lunch in Hedlington."

"Stella won't go out," Cate said heavily. "She'll stay in the house, looking out of the window, but not seeing what she's looking at. But you go. John needs to talk to someone his own age . . . someone like you . . . Here, here's my first letter from Richard and Susan in America. They seem to be enjoying themselves."

"That's more than Aunt Louise is," Guy said, picking up the letter with a laugh. "I don't think she realized what little tartars Sally and Tim are, when she volunteered to "mother" the children while Uncle Richard and Aunt Susan were away. She's had to go to Cheltenham Ladies' College once already, to get Sally out of trouble there—she was caught running round the hockey field naked, for a bet . . . and Friarside School is threatening to sack Tim if they ever catch him making stink bombs again . . ."

March 1919: The United States of America

21 Blustery winds blew intermittently up the Hudson from the south, causing green-brown waves to lap over the pilings at the foot of the lawn. A sheen of spray hung over the river, here three miles wide, sometimes fully hiding the Westchester shore opposite, sometimes clothing it in a gauzy curtain, like a woman in a tantalizing gown, now revealing, now hiding. Isabel Kramer sat in the window of the sunny room, facing down the lawn and across the river, the *New York Times* folded in her lap. WILSON ARRIVES IN PARIS, the headlines had said. Poor Mr Wilson was spending most of his time on shipboard these days, flying back and forth like a shuttlecock between the Peace Conference in Paris and the Congress in Washington, both equally turbulent, both equally hard for him to manage.

Her brother came, *The Wall Street Journal* in his hands. He had breakfasted in bed, sending word to her that he was feeling a little under the weather and did not intend to go into the city today. So now he sat down in another easy chair, and began to open his paper. Isabel said, "Are you feeling a little better, Stephen?"

"Oh yes," he said, "But I think it would be wise not to face the Erie Railroad and the ferries today . . . I see Wilson's reached Paris. I hope he's taken a long spoon with him."

She said, "Come now, it's not fair to call Mr Lloyd George and Monsieur Clemenceau devils."

"They will be, in pursuit of what they want for their countries," Stephen said gloomily. "They're very tough-minded, able, and ruthless politicians, and Wilson is . . . a high-minded schoolmaster. It's no contest. And to make it worse, they both have enormous popular backing in their own countries, while opposition to Wilson has been building up ever since the last elections . . . and it's grown by leaps and bounds since the armistice."

"Do you think the country wants this League of Nations?" she asked.

"No," he answered without hesitation. "And the Senate will reject it, however hard Wilson tries to ram it down their throats. Keep the country free from foreign entanglements, George Washington said, and he was right."

She sighed—"But what if our help is needed to save something worthwhile? As it was in the war, really, wasn't it? Suppose it comes about that we have to fight anyway, but if we'd had this League of Nations, properly backed, no one would have dared to start the war in the first place."

"That's a hypothesis," he said. "We're going to keep out of Europe and make sure they keep out of us . . . And obviously we shall insist that the League of Nations treaty has no effect in the Americas, because it would conflict with the Monroe Doctrine. We're going to build a navy as big as the British, whatever they say. They're never going to be able to force us into another war by blockading our trade . . . we're going to look to our own country."

"*Il faut cultiver notre jardin,*" she murmured.

"Yes," he said. "We must . . . Heavens, when I think of the opportunities here now, and the much greater ones that lie just around the corner, I could kick John and Betty for staying over there in England. The future lies here! They are staying in the past . . . the sick, diseased past . . . And now Betty's apparently made up her mind to marry that young man, the poacher's grandson, Fletcher Gorse . . ."

Isabel said, "He's a very good poet. And quite the lion of British Society."

"For the moment," Stephen said. "But being lionized isn't the basis of a marriage . . . it isn't a way of life."

"It can be," she said. "Though I don't think either of them will want it for long . . . She'll never come back here to live, Stephen. She'll visit, I'm sure—but live—no."

"Why not? We have poets here. Our publishers will pay him as much as British ones."

"Yes, but he's English, to the core. I know him quite well. He can't be uprooted, brought over here, and expected to flourish. The soil's not his, nor the water, nor the air . . ."

"Then John won't either, because of Stella. She's just as English as Fletcher Gorse."

"Yes, but Christopher told me in his last letter that John's beginning to understand that in her case, the roots are sucking in something bad, something rotten. If they can be broken, she'll grow new sound ones. I think he *will* come . . . When are Richard and Susan due?"

"Tomorrow, 10 a.m."

"I shall meet them at the White Star pier and drive them out myself. Will you be going in tomorrow?"

"Probably. I'll be back at the usual time, though."

*   *   *   *

Isabel Kramer sat in the back of the big Packard tourer with Susan and Richard Rowland, while the chauffeur drove from in front. The canvas top of the car was folded down, and a fresh spring wind whistled round their ears and the turned-up collars of their overcoats. Susan had visited New York once with her parents while in her late teens, and had sailed from the city on the trip where she met Richard Rowland; but on neither occasion had she left the city, or, more precisely, the Borough of Manhatan. Now they had crossed the Harlem River on a crowded bridge and were winding through narrow lanes in Westchester County, the woods glowing a delicate green under the spring sun. It was a sort of countryside she had never associated with the words "New York" . . . rolling woodland, cattle grazing in quiet fields, rocky outcrops, bright-painted wooden houses; and there, looming up across the river, the great dark brown cliff wall of the Palisades.

Now William the chauffeur had driven them onto the little ferryboat; its siren boomed and they throbbed out into the stream, and started across, crabbing to counteract the strong combined flow of the river's current and the ebb tide.

Her husband whistled softly—"What a magnificent vista! . . . Look, down river, you can almost see the sea . . . and up . . . there's another sea!"

"The Tappan Zee," Isabel said. "Up there, on the right, that grey building just coming into sight is Ossining prison . . . Sing Sing."

"It's like the Rhine!" Richard exclaimed. "Why don't we hear more of it? Why don't people come here from all over the world to see it?"

"Oh, some do," Isabel said. "But mostly Americans, and mostly Easterners at that. We don't get many foreign tourists. Europeans are afraid they'll be scalped by Indians, shot by outlaws, or poisoned by American cooks . . . And now Prohibition will be in force by early next year, and that certainly won't help to attract tourists."

Susan said, "I wish Sally and Tim and Dicky could see this."

Isabel, standing beside her on the deck of the ferryboat, noticed a

383

tear in her eye, and took her arm—"They will, dear, one day soon. Dicky's a little young to appreciate it all, anyway."

"Of course," Susan said, dabbing at her eye. "It's just . . . I miss them."

Isabel said nothing. Dear God, how she missed Christopher, her lover and *preux chevalier;* and that was a deeper and longer-lasting hurt than Susan's; for all she knew, it might last to her death.

Soon they were bowling northward on the Rockland bank of the great river. Richard leaned back between the two women, his gloved hands resting on his kness. "Just driving through New York City was exciting," he said. "What energy . . . everyone working, hurrying, not wasting a minute! I could amost feel the city throbbing with electricity. As though it might generate a tremendous flash at any moment."

"Mettlesome, mad, extravagant city," Isabel quoted—"We'll spend the day there the day after tomorrow, if that suits you."

"Wonderful!" Richard said. "I want to see Wall Street, the Stock Exchange . . ."

Susan said, "The Statue of Liberty . . .   the Metropolitan Museum . . ."

"Macy's . . . the Brooklyn Bridge . . ."

"A theatre . . . dinner at Luchow's, if the mob hasn't burned it down for being German . . ."

Richard said, "Stephen will be back this evening, won't he? I'm very eager to find out what he has arranged about our visit to the Ford factory. I do hope to meet Mr Ford himself, if it is possible."

"It has all been fixed," Isabel said. "Stephen knows Mr Ford quite well."

"I also hope to see the Jones & Gatewood plant . . . and Armbruster's."

"Bridgeport, Connecticut, and Columbus, Ohio, respectively. You'll visit Columbus on your way to Detroit by train. You'll visit Bridgeport by car. It's only two hours' drive from here, or less if the traffic isn't bad. Now that the war's over more and more people are buying cars, but the roads aren't keeping pace. When summer comes, the roads to and from the beaches will be a nightmare, on weekends."

"What a country," Richard said dreamily. "What a market! And all the capital you need . . . all the skilled labour . . . all the resources. Already England seems like a quiet little backwater in a forgotten continent."

"Yet England still holds the world's sea trade . . . insurance . . . international banking," Isabel said.

"America is the future," Richard said. "Everything's so big, so *forward*-looking!"

384

"We have our problems," Isabel said. "Some of them we can cure, with money. Some we'll have to cure with things we seem to find more difficult to come up with . . . patience, sympathy . . ."

The car was running along the bank of the river. "Grandview," she said. "About two miles to go . . . That was Piermont we went through just now. That little stream we crossed was where Henry Hudson got fresh water for his crew, in 1609."

The Hudson was as wide as the sea here, and Richard gasped again, stretching out his arms as though to embrace the great river and the spreading land—"America," he murmured. "America . . ."

*   *   *   *

"History is bunk," Henry Ford said, tapping one of his long, strong, bony fingers on the desk top.

Richard gazed with awe at the thin face with the clear, wide-set eyes. This was one of the richest men in the world, richer perhaps than even the Nizam of Hyderabad, or the Aga Khan. But he had made it all himself, by *producing*. He had almost single-handedly changed the face of the world, not by waging war, but by producing. Others had invented the internal combustion engine; Henry Ford had put it in the reach of the common man. In so doing he had created more work at better pay, more leisure, and more things you could do with that leisure. These benefits had gone not merely to the workers in the car factories, but—as Isabel had pointed out one day when they were driving down to New York—to road builders, which meant to a mass of unskilled labour; to all who produced and refined oil; to the whole recreation industry . . . to the makers of beach towels, bathing costumes . . . to house builders, for many would now keep beach or lake houses, which could easily be reached by car, but before would have been inaccessible . . . The chain went on endlessly, ascending ever higher into the clouds, of light and gold.

Henry Ford said, "You people in Europe look back too much. What does it matter what King George IV said or did? It don't apply now. But it'll take years, centuries perhaps, for those Europeans to understand that, because their feet are in the mud . . . in history . . . And if we're not careful, we'll get stuck down there with them."

"So you are against the League of Nations?"

"Sure thing!" Ford said. "No foreign entanglements, that's what George Washington said, and he knew what he was talking about, which is more than I can say of President Wilson."

Richard thought, but George Washington is history; was that part of it not "bunk" because it was American? He held his tongue. Mr Ford was probably right; he was seldom wrong, and in any case it would be rude and tactless to argue the point now. Ford said, "Go take a look round now. Hindle is waiting outside." He stood up and held out his hand. Richard grasped it and winced. The automobile magnate was in his high fifties, but his grip was that of a strong young man, a mechanic.

Richard returned to their hotel in downtown Detroit at half-past six. Susan met him with an anxious look—"Are you all right, dear? I thought something must have happened to you . . ."

Richard flung himself into a chair saying, "Ring for room service, Susan. I need a large whisky and soda. Mr Ford wouldn't approve, but . . ." He jumped up and started pacing the room with an almost febrile energy—"Something has happened to me. I've seen . . . I was about to say, the future, but that's not right. I've seen the 'now' as it is and ought to be . . . five thousand men in certain, exact places, each doing a certain exact task, all arranged so that there is no possibility of mistakes . . . no one moves from his place, because the tools and materials he needs are brought to him, and placed precisely where he wants them at the precise instant that he is ready to deal with them . . ." He paused to draw breath, and Susan said, "But you saw this in Manchester, just before the war, didn't you, when you went up to look at Mr Ford's English factory?"

"The small, pale shadow of this!" Richard exclaimed. The door opened and a waiter brought in a tray, ice, glasses with whisky, club soda. "I don't want any ice," Richard said impatiently. "Why must we ruin the taste of good whisky . . . oh, leave it. Here."

When the waiter had gone he drank deep and said, "The plant out here is the greatest thing on earth, Susan. Mr Ford's making a new world, and he's not making it at a conference table, or at the point of a gun, but there, in that factory, turning out good cars for less than fifty pounds apiece. It's unbelievable! The place where the employees keep *their* cars—the parking lot, they call it—is incredible. Thousands of cars belonging to the men who work on the production line! Because he pays them enough so that they can afford to buy a car. Of course they get the sack on the spot if they buy any car but a Ford . . . I am beginning to feel that I can never live in England again without going mad at our slowness, our backwardness, our inefficiency."

"But they don't put ice in your whisky there," she said.

"Oh, that . . ."

"There'll be lots more of the same . . . I don't know very much about production lines, but surely it must be very boring for the workmen. Can they possibly find their work satisfying if they don't make anything, but merely make small parts of something, over and over, and never see the end product?"

"They're not educated men," Richard said. "Or they wouldn't be on the production line. They don't have the imagination to be bored. All they look forward to is their pay, and a pub afterwards."

"Not a pub, Richard, a saloon. They're rather different."

"Or jump into the car and go to the lake, or a dance hall, or a cinema . . . it can be twenty miles away, that's nothing nowadays. I tell you, the whole face of society will change. It *is* changing . . . and here, America, is at the front edge of that change."

She said quietly, "I know, Richard. I'm American, and I see that very clearly. But in spite of what Mr Ford said about history, there are many things from our own American past that I shall be very sorry to see go . . . and I am afraid that Mr Ford's revolution will do just that."

*   *   *   *

"But . . . but this is a foreign country!" Richard exclaimed.

"It is," Susan said, half-smiling.

They were standing on the corner of Washington and Grant in the heart of San Francisco's Chinatown. The smells of savory rices, of roasting duck, of scallions and sesame seed oil and thousand-year-old eggs were mingled in a single brew with the smells of the people, the peculiar odor of the pipes and little cigars many of the men and women were smoking, the smell of the sweat of the coolie struggling up the steep hill, a huge basket of vegetables on his back, his feet bare; and the sounds mingled with the smells—the high-pitched guttural voices speaking a dozen of China's dialects, the cries of street vendors, the rumble of the trams grinding and squealing on the steep tracks, the honk of an occasional motor horn and the growl of its engine as it faced the slope . . .

To Susan, all this was familiar, but not to Richard. He was agape, aghast. "But this is not America!" he cried, almost shouting to be heard above the din.

"Yes, it is," she said. "This and all the rest—Nyack, Columbus, Detroit, Bridgeport, and Daddy's house here on Nob Hill."

They started slowly back, easing cautiously through the crowds. "It's so unsanitary, for America," Richard said, as they began to leave Chinatown behind, heading for Nob Hill. "It's so incredibly different from Nyack, and New York, and those other places."

"And they were all different from each other," Susan said.

Then they said little more till they reached the big comfortable house with the view over the Golden Gate, Alcatraz, and the distant Marin shore. There, in the empty drawing room—Susan's old parents were out—they picked up the *Chronicle* and glanced at the front page. "Hoggin," Richard chuckled, pointing at the lead article—"Hoggin's making his presence felt." The heading over the brief article read BRITISH PEER PRAISES YANKEE GET-UP-AND-GO. The article related details of Lord Walstone's visit to a refrigeration plant. His Lordship, it appeared, was hoping to introduce similar plants in his chain of food stores in Great Britain, to retard spoilage and increase the shelf life of many foods. "And cut down on waste, in things like bread and greengroceries," Richard said. "There are no flies on Hoggin . . . but I wonder if the British will accept frozen foods?"

"Fishmongers use a lot of ice," Susan said. "And no one minds."

"This will be different." He put the paper down—"Susan, I've been thinking. All the way here on the train . . . what a journey, what great spaces, what mighty rivers . . . I was thinking, why shouldn't this be our home? America. It was yours, why shouldn't it be Sally's, Tim's, Dicky's . . . mine? The idea wasn't really formed until we got on the ferry at Oakland. Then, coming across the Bay, approaching San Francisco, with the Golden Gate like an opening to a promised land beyond . . . and the sun on all the towers and roofs . . . it became clear to me—let us stay. Bring the children and stay . . . You'd like it, wouldn't you?"

Susan got up and walked toward another window, this one looking South toward the crowded hills of the back part of the city. She faced her husband—"You know there are many things in England that I have never agreed with . . . the class system . . . the insularity . . . the way you are all so sure that everything English must automatically be best . . . insensitivity to foreigners' feelings and opinions, which really stems out of the insularity . . . I have often thought that we would all be better off over here. You would be in your element. Here, the business man, not the aristocrat, is king. You want to produce things—cars, aeroplanes, whatever. *Here* you'll be given the chance and the money to do it. But . . ."

"But what?"

"It's not your home and I don't think it ever can be. It could be some people's . . . Louise would settle here easily, become a Quaker perhaps . . . Virginia could have, she hates the class thing, and she might just as easily have married an American artisan as that sergeant major . . . Naomi could—she is self-contained and isn't really attached to or rooted in any place . . . But you can't. Suppose Dicky married a Chinese girl . . ."

"He wouldn't do that!"

"He might, easily. Or a Negro."

"But . . . but Stephen Merritt wouldn't be happy if Betty were to marry a Chinaman or a Negro, either. He's absolutely horrified that Stella should have let a brown or black man make love to her, even under the influence of drugs, however frantic to get more. And he's American."

"He's old-fashioned . . . and prejudiced. Stephen *would* be very unhappy, but as an American he has no right to be. We are all supposed to be born free and equal. A Chinese American or a Negro American should expect to be able to become president as much as a white Protestant like John Merritt. It's not the case now, but it should be."

"One would never be prime minister of England," Richard said.

"Exactly . . . Let's discuss it later. After we've finished our tour. On the ship on the way home, eh?"

"I'm fed up with England," Richard said. "People like Bert Gorse, Ramsay MacDonald, Snowden . . . those are our masters now. They'll bankrupt the country, and tax us out of existence."

"Let's talk about it on the ship," she urged again. "Daddy and Mommy are back . . ." She went to the door and opened it—"What did you buy? Ah, an Easter bonnet! Let's get it out of the box and have a look at it."

*   *   *   *

The huge 4-8-4's whistle chimed out over the red rocks, the desert, and the huddled houses as the Grand Canyon Limited began to glide out eastward, facing the long climb to the Continental Divide, the Rio Grande, and Albuquerque; but for now, as the train drew away under a drifting cloud of dense black smoke, they were standing on the low platform at Gallup, New Mexico, their suitcases piled beside them. The platform was slowly emptying—half a dozen Indians in bright blankets, another in a big black hat with many turquoise and silver ornaments on his arms, two white business men, some Mexican-seeming women and children . . .

"Good God, look!" Richard exclaimed. "That poor man there . . ." They stared at the shape sprawled flat at the far end of the platform, arms outstretched. "Perhaps he's been taken ill," Susan said. "Or had a heart attack." A railway servant in a blue peaked cap passed, and she said, "That man there . . . perhaps he's in trouble."

The railway man glanced over his shoulder—"No, ma'am, he's just drunk . . . We'd 'a moved him out sooner only it don't pay to fool with drunken Indians. They're crazy any time, but when their bellies are full of whisky . . . look out!"

He moved on. Richard pulled out his watch—"A quarter to eight," he said. "How can anyone be drunk at a quarter to eight in the morning?"

"He hasn't had time to sleep it off, perhaps," Susan said. "He must have been drinking late last night . . . but why here?" She looked across the rail lines at the road beyond and exclaimed, "Look, there are more . . . I can see four, five lying in the gutters or in front of the stores. And it's Sunday!"

Richard said, "Last night was Saturday, then . . . Our car should have come by now. Your father swore they were a reliable company."

The Indian at the end of the platform was struggling to his feet. Swaying, he propped himself against a lamp post for a while, then came down the platform, at first staggering, gradually regaining his balance. He passed them, reached the far end of the platform, and, scooping up water from the overflow from the station's water tank and tender feed hose, that lay in puddles among the ash and clinker, dashed it on his face. Then he found a cigarette in his pocket, lit it, and came back. He passed them again, then turned, and stood before them, swaying, a short, dark, strongly built young man whose exact age they could not tell. His dark eyes were bleared, and he was un-shaven, but the stubble was very short. He said, "Are you Mr and Mrs Rowland? Friends of Johnny Merritt?"

"Why, yes," Richard said. His heart sank—"You aren't the man from the motor car hire people, are you?"

The Indian shook his head—"Chee Shush Benally," he said. "John write, tell me you come . . . I got letter yesterday, came in . . ."

"But," Richard exclaimed, "we were coming out to see you! We understand there's a place where we can stay in Fort Defiance, and from there we were going to drive out to you at Sanostee."

The Indian said, "I come with you . . . Here's driver." He pointed to the exit from the station, where a young man was hurrying toward them. "Mr Rowland?" the latter said agitatedly. "I'm from the Gallup Automobile Livery . . . I'm sorry to be late but we found a slow puncture in one of the tires just before I was due to set out, and we had to fix it. You need all your spares in the Navajo country." He picked up two of the suitcases and Benally picked up the others.

Richard thought, what can I do? John Merritt particularly asked me to go and see this man, in his home. He swore he was a wonderful fellow, once you got to know him; though, he warned, all Indians are very reserved . . . And the fellow turned out to be a drunkard!

He said to the chauffeur, "Mr Benally is coming with us." The young man looked astonished, but said nothing. Soon they were all seated in the big Buick, and heading north toward Fort Defiance. The air blew fresh and keen, for they were 7,000 feet above sea level; and they were glad of it, for Chee Shush Benally smelled of stale liquor.

He pointed out places and things as they went—"Those sheep belong my grandfather's brother . . . that's his daughter on the horse

. . . That hogan built by my uncle and me, just before I went army
. . . You got any whisky on you?" he turned to Richard.

Richard said stiffly, "No . . . and don't you think you had enough
last night?"

Chee smiled, a sudden warm, wide smile that in that moment
wiped away the blear from his eyes, and the grimness out of his face—
"Just about," he said. "Bottle and half . . . tequila."

"A bottle and a half!" Richard cried. "But . . . you might kill
yourself!"

"Plenty Navajo do . . . whisky, tequila . . . freeze in the street. No
room in the jail for all Navajos, and in winter . . . plenty cold."

"Can't you get a beer or a drink at home?"

Susan cut in, "No liquor is allowed on any Indian reservation,
Richard. They asked for that law themselves."

Chee said, "Right, madam . . . so no bars. Nearest bars in Gallup,
Flagstaff, Cortez . . . white man make plenty money out of drunken
Indians there . . . But it take me two days to walk to Gallup. So, when
I get there . . . once a month . . . drink for whole month, eh?"

Richard gazed around, at the barren landscape, the slow-moving
flock of sheep in the distance . . . no electric light, no running water,
very little cultivation . . . and apparently the only escape in faraway
bars, and oblivion.

He said, "Are there any doctors, here? Nurses?"

Chee said, "One doctor, Fort Defiance . . . Indian Service."

"And how big is the reservation?"

Chee shrugged, "Big . . . two hundred miles each way."

"Forty thousand square miles!" Richard gasped.

"Two hundred and fifty thousand Navajo, thirty thousand Hopi
live here."

"It's . . . disgraceful!" Richard cried. "How is it possible, how can
the Government allow it? Babies must die of all sorts of curable and
really quite minor diseases . . . women in childbirth . . . men from
small cuts that must go septic . . . gangrene . . . accidents."

Chee said, "Yes."

After a long time, as the Buick passed on over the dusty road,
climbing gradually to pine-covered hills, Benally groped in his pocket
and pulled out a pale blue ribbon, the blue studded with white stars, a
medal clasp dependent from it. He hung the whole round his neck.

"What's that?" Richard asked.

"The Congressional Medal of Honour," Susan said. "Did you win
that, Mr Benally? John didn't tell us."

Chee smiled again, "Yes, I win it . . . Isseaudun, some name like
that . . . I wear it when I go Fort Defiance. Then the clerk in Agent's

391

office feel bad . . . so he lend me some money for Gallup . . . I come back with medal on, he don't ask for money back . . . Fort Defiance," he said, pointing—"Sanostee, fifty miles, that way. We go tomorrow? Road bad, but this car go. I show you how Navajo people live . . . and die. Everyone near starving in Sanostee—bad snow, bad rain, bad crop, sheep dying . . . people dying, flu. Only one cure."

"What's that?"

"Whisky."

*   *   *   *

They were walking down Iberville Street, in the New Orleans dusk, the gas lamps bright. Sounds of a trumpet playing ragtime rang out loud and demanding from behind drawn curtains on an upper floor, the curtains back-lit by a reddish glow. Women in dresses cut so low as to reveal the whole outward swell of their breasts, including the nipples, hung over second-floor wrought iron balconies. "You want to hear some real good music, doctor," one cried, in a hoarse sensuous voice, smiling down at Richard. "C'mon up. And you'll be able to see me without those glasses . . . all of me."

Richard and Susan hurried on, heads bent. A saxophone from another tall house joined the trumpet. Half a dozen Negro youths stomped down the street, clapping hands and dancing with a powerful tribal rhythm, shouting in a syncopated beat, and the shouts were not words, but more like exclamations of ecstasy or uncontrollable excitement. Behind the steamy plate-glass windows at street level, men in white aprons were shucking oysters over great barrels of ice. There were women in the street doorways now, beckoning, flaunting their over-ripe bodies, painted faces, painted lips, dyed hair . . .

"It's . . . like what I've heard about Port Said," Richard said hoarsely. "Or Rio de Janeiro . . . some Latin or Arab country. Not a white one . . ."

"We aren't," Susan said.

"Look," Richard pointed. "The Negroes have to get in the back of the buses . . . there are signs everywhere, even in the W.C.s— Coloured, White . . . yet some of these street women are black, or mulatto. That was a Negro with the trumpet, who pulled back the curtains and looked out while he was playing, and I saw white men behind him. Everything's mixed up . . . Do they have many riots here?"

Susan said, "You don't feel safe? No, they don't, as far as I know. There's a time when everyone goes mad—Mardi Gras—but it doesn't get out of hand."

"I don't understand why not," Richard said. "There are a lot of things I don't understand,"

"And not only about New Orleans?"

Richard said, "Yes . . . Look let's go in here and have some oysters."

Five minutes later they were sitting at a table in a small oyster house, two dozen oysters on the half shell before them. Richard took an oyster, tilted the shell, and swallowed. "All right," he said after a while. "Not as good as a fresh Whitstable or Colchester, but . . . one can eat pretty well here, in New Orleans. A bit of a change from the rest of the country, except San Francisco . . . no decent bacon, no decent puddings, the beef always overdone, salads instead of good hot vegetables."

Susan looked at him over the rim of her wine glass, smiling—"And tomorrow we leave for Atlanta. More segregation, more signs—White, colored. And the food will all be Southern Fried, in deep fat." Richard shuddered and murmured, "Don't!" She continued, "How do you feel now about bringing the family over here to live?"

Richard said nothing, ate two oysters, took off his glasses, polished them, put them back on, and looked at his wife: at last— "I don't know how you, as an American, were able to accept us—the British—as thoroughly as you have. We are apt to think of Americans as Englishmen who boast a lot and speak English very badly. But . . . this is a foreign country, and Americans are foreigners, just as much so as Frenchmen or Egyptians."

Susan said, "Women are adaptable. They have to be. And we were both a lot younger. I wouldn't mind coming back to live . . . after all, it was my home . . . but I didn't think you realized what was involved. I didn't think you would be happy, once you understood that we have as many problems, and as serious ones, as you do . . . only in different areas. You don't have a Negro problem, because you don't have any Negroes. Same with the Indians. Our real trouble is that we've set ourselves certain goals, as a nation, and we're not living up to them . . . one nation indivisible, with justice for all. We say it, but we don't live it. You know that now. We've always known it, and under the bustle and bluster there's a guilty conscience. It'll change, but not without tears . . . and years."

"We'd better go home," Richard said. "Heaven knows how I shall manage to survive with the unions . . . with a Socialist government likely in a few years . . . with wages going up all the time, costs too . . . Well, we've faced worse things before, and we'll have to face these, too, as best we can . . . Let's have some more oysters.

You know what they're supposed to do. I feel like testing it out tonight."

She blushed, smiling, and put her hand to his.

Daily Telegraph, Tuesday, April 15, 1919

INDEMNITY MODIFICATION

From our Special Correspondent, *Paris,* Monday.

A statement has reached me to the effect that the arrangement concluded on Saturday about the payment of a war indemnity by Germany has been modified. According to what I was told, Germany would have to undertake to pay all war damages and destructions by fifty annual sums, the total exceeding by far the provisional 150 milliards (£ 6,000,000,000) already mentioned. At the same time the first instalment of 25,000,000,000 francs would have to be disbursed within the next eighteen months.

Cate thought, that's all very well, but how in fact do the Germans pay? Before the election the politicians were all shouting for blood. Now they were beginning to hedge, but their electioneering speeches hung round their necks, like dead albatrosses. Suppose coal from the Saar, which was being seized, was sent to Britain to pay part of the indemnity . . . what would happen to British coal, and British coal miners? The same applied if German steel was seized, German ships and shipping taken to carry British and other world trade. Yet . . . yet, he felt as strongly as anyone that the Germans must be made to pay, somehow, for all the misery they had brought upon the world. But how?

He turned to another page

SERIOUS RIOTS IN INDIA

EUROPEANS KILLED

Mr Montagu, Secretary for India, replying in the House of Commons yesterday to Colonel Wedgwood (C.L. Newcastle-under-Lyme), said he regretted to have to state that there had been further riots at Lahore and slight rioting at Allahabad, where the city telegraph office had been burned, and at Amritsar where the telegraph office and other buildings had been destroyed. There had been some loss of life, including Europeans . . .

Replying to a further question, Mr Montagu said he did not think it would be safe, in the present condition of the world, to attribute these riots to any one cause.

Didn't he indeed, Cate thought. Gandhi's movement to end British rule by passive resistance, which they had all been hearing about for some time now, had obviously turned violent. Quentin was out there, now, so they might learn more about it from him; but whether his station of Hassanpore, was anywhere near Allahabad, Lahore, or Amritsar, he had no idea. In some ways, the war communiqués from all over the world had been one long, ghastly geography lesson. Now it looked as if the British were going to get another one, this time to teach them more about the sub-continent they ruled—and, he admitted, knew next to nothing about.

Hedlington, Kent: April 1919

22 Richard Rowland, two days back from America, looked up from the piece of paper in his hand—"Nineteen percent absent today. What is it at H.A.C.?"

John Merritt said, "About fifteen. All flu, I suppose."

"Some damned shirkers among them, too, I'll bet," Richard said. "I'm going to demand doctors' certificates from every one of them when they come back, or they'll get docked all pay."

"A lot of them don't go to doctors," John said. "They don't think the doctor can do anything. And they can't afford it." He spoke seriously, and the expression in his face was of its now habitual grimness, mouth in a straight line, eyes level under straight brows.

Richard said, "I'm going to get some sort of proof, or"—he made a cutting motion with his hand—"out! There are five men ready to take every job that becomes vacant. Next week I'm going to cut pay, in accordance with the productivity study Overfeld and I made before I went to America. Overfeld's had time to check it out thoroughly in practise, and it works."

John said, "We'll have trouble, Richard. The union has amassed enough funds to hit us with another strike. And this time, it could last much longer."

"Let them do it," Richard said. "We'll just hire new men . . . You and Stella are coming to dinner tomorrow night, aren't you? Good. Well, we'll tell you all about our trip then, but I want to tell you about your Indian friend now . . . We were on the Navajo reservation three days—two at Fort Defiance and one with his people at Sanostee. Benally was drunk all the time . . . either just recovering, actually drinking, or in an unconscious stupor. One of his brothers was the same. He wants to marry but none of the other families will let him have one of their daughters. He's in a bad way." He paused, and took off the thick spectacles that had earned him the nickname, from boyhood, of Giglamps; and said, "If you ask me, John, the whole Navajo tribe is in a bad way. All the Red Indians we saw are. I don't know much about American history, or exactly why the Indians have to be kept on these reservations—but they seem to be mostly desert. A lot of Indians starve whenever there's a bad crop, or anything goes wrong with the grazing for their sheep. The Indian Service people we met at Fort Defiance were treating them like children, or savages—enemy savages. They're in despair. Particularly the young men who went to the war. They've seen the rest of the world, and they've fought for their country, and then they come home to . . . that."

John said heavily, "I know. It's as bad . . . or worse . . . for our Negroes and Mexicans."

"Perhaps," Richard said. "But somehow that didn't bother me half as much. But the Indians . . . damn it, it's their country! They need help, but heaven knows where it's going to come from. Not from Washington, obviously . . . Only from the bottle, Benally says."

The door opened, bringing in Miss Harcourt and a rumble of noise from the plant across the hall and beyond the wall. John got up—"I'd better get back to H.A.C. Frank Stratton's taking over again as works foreman today. He was demobbed in January, but he took a long holiday actually he went to a motor car racing track outside Paris and worked on his motor cycle for two months . . . then Guy had him taught to fly, but now he's back."

"He's separated from his wife, isn't he?"

John nodded—"Yes. They're both miserable."

*   *   *   *

John thrashed and turned in bed in increasing pain. His back hurt, with acute stabbing sensations that were beginning to spread into his loins. He felt dry and hot, his head throbbing and aching, his eyes sore and scratchy. From downstairs he heard the clock in the hall strike two . . . two o'clock in the morning. Stella slept beside him, calm, unmoving . . . she'd had her injection just before bedtime. God knew what her dreams were, but whatever they were, she was unaware of him or his pain.

He struggled out of bed and sat a moment on the edge, his head in his hands. Got to take my temperature . . . or throw up . . . both . . . He rushed to the bathroom, switched on the light, and hung over the toilet bowl, retching. Nothing came. After five minutes of struggling to conquer the nausea, he found the thermometer in the medicine cabinet, put it under his tongue, and looked at his watch. Three minutes. . . 103. He took it out, washed it in cold water, shook it down, and replaced it. He had the influenza.

He crawled back into bed and waited for the light to come. Before dawn he developed a dry cough, that possessed him in short, desperate paroxysms. Stella did not stir. He'd have to call Dr Kimball . . . or a doctor from Hedlington might be younger, and more up to date with the treatment for flu. They'd all had enough practise since it first hit a year ago, heaven knew.

At last she awoke, and said, "Good morning." Her voice was hoarse but otherwise she seemed all right. He mumbled, "Darling . . . I think I have flu. Call a doctor, please."

She slipped out of bed and for a moment, as she adjusted her nightdress, he saw the many dots and spots of the needle marks inside her left arm—and she had as many on the right. She said, "You lie back."

The hours passed. Dr Kimball came, harried and curt from overwork. John's temperature hovered close to 104 and he felt that he was slipping beyond reach of human help. Not many people had died in that first wave of the epidemic, back in May and June last year; but millions had in the second wave, about the time of the armistice. This third wave seemed to be more like the first . . . so far. But one of the facts everyone had noticed about the epidemic was that the fatalities were mostly where one would least have expected them—among otherwise strong and healthy young adults. Such as himself.

Stella stayed with him all the time. The cook came up to receive orders and through his haze of fever and pain, John heard the note of decision in Stella's voice as she told Mrs Hackler what to buy, what to cook, and how to cook it for the invalid . . . though he ate precious little that week except soups and broths. At night she sat up beside him in bed, propped by pillows; and whenever he was awake, which seemed to him to be most of the night, she was. She must have slept, but he did not know when. If she was taking her regular doses, and he thought she must have been, he did not know where or when. His cough got worse, and Dr Kimball looked grave and talked of moving him to Hedlington General Hospital; but John shook his head wearily and, through the waves of misery, he heard Stella say, "I can look after him better, Doctor, because I'm here all the time. Just give me the right medicines . . . tell me what to do if he starts coughing blood, or gets the 'wet lung.'"

He heard the doctor's old voice, thin and miles away now, "You are a wonderful woman, Stella . . . We should have remembered . . . during your troubles . . . what sort of a girl you were . . . brave as a lion."

She had not said anything and he thought he had fainted . . . to return to a change in the pattern of his pain. The cough had moved down, and he was coughing up gobs of phlegm. His fever reached 105, and then suddenly he was sweating, soaking the sheets, and even the blankets, and mattress. Stella mopped his forehead with damp sponges; and three times that night changed his pyjamas and sponged down his whole body. Her intense face as she worked swam in and out of focus . . . lovely, the complexion as velvet smooth as it used to be . . . or was that only because he was too tired to exert his optic muscles, so that she swam over him against the light, a pink madonna face under a golden halo . . .

At last, Dr Kimball came and tapped and thumped and listened to his stethoscope and after fifteen minutes said, "You're over it, John. For a time you were beginning to develop symptoms of 'dripping lung,' but you fought it off, thanks to her." He nodded toward Stella. "You're a lucky man . . . I won't be back unless there's some drastic change for the worse. But stay in bed for three days, and then start taking gentle exercise. Do *not* go back to work for at least ten days from now, and then make your days short . . . You have recovered from a very dangerous and debilitating disease . . . I know the way out, thanks."

When he had gone Stella knelt slowly beside his bed and buried her head in his side. He heard her voice, muffled and distant—"Please, God, I want to be cured . . . please, John darling . . . but do it quickly . . . or it'll be too late. Again."

She struggled to her feet before John could say anything, and he heard her footsteps going fast downstairs. He lay back, exhausted— mentally, spiritually, and physically. She had cried for help . . . to him, and to God . . . a woman's cry: he for God only, she for God in him . . . But he was too tired. The pain had gone, but not very far. It was just below the surface of his being, transmuted from acute stabs to a universal dull ache of utter weakness. He closed his eyes and, against his will, for he was trying to keep Stella in his thoughts, he fell into a deep, untroubled sleep, and did not awake for ten hours.

When he opened his eyes, Stella was there beside the bed. The pupils of her eyes were pinpoints, and her whole being radiated warmth, excitement. She was still on the heroin, and had probably taken a double dose. She held a pink telegraph envelope in her hand and said, "Oh darling, this came this morning . . . Shall I read it to you?" John nodded and she held up the paper, moving it back and forth in front of her eyes to get it in focus. Then—*"Chee Shush Benally killed by train Gallup Tuesday—Hakis Benally."*

"That's his eldest brother," John said.

"Poor old Chee," Stella said brightly, smiling wide. "Gone to the happy hunting grounds, eh? That's what Red Indians say, isn't it?"

John did not answer, feeling sick, and just as exhausted as before his sleep, and now experiencing a return of the pain in his eyes. Killed by a train. He did not have to ask what had happened. He knew Gallup—had been there with his parents and sister several years on summer vacations. Richard had described it, very well. Chee had gone into Gallup for his monthly bout with drink . . . though he had also been managing to smuggle some liquor into the reservation, from time to time, according to Richard . . . and he had staggered out from one of those Main Street bars and across the Santa Fe tracks as a train was pulling in . . . or perhaps he'd tripped over the rails, and just lain there, dead drunk, until a train came, cutting him up . . . he shivered, thinking of the corpses by the guns, after the big German shelling attacks on the Chemin des Dames. Chee had gone . . . probably wearing his Medal of Honour . . . with no mourners, no bugles, no decorated caissons. And no help from those whom he had helped—Americans, his countrymen.

*   *   *   *

April was the breeding month for the pheasants. All the hens had been trampled by the cocks, and were laying. There was an old shed across the yard from the head gamekeeper's cottage of Walstone Park, and there the eggs were hatched, partly by incubators and partly by ordinary broody hens. The hen pheasants seldom sat themselves, because they were careless and after laying a batch of a dozen eggs didn't seem to care very much whether they hatched or not. But the broodies, when Probyn could get them, sat patiently and with intuitive skill and care, turning the eggs under themselves every twelve hours, never breaking any with their own weight, never allowing one to roll away from under and grow cold in a corner of the nest, or worse, roll onto the open boards between one nest and the next.

Probyn had started making the nests late in March, to be ready for the hatching, cutting out bowls of turf and lining each with hay, the bowl not too steep-sided and not shallow—all designed to give the eggs the best chance, and the hen the best chance of hatching them. The incubators were heated by oil lamps, but Probyn did not like them. There was always the risk of fire, which would have destroyed all the eggs and chicks, and with them a whole shooting season for His Lordship and his friends . . . right funny it had been, at the end of the season, to see Florinda, his granddaughter, out there with the guns, wearing a tweed skirt and jacket, sitting on a shooting stick behind that young Bidford fellow as though she'd been doing it all her life. She'd given him a big wink first time he passed her but he just touched his cap and said, "Good morning, milady." She was a marchioness and just as good as plenty of others that had the title. She was a Gorse.

He was turning the eggs in the incubators now. Next, he'd give grain and water to the broodies. Then . . . better go over to Beighton and see if he could find some more broodies there. There was so much damn money about that a working man didn't need to be given a pheasant or a rabbit—he could go and buy one: so it was hard to persuade men who kept hens to sell a broody . . .

His grandson Fletcher came in, preceded by his shadow falling through the open door and across the incubators. Probyn said nothing, while Fletcher, leaning against the doorjamb, watched, equally silent.

At length Fletcher said, "I found four eggs in the laying pen. Got 'em here."

Probyn grunted. They'd have to be cleaned, washed, and put in the trays for transfer either to the incubator or a broody. One thing at a time. Fletcher said, "There was a broken egg, too. Half-eaten."

"Crow?" Probyn said.

"Maybe. But a crow would have eaten the lot. 'Twas most likely one of the layers."

Without a word Probyn reached up on the wooden shelf over the incubators and felt inside a cardboard shoe box. It contained half a dozen cold eggs—last year's eggs, that for one reason or another had not hatched. He picked out one and gave it to Fletcher, who went out, opened the gate into the wired laying pen, put the egg on the ground close to where he had found the broken egg. Soon the hen pheasant which had probably by accident pecked the first egg—and found food in it—would find this, and this time peck deliberately . . . to have its beak buried in the foul, black, stinking slime of the year-old egg. It would not break any more pheasant eggs . . .

Fletcher returned to the shed and said, "I'm going away for a bit, Granddad."

Probyn grunted. Fletcher had been back from the army near three months, living in Probyn's old cottage by the Scarrow. The roof had burned off, but Fletcher had thatched it again, fresh; and put chicken wire over the thatch to stop starlings from nesting in it; and cleaned and painted the place up . . . worked like a nigger he had, all those weeks. Now Probyn hardly recognized the cottage when he went by, or dropped in to have a talk with his grandson. Fletcher had got everything a man could want—his own rabbit nets and snares, wire for running loops, fishing spears, a pair of ferrets . . . but no dog. And he didn't seem to know what he wanted to do, 'cept spend his bounty. The American girl had been there sometimes, evenings and weekends, and Fletcher he been up to London and all over. He had money.

Fletcher said, "I'm going to France . . . Spain . . ."

"Thought you'd 'a seen enough of them places, in the war. You said they was right greedy folks."

"That was the Frogs," Fletcher said. "Betty says they're different in Spain. She's never been there, either, but she knows Spanish . . . learned it when she was a kid, on holidays somewhere . . . We'll be married afore we come home."

Probyn grunted again. The girl was going with him, then. Good thing. Better take your own woman on a long trip than get into trouble finding one. That got their men angry, and besides, you didn't know what you was getting. As to the marriage . . . well, wait and see.

Fletcher said, "I came through Earl's Wood. You had two traps there, and a big log tied to them."

Probyn grunted. He had two steel-jawed traps in Earl's Wood that had to be taken out before the hunting season, in case a horse trod in one. But the rest of the year, especially now when the pheasants were laying, the foxes had to be kept off by any means. Those traps were agin the law, but every keeper used them . . . not tied to a stake, for a strong fox in its desperation might jerk the line so hard as to break it, or even pull the stake out; but tied to a heavy log, that the fox could drag, but not far, and only with great effort.

Fletcher said, "One wasn't there . . . So I followed the trail . . . broken bracken, earth scratched . . . found it a hundred yards away."

"A hundred yards!" Probyn cried. "That's . . . !"

"With a vixen in the jaws," Fletcher said. "In milk. She'd pulled that thing a hundred yards, with two legs practically off . . . She wasn't dead, either. I bashed her head in . . . We're leaving tomorrow. Back in a month."

Probyn grunted and Fletcher left, easing himself off the doorjamb and striding leopardlike, his movements flowing one into another, across the yard and out onto the back drive, behind the bulk of Walstone Park.

In the shed, Probyn straightened his back and stretched. He felt restless. This job was too easy . . . and it wasn't as much fun as poaching, to tell the truth. There was something wrong, too, about a

Gorse preserving some man's game, instead of taking it. The poachers nowadays were ruddy useless.

He yawned . . . never used to yawn. Probyn Gorse, gamekeeper. Well, it was better than pleaching hedges . . . and there weren't no damn women doing it, either.

*   *   *   *

On Beighton Down it was a perfect spring day, two earlier showers having passed over to the east, leaving the short grass pearled with drops of moisture that imprisoned the sun, dappling the down with points of fire. The clouds overhead moved like lazy sheep, and between them the sky was pale blue; but now there were no real sheep on the Down, as there used to be before the war. The economics of sheep rearing in this part of the world, where the flocks had never been very large because the amount of open space was not large, had destroyed the industry. Hedlington Sheep Fair was to be revived this coming July; but there would be no buying or selling of sheep, no competitions of skill among sheep dogs and their masters . . . The air was slightly hazy as it is in so many Canalettos and Constables, the Weald spread out below like such another vision as that vouchsafed to Christ on the mountain . . . a vale flowing with the riches of earth, dense green, well-watered, spaced with great mansions, oast houses, cattle sheds, tithe barns, and the towers of Saxon and Norman churches. Far to the east lay Canterbury . . . to the west, Hedlington—the twin capitals of this ancient kingdom.

John Merritt walked beside his sister, swinging an ash plant in his hand. It was eleven days since the fever of his influenza had broken, and most of his strength had returned, brought back by steady and careful exercise, the right food, plenty of sleep, and some suitable medicines. Stella had relapsed, as soon as the crisis was over, to her place as a gently smiling presence, doing nothing . . . only frowning, and so becoming real, in the space between one dose of her drug and the next.

Betty said, "Tomorrow Fletcher and I are going to Spain for a month."

John had only been back at the factory one day, but Ginger Keble-Palmer had mentioned nothing of this, thinking, presumably, that as it was his own sister she would have told him.

She said, "There's nothing for me to do now that the modifications to the Buffalo for passenger and goods service have been completely worked out . . . We're well advanced on the one Guy's going to use in

June. It's been registered as G-BGR . . . Fletcher and I need to be together, and alone, for at least a month."

"Are you going to marry him before you go?"

"No. But before we come back, probably . . . I've learned what he wants to do, or be, at least. Poet Laureate of England."

John said, "Are you sure that's not what *you* want him to be?"

She hesitated, then said, "I suppose there's some of that in it . . . What he has to have before he can achieve that, or any other goal as a poet, is education. Oh, I don't mean that Oxford or Harvard sort of education. He *doesn't* need that, any more than Isaac Rosenberg did . . . He has to realize what this world he lives in, is—not just the Weald and soldiers and the war. He has to meet all sorts of men and women, *feel* their lives . . . miners, dons, fishermen, milliners, bankers. He needs a guide in that world."

"And you're going to be it? Married or not?"

She said, "Yes. And when we come back, we'll be living in London for a time. So I'm leaving the H.A.C. I've spoken to Richard about it."

A skylark burst from the grass at their feet and towered into the sky, rising, pouring out its song against the moving clouds above.

John said, "I think you're doing the right thing, Sis. Anything I can do to help . . . I will."

He walked on. He was feeling a little weary already; he would be very tired by the time they got back to the cottage, in a couple of hours' time.

He said, "I've made up my mind, too. I'm going to take Stella to America."

"Oh!" his sister cried. "Good! . . . You may have some trouble getting her to agree. And I suppose Father Christopher will be sad."

"I'll do whatever is necessary," he said grimly, his mouth shutting like a trap. "She is my wife. I have talked to doctors, friends, relatives, an alienist. I am sure that this is the only course that might lead to a cure. I don't think Father Christopher will be upset. He understands."

"They have good alienists in New York," Betty said.

"I'm not going to New York," John said, "except to see Dad and make some arrangements. I'm going to join the Indian Service, and work for the Navajos."

After a long pause she said, "Is this anything to do with the death of your Indian friend?"

John said, "Yes. All the time I was in that bed . . . all the time I was walking round and round the garden, up and down the road . . . I was thinking. At length I knew what I had to do. I had to devote the rest of my life to those people, for Chee's sake. He saved my life, a couple of times, in France. I couldn't save his. But I can try to save his people."

"Stella's going to find Fort Defiance pretty lonely," Betty said dubiously. "She'll be lonelier even than she was here, while you were working so hard."

"She's my wife," he said, "and she must share my life. We're not going to be in Fort Defiance any longer than I can help. We'll go out to whatever post I can find among the Navajo . . . I want to take my help to them, not have them come into Fort Defiance to beg it from us."

"Stella . . ." she began.

John interrupted curtly—"I am selling the Cottage, and we are leaving England, for good. We will start a new life, in a new world, among new people, new customs, religion, air, water—everything. The Navajo country, and the Navajo people, can cure her, if anyone can. This will either make her or break her. And if it breaks her, she might as well be dead . . . as she is now . . ."

* * * *

As soon as he came into the room he knew that her nerves were on edge, her body palpitating, aching for the next dose. It would have been easier if he had caught her after she had had it; she would smile then, and agree; but the spell would not last long enough for him to take her even to Liverpool, let alone across the Atlantic and most of the United States. It was a sign of improvement that she was fighting, watching the clock but not surrendering. It would be so easy for her to shorten the wait, take the dose, stay for all the time in that warm, floating world. But now she had to be told, and conquered; and now was the time

She was sitting up in a chair by the fire, which was not lit, staring into the empty, cold grate, smoking a cigarette, puffing at it with quick, nervous puffs, taking it out of her mouth, exhaling a little stream of grey-blue smoke, putting it back, puffing. He said, "I am resigning from Hedlington Aircraft. Ginger is taking over from me. I have cabled my father that we are sailing for New York on Monday. We have a first-class cabin on the main deck."

For a time she did not appear to hear, then she threw the cigarette into the grate and snapped, "Don't be silly, John."

He stood opposite her, looking down. She looked so vulnerable that his will almost failed him. How could he really know, after all, what was best for her?

He steeled himself again, and said, "I have consulted everyone who knows about your position—they all agree that you must make a complete break with your past, both the near and the distant. Your father . . ."

"*He* wants me to go? I don't believe it!"

"Of course he doesn't *want* you to go. He thinks you must, for your sake . . . and mine. Dr Irwin will give me a six months' supply of heroin for you as long as I promise to see that it is guarded, and given to you only in the doses he is prescribing for you now. Betty . . ."

"What does Betty know about me? She's not my keeper!"

"She loves you," John said. "And she has been watching you for several years now, hasn't she? She understands you better than I do . . . she is a woman, after all. She is sure it's best for you to break away."

"I don't care. I'm not going."

"Dr Deerfield . . ."

"You saw Charles . . . Dr Deerfield?"

John nodded—"Yes. He didn't want me to tell you—because he knew you socially, I suppose . . . but now I feel it's important for you to understand that an alienist, who had known you, agrees that the only way you might be cured is to make a clean break."

She began to laugh, at first quietly, soon maniacally, loud, shrieking, stuffing her clenched fists into her mouth, at last rolling out of the chair onto the floor and there kicking, biting, coughing, and beating the carpet with her fists. John stooped and pulled her upright. She was having a hysterical fit. He slapped her across the face, not gently. She fell silent at once, breathing deeply from her exertions, crimson in the face and neck.

Without warning, she attacked him, kicking out with her pointed shoes, scratching and clawing at his face with her nails. He struggled to enfold her in his arms, so that she would have no room to strike. She was as strong as a little horse, lithe as a jaguar, hissing now with fury. The eyes, the pupils dilated, glared close into his, the open mouth slavered and shrieked. She lunged forward unexpectedly and buried her teeth in his neck. With difficulty he brought a hand up and pressed it over her nostrils so that she could not breathe. After a long minute she fell back, sucking air into her lungs. The blood ran down John's neck onto his collar and down his shirt. He ran at her, grabbed her, threw her to the floor and knelt astride her—"You're coming home!" he shouted. "Home! Your husband's home! Your home!" He had her by the throat, hard enough to check her breathing, shaking her to and fro, every now and then banging her head on the carpet. "You're going to keep house for me in the Arizona desert . . . raise Peace to be a man among the Navajo . . . protect him from rattle-snakes and dust storms and Black Widow spiders . . . learn to weave

. . . to speak Navajo and Hopi . . . understand sand paintings . . . work, work, fight for the Navajo—men and women . . . fight the elders, the government, anyone we have to fight . . . do you under stand? DO . . . YOU . . . UNDERSTAND?"

She said nothing for a long time, her teeth locked together, eyes glaring up at him, like a caged, furious animal. Then she went limp and said, "I understand. I'll come. I'll try . . . Now, can I have my dose? It's time."

He pulled her to her feet and held her tight, caressing her disheveled hair, and said, "Of course. I'll give it to you. Then we'll start packing."

Daily Telegraph, Tuesday, May 13, 1919

MADRID-LONDON IN TWELVE HOURS

A record flight from Madrid to London, a distance of 987 miles, was accomplished yesterday in less than twelve hours by Lieut. Colonel W.D. Beatty, accompanied by Lieut. Jeffrys as observer.

Ah, Cate thought, I wonder whether Guy will take that as good news or bad. It was good in that it showed what modern aircraft could do, over long distances; but perhaps it would spur Colonel Beatty or others to perform other, similar feats, stealing some of Guy's thunder. There was already a plan afoot, Guy had told him, to fly a machine non-stop from the American continent to Europe, over the North Atlantic, at about the same time that Guy hoped to traverse the South Atlantic. He turned to another page:

MR BONAR LAW AND THE PEACE TREATY

THE INDEMNITY CLAUSES

In the House of Commons yesterday Mr Bottomley (Ind. Hackney, S.) asked whether it was correct to assume from the official summary of the Peace Treaty that the only cash payments to be made by Germany were as follows: That she is to make reparation for damage to persons and property under the seven heads enumerated in the summary, the total obligation in respect of which is to be notified to her not later than May 1, 1921; that she is to reimburse Belgium by means of bonds falling due in 1926 all sums borrowed by that country from the Allies; that within two years she is to pay

---

> the sum of £1,000,000,000 sterling, a further £2,000,000,000 in
> bonds at varying rates of interest with a sinking fund beginning in
> 1926, and a further £2,000,000,000 in Five per Cent bonds under
> terms . . .

Cate's head spun. It didn't make sense. Such sums of money did not actually exist, the figures were just that, exercises in pure mathematics . . . or fantasy.

"More coffee, sir?"

"Thank you, Garrod," he said, nodding as she bent over to pour the coffee.

He began to re-read the long letter from Isabel Kramer that had come in the morning's post. They—she and her brother Stephen Merritt—were eagerly awaiting the arrival of John and Stella on the 13th—today, Cate thought: perhaps they'll cable when they've arrived safe and sound. Stephen was pulling strings to get John into the Indian Service, among the Navajo, while at the same time ready to try to persuade him to stay in New York with Fairfax, Gottlieb. They'd have to await their arrival and find out how deep John's determination really was. What Stephen could offer him in New York, in the booming postwar business world, was enough to make any man, especially a young one, think very hard; but—Stella was the key, Stella, and what John had decided was best for her. There, Isabel was on John's side, whatever Stephen said. Otherwise, she was well . . . lonely . . . kept thinking of the wild flowers in the woods in the Weald, in May . . . of the Manor, the music room, of him, playing his violin, sometimes at night, sometimes putting down his bow so that they could listen to a nightingale. Her love, as always . . .

North-West Frontier, India: May, 1919

23 The officers' mess was an old building made of large bricks of dried mud, flat-roofed, low, long, the walls nearly two feet thick to keep out the sun of the hot weather, now full upon them. It had been very different when the battalion arrived, late in November '18. But now all day, every day, the sun beat down like a club, without mercy, the shade temperature hovering between 110 and 120 Fahrenheit. The thorn trees in the mess garden offered no protection, and the grass was parched, though the mess *malis* watered it from the irrigation ditches as soon as the sun went down. Then the earth smelled damp and the drooping zinnias raised their heads, and stood tall, unseen, in the tremulous, scented heat of the night. All round, the mountains, ribbed with rock, skimpily garbed with holly oak, shimmered in the sun; and, at midnight, were still too hot to touch with the bare knees, which showed between the bottoms of the soldiers' khaki drill shorts and the tops of their rolled khaki puttees.

Inside the mess the officers of the 8th Battalion the Weald Light Infantry had finished dinner, and were standing or sitting round in the anteroom, talking and drinking, or playing snooker in the separate mud building nearby, which housed the billiard room and the *ghuslkhana* . . . which might be translated as "W.C.," except that there was no running water, only a row of enamel chamber pots on a wooden shelf at the appropriate height, and two cubicles containing wooden "thrones" and deeper pots. Outside the back door, the mess sweeper squatted, waiting to clean out the pots as necessary. Outside the mess building itself, two small brown boys leaned back against the outer wall, strings attached to their toes. As they swung their legs back and forth the strings pulled a series of short blue curtains hanging over the heads of the officers inside, so stirring the hot air . . . and gently showering them with almost invisible dust.

"Roll on, as the soldiery say, roll on," Harry Garth said dreamily. "A boat! England! Blighty! Beauty!"

"Less than four weeks to go," another officer said. "Has it been decided who we're handing over to?"

The adjutant, Lieutenant Claude Mitchell, said, "2nd Battalion, South Wales Borderers. From Germany."

"Why not *our* 2nd Battalion? They're coming out about the same time, aren't they?"

"Yes, but they're going to Hassanpore. Lots of jolly Aid to the Civil there. With luck they'll be able to give the blighters another Jallianwala Bagh."

An officer reading a newspaper in an easy chair by the big, wide, empty fireplace lowered his paper and said, "That's a very unfortunate remark to make, Mitchell." The speaker was a dark-skinned Indian, tall, thin, wearing the lapel badges of the Indian Medical Service on his white mess jacket, and the three stars of a captain on his shoulders.

"Sorry, Govind," the adjuant said, "I didn't know you were there."

"That has nothing to do with it," the Indian said. "A great many Indians fought loyally for Britain through the war. Many died in France and Flanders. The campaigns in Gallipoli, Mesopotamia, and Palestine would have been impossible without them. We had a right to expect some reward for this loyalty. What did we get? Three hundred and seventy-nine of us massacred at the Jallianwala Bagh . . . and every British officer and civilian in the country going out of his way to praise the butcher, General Dyer, as the savior of India."

A voice from the corner of the big room said, "Not the fair word to use about a senior officer, Govind." It was Major Schofield, the 2nd-in-command. "Get on with the argument."

"Sorry, sir . . . As I was saying, we expected more . . . That slaughter of innocent civilians in Amritsar is the worst thing that's happened since the British came to India . . . for you, not for us. Waiter . . . lemonade please." He raised his paper and continued reading.

After an awkward silence, a young subaltern said, "I want to get home. No job's waiting for *me* . . . I'll have to get out and find one. And what training do I have? Joined up when I was eighteen . . . no degree, no skill . . . except commanding a platoon out here."

"The men are very restive," another, older man said. "I hope to

410

God we don't have any trouble here before we're relieved. Their hearts are not in it . . . they want to go home, now!"

"One column," Mitchell said, "next week. And that's our last. It took Army Headquarters long enough to sort everything out after the armistice, but they finally did it . . . Care for a game of billiards, Stratton? A pice a point?"

The newspaper in the corner was lowered again, "You appear to have forgotten, Mitchell, that no gambling is permitted in the mess, except bridge, at the rates specified in Regimental Standing Orders."

"Sorry, sir, I forgot."

Fred said, "All right." He had learned to play quite well when he was living in Mess, before his marriage. There wasn't much else to do, after dinner. And immediately afterwards the battalion came up here, a non-family station, so he had, of course, dined in every night. That month's leave in Bombay with Daphne had been a nice change—*and* she'd got pregnant—but otherwise this Frontier routine was all right and had become familiar: the voices of men, and only men, the camaraderie . . . no one to order him to sit up straight, or correct his accent, or tell him he'd never get on if he didn't learn to play bridge, or . . . or, face it, nag. Oh well, column next week, then . . . what?

*   *   *   *

The battalion was acting as rearguard this third day of the column. A "column" was normally merely an excursion into tribal territory to show the flag, and to exercise the troops—on this occasion one Indian, one Gurkha, and one British battalion, with mountain guns, Sappers and Miners, Signals, and the usual services. The force had marched twelve miles the first day, mostly on a dusty road into the foothills west of Ghazi Khan; the second day eleven more miles on narrow tracks in ever-rising mountains thinly covered with scrub. The heat had been tremendous, the water scarce. All the men had suffered, the British troops the most, with six cases of heatstroke on the first day, all evacuated by motor ambulances, which had accompanied the column that far. From there on any sick had to be carried with the column in *khajawas,* the awkward stretchers hung one to each flank of a camel.

Colonel Pulliam stood at the rear of the winding column, staring up through binoculars at a rocky ridge about half a mile to the north of the path. Close to him a corporal carried a huge red flag, denoting the official rear point of the column. To one side signallers wig-wagged messages in morse with blue and white flags.

Pulliam lowered his binoculars—"They're moving . . . took 'em long enough. Damned Jats! I'll give the platoon commander a rocket when he comes in. He can't have had anyone watching for signals."

411

He raised his glasses again. The rearguard artillery officer turned to Stratton, "Heard the latest? The Afghans have crossed the border . . . Unless they go back, *ek dum,* we have the 3rd Afghan War on our hands."

"Won't make any difference to us," Fred said. "We're going home. And our tribesmen hate them, as far as I can make out, even though they're all as good as cousins, or closer."

Mitchell, nearby, said, "Don't you believe it. We're infidels. The Emir's started something, because he thinks we're weak, and our tribes will join in."

A loud fierce rattling cracking rent the air over their heads and Fred dived to the ground. He had served on the Western Front three full years, and he recognized concentrated rifle fire when he heard it. One or two more in the headquarters group were also flat by now, others staring vacantly up and around as though asking, what's that funny noise. Then one of the signallers fell, clasping his stomach, the flag dropping from his hand. At the same time Colonel Pulliam, his glasses still to his eyes, exclaimed, "By God, a man of the picquet's down . . . and another!"

Stratton shouted, "They've ambushed the picquet, sir . . . And they're firing at us!"

The gunner officer shouted to his own signaller, who began to wave his flags frantically. The gunner, a captain, knelt beside Pulliam, now also kneeling. "We have one battery with trails down, sir . . . We ought to have fire within a few seconds."

The little khaki figures on the hillside were running faster now . . . another man had fallen. Still no sign of who was shooting, either at the picquet, or at the headquarters group round the red flag. Shells began to whine overhead to burst thunderously on the hillside behind the running soldiers. Colonel Pulliam was pale and disconcerted. Stratton, watching him, thought—he doesn't know what to do. He was a stockbroker in peace time, a Territorial part-time soldier; he'd never served in France; and what of battle had he learned in India? Nothing. He shouted, "Sir . . . they've had at least four wounded out there. I'll counterattack and get them in as soon as I can fix artillery support."

"Carry on, yes, yes, carry on," Pulliam said.

The gunner captain turned to Fred, "Which way are you going to go? . . . It's Stratton, isn't it?"

Fred nodded, surveying the terrain in front of him with his binoculars. The enemy was to the right . . . might be some to the left and some straight beyond the picquet, but mostly on the right . . . The nullah down the middle offered a little cover, in fact the Jat platoon was in it now, taken position, and returning the enemy's fire. A low

ridge of rock ran from a hundred yards to his left up to the crest line
where the picquet's position had been. It would do. Nothing better
. . . so, get to the rock line, go up, two platoons up, two back . . . get
the guns to protect his right flank . . . retake the crest, then clear out
the wounded. Once that was done . . . it would be three o'clock.

He ran to the C.O. and gave his plan, adding, "I'll need another
company to get me out, sir . . . and all the artillery and machine-gun
fire we can muster . . . There must be a hundred and fifty of them up
there."

Pulliam said, "Good, good . . . Arrange your start time with the
gunners . . . Mitchell, tell Sergeant Grundy to fix machine-gun support with Stratton. And send for Major Tomlinson and D Company."

Fred sent his runner to bring back his company, waiting 300 yards
forward of the red flag as battalion reserve for just such an eventuality
as this. Then, crouched behind the rocks with the gunner captain and
Sergeant Grundy, he explained his plan, and fixed support from the
mountain guns and the machine guns. He looked at his watch—
"Starting line, here . . . Zero hour, twelve noon."

The gunner said, "Send down a signal as soon as you're on the
crest, Stratton. We'll be firing on it until then, but as soon as you have
it, I'll lift a hundred yards, to stop any counterattack."

"Right . . . I'll wig-wag back P K . . . or green over white."

"Right. Good luck. We ought to have another battery's trails down
in ten minutes. They were well forward and on the move when this
blew up."

Stratton nodded and stood up. Here was his company. The platoon commanders were running forward, the men crouched low,
spread out. He looked at them carefully . . . hot, tired, sweaty . . .
and nervous. Christ, they ought to have been at Loos . . . Fricourt
. . . Contalmaison . . . Passchendaele. This was a joke. Still, you
could get killed by these ragged-arse barnshoots just as dead as by a
Hun: one bullet was all it took.

The platoon commanders and the C.S.M. were round him, all
kneeling, big flat-topped solar topees like inverted dung baskets on
their heads, walking sticks in their hands. He looked at them one by
one and at last said, "Calm down . . . Number 11 Picquet ran into
trouble as it was being pulled in. It's from the Jats. Some wounded,
probably some killed. We are going to retake the picquet's position on
that ridge . . . *that* one . . . so that the wounded can be brought out."

"We'll only get some more wounded," a 2nd Lieutenant muttered.

Fred said sharply, "Shut up, Greville! We don't abandon wounded
to the tribesmen, and that's all there is to it. Nor the dead, if we can
help it. How would you like to go to heaven with your prick and balls

413

cut off and sewn into your mouth? . . . We'll attack up that ridge line, two platoons forward, then my headquarters, then two platoons, abreast, in reserve . . . 5 left front, 7 right front, 6 left rear, 8 right rear. Platoon formations—sections in arrowhead, men in arrowhead. Move steadily, not too fast, that's a 500-foot climb . . . no stopping for casualties . . . supporting fire . . . the mountain guns are . . ." He went on for five minutes. And, at the end—"Any questions?" No one spoke. Fred said, "The time is . . . eleven forty-two . . . now! See that every man thoroughly understands the plan. Good luck."

*　　*　　*　　*

The camp was dark, all the hurricane lanterns that had been carried on camel back, or strung round transport mules' necks, extinguished since an hour after nightfall. The tents were up, in long rows, each full of sleeping men except where the occupants were on sentry duty round the low stone wall that marked the boundary, a bigger stone set up as headstone every five paces all the way round the three-quarter mile of perimeter. The night had started hot, a wind blowing dust across the little valley and into the men's eyes as they worked at their myriad tasks—putting up the tents, collecting the rocks, building the wall, digging down some cover for the wounded in the Field Ambulance area. The brigade had suffered twenty wounded, besides seven left dead on the ridges three miles to the east, where the afternoon's battle had been fought. Fred and B Company had reached the crest with little trouble, and no more casualties than one killed and four wounded. Other troops below had come in and taken out the wounded from the Jat Picquet; that picquet itself had finally rejoined the column; and there B Company was, still up, and the tribesmen gathering, for they knew that the soldiers had to go down. The screw guns had performed marvels of accuracy, dropping a hail of shells within fifteen yards of the crest when the tribesmen started an attack; and Fred had done well, pulling out at full speed while the enemy were still confused by that setback. Even so, he twice had to halt the withdrawal, fight back fifty yards, and wait five minutes, till another newly wounded man was carried out. The dead, he left. With this number of Pathans against him, and coming on much more openly than they were supposed to, it wasn't worth it. The dead would have to face St Peter without their balls. St Peter would understand, being a sort of tribesman himself.

The medical orderlies had scrubbed the blood-soaked *khajawas;* the tents smelled of ether from the operations; one wounded man had died. While they were setting up camp the tribesmen had sniped continuously, but not very heavily. Everyone was dead beat—too tired to eat much. They prayed for beer but there wasn't any . . . not much water, either. No more washing of filthy clothes, or even *khajawas,* now . . .

The C.S.M. shook Fred awake at two in the morning. "You wanted to go round the sentries, sir."

Fred struggled up from mile-deep dreams, his mouth dry and harsh, sweating. There was a little chill in the air at this hour, 6,000 feet above sea level; but, like every other soldier, he had been sleeping fully dressed. He buckled on his belt and equipment and started out, following the C.S.M. The sentries were dimly seen shapes against the faint stars, their bayonets sticking up if they were patrolling; but rested against the wall, only the tip showing, if they were on guard, leaning behind a headstone . . . Here was a machine gun, the sentry sitting behind it, the rest of the crew sprawled asleep on the ground all round, the corporal leaning against the wall, asleep.

Fred stooped, "Seen anything?"

The man didn't look up—"No, sir."

"What are you loaded with?"

"One in five tracer, sir . . . standard for night."

Fred moved on. They were very tired, half-asleep, yawning. Three hours to first light. He paused, peering out, trying to make sense out of the shapeless dark beyond the wall. By God, there might be no shape, but there was movement—close! "Stand to!" he yelled at the top of his voice. "Stand to!" He ran back to the machine-gun sentry and shouted, "Open fire, man! On your fixed line!"

The man hooked his fingers up under the safety bar and pressed his thumbs on the trigger. The gun began to rock and shudder, spitting out a stream of bullets, every half-second a tracer blazing into shooting light as it slammed across the dark. The rest of the crew were tumbling into position. Others had taken up the shout "Stand to! Stand to!" From brigade headquarters an artillery trumpeter was blowing the call. And now out of the dark Fred heard the wild, falsetto screaming of the tribesmen, coming in for the attack. He could see the glitter of their long knives. Where the hell were his men? Coming . . . the C.S.M. was beside him, roaring like a bull, firing across the parapet . . . more men were rushing to the wall, taking position, firing. Some of the Pathans were firing now, but not many: they were going to trust to cold steel. He hitched his revolver round, drew it, and checked that it was loaded in every chamber.

They were coming over the wall to his right—D Company's area—shadowy shapes in black and dark grey, fluttering like moths, steel flashing. And D Company was breaking, taken by surprise in the middle of the night, overwhelmed by this horribly personal war . . . not

415

shells or machine guns or impersonal explosions, but dark, white-teethed men, mouths wide, coming at them, screaming. He saw a soldier go down, his belly ripped open, and fired carefully at the Pathan kneeling over him. The Pathan fell. "Hold tight, B!" he yelled. "Hold tight!"; and ran toward the centre part of his company, where one of his platoons was the Inlying Picquet. In a few moments, he'd take them up to sweep along the wall to the right, where D was no more than a fragment. Better do it now, and cut off the tribesmen's retreat. A shadowy figure appeared beside him and said, "Who are you?"

"Stratton . . . Wealds."

The other said, "I'm Graham, commanding brigade reserve—A Company, 4th/4th. What's happened?"

"They're in to my right . . . overran our D . . . I'm going to take my Inlying Picquet and seal them off."

"I'll follow you . . . Once we've made contact the other side of the gap, you cover the gap and I'll sweep through the camp . . ."

"Better use bayonets only," Fred said. "There'll be a godawful mess inside, everyone mixed up."

Graham said, "Bayonets and kukris . . . My subadar will be pleased."

The Wealds' Inlying Picquet was ready . . . jittery, Fred noticed; this was bad luck, so near to going home.

"Ready?"

"Ready."

"All right. Advance!"

The British soldiers moved slowly forward, rifles and fixed bayonets outthrust, the points at chest height. Here was a dead man—British . . . another—Pathan . . . a wounded Pathan. A soldier bent over and drove his bayonet through the man's ear and head. Fred said, "Well done." Another, this one also wounded, swinging round, pointing a long musket. The musket flared, a soldier beside Fred fell. Others ran forward, bayonets stabbed down . . . more dead . . . British—two, three, two here wounded, one in the neck, his head nearly off, he wouldn't last; the other in the belly—hard to tell how badly. "No!" he shouted. "Don't stay with him! We've got a fucking job to do, man! Get on!"

On . . . more dead along the deserted wall . . . now dark, living faces, turbans, the Jats. Fred found a British officer and said briefly, "We've cleared the wall. I'm going to take it over into my area . . . How many Pathans broke in?"

"God knows. My subadar here thought about a hundred."

The Gurkha captain Graham said, "We'll try to reduce that in the next half hour or so . . . I'll wait until you've got the perimeter wall properly covered, Stratton, then . . ."

A man staggered out of the darkness and Stratton, peering, cried, "Govind! Are you all right?"

"Knife wound in the neck," the doctor gasped. "They're in the Field Ambulance . . . killed all the wounded . . . butchers . . . bloody barbarian devils, Muslim swine . . ."

"You rest here," Fred said. "Sit against the wall until we've had a chance to tidy things up . . . Looks as though you'll have something to avenge, Graham. Didn't you have some sick in the Field Ambulance?"

"The men know," Graham said briefly. "*Tayyar chha, subadar-sahib? Advance!*"

*   *   *   *

The Mess was nearly all packed up. As a Territorial battalion the 8th did not have much silver or other trophies. The furniture was not its own, but had been hired here, as at every other station it had occupied since being embodied in 1914. The 2nd-in-command, Quartermaster, three sergeants, and a clerk of the South Wales Borderers had arrived, and had agreed to take over most of the barrack fittings. Stores were now being counted, from *tables, office, I.P.—10* to *Lanterns, hurricane—143* and *Paper, toilet G.S., rolls—1,489.* The officers were again in the anteroom and billiard room, talking, drinking. There was a different look in most of their eyes now. They had seen war, in its Indian form, and it had marked them.

Major Tomlinson's hand still trembled; and a livid, hidden scar down his back marked where a dying Pathan, shot by his Webley, had yet managed to stab him. It was his company that had broken in the night attack at Khaza Toi. Tomlinson would never be fit to command troops in action again. It didn't matter; in a month or two he'd be back in Canterbury, at his profession of assistant bank manager, whence patriotism had dragged him five years ago. Stratton, sitting next to Tomlinson in the anteroom, said, "How's Private Balchin, sir?"

Tomlinson said, "Died half an hour before I came to mess . . . poor devil. I don't know how he survived this long, seeing what those devils did to him." He shook his head, trying to blot out what he remembered. I've seen worse, Fred thought grimly—at Passchendaele. A few thousand heavy shells can do worse things to the human body than knives or bayonets or kukris can. But the scenes in the Field Ambulance and along the perimeter wall, when the 4th/4th Gurkhas were cleaning up, had been different . . . Pathans, stabbing for God, ripping open bellies, slashing off genitals, slitting throats, holding a man from behind, drawing the knife deep across his throat so that the blade grated against the vertebrae . . . and the Gurkhas, rifles slung, kukris dripping in their right hands, slashing, a turbanned head rolling here, another jammed under a tent fly there, a third being kicked like a football across the barren earth, blood like a river, the Gurkhas laughing and shouting . . . *"Ayo Gurkhali!"* they'd yelled, and he'd remember the gleaming red in their eyes, till the day he died . . .

Mitchell said, "Shan't be sorry when we leave . . . I never expected to feel *that.* How many servants will we have when we get back to Blighty? Will the lads of the village lower their umbrellas and get off the pavement when we pass? Who'll knuckle his forehead, and call us Sahib, father and mother, protector of the poor, light of heaven?"

"I'm not worrying about servants," another said. "Getting a job's going to be hard enough."

"Stay here, then," Mitchell said. "Or come back again after you've been demobbed. Lots of jobs going here, there'll be . . . police, railways, telegraphs . . . and you don't have to start at the bottom. They've got jobs reserved for chee-chees and old soldiers, and put them in above the Wogs . . . us above the chee-chees, of course. Or you could plant tea, or coffee. Or go into trade. Once you've taken those pips down, trade won't look so bloody low as it does now."

Stratton drank deep of his whisky and soda. It was long and weak, as one drank it out here; and it was cheap. He'd come to depend a lot on his daily *chhota pegs* and the occasional *bara.* Life was all right in India; but it wasn't exciting, once you got away from the Frontier. You felt cut off, and the letters from home didn't help much. In fact, they made you feel worse, reminding you that you were in a hot, barren country full of niggers, while back at home, everyone had forgotten you . . . Frank was home; or rather was back at H.A.C., but not at home. He was living in a little room off High Street; he hadn't seen his kids and didn't mean to; and he had learned to fly . . . Carol Adams was married to one of the Woodruffs in Walstone and had had a baby . . . about three months after the wedding. Well, she'd had a hot twat in '14, and it obviously hadn't cooled. Fletcher Gorse had married the American girl Betty Merritt, daughter of the American banker . . . trust Fletcher to land on his feet . . . Fagioletti had been home from Germany for a 96-hour leave, but though Ethel said they'd done their best, she wasn't pregnant yet—but next month she'd be joining him in a sergeant's married quarter in Cologne . . . Mother hated living in that bloody great palace with the Hoggins, but where else could she go? Ruth was good to her, but so busy with all her important affairs.

Important affairs? Ruth? Well, as Lady Walstone she probably opened bazaars and dished out pies at the Workhouse . . . But hearing about all this, reading about it, didn't bring it closer—it took it farther away . . .

Major Schofield said, "I have work to go back to . . . and I'll be glad to, I can tell you. Over four years out of my life . . . can't call it wasted, but it's enough . . . more than enough. It's you younger fellows I'm sorry for. And I'd recommend you think carefully about what Mitchell said just now. There are jobs here in India, and they pay well."

"How long for?" Lieutenant Booth asked. "After the Amritsar business, I can't see us staying in India for long."

The Regimental Medical Officer looked up from his paper—a Hindu weekly from Bombay, published in Gujrati and Hindi in the Devanagari script—"The jobs'll last you out. You aren't going to pack your bags overnight . . . Amritsar proved that."

"Well, I don't want to hurt your feelings, Govind," another young officer said, "but I wouldn't take a job in this bloody country if they paid me five thousand chips a month for it. If I never see India again, it'll be too soon."

"Tell that to your politicians in Parliament," Govind said. He returned to his paper.

Mitchell said, "Well, I'm off to bed." He turned to Fred, and said in a low voice, "Sorry to bring up shop, Stratton, but I forgot earlier. The C.O. wants to see you tomorrow, at nine o'clock."

*   *   *   *

Fred stood stiffly at attention in front of the commanding officer's big desk in the orderly room, Colonel Pulliam sitting at the desk, Mitchell standing behind and to one side of the C.O.

Pulliam said, "We're off the day after tomorrow and I have to tell you that I've put you in for an immediate bar to your M.C. . . . you and Govind, who did magnificent work in the Field Ambulance before it was overrun . . . must have killed half a dozen of those swine himself with someone else's revolver he'd grabbed. I don't know when the awards will come through, but I have the Brigadier General's word that they will. So, congratulations."

"Thank you, sir." A silver rosette on the purple and white, Fred thought; very pretty.

Colonel Pulliam continued—"I have been ordered to transfer one captain to the 2nd Battalion, which, as you know is already in India, at Hassanpore in the Punjab. Would you like to go?"

Fred didn't answer for a moment. Within the week he was supposed to be boarding a troopship in Karachi, bound for home with Daphne. Then . . . what? Finding a house in Hedlington . . . looking for a job . . . what sort of a job? She would never let him take a job in a factory, and he didn't want to. He was a sahib, and by Christ he'd worked for it, learning how to speak properly, how to play billiards, ride a bloody horse, eat with the right knife and fork. But there weren't really any sahibs in England, only the gentry, and that was different. What would Daphne say? She talked of England all the time, though it was the hell of a long time since she'd been there . . . and she'd miss the servants much more than he would. He sometimes wondered if she really wasn't a little bit afraid of going back home.

To the colonel he said, "Well, sir . . . I've been away from home for four and a half years . . . When would I be demobbed, if I was transferred to the 2nd Battalion?"

Colonel Pulliam said, "You wouldn't . . . You see, I have been thinking about your future, Stratton. I know your background. You have made yourself into a good officer . . . an excellent officer, as your two M.C.s attest . . . and also, if I may say so, a gentleman. I do not know what career you were thinking of pursuing, or returning to, in civilian life . . . but I can not think of any that would suit you better, or half as well, as the one you are now engaged in . . . an army officer. I am suggesting that you apply for a regular commission. If you agree, I will send it forward this very afternoon, with my strongest recommendations. Then, when you go to the 2nd Battalion, you will be joining a Regular battalion of the regiment, which is badly in need of officers. They are five short on the Peace Establishment. I will send Colonel Trotter, their C.O., a copy of my recommendation about you for his information, and I do not doubt that he will be as eager to support it as I am to initiate it. Incidentally, the Brigadier General in Hassanpore is Quentin Rowland, of ours. I know he will support you if the application needs more support. What do you say?"

Fred did not wait long. He must have been thinking along these lines for some time, but he didn't want to push himself forward. The Regulars were a snooty lot, and he didn't want to risk being snubbed . . . mechanics' sons never became Regular officers of the Weald Light Infantry before the war. Daphne? She'd be happy; she'd be staying in India, at least for six years, with all the servants. The baby would be born in India, and there'd be an *ayah* to look after it. After that, when the battalion's tour in India was finished, and it was sent to God knows where—Rangoon, Jamaica, Khartoum, England perhaps—well, time enough to worry about that when it happened.

He said, "Thank you very much, sir. I'd like that."

*   *   *   *

The adjutant of the 2nd Battalion was a tall, fairly senior captain, George Clifford, who wore a black patch over one eye socket, the eye having been blown out at Arras late in 1915. He had spent the rest of the war as adjutant of the Regimental Depot in Hedlington. He had seen no more active service, which he genuinely wanted to, and his temper had soured considerably. Now, as Fred Stratton stood at attention in front of his desk, Clifford's one dark eye wandered stonily up and down his person, but there were no words until the inspection was finished. Then he said, "We wear polished brass buttons, cap, and rank badges, not bronze ones, when serving outside England. We do not wear long puttees, but khaki hosetops with green turnovers, and short puttees—you can have your batman cut them down from the long ones—three and a half folds. Your Sam Browne is nowhere near the right colour—it should be like mine. You can get all those fixed through the dry canteen, or at Ranken's in Lahore."

"Yes, sir," Fred said. Clifford was a captain, like himself, but the adjutant was always addressed as "sir" in his office, by officers of equal or lower rank, as the personification of the commanding officer. Clifford now rose and went through a door behind him, closing it. Fred heard some mumbled conversation and wondered if he could stand at ease, or easy. But Clifford returned and said, "The C.O. will see you now." He stood aside and Fred marched in, halted with a clash of boots, and saluted, his left hand holding his sword a little below the hilt.

Lieutenant Colonel William Trotter stood up and came round the desk, his right hand out, "Glad to see you, Stratton . . . Did you see the 8th Battalion off satisfactorily?"

"At Mari Indus, sir. They had a bit of a party."

"Well, I suppose they're happy to be going home. I'm glad to be out here again, and doing some real soldiering. I was afraid they'd keep us in Germany, or, God forbid, send us to Aldershot or Ireland." He returned to his desk and sat down, saying, "Stand easy, Stratton . . . I'm putting you in A Company, as 2nd-in-command to Major Featherstonehaugh"—he pronounced it Festonhaw, but Fred had seen the name in the Army List and knew how it was spelled. The C.O. noticed a shadow cross Fred's face, and went on—"I know you have been commanding a company in the 8th since you arrived there from the 1st Battalion—over a year ago, wasn't it?—but this is a Regular battalion, the war's over and all our surviving Regular officers are coming back from the war-raised battalions, Territorial battalions, staff jobs, secondments. I'm still short, that's why I wanted you—but I

421

do have several officers senior to you, so . . . You're married, aren't you?"

"Yes, sir."

"Do you want your wife to join you here?"

"Yes, sir," Fred said.

"Well, when you leave me talk to the Quartermaster. He's found an old friend in the M.E.S. man here . . . and of course, the Brigadier General is one of ours. You'll get a suitable bungalow in no time, then you can settle in. Is there anything you would like to ask me?"

Fred hesitated, then said, "Did my application for a regular commission go forward, sir?"

Colonel Trotter smiled—"It went forward, Stratton. And General Rowland has sent up a strong endorsement. The rest is only a formality. You can count yourself one of us, from this moment."

"Thank you, sir," Fred said. He wondered why he felt a sensation as of an ironbound door closing heavily behind him. The C.O. nodded and Fred saluted, wheeled round, and marched out. As he passed through the adjutant's outer office Clifford said, "One moment, Stratton. Here's a specimen visiting card. Have some printed—Vail Chand on the Mall—precisely like this and make your calls before the end of the week . . . on the other two battalions—one card for the C.O., by name, one for the officers . . . also the brigade commander and Mrs Rowland . . . and the D.C. and Mrs Laslett."

Fred said, "I have cards, sir. I had them printed when I joined the 8th Battalion."

The adjutant held out his hand—"Let me see one, please." Fred found a card in his wallet and handed it over. The adjutant read, and said, "What's your club?"

"I don't have one."

Clifford's one eye blinked and he looked as if he had been shot. His mouth turned grimly down—"In this regiment all officers are required to belong to a London club. You'd better see about it at once."

Fred felt the colour rising in his neck. Daphne's father had brought up this subject before they were married . . . why the hell should he join a London club? But he was a Regular now. He said, "I don't know anything about clubs, sir."

Clifford glared for a moment; then his manner softened. He said, "Apply to join the Rag, Stratton. I'll propose you and that'll be enough. It's very reasonable, and very comfortable . . . and it'll save you money in the long run, as you can spend a night or two in London—we never refer to it as 'Town' in this regiment—much more cheaply than in a hotel . . . That's all. Wait . . . the Brigadier General's *chaprassi* delivered this note for you while you were in with the C.O."

Fred pocketed the envelope, saluted, and went out. Outside, standing close to the sentry at the end of the Orderly Room verandah, both sheltered by the overhang of the roof from the blinding sun, he read the letter—*Dear Captain Stratton—My wife and I would be pleased if you would come to tea next Thursday. Plain clothes.*

The letter was on heavy paper stamped in deep blue: *Flagstaff House, Hassanpore.*

      *   *   *   *

Inside the sprawling bungalow it was cool and almost dark, at first, when you walked in from the glare of the afternoon sun. Two *malis* were working in the garden and the Union Jack fluttered from a tall white pole in the middle of the circle of the graveled drive. An empty sentry box at the outer gate contained a box for calling cards, but Fred brought his in, and left them on the hall table while the khitmatgar in his high turban and kullah, white achkan and green cummerbund went to announce him. The general came out, rubbing his hands. His blue eyes were a little more protuberant in the plump face, Fred thought, and there was a little more belly under the white duck suit—he was wearing a coat and tie, of course, as was Fred . . . but it was Old Rowley.

The general shook his hand vigorously—"So glad to see you, Stratton. It's been a long time . . . not so long, really, I suppose, but so much happened after you left."

They were walking into a big room, again nearly dark, curtains drawn, but still some light filtered through from the furnace of the day. There were flowers in vases, polished tables gleaming, silver-framed photographs on them, a mantelpiece, a fireplace . . . they'd need that in the cold weather, for a couple of months. A woman came forward—"My wife," Quentin Rowland said. "Captain Fred Stratton, my dear."

"We've met," she said. "Your father used to work at the factory . . . and you were manager at High Staining, weren't you?"

"Yes, Mrs Rowland," Fred said. He wondered if she knew how he had left that last job . . . found on top of Carol Adams, fucking away in the hay, by John—the general's brother—and his wife, on a rainy afternoon when they came back early from a trip into Hedlington. A long time ago now.

He was beginning to see more clearly as his eyes became accustomed to the twilight in here. He was also becoming aware that it was not as cool as he had at first thought. The punkah swinging overhead was stirring hot air, not cool. Someone was bringing in a loaded silver tray, another carrying forward a small tea table. Mrs Rowland was wearing a long, cool, white dress. She was tall and thin, hair fair, greying, eyes grey: she looked strange, wild . . . must be in her mid forties, and Old Rowley the same. She was wearing a man's wristwatch. It looked huge and out of place on her bare, slender wrist.

They were asking him questions about his wife . . . who she was, when she was coming. He answered the questions, noting the pictures round the walls. Several scenes of the trenches. He knew who'd done them—Archie Campbell, the 1st Battalion adjutant after Boy. He'd seen Archie making the sketches often enough in the line, in billets, in a rest area, anywhere, everywhere.

The general said, "We'll try to get you a bungalow in the lines, Stratton. Wouldn't want to leave your wife alone all day out near the bazaar these days. Especially as she's going to have a baby."

Fred said, "Why not, sir? Isn't it safe?"

Quentin Rowland said heavily, "This province is in a bad mood. You'd have thought they'd calm down after what General Dyer did to them in Amritsar, but it's the opposite. More hostility. More subversive pamphlets . . . terrorism . . . Why, the swine attacked and murdered a canal engineer in a canal bungalow last month."

"I read about it," Fred said. "They said it was dacoits, who did it for money."

The general shook his head—"Nonsense. It was some damned fanatics . . . We'll have to be on our toes here. And if there's trouble, it'll fall on the battalion. We don't want to use the Indian battalions in aid of the Civil Power unless it's absolutely necessary."

Fred sipped his tea with a sinking feeling. Riots, terrorism, his wife behind bars all day, a knife in the back any time you went shopping out of the military lines. This was not what he had thought of when he looked forward to being a sahib, a ruler. Too bloody late now.

He half-turned his head to hear something Mrs Rowland was saying to him and caught sight of a portrait lit by a shaft of light from a side window—Archie Campbell, a self-portrait, looking weary, tin hat on the back of his head, in a dugout, just the head and shoulders, and—this was typically Archie—the neck of a whisky bottle showing level with his chest, as though on a table beside him.

Fiona Rowland saw the direction of his glance and said, "Archie Campbell . . . but, of course, you knew him."

"Very well, Mrs Rowland."

"He was our best friend." Her hand went out and the general's hand crept out to cover it. They sat there, looking at each other, oblivious of him for a while; until at last Mrs Rowland eased her hand

424

away and said brightly, "Another cup of tea, Captain Stratton? And as soon as your wife comes, you must bring her round, and I will help her furnish your bungalow . . ."

*　　*　　*　　*

Quentin and Fiona were having a last weak *chhota peg* in the drawing room before going to bed. The servants had been dismissed, the bungalow closed down, the night sentries posted. Fiona, leaning gracefully back in an armchair, said, "Well, Quentin, we are well settled in here now . . . so, what do we have to look forward to? How should we plan for the future?"

Quentin stood by the mantelpiece over the empty grate, looking down at her—"Retire in three, four years," he said. "I'm very lucky to have got a brigade, not being p.s.c. . . . but I won't go any further. Retire to Hedlington . . . see if I can do something to get the recruits and Depot staff a better time when they're not on duty . . . try to get the town to know more about the regiment, and the men who make it . . ."

"The regiment, always, all the time," she said, smiling.

"What else is there for me—except you?" he said. "I'm not a brainy chap . . . my job's been to teach everyone his responsibilities . . . make them all understand that they depend on each other, all doing their job, up and down the scale . . . spotting brainy fellows, seeing they don't forget that their brains won't be any use unless they understand the men who're going to have to carry out their plans . . . understand them, and love them . . . Then, when they go on up and become generals, they'll have their feet on the ground. I'll never be a general and make great plans . . . wouldn't know how to do it . . . and I can't save the men from being killed, wounded . . . but I've tried to teach them a spirit, a feeling that it's worth it, for the comradeship, the trust . . . and that's all in the cap badge. There are lots of fellows like me, who've been doing that all their service . . . no one's ever heard of 'em, nor ever will. And it'll always be the same, in the army. We haven't succeeded always, everywhere, none of us . . . but we've tried."

She whispered, "My dear, sweet, great Quentin . . ."

Daily Telegraph, Tuesday, June 3, 1919

SOCIETY WEDDINGS

LORD RIBBLESDALE AND MRS ASTOR

Lord Ribblesdale was married very quietly on Saturday, in St Mary's, Bryanston Square, to Mrs John Jacob Astor, widow of Col-

> onel Astor, who was drowned in the *Titanic* when the vessel went
> down on April 15, 1912, in the Atlantic on its first voyage to New
> York. Lord Ribblesdale is the fourth holder of the title and suc-
> ceeded his father in 1876. He was Master of the Royal Buckhounds,
> which have since been given up, from 1892 and 1895, and before
> that was a Lord-in-Waiting to Queen Victoria for five years. He is a
> very popular member of the House of Lords. His first wife, who
> died eight years ago, was a sister of Lord Glenconner and of Mrs
> Asquith. They had two sons and three daughters. The eldest son,
> who served in the 10th Hussars, was killed in action in Somaliland,
> and the second son, The Hon. Charles Lister—a brilliant scholar
> who entered the Diplomatic Service—lost his life in the present
> war, leaving many most interesting letters, which were subse-
> quently issued in a volume edited by his father. His daughters are
> Lady Wilson . . . Lady Lovat . . . and Mrs Capel, who married as
> her first husband, Mr Percy Wyndham, Coldstream Guards, who
> was killed in the retreat from Mons.

Cate thought, there is a noble family that has given generously of its
blood to the country: Lord Glenconner's son, a war poet almost of
Fletcher Gorse's class, had also been killed in the war. They had done
no more than humbler folk, but the Ribblesdales were certainly entitled to say that they, unlike some, had not sheltered behind their
wealth and position. He remembered seeing Sargent's portrait of the
Marquess in a Royal Academy summer exhibition, some years back: a
technically brilliant work, and also extraordinarily searching in the
way it had captured the nobleman's very English face and manner, the
careless, slightly bored, grace . . . He wondered if Ribblesdale would
now have to forgo his cosy rooms in the Cavendish, and his cosy,
unplatonic friendship with its owner, Rosa Lewis. The first Lady
Ribblesdale had been a Tennant, as eccentric and original in her way
as Margot Asquith, her sister. She had had other, perhaps higher,
things on her mind than worrying about her husband's affair with the
cockney Mrs Lewis. But Mrs Astor . . . ?

His fellow passenger in the first-class compartment coughed, and
he lowered his paper. He was taking the train up to Town to watch
some cricket at Lord's. Lord Walstone, who nowadays usually had his
chauffeur drive him to London in one of his Rolls Royce motor cars,
was also taking the train today, because of the filthy weather, lowering
clouds and heavy rain: no cricket until after lunch, for certain.

Walstone cleared his throat again, and said, "Cate, you're a gent,
born one, I mean. You always know what's right . . . I don't . . . My
wife—you know what women are—my Ruthie told me months ago
I've got to *do* something, because I've made a lot of money, and I've

got a title . . . but *what* does she want me to do? What should I do? I've been thinking about it ever since, but damned if I can find an answer. Tell me, Cate."

The man was pleading, Cate thought, pleading rather touchingly, his fat, strong hands outspread, they two alone in the compartment, the slashing rain blurring the windows, the train rocking on toward London, the engine ahead whistling for a level crossing.

"Is that all she said," he asked cautiously, "just that she wanted you to do something?"

Walstone said excitedly, "She said we could only eat so many pounds of caviare a day—I *hate* the ruddy stuff, fish jam, I call it . . . only sit in so many motor cars at once . . . buy so many fur coats . . . and once we'd got enough money in the bank to do everything we *could* do, we ought to look for something more. But what, eh, tell me that?"

Cate began to say something, but Walstone overrode him, continuing, "I don't mean being Lord and Lady Bountiful in Walstone . . . we're doing all what we can there, without getting the folks' backs up."

Cate said, "Perhaps she had in mind some sort of service . . . to the country, or to some particular segment of it . . . Have you ever thought of devoting yourself to politics? You would do very well."

"Spent too many years hating politicians," Lord Walstone growled. "No, that's not for me . . . I suppose starting the 'Ounds again doesn't count, though it's going to take up plenty of my time, I can tell you."

"The R.S.P.C.A.," Cate said. "But you're not particularly interested in animals, and one has to be . . . the R.N.L.I., but you are not a man of the sea . . ." He felt a wild desire to go on dredging up unlikely causes for Hoggin to serve—unwed mothers, maltreated songbirds, distressed gentlewomen; but held his tongue. The trouble was that there didn't seem to be any cause large enough and general enough to harness Walstone's tremendous energy.

He had an idea, and said, "Look, Walstone—you have a skill, a talent for making money . . ."

"I do, and that's the truth," Walstone said.

"Your wife's pointed out that you've made enough for yourselves, and your children. But if that is your skill, your vocation—as well as your avocation—you obviously ought to go on doing it . . . for someone else, some worthy cause . . ."

"But what?" Lord Walstone wailed. "New hospitals, universities, houses for poor folks—I've thought of 'em all. None of 'em's lit a fire yet."

Cate said nothing and after a time Walstone said, "Well, I'll just have to keep on thinking, won't I? And hope something turns up."

427

The Great Air and Road Races: June, 1919

Thursday, June 12

24 In the west the full yellow moon was sinking into the dawn haze. From the east daylight was spreading across the grass, delineating the shape of the great hangars, gleaming momentarily in the windows of the hutments beyond, and, at last, picking out in sharp detail the bulk of the Hedlington Buffalo standing outside a hangar, like a great winged beast ready to charge and, perhaps, seize some object off the airfield ahead—the control tower, or one of the cars drawn up at the side—some prey larger than the men around it, whom it dwarfed.

"Wind's good," Guy Rowland said to his co-pilot and flight engineer, Frank Stratton.

"The weather report from France is good, too, sir. It just came in on the wireless. All clear as far as Bordeaux."

Beside Guy, Florinda Lady Jarrow said plaintively, "When are you starting, Guy? I have to be in Piccadilly Circus by eight."

"As soon as the tanks have been filled, and Frank's measured them with that rod in his hand," Guy answered. He knew that Florinda had promised to attend the start of Billy Bidford's motor car race from London to Constantinople . . . but why did they have to start their race so early?

Florinda answered his unspoken question—"They want to get out of the West End before the traffic gets really heavy . . . but not before people can see them, and the newspapermen can take photographs. The sponsors insisted on that, for the publicity."

"So do ours," Guy said. "But we're taking off as soon as we can." A mechanic came up and said something to Frank, who went with him and climbed up onto the great machine. Frank began thrusting his measuring rod into the tanks, one by one, and checking that they were as full as the gauges stated.

Florinda said in a low voice, "Come home safe, Guy."

He bent down and kissed her on the lips, his raised goggles brushing her forehead as he did so. She put her arms round his neck and returned the kiss with warmth and affection. Major General Sykes came up and Guy, breaking free, saluted—"You know Lady Jarrow, sir . . . Any news of Alcock and Whitten Brown?"

"They haven't taken off yet . . . Still not quite ready. For your sake, I hope . . . no, I can't take sides. Just as long as it's one of you and not a Yank or a Frenchman. Nungesser's dying to have a go, I know, but I don't think they have a machine capable of it."

Frank returned from his mission—"Tanks full, sir. Food and water checked and properly stowed. Compasses checked . . . The machine was under guard all night, just in case. We're ready."

Guy said, "Well then, let's go. Bye, Florinda. Give my good wishes to Billy . . . Good bye, sir."

He climbed laboriously up the stepladder onto the lower wing and then crawled into the fuselage through the entry port on that side, and so into the second cockpit, which he would share with Frank Stratton. The forward cockpit was, in service use, the gunner's place, but the Scarff ring and the twin guns had been removed, as also the tail gunner's turret, with its seat and guns. All the weight so saved was used for the extra fuel and oil; spare sparking plugs, contact breakers and other spares, including two huge tires for the landing gear; food, water . . . for drinking, not for the engines as they were radials, air-cooled; a first-aid kit.

The ground crew came up to their places. The propellers were laboriously turned one by one by ground crew standing on the wing and using starting handles geared to a 10:1 ratio, while a starter magneto provided the spark. In five minutes all four propellers were whirling slowly. Ready to go, G-BGR throbbed and shuddered mightily. Guy thought, we ought to have named it . . . but what? Why hadn't he named it "Florinda"? Because it would seem like begging. Billy hadn't named his racing Sunbeam "Florinda" either—just "148," the number of his C.M.B. at Zeebrugge.

"All ready?" he asked. Frank raised his right thumb and Guy pushed the four throttles slowly forward. The engine sound rose in pitch and the great craft began to move. They taxied slowly up to the far end of the field, turned into the wind, and stopped. One by one

Guy ran each engine up to full throttle, while chocks inserted by ground crew held G-BGR steady, and Frank scanned the oil-pressure gauges. Then Guy ran all four engines at once, full throttle, while holding back the control column with all his strength to prevent the machine from keeling over onto its nose. The roar was deafening, even through his fur-lined leather flying helmet. The wind sock was flaring straight down the field toward him. The controller was leaning out of his tower, a green Very light flashing up against the dawn sky. Guy glanced down, raised his thumb, and eased back the throttles. The ground crew jerked out the chocks. Guy pushed the throttles forward against the stops. G-BGR started to rumble down the grass, its speed rising steadily.

*   *   *   *

Friday, June 13

This was a breeze after yesterday afternoon, Guy thought. As the forecast had promised, they'd had plain sailing as far as Bordeaux, where they refueled. But soon after takeoff, crossing the western Pyrenees, they had run into an Atlantic low-pressure system that had thrown the great machine all over the sky, set the long wings to creaking and waving, ripples of stress moving along them, while torrents of rain dashed them in the exposed cockpit and blurred their goggles, so that at times they could hardly read the instruments in front of them. They'd climbed to the Buffalo's ceiling of 18,000 feet, even pushing her a little higher—to no avail: the cumulo-nimbus still towered thousands of feet above them. So, setting his teeth, and easing the throttle back a little to reduce the strains on the fuselage and wings as they bucked in and out of the turbulence, Guy kept his course, plunging, rising, falling. Through everything the four engines purred contentedly on between the wings, the four four-bladed propellers turning steadily, a shower of water spinning from the tips into the dark void beyond and onto the fuselage behind the cockpit.

But today, after a stopover in Madrid, with the Spanish air force at Carabanchel, what a change! The edge of the Atlantic ran like a ruler below them into the hazy south-west—Gibraltar passed, then Ceuta, and a landing for fuel for the long leg to Ifni . . . and now, blue sky, cool at this height of 8,000 feet, no turbulence, only a gentle rocking, a slow rise and fall as though the Buffalo was cradled by the ocean far below there, not by the unstable air. Guy leaned back, his hands light on the control column. Yesterday he'd flown from England, over all France, and half Spain. How much history had passed beneath his wings without affecting him, or his machine? Down below, if he had made the journey by land, as Billy Bidford was doing to Constantinople, he would have passed through ruined towns, pockmarked fields, forests ripped by shell fire, acres of crosses marking millions of dead, smashed factories, starving children, women prostituting themselves for a loaf of bread. But up here . . . only now and then the outline of an ancient city beneath the sand, the line of a Roman road across the land . . . cleanness, light, speed. Perhaps he should try to live in the air all his life. Was it possible? And take whom with him? And so avoid all fear, pain, worry, responsibility? Frank was surely flying away from his wife and the baby that was not his, the sense of being soiled, betrayed . . .

Some strange rhythm intruded on his thoughts and he sprang back to where he was. What was wrong, or different?

Frank said, "One of the starboard engines is misfiring, sir . . . It's the pusher. See, now she's throwing oil all over the place."

Guy glanced to his right and back and saw oil spewing from the pusher engine. Frank said, "Better cut it out, sir."

Guy nodded and pulled the engine's throttle back. The propeller whirled more and more slowly but did not stop, until after a minute it was windmilling round and round, still throwing oil. The loss of the engine's power, and the drag of the propeller, dropped the airspeed to 80. Guy shouted, "We won't be into Ifni before dark now. I could land. The desert looks quite hard down there. What do you think's wrong?"

Frank said, "Don't know, sir . . . There's an airfield at Agadir, and that's close."

"All right. We'll land there . . . unless another one goes." He pointed down to the earth, smiling—"Thank God for a full moon."

But another engine didn't go and the Buffalo ground on above the edge of the sea. The air began to stir and the skies to darken. Below, a circular sandstorm took possession of the western rim of the Sahara; and Guy thought, if we have to land in that, we'll be in trouble. But the storm whirled and danced far below, its only effect being some jerky movements of the plane, as invisible arms of the cyclone reached up into the middle air and tried to drag it into its heart. Then as they left the storm behind, and the air grew calmer, Frank said, "Wind's moved round, sir . . . on the ground at least."

Guy glanced at the panel—air speed still 80. But if the wind was behind him at this altitude, as it seemed to be at ground level, then he might be making more than a hundred, ground speed.

They were passing over a spur of the Atlas that ran down in steep crags into the Atlantic. The air became turbulent again, calming as soon as the mountains had passed behind the wings. "That's Agadir," Guy said, "straight ahead." He could almost glide in from here.

He leaned back. Billy Bidford would be somewhere in Germany now, depending on the state of the roads, civil wars, riots . . . and how the Sunbeam went, of course. It was great fun, these races . . . exciting, worthwhile for England, worthwhile in themselves. And when they were over, and they'd drunk the victory champagne, then what?

*　　*　　*　　*

Saturday, June 14

Guy gave the starboard engines more throttle to turn the big plane more sharply on the tall, lush grass. Aside he said to Frank Stratton, "We must get the grass cut before morning. This'll add 5 or 10 percent to our takeoff run, and we don't have the room."

Frank said, "You'll have to get it done, sir. I've got to find out what makes that starboard pusher misfire."

Guy nodded. The starboard pusher had started misfiring again, but only half an hour before the end of the day, so it had hardly marred an otherwise perfect day. And now they were in Bathurst, taxiing through the grass over the rich, light red soil below, a row of tall palm trees shielding the field from the ocean, a small hut at one end, the tropical sun sinking fast into the ocean behind the palms.

Guy swung the Buffalo round and cut the engines. The wind was warm, soft, and damp, blowing down the coast in the North East Trades. He'd have it more or less behind him for the first three hundred miles tomorrow, and then, after crossing the equator, nothing as he reached the Doldrums . . . but no one really knew much about the air patterns in the upper air, only on the surface, where the information was vital to sailing-ship captains.

Frank was already down, reaching up to give him a hand. He jumped to the ground and went forward, pulling off his helmet and goggles. A thin man in a white suit and white solar topee was waiting at the hut, several big Negroes behind him. He came forward now— "Lieutenant Colonel Guy Rowland, I presume." The remark was meant to be a joke, but it didn't come out that way because the man's personality was obviously as cold as a fish's. He said, "I'm Dragee, Deputy Commissioner . . . in charge of making all arrangements here for your little venture . . . at the orders of the Governor."

"Glad to meet you, sir," Guy said. He didn't really have to call a deputy commissioner "sir," but this man would probably relish it. "It's getting rather dark, and there are a couple of things that need doing urgently . . . Could you have the grass cut? It's so heavy that it will affect our takeoff."

"I don't see any difficulty," Dragee said, "but there's no hurry. The petrol for your machine has not arrived."

Guy said tensely, "It was supposed to come in on S.S. *Kalahari* two weeks ago."

"Quite," Dragee said, "but the *Kalahari* was delayed ten days in Dakar with engine trouble."

"That's only just up the coast. We could have landed there," Guy exclaimed. Damn the man! Why hadn't he cabled London days ago, so they could make other arrangements?

Dragee said, "Quite. But the *Kalahari* was then in collision—only a small one—when leaving harbor—and she had to return to Dakar, and is not here yet."

"When do you expect her?"

"She has no radio," Dragee purred. "I really couldn't say. But it could be tomorrow."

For a moment Guy glared at the man as he had glared at German pilots in the air over the Western Front. Dragee blinked. Guy controlled himself and found a smile. Dragee looked alarmed. Guy remembered that his smile looked worse than his frown, because of the severed branch of the mandibular muscle on the right side of his face, which held that side of his mouth down, even when he was smiling. He said, "I hope you have someone at the docks to unload the petrol and bring it up here as soon as it does come in."

"Of course," Dragee said. "One other thing . . . This came for you two hours ago." He held out a slip of paper. Guy read aloud: "To Rowland . . . From Sykes, Civil Aviation. Alcock and Brown took off early this morning from Newfoundland."

Guy scrumpled the paper furiously in his hands, crying fiercely, "Christ, I hope they don't make it!"

Stratton said, "Sir, you can't mean that!"

Once again Guy controlled himself, and said—"Of course not. Can we send a cable from here, sir?"

"Certainly. I have a car here to take you to my bungalow. These men are from the Royal West African Frontier Force, our Gambia Battalion. The native sergeant there will see that your machine is safe."

"I'll get them to help me tie it down, sir," Frank said. "And then I'll stay and work on that engine . . . I can sleep here, I suppose."

Guy said to Dragee, "I'd welcome a bath and a bite, then I'd like to come back here and stay with my mechanic, if you don't mind."

"That can easily be arranged," Dragee said. "And perhaps you'd like to see the paper . . . The road racers are in Hungary, and running into a revolution. Bidford and a Frenchman are in front by several hours, apparently."

Guy grunted non-committally. He really must rid his mind of the idea that any race would decide Florinda's love.

*   *   *   *

Sunday, June 15

Guy and Frank dozed under the wing of the Buffalo all night in the still, dense dark, hearing the distant rumble of the sea on the beach beyond the palms. Soon after dawn the sergeant brought them cakes of unleavened bread, and fruit, and they ate. Guy said to Frank, "The ruddy *Kalahari* may dock at any moment . . . wish we could see the harbor from here . . . not that it would help."

The hours passed, the heat increased, the sun rose. Guy strode up and down, swearing. The soldiers scythed the long grass. At last, at one o'clock, the sergeant returned, running, to announce "Sah, ship at dock now!" An hour later two battered lorries ground up, loaded with tins of aviation fuel; then Guy, Frank, and the soldiers worked for another hour and a half filling the Buffalo's tanks.

Finally G-BGR stood ready, fully loaded. It was a few minutes before four in the afternoon, and a slow, wet, hot wind was blowing straight down the field from the sea.

"Estimated flight time to Natal is nineteen hours, ten minutes," Frank said. "If we take off now we should be landing about eleven in the morning Gambia time . . . ten, Natal time."

Guy followed Frank up the portable stepladder onto the wing, through the port, into the cockpit. Two soldiers followed, each carrying a starting handle. One by one the four engines coughed and sputtered to life, one by one the four propellers started to rotate. The soldiers pushed their starting handles back into the plane through the entry ports, and then clambered back to earth. Frank recovered and stowed the stepladder and closed and fastened the entry ports.

Guy said, "All ready?"

Frank tugged at his sleeve and pointed. A small old Rowland Ruby was puttering toward them across the field. It stopped beside the Buffalo and Dragee jumped out. He cupped his hands to his mouth and shouted something; but they could not hear against the thunder of the engines. Dragee dived back into his car and came out with a big notebook. He wrote in it, and held it up to them, close under the cockpit. Guy read aloud—"Alcock and Brown landed Ireland this a.m."

Guy raised a hand in acknowledgment, his lips tight. To hell with Alcock and Whitten Brown! He pushed the four throttle levers slowly, firmly forward. Buffalo G-BGR lumbered down the field, as ponderous as its namesake in the hot afternoon light. She's never going to get off, Guy thought grimly, his right hand pressed forward against the throttles, his left firm on the half-wheel of the control column . . . there must be something in heat and damp that made engines work less efficiently . . . it needed working out, scientifically, not this by-guess-and-by-God method . . . "56, sir," Frank shouted. That was takeoff speed at this weight . . . the end of the field was coming fast, marked by the sergeant at one side and a soldier at the other, "60," Frank said, " . . . 62 . . ." Guy eased the stick back and the Buffalo slowly, unwillingly, lifted off the ground on its 1,850-mile flight to Natal, Brazil . . . climbing heavy-laden now toward the brighter air of the sky, through a yellow band, through scattered playful little clouds, the sea below ironing out to a blue sheet, the palms and houses falling back . . . now only the sea.

"Phew!" Frank said, grinning at Guy. "Glad we had the grass cut."

Guy nodded. "Let's have some coffee, Frank. I was too busy on the checklist before we took off." They passed the Thermos back and forth; then settled down. The sun sank deliberately toward the sea. It was pleasant and cool at 8,000 feet, the engines thrumming, the big blades turning lazily, the air rushing past.

After an hour of silence, Guy said, "Frank, I love one woman, but feel it is my duty to marry another . . . who is also a very attractive, and good, lady. What should I do? Or should I not marry at all? I'm the Butcher, remember."

Frank's face showed his startled astonishment. The colonel was years younger than himself, but he was the colonel. He himself had told the colonel of Anne's unfaithfulness, but . . . this was different. He said at last, cautiously, "I suppose one is Lady Jarrow, sir."

Guy nodded, "Just as the *Daily Mail* trumpets. I've known her since we were children. I've always loved her, too, I realize now, though there has always been so much affection, as well, that I didn't know it until recently. But am I the right man for her, even if she'd have me? She likes the theatre . . . society, Ascot, the London season . . . all the things she didn't have as a child, but thought she was entitled to for being beautiful."

Frank said, "Why, sir, you could give her all those, with what you've done."

"I know," Guy said, his mouth grim, "but *I* don't like any of it . . . The other lady is Maria von Rackow, Werner's widow . . . *and* her baby. She had a boy on the 20th of May—and is calling it Guy."

"But you don't—er—love her?" Frank asked. "You can't have seen very much of her, can you?"

Guy said, "No, but isn't it my duty? I am Werner's reincarnation, as well as his executioner."

"I don't think any man should marry for a sense of duty, sir," Frank said energetically. "Except p'raps those blokes that get girls in the family way. But even then, it's not the right way to start off, is it?"

Guy said, "But perhaps it's duty that we're missing now. We had duty for four years, and now . . . it's gone. Everyone for himself. Fuck you Jack, I'm all right. I might be happier knowing that I had done my duty rather than doing what I wanted to do. I know plenty of people who are looking for happiness, at the expense of duty or responsibility . . . and do they find it? Never!"

"Wait a mo'!" Frank exclaimed, half-rising against his seat belt, and staring at the port pair of engines. "Revs irregular, pusher," he said. Guy could hear it now, and looking at the r.p.m. counter fixed to the inboard side of the strut by the engine, saw the needle wavering. Then Frank exclaimed, "She's leaking petrol, sir . . . quite a stream." Quickly Guy switched off that engine. A spray of petrol was still flying back over the cylinders and propeller boss, but the engine, thank God, had not caught fire, though it still might. They waited tensely, staring. The cylinders cooled fast in the rush of the cold air. At last Guy said, "Pheew! . . . It still might catch fire, but not very likely now." Seventeen hundred miles to go, speed down to eighty, and petrol being lost steadily . . . Alcock had already beaten him. Better turn back to Bathurst.

Frank had undone his seat belt and was taking off his flying boots and getting into a pair of thin rubber-soled gym shoes. Then he began to fasten himself into a sturdy webbing harness. The straps were four inches wide, with strong brass hook-and-eye fastenings. From the side of it dangled more webbing straps and hooks. Frank shouted, "I've always thought I might have to go out on the wing if we had engine trouble in flight. So I made this harness, and tested it out in secret, because I knew you'd say no . . . But it holds me safe. And I can take all the tools I need, and a spare timing arm, and a file in my pockets . . . Now sir, if you'll throttle back as slow as you can."

Guy stared at him. He was going to walk out on the wing, held against the slipstream by that harness attached to the struts. He could step on the walkway, as the fitters who started the engines on the ground had to; and the belt looked strong enough, but . . . 8,000 feet up! It would be wiser to turn back . . . Frank pleaded, "Don't turn back, sir! I want to make it just as much as you do . . . There's no danger. The gym shoes stick like gluc."

Guy made up his mind and put his hand to the throttles. Stalling air speed would be 45 with that dead propeller . . . he watched the needle circle round . . . 70 . . . 60 . . . 55 . . . that would do. She was like a lead balloon on the controls, but she wasn't heaving; the air was still and she'd make a good steady platform. "All right," he said. "Be careful."

Frank crawled back into the tunnel of the fuselage; for in the cockpit they were twelve feet out in front of the leading edge of the wings; and Guy did not see him until, leaning out, at last he saw Frank's arm and head appear out of the fuselage's port hatch. Reaching out from there, Frank hooked one of the loose straps of his harness round the nearest strut on that side. Once it was secure, Frank followed, standing upright, pulling himself forward by the harness until he reached the strut. Then he took the second loose strap, and working round the first strut, and reaching as far out as he could, fastened it round the second strut. There, held now by both extra straps to the second strut, he began to work with a screwdriver and spanner on the nacelle casing of the port pusher engine. The slipstream from the tractor engine ahead roared past him, tugging at his clothes . . . but his feet were secure, Guy thought, and that was the big danger. If they slipped out from under him he'd have the hell of a job getting back upright . . . He had the aluminum casing open; it suddenly blew away on the wind and vanished astern . . . no great harm done . . . the propeller of the dead engine was windmilling gently, the cylinders spitting oil. Frank was feeling in his pocket, pulling out something—a roll of adhesive tape. He was leaning into the engine, working with both hands, braced against the cylinders. Guy couldn't see what he was doing, but could guess—sealing a break in a fuel line with the adhesive tape; the jarring of an aeroplane in flight was always cracking or breaking the rigid metal tubing, usually where it connected with another part of the machine . . . Frank was turning, one thumb raised. Done! He made a motion of starting the propeller and Guy thought, is that safe? If he slips he's so damned close to that pusher . . . but Frank was right; there was less danger than in him coming back, and then going out again if the trouble hadn't been cured. He switched on. The windmilling propeller dragged in fuel, the spark fired it, and the exhausts puffed out dense blue smoke. The engine whirled into life, and Guy at once throttled back. Frank waved, and, as carefully as before, made his slow way back to the cockpit. Guy waited until Frank crawled out of the fuselage and took his place in the other seat. There he sat silent for a long time, until Guy said, "That was a good job, Frank . . . You all right?"

"Yes, sir. Just thinking." Ahead, gathering blackish clouds blocked the south-western horizon. To the west, the same layer of cloud glowed blood red from the sun setting behind it. Frank said, "I think I'll have a tot of rum, sir."

"Of course."

Frank found his flask and took a small swig. Holding the flask in his hand he said, and his voice was puzzled—"You know what I was thinking about out there, sir? Not when I was working—on the way out and back, with the sea all that way down below, and the wind trying to pull me off . . . I was thinking of Anne, and my kids . . ." His voice grew very intense—"And I was thinking of Anne's new baby. I haven't thought of any of them for months . . . since I knew about it. What does that mean, sir?"

Guy watched the sun as it seemed to dive in toward the sea, so rapidly did it pass through the cloud layer; compass bearing south-west by south; all instruments reading normal. They'd have some rough weather during the night, but she was a good machine. He said, "It means you love them all. And want to go back to them."

It was full dark when Frank spoke, nearly a quarter of an hour later—"You're right," he said, his voice choking—"Poor Anne."

"Poor Frank," Guy said softly. "It's all over now though—war and all."

* * * *

Thursday, June 19

At almost the same hour, allowing for the difference in time zones, Billy Bidford was driving his Sunbeam across the Golden Horn, by the Bridge of Boats, into Constantinople; while Guy Rowland was bringing G-BGR in to land at the Argentine Army airfield outside Buenos Aires, to be greeted by a huge crowd, mostly of the British colony; but also containing many Argentine officials, ambassadors, consuls, and common people. G-BGR had covered the 8,349 air miles in 85 hours 14 minutes flying time, spread over eight flying days.

* * * *

Saturday, June 21

On this day Guy Rowland received a cable from Florinda, Marchioness of Jarrow—CONGRATULATIONS COME HOME QUICKLY. In Buenos

Aires Guy read it, scrumpled up the paper, and threw it into the corner of the big hotel room, where it fell among a huge pile of similar cables and telegrams; he rang the bell for service and said, "Another bottle of champagne . . . whass your name? Manuel? Pedro?"

"*En seguida, señor,*" the waiter said, disappearing. Guy's head slumped onto the table, and he began to snore. Frank Stratton came through the open door from his connecting room in the suite, stopped, stared sadly, and returned to his room.

*   *   *   *

Wednesday, June 25

At noon, Guy and Frank were making ready to board the Royal Mail Steam Packet vessel *Andorra*, bound for England. Buffalo G-BGR was being flown to another base by pilots of the Argentine Army, which had bought it with the intention of buying half a dozen more, and using the big bombers in their next border dispute with Chile. Guy was drinking champagne before setting out to the docks. He was not drunk this time, nor was he euphoric, just morose. What the hell was the good of champagne and brandy if they didn't make you feel better, forget things, solve problems?

There was a knock on the door and Guy said curtly, "Come!"

The hotel manager entered, bowing—"Sir," he said. "The British Ambassador is here. He wishes to see you, and Mr Stratton."

"Show him in," Guy said. "Frank! Big cheese to see us. Come through."

The manager re-entered with the ambassador. He had been at the airfield, and seemed a decent enough old stick, Guy thought; but he wanted to get off, to the ship, to his berth, to sleep.

The manager went out, closing the door behind him. The ambassador said, "I have a message from His Majesty's Private Secretary . . . It is personal and for the moment, its contents must remain secret."

He paused impressively. Get on with it, Guy thought. The King had probably sent a message of congratulations; Billy was probably getting one, too, in Constantinople.

The ambassador said, "His Majesty wishes to invest you both with the honour of Knighthood in the Order of the British Empire, as he has done to Captain Alcock and Lieutenant Whitten Brown. Before any announcement is made, I am instructed to ascertain that you will both accept."

Guy shrugged, "Delighted . . . an honour."

Frank's jaw had dropped, and his eyes were popping out of his head. He stammered, "Me? Sir Frank? . . . Oh no, sir! I'm a mechanic. I don't want to be a knight. I'd feel real daft!"

"His Majesty knighted both members of the other crew," the ambassador said.

"Yes," Frank broke in, "but Mr Whitten Brown's an officer. You can't knight a *sergeant!*"

The ambassador said, "His Majesty can dub or ennoble anyone he chooses, Mr Stratton"; and Guy said, "Accept it, Frank. If you don't, I won't."

Frank turned on him, beseeching—"Oh, please sir, don't say that. We'll all be so proud of you, but it's different for me. You *know* it is."

"Times are changing," Guy said. "They *have* changed. The war saw to that. If you've done the job, you should get the reward, whatever your rank or station. And you're not a sergeant, you're a civilian."

Frank said, "Some other time, perhaps, next century perhaps, if they still have knights by then. Some other bloke, perhaps . . . but not me. I'd feel like a proper twerp, people calling me Sir Frank, with my head inside an engine and oil all over my face. No, sir, I don't want it, and Anne would feel worse . . . *Lady* Stratton! Why, the other women would be laughing at her up their sleeves every time she went out."

Guy said at last, "All right, Frank. But you *are* a ruddy knight, even without the K—a *preux chevalier* . . . I suppose Frank will get a C.B.E.?"

The ambassador nodded, "That is what I was advised, if . . . as the Private Secretary's cable put it—either of you did not think the knighthood appropriate."

"All right, then," Frank said, albeit still grudgingly. "I'll be a C.B.E. Thanks."

"Thank His Majesty."

The manager appeared, bearing another bottle of champagne. The ambassador said, "A toast, Sir Guy, and Mr Stratton . . . The King! God bless him!"

Daily Telegraph, Monday, June 30, 1919

SIGNATURE OF THE PEACE TREATY
AT VERSAILLES

GREAT CEREMONY

From Perceval Landon. *Versailles,* Saturday.
The treaty is signed. After seven months of labour and anxiety unspeakable the great work of human regeneration which the Allies set before themselves in 1914 had been accomplished. Militarism,

with all its disciplined brutality and unbridled lust of conquest, is at an end. At an end, too, is the German Empire. The world looks forward from today not only to a full generation of peace but to the hope of rising, during that generation, to a higher place, and, so far as human effort can attain that end, looks forward to the end of warfare itself. The signature of the terms of peace in the "Hall of Mirrors" at Versailles today marks the close of an epoch as clearly and as certainly as did Wolsey's great puppet show of the Field of the Cloth of Gold . . .

AT THE SIGNING OF PEACE
KING AND PEOPLE

Peace is signed.

The greatest war in history is over.

I join you all in giving thanks to God.

These "straight-flung words and few," uttered by the King from the balcony of Buckingham Palace, formed the climax of a great and memorable scene on Saturday . . .

Over, Gate repeated to himself. In France, and Belgium, Mesopotamia and Palestine, East Africa, Roumania, Italy, Austria, Russia . . . but not in Ireland. Nevertheless, the greater cloud had lifted. During the war he had felt tied to Walstone, to the people of the village, to the land itself. Now the war was over; he had much less land; and his responsibilities as squire seemed to have diminished— the people wanted to look after themselves, and were doing so. So he could get away for a time. He must take a holiday. The South of France? . . . not in the middle of the summer . . . Norway, Sweden, Finland perhaps, to see Lapps and reindeer? But it was impossible to think of such a journey without Isabel. He would not enjoy himself because he would be thinking of her, what she would have said, what she would have done.

What he must do, instead of taking a holiday, was to make another determined effort to find Margaret, tell her his situation, and beg her to divorce him. The first step was to send her a message through the Agony columns of the *Irish Times*. She would see the message herself; or others would pass it on to her. And he must go to Ireland, and stay until he had seen her.

He returned to the *Telegraph*.

And yet there was no sense of rejoicing in the Galerie des Glaces; there was scarcely even a deep feeling of relief. Only the night before last the President of the United States had well said that whatever had been accomplished, there remained still more to do.

Dublin: Friday, July 4, 1919

25 "We will have nothing to do with Dominion Home Rule, or any other Home Rule . . . We avoid it as a thing unclean, we fling it back at them . . ." Christopher Cate read on gloomily, the *Irish Times* reporting a speech made by Sir Edward Carson, the leading Ulster "Covenanter," the day before; but a couple of days before that J.L. Garvin, in the *Observer*, had written that the Covenanters' policy of "won't have it" was as dead as King William, and that the small Protestant minority had no right to stand for ever blocking the unification of Ireland, perhaps in some form of separate Dominion status subservient to a free Dublin. But . . .

The telephone rang and Cate hurried to the desk and lifted up the receiver. A man's voice said, "Is this the party that was advertising in the *Irish Times* to get in touch with Mrs Margaret Cate?"

Cate said, "Yes. I'm her husband," thanking heaven as he did so that he had booked himself into the most modern hotel in Dublin, and perhaps the only one that had telephones installed in all its rooms.

The voice, which was that of an educated man, for all its slight brogue, said, "And what would be your purpose in wishing to see the Lady?"

Cate knew, from the papers, that Margaret had long been called the Lady among Irish revolutionaries of all shades, so he said, "I wish to marry another lady, and propose to ask Margaret to divorce me." He was tempted to give more details, in the hope of persuading Margaret to come to a meeting; but he had no guarantee that this caller was not in fact an agent of the Irish police, of Scotland Yard, or of M.I.

442

5. Margaret was wanted by practically all the law enforcement and intelligence agencies of the Crown, for one reason or another.

The man on the telephone was silent for a few moments, then said, "Ah, personal."

"Yes."

"Well, I'll get the message to her. You understand that it will take some arranging to keep any meeting free of the R.I.C., or G Branch of the Dublin Police . . ."

"I understand," Cate said, thinking, of course, this may be G Branch speaking.

". . . which means time. How long will you be in Dublin?"

"As long as necessary. This is a matter of the greatest importance to me. Do please impress that on Mrs Cate . . . And tell her, in case she may not have heard, that Stella—that's our daughter—went to America in April with her husband. They are now living in Arizona, among the Navajo Indians. I can give her the address if she wants it."

"Very well, sir . . . I hope you will hear from your wife, through us. But that's up to her, you understand."

"I understand," Cate said again. The man at the other end hung up. Cate followed suit. How long, O Lord, how long?

*　　*　　*　　*

Margaret sat alone in a little back room with Michael Collins, their revolvers on the table, loaded, and two sawn-off shotguns propped against the walls close to hand. These were not loaded, but a bag of 12-bore cartridges, No. 3 shot, hung over the back of Collins's chair.

"It can't be helped," he said quietly. "It was just a mistake."

"Don't say you can't make an omelette without breaking eggs," Margaret Cate said. "If I've had that said to me once, it's been said a hundred times."

"It's true, even so," Collins said. "But this time it's fairer to say that we all make mistakes sometimes. British secret agents have shot three of their own supporters, to my certain knowledge."

"But I was positive it was Loughran, the informer," Margaret said. "I *couldn't* be mistaken."

"Well, you were, and it was poor Mr Ryan of Kilkenny, visiting his sister in Dublin, that got shot. He died for Ireland, though he didn't know it. He knows now." He crossed himself with real reverence.

Margaret said, "Is there no hope for some middle way? You know, I felt the same as you do . . . but since last Friday, I can't live with myself. There *must* be another way."

"Moderation is . . ." Collins stopped, searching for the right word—"I was going to say it's useless, but the truth is that it's irrelevant."

"Only as long as we—you, your wing of the Volunteers—go on murdering police—Catholics, Irishmen—and the British answer with more repression, more martial law, and God knows what next . . . it's irrelevant—but what if we stop, negotiate?"

"Then you'll be the ones we'll be killing," Collins said grimly. "Ours is the only way. Believe me. You *did* believe me—you're my best right hand, because you understood and had the guts to come and shoot . . . so many of the blatherskites just talk talk talk . . . I'm not giving guns to anyone unless they take the bloody things and *shoot* . . . If the British had any sense they'd go softly, understanding what the people are thinking, how their loyalties are torn. The Church thunders against our killings, at the same time prays for freedom for Ireland. The people would listen to the Church, turn against us, if they were given half a chance . . . So what do the British do? Suppress this, abolish that, arrest everyone in sight. If the people have to choose between us, for all our killings—and systematic, universal British oppression, there's not much doubt which way they'll go . . . especially if we can frighten them more effectively than the British can."

"How long will it last?" Margaret said. "It's getting like the war, going on forever . . . killing, killing."

"A long time," Collins said flatly. "The British aren't called bulldogs for nothing. But the time will come when even they will realize that they can't win here . . ."

"Then the real fight will begin," Margaret said. "Irishman against Irishman."

"If it comes to that, so be it," Collins said. "We're going to make an independent Irish republic, encompassing all Ireland, whatever it costs . . . You've got to get out of Dublin. G Branch have learned that you were the flower seller on O'Connell Street who shot Mr Ryan."

"I'm leaving tomorrow," Margaret said. "As a Red Cross matron with some nurses—all Auxiliaries, of course."

"Where to?"

"Westport, in Mayo. There are half a dozen good men there, who spent the war running out information and supplies to German submarines. They're itching to get back into action . . . the British Navy caught one of their skiffs late in '18 and sank it, killing all four men on board."

"I remember."

"Well, they want their own back. I'll arrange it."

"Good . . . What about that message from your husband?"

444

Margaret said, "I don't know. If it was anyone else but Christopher he'd just set the other woman up as his mistress."

"It won't be easy to arrange a meeting, with the R.I.C. so stirred up about the killing of Mr Ryan . . . but it can be done. I'll guarantee that if he comes it'll just be him, no police or agents . . . and no one'll know where he's gone either."

She stood, undecided. At last she muttered, "It's so damned unimportant . . . so far away . . . unreal . . . Leave it for the time being. He said he'd wait as long as he had to. I'll send a message from Freeport, in about ten days."

*   *   *   *

Margaret, dressed in trousers and a light grey shirt, a man's peaked cloth cap pulled down over her hair, followed Sean and Eamonn along the rough track leading to the cliffs. If she were interrogated now there would be no hope of escaping recognition; women in Ireland did not wear trousers except on some dangerous and illegal mission such as this.

Sean, close in front of her, threw over his shoulder, "There's Clare Island, out in the bay, see? Five miles from shore . . . The U-boats used to lie up in the lee there, and we'd be fishing on the island, with our boats pulled up and out of sight in the rocks. Then we'd row out to them . . . spend half an hour on board, down inside . . . they had some good gin, those German skippers . . . schnapps, they called it."

They paused at the poor fields marking the edge of Clew Bay. Dry stone walls divided the little patches of cultivation one from another; and another wall ran along the top of the low cliffs, leaving room for a rough stony track, twenty feet wide, for ox carts and jaunting cars.

Eamonn said, "The constables patrol this regularly. They might be on their way now, but we'd know because . . . see that little bothy up there? My uncle lives there and he has nothing better to do than work in the cabbage patch out front, and if he sees anything along the coast, he hangs a length of peat over the way to dry . . . There's no peat there now, so . . . The constables are from Westport. They use bicycles, for they've a powerful long stretch to cover from outside Westport to Killary Harbour."

"Why do they patrol at all, when the war's over?"

Sean chuckled, "Smuggling, Lady . . . trawlers up from France with perfumes and brandy and silk stockings, though precious few of the colleens round here would be seen in them—the marks of a whoor, they think . . . Right after the armistice they did catch some arms . . . German machine guns for the Volunteers that had been transferred to a Dutch ship and no one really knew what to do . . . so the R.I.C. got 'em . . ."

Margaret stood, rubbing her cheek in thought, staring out over the heaving sea. It had been blowing hard from the west for two days and the sea was a tumble of grey-green water and white foam under low, hurrying clouds. She said, "Is there any way we could get more than two?"

It was Eamonn's turn to scratch his head—"Well . . . we've never seen more'n just the pair . . . there's ten of 'em in the barracks at Westport, that do this patrol, the same pair for a week at a time, as far as I can make out . . . and once a week they have to do it twice in the day—they choose their own day for that."

"What about today?"

"They've been round once . . . can't say whether they might make today the day for the second patrol. It's getting late."

Margaret said, "Suppose we let them learn that some more arms are coming in, one day . . . or that I am to attend a Volunteer meeting."

Eamonn nodded—"If they thought you were going to be there, Lady, they'd bring up a battalion."

"No," Margaret said. "They'd want to keep all the glory for themselves. Especially if the information reached them late enough so that they couldn't get reinforcements. If it were a question of just getting together whatever men they have on the spot and rushing out there, how many would it be?"

Sean said, "A sergeant and ten."

"And we're seven, with me."

"You mustn't come out, Lady."

"I'm coming, and I shall be in command," she said briefly. "Now, what night?"

"We could do it the second night from now," Sean said. "But how do we let the sergeant know?"

"Don't they have any spies in town?" she asked. "You must know who they are."

Sean nodded—"We know two for sure."

"But they don't know you know?"

Both men shook their heads.

"Tell one, then, under oath of secrecy, that . . ."

*   *   *   *

It was a dark night, the moon hidden by clouds, rain falling intermittently in warm, slashing showers from the invisible sea—invisible, but fully known to the nostrils from the reek of the piled seaweed along

446

the rocks, the smell of tar from fishing boats hauled up above the high-tide mark along the strand . . .

Margaret waited with the six Volunteers from Westport. They'd be outnumbered if the whole eleven of the R.I.C. came, but she didn't think they would. The sergeant would have to leave at least one to answer the telephone and take urgent messages; and probably another to keep him company—and one was ill with flu. So she would probably face eight—almost equal numbers; but the Volunteers were in position and they had two Lewis guns, which had spent the last six months buried under floorboards in cottages in Westport, waiting for just such a night as this; and two men, both ex-Lewis gunners with Irish regiments on the Western Front, who knew how to use them.

She waited, tranquilly. Peace had returned to her soul since she came to Westport, and the sea. Dublin was not a good place for a revolutionary; one thought too much, worried too much; there were libraries and books and courts and churches everywhere to confuse one's directions. As soon as she arrived here she felt that the wind had blown the cobwebs out of her mind; and all she saw was the land, the bare rock and tilled earth and purple heather of Ireland . . . and on that harsh soil, against that unforgiving sea, the people bent, struggling . . . only the distant sound of a church bell, borne down on the wind from Killary Harbour, disturbed her. As to Christopher—she would not see him, or send any message. He was irrelevant.

Sean, beside her, said, "They'll have left the barracks by now . . . Sergeant Doyle's no fool. He'll come on cautiously . . . and from both directions."

Margaret said, "We're ready for them, however they come. Go round and remind them all again that when I fire the Very light, they are to disperse, as planned . . . it doesn't matter if we haven't killed them all . . . though I think we will . . . And Sergeant Doyle will surely have telephoned for reinforcements as soon as he got the information . . . so more may be coming, later, and our men have to be reminded to look out for them."

"They've all been told," Sean said.

"People forget things when they're excited," Margaret said. "Particularly Irishmen."

Sean disappeared silently into the darkness. The clouds seemed to be dispersing, and some stars appearing, shedding a faint light over the still land and the heaving sea. Margaret sighed contentedly; this was better; her men, hidden among the rock walls, invisible against their background, would have a little light to aim by.

A Lewis gunner, ensconced beside her in the corner of a wall, big rocks hiding them from directly in front, muttered, "Someone coming, Lady."

"How many?" she whispered.

"One," he said, ". . . if he's got a gun he's holding it low . . . can't see it against the stars . . . he's gone."

"Wait, wait," she whispered. "He's a scout . . ."

A heavy explosion rocked the air and seemed to shudder in the ground immediately beneath her where she knelt by the wall. The Lewis gunner muttered—"Can't see the fellow now . . . must'a ducked down when he heard the bang. What was it?"

Behind them someone was moaning in pain, trying to suppress it but unable to do so. Another explosion roared out in the night, with a momentary flash of orange flame. "Grenades," Margaret said.

"The R.I.C. don't use 'em much," the gunner muttered.

A stream of machine-gun bullets ripped down the track in front of them, some ricocheting off the walls, others striking sparks from stones and then leaping toward the sky with a clatter and a whine.

Another machine gun opened up from behind—her other Lewis, Margaret thought. The gunner beside her opened fire suddenly, sending short hiccoughing bursts down the track. "Saw something move," he shouted to her above the rattle of his own gun.

A voice from the darkness called, "Sean? How do you like it now?"

He was answered by a few single shots from a revolver. The speaker chuckled—"Missed!"

The Lewis gunner said, "That's Lynch . . . recognize his voice anywhere."

The voice cried, "There's me and my father and uncle, me brother, and three cousins here, Sean . . . and these are for the other three brothers you dirty bastards sent to the bottom in the *Leinster*." Four grenades exploded one after the other among the walls behind them, followed at once by screams, gasps, curses.

Sean the gunner said, "I don't think the constables have got here yet, though they'll be coming as fast as they can, 'cause they'll hear the shooting."

Eamonn came, crawling, his face a mask of blood—"They got us, from behind . . ." he coughed, "and now the R.I.C's coming to finish us off."

Margaret thought, we must charge; they are no more than we are, and we must get away before the R.I.C. come. She leaped to her feet, to be struck at once by a savage blow in the stomach and another in the chest. The force of the bullets hurled her back four feet against the stone wall where she lay, crumpled, on her back, blood filling her mouth and lungs.

From a mile away she heard Eamonn say, "Christ! Lady's hit . . . Paddy, pick her up . . . Drag her, drag her . . . they mustn't know they got her."

"I'm . . . I'm . . ." she gurgled through the blood.

They were dragging her, her feet sliding over the grass, over the pebbles, to the steep path down the cliff, to the sand, hitting rocks, bouncing off, to the sea, her feet wet and cold in the sea, under the vagrant stars, clouds sliding over again, darkness containing the stars, to the boat. They dragged her over the gunwale into the coracle, and jumped in after her, Eamonn bleeding, Sean the gunner rowing strong, for he was untouched. Behind them Margaret Cate stared at the dark sky, eyes wide open, seeing nothing.

*　　*　　*　　*

The guard at the window said, " 'Tis a priest, general . . . They'll search him downstairs, but he looks . . . well, like a priest, bejasus."

Collins frowned. He did not approve of blasphemy. He said, "You've never seen him before?"

"No."

"Then how did he find his way here?"

"Sure, and how should I know? Wherever he came from, it was a long way, and in the bogs . . . there's mud and peat on his shoes, and shameful old trousers sticking out from under the cassock . . . I can't see him any more—they've let him in."

Collins waited. His quick mind, searching the past week or two, had already come to the conclusion that the priest's visit—especially if he was from the countryside—was connected with Lady's death. From outside the door a low voice called, "There's a priest come to see you, general. Won't give his name or say where he's from. He has no weapons."

"Let him in."

The door opened and the priest came in, a man of medium height with a very Irish face, a long mobile upper lip, bright blue eyes, about forty, but looked older, yet serene.

He said now, "I do have a weapon, general . . . my crucifix." He held it up deprecatingly from where it hung on the chest of his black cassock. "May I speak to you alone?"

Collins stared a few moments, wondering. Was it a trap? But if he was unarmed . . . and the house was full of his men, all armed . . . He said, "All right. Wait outside, Mick . . . and don't listen at the door." The guard nodded and strolled out, putting his pistol, which he had been carrying negligently in his hand, into the pocket of his old tweed coat.

As soon as the door had closed behind him the priest said, "I believe you were visited by Cathal Donoghue from Westport a few days ago."

Collins nodded. His guess had been correct; Donoghue was the man from Westport, who'd found his way up through the channels of the extremist Volunteers to tell him that Margaret Cate was dead, and buried; but that so far only he, two others, and a priest knew it. Margaret had been killed, apparently, in an internecine feud caused by the fact that two Westport families—Sinn Feiners but not Volunteers—had lost three sons in the torpedoing of the Irish packet boat *Leinster* shortly before the end of the war; and of course had held the men who had been supplying U-boats to blame.

The priest said, "I am Father Caffin."

Collins exclaimed, "Are you Padraic's brother, that was shot after the Rising?"

The priest nodded and said, "I served in France as padre to the 1st Battalion the Weald Light Infantry. Their C.O. was a man called Quentin Rowland, and I soon learned that Margaret Cate, the Lady, was his sister."

"Are you for us or against us?" Collins broke in roughly.

"I am for Sinn Fein—ourselves alone, one Ireland, independent, united. I am not for murder . . . on any grounds, for any reason."

Collins said at last, "That's your right, father. We don't have the privilege of choice."

The priest said, "Colonel Rowland told me that his brother-in-law, Margaret's husband, had heard nothing from her for a long time. And that he—Cate—has for years been desperate to marry another lady. But he could not, because she was still alive, and had not committed adultery, that could be proved."

"She hadn't, at all," Collins said shortly. "She wasn't that sort."

"I buried her," the priest said. "On the Island of Inishturk, in Clew Bay, where two of the Volunteers took her. One has since died of his wounds. Now only four men know that she is dead—myself, and the other Volunteer, Cathal Donoghue, and you."

Collins said, "They did good work, great work, to bury her without anyone knowing. Why had they to bring in a priest? . . . Sorry, father, but it is absolutely necessary for our cause that the British continue to believe she is alive. Her name is worth a thousand men . . . The Lady, the woman they can not catch . . . the Will of the Wisp . . . the Angel of Death, for them . . ."

The priest said, "It is wrong that Mr Cate and the woman he wishes to marry should suffer for such reasons, born of hatred."

Collins said angrily, "Anyone who publishes the fact that the Lady is dead will be punished."

The priest said, "That is a pity, general. The green flag can not stand much more Irish blood on it, shed by other Irish, without bearing the stains for ever . . . I am now going to the hotel where I have reason to believe that Mr Cate is still waiting for an answer from Mrs Cate to his plea. Good day, and may God bless you and forgive you your sins, as I pray that He will forgive mine."

He turned and went out, without looking back.

Collins went to the door and watched him go down the stairs. The guard was there, five feet away, leaning against the wall. Mick was a man who didn't give a damn for the Church, or priests.

He said in a low voice, "That priest's going to the British. Stop him!"

At this the guard looked up, touching the pistol butt in his pocket. Collins nodded and the guard said, "Better wait till dark, general. The people won't stand by when a priest falls."

"It doesn't matter! Get him!" Collins cried in a hoarse, low, agonized whisper that could not be heard above the thud of the outer door being shut. The guard started down the stairs. When he was near the bottom Collins cried in a terrible voice, "Stop! What am I doing? No, no, no!" He made the sign of the cross and bowed his head a moment, praying; then went back into his room.

Daily Telegraph, Monday, July 14, 1919

NEW BEER ORDER

The Food Controller has made an order amending the Beer (Prices and Description) Order, and fixing a maximum price of 2d a pint in a public bar for any beer sold below 1020 deg. The maximum price of this beer was formerly 3d.

Other alterations in the order provide that beer of any price must now be of a greater strength than previously, e.g. a beer at 5d a pint in a public bar will now be of a gravity 4 deg. higher than before, and the same applies to the other prices. This is in accordance with the decision of the Cabinet that brewers must give better quality for the same money instead of further taxation being imposed on them. The order takes effect on Aug. 1.

Stronger beer at the Arms, Cate thought, that'll please our many beer drinkers. They'd been complaining bitterly since 1914 that they didn't mind any other sacrifice for victory, but why did the beer have to taste like dishslops? P.C. Fulcher might have to deal with a few more drunks on Saturday nights from the stronger beer, but they'd probably be visitors from London. The men of Walstone knew how to hold their beer.

He put the paper aside and read the letter from John Merritt for the third time. John had written the letter, and Stella had added a postscript about how the countryside was impressing her—the silence, the distances, the pale gold and yellow and red of the earth, the upthrusts of rock—mostly places sacred to the Navajo. She could not, or would not have written so much, or so lucidly, three months ago. John was more matter-of-fact, and dealt more with the people than with the land. "I am enjoying my work here," he wrote, "because I am learning—the language, which is very difficult for me; the religion; the customs and manners; the working of the economy; above all, the way of life. I doubt if I shall enjoy myself much longer, as I disagree with the Indian Service's policy toward the Navajo. I am continually having arguments—fights you could call them—with the Agent here over programmes, policies, and people. One day they will throw me out, or I will get out myself. But we will not leave the Navajo. Or the Hopi, whose reservation is entirely surrounded by the Navajos'. They are a very different people—inward-turned, while the Navajo look out; peaceful and pacifist where the Navajo are warlike in their hearts . . ."

Cate read on, finally putting the letter aside and pulling toward him a rolled blueprint. He unrolled it and began to study it carefully. It was the final plan for the Walstone War Memorial—a simple obelisk in local stone, a sword carved in bas-relief on one face, the hilt garlanded with laurel; on either side the dates 1914–1918; and on the other side of the obelisk the names of the fourteen men of Walstone who had been killed in the war. It was very simple, because Walstone could not afford anything more elaborate; nor would that be proper: remembrance should be austere.

The names on the back were pencilled in, on the blueprint; the official list was pinned to one side. There, in his place in alphabetical order, was *CATE L.H., Lieut.; Weald L.I.* But Laurence had been cashiered, and shot by a firing squad for desertion in the face of the enemy. Was it right that he should be remembered with these others who had died doing their duty? He ought to cross Laurence's name out. He wouldn't have to say anything. They'd understand. Just cross it off.

Laurence had died doing his best. It was a tragedy that his best was not enough, in war. But he had tried, and suffered—far more, and worse, for months, before the firing squad relieved him of his misery. Let the name stand; and be remembered.

Garrod came in with a pink telegraph form. "The boy just rode up with it," she said. "He's waiting in case you want to send a reply."

Cate ripped open the envelope and read aloud: OF COURSE ARRANGE WEDDING SOONEST CATCHING FIRST BOAT LOVE LOVE LOVE ISABEL.

Cate leaped to his feet with a yell and, grabbing Garrod by the shoulders, swung her round the table in a waltz, finally kissing her roundly on the lips. Tears were in her eyes as she gasped, "Oh sir, oh sir, how happy we are!"

Cate felt in his breast pocket and found his wallet. "Here," he said, "give the boy this . . . They used to execute the bearer of bad news, so the bearer of good news ought to get his desserts, too."

"Five pounds!" Garrod gasped, tucking up her now disheveled grey hair under her white maid's cap—"Well, all the other boys will be touching him for luck, when they hear of this!"

Cologne, Paris, London:
August, 1919

26 The 1st Battalion, the Weald Light Infantry, was parading through Cologne, in honor of Minden Day, every man wearing a red rose tucked into the right side of the chinstrap of his peaked cap—for steel helmets were no longer worn on ceremonial occasions: the Germans no longer needed reminding that there was a war on, for with the signing of the peace treaties in May, it was over.

The colonel led the parade, followed by the adjutant, both with swords drawn; then A and B Companies; then the Colours, carried by two 2nd lieutenants, with an escort of two sergeants with fixed bayonets, but the scabbards still on the bayonets so that the fluttering Colours would not be ripped by naked steel; then C and D Companies, and finally the battalion's 2nd-in-command, and the R.S.M.

Sergeant Fagioletti, M.M., and a private soldier, the former wielding a swagger cane, the latter a short heavy club, marched fast along the sidewalk behind the spectators. The roadway had been cleared by the German police fifteen minutes ago, and the sidewalks were crowded with Germans, perforce spectators of the parade. Fagioletti and the soldier kept level with the waving Colours; and most German men took off their hats as the Colours passed. They had been raised in a militaristic country and they knew that that was an honour due to them. Some did not raise their hats, and here Fagioletti tipped their hats off their heads with a quick flick of his swagger cane. When the man turned angrily round, to see who had done it, he was confronted by the private soldier, the club rested on his shoulder and a cold look in his eye.

454

This was being done on the direct orders of Regimental Sergeant Major Bolton. "These buggers know they're supposed to salute Colours," he'd said, the points of his waxed mustache twitching. "And they're bloody well going to salute ours, just the way they'd make us salute theirs, if they'd won. Besides, Minden is only a hundred miles away, the colonel says, and then they were on our side . . . So, don't let anyone get away with anything."

Fagioletti didn't have to tip off many hats. The regiment was popular in Cologne; fraternization had become a way of life, as the German economy grew worse. The naval blockade had finally been lifted, but irreparable damage had been done to the health of most of the children, and the minds of most of the adults. The conquering nations had won the war, but were now hard and successfully at work losing the peace.

The battalion dismissed on the barrack square, and as the Colour escort marched the Colours off to the Officers' Mess, where they were kept, Fagioletti walked to his married quarter . . . What would Ethel want him to try today? Yesterday it was some bloody stuff she'd made him drink. It tasted so awful he'd had to rush to the bathroom and be sick. She'd never get a baby from a man who was busy sicking his guts out. Day before he had to fuck her from behind, like a dog; and she'd stayed on the bed for an hour afterwards, her bare arse stuck up in the air, mumbling some sort of prayer or magic. And sometimes he had to rub his prick and her cunt with butter, and put on a green shirt before beginning to fuck . . . And whenever there was a thunderstorm she'd grab his hand, even in the middle of breakfast, and drag him upstairs, and wait till the lightning was flashing and the thunder crashing all round the house, then shriek, "Now, now, Niccolo!" like a mad woman, her legs round his neck . . . Another time she'd set the alarm for midnight, and he'd had to do it three times before one o'clock in the morning, holding a big chunk of seaweed; God knew where she'd got that from, but it smelled horrible. The whole house smelled pretty funny, come to that, with the things she was cooking up for him, or her, or both of them to drink, facing east, one foot on a bed . . .

She was waiting for him at the door, her arms out, face up for a kiss. "Everything go off all right?" she asked.

" 'Course," he said. "I knocked a dozen caps and hats off . . . didn't have any fights. Brennan's a big man and that was a big club he was carrying . . . What's for dinner?"

"Spaghetti and meat," she said. "Bolognese."

He rubbed his hands—"Good! You're learning . . . But don't go putting any of your potions into the meat sauce, now."

Her face fell. "There's a little special stuff in it, dear. Probyn's Woman said to be sure to give it you every Friday in August . . ."

"What's in it?"

"I can't tell you. It's a secret."

Mama mia, he thought, it'll be frogs' eyes, and cats' livers . . .

"You won't be able to taste it, I promise . . . There's a bottle of beer in the larder for you."

"German beer? I'd rather have some wine. German wine's not bad."

She went out, returning soon with a bottle of white wine and a glass. "Sit down, dear . . . drink up . . . I'll have some too. This is my first Minden Day with the regiment."

"Didn't know you were becoming so G.S.," he said. "I remember when you wouldn't 'a given a fig for the regiment."

"Ah, but that was before you became a soldier—a real soldier. And now you're going to stay on, as a Regular . . . so it's my life, isn't it, as well as yours?"

"Suppose so," Fagioletti said, drinking some wine. "Who'd 'a thought it would ever come to this . . . Sergeant and Mrs Fagioletti!"

"Sergeant Major soon."

"Not a hope yet. Too many sergeants senior to me soldiering on. It's not so easy to get jobs back home as they thought, when they was all so eager to get demobbed."

"Perhaps the battalion will go to India."

"No, the 2nd battalion's there," he said. "We'll stay back till they come home . . . but *I* might be sent out to them. There might be a vacancy for a C.S.M. out there. But I don't *want* to go to India. In your brother Fred's last letter he said it was 121 in the shade where he is, in Hassanpore . . . only there isn't no shade. An' if I went out p'raps Fred would be my company commander. Don't know 'ow you'd like that."

He drank again. Ethel watched him and when he had drunk about a third of the bottle touched his sleeve and whispered, "Let's go up-stairs . . ."

He said, "You'll kill me, Ethel." But his body was responding to her invitation; and in a moment he followed her up the stairs.

Later that day, when Fagioletti was out on the sports field, playing soccer with men of his platoon, Ethel was receiving three other women in her front parlor. One was the wife of another sergeant, one of a corporal, and one of a long-service private: very few private soldiers were eligible for married quarters, but this one was.

The sergeant's wife said, "We all have the same problem, Mrs Fagioletti. We found out about it by accident. Mrs Palmer 'ere caught me crying when she came over to borrow a cup of sugar, that's the truth . . . and Mrs Jones was with me, chatting, like . . . so it all came out. That was months ago, soon after we was allowed out to join our 'usbands . . . It's money, Mrs Fagioletti. Our 'usbands don't give us enough of their pay to run the house properly. An' we all got kids . . ."

"I haven't," Ethel said sadly.

"Oh, you will, you will, Mrs Fagioletti, we're all praying for you . . . So, we talked round and round and up and down, but our 'usbands get angry, really lose their tempers, if we say anything to them, so . . . we come to you."

Ethel thought, to me? Why me? How can I help? No one's ever come to me for anything before: I've always been told what to do, by Mother, or Father, or her brothers, even Ruthie, and finally by her husband.

The corporal's wife answered her unspoken question—"Everyone respects you, Mrs Fagioletti . . . and your husband. We all know what he did in the war, and you . . . you haven't been out here long, but you're kind, you listen. We 'oped you would speak to our 'usbands. Or get your 'usband to do it, off the square, like."

Ethel said slowly, "I don't think it would help if Niccolo did. That might make your husbands feel that everyone was against them . . . You could go to your husbands' company commanders, couldn't you?"

The women chorused—"We could, but . . ." They all stopped; then the private's wife said, "That's worse than having Sergeant Fagioletti speak to them . . . All G.S., caps off, it would be. They might 'ave to pay up the extra money, but they wouldn't be loving husbands."

Ethel said, "I could try, myself . . . but it would have to be alone, with each of your husbands, one at a time, in your house . . . You'd have to trust me alone in the house with him for half an hour."

"Of course we trust you, Mrs Fagioletti," the women chorused.

"Well, we must fix times . . . make the opportunities," Ethel said. She could help, after all, she thought. She was respected: and in the army, which she had once thought of as so standoffish. "Now," she said, "Let's have the details . . . what money you are actually getting, what your husband's pay is, what you think he's spending it on, and how much you must have . . ."

*   *   *   *

"What on earth are we doing in a Parisian night club, in the middle of August?" Noel Coward cried theatrically, his questioning arms embracing all the others at his table—two young actresses, Tom Rowland, and Charlie Bennett, English all.

Tom said, "If it has to be a night club, better here than in London. Here, it's sort of natural—there . . . well, imagine ex-Guardees managing places like this, before the war . . . the police extorting large bribes to look the other way as the licensing laws—and a lot of other laws—are being broken . . . our sacred incorruptible bobbies!"

"It's the war done it," Charlie said phlegmatically.

The girls did not appear to have been listening, for one, giggling, cried, "If it wasn't August this place would be full of Frenchmen, and there wouldn't be *any* room for us."

"I'd rather be in Deauville or Quimper, where *they* all are," Coward said, pouring more champagne from the magnum in the silver bucket beside him. He began to hum in tune with the tall thin Negro at the piano a few feet away, in the Montmartre cellar that was Rum à Gogo, the newest and most fashionable *boîte* in Paris, and crowded even in August. The Negro, catching his eye, raised one hand momentarily off the keys in salute, then began to sing a very dirty ballad, in French. Coward's party bent forward, listening and chuckling. Every now and then Tom would translate to Charlie, while Coward did as much for the girls.

The door at the far end opened and four people in evening dress came in, wending their way through the haze of cigarette smoke, between the crowded tables, round the tiny dance floor, toward a vacant table close to Coward's. Tom looked up as the party came close and exclaimed, "Guy! It's my nephew, Noel—the tall one with the sandy hair." He rose, smiling, Guy Rowland saw him and cried, "Uncle Tom! I haven't seen you since, heaven knows when! You know Billy Bidford . . . and Florinda, of course . . . Maria von Rackow."

Coward stood, hand extended, as Tom made the introductions—"Sir Guy Rowland . . . Noel Coward . . ."

"Ah, the South Atlantic hero! Congratulations! Why don't you join us . . . if you don't mind sitting with commoners?"

Guy laughed and said, "Delighted." Two waiters bustled up and moved the other table up to Coward's; they all sat, while Guy beckoned imperiously, and called "Champagne!"

He's a little drunk, already, Tom thought; the eyes, usually so disconcerting in their disparity of blue and brown, now disarmed by a sort of blurry film; the grin more lopsided than ever, from a slackening of the jaw. Well, it was one o'clock in the morning. They'd probably been on the binge since eight or earlier.

Coward said to Florinda, "What brings you over to Paris in August? Ah, I remember, you're opening in a revue next week, aren't you?"

Florinda nodded and said, "Yes, and Billy came over to chaperone me, I don't think."

Coward turned to Guy—"And you?"

"Consultation with the French on a joint bombing policy, in case the Germans start the war again," Guy said briefly. "And Maria's chaperoning *me* . . . What are we talking about that for?" He stopped, listening—"Hey, that's a filthy song . . . jolly funny, too!" He clapped loudly, interrupting the singer at the piano. Maria von Rackow tugged gently at his arm, muttering, "Not so loud, Guy. The poor man can't hear himself . . ."

Guy patted her hand and said, "Sorry, Maria . . . Gimme a little more champagne . . . I thought you were slaving for Arthur Gavilan, Uncle."

Tom said, "For God's sake call me Tom, or I'll have to call you Sir Guy . . . Business is always very slack in London during August and Arthur closes the place down for the whole month. He usually goes to Spain to watch bullfights—his family was originally Spanish and, well, I thought we'd come to Paris . . . Charlie and I . . . then probably Scandinavia."

"He's showing me the world," Charlie said, grinning. "Bit different from what it looks like from the lower deck."

Nice man, Guy thought lazily—a Geordie, probably a miner's son, and doesn't try to hide it or pretend otherwise; or about the nature of his relationship with Uncle Tom. And Uncle Tom was so much less tense than he used to be . . . the navy was slowly being leached out of him, for better or worse. His mind was blurring and he took another drink of champagne. Good old Uncle Tom . . . *he'd* found what he was.

Florinda said to her escort, "Let's dance." Billy escorted her to the floor, where they sank into the close embrace of a slow foxtrot, as the pianist was joined by two other Negroes, one with a saxophone and one with a banjo. Maria muttered, "I'm feeling quite tired, Guy . . . Could we go home soon?"

"In a minute," Guy said, "Let's have a dance." He stood up, controlling his balance with difficulty. On the floor Maria guided him in the steps. He felt her firm full-breasted body conforming to the contours of his. She was good and kind, and she loved him. But he didn't love her. He loved Florinda . . . dancing there with Billy Bidford. What sort of understanding did *they* have? Was she as torn as he himself was? Was she wondering about the true situation between himself and Maria? In fact they were both staying at the Meurice, Maria in a connecting room with her three-month-old baby boy, Guy von Rackow, and his old English Nanny. Guy and Maria had not made love; and would not do so unless he asked her to marry him. She had come to Paris so that they could talk, feel, think, decide . . . Not yet. Just more champagne. Answers used to come so clear and fast to him, in the air, in the cockpit of a Camel. Not now . . .

After fifteen minutes, dancing two foxtrots and a new dance Guy didn't know, called apparently the Bunny Hug, they returned to their tables. The pianist stood, announcing, *"Mesdames, messieurs . . . quinze minutes de repos pour le personnel. Merci . . .* As I see English and Americans here . . . fifteen minutes break for the musicians. Thank you."

Coward was on his feet, calling—"Hold on a minute, Henri . . . I've been composing a little poem myself. What else is there to do in Paris in August? While you're having a rest, I'll recite it."

Henri grinned and indicated the piano stool—"Be my guest, Noel."

Coward sat down, sweeping up his tailcoat with a flourish. He played a few chords on the piano then swung round to the audience— "Esquimo Nell . . . or, Pride Goeth before a Fall . . . with apologies to Mr Robert Service . . ." More chords, then a low, gentle massaging of the keys as he swung back and in a clear, slightly nasal tenor began to declaim:

Now Dead Eye Dick & Mexican Pete had been working Wild Horse Creek
And they'd had no luck in the way of a fuck for well nigh over a week,
Except for a couple of caribou, and a bison cow or so—
And Dead Eye Dick had an itching prick, and he found life fucking slow.
So Dead Eye Dick and Mexican Pete set out for the Rio Grande,
Dead Eye Dick with his cast iron prick and Pete with his gun in his hand.

The young actresses gasped, one muttering, "Oh Noel, you are awful!" Maria whispered to Guy, "What's prick?

He said, "You'll guess."

The outrageous verses poured out, all in the rhythm of Service's Yukon ballads. The audience was slow to catch fire, partly because it could not believe what it was hearing; but soon it began to respond to the wealth of Coward's comic invention, the wonderfully evocative lines—

All the ladies knew his ways, down there on the Rio Grande,
So forty whores tore down their drawers at Dead Eye Dick's command.

460

As forty arses were bared to view, with lecherous snorts and grunts,
Did Dead Eye Dick start breathing quick, at the sight of forty cunts.

Now forty arses and forty cunts, you'll know if you use your wits,
And if you're slick at arithmetic, also means eighty tits.
And eighty tits is a gladsome sight to a man with the hell of a stand.
It might be rare in Berkeley Square . . . but it's not on the Rio Grande!

Guy was laughing outright, tears rolling down his cheeks. Florinda was doubled up, holding her sides, Billy staring openmouthed, Maria giggling helplessly.

She shed her garments one by one, with a smile of conscious pride,
Till at last she stood in her womanhood, and they saw the Great Divide.
They laid her down on a table top where someone had left a glass
She wriggled her tits and smashed it to bits between the cheeks of her arse.

The recitation marched relentlessly on to its ordained end—the complete discomfiture of Dead Eye Dick and Mexican Pete by the iron lady, Esquimo Nell.

Coward stood up, with a final glissade up and down the keyboard. The audience was on its feet, shouting "Encore, encore!", stamping, yelling, gasping with laughter, except for some Frenchmen who had not understood a word.

Coward bowed and raised his hand—"No encore, I'm afraid. I can't write another till tomorrow." He stepped down and returned to their table. There, while they stood and applauded him, he looked at his watch—"Time for my beddy byes. Work tomorrow, early . . . ten o'clock. Are you coming, Tom?"

Florinda said, "I have to go, too. You needn't see me to the hotel, Billy."

"I will, though," Bidford said.

Guy sat, his shoulders hunched, staring at the tablecloth. The little band was back, playing. The dance floor was crowded. Billy was taking Florinda to her hotel—their hotel. He was alone at the table with Maria.

He said thickly, "More champagne, Maria?"

"No," she said. "And not for you, either . . . I'm really tired, Guy. And I have to give that baby a feed, or I'll burst. Let's go back to the Meurice now. Please."

"I'll take you," he mumbled, "then . . . I'll come back here . . . won't be able to sleep."

"Champagne won't help."

After a time he said, "I know."

461

A little later he said, "Home, James. I might as well lie awake in a comfortable bed as suffocate in this tobacco smoke. Come on."

*   *   *   *

Fletcher Gorse swung round after the rocketing, drumming grouse and fired, first the left barrel and then the right. Both grouse arched into the heather with audible thumps, feathers flying. "Good shot, sir!" the loader behind him cried, and on the other side, "Good shot!" his wife Betty cried.

They were part of a shooting party at Lord Keighley's estate on the edge of the Yorkshire moors—six men and their ladies; but none of the latter, it was understood in the invitation, would do any shooting. Lady Keighley didn't like shooting; her hobby was collecting literary lions, and she had had a great tussle with her husband to be allowed to invite Fletcher, still the rage of literary London. The viscount had given in grudgingly, grumbling, "Ruddy long-haired johnny, I expect
. . ."

"His hair's a perfectly reasonable length, as you would have seen if you ever read the magazines."

The viscount had grunted, "And can't shoot for toffee."

"Probably not. But you can afford to have one poor shot with the others you have invited."

But Fletcher had outdone all but one of the other men, Sir John Haycraft, reputed to be one of the half dozen best shots in England; and his loader, one of the viscount's gamekeepers, had quickly changed his tone from suspicious scorn, at the sight of Fletcher's cheap guns, recently bought, to respectful admiration, going so far as to say, "If you had as much practise as Sir John . . . and had his guns . . . you'd be the best in England, sir."

Fletcher threw over his shoulder—"Don't call me 'sir' . . . I'm a poet, not a ruddy gent."

The keeper grinned at Betty, and said nothing, while Fletcher took down another brace of grouse with another right and left. Then there was a pause while the beaters took up a new line, and Fletcher said, "I like this better than watching the insurance blokes at Lloyds . . . even though they did give us a damn good lunch . . . And do we have to go to that mine on Monday? Haven't I learned enough for this month?"

"No," Betty said firmly. "It's all arranged and they'll be very disappointed if you don't go. And on Wednesday to Grimsby, and out in a trawler for a week."

"What'll I do without a woman for seven days?" he said. The loader tried to keep his face straight. Betty said coolly, "Practise continence . . . Poor darling . . . but when you come back, we'll have a month together in Wolverhampton."

"That's going to be bloody hell," Fletcher said. "Smoke, machines, noise . . . everything I can't stand, and never have been able to . . . everything Granddad taught me was bad."

She said patiently, "You can not understand your own country unless you see how its people live. There are far more men and women in heavy industry than there are in farming, you know. Their life is so different from what yours used to be that you can't imagine it. You have to go and *live* it."

The loader said, "The beaters are ready again . . . The birds'll start breaking out of their cover in a couple of minutes."

"Thanks . . . Can I rest in October than?"

"No," she said. "Parliament. Coutts Bank The Stock Exchange. And Captain Kellaway's taking you round the art galleries most of that month . . . And there are the Queen's Hall concerts . . . And you ought to think again whether you shouldn't go to Oxford or Cambridge for a year."

Fletcher stood up off the shooting seat and swung at two grouse, fired; got one . . . then a right and a left . . . missed one clean . . . another right and left . . . two singletons . . . three more . . . firing the gun, passing it back without looking, receiving the other ready loaded, all as smooth as though he'd been doing just this all his life, in just this manner.

He's a genius, Betty thought comfortably: a lover as strong as a stallion and as tender as a dove; swimming up in the world with the ease of a fish, looking into the experience of others, seeing, feeling, recording, remembering . . . and everything one day to flow out again in strong, lovely rivers of poetry.

*   *   *   *

It was a warm, dry, sunny Sunday near the middle of the month and Helen Rowland was riding with David Toledano in Hyde Park, walking their horses now along the dusty riding track between the Serpentine and Knightsbridge Barracks. Ahead of them two Corporals of Horse in undress uniform were exercising their horses. The spring's ducklings were almost fully grown and no longer trailed behind their mothers in anxious little flotillas, but wandered off in ones and twos, looking for food.

David said, "What news from Ethel?"

Helen said, "She's very happy in Cologne, but not pregnant. It isn't as easy for some women to get pregnant as it is for others."

David said nothing. They had never discussed the intimate details of her affair with Boy Rowland but it was clear from the circumstances that they could not have made love more than three or four times. Helen said, "This dust is making me cough, David. Let's get ahead of the soldiers."

She eased the bay mare she was riding into a trot, posting comfortably with her stride; and David followed suit on his big chestnut gelding—both horses hired from the Watkins' livery stable.

David said, "Any better luck with the Boutique?"

They passed the Corporals of Horse and Helen said, "No. Worse . . . This is a very dead season, with so many fashionable women in Yorkshire or Scotland, or at Cowes . . . I miss Ethel, too, though I've got a bright girl of about twenty to help . . . but none of that explains it all. I've done everything you advised—about economizing, keeping better books, watching the inventory, but it isn't enough." They eased back on the reins together, bringing the two horses down to a sedate walk. The dust rose in little puffs from their hoofs, but the soldiers were far back, and would not suffer from it.

Helen continued, "It's a knack . . . a flair . . . Florinda could open a boutique tomorrow, and have it clearing fifty pounds a day by next month. She is really excited by clothes, hats, shoes, bags. She could not only follow fashion, but lead it. She has the looks, and . . ."

"So do you," David said quietly.

"Oh, I *look* all right," she said, "but I don't have the proper feelings in here." She raised her free right hand and momentarily tapped her bosom. "There's no one close. Let's open up their lungs . . . and ours."

She touched the mare's flanks with the heels of her riding boots— she was not wearing spurs—and the well-trained animal stretched into an easy canter, and David's gelding followed suit. As the hooves bit deeper into the dust little clods of hard earth flew back, and the dust lay in a trail two feet above the ground for a hundred yards behind them. David thought, the earth's a little hard for this . . . don't want to damage the beasts' hooves. But Helen knew her horseflesh and was holding the pace to a very gentle canter. They rode on, not talking, easing comfortably back and forth in the hunting saddles, both tall—Helen the picture of English beauty with her deep blue eyes and fair skin, David like some warrior Saracen, olive-skinned, dark-eyed, a powerful man on a powerful horse.

Having reached the end of the Row, they slowed to a trot, turned, and started back eastward.

Helen said, "I don't know how much longer I can hang on—with the Boutique. We're simply not making enough money. The debts are piling up . . . nothing serious yet, but I don't like *any* debts."

After a while David said, "I would be happy if you would let me pay off the debts, at least. How much are they?"

"Oh, a little over three hundred pounds, so far. But I can settle them easily. I have jewelry worth several thousand."

David thought, at least she didn't react with horror to the very idea that I should help her. She was a very sensible and practical woman, for all her rank.

She said, "Mummy knows we're in trouble. She says she can get a job for me managing one of Lord Walstone's H.U.S.L. stores . . . probably not in London, but that wouldn't bother me, if . . ."

"If what?"

"If I hankered after that sort of life. I don't . . . I ought to go back to High Staining . . . well, to a farm. That's what I really like. That's what I really want to do."

"Then why don't you?" He hesitated, then said firmly, "I would be honoured to get you started. I know you're a good farmer . . . Guy's told me often enough. I'd get my money back. I'd really like to do it. And I hope you wouldn't mind if I came down to look at my investment now and then . . . but I'd stay in the nearest pub, of course."

She said, "I wish I could accept your offer, David, but . . ."

This time the silence was much longer, until finally he said gently, "Is it because your parents disapprove of your seeing me?"

She said, "Mummy doesn't mind. She approves, in fact. But Daddy . . . he hates Jews. He always has. Heaven knows who taught him to . . . his father, I suppose. Though he doesn't really know anything about Jews. But that's not really it. I couldn't take that much money from you, David."

Now, he thought, I should say, would you take it if you were my wife? He should say, Will you marry me? Then all her problems would be solved; but it was not yet quite time. Her father's disapproval mattered to her, and that was proper. His own father regarded Gentiles like an infectious disease, but he *was* his father. He, too, might have to be disregarded . . . some day. David was doing his best to see a potential wife in the parade of beautiful young women his father and sister were conjuring up out of all the great British Sephardic families; but so far none had made a dent in his growing conviction that Helen Rowland was the only woman he could marry. And then, when he did, he would have to spend years erasing the memory of Boy Rowland from her mind. Ah, that was wrong. She would not, and should not, forget that love. Somehow she must be made to accept his own love as a complement and partner to it . . . perhaps, for a start, if he became a real father to young Boy, fruit of the old love.

*   *   *   *

The four men were met in the big room of the Secretary of State for War and Air, in the War Office, on Whitehall, opposite the pale grey stone arches of the Horse Guards. The Secretary, the Right Honourable Winston Spencer Churchill, was standing in the window, looking out at the resplendent breastplates of the two mounted troopers of the Life Guards on sentry duty in the high boxes to either side of the gate. They were well nicknamed The Tins, he thought; for the sun was reflecting the glitter of one cuirass straight into his eyes. He turned back to face the others, seated round the table—and said, "The plain fact is that Admiral Kolchak is being beaten. The Bolsheviks have had him on the run for the last two months and his men are deserting in droves. There is no practical possibility of saving him unless we—the Allies—send troops . . . a great many of them, with all necessary support—tanks, artillery, aircraft, engineers, experienced commanders, a proper train of supply . . . which means all-out war. Now, what are your attitudes?" He looked straight at Lord Swanwick.

The earl said, "We've got to beat the swine . . . damned murderers . . . nothing will be safe if they are allowed to survive . . . We'll have Bolshevism here . . . they'll hang the King and the Prince of Wales . . . shoot the Queen . . . take all our land, our savings . . . abolish property, foxhunting . . ."

Churchill said patiently, his lisp very apparent—"Then you would vote, in the Lords, for such measures as I have stated will be necessary? The cost, I may add, will be enormous, but in essence incalculable because we do not know where or when any such action would end." He looked at Wilfred Bentley, and added, "I presume your party would be against any extension of aid to Admiral Kolchak."

Bentley said quietly, "Of course. We were against interfering in Russia's internal affairs from the beginning."

Churchill cut in—"But the Bolsheviks have been interfering in everyone else's—where they could . . . Poland, Esthonia, Latvia, Finland, Lithuania . . ."

". . . which were all Russian, before the war," Bentley said. He raised a long hand as Churchill opened his mouth—"But, Mr Churchill, we do agree with the Peace Conference's decision to create those countries . . . we only wish it had created an independent, united Ireland, too—thus taking an insoluble problem out of *our* hands . . . But we must understand the Russian point of view in this matter. They had no say in the writing of the clauses that tore these new countries out of what they—even the Bolsheviks—regard as Holy Russia."

"Do you think that your party would so vote if it came to the test?"

Bentley said, "I can not speak officially for the Party in the Commons, but unofficially, yes, I can assure you that that is what we all feel. It is the Socialism of Russia that our Government is trying to stamp out and, of course we, as Socialists, want that to end at once."

Churchill said softly, "Russian Bolshevism is a little different from British Socialism, my dear Bentley. Or does Snowden really keep a guillotine in his tool shed, for use on such as me and Carson and . . . Lord Walstone?"

Bentley laughed and Lord Walstone said, "Snowden? Chop my 'ead off? Not bloody likely! . . . How much would this cost? Sending a big army to smash the Bolshies?"

"Millions . . . every day," Churchill said. "The reimposition of wartime controls . . . and the very strong chance that we would in any case fail. Russia's a big place. Napoleon learned that, and it hasn't grown any smaller since 1812."

Lord Walstone said, "I say we must get out. Whatever happens it can't be worse than if we go in there and start the war over again."

"Damned Bolsheviks," Lord Swanwick muttered.

Churchill said, "Well, that's all. I think that when the moment comes, and it will be soon, the majority in both Lords and Commons will support our actions. For the Prime Minister's mind is made up. We are going to withdraw all support from Admiral Kolchak. Good day, gentlemen."

The others filed out. Two backwoods peers and one bright intellectual Socialist; you got as good an idea from them as in most other ways. He returned to the window. They were changing the guard. It had been only eight, nine months since there'd been a mob of mutinous soldiers out there, on the Horse Guards parade . . . and himself, here, asking whether the available battalion of Guards would obey their officers if ordered to disperse the mutineers. From that point of crisis, England had subsided, back to safety, ceremony . . . the new guard was from the Blues, he noticed—dark blue tunics under the cuirasses, red plumes on the helmets . . . decency, form, custom. The Russians—into an abyss, of fire, hatred, blood . . .

He pressed the bell on his desk and in a moment his secretary came in. Churchill said, "Take a telegram, Charles. To Mr Balfour, in Paris. After discussing the situation about German prisoners with General Asser I am convinced that their repatriation should begin immediately. Their work is done; they are costing us more than £30,000 a day. A fine opportunity for repatriating them is afforded by using the return trains which are bringing back the British Divisions from the Rhine to French ports. In addition . . ."

* * * *

Guy Rowland waited at the barrier, his head throbbing, watching as the train chuffed slowly up to the buffers at No. 20 Platform, Waterloo Station. His sister Virginia and her husband Stanley Robinson were in the front coach, and he saw them at once, as they came toward him among the crowd getting off the train. Stanley was wearing a blue suit with the zigzag-striped red and blue tie of the Royal Field Artillery, and a cloth cap, Virginia a plain blue cotton dress, and a wide-brimmed straw hat, and long white gloves. Guy kissed her and shook Stanley's one hand—"You both look well," he said. "When do the boys come back?"

"September 19th," Stanley said. "Guy, will they let me into Buckingham Palace with this cap? I just didn't have the brass to buy a bowler."

"You'll be taking it off as soon as we go inside," Guy said. "Where are your ribbons? In your pocket? Well, pin 'em on."

He was in the new blue-grey uniform of the Royal Air Force, on his left breast the embroidered wings of the albatross, the bird that flies o'er land and sea, below it three long rows of ribbons denoting his British, French, Italian, Serbian, Portuguese, and Belgian decorations. They climbed into the waiting hired limousine and Guy said, "Frank and Anne Stratton are waiting for us at Victoria. We pick them up there and then go on to the Palace."

"What'll the King say?" Virginia asked excitedly. She was plumper than ever . . . and obviously pregnant again. Stanley looked at her now with the same love, but now more coloured by proprietary pride . . . that's my wife . . . she bears my children . . .

"How do I know what the King will say?" Guy said. "He didn't say anything when he pinned on my V.C. and D.S.O.s . . . except 'Well done.' Too many others in line." Privately he thought, this time the King might say, You have a hangover, young man, your hand's trembling, your eyes are bloodshot.

"This'll be summat to tell our bairns," Stanley said. "How we were *that* close to King George the Fifth. It's a shame my mum and dad couldn't be here."

"Even more, that all the chaps who went down in flames can't be," Guy said shortly. Then they spoke very little until, having picked up Frank and Anne Stratton, they showed their command letters at the gates of the Palace, and were escorted to an inner courtyard, where they climbed down.

An equerry came forward—"Lieutenant Colonel Sir Guy Rowland and party? His Majesty wishes to see you in private, before the main investiture. This way, please."

They followed the equerry into the building, up stairs, along passages, to a small drawing room facing out over the Palace garden. They waited, standing, the two women muttering to each other in low voices. After five minutes the King came in, accompanied by the Queen, his youngest son Prince George, two equerries, and a Lord in Waiting, bearing a sword. The men bowed, the women curtsied.

An equerry led Frank Stratton forward and he bent his head as the King hung the insignia of a Commander of the Order of the British Empire round his neck. Stanley followed, to receive his Distinguished Conduct Medal. Then, at a sign, Guy knelt, the King drew the sword from its scabbard, and touched him with the blade on each shoulder, saying, "Arise, Sir Guy." He handed the sword back to the Lord in Waiting, who returned it to its scabbard. Then the King said, "Sit down, everyone, please. Hatfield, do you think you could find us some sherry?"

"Certainly, sir."

"I want to hear all about your flight, Sir Guy. And where did you lose your arm, Mister—what was it?"

"R-r-r-obinsson, Y-y-your Mamamamajesty, B-batcry S-s-s-ergeant M-major, Royal Field Artillery . . . I l-lost it at L-l-loos."

"When you were winning your D.C.M.?"

"Y-yes, Your Majesty . . . sir!"

"Fill the glasses, Hatfield. Here's to all of you. There'll always be an England as long as we have men like you . . . who are supported by ladies like you, Mrs Robinson, Mrs Stratton . . . and my own wife here."

The Queen, who had not taken any sherry, said, "I assume you are not married, Sir Guy?"

"No, madam," Guy said.

"You should get married, at once," the Queen said severely, admonishing him with a wagged forefinger. "Men need wives, otherwise they get into all sorts of stupid scrapes, and do all sorts of stupid things."

"Yes, madam," Guy said. Her Majesty had seen the shaky hand, the bloodshot eye. The sooner he got to a pub and downed a couple of Horse's Necks, the better.

Daily Telegraph, Saturday, September 13, 1919

WIDNES BY-ELECTION

MR HENDERSON RETURNED

The result of the Widnes by-election was declared yesterday, as follows:

Mr Arthur Henderson (Lab)	11,404
Hon. F.M.B. Fisher (C.U.)	10,417
Labour Majority...........................	987

This was the seventh by-election since the new Parliament was formed, and in five cases the seats have been lost by the Coalition.

A LABOUR GOVERNMENT

After the declaration of the poll at Widnes, Mr Arthur Henderson, addressing the crowd, declared that the result was a magnificent victory after only eight days' campaign, and a fight against a powerful organisation belonging to a party that had held the seat for some thirty years . . . It would not be his fault if he could not influence the public of the nation and the wage-earning classes from one end of the country to the other . . . Sufficient had been heard about Reconstruction, but Labour wanted more than words, it wanted deeds. They were not going to be content with patches and poultices. The present system was like putting poultices on wooden legs. Labour believed that the people, having won the war for the nation, should win the nation for the people . . .

A Labour Government, Henderson was promising, Cate thought. It would have seemed like promising green cheese from the moon, a year or two ago, even a few months ago; but there was no doubt that Mr Lloyd George's Coalition Government was fast losing the immense popularity with which it had gone into the Khaki Election. The working people no longer believed that either the Conservatives or the Liberals had their interests at heart . . . and perhaps it was true. Still, it was very difficult for him to imagine that such innocents as Ramsay MacDonald, Snowden, and this Arthur Henderson could ever be a match for the Clemenceaus and Bismarcks of the world in foreign affairs. Perhaps the Labour Government would more or less withdraw Britain from the world arena . . .

Garrod came in and said, "Telephone, sir. It's Sir Guy."

Cate pushed back his chair and hurried out, picked up the receiver and said anxiously, "Guy? Is everything all right?"

The voice at the other end was laughing, "Calm down, Uncle. I have the ring. Everything's fine. I am calling just to let you know that we're taking off in half an hour from here—Hendon. We're flying a passenger version of the Buffalo, so there'll be plenty of room and we ought to be landing at Hedlington in an hour from now."

"Who's coming?"

"Everyone . . . David Toledano, Helen Rowland—with the baby, Boy—Lord and Lady Swanwick, Lady Barbara and her husband, Virgil and Jane Kramer, the Ambassador and his Mrs, Fletcher and Betty, Florinda . . . Oh, yes, and Isabel."

"Good heavens! Are you sure you'll all fit in?"

"With room to spare. It's a big machine, Uncle . . . Who's meeting us at the airfield?"

"Your Aunt Louise, with a fleet of hired cars. Isabel's being married from High Staining."

"All right. I'll drive over to the Manor as soon as I can . . . and we will share a few French 75s to strengthen you for your ordeal. That's the least your best man can do for you."

"Good heavens!" Cate said again. "What are they?"

"Half cognac, half champagne, with a drop of bitters, all on ice."

"Well . . . do fly carefully, Guy. She's awfully valuable to me."

"Some of the passengers are to me," Guy said briefly, hanging up.

Behind Cate, Garrod said, "Why don't you take an aspirin and lie down a bit, sir? It's too early to dress, but everything's ready . . . clothes pressed, carnation in a glass of cold water in the larder, shoes polished, church decorated—the Rector called half an hour ago . . . so do rest. Mrs Kramer wouldn't like to see you looking nervous at the prospect of marrying her, now would she?"

Vale of Scarrow, Kent:
September, 1919

27 Christopher Cate and his wife Isabel were walking back home from Walstone Park, where Lord Walstone's team had narrowly beaten a Babes' Team to mark the end of the cricket season in the village. The leaves were beginning to turn on the trees and the air had the peculiarly heavy feel of dying summer. With the couple walked Guy Rowland, on a month's leave from the Air Ministry before taking up his next post, as commander of 84 Squadron, Royal Air Force, in Mesopotamia.

"I suppose you'll be promoted to full colonel, or brigadier general."

Guy laughed, "Not a bit of it. When I get out there I'll drop to Major . . . well, the rank is now called Squadron Leader. We're all losing rank as the R.A.F. finally wastes down to its peacetime strength." He looked across the river at the slope of Lower Bohun Farm and said, "What's going on there, Uncle Chris?"

Cate said, without looking, "Building . . . The bank foreclosed. I tried to save the farm, but couldn't manage it."

"Because he wouldn't let me help," Isabel murmured.

Cate said, "They're going to build rows of little houses, each to contain a little stockbroker or a little bank clerk, with a little wife and a little family and a little car in a little garage. They're going to electrify the railway to Hedlington and London soon. Then we won't be a village any more. We'll be a dormitory."

"I suppose the village people hate it all."

"Some do," Cate said grudgingly, "but most don't. They expected to, but they're all making money hand over fist. Especially

Woodruff—the garage man, and his elder son, who was in the Wealds with your father . . . he came back a captain. They're the most important people in the village now—not me, not Lord Walstone. I've been simply passed by as, well, irrelevant. Hoggin's powerful, all right, but his influence is not particularly here, it's all over the country."

A few moments later, by the half-completed war memorial, they heard singing and edged off to the side of the road as a mob of young people came up, mostly girls, but liberally scattered with a few old men and older women. They were singing "Knocked 'em in the Old Kent Road" at the tops of their voices, carrying unwieldy sacks slung over their shoulders, with here and there a battered suitcase, and a few classic tramps' bindles slung on sticks.

"Wotcher, dad!" they yelled at Cate as they passed; then " 'Ere, look at *'im!* Give us a kiss, ducks!" A young woman with big dark eyes put up her face to Guy to be kissed and Guy obliged. He had to kiss a dozen more before they passed on, still singing.

"Now what on earth was that?" Isabel gasped.

"Hop pickers," Cate said briefly. "Our annual invasion from the East End of London. They live in camps and work about ten days during the hop harvest. I'm surprised you haven't seen them before."

"*Plus ça change, plus ça reste la même chose,*" Guy said. "I could swear some of those were the same girls who were demanding kisses when I was sixteen."

Isabel laughed then, and they walked on, the older couple holding hands. They entered the footpath along Scarrow bank and soon came to a thatched cottage half-hidden by a dense wall of hazel and bramble. Guy said, "Are Fletcher and Betty still living in there—Probyn's old cottage?"

Cate said, "Yes, when they're here. But most of the time they're in London or she's dragging him round the country, educating him. She's very American."

"Now, now," Isabel said comfortably. "She's not ramming book-learning down his throat. She's just trying to widen his horizons so that he will have more background . . . more depth of experience to quarry his poetry out of."

A boy of about eleven popped out of an invisible gap in the brambles, crying, "Uncle! Uncle Christopher!"

Cate turned, "Hullo, Tim. What is it? What are you doing here?"

"Come and see my nets and traps, Uncle. You, too, Guy." He looked at Isabel and added grudgingly, "You can come too, if you want."

"Oh, thank you, sir," she said mockingly. "Do we have to dive through the hedge?"

Tim shook his head and led them to the real entrance. The "garden" inside was full of weeds of all kinds, but the house was in good enough shape outside and, when they entered, inside too. Cate said, "Who's keeping this clean, looking after it?"

"Probyn," Tim said, "but he lets me look after all the guns and traps . . . and feed Fletcher's ferrets."

Guy thought, his voice is hushed when he talks about Probyn; he thinks he's the greatest man in the world. Well, he thought about the same at that age.

Cate said, "What's going to happen when you go back to school in a few days? And what school will it be this time?"

"St. Swithin's, near Hindhead. I expect it'll stink." Tim frowned and his lips curled in an angry pout. "Probyn'll have to do it till I get back . . . I've made some gunpowder and I'm going to blow up the bogs at school. Or make stink bombs and leave them about in chapel, in the dining hall, in class—everywhere. They'll think the whole school has farted . . ."

"Tim!"

"Sorry, Uncle . . . Anyway, they'll sack me and I'll be home again in a couple of weeks."

"Tim," Cate said, "your mother and father are spending a great deal of money giving you an education which will enable you to do and be whatever you want to do or be when you grow up. Now you have been sacked from two prep schools already, and . . ."

"I want to be a poacher," Tim said defiantly. "I want to be like Probyn . . . What's the fun in getting up at seven o'clock, taking a train somewhere and coming back at five, every day?"

Guy said, "You'd better get your schooling over, Tim, then you can decide . . . That's a good decoy there. Did you make it?"

"Yes," Tim said eagerly.

"Well, sign it," Guy said, and tousled the boy's unruly hair, as he went out, following the Cates.

In five minutes the party left the Scarrow bank woods and came out on a country road, to confront an unexpected scene—a police constable and three other men standing outside the gate to a little cottage; and facing them, inside the gate, a middle-aged man with a double-barreled shotgun in his hands, while a woman and a small girl stood in the doorway of the cottage, hands defiantly on hips.

Cate stopped and said, "What's going on, Fulcher? What's the matter with Hawthorne?"

The constable turned, touching the peak of his helmet, "Mr Moore wants to sell the cottage, sir, but Hawthorne says he can't, because it's a tied cottage. Hawthorne says the only way Mr Moore can get him out

474

of it is to sack him . . . but Mr Moore doesn't want to do that, because Hawthorne's a good, experienced man."

"And who are these men?"

"Lawyers, sir . . . One for Mr Moore, one for Hawthorne—he was sent down by Mr Bentley, the M.P., when Hawthorne wrote to him about all this . . . and the third lawyer's for the people who are buying the rest of Mr Moore's land, and want this cottage."

Cate said, "Well, let me know if you need any help. Though I have no idea what I can do . . . or should."

He walked on. Isabel said, "A tied house is one that belongs to a farm, specifically for a labourer who works on that farm, isn't it?"

Cate nodded—"It was a necessity once. Now . . ." He shrugged— "I don't know. All I know is that this sort of argument has been going on over tied houses ever since I was a boy . . . and long before. As Guy said, in the country here, *plus ça change, plus ça reste la même chose.*"

*   *   *   *

It was a small house in a row, in the unfashionable northern part of Hedlington, but not quite so far north as to be in North Hedlington, the district of factories, wasteland, and actual slums. Guy sat in the front parlor with his Aunt Alice and Dave Cowell, drinking tea. The mousey little Mrs Cowell bustled in and out with plates of sandwiches and cake.

"You made all these scones?" Guy asked.

"Oh yes, Sir Guy," she said.

"Well, they're very good."

"Thank you." She stopped. "If it isn't impertinent, Sir Guy, what did the King and Queen say to you when you went to Buckingham Palace?"

Guy said, "The King asked about the South Atlantic flight, and what I was going to do next. The Queen told me to get married, at once . . . How's the partnership going?"

Cowell said, "Very well. I'll be passing my finals—for F.I.C.A.— next year, and Alice a couple of years later—unless she decides to spend more time at home."

It was apparently a loaded remark, for Alice looked at Dave, then at Daisy Cowell, standing behind her husband's chair, arms folded. Alice said, "I'm pregnant, Guy. By Dave. The baby's due in March next. Everyone will know soon enough and we have been deciding how to face it . . . how to control our lives, in fact."

"I wanted Miss Alice to have the baby," Daisy said. "We can love each other without being jealous. Dave and Miss Alice will work to bring the money in. I'll look after the house, and the baby when it comes."

Guy said, "You'll get some nasty looks and words from your neighbours, I suppose. Unless you pretend you had a husband who was killed in the war . . . too late for that now . . . drowned at sea, perhaps?"

Alice smiled—"We're not going to pretend at all, Guy. We just say nothing. Dave and Daisy will officially adopt it. As to what others *think* . . ."

"They can go to bloody hell," Daisy Cowell said suddenly, with great vehemence.

"Good," Guy said. "At least *you* three know what you're doing, and going to do, and why."

*　　*　　*　　*

Guy stood at the top of the steps looking down the length of the huge room. This was where his grandfather and old Bob Stratton used to make Rowland Rubies and Sapphires . . . there were overhead cranes then, put in when he was a kid; and lots of men in cloth caps, and smells of hot steel, oil, noises of lathes turning, and whining metal . . . a masculine, engineering place. Then, during the war it had turned to filling shells, and nearly all the men disappeared—transmuted to mud in the trenches—and the place had become a flowerbed of women's blue mob caps, and it smelled different; the toluene had its own, chemical smell . . . there was steam everywhere, and water on the concrete floor; and though they did not use much perfume, the smell of the women themselves, a femininity. Then there had been the explosion . . . and the rebuilding . . . the final closing down . . . and now . . .

Beside him, his cousin Naomi Gregory said, "We're following the same rule as Mr Ford does in his factories. Everything must go to the man—the woman mostly, here. No one needs to turn away, or move a step, for material or tools."

"Just like the army," Guy murmured. "How many are you employing now?"

"Two hundred and twelve," Naomi answered at once. "But I hope to expand to four hundred as soon as we've built up a name for ourselves in the industry. We only completed the factory in all particulars four months ago . . . And our unit cost is too high still, solely because of our small output . . . comparatively small. We've got to get more orders."

"Going to do poor Champion and A.C. and Lucas in?" Guy said.

"We'll try," Naomi said, smiling. "What was the figure we expect the motor car industry to expand by, Ron?"

Her husband, the tall quiet man walking behind them, a big clipboard in his hand, said, "Six percent this year, fifteen percent next . . . perhaps more when we're definitely out of Russia . . . twenty percent, perhaps. It depends on how soon, and how much, taxes come down, releasing money to buy such items as cars."

Naomi did not acknowledge the information, but said to Guy, "Fifteen percent for the whole industry! There's enough there for all of us . . . but I'm going to make sure that we get at least our share of it. If the others can't keep up with us, we will get their share too."

"Are you going to go public?" Guy asked.

"We think . . ." Ron began; but Naomi overrode him, saying firmly—"Not yet. We have approached Lord Walstone—Hoggin—for capital and he will probably lend it to us—he doesn't know what to do with his money. With that we can expand a bit, and still be a partnership. Then, once we have established a profit record, and a sales base, we can capitalize and become really big . . . We could raise twenty times earnings, easily . . ."

They moved out of the big room, across an open space, and into another—"Accounts and records," Naomi said. "Adding machines . . . automatic registers. No more quill pen offices for us. That's Carrie Houlton, she was at Girton with me, a real whizz at math, she's head of the department. Good morning, Carrie. This is my cousin, Sir Guy Rowland."

"It's an honour to meet you, sir. Good morning, Mrs Gregory . . . Will you be in your office at the usual time?"

"Yes," Naomi said, moving on. "Ron's department is the technical side . . . keeping up with inventions, making some of our own—physics rather than manufacturing. He brings me his ideas, and we discuss how the thing, whatever it is, can be most efficiently manufactured and sold . . . Don't we?"

"That's right," Ron said.

"He's away a lot . . . scientific meetings . . . talking to inventors . . . sneaking looks at what our competitors are up to." She stopped, sniffing the air like a conqueror savoring victory after battle—"We're going to make two hundred thousand for ourselves by the end of next year, Guy—two hundred thousand, after all expenses, after we've paid the interest on Lord Walstone's loan! A year later we'll be the second biggest automobile electrical engineering and manufacturing firm in the country."

"And what happens if you have a baby in the meantime?"

477

"I won't," she said forcefully. "Not till 1925. Then we'll have two, a girl and a boy. The boy will go into politics . . . and the girl will take over this from us when we're ready to retire."

"Where are you going to retire to?" Guy asked.

She said, "I think we'll . . . Oh Guy, you're pulling my leg again! Just like the horrible little boy you used to be, even though you are a knight."

"Can't help it," he said. "I was born that way. Well, good luck in your great career . . . I mean it, Naomi—so, do you have any champagne in your office? . . . Whisky, then? Let's drink a toast to both Gregorys, and to Gregorys', your firm . . . several toasts."

*　　*　　*　　*

The pheasant season was close, the birds were in fine shape, and Lord Walstone was pleased. A few successful shooting parties would bring him considerable prestige. Probyn Gorse, walking the outer boundaries of the Park, was not thinking of prestige. He was watching for signs of predators . . . crows, rooks, hawks, foxes, kids from the village, poachers. He carried a double-barreled 12-bore under his right arm, broken but loaded . . . for a fox would not wait while he loaded the gun . . . He'd have to be careful what foxes he shot, though, for His Lordship was just as keen on the hounds as he was on the pheasants . . . more prestige. It meant a lot in England still for a man to have the letters M.F.H. after his name. It meant a lot to him, Probyn thought, though danged if he knew why, really, when His Lordship sat a horse like a sack of mangold-wurzels and knew less about hunting hounds than he did about breeding pheasants, and that was nothing at all.

It was near twilight, and Probyn thought, I'll go round the top of the next wood and then home by Ten Acre and Fawcett's Copses. The sun was setting earlier each day now . . . why, last time they'd played cricket at the Park, the last ball had been bowled almost in darkness . . . He paused, his eye caught by something in the edge of the wood, where a rabbit trail ran in from the field to a small warren just inside: a running noose, brass wire that had been dulled by rubbing with earth . . . stick firmly thrust into the hard ground . . . dang it, this was his own wire, and one of the sticks he'd whittled a couple of years ago. Young Tim Rowland, that's who it was, who'd set the noose . . . and another ten yards farther on. He stood a moment, looking. These were His Lordship's rabbits, which he was supposed to be looking after. Let the boy set his nooses on someone else's land, land where there wasn't a gamekeeper. He pulled up the sticks and put them in his capacious pockets, wire and all.

Five minutes later, as he entered Ten Acre Copse, a man rose from the bushes beside him and swung at his head with a big wooden club. The club hit with a hard smash to the left side, above the ear, and he fell, the gun falling from his hands. He was fighting for consciousness as he heard a man's voice nearby—"Tie him up . . . to the tree, Bert . . . Tight, man." They were dragging him along the ground, supporting him half-upright, tying a rope round him. He mumbled, "What . . . wha' . . . ?"

"Shut up, you old fart, or you'll get hurt."

He said no more; but as he slowly swam back to consciousness and overcame a strong desire to vomit, he kept his eyes all but closed, and listened. There were five of them . . . no, six. They were beginning to shoot up into the trees with silenced .22s . . . There was a little wind, but those small *phuts* would not carry far. The pheasants were not frightened, seeing no connection between their comrades falling off their perches, and their own situation. After a time the men moved on, and Probyn heard no more; but he could guess. They were going to the other copses where pheasants were roosting. They worked fast . . . He began to pick at his bonds with nimble fingers, and in ten minutes had freed himself. His gun was gone—stolen, of course. He staggered through the Ten Acre, and, listening, heard the faint *phuts* from Fawcett's; and started to run across the field toward it, croaking, "Stop! Help, help!"

He heard sudden cracks by his head . . . bullets, passing close through the air. The poachers were firing at him. They were trying to kill him! He flung himself to the ground twenty yards from the edge of the wood, and a bullet kicked up dust a foot from his head. A voice snarled, "Lie there, you bastard!"

"Kill him and be done with it," another said.

"In another half hour we'll just about have the place cleaned out. Bring the vans up to the crossroads down there."

"All right, Jim."

Probyn lay still, listening. More steady *phuts* . . . pheasants being killed by the hundred. His pheasants. And they wouldn't hesitate to kill him if he got in their way. Vans to take the birds to London. He might sneak down the field and get their license numbers. He moved a foot cautiously as he lay, and a voice said menacingly, "Move and you're a dead man, Gorse."

So they knew his name . . . must have; this had been planned like one of them military operations you read about during the war. He lay still, waiting. At last they went, in the darkness, slowly under heavy sacks. He heard the sound of motor engines from the road below. Then he got up and staggered as fast as he could toward the Big House.

Close to the bulk of it he turned into his own cottage, stopping short in the doorway as he saw Guy Rowland inside, talking to his Woman. They looked up and Guy's expression changed. He sprang to his feet and came forward, saying, "What happened, Probyn? You're bleeding."

" 'Course I am," he said. "Set on by half a dozen blokes from London. They've taken half the pheasants." He went to the sink, washed his face, and ran his hands through his henna-dyed hair— "Got to go and tell His Lordship."

"I'll come with you," Guy said. They went out together, and to the back door of the Big House. Probyn rang the bell and waited till a footman came; then he said, "Got to see His Lordship, James, in a hurry."

"They are in the Gainsborough Room," the footman said. He led along the passage, knocked at a door at the front of the house, and went in. A moment later he came out, saying, "Please go in, sir . . . and you, Probyn."

Lord Walstone was on his feet by the fireplace, his hands behind his back, his ample belly outthrust. Lady Walstone was knitting, in a chair the other side of the fireplace. Her mother was sitting beyond, her gnarled hands folded in her lap, doing nothing.

"What is it, Probyn?" Walstone asked. "Out with it, man."

"Poachers, my lord," Probyn said. "Knocked me out as soon as I went into the Ten Acre . . . shot a lot of pheasants with silenced .22s . . . tied me up first, then threatened to shoot me when I got free . . . they was in Fawcett's by then. Took away the birds in two vans."

"Poachers, eh?"

"They aren't poachers!" Probyn burst out. "They're . . . soldiers! What do they call 'em in America? Gangsters! I seen nothing like this in seventy-four years. Nor my father before me. It's . . ."

"It's war," Walstone said. "That's what it is. And you're not a soldier. You're a gamekeeper." He went to the corner where a telephone stood on a round marble-topped table, picked it up, and said, "Trunks, please miss . . . London, Gerrard 0433 . . . 'Arry? Bill Hoggin here. Seems a bunch of boys from the Smoke have come down and nicked half my pheasants. You'll see 'em coming onto the market in a few days. Find out who done it, and let me know right away. Yes, you can spend some money. A hundred quid. No, I'm not going to prosecute. That's a mug's game."

He hung up and returned to the fireplace, nodding to Guy—
" 'Ullo, Sir Guy. Nice to see you."

"I was paying a call on Probyn, waiting for him to come home."

Lord Walstone turned to Probyn—"You're sacked, Probyn. It takes more than *know*ing about pheasants to look after them these days. I'm going to find the bloke who fixed this raid, then I'm going to hire *him*. You go back to your cottage and take a few of my rabbits and birds now and then, like you used to. These blokes won't mind about that, because they think big, see? Any time you want any money, come and give 'em a hand with the breeding, getting beaters, all the stuff they know nothing about . . . but they'll defend this place like it was Verdun, see. Just remember that, when you want to come out on a moonlight night. This is 1919, Probyn."

*　　*　　*　　*

Guy Rowland walked carefully out of the Saloon Bar of the Lord Nelson about half-past eight in the evening and stood a moment, swaying on his heels, looking around him, seeing nothing. He became aware of sound, an awful scraping, whining, tinkling sound. He gazed blankly about and finally saw that a trio of ex-servicemen had taken position at the corner of the building, begging. One, who appeared to be blind, with patches over both eyes, played a cornet, out of tune. Another, with one arm, played a fife, holding the instrument ingeniously in the hunch of his shoulder. The third was without both legs, and squatted in a child's cart; he waved a tambourine in one hand, and sang. They were all wearing their medals and the tune they were singing and playing at this moment, in the near dark, was Tipperary.

The whisky he'd drunk was swimming in Guy's head and it took him a minute to find his wallet, pick out a ten-shilling note, and drop it into the cap set beside the man in the cart. "Thank yer, sir, thank yer," the legless man cried, breaking his song for a few beats . . .

> *Goodbye Piccadilly, farewell Leicester Square,*
> *It's a long long way to Tipperary, but my heart's right there!*

Guy wandered off aimlessly. The Lord Nelson was in the older part of Hedlington, the streets narrow, the houses close-packed; but, partly due to the bombings in the war, and partly to condemnation of some old buildings in a dangerous state, there were also open spaces, mostly littered with paper, tin cans, bottles, and other debris. The Scarrow, here murky and sluggish, flowed past the end of one of them. His head ached but not very badly. He had been thinking about Maria and Florinda, and had still reached no answer.

481

A boy darted toward him, followed by a bellow of rage and, a moment later, a man with no trousers on, weaving out of an alley, waving his arms and shouting, "Stop him! Thief! Thief!" Instinctively Guy shot out an arm and grabbed the boy by the throat. The boy struggled and tried to bite but Guy had him firm, and said, "Quiet now, or I'll strangle you!" Behind the bare-bottomed man a girl darted out and away; but the man was not as drunk as he seemed, and he turned quickly and had her before she could escape.

"What's the matter?" Guy asked.

"Bloody little whore," the man said. "And that's her mate, takes my money while I'm fucking her in the alley there."

"I ain't done nothing," the boy whined, making a sudden jerk for freedom. Guy tightened his grip until the boy was choking—"Aaahah . . ."

The girl whined, "I done nothing. I earned that money."

But the boy was feeling in the pocket of his ragged coat and pulling out a few coins. " 'Eere, take 'em mister," he gasped. "Just let us go. We got to make money, some'ow, ain't we? My Dad got bofe legs blown off in the war and . . ."

"Was that him playing outside the Lord Nelson?"

The boy said, "Yus. That's 'im. Willum Gorse. My Dad."

The bare-bottomed man grabbed the money and, giving the girl a final shake, threw her to the ground and hurried back into the alley in search of his trousers. Looking round, Guy thought, perhaps someone has seen all this; perhaps not; whether or not, it is certain that no one cares. He said to the girl, "Don't run away."

She began to dust herself off, saying, "Five shillings it is, for a toff like you. Money first . . . And I'll send Rupert away so's you won't worry about 'aving your wallet pinched."

Guy said, "I know your father well. I don't know why I didn't recognize him just now."

" 'Ad a bit too much wallop?" she said, slyly—"But I can smell yer breath, and that's not beer. That's whisky."

Guy said, "Why does he have to beg? Doesn't he have a pension?"

"Not enough," the girl said at once. "Muvver takes in washing . . . Violet's left 'ome and lives with a fancy man in Chatham . . . but she 'ad a baby wot's now nearly four and she left that for us to look after. Rupert 'ere's a proper little Artful Dodger, a real expert 'e is. 'E'll get to the top of the tree in his profession in no time . . . or the top of the gallows."

"And you're . . . wait a minute—you're Betty. You're about . . ."

"Thirteen," she said.

"And there was another girl, who'd be about eleven now."

"Jane. Died of the influenza, last year. You do know a lot about us."

"I . . ." Guy's head was throbbing and he sat down suddenly in the dirt, beside the dark quivering surface of the river—"I don't understand . . . Florinda's your sister. She has plenty of money. So does Fletcher, now. Why are you all so . . . wretched?"

"Ma won't take money from either of 'em," Betty said indifferently. "Though I know Florinda sends quids and 'alf Bradburys and 'alf crowns to people 'ere, for them to drop into Dad's cap . . . which they *sometimes* do. But this is more fun . . . much more fun. 'Oo the 'ell wants to be a fucking skivvy in some toff's 'ouse? Or work like a ruddy nigger in a H.U.S.L. shop? Not me!. . . C'mon, Rupert. Let's go down to the South Eastern."

They disappeared into the gloaming. Guy slowly rose to his feet and staggered back toward the Lord Nelson. The ex-servicemen were still playing on the corner, now "Keep the Home Fires Burning," as dreadfully as ever. He stood a few feet from them, recognizing Willum clearly now . . . staring, thinking. Why did everything have to be so . . . so debased, so miserable? Why did no one care? Tears began to flow into his eyes and sobs choked him. He began to fumble for his wallet; but at once gave that up. Money wasn't enough. Money would never be enough. The cripples played on, and men and women passed, going in and out of the pub, and some dropped pennies into the cap, or now and then a tanner . . . Guy waited, watching relentlessly. What did they want of him? But they did not answer, only played on, as relentlessly, and terribly . . . *All the nice girls love a sailor* . . . *Pack up your troubles* . . .

*   *   *   *

Florinda rang the bell outside the street door of the flat, and waited. It was four in the afternoon, teatime; but for him, these days, it might be champagne or brandy time. He might be asleep, or quarrelsome. It didn't matter; she had made up her mind that the time had come for her to act. Good heavens, in her own way she had been dithering and drifting just as much as he had.

The door opened and he stood there, one hand on the jamb, staring down at her. He had not shaved, but the fair stubble barely showed. He was sober, she thought, and said, "May I come in?"

He stood back without a word and she swept in and up the stairs and into the flat proper, threw her sable into an armchair as she passed, sank into another, and lit a cigarette. He came and stood in front of her, blocking out the light from the windows that overlooked the small park in the centre of Greeley Crescent. She got the cigarette drawing and blew out a long stream of smoke. She said, "I'm going to get married."

He seemed for a moment to shrink, and said, "I see. Congratulations . . . but I'm supposed to say that to Billy, a'n't I? All good wishes, then."

Her heart sank, but she gathered her inner determination and said, "I love him. And he's handsome, brave . . . and good in bed."

He stooped suddenly, and said, "You *don't* love him! You're going to throw away the rest of your life just for money, and good fucking? You're a bloody stupid cunt, that's all you are! You never had a brain in your head and you've never learned anything!" He seized her by the neck and shook her furiously. Oh dear, she thought, this is getting a bit close to the bone; he is a killer, and has proved it over and over again; but she felt much better. She kept her eyes unblinking on his, as best she could, while her head bobbed fiercely back and forth. His face was close on top of her, his teeth bared, as he snarled, "I won't let you do it! I'll strangle you first!"

"Why?" she managed to gasp. "What's . . . it . . . to do . . . with . . . you?"

He was sweating, the skin of his face livid and gleaming damp, as he grated, "Because *I* love you . . . *I* need you . . . *I* want you . . . You belong to *me* . . . You always have, and always will. Do you understand?"

She waited, holding her tongue, until he had shaken her for another half-minute, all the time repeating, "You're mine! Do you understand?"

At last she said, "That's better . . . Now, let me go . . ." His hands slowly released their grip on her shoulders. Cor, she'd have deep purple bruises there soon—no décolleté dresses for a month. She stood up and said, "So, I'm going to marry you, am I?"

He said, "Yes." He was breathing deeply, and wiping the sweat off his forehead with his handkerchief.

She said, "Good. That's what I came to tell you. *I* never mentioned Billy Bidford. I only said I was going to get married, and I loved the man, and he was handsome and brave, and good in bed . . . Guy Rowland. Now . . ." She held out her arms, and Guy slowly came to her, and held her loosely, laying his head on her shoulder, where so recently his iron fingers had dug into her flesh. She felt his tears on her neck, and patted his shoulder, but said nothing.

At last he stood away, but still held both her hands in his, "Flo, I don't know what prevented me from saying it months ago . . . a year ago, really, except that killing Werner . . . leaving Maria a widow . . .

the awfulness of what the war had done to the world, even after it was over . . . I was paralyzed."

She said, "I realized that, and it took me long enough to understand that if you couldn't act, it was up to me. So I did. Now, let's sit down, Guy . . . you there, me here . . . We've settled one thing—we love each other, and no one else. You'll have to tell Maria."

"Yes."

"We're going to spend the rest of our lives together."

"Yes."

"Doing what?"

"You have a career, on the stage. I don't want to stand in the way of that."

She gestured impatiently—"Career, my foot! Or rather, my legs. I can wave my legs in the air, in silk stockings, and men will pay to see me doing it. But I'm not and never will be a great actress. My career is going to be, being your wife. Cor, I'll still have a title! What fun! . . . So, what are *you* going to do?"

He said, "I've learned what I don't want to be . . . a banker . . . a politician . . . not even an officer of the R.A.F."

"But you're still in it. You're due out to Mesopotamia soon."

He nodded, saying, "But that's not what I *want*. I'm accepting it because it's been pressed on me. It didn't require any decision. I already was an R.A.F. officer."

She said, "Well, decide now that you're going to resign your commission. So, what's it to be?"

He said slowly, "All I've been seeing, for a long time, is the misery caused by the war . . . separation, mutilation, death, loss, cruelty, deprivation. And I've felt that I am responsible, because I survived, and did well out of it—all those jobs offered to me, all those women, all that money—I have wished I could do something to atone."

"Not atone," she said quickly. "You may *feel* guilty, but you're *not* guilty."

"To make things better, then," he said. "To help people . . . I could help people as a politician, or a banker, in a way, but I mean in a more personal way, face to face, hand to hand."

She sighed, "Aaaah . . . now we're getting to it. You want to help my Dad, sitting in that bloody little cart, begging, and men who can't see any more . . . and men who can't sleep, for their dreams . . ."

"Yes," he said eagerly. "All that, and more."

She said, "We can do it, Guy. Let's work it out together first, boil the idea down into something solid, that we can go out to the world and say, this is what we're going to do—come and help."

"Right!" he cried enthusiastically.

She held up her hand, "We start on that tomorrow. First, you telephone your general and tell him you're resigning from the R.A.F. Then we go out and buy an engagement ring—not too expensive, mind, we'll need all your money, and mine, soon. Then we stop off at my car, which is just round the corner, and pick up a little case there's in it, with my nightie and toothbrush and a change of clothes for tomorrow. Then—bed, and don't set the alarm. Tomorrow can wait, on love . . . Your eyes are dry. You look different. Have I got my man back, my strong, hard man, that always looked after me, and told me what to do, and held me tight, and kissed me gently?"

He took her in his arms, smiling, whispering, "Yes."

Daily Telegraph, Monday, September 15, 1919

DRAMATIC COUP BY ITALIAN ARMY
D'ANNUNZIO'S RAID

Rome, Saturday.

The following semi-official Note has been issued here:

"According to news received yesterday afternoon, some detachments of Grenadiers and bands of Arditi (storm troops), with machine guns and armoured cars, which started from Ronchi—on the old Italian frontier—arrived at Fiume at noon. Gabriele d'Annunzio was amongst them. No disorder has been reported from Fiume up to midnight tonight. The Government will take the most energetic steps in order that the movement may be checked at once, and that those who were responsible for an act which is as rash as it is harmful may be discovered."

Cate read on. The Italian Prime Minister, Signor Nitti, was disclaiming all responsibility, and denouncing the raid. But Italy, one of the Allies in the late war, had now set itself in conflict with the Kingdom of the Serbs, Croats, and Slovenes, another Ally. The wartime alliances were already beginning to break up, as was Lloyd George's Coalition, the heavy chains of the war now loosed.

From across the table his wife said, "When is the war memorial being dedicated, Christopher?"

"On the anniversary of the Armistice—November 11," he said. "Old Kirby's doing it, with the assistance of Father Caffin. He's the Irish priest who served with Quentin's battalion, and the man who told me Margaret had been killed. He wrote to me the other day asking if he could help to officiate. Why do you ask?"

"There's going to be a memorial service at Arlington National Cemetery near Washington, in February next, for our American war dead. I'd like to go. Walter's buried there."

"Of course."

"I'd like you to come with me. After the service, it can be our honeymoon. Let's leave in mid-January."

He hesitated, thinking, can I be away for so long? Something always crops up . . . emergencies, trouble, floods, feuds, tenants' roofs falling in . . . Then he thought again—but this is a new England, a new Walstone. I am the squire, but I'm no longer the bountiful and all-seeing lord of the Manor. They do not depend on me . . . rather, I depend on them; and really it has always been like that.

She interrupted his chain of thought—"And there's another reason, Christopher, why I think you ought to come . . . For a long time your England has been a tight little island, secure against infection and the hand of war . . . especially infectious foreign notions. You have ruled your own destinies—you have sent out men and ideas all over the world, and have by that greatly affected the way other people live. You have imported goods, but not many ideas. The time is coming when you will, willy nilly. And in the nature of the present circumstances, many of those ideas are going to come from America . . . for better or for worse. America's going into the export business. Come with me. Travel over my country. I think that when you come back, you'll understand better what is happening to your country . . . and what is going to happen . . . and why."

"We *will* be coming back, won't we?" he asked anxiously.

She blew him a kiss across the table—"Of course! Englishmen like you don't transplant at all, my dear. Besides, I want to live with you, and I know that *you* can only *live* here."

Fort Defiance, Arizona:
Thursday, September 25, 1919

28 Stella Merritt wiped her dirty hand across her forehead and returned to her work, of scrubbing the floor of the little one-storied house on the outskirts of Fort Defiance. Mary Begay, the Navajo girl who usually came every day to clean, had not come today; and the house was filthy from the dust and sand that had been blowing in all week from the northwest, out of the stark landscape of the Navajo Reservation. John was due home this evening . . . but nothing was certain out here. They had arrived at the beginning of summer, too late to experience the spring mud which everyone talked about, when the few roads, none macadamized, would turn into quagmires that even the high-wheeled Navajo wagons could not negotiate; and the little settlements of hogans scattered through the reservation, which was as big as Ireland or West Virginia, were as cut off as though they had been islands in the middle of the ocean. The summer was better than she had expected . . . many days of wind, many vivid thunderstorms, and always the pink, orange, and blue-grey colours of the rock, the sense of shimmering light on far horizons, and at night the cold breath in the air that reminded her she was at 7,000 feet above sea level. Now fall was upon them, and in the woods west of the Fort some of the few deciduous trees were turning to gold and yellow. She knew what to expect, for she had been told many times—a month of perfect weather, and then, any day, the white flakes swirling out of the sky; the women wrapped in bright blankets, sitting high on their horses, bringing the flocks in toward the settlements, the dogs running behind, often a sick sheep across the saddle . . .

488

She scrubbed carefully. When this was done she'd carry coal in from the yard and stack it close to the stove. She would have preferred wood, for the wonderful tangy scent that piñon gave out; but there was plenty of cheap coal at Gallup; and the Indian Service had it brought in by the wagonload for its employees. The water came from a tank on the hill behind the Fort, after being pumped up there by a gasoline engine from a nearby spring . . . which often froze in winter, the Agent's wife had warned her.

Peace was crawling about in the back room. Mary Begay loved him and spent more time with him than she did at the work she was being paid for. If Mary were here he could have played in the yard; but without her, it was too dangerous, for this was rattlesnake country. That danger would soon be over, they said, while the snakes hibernated through the winter. At two, she'd eat . . . beans, canned beef, canned tomatoes. Fresh vegetables were hard to find, fruit still harder. You could drive to Gallup, but the road was bone breaking—and axle breaking. At three Philip Nakai would come, to give her her daily Navajo lesson . . . And that was the end of the real work for the day . . . except for cooking supper, washing up, cuddling Peace, and crooning to him one of the Navajo cradle songs which Nakai was teaching her, at her request. Peace was only eleven months old, but he always listened intently, and sometimes seemed to be trying to croon along with her. These days she took her daily dose of heroin in the morning; and it lasted comfortably through the day. The physical effects wore off in a few hours, but she was too busy to notice, or feel anything more than quite minor discomfort.

John was away a great deal, and there was always so much to do, for herself and Peace. Perhaps it was for the best; she had no time to think, to worry, to miss her past. She thought, with some surprise, that it must be two months since she had consciously "missed" Walstone.

She got up and went to refill the bucket with clean water. "Water—*toh*," she said aloud. The bucket was red, and she said, "*Chee*" . . . "*Hago!*" she added, imagining she was calling Mary to come to her—"*Ya-ateeh!*" That was a greeting. She sighed. It was a difficult language.

She returned to the living room, knelt, dipped the scrubbing brush in the soapy water, and continued her work on the knotty-pine planks of the floor.

*   *   *   *

John Merritt walked toward the New Yorker Bar & Grill, across the street from the Santa Fe Railroad Station in Gallup, New Mexico, frowning to himself, for he did not feel happy. He opened the front door, passed through the hall where electric fans whirled slowly to disturb the air and the dust, and pushed through the swinging half-doors to the bar. At first, he thought there was no one in there—it was just past eleven—but then, beyond the big sign set in the middle of the bar, reading NO INDIANS SERVED, he saw a shape hunched over a tall beer and a shot glass of tequila. John sat down on a stool at the near end of the bar and said to the barman, "A beer please . . . good and cold."

The man at the far end peered round—"Well, if it isn't Sir Galahad . . . the Straight Arrow from Harvard!"

John stared then said, "Mr. Reinhart . . . I thought you'd gone back east."

"I did," Reinhart said, "but after a few weeks I couldn't stand it any more . . . prissy New Englanders . . . fogs . . . beans . . . chowder and scrod . . . I came back."

The bartender brought John's beer and he drank appreciatively. It had not been a long drive down to Zuni yesterday; but it had been a very long afternoon talking to the tribal chiefs there, trying to find out why they were having such a high rate of infant mortality . . . trying to help, but not interfere. And he'd slept badly. And he'd had a puncture on the way back . . .

Reinhart had been an Indian Service assistant at Fort Defiance when John first arrived with Stella and Peace in June. A month later the Agent had fired him for drunkenness. At the time John had felt no emotion; it was obviously impossible to keep a man whose trouble was the same alcoholism that afflicted the Indians themselves. But in the ensuing months he'd learned that Reinhart knew more about the Navajo than anyone else at the Agency. People from the Agent down had kept saying, "Ask Reinhart . . . Reinhart will know . . . oh damn, he's gone, hasn't he?"

"Still all gung-ho for the U.S.I.S.?" Reinhart said. Watching him, John remembered that tequila boilermakers had been his favorite drink; he was sober now, but they'd catch up with him in an hour or two.

John began, "The work's important . . ." What the hell, he thought? Why am I pussyfooting around to a straight question? He said, "But I think we're not doing the right things, at all. And when we are, by chance, then we do them the wrong way."

The barman had poured Reinhart another boilermaker without a word; and Reinhart now raised the shot glass and said, "The beginning of wisdom! You're dead right. The U.S.I.S. has no reason for its existence, as it now operates . . . except to perpetuate itself. It does no good to any Indian in the country. In most cases it does actual harm."

"What can we . . . I . . . do about it?" John said. "I went to the Hopis last week and got a whole lot of ideas from them . . . about what could be done, in our administration, by giving Indians more responsibility, fundamentally letting them grow their own way, while offering them opportunities to learn and use the white man's skills, and knowledge, *if* they want to . . . The Agent listened to me for half an hour; then said I was wasting my time—I knew what the Government's policy was and I was to follow it, and he was there to see that every employee of the Indian Service did the same. I damned nearly called him a narrow-minded idiot. Then I would have been fired, and been able to do still less for the Navajo."

Reinhart said, "You're wrong, me boyo. You *can't* do less than you are now, can you? . . . How are you coming along with the language?"

"Pretty well. My wife, too."

"Ah, Stella, isn't it? . . . Good. Well, if I remember right your Dad's a banker in New York, eh? Get him to put up the money and buy Hurford's Trading Post."

"Between Two Grey Hills and Sanostee, in the Chuskas?" John exclaimed. "But . . ."

"Hurford wants to retire. You'll be your own boss. And you can do something for the Navajo. Look . . ." he leaned toward John along the polished expanse of the bar, and raised his voice to be heard above the rumble and roar and staccato exhaust thunder of an eastbound Santa Fe freight grinding out of the yards, double-headed, bound for the Continental Divide—"The Navajo are poor. Very poor. The reservation can hardly support them . . . but if they leave the reservation, they cease to be Navajo, because they are bound up with their land in a way white men don't understand . . . and never will . . . the Hopi even more than the Navajo. So the first thing we have to do is find ways to help the Navajo survive, in his own way, on his own land. You could discover coal . . . but that would mean scarring the sacred Mother. You could do something by staging dances and sings for tourists . . . prostitution and sacrilege! So what's left? What do the Navajo do well now?"

"They're great sheepherders," John said, "though they need veterinary help here, and they should investigate whether they can't breed a strain of sheep that'll do better in this country and climate than what they have now . . . Their silver and turquoise jewelry is barbaric, but . . ."

491

"Why call it barbaric?" Reinhart cut in—"It's different, that's all . . . and it's not very different from Tibetan and Chinese work, I can assure you. Their rugs are superb . . . but no Eastern carpet expert recognizes the weaver and the patterns, and can say, 'That's a Two Grey Hills, that's a Toadlena,' the way they say 'That's a Meshed, an Isfahan, a Turcoman' . . . The Navajos sell them at the Trading Posts for next to nothing. They get next to nothing for the priceless old jewelry at pawn. But they should not be encouraged at all to find cheaper or easier ways of making these things. They must stick to their own ways, in their own land . . . Buy and run Hurford's, so that you are in touch with sources . . . so that you learn about all the artists, all the silversmiths, all the weavers . . . who's good, who's lazy, who copies, who's original . . . get to know the metals, the stones, the wools. Then work to create a demand for this art in the East . . . New York, Philadelphia, Washington . . . Do you realize the effect if the President's wife were to be photographed at just one big function wearing a Navajo brooch? Or suppose there was a great Navajo rug spread in the main entrance hall of the White House . . ."

John whistled softly through his teeth. Reinhart's face was red, his eyes shining; partly the boilermakers, of course; but what he said made sense. He himself was fed up with the Indian Service; but he had fallen in love with the land, and the people; and Stella was improving, slowly but surely, clawing up from her world of hallucination to the hard pure reality of this country, these people.

Reinhart said, "Work on the legislatures of New Mexico and Arizona . . . and on Congress too . . . to protect the real Indian artists against white imitators. No one yet knows the difference in New York, and your people will suffer . . . because the imitation stuff won't *feel* good, it won't last, and a lot of it won't even be of genuine silver or turquoise . . . and you'll be blamed."

John said, "I'll resign from the Service right away."

Reinhart said, "Now you're talking! Send your father a wire. But don't get Hughes mad. He could stop you buying Hurford's . . . or at least see that you were never allowed onto the reservation to run it. Now he probably thinks you just need some moulding to become a good bureaucrat."

"I'm not so sure," John said. "Anyway, I think Dad has enough clout in Washington to fix anything with the U.S.I.S., if he agrees with me. But if I'm fed up with the Service he'll want me to go back to Fairfax, Gottlieb in New York."

Reinhart was on another boilermaker; but he became calmer, and spoke more deliberately—"Get him to come out here. Show him what

you want to do for them . . . If he's worth anything, if he can understand men, he'll see."

*   *   *   *

John was away in the western end of the reservation, and would not
return for three nights. Mary Begay was eighteen, dark-skinned, her
hair braided, full-breasted. She was distantly related to Chee Shush
Benally, John's dead friend. She usually left the house at four o'clock
to walk three miles across the foothills to the hogan of another relative, west of Fort Defiance, where she had lived since starting to work
for Stella and John. But this day she said, "Missis . . . you are alone
with Ké"—this was the Navajo word for "peace" and also Peace's
Navajo name . . . She had little English, but her message came
through, in Navajo words, some English, signs. Stella wanted to stop
using the heroin. She knew of it. Who could miss the needles, the
marks of them? She had thought of taking the missis to a sing . . . that
might be good later, when she knew more . . . Now, she should take
peyote, alone, thinking of what she wanted to be. She held out her
hand, open.

Stella knew peyote by sight and name. The button heads of the
mescal contained a hallucinatory drug as strong as hashish or bhang.
She stared at the buttons now, without fear, yet she had lived in terror
of all drugs, even heroin, since she had become an addict. She asked,
"Will I . . . have to have it always?"

Mary said, "As you wish."

It was dark outside, a wind blowing in from the mountains, stars
brightening as the darkness grew more dense, closing down on the
little house at the edge of the government settlement. Mary moved
silently about, putting out the oil lanterns by laying a flat cardboard
over the glass, so that the flame in each died but left no reek of
kerosene. The house was bare, smelling only of dust. Peace was asleep
in his crib at the back, and in sudden panic Stella cried, "What about
Peace? What if he wakes . . . falls?"

"Shh! Peace, peace," Mary said, almost chanting. Stella pulled back
a chair, to sit at the table, but Mary motioned toward the fireplace, and
said, "Sit on floor . . ." Stella sank down, her back to the wall beside
the fire. Mary took a few of the buttons and mashed them with her
thumb into a bowl she had brought from the kitchen and set on the
table, mixing them with a little water. Then, again with thumb and
fingers she rolled the small greyish mass into two balls and handed
one to Stella. She murmured a long phrase in Navajo, that Stella could
not understand, and swallowed the ball she had been holding in the

palm of her hand. Stella stared at her own palm in the deep gloom and thought, to sleep, perchance to dream, but in that sleep, what dreams? She swallowed the pill and waited.

Mary Begay sat on the floor opposite her, cross-legged under the long blue velveteen skirt, nothing to support her back, staring wide-eyed at Stella, six feet away. At first Stella did not think she could make out the girl's features at all, as she seemed to sink slowly back into the darkness. Then gradually her mind, the inside of her head, began to lighten, and as it did Mary's dark eyes swam up out of blackness to become glowing, then shining lights . . . the colour of them a deep gold, each two inches across, and wider set than they could have been in real life. Inside, the scattered amorphous lights were taking form . . . the red cliff escarpment along the railroad tracks by McCartys, in New Mexico. The rocks towered up, and there was a white road, pale, winding down out of the high desert behind, and a single figure riding a white horse, a child on the saddle bow. Herself. And there was water, a house tucked under the cliff . . . above, vigas sticking out from under the firewall . . . the whole sheltered by the smooth upward and outward sweep of the cliff. The grey rock was marked with vertical black lines, where water had run down for millions of years . . . John was running toward her, striding like a stallion, fleet as the wind, running across the desert, against the cliff . . . She was with him, making love, but a love so powerful their whole bodies were engaged in it, melting into each other, not only their sexual parts, she was floating away, not with orgasm but with the power of her own imagination, going, where? It did not matter. She knew, but was sworn not to tell . . . on, up, through groves of cottonwoods, a river running shallow by tall cliffs—that was Canyon de Chelly, but infinitely bigger than when she had seen it, and peopled now by ancient people, they whispered to her their name—Anasazi, Anasazi, Anasazi . . . words hovered over her, Shongopovi, Betatakin, Oraibi, Biklabito . . . and with each name, an image, as though the word possessed the power of creating the reality as she repeated it . . . From a distant star, sweeping slowly past the face of a yellow planet, she heard a woman's voice cry, "The Peyote Road . . . !"

About two o'clock in the morning she vomited and went to bed, while Mary curled up on the floor of the passage outside Peace's room. The two women had said nothing to each other, as Stella sank slowly down to the consciousness she had called being awake, before; and Mary's eyes had burned bright again, and dimmed to a glowing, and from that to the nondescript darkness of the night; but Stella could see everything much more clearly now than she had in the day.

In the morning she took out her needle and syringe and heroin, and stared at them a long time, wondering. Then she put them back in the medicine cupboard and locked the door. But at midday she was sweating and her mouth was dry and she went to the bathroom again, unlocked the cabinet, and did what she had to do. Not yet, not yet.

*   *   *   *

They were riding on three Navajo ponies, all three buckskins, two stallions and a mare, followed by Mary Begay on a fourth, the baby Peace rested in front of her, enfolded in her blanket as well as supported by her arm. The Benallys had brought the horses to the road, near Tocito, and waited a day, two days, perhaps, for John had not been able to tell them exactly when his father was coming, until he had wired from Chicago. Stella, on John's right, rode in a strange awareness that she had been here before . . . not just this road, this dusty cart track, but in this cavalcade, with John and his father, and Mary and Peace. She had taken her day's dose of heroin a long time ago now, but the effect was not wearing off. Or had it been replaced, without her noticing, by some other equally powerful presence, an Indian presence, first revealed to her in the peyote two weeks ago, since then often manifesting itself without the introduction of the mescal buttons? She had taken them twice since, both times when alone in the house; for now she had no fear of them.

John said, "Rein in, Dad." He pointed, as the horses dipped their heads and tugged at the reins, searching for grass among the desert scrub and straggling vetch—"There's Hurford's."

Stephen stared. He had visited the Navajo reservation several times, but never precisely this part of it. He had heard of Hurford's Trading Post, which John now wanted to buy, but had never seen it. Now, across three miles of slightly rolling desert split by a wide sandy wash, he saw a red cliff wall, climbing up and out from the pale earth 400 feet, its glowing surface marked by the usual black water stripes; and under the overhang, the long line of an adobe building . . . a corral to the right . . . two, three hogans to the left . . . smoke rising from the low chimneys of the main building. He thought there were some wagons and horses drawn up outside the Post, but his eyes were not as good as they used to be. He said, "It looks rather like the White House ruin, in Canyon de Chelly."

Stella cried, "That's the place!" She passed them, forcing her pony to walk faster. Mary drew up and past too, finally kicking her pony into a canter to catch up.

"It's absolutely isolated," Stephen said. "Fort Defiance would seem like the back of beyond to most Easterners—it would to me if we

495

hadn't visited this country before . . . but this, this really is. What on earth is Stella going to do with herself here?"

"Help me," John said briefly. "Help the Navajos. We'll both be up to our ears in work, soon enough . . . Not right away. The people will take time to trust us. But the Benallys will help to persuade them, simply by coming . . . by trusting."

Stephen said, "John—listen . . . Are you sure you're not hiding away here for something more than to help Stella, and the Navajos? Are you sure you aren't trying to escape from the war?"

"The war was a humbling experience, Dad," John said briefly.

Stephen said, "You are fit . . . and have fitted yourself . . . to help many, many more people than one, or even one tribe. You, who have a dozen talents, will be using only two or three."

The two women ahead were growing smaller as they dropped over the rim where the rock dipped down to the wash, Mary in bright blue and pink, her skirts billowing out on both sides of her horse, Stella harder to see in her wide-brimmed hat, tan shirt, breeches, and riding boots.

John said, "I have thought of all those things, Dad. All that you say is true, and I know it. But I am not *called* to anything else . . . When I went off to the war, it was because I felt I ought to, but I certainly did not feel *called* to it, as I think Guy Rowland was. And all those months I was in France, or at Fort Sill, or back in France, I was thinking, what happens after this is over? What do I do then? . . . I didn't know . . . and when at last a call came, it was strong but not very clear . . . first I knew I had to get Stella away from Europe, from England, her home . . . break that whole life pattern. And I did. But months later, here, I was wondering what I was really here for . . . then the second call came: *this* is what you have to do. It was just a few weeks ago, and the voice was the voice of a drunken old man in a bar in Gallup— Reinhart. He's going to come and work for us here—teaching us how to value pawn, rugs, silverwork, turquoise, sand paintings . . . But this is it, Dad. I know that."

Stephen said, "For now, then, I'll have to accept it. And do. You can count on me for whatever financial and other help that I can give."

*   *   *   *

They had been settled into the Trading Post, now called Merritt's, for six days. Stella was alone, for John had gone to the Hopi territory to buy their silverwork. Autumnal thunder crashed against the face of the cliff and reverberated through its solid rock, shaking the vigas in the ceiling and sending trickles of dust to fall through the latillas, the pale aspen boughs that were laid herringbone fashion between the vigas. Stella lay awake, shaken by the thunder, dazzled by the flashes of lightning that painted the whitewashed adobe walls with sudden brilliance. It was colder, much colder than when she had gone to bed four hours ago. She had no clock beside her but she knew the hour, exactly. She was uneasy, too, feeling that something had gone amiss in the plan of the universe, and of the land; but as yet she did not know what. She would know soon. She did not need peyote to come to that awareness, it would come to her.

Rain lashed across the windows, onto the earth . . . she heard it, felt it . . . it was running down the curved face of the red cliff over her head, too, pouring into the trenches beside the Post, running out onto the plain, some falling in a curtain direct from the outermost point of the curve to the ground ten feet in front of the front wall of the Post.

It was a hurricane, Reinhart had told her—a deep disturbance either in the Gulf of Mexico or off Baja California that carried swirling water-laden winds a thousand miles, far up over the high desert lands, and when they struck the rise of the Arizona and New Mexico mountains, dropped their heavy load of water. Such storms moved slowly, Reinhart said, sometimes taking three days to move off a particular part of the country.

Someone knocked on the door . . . their bedroom was at the end of the long low building, next to it the living room, beyond that the big kitchen, through which they must pass to reach the Post. At the other side of the bedroom was a small spare room where Peace slept, with Mary Begay, for the Post was too far from her home for her to return there every night, as she had done in Fort Defiance.

Stella called, "Who is it?"

A man's guttural voice grunted, "Hoskie Tsosi." She swung out of bed. Hoskie Tsosi was the head of one of the families that lived in the hogans beyond the Post. She struggled into a robe, and when she was ready, said, "Come in."

It was very dark, but she heard the door open and sensed the silent passage of his moccasined feet across the rugs; then she heard the dripping of water. He said, "Boy come . . . sister having baby . . . baby not come out."

"Where?" Stella asked. Behind her she heard the other door open and heard Mary say, "Where live woman?"

The man answered quickly in Navajo and Mary turned to Stella— "It is Ason Atsiddy. Their hogan is by the Turkey Spring . . . nine miles, ten miles. Two hours on horse."

497

"What can I do?" Stella cried. "I'm not a doctor. Have they no midwife? Or experienced women?"

Mary and the man were talking rapidly as Stella cried out, and between their staccato sentences Mary threw out words and phrases to her . . . "No woman there, only children . . . eldest boy came here."

"What about the doctor at the Fort?" she cried. "Can't you get him?"

"No time . . ."

"But . . . I don't know what it is . . . is it something to do with the baby? Has she got a stomach illness?"

"Don't know . . . need help."

A tremendous flash of lightning lit the room brighter than day and she saw their faces, the dark brown turned to pale green. She said, "I will dress. Bring horses. The boy will return with me as a guide. And wake Mr Reinhart."

Tsosi said, "He drunk. No good."

"You come with me then."

Mary said, "He will go with you. I stay with Peace."

Tsosi went out toward the Post and Stella, lighting a lamp, dressed hurriedly. She had thought her fingers would be trembling, her whole body shaking, but they did not. In five minutes she was ready, dressed in riding clothes, a heavy poncho over all, in her coat pocket the first-aid box they kept in the Post, inherited from Hurford.

The horses were already saddled, waiting outside the Post door, the curtain of water from the cliff falling beyond them, all round a sea of water appearing and disappearing with the lightning. Stella took the reins and swung up into the saddle. The boy led off, she followed, then Tsosi. Every few seconds the lightning delineated the valley, the wash ahead, the distant rocks. They went up the near side of the wash for ten minutes. By then she was soaked through the poncho, and the temperature was dropping behind the weather front. It was a cold rain that slashed across her face and shoulders, cold air driving through the wet clothes.

The boy reined in his horse and Stella and Tsosi came up beside him. He pointed to the water in the wash and said something in Navajo. Stella shouted, "What?"

Tsosi said, "He says, cross."

Stella hitched down more firmly in the saddle. The water was deep, how deep the lightning did not tell her, but it was running now from bank to bank, 300 yards, which she had only known as so much sand, twisted roots of greasewood, and sage. But the banks were three to four feet high, and the wash was up to them, and in places over. She did not know the hogan they were going to, but it must be on the other bank; and they were crossing here rather than wait, when two more hours' rain would have swollen the river even higher.

They entered the water together, all three horses side by side. The ponies stepped carefully, bracing their legs against the rush of the water, dirty brown, swirling past in the lightning . . . a whole sage bush raced by . . . here something dead, a cow, perhaps, from higher up, or a sheep—she could not tell. Her pony stumbled and Tsosi's hand reached out at once, gripping the reins by the head as he leaned over and spoke to it in Navajo—"Steady! Do not be afraid . . . Careful!"

The water was forcing against her boots . . . trickling in over the top of the left one, on the upstream side. To her right the boy suddenly vanished into the darkness. A flash of lightning showed him momentarily, twenty yards downstream, the horse fallen sideways, his face white, mouth open, teeth bared . . . then darkness—"Can't we . . . ?" Stella cried.

Tsosi shouted "On!"

Pace by pace, the ponies crabbing diagonally across the flood, as they were unable to keep their balance while walking directly across, they reached the farther bank, scrambled up out of the bed of the wash, and turned again westward. The lightning was becoming less frequent, but the rain fell just as hard, and even colder. Stella again wondered, why am I not strangled by fear, paralyzed by cold? She knew, but could not explain.

They struggled on in the rain, the ground under the horses' hooves now a quagmire that gripped them, and held them, only to release grudgingly, hurling mud into their faces. Near dawn, they came at last to the place where the woman lay.

Stella swept aside the blanket that curtained off the tunnel entrance, and stumbled into the hogan. It was no different from any other hogan but, coming in out of the cold and the wet, the heavy, warm atmosphere, compounded of the odors of piñon and juniper smoke mixed with mutton fat, nearly overpowered her. It took her a few seconds to adapt to the extreme contrast of the cozy haven and the sodden chill outside. Ason Atsiddy squatted on sheepskins, completely enveloped by a Pendleton blanket. Only her face was visible in the fire glow, but its sweaty grimace told the story of her agony.

Stella set out to persuade the woman to lie down, recumbency being unheard of among the Navajo as a position for delivery, and at length succeeded. As Stella's hands warmed on her patient's belly, which relaxed after a long contraction, she felt the unmistakable contour and reverberation of the infant's head low on the right side. She dredged urgently back into her memory, of her training and experience as a V.A.D. . . . . what was it the doctors called that slight inner reverberation on palpation? . . . ballottement. This head was very low in the right iliac depression. Her heart sank. It was a transverse presentation, probably a shoulder jammed into the cervix. She could not remember all the complications that might also be present, but she knew the condition was an obstetrical nightmare. The doctors and nurses had always looked grave when faced with it. She had been present at two deliveries from transverse presentations, of which one baby had died. Now she was faced with it again, alone, under the worst possible conditions.

The children had kept the hogan fire going through the storm, and there was a smoke-blackened galvanized bucket half-full of water next to the ashes. Stella hoped it had boiled, for there was no time to boil it now. She took the small piece of yellow soap from her first-aid box, and had the oldest child pour water onto her hands and forearms, as she washed carefully, consciously trying to make haste slowly. Dawn filtered grey through the still-falling rain, and threw a soft illumination down from the smoke hole in the roof. Stella's purposeful activity seemed to trigger an immediate sense of confidence in Ason Atsiddy, more than any words could have, and she allowed Stella to insert her still soapy right hand into her vagina without question. Stella felt carefully . . . the cervix was fully dilated and almost completely thinned—effaced . . . it was the infant's left shoulder being presented. Now she knew what she must do to give mother and child a chance of survival, for she had seen it done. Whether she could actually do it . . . she would, she would!

First, left hand on the belly, for she could only work when the uterus was relaxed. The hand signaled when a contraction was ending . . . Stella pushed up on the presented shoulder, trying to rotate the head into the pelvis, and so convert this into a normal headfirst presentation. It was hard work, and on the third attempt Stella found she was sweating in spite of her cold, wet clothes.

The head would not move. She must try something else. Pausing a moment and getting the eldest child to mop her face, she began again. This time, when she dislodged the shoulder she inserted her hand well up into the uterus, felt for, at last found and identified a foot. She pulled gently, bringing it down. Then the other foot, and as she pulled the baby slowly rotated into a classic double footling breech. This she'd seen a dozen times, and though it was a difficult presentation, particularly during the delivery of the head, it seemed like nothing after the long agony of the shoulder arrest.

An hour later, the baby was born—a boy, who cried loudly on greeting the Navajo world of his inheritance. Except for a bruised left

500

shoulder he seemed none the worse for wear. Ason Atsiddy, totally exhausted, gave Stella a faint, eloquent smile of relief and gratitude, which, again, said what no words could have.

For the first time since she had first taken heroin, at the hands of Dr Deerfield, Stella felt a slow warming flood of pure, clean excitement and equally pure joy welling up in her, to overflow into a low cry of gratitude to the Navajo land, this woman, this baby, for giving her the opportunity, and the power, to break free. John worried about the Trading Post, whether it would succeed, how all his plans and hopes would go . . . but she knew. They were of the Dinneh, and they would go on, together now, she and John and Peace, and the People.

Daily Telegraph, Tuesday, October 14, 1919

NORTH RUSSIA EVACUATION

The War Office announces that the evacuation of North Russia has now been completed. The last transport sailed from Murmansk on Sunday afternoon.

His Majesty the King has sent the following telegram to General Rawlinson:

On completion of the evacuation of the Allied troops from North Russia I desire to congratulate you and all ranks under your command on the successful manner in which this difficult operation has been accomplished.

I wish to express my appreciation of the skill displayed by the commanders, and the courage, discipline, and power of endurance of all ranks. These qualities have enabled the forces both at Archangel and Murmansk to be withdrawn from their advanced positions in contact with the enemy, transported over great distances to their bases, and embarked with practically no loss of life . . .

General Rawlinson . . . arrived at Glasgow yesterday on board the troopship *Toloa* . . . Over a thousand troops, including Russian and Serbian officers, also arrived by the same boat. After inspecting the guard of honour, composed of a detachment of Argylls, General Rawlinson motored to Kelvingrove Park, where he viewed the equestrian statue of Earl Roberts. The General was an intense admirer of the late Field Marshal, on whose staff he served for a quarter of a century . . . He subsequently left by train for London.

The Bolsheviks were lucky they had had their revolution toward the end of the war, Cate thought. The world was on the edge of bankruptcy, and above all, war weary. If this had happened in 1912, say, half a dozen countries would have banded together to intervene with overwhelming military strength, and strangle the revolution before it could gather strength. But that was a fruitless speculation: it was the war which had caused the revolution; without it, the Romanovs would have struggled through another half-century, at least, with nothing worse than an assassination or two, and some scattered peasant revolts.

"More coffee, madam?" Garrod said, leaning over Isabel, at the other end of the table.

"Please," Isabel said, smiling up at the old maid—"That's enough . . . thank you." She drank, and looked across at Cate, "Did you see the bit about the troops returning from Russia?"

"I'm reading it now."

"Well, you remember I was saying, the other day, that the U.S.A. was going to go into the export business? What I meant was that Britain was going to go into the import business, importing ideas from all over, trying to change things for the better after the miseries of the war . . . and that a lot of these ideas were going to come from the U.S.A., for better or for worse."

"I remember," he said. "And that's why I ought to go over with you, to learn, you said."

"Quite. But you are now reading about another country from which you—and all of us—are going to import ideas, willy nilly."

"Russia? The Bolsheviks?" Cate exclaimed. "Well, I suppose you're right. I was just thinking that if their revolution had taken place at some other time, the rest of Europe would have strangled it at birth . . . and they wouldn't bother to do that unless they were afraid that the Russian revolutionary ideas would be infectious."

"Quite," Isabel said again. "Forewarned is forearmed."

"Do you mean we ought to visit Russia, too? To learn what influences we might expect here?"

"It wouldn't be a bad idea," she said. "It's hard to tame a horse if you don't know its strengths and weaknesses . . . but one thing at a time. We'll wait till the dust has cleared over there . . . a couple of years, at the least, I should think."

England and Germany: October, 1919

29 David Toledano moved out from behind his tall little desk at the end of the crowded room, and bowed deeply—"Good morning, Sir Guy. To what do I owe the rare honour of this visit?"

Guy said, "Cheese it, David . . . Don't you have a private office?"

David grinned, "No. Only my father . . . but I shall have one on January 1, 1920. My father's retiring the day before . . . Have you come to tell us that you will accept the offer he made to you, to come in with us? I wish you would, Guy. I'm going to feel awfully lonely in there, in spite of all the earnest old men in yarmulkas who will advise me."

Guy said, "Sorry, David. I'm out of the R.A.F., but I have other plans. We—Florinda and I—are starting an organization to repair people physically or psychically destroyed by the war. We need money. Lots of it."

David leaned back against his desk. "Pheeew," he whistled softly. "What's the plan?"

Guy spoke slowly and carefully. "There are four organizations trying to help look after ex-servicemen . . . see that they get their disability pensions, help them find jobs—create jobs, even. I know that Field Marshal Haig is very concerned about all that, and will take an active part once he retires, or resigns from the ridiculous job Lloyd George has shunted him into—Commander-in-Chief, Home Forces . . . What we want to do is something more ambitious. We want to take these wrecks . . . these people whom the war crushed under its tracks . . . and, if we can, make them more than they were before. We think—Florinda and I—that there is music in the souls of many men who have never had the chance to let it grow, flourish, take over. Art, too . . . how many men—cripples even—might be able to paint really well if we can open their eyes to the whole horizons of art, and all its nooks and crannies, and give them what skills they will need—and have the capacity to absorb? Why should such people not formulate ideas about the way we should reorganize the world, using what we have learned in the war, studying the changes that have come about, and the reasons for them . . . ?"

He paused for breath and Toledano said, "What are the mechanics of all this? How are you going to set about it?"

"Get an estate, with a big house, and room to build more . . . or to put up Nissen huts . . . then take in the wounded, the sick. Find the teachers. Knock down barriers. Build roads back to ability, pride—and beyond."

"You'll have a resident staff, then? A pretty big one."

"No larger than it has to be . . . We need to be reasonably close to some biggish city, so that local doctors, alienists, specialists and experts of all kinds, can devote half a day or a day to us without spending several more hours traveling . . . A lot of the staff will be the patients themselves. We might be able to use Willum Gorse—he lost both legs at the end of the March '18 retreat—as a telephone operator, for instance . . . Will you help?"

"Of course," David said slowly. "I might have guessed that you would do something quite unexpected. That was how you fooled Wokingham, that match in '14, when you won for us with a dropped goal . . . And that day you twice got C.B. Fry out for a pair of spectacles . . . I've been imagining you in a frock coat and top hat, refusing to lend the Government a penny more than a hundred million . . . or, if you wouldn't come in with us—and privately I never thought you would—then as Marshal of the Royal Air Force, sending great bomber fleets out over Germany . . . or perhaps it will be France next time . . . How much do you need?"

"I have no idea, David. Suppose we start with a million. And you have to agree to be on the Board of Governors, and for the moment to act as Treasurer."

Toledano threw up his powerful hands, "Me? I'm a banker, Guy, not an accountant. I can't add or subtract for toffee."

"But one of your old men in yarmulkas could do it?"

"Of course. All right. Done! Tell me when you actually want the money. Meanwhile I'll get the right sort of bank account started for you. What's the name of your organization?"

"We don't have one yet. We have an idea, but I can't tell you for sure for a couple of weeks yet. We want the organization to spread beyond England—to be world-wide . . . Thanks, David."

Toledano held out his hand, saying, "You've lit a spark, Guy. I was feeling guilty . . . I personally had a jolly interesting war. We took Jerusalem, so now we really can say, 'Next year, in Jerusalem,' at Passover . . . The bank made hundreds of millions out of the war. Oh, we earned it, but nevertheless, we made a lot of money . . . And I, at least, haven't slept too well since, thinking of those who didn't have a jolly good time. I'm with you all the way."

"Thanks, David. It'll cost you a lot."

"Not as much as two legs, or two eyes, or a sound mind."

*   *   *   *

Lord Walstone spread his legs a little wider in front of the fire, holding his thumbs tight in his waistcoat pockets, below the gold chain and fob. He said, "I will give you an answer as soon as I can, Sir Guy. Perhaps a week. Your proposal needs some thinking over, you know. Millions of pounds don't grow on trees. Not in this country, mate. Let me show you out."

He unhitched his thumbs and strode purposefully ahead of his caller to the door, opened it for him, and went with him down the long parquet-floored passage to the front door of Walstone Park. Then he returned, to find his wife Ruth standing by the fireplace.

"That was young Rowland, the airman," he said. "Sir Guy, and him only twenty-two! Come here on some harebrained scheme to help ex-servicemen, as far as I can make out. He has his nerve . . . asked me for a cool million, right out, just like that! Well, I s'pose if you've shot down seventy Jerries and flown across the ruddy Atlantic without stopping, you have to have a nerve. But get a million from yours truly? I'm a wide boy, I am. Not bloody likely!"

Ruth said, "I was listening from the Blue Room, Bill. The connecting door was open."

"Why, you little eavesdropper . . ."

"I want you to give him the money. And be on his Board of Governors."

Lord Walstone roared, "D'you think I'm out of my fucking mind, Ruthie? Here I work . . ."

"Do not swear, Bill."

"Here I work like a bloody nigger to make money for you and Launcelot and Christine, so you won't have to beg in the streets, or go to the workhouse, and have a roof over your heads and good clothes on your backs, and now you want me to give it all away for . . ."

She said quietly, "You know we've gone far past worrying about shoes and shirts and food, Bill. We've talked about this before, remember. When I said you must find something else to do with your brain than make more money. Well, here it is."

"But . . . give it away!" Hoggin wailed. "That's not right."

"It's the only thing that is right, for you, now. To give, not take. Give your money . . . and yourself. You've done what you set out to do. You're rich. You have a title. But how much have you enjoyed your money, since the end of the war, say?"

Hoggin went to the sideboard, opened it, and poured himself a bottle of Bass. He said, "Not so much, that's a fact. Don't know why . . . I've made some big deals . . . spent a lot of money and energy getting the Hounds started again, but . . . I think I'm bored. I'm not sure, 'cos I've never been bored before, so I don't know what it feels like, really."

She said, "This is the cause, the new task, you've been looking for. Sir Guy will need a great deal of practical help, when he starts his house . . . purchase of food, furnishings . . . bookkeeping, pay of staff . . . You could allot one day a week to him. And it wouldn't be far for you, if he does get Scarrow Hall."

Bill said, "He ought to. Beacham's dead broke, and has to sell. Who's going to buy a barrack like that, except some organization? Christ, it's bigger than this place . . . More modern, though. All the floors level, at least, and there's room in the stairwells to put in lifts . . . bloody great kitchen . . . only a mile and a half from Hedlington Station."

"With bus service to the cinnie, for the girls working there," Ruth said. "Make this your new goal, Bill. Make it work, work as hard for it as you did for yourself and for us. Sir Guy's going to get some very important people in with him, you know. You'll be working with them. Next thing you know you'll be invited to join their clubs . . . The King might make you a viscount, even an earl."

"Well . . ." Bill began.

She interrupted, "You owe it to the people who fought while you were making money. And I want Launcelot's and Christine's father to be a very respected man, working hard for those less fortunate than he."

"All right," Hoggin said at last. "All bloody right! I give in. One million spondulicks to begin with . . . I'll telephone him this afternoon, when he's back in London." He began to stride up and down the floor—"We ought to be able to buy Scarrow Hall for under a hundred thousand. I'll see if I can get the Building Inspector to declare it's unsafe. Might cost me a thou, but . . ."

"Bill!"

*   *   *   *

Guy and Florinda were sprawled on the huge sofa in Florinda's Half Moon Street flat, kissing comfortably. They had been at it for half an hour when Florinda slid her tongue into his left ear, searched around inside, then leaned back, saying, "That's so you can hear me better, cock o' my 'eart. I am about to say something important . . . It's about this thing we're doing, helping the people broken up by the war. I'm not going to have you spending the rest of your life feeling guilty, you know . . . going around moaning and moping because you're so wicked, you blew up all those blokes and houses and starved all those women and kids personally, yourself."

He leaned away from her—"I don't feel like that, Flo. I did feel guilty, but this work, this plan we have, is changing that. I feel really good, really happy, for the first time in years. War humbles you, and I'm feeling humble—it was about time—but good, too, now."

She said, "All right, but if I ever catch you crying in your beer, I'll give you a swift kick in the pants, got it? Now, another thing . . . You were a major when you were twenty, commanding that squadron. That took more than guts, it took brains. And then the generals picked you to make reports on bombing policy, and they sent you to Paris, and all over, to talk with big cheeses about things that were going to cost millions, and affect all of us, and England. Now you're devoting yourself to this Scarrow Hall, and the comparatively few people who are going to come to it . . ."

"And to the other branches we hope to found all over the world," he said.

"Yes," she said impatiently. "But in three, four years it's all going to be running like clockwork—you'll see to that. Then what are you going to do? Start a harem to keep you busy? Collect stamps?"

"Play some cricket, perhaps," Guy said.

"Garn!"

"This is all I want to do," he said. "I'm happy, and that's all there is to it. And I'm going to do this right, with everything I have and am."

She said, almost to herself, "Overstretched, and overworked, at twenty, now you want to lie fallow, or just grow hay . . . need to, probably . . . doing a good job down among the worms instead of the eagles." She spoke up—"A time will come when you'll need to fly higher again, Guy. Don't fight it. Everyone will be behind you . . . especially the blokes . . . By the way, what did General Trenchard say when he sent for you, after you'd resigned your commission?"

Guy said slowly, "He said he was accepting my resignation, though he needed me, because he didn't want any unwilling officers in the R.A.F. . . . but if the time came when *England* needed me, he would call me back—'even from my grave,' he said, looking coldly at me from under those great, grey eyebrows. Then he said, 'That's all,' nodded curtly, and I was out . . ."

"If England needs you," she repeated, shivering suddenly.

*　　*　　*　　*

Billy Bidford was sitting in his suite at the Ritz, reading the *Times*. It was nearly eleven o'clock in the morning, but Billy had been motor racing in Surrey the day before, and that had been followed by a late party at the Cat & Mouse in Albemarle Street with a Miss Maxine Merlin—her real name—an American film actress on a visit to England; and she had not left him to return to her own room in the same hotel until four o'clock . . . so he had slept in; and now, wearing a Chinese silk dressing gown of red and gold, was smoking a Turkish cigarette in a long holder, drinking coffee, and eating a croissant. He looked up as Guy entered and said, "Coffee? A croissant? . . . Or I could get you some Nice biscuits. That's what you used to eat in the air, wasn't it?"

Guy said, "Yes," smiling. "A croissant will do me fine."

He sat down opposite Bidford, noticing that the tray had been set for two. Billy poured him coffee and told him to help himself to the pastry. Then he said, "I saw that you had resigned your commission. I thought the air force was your dream."

Guy said, "I did think, once, that the air force would be my life. But then, when it was being offered to me on a plate . . . when first General Sykes and then General Trenchard told me the R.A.F. was mine for the taking, I found I'd lost interest . . . You haven't heard what I'm doing?"

Billy shook his head, "I don't read the papers . . . except the racing pages."

"I'm starting an organization to mend people broken by the war."

"Just in Britain?" Billy said quickly.

"At the moment. But I want to expand it world-wide . . . Will you help—with money, and if you can spare it, time?"

Bidford laughed loudly, throwing back his head and laughing at the high Corinthian swirls of the ceiling plaster.

"I didn't know you were a wit, Guy," he said at last. "Do *I* have the time? You mean, from racing at Surrey Park? Moving my yacht to Cowes? Flying to Paris for the Longchamps meet? Driving up to Rannoch Moor on August the 11th? . . . But what the hell can *I* do for you?"

"I need money and publicity," Guy said. "Could you race for us, sometimes? Fly for us? Nobble your friends. Pass the hat round. Be our herald among the idle rich . . . the people who literally don't know what to do with their money? Give up a few hours a week for us . . . and some cash now, if you can spare it?"

Bidford wagged a finger at him—"There you go again, Guy. Sarcasm ill becomes you. Yes, I can spare a few quid. How about a million? Or two?"

"One would help a lot now, when we're just getting set up."

"What are you going to call your organization?"

"Don't know yet. But we'd like you to be a Governor."

"Fine. And I'll do what you say . . . It'll make me feel a little better for having come out with a V.C. and a big reputation, while . . ." He didn't finish the sentence, but emptied his coffee cup, and said, "When's the wedding?"

"Wednesday week, in Hedlington."

"I suppose I ought to be as jealous as hell, but since Flo told me, I've had time to think it over. I'm not really the marrying kind. Any woman I marry is going to be very bored. She'll fall for other men, because she's lonely, because I neglect her. Flo might have been strong enough to make me realize that I have to share my life . . . but I didn't get her, so . . . good luck. Damn your eyes."

Guy said, "Will you be my best man?"

Billy sat back—"You really are the most underrated wit in England . . . Why not? Yes. An original idea, but you always were an original fellow, weren't you?"

*   *   *   *

"We are being married next Wednesday week," Guy said. "Nine days from now."

Maria von Rackow said, "I'll come, if you invite me."

"Of course."

"I cried all day, and all night, when I got your letter, that you had made up your mind. At first, you were simply a sort of image of Werner . . . Werner himself, in another body—another eagle. But gradually, as we corresponded, and met, and talked, you became yourself, Guy Rowland . . . and I fell in love with you, yourself. It was treachery to Werner's memory, but I couldn't help it."

They were in the big living room of the schloss, terraces sweeping down to stone balustrades, manicured lawns, and beyond, the dark pines of the von Rackow forests, stretching twelve miles to the Elbe. She was standing by the window, Guy at her side, both looking out. Two deer were feeding at a high trough set up near the foot of the main steps. "Pakli will not feed them after this week," she said. "The season begins . . . Can you stay for a boar hunt on Wednesday?"

He shook his head, "A meeting in London . . . Work in Hedlington. We got Scarrow Hall for 100,000 pounds, thanks to Lord Walstone. It'll cost us another 45,000 to make the essential alterations, but after that, I want to build afresh if we need more space . . . a completely modern, automatic dwelling and working place, leaving people free to learn, to create. I don't think a crippled man's going to regain his pride by washing dishes or scrubbing floors."

"Leave some of your time for us, your friends," she said, laying a hand on his elbow—"Florinda, even. She will be jealous of it, if you let it come to that."

Guy nodded, and after a time, said, "I'm trying not to let that happen. She's very much involved . . . I want to make it a world-wide organization. After all, it was a World War. I want you to start a German branch. And I want your permission to call it the Von Rackow–Rowland Foundation. I tried to think of another name than my own, but I couldn't. And it does have value, in raising money—for now at least."

She turned to him, tears welling up in her grey eyes—"Of course . . . Von Rackow–Rowland. It'll make a nice monogram, with the F . . . or perhaps we can leave out the 'Foundation.' Then there won't be any difference in title between British, German, French, Italian, American branches. You just say, 'This is Von Rackow-Rowland.' "

"Good idea . . . Have you any thoughts about who might lead the French branch?"

"I would have said Guynemer, before he was killed . . . Nungesser?"

"He's great," Guy said. "But he's such a show-off. It was all right in the war, to fly into battle wearing full dress and all your medals—the actual medals, not just the ribbons—but in peacetime that attitude would make us a laughingstock. I think I'll approach Daniel Vincent. He was high up, and a really great organizer . . . perhaps a little cold-blooded, but we'll see."

"Italy?"

"Gabriele d'Annunzio," Guy said, laughing. "We'd welcome his support as a national hero. But not as a Governor, or actually associated with us. Baracca? If he's alive . . . I'll talk to the Italian Ambassador . . . Florinda knows him well."

"Ah," she sighed. "She will be much more useful to you than I could. You chose well, Guy . . . No, no, please don't thank me, or I will break down and disgrace myself."

He stood away from her until she had put away her handkerchief, then said, "Come over, for the wedding, Maria. We're having a meeting of the Board of Governors the next day, at Scarrow Hall. The meeting is at 10 a.m. punctually, to be followed by a buffet lunch served through the courtesy of Lord Walstone."

"Good heavens!" Maria said, summoning a laugh—"We will all be poisoned!"

"I shall have a dog under the table, and we can test the sandwiches on him first."

"Well, that's settled. Now come and see Guy. He's grown a lot since you saw him in Paris."

* * * *

Lady Rowland, Florinda, married two days, no longer the Dowager Marchioness of Jarrow, faced her mother in the little kitchen. It smelled of soapy water, and her mother was working over a washtub, pushing the soiled shirt up and down in the suds. Her face was paler than it ought to be, Florinda thought, and her arms thinner, her neck too. She was overworking, and not eating enough. None of the girls was here to help her today . . . out on the streets, earning easy money, stealing food, ladies' handbags, anything. Violet's baby by old Bob Stratton was over four now, and talking to her dad, Willum, in the front room; while Dad was probably trying to read the newspaper—a day old; they couldn't afford to buy one, so picked yesterday's out of some dustbin every morning. Soon Dad too would be going out to work, pushing himself along in his cart, until at the corner outside the Oddfellows' Hall, one of the others would meet him, and push him to their first stop. The padded gloves he wore were not thick enough. He was growing hard calluses on his knuckles, from pushing himself along the stone pavements.

She said, "Mother, why didn't you come to the wedding?"

"Couldn't afford the time," her mother said, gesturing toward the pile of laundry behind her. She did not sound angry, Florinda thought, just stating a fact. She went on—"Your dad said it was very pretty. He was sorry the colonel . . . or what they call him now . . ."

"Wing Commander," Florinda said.

"That's it . . . wasn't wearing his uniform and medals. Still, you both looked very nice in the paper."

Florinda said, "You know what we're doing?"

"Not really. Don't have the time, and your dad can't really explain . . . He says the Wing Commander was telling him at the wedding he'd have a job for him soon."

Florinda said, "And one for you, too, Mum. We've bought Scarrow Hall—you know it—and there's going to be a lot of laundry there. We've found out about laundries . . . big ones that do most of the

511

work automatically. But there has to be someone in charge of it. We want you."

Her mother stopped her kneading and straightened her back painfully. She said, "You are just trying to give me money, Florinda Gorse, and I won't have it. I won't beg, and I won't take any of your money."

Florinda said heatedly, "Now you listen to me, Mother. I lived with Lord Cantley because he was kind to me, and taught me how to live, and about art . . . and he gave me money, and paintings. Then he went to the war, and was killed. Then I married old Jarrow, because I wanted to live how Cantley had taught me I could. He gave me money and left me money. Then *he* died, and now I've married Guy Rowland. I'm a respectable woman now, whatever you think I was before, and Guy and I are trying to do something for people who were hurt by the war. You've been hurt—Dad losing his legs, what the girls and Rupert are doing, because the war made anything seem all right."

"What are they doing?" Mary said, hands on hips, belligerent.

Florinda said, "You know, Mum, but you've closed your eyes and ears. I don't know that we can help Violet, but the others . . . You'll get a decent salary. A place for you and Dad to live. Work, but not this slavery day in, day out. We can teach Betty something useful—to cook, perhaps . . . and Rupert, too."

Her mother was crying now, her reddened hands to her face, the tears pouring down behind them. Florinda couldn't remember ever seeing her mother cry. She moved round to her and held her by the shoulders, murmuring, "Let's start again, Mum. I need your help, up there . . . someone to talk to, someone who'll help me understand what the men, the broken ones, are feeling. Come on, it's not charity. And whatever it is, it's honestly come by."

At length, "All right," her mother said; and then, "I've got to get on with this. You let me know when I'm to start. And talk to your Dad. He has to go out in half an hour."

*　　*　　*　　*

Guy Rowland wrote quickly in pencil at a deal table, dusty autumn sunlight streaming in over his left shoulder. He was sitting on a kitchen stool in the huge main drawing room of Scarrow Hall, a plan of the great house beside him, and sheets of paper under his hand, making a general scheme for the allotment of the rooms. The most urgent need was to get the lifts put in at once; otherwise, with crippled men, each floor would be isolated from the others. He wondered whether the lifts could be of a sort that could be operated by the men themselves. The normal type needed an operator, and that could be a job for someone with, say, one leg, or blind, perhaps. But it wasn't really fulfilling work . . . he'd have to get the committee to think about that. And very soon, as the orders for the lifts must be placed within a week or two. And who was going to be on the committee which actually ran the place? Perhaps there shouldn't be a committee, but a Resident Governor—himself, obviously . . . with heads of departments, like, say the Housekeeper, the Accountant, the Controller, the Groundsman, the Doctor, the . . . what would you call the fellow in charge of rehabilitation, of the programmes for them . . .?

He heard footsteps and looked up. The door was open and two men came in, one tall and thin, with a black patch over his left eye, the other a slender Roman Catholic priest of medium height, in his forties, with greying hair. He was wearing the long cassock and wide-brimmed hat that Roman priests seldom wore in England. The tall man said, "Wing Commander Rowland?"

Guy stood up—"Yes." He looked more closely—"Haven't we met? You're . . ."

"Charles Kellaway. We met briefly in '16 when you visited the battalion on the Somme. I was commanding B Company."

"My name's Caffin," the priest said. "I had the privilege of being padre to your father's battalion for over two years."

They shook hands and Guy, looking round, said, "I'd ask you to sit down only there aren't any chairs in here yet. What can I do for you?"

Kellaway looked at the priest, the priest looked at Kellaway; then said, "I'm parish priest of Westport in County Mayo. I saw in the *Irish Times* about what you and your wife are going to do . . . and I thought, that is God's work, if ever anything was. So I came over to London, to see the Captain here, and ask him if he had heard about Von Rackow–Rowland—we've been corresponding regularly since the end of the war . . ."

"I had heard, of course," Kellaway said. "And . . . I felt the same as Father Caffin. I dabble in art, you know . . . collect a few paintings, first editions, chinoiserie . . . whatever takes my fancy. It keeps me busy . . . and surrounded by beauty. That's important to me."

"I don't know how you survived the trenches, then," Guy said, smiling. He remembered his father's letters had mentioned Kellaway a few times; and Caffin quite a lot. Kellaway was perhaps a fairy, but probably not actively: a dilettante, but . . . he'd been through the trenches.

Kellaway said, "The men were the only thing that enabled me, and plenty of others, to retain our sanity . . . their spirit . . . their courage . . . endurance . . . their jokes, in the face of unspeakable horror. What can I do?"

"Do you have any particular skill, or training?" Guy asked.

Kellaway shook his head—"No . . . I went to Oxford, but nothing specialized . . . except perhaps books. I'm quite knowledgeable about books, printing, binding, all that."

Guy thought and said, "Could you teach men bookbinding? High-quality work? So that we might start a binding shop and then advertise that we would bind books in leather, gilt, whatever, as gifts or heirlooms . . ."

Kellaway said, "Yes, I think I could do that for you. I studied it for a time when I came down from Balliol. I'd need to refresh myself, but that's no problem."

"Well, give me an idea of what we would need to set up such a programme . . . what space you need, power, tools, machines, materials . . ."

"I would pay for all that myself," Kellaway said. "And I'd like to run it, say, three days a week."

"Good," Guy said. He turned to the priest—"We won't be getting many Catholics, Father . . . just the usual proportion of the population."

"Och!" the priest said, suddenly very Irish in his brogue and intonation—"I was a teacher at the seminary at Drogheda for nine years . . . till I decided I had to go to the war . . . and sure, I'm a Catholic, but I'm not cut out for saving souls for the Church. I . . . I just thought, out there in the trenches, when I spoke to the men— Jews, Catholics, Protestants . . . that I was speaking to Christ on His Cross. It was not I forgiving or helping them. It was them forgiving me, lifting me up . . . I want to come back to them. Your men here will still be on the Cross."

Kellaway said, "He was the best padre any battalion ever had. Your father told me once he was worth an extra company, or two rum rations."

Guy laughed, thinking, we'll have to pay him . . . not much, but something. Can we afford it? What is he actually going to do? He made up his mind, and said, "All right, Father."

"Call me 'padre,' please. It takes the curse off the word, for the Nonconformists. It's regimental, not religious."

"Very well, padre. We'll pay you the same as you get at your parish. And for a start I'll leave you to find out what exactly you should do."

"One thing he can do better than anyone," Kellaway said, "is tell you what the men are feeling . . . really feeling."

"When can you come back?" Guy asked.

"I can stay," the priest said, smiling. "I told my bishop I had had a Call . . . I had a young curate, who was painfully eager for me to die or be made a bishop, so that he could take over the parish. My belongings are in the Captain's flat. Whatever I am in Von Rackow–Rowland, I'm at work now, Guy."

The telephone on the table rang and Guy picked it up—"Von Rackow–Rowland."

A woman's voice said, "Guy? I'm Dorothy Norvell—Arthur Durand-Beaulieu's widow."

Guy exclaimed, "Good heavens, Dorothy, it's ages since we heard of you. You remarried, didn't you?"

The voice was soft but firm—"Yes. Jim Norvell, in '17. He was killed, too, a month before the armistice. He left me a baby . . . a girl. She's a year old now . . . I was a qualified nurse before I married Arthur, and am now a matron. Since March '17 I've been working with shellshock victims and learning psycho-analysis. I have no money beyond a little pension. I want to help you, and I want my little girl to grow up helping. Will you take me as head nurse, or matron, at your Foundation?"

Guy didn't hesitate, but said, "Yes. Give me your address and I'll write or call when we have a place for you."

He jotted down what she told him, replaced the receiver, and turned to the two waiting men—"Let's find the kitchen and make ourselves a sandwich or two, eh?"

*   *   *   *

The two men in the corner of the saloon bar of the White Horse were drinking beer out of pint tankards, bitter for the taller and younger of the two, old and mild for the other.

Guy, the taller, said, "I'd give anything to have you with us, Frank, but we can't pay you anything like what you deserve because we don't have a big enough job. We need someone in charge of machinery of all kinds . . . the boilers for the central heating, and for the laundry, the laundry machines, the mechanism of the lifts . . . the cars and lorries, and I suppose we'll have to have an ambulance . . . perhaps a fire engine of our own . . . I suppose things are about the same at H.A.C.?"

Frank nodded—"Winding down, sir, that's it. They can't get orders. Civil flying's not coming along as fast as it should, not in this country anyway, and the Americans and French have their own machines. No one wants to even think about new bombers, let alone actually order them . . . I've been offered the works foreman's job at Bristol. They are doing well—much better than us."

"Are you going to take it?"

"No, sir. Unless you really won't have me."

Guy drank and put the tankard down. He rubbed his wounded ear and stared at Frank across the little table—"Damn it, Frank," he began. Then he remembered Kellaway and said, "What could you teach crippled men, that would be profitable?"

Frank scratched his chin and at length said, "If you could put in a power saw or two . . . some lathes, turning machines, we could make furniture. I don't know as much about woodworking as I do steel and metals, but I know enough. We could do the whole thing . . . from design to varnish, painting, and selling. That'd pay my salary."

Guy said, "Anne has always made her own and the children's clothes, hasn't she? And she's an expert at working from patterns, using the sewing machine? And even making patterns?"

Frank nodded—"That she is. And loves doing it, too."

Guy said, "Bring her along then. She can teach the men. Find a house nearer the Hall than your old place."

Frank said, anxiously, "Can I bring my bike—Dad's bike?"

"Victoria?" Guy said. "Of course."

"There'll have to be a workshop where I can fix things and make things . . . and I could work on Victoria there. They're going to open Brooklands again next year, and then . . ."

"Of course," Guy said.

Daily Telegraph, Tuesday, October 21, 1919

BOXING DRAMA

DEFEAT OF JIM DRISCOLL

By B. Bennison

Seldom, if ever, has boxing produced a drama so thrilling and so tragic as the contest at the National Sporting Club last night between Jim Driscoll, "incomparable Jim" we shall always know him as, the retired feather-weight champion of the world, and Charles Ledoux, the best bantam (albeit a heavy one, and maybe unable to do the stipulated poundage) of Europe. Here was an old man, old as boxers go, for Driscoll is in his fortieth year, who dared to get into the ring and gamble in his knowledge of ringcraft against a man twenty-seven years of age, who, by common consent stands alone as a fighter, as distinct from a boxer. And yet for fourteen and a half rounds this Driscoll, toothless, grey-headed, wrinkle-faced, often bewildered and bamboozled his opponent. He introduced to us the straight left par excellence, a defence wonderful, and hitting done as if by measure.

But he could not survive against irrepressible youth and viciousness, as personified by Ledoux . . . . The defeat of Driscoll was

> glorious, yet pathetic. He showed us the magic of boxing; he only
> lost because he believed that he was young when he was really old
> . . . Ledoux, as he went to his dressing room, sought to make it
> known, in the best English at his command, that in Driscoll he had
> encountered an opponent who was marvellous in every way. Said
> he: "I was losing nearly all the time, and yet I won. Great is
> Driscoll."

It must have been a sad sight, Cate thought; but at that moment
Charlie Bennett, reading another newspaper, exclaimed, "That must
'a been a bonny fight! I wish I could 'a been there!"

Tom Rowland, across the table, said smiling, "Charlie was a good
little boxer, in the navy. I think it's a bloodthirsty brutal sport, myself."

"Haway wi' you, Tom," Charlie cried. "It's a science . . . an art
. . ."

"The Noble Art of self-defence," Isabel murmured. "And it may
be so, but I don't think I could bear to see men battering each other
into insensibility, however scientifically or artistically it was being
done."

"It's not a sport for ladies," Charlie said.

Cate spread marmalade on a piece of toast. He had invited Tom
down for a few days in the country; but before sending up the invitation, Isabel had persuaded him to make quite clear that Charlie Bennett was included, as a guest. He had had a struggle; for Charlie was,
to put the best possible interpretation on it, Tom's valet, and accordingly could certainly come down; but as such would eat in the servants'
hall with Mrs Abell, Garrod, and Tillie. But of course Bennett was
actually Tom's homosexual paramour . . . "lover," Isabel had said,
but Cate could not use the word for such a relationship. Reluctantly,
he had given in; and they had been down three days—Tom was going
hunting tomorrow; then they'd return to London on Thursday . . .
and to his surprise it had gone well. Charlie was a Durham miner's
son, pure Geordie, and a most likeable young man. It was touching to
see the real affection he had for Tom, and Tom for him. Isabel was
teaching him a lot, and it was doing him good. What an old fogey he'd
been . . . a blind, narrow-minded old fogey . . .

He turned to Isabel, "What are we doing this morning?"

"Nothing is fixed, darling. But I thought it would be nice if we
called on Mr Brewster. He's an artist . . . young, fought in the war,
but is a rebel. Quite a few people like that have come to Walstone since
the war—and we ought to get to know them . . . what they think, how
they see things. Or they'll stay convinced that we are just old-
fashioned fogeys still living in the nineteenth century."

"I wish I was," Cate said.

"No, you don't," she said, smiling. "And you can give them as much as they can give you. They must learn to live with and in Walstone's past, just as much as we to live in its present and future."

"All right," he said.

"And tomorrow we are going up to London to hear the new Sibelius Symphony at Queen's Hall . . . and meet Betty and Fletcher and David Toledano and Helen for dinner."

Cate sighed, and Tom, laughing, said, "Now I've got some news for *you,* Isabel. Skirts are going to go up . . . up . . . up . . . up . . ."

"Good heavens!" she exclaimed. "How far . . . and when? I don't want to have to buy a complete new wardrobe."

"Above the knees, in a year or two . . . You can always stick with the length you wear now. Old ladies . . ." He smiled mischievously.

Isabel cried, "Tom Rowland! I *am* an older lady, but I am *not* going to be branded as one. I'll have to go and look at my legs in the mirror. What an evil thought!"

Hedlington: Wednesday, October 22, 1919

30 Richard Rowland was not feeling very well, and though he did get up and get dressed, he did not go to his office at the Jupiter Motor Company, but stayed at home, reading some financial statements he had brought home with him the night before. At ten o'clock the telephone rang. It was Morgan, the works foreman at J.M.C. Overfeld had at last left to return to America, and Morgan was now in charge, under Richard's supervision. "They're going out on strike, Mr Richard," Morgan said.

"Who is?" Richard said irritably. "Why?"

"About three-quarters of the men—women, too. It's the closed shop thing again, same's we had a year ago. Now they've built up a big strike fund, and they're ready again."

Richard felt his anger rising like a tide in him. That bloody Bert Gorse and his union . . . cancers, they were, nothing less.

"Swine," he grated. "Without any warning."

"Well, Mr Richard, they always said they'd strike some time, if we didn't agree to the closed shop."

"I'll never agree," Richard said. "Can we keep the place going with what we have left?"

"Just. We'll have to shift some men onto work that's new to them, because in some departments practically everyone's going out. We can work at about 20 percent capacity."

"I'll be right down," Richard said. He hung up. Immediately the telephone rang again. It was Ginger Keble-Palmer at the Hedlington Aircraft Company.

"They're going out on strike, Richard," he said.

"How many?"

"About half."

Good, Richard thought. Not as bad as J.M.C. He said, "Can we keep going?"

"Yes. Because we're really not doing very much, are we?"

"I'll be down as soon as I've been to J.M.C. They're out, too." He hung up again.

Twenty minutes later, driving through the gates of the J.M.C., he passed a line of men and women carrying placards, handwritten—ON STRIKE FOR A UNION. They glanced at him, sitting in the back of the big car behind Kathleen the chauffeur, but did not show any sign of recognition or anger.

In the factory Morgan was waiting for him with the five department foremen. He sat down at his desk, they all standing, all wearing their caps, Morgan his ceremonial bowler. He said, "Now let's get one thing straight—we're not going to have a closed shop of the Union of Skilled Engineers here, or any other union. We pay as good as the best wages in the industry, we give good holidays, we pay compensation and doctors' bills for any injury incurred at the plant . . . and that's that. Second, none of those people who've gone out are to be re-employed here. So start hiring men and women to replace them. But first hire half a dozen men . . . big men, to see that no one who wants to come in and out of this factory is prevented from doing so by the pickets."

"Using just their fists, Mr Richard?" one of the foremen asked.

"Get them rubber clubs," Richard said shortly. "And knuckle dusters . . . there's a lot of unemployment everywhere. You won't have any trouble getting the numbers we need in the factory."

"Not the numbers," Morgan said, "but the skills. The car business is doing pretty well."

"If you have real difficulty, we'll think about offering more pay," Richard said. "The main thing is to remember that we're in a war. They mean to bring us to our knees. But, we're going to fight back, and force them to theirs."

A woman rushed into the room without knocking, and screamed, "Fire! In the paint shop!"

"Christ!" Morgan said, and dashed out. Richard picked up the telephone and hurriedly wound the handle. There was no sound. The telephone was dead. The wires must have been cut! Bloody swine! He followed the foremen, and now a stream of men and women, to the paint shop.

One corner of the shop was on fire, flames licking toward the roof and dense black smoke, chokingly acrid, billowing through one window, which was half-open. Morgan and two other men were already up close to the fire with fire extinguishers, squirting streams of foam at the flames. Richard, looking round, saw that the flames were licking close to the three overhead paint tanks, which were used with sprays to paint the lorries. He shouted, "Smith, empty that first tank . . . run the hose through the door and empty it. Hurry!" More men hurried in with extinguishers from other parts of the factory. One of the foremen came up, panting, "I tried to telephone the fire brigade . . . couldn't get through."

"So did I," Richard said. "Wire's been cut."

"I went out . . . phoned from a house down the road. They're on their way."

Richard nodded. The firemen would arrive just in time. Meanwhile they could hold the fire with what they had here. Paint was damnable stuff . . . the most dangerous place in the factory for a fire to start . . . to be started, obviously, he thought, possessed anew with an almost blind fury. This was arson. By those bloody strikers. Now he'd really start fighting. Two could play at that sort of game.

*　　*　　*　　*

"All ready?" Richard said.

"We're ready," the man said. He was wearing his usual working clothes, with the addition of a steel helmet, just like the one he had worn in the trenches a year ago. But they weren't in Flanders now, but at the works of the Jupiter Motor Company, in Hedlington, Kent, the Garden of England, preparing to deliver a dozen 3-ton J.M.C. lorries to a jam factory in Lincolnshire. The lorries were inside the main storage garage, all work done on them, including the painting of their future owner's name, address, and advertising slogan. It was dark, the street lamps lit, and forty pickets waiting outside the main gate.

"All right then," Richard said. "Go ahead."

Men swung open the gate of the storage garage and the leading lorry rolled out, followed at a distance by another. At the gates of the factory a man who had been walking beside the lorry made to unlock the gates, which were of wire mesh, ten feet high. The pickets stood in dense rows outside, blocking the roadway. They began to shout in chorus, "Blacklegs! . . . Blacklegs! . . . Blacklegs!"

Richard, watching from inside the garage, said, "Ready, Manning?"

"Aye, sir."

"Go, then." Two men waiting beside him went out of the side door of the big shed, heading in the darkness for the wire fence at the east side of the plant, hidden from the main gate and the pickets by the factory's many buildings. They carried in their hands big, long-levered wire-cutters, a pair each, but held close to their sides in case some stray strike sympathizer should see them before they got to work, and made the right deduction.

At the fence they set to at once, cutting a gap twelve feet wide in it. As they dragged the wire aside, they heard the sound of approaching engines; and at that moment the factory lights went out, and the street lights.

Richard, in the leading lorry, drove out of the storage garage, but instead of making for the main gate 200 feet ahead, turned right, and driving between the factory buildings, headed for the newly cut gap, seeing only by the stars but making no mistake because he and the other drivers all knew this area like the back of their hands. He smiled grimly, muttering under his breath, "That'll teach you, you damned swine."

He drove through the gap in the fence, and one by one the other lorries followed. Now the pickets were coming, running down the side street, shouting. A half-brick crashed through the windshield six inches from his head, shattering the safety glass. Someone was trying to climb up on the other side, screaming "Blackleg!" The guard sitting beside Richard leaned out and smashed his knuckle-dustered fist into the picket's face. The man fell off and a moment later Richard felt a heavy bump. The guard muttered, "Ran over his leg."

"Good!" Richard said. If this was what they wanted, this was what they'd get.

*   *   *   *

"Runover Rowland! Runover Rowland!" they were shouting outside the gates as he drove up, some shaking fists, most making the thumbs-down sign. Richard kept his eyes straight ahead. The picket who'd tried to hit his guard that night last week had had his leg crushed; it had had to be amputated. He'd also had his nose broken by the guard's knuckle-duster. Serve him right.

The four police standing majestically in front of the gate stood aside. The watchman inside opened it. The crowd of pickets and idle spectators—again about forty strong—booed and hissed and chanted, "Runover Rowland! Runover Rowland!" One of the constables touched the peak of his helmet to him as the car passed. The others maintained their appearance of stolid indifference.

Richard got out and stalked into the plant and to his office. Morgan had been waiting for his arrival and came in at once—"Morning, Mr Richard . . . twenty-six more haven't shown up for work today."

"Why?"

Morgan tipped his bowler a little farther back on his head. *"They* don't say. But others have said they're not happy about Freeth losing his leg."

Richard said, "He was trying to punch up my guard, and he got what he deserved . . . Anything else?"

"We're due to get thirty tons of sheet steel from McGarvie's today. It's coming by road. And I told their foreman on the telephone to be sure that the drivers were picked, non-union men, and had guards with them. We'll be paying for the guards' time."

"Right."

Richard picked up a paper from his IN tray and started to read. Morgan said, "Charltons called . . . their foreman . . . and said they'd decided not to try to deliver our last order of lamps to us. Said their drivers were all union men, and even if they weren't, it would be too dangerous for them to try to get through the picket line here."

Richard said, "Bloody cowards." He took off his thick glasses and polished them angrily—"We'll go and get them, then. Work out what lamps we'll need for the lorries that we'll finish in the next month— make it two months . . . Send our lorries out tomorrow, at nine o'clock. I'll see that there are plenty of police on hand then. And tell the lead driver . . . send a good reliable man . . . to be back at the station, Hedlington Station—at exactly four o'clock in the afternoon, of the day after. We'll have police and our own guards there to escort them back into the factory . . . And as soon as we have taken delivery, I'm going to cancel any outstanding orders we have with Charltons. They're breaking the contract and they can't give me any argument."

"Where are we going to get electrical gear from then, Mr Richard?"

"We'll try Gregorys' first. It's a Hedlington firm and I've had good reports of them. Of course Mrs Gregory is my niece, but if they don't come up to scratch, we'll drop them. And we'll drive a hard bargain in the first place."

The telephone rang and Richard picked it up—"Rowland."

"Frank Stratton here, sir. One of our aeroplanes has just crashed. You'd best come up."

"What happened? Was the pilot hurt?"

"Mr Vinton was flying it, Mr Richard . . . an old Leopard we were experimenting on with the new ailerons. He'd been in the air about fifteen minutes when first one engine failed—I heard it, he was still circling round quite close . . . then in a minute or two, the other, and he had to make a crash landing . . . broke some ribs, I think, and his wrist. The machine's a wreck."

"But what made the engines stop? They didn't catch fire in the crash, did they?"

"Fortunately no. I'm not sure yet, but I have a good idea what happened."

"What?"

"Someone put sugar into the fuel tank . . . the big one by the hangars, that all the machines fill up from."

"Who? . . . The strikers!" Richard gasped. "But how did they get at it?"

"At night, probably, sir. It's not too difficult to climb over the fence. We have two night watchmen, but they can't be everywhere, and it doesn't take long . . . just empty twenty pounds of sugar in there . . . The engines are seized up, sir. I'm still working on it, but that's what it was."

"I'll be right up. And hire four more guards."

He hung up, thinking. He said, "What about dogs? Why don't we get some big fierce dogs . . . keep them hungry and bad-tempered, maltreat them so that they associate humans with pain? No, that won't do, they'll be frightened . . . We could teach them to bite anyone, using dummies . . ."

"Except the people who feed them," Morgan said drily.

"Feed them mechanically," Richard said. "We'll work something out."

He hurried out of the office toward his car. Morgan, looking after him, shook his head slowly. The Boss was going nuts about the strike. He was taking it all as a personal insult, and he wasn't thinking of anything else. All this business was costing money—guards, more guards, rebuilding the paint shop, doctors' and hospital bills for workers injured by the pickets . . . he was suing the union for those . . . lawyers' costs. If the strike didn't break J.M.C. and H.A.C., bankruptcy might . . .

Later, at the aerodrome, Richard inspected one of the Leopard's engines, which had been lifted out of the wreckage and taken to a bench in a hangar. The cylinders were black, the pistons stuck firm in a black glue the consistency of baked tar—the sugar, melted and burned in as the petrol ignited. He could claim from the insurance company for the aircraft, and for Vinton's hospital bill; but they wouldn't like it. Aircraft insurance was risky enough, the agent had said, without them having to be concerned about industrial unrest as well. They'd pay this time, but they might cancel the policies after that; or hold them in abeyance until the strike was ended . . . or renew them only at higher premiums. Damn them all! He wasn't going to give in.

"What about the police?" Keble-Palmer asked anxiously. "We ought to tell them. Vinton could have been killed."

"We'll tell them," Richard said. "And see that it's published in the local paper, including Vinton's injuries and what a narrow escape he had . . . with pictures of his wife and little children. Make the union unpopular."

A man came in and said, "Telephone for you, Mr Richard, in Mr Keble-Palmer's office."

Richard hurried off, throwing over his shoulder, "Call the police as soon as you can, Ginger."

In the other office Richard picked up the dangling instrument. The voice at the other end was the unmistakable Welsh lilt of Morgan—"They've got our sheet steel, Mr Richard."

"What do you mean, they've got it?"

"They had a man at the edge of town—who stopped the leading McGarvie lorry and told them he was from you . . . they were to take a secret route to the factory because the pickets were blocking the direct road, with crowbars and steel spikes . . ."

"God!" Richard gasped. "And they believed him?"

"Yes. He was well-spoken, they said. Wearing a blue suit and bowler . . . told them his name was Morgan, the works foreman . . . Well, the bloke, whoever he was, led them to North Hedlington, out on the Chatham Road, and into a field by the river, where they had fifty men waiting, hidden behind one of them old brick kilns. And chucked all the steel into the Scarrow . . . Then they roughed up the McGarvie drivers a bit . . . and the guards . . . told them not to be blacklegs, and sent them off, with their lorries. The McGarvie charge hand called me from Rochester."

A thousand pounds worth of steel gone, Richard raged inwardly. More insurance problems. More delays. "Very well," he said, "re-order. Tell Miss Harcourt to start making out the insurance claim . . . The next order we have for over a hundred pounds, of anything, send a man with an identity card to the supplier, to come all the way back here with the goods." He hung up as Keble-Palmer came in—"What do we do next, about the fuel?"

Ginger said, "The fuel tank is being pumped out now. Then it'll have to be cleaned of all trace of sugar in the residue. We'll have to stop flying for two or three days."

"No, we won't," Richard snapped. "Call B.P. and tell them to send a tank lorry here, and keep it here. We'll fuel direct from that. Tell them we'll want another tanker when the first one's three-quarters empty. And see that the tanker is guarded day and night."

More money, he thought. Damned swine. What could he do to get back at them? He wasn't just going to react to their filthy deeds, but do something on his own. But what? They'd lost their jobs already . . . and all other benefits, of course . . . Perhaps he could see that they didn't get any other jobs, at least in Hedlington. It wouldn't be easy, but he had a lot of influence, and all employers ought to stick together . . . a sort of union. Why not? Those bastards had one.

What a damned mess! And on top of everything else, he was going to lose Frank Stratton to Guy's Foundation . . . damned waste of a superb mechanic, in his opinion—but there it was.

$$*\quad*\quad*\quad*$$

Wilfred Bentley M.P. sat back in the passenger seat of the old Rowland Ruby . . . time he got a new car; but the Ruby ran perfectly, for all its old-fashioned appearance. It was ironic that he should be going to Hedlington in a Rowland car to tell another Rowland—the son of the original Harry Rowland—how to run his business . . . ironic, but fitting, perhaps. His wife, Rachel Cohen, was driving. She had insisted on being taught as soon as he became an M.P., and had warned him that as of early 1920 she was going to need a car of her own, as it would save a great deal of money in taxi and train fares. In London one could usually use the bus or tube, but his constituency was Mid Scarrow, and that took a lot of covering . . .

Rachel said, "We're seeing Rowland first, then Bert. Lunch between, with the Mayor. He's a Conservative, but several of the town councillors are Labour. And they're all worried about the strikes."

Wilfred nodded, but said nothing as Rachel slowed down, for they were entering Hedlington, coming up the Scarrow from Rochester. Fifteen minutes later the two of them were in Richard Rowland's office at the Jupiter Motor Company, with Richard and Morgan, the latter standing behind Richard's chair, his bowler hat very straight on his head. They all shook hands, and Richard said, "Please sit down." All sat, except Morgan. Richard said, "I appreciate your coming down, and hope you can help us end this strike and the violence that the strikers have been using against our loyal workers."

Rachel said tartly, "I hear there's been some violence on management's side, too."

"Nothing that was not in self-defence," Richard snapped back.

Wilfred cut in, soothing—"We can discuss these things in due course. What I think we should look into first is the cause of the strike, as seen from both sides."

Richard said at once, "They went on strike because I refuse to permit the Union of Skilled Engineers to make this factory and Hed-lington Aircraft closed shops. That is my right. This is my factory, founded with my family's money . . . and some American capital . . . not theirs."

Bentley said, "The U.S.E. is very strong in the car business, Mr Rowland. They have a good reputation in Wolverhampton and Coventry and Birmingham, where most of the factories are. The own-ers I have spoken to say they provide an element of stability in the labour force, and that they live up to their side of contracts."

"They won't take over here," Richard said. "I'm not going to be told what to do by the likes of Bert Gorse. Or have the whole works shut down because we sack a man for petty thievery."

Rachel said, "All these things can be covered in a good contract with a good union, Mr Rowland."

"They can be," Richard said, "but that has never stopped the unions protecting thieves, scoundrels, and plain incompetents among their members . . . In this factory a worker's loyalty will be to his work, not to a union official."

The talk went on, round and slowly round in circles. Would he take the strikers back if the whole question of unionizing was shelved for say a year? Would he meet with a member of the national board of the U.S.E. to discuss what sort of a contract he would consider making with them? Would he accept arbitration by the Government? By any other body?

At last they broke up, Rachel and Richard both out of temper and worn with frustration. He/she *would* not see her/his point of view. Morgan went to his little office, put up his boots on the table, and ate a cheese sandwich. Richard drove home and railed on to his wife about the iniquity of the union, the stupidity of Labour M.P.s. . . .

Wilfred and Rachel had lunch at the South Eastern with the Mayor and the two Labour councillors. Rachel said, "He's like Haig . . . It's the Western Front mentality all over again. Dig your toes in, close your eyes, refuse to try anything new . . ."

One of the councillors said, "He ought to be made to back down. There's too many men out of work . . . kids near starving . . . and winter coming."

Wilfred said, "He can't be forced to accept a union. He can be persuaded."

"But he can't," Rachel said heatedly. "That's what we have just spent the morning discovering . . . which I knew already."

"We have to try," Wilfred said. "I should think the financial situa-tion will do some persuading for us soon. And he must be having difficulties getting supplies of material, for both factories, as long as the picket line is up."

Later, they met Bert Gorse and a man from the central headquarters of the U.S.E., in the local branch office, H.E.16, in Stalford Street. Bert said, "We've got him on the run now. He doesn't know where to turn. He's running round in circles . . . hiring more guards here, putting up more fences there, sending his own lorries as far as Newcastle-on-Tyne for materials. We'll break him soon."

"Meantime, a lot of people are going hungry," Wilfred said. He turned to the union representative—"I don't like the reports that we have been hearing of violence . . . arson, deliberately sabotaging aviation fuel with sugar, bricks thrown through windscreens, tyres slashed . . . physical beatings of workers . . ."

"Blacklegs," Bert said.

"Nothing's been proved against any member of our union," the official said.

"You know that's almost impossible," Wilfred said. "You'll lose sympathy if it goes on. And it can be stopped."

"It won't stop as long as Rowland's men use knuckle dusters and run over pickets," Rachel said.

"It has to stop somewhere," Wilfred said. He spoke directly to the union official—"I rely on you to see that all violent action by the union, or its members, is stopped. You don't need it. Just see that the picket line is maintained, day and night, round both factories. Make it clear to Mr Rowland, as we already have, in your name, that you are willing to negotiate a contract with him as soon as he wishes to . . . and that everyone will go back to work while you're negotiating."

"He won't take anyone back, who went out," Bert said.

"Sooner or later, he'll have to . . . You have plenty of strike funds?"

The U.S.E. official nodded—"Through January . . . providing we don't have to back any more major strikes in other parts of the country."

Rachel said, "See that you don't. Tell your other branches to postpone any strike action till you give the go-ahead . . . and tell them why. They'll understand, and hold back until you have J.M.C. and H.A.C. in the fold."

*   *   *   *

Naomi Gregory paced up and down the big office, from the desk at one end, where her husband Ron sat, to the other, where an exactly similar desk faced his across the breadth of the carpeted floor. "What are we going to do about Uncle Richard's letter?" she said.

"The specifications are simple enough," Ron said slowly. "I've been through them with Reynolds and he agrees there's no difficulty at the shop end. Prices . . . if the order's big enough we could shave a few pennies off the regular quote, but not many. We're already bidding very low, to get ourselves established."

"You don't have any new methods yet?"

"Not for headlamps or sidelamps. I'm working on a new magneto, but it won't be ready and tested for six months yet."

"Well, let's fill out the forms in pencil and take them to all the foremen and then to the buying department to see that we haven't overlooked anything. It's a good order, if we get it."

Ron leaned back in his swivel chair, and said, "If your Uncle Richard gets it, Naomi. His people are on strike, and there's a picket line."

"I know *that*. But we'll find a way to deliver the lamps, if they accept the models we're offering. I don't see why they shouldn't. They meet all the specifications for size, shape, waterproofing, bulb types, glass. We can find a way to deliver through the picket line."

Ron said, "I don't think we should." He got up and joined her in the middle of the floor, as though they were two boxers meeting in the middle of a ring—"I know your family's dead set against unions. But I think they're here to stay . . . to take a much bigger part in running industry than we ever expected . . . bigger, probably, than they did, even. A man from the Union of Electrical Engineers approached me yesterday, and told me they would like to organize us. He said that he'd had messages from some of our staff that they wanted a union, and the U.E.E. was the obvious one."

"What did you tell him?" Naomi demanded.

"I told him I'd talk it over with you. And Reynolds, of course."

"The U.E.E.," she said. "They're very Bolshie, aren't they?"

"Not really," Ron said. "They're tough bargainers, I know that. And they usually stick by their contracts . . . they don't tolerate any unofficial actions at all. They've got some very able men in the central organization . . . some of them are heading for Parliament, and if there's ever a Labour Government in this country, one or two of them may well be in the Cabinet."

"Let the union in, without a fight?" Naomi cried. "It's . . . it's treason! What will Uncle Richard think of us?"

Ron stood his ground manfully—"We can't afford to worry about what Uncle Richard thinks, darling. Our whole business is at stake.

529

How long could we last if there was a strike here, backed by the U.E.E.? We're just getting known, just getting on our feet financially, just building up a reserve, getting ready to expand . . . we'd drop back, down, down, and out. And don't think the U.E.E. don't know it. The man I saw was really saying, in a nice way, look, come in easy, now . . . or we'll come and get you the hard way, later."

Naomi pursed her lips, glaring at him. He was willing to surrender their rights as owners of the business . . . all that she had worked for, that both of them had worked for. But what he had said was true. It was no use denying it. She hated the idea, but there it was. If they started now they could get a favorable contract. And for everything the union demanded she would see that Gregorys' got something cast-iron in return. She said, "All right, Ron. Let's get specimen contracts from the union, and find out from, say, Charlton and Lucas what their contracts give—and don't give. If they won't lend us copies, have them stolen."

Ron said, "I'm sure you're doing the right thing, Naomi . . . And we'd better tell Uncle Richard we can't bid on the lamps until his strike is over."

She nodded—"He'll call me some names I didn't think he knew. But it has to be done."

*　　*　　*　　*

Willum Gorse shouted upstairs, "I'm going out, Mum!"

"Where to?"

"To the Rovers' ground, of course. There's a match on between the strikers from Mr Richard's factories, and the extra police they brought in from Canterbury and Margate and Rochester after that aeroplane crashed."

"Well, go along then. Betty! Push your father to the Rovers' ground . . . Here's a tanner for each of you to get in . . . And another for a beer on your way home, and a lemonade for Betty."

"Ay, you're a good wife, Mary."

"Go on with you. And no betting, mind."

Upstairs, she cocked her head, listening for the rumble of the cartwheels on the hall linoleum, then the crash as Betty pushed the front door shut behind her with her boot. Funny, she hadn't complained at all about having to push her dad all that way, and watch the game, too. Ah, there'd be men there, lots of men. But she couldn't be going off with any of them when she had her father to push along . . . She shook her head. It was terrible to be worrying about your daughter like this, and she only thirteen. What could they find for her to do, that would save her from what she had fallen into, when they moved to Scarrow Hall, and Sir Guy's Foundation?

Daily Telegraph, Saturday, November 8, 1919

FOOD PRICES AND PROSPECTS

WORSE THAN WAR TIME

It is little consolation to know that the people of the United Kingdom are better off than the inhabitants of some other countries, but it is due to those who have organized our food supplies that the following percentage increases since July, 1914, should be tabulated:

Belgium (Antwerp)	278	Norway	171
Belgium (Brussels)	267	France (Paris)	150
Italy (Milan)	226	France (other towns)	188
Italy (Rome)	107	Portugal	151
Sweden	209	Switzerland	151
United Kingdom	122		

After these figures the rise continued, the higher price of meat carrying the percentage of 122 to 128, and further increases have been estimated to bring the cost of food to about 133 percent above the pre-war figure . . . Further increases are regarded as inevitable—a disturbing situation considering that prices of necessaries are already higher than in our darkest days of war . . . Mr J. O'Grady, M.P. is urging that the Government should promptly release all its stocks of food, placing the whole on the market at reasonable prices. Such a suggestion as that naturally demands consideration from the point of view of ability to replenish our stores.

ANTI-CONTROL TO THE FORE

There is a revival of the opposition to control of various foodstuffs, particularly as regards meat and milk. It is asserted by traders that imported meat would be 3d per lb cheaper and milk a similar sum less per quart if control were removed. The meat trade also differs from the pessimistic view of the Ministry of Food on the subject of future supplies . . .

Cate thumbed gloomily through the rest of the paper . . . dock strikes in America, coal strike feared here, railway strike not long over . . . both Richard's factories on strike in Hedlington . . . President Wilson apparently unable to exercise the functions of his office and many Americans suspicious that his wife was usurping them. He looked at his own wife across the table—"What is the world coming to, Isabel?"

"A period of lancing boils," she said. "It's not a very pretty simile for the breakfast table, I know, darling, but it's accurate, I think . . . The war was like a huge malady in the body of the world, causing all sorts of illnesses, ailments, ulcers, sores, poisonings . . . but few of them visible or treatable, because the body was wearing armor, to fight the war . . . Now the armor's been laid aside, and the boils and sores are being bared, and must be treated, or burst . . . And while we are on not very pleasant subjects, I think Fletcher is having an affair."

"Oh dear," Cate said. "They haven't been married very long."

Isabel said, "I'm sure that women throw themselves at his head—he is so good-looking, in that wild animal way . . . and now he's famous, and a poet into the bargain. He has no armor to resist . . . When I went up to London yesterday I had lunch with Jane in the Coq d'Or, and Fletcher came in with a very pretty and expensively dressed young woman. Their table was at the front and ours at the back, and they never saw us. Anyway, they only had eyes for each other . . . they were holding hands, stroking each other . . . everyone else noticed, but they didn't notice . . . or didn't care."

"Poor Betty," Cate said after a while.

Isabel said, "If she ever gets to know. Though I think she will . . . she's very sensitive. And it's perhaps as well that she has to face it now, and come to terms with it, and with Fletcher, so early in their marriage."

"Let's hope it isn't also rather late in their marriage, then," Cate said.

Hassanpore, India: October, 1919

31 "Next detail—ready!" Company Sergeant Major Lodge barked. The twelve men fallen in behind the firing point marched forward. "Halt! Number! Right turn! For inspection, port arms! Ease springs!"

Fred Stratton, standing with two of his platoon commanders at one flank of the firing point, stifled a yawn. This was the last detail, about to fire its last practice—five rounds snap-shooting at 400 yards.

"Five rounds—lying—load!"

It was eleven o'clock and they'd been here since seven-thirty in the morning. Early on it had been almost fresh, but as the sun climbed it grew hotter, and the sun beat relentlessly on the back of his khaki cotton shirt, and the shade of his pith helmet grew smaller and thinner and at length seemed to vanish. Still, it was nothing like as bad as it had been in June. Half a dozen palm trees forty yards off gave some respite, and the men who were not actually firing were lying and sitting there, huddled together, smoking, waiting.

"Ready in the butts, sarn't major."

"Detail—fire each time the targets appear . . . one round each time."

Fred looked toward the butts, a wall of earth and sand twenty feet high standing isolated out in the semi-desert two miles south of Hassanpore. Every now and then a firer's arm would slip and the bullet would hit the hard ground between the firing point and the butts; and every now and then one of those bullets would ricochet over the top of the earth wall and whine off into the nothingness beyond. There were a few fields in that direction, and a mud hut or two, but it was practically desert, for most of the cultivation was done in the zone fed by the Doab Canal: this was not.

Twelve rifles cracked . . . nine of the black and white disc targets were rotated gently . . . Damn, three misses. The targets sank down, as the butt detail lowered them into the trench where they stood. Suddenly they all came up again. Again the twelve rifles cracked . . . eleven hits . . . No. 4 had missed again. Who was it? Fred peered— Private Denton: very young, seemed to be afraid of his rifle. He'd not get his proficiency pay unless he improved. The C.S.M. was yelling, "Don't jerk the bloody rifle, Denton. Squeeze! It's not going to bite you!"

But that's just what Denton believes it will, Fred thought. Well, Mendoza was Denton's platoon commander and he was here. It was his business.

Cracracraaccraak . . . Denton had a hit this time. He turned away, looking at his watch. Forty minutes' march back to cantonments, just time for a beer before lunch; and in the afternoon, go through all the morning's results and enter them in the men's records. He yawned again, pulled out a big khaki handkerchief, took off his helmet, and mopped his forehead.

"Firing programme completed, sir." The C.S.M. was at his side, saluting.

"Very well, sarn't major. Get them fallen in."

The road was a dusty cart track for the first mile, then they joined the Grand Trunk Road, and the men's nailed boots bit rhythmically into the packed macadam of the surface. Fred, marching at the head of the company, did not speak while they were on the cart track, for the wind was behind and the dust kicked up by the marching feet eddied forward and hung round all the way. Today it would be better for him to be where he would normally have been, at the rear, as 2nd-in-command: but Major Featherstonehaugh had gone on leave to shoot bison in the Nilgiris, and Fred would be commanding the company for the next four months. It was an odd feeling, strangely unlike commanding a company in battle. Of course you might have to do some fighting—he'd learned *that* on the Frontier, but that wasn't the real substance of soldiering: this was—drill, annual musketry course, ceremonial parades, the C.O.'s lectures on map reading, the adjutant's on regimental tradition and customs. A Regular battalion in peacetime was a sort of large family, with no real job to do, except live together—ready.

They swung onto the Grand Trunk Road and the C.S.M. sent two men doubling on a hundred yards ahead to turn any wandering bullock carts off the road. Often, even at this hour the carter would be fast asleep in the back, or even perched on the swingletree. Stratton glanced round. No. 3 Platoon was leading, so 2nd Lieutenant Mendoza, its commander, was marching just behind him. He dropped back level with the young man and said, "How did your fellows do?"

"All right, sir, except for Denton . . . and even he can hit a native at fifty yards."

"What do you mean?" Fred asked. Mendoza was tall and swarthily handsome. Must be a lot of Spanish or Portuguese blood in the family; lots of money, too. He was always nipping into Lahore to buy more boots and clothes at Ranken's, and he owned a very large American Buick car.

Mendoza said, "I heard last night that the Hindu procession is coming off next week. They've refused to cancel it. So . . . don't you think there'll be trouble then, sir?"

Fred said, "These silly buggers are capable of anything. What's it all about, anyway? I don't read the papers much."

Mendoza said, "Well, some Hindu saint was killed here by Muslims a long time ago . . . eight or nine hundred years . . . and every ten years the Hindu community takes a sacred image in a big cart to his grave. It's right in the middle of the bazaar . . . but to get there they have to pass a certain tree, and the tree's branches now stick out across the road. The Hindus' cart won't pass under them."

"They can cut the branches off," Fred said.

"The tree is sacred to the Muslims. Some mullah used to preach under it in the fourteenth century. They won't allow it to be touched."

"Bloody fools," Fred said. "Why don't they take the cart round another way?"

"Ah, but they must use the exact route, saying mantras at certain points. That's the tradition."

"Well, if it does come to trouble, they won't need the whole battalion. Let's hope the C.O. sends some other company. The bazaar stinks, and we'd be standing about all day among the flies and rotting food and shit, in the sun . . ."

"It's quite interesting though," Mendoza said diffidently. "Muslims saying their prayers in the middle of the street . . . whores looking down at you from some of the high windows . . . a Jain with a little whiskbroom sweeping the dust in front of him so that he doesn't by chance tread on an ant . . . India's absolutely fascinating."

"You'd better join the Indian Army if you think that," Fred said grumpily. They had entered the cantonments and in a moment would turn onto the road into the regiment's lines. He stepped aside, and shouted over his shoulder, "March to attention!"

The rifles were unslung and carried at the trail. The C.S.M.

barked the faster cadence. Outside the Orderly Room the Quarter Guard turned out, and fell in in two ranks. The guard commander yelled, "Quarter Guard, attention!"

Fred called, "A Company . . . Eyes *right!* . . . Eyes *front!*" Three more minutes to "Dismiss," six to beer. Christ, the Light Infantry pace made you sweat, in this Indian heat.

*　　*　　*　　*

But, when the time came, Colonel Trotter did not choose B, C, or D Companies; he chose A; so Fred Stratton found himself the next Tuesday morning, at 9 a.m., marching toward the city. The cantonment roads were always wide, straight, and sparsely occupied; and so they were today; but as one neared the city, across the half-mile of wasteland and smoking piles of garbage that separated the two, one normally ran into more and more people until, entering under the old Mogul brick arch, one passed into a world of Harun al Raschid, smelly, noisy, teeming with life, movement, and colour. Not this day, though . . . the narrow street inside the arch was not deserted; it was just not packed, and the people who were there seemed to be going about definite tasks, then returning to the shelter of their houses. Very few people seemed to be merely wandering, looking, haggling, or chattering.

The company marched 400 yards into the city, then turned into the Kotwali, the city police station. Here Fred ordered them to pile arms and rest, in the capacious garden behind the building. When that was done he went into the Kotwali itself, as ordered, to report to the Deputy Commissioner, the head of the local civil government. Mr William Jordan, Indian Civil Service, was about his own age, thickset, smoking a pipe and wearing a large pair of horn-rimmed glasses, a white suit, and a small white sun helmet, the latter set on the table in front of him. He got up as Fred entered, saluting—"Ah, Captain Stratton, we've met . . . and your good lady and mine share an enthusiasm for horses. Do sit down . . . Now, there seems to be no doubt that there's going to be a confrontation. What we have to ensure is that there is no, or very little, bloodshed. Obviously that means that we ourselves must not shed more blood than is necessary, or we'd be defeating our own purpose—wouldn't we?" He shot a keen glance at Fred, his eyes seeming to bulge behind the lenses.

"I understand," Fred said shortly. He knew perfectly well that he must use minimum force; to that end, the Lewis guns had not been brought out, and the cutoffs on the rifles would be used to ensure that each man could fire only one round at a time.

The D.C. repeated, "No more blood than is absolutely necessary.

536

The province . . . and the country . . . can't afford another Jallian-wala Bagh. So, I propose to use all the police in the first instance. On my orders, they will physically prevent the Hindus from cutting down the branches. The Assistant Commissioner will read the Riot Act and declare that the tree is government property . . . There's a perfectly good way up an alley and round the tree, so the procession can go on to the Saint's Tomb . . . Now if the Hindus press forward and over-run the police, I shall have no alternative but to call on you to disperse the crowd. Because, once damage has been done to the tree, the Muslims will attack . . . they will be there, waiting, of course. So, how many men can you use, do you think?"

"I'll go and look at the tree, sir, and the whole position. But I doubt if I'll need more than a platoon—twenty-five men—at the tree."

"They should be visible, but not aggressively so. And they must be able to act fast, once I hand over to you. Remember that the Riot Act will already have been read. I will be there, and I will give you the authorization according to the Riot Act, and it will be signed—here it is"—he produced a square card from his pocket; Fred, reading it, saw that it was in the proper form, from the Civil Authority, for military intervention, as the situation was beyond its own power to control; and the D.C. had signed and dated it.

The D.C. put the card back in his pocket and said, "So, when I give you this, just step up and start firing . . . I wish to heaven you could fire a few rounds over their heads."

"We are not allowed to do that, sir," Fred said. Colonel Trotter had impressed on him that the army must never threaten—it must shoot, to kill, first time; nor must it let the crowd get close; nor must it make arrests, for it had no power of arrest, nor training for it. He said, "Some of the police have rifles, don't they, sir? Why don't they fire a few rounds over the Hindus' heads . . . or everyone's, if the Muslims look threatening, before they give up and hand over to us?"

"I'll probably have them do that," the D.C. said. "But it isn't effec-tive because the crowds know they won't actually fire into them. God knows what relatives they might be hitting. Their rifles are for use against dacoits, not crowds. You don't live among the people, as the police do. They know you *will* shoot, and they know, really, that you are quite impartial . . . so the dirty work will fall to you. But we will really do our damnedest to see that it doesn't get that far."

Fred had a brainwave—"Sir, would it be possible to dig the road down at the tree, so that the Hindus' cart can pass under the branches?"

The D.C. stared at him, and cried, "By God, you're a genius, man! How much time do we have? Two hours before they're due to start out. We'll need every man we can get . . . Can some of your fellows help?"

"I can send three platoons—seventy-five men, sir," Fred said. "But they don't have picks or shovels here."

"I can . . ." the D.C. began; when a police havildar burst into the room, and gabbled rapidly in Hindustani. The D.C. stood up, and took off his glasses—"The best laid plans," he said. "They've cut the branches. A big crowd of Muslims is gathering there. Let's see. They'll go through the bazaar to the Raj Mandir—that's where the image and the cart are being garlanded. There'll be several hundred, or thousand, Hindus there."

Another Englishman came in, and the D.C. said briefly— "Simpson, the D.S.P. . . . Simmy, have your men block all streets between the tree and the Raj Mandir, to the north of Hanuman Road. Captain Stratton, will you please help us by blocking all streets to the south of Hanuman Road—that is, this side? Just don't let anyone pass."

"Can we shoot, if they won't stop?" Fred asked. He wished the C.O. was here; this was not at all the sort of situation they had been discussing and planning for.

The D.C. said briefly, "Yes, once the Riot Act has been read and your card signed. I'll send the A.C. with you—he'll do those, instead of me."

"I'll need three more interpreters," Fred said. "One with each of the other platoons."

"Simmy, find some, quick . . ." The door opened and Brigadier General Quentin Rowland, commanding the Hassanpore Brigade, strode in. "Morning, Jordan," he said briskly. "Morning, Stratton. Colonel Trotter told me he'd sent you down. Everything all right?"

The D.C. said, "The Hindus have cut the mullah's tree."

"No time to waste then, eh?" the general said, his blue eyes bulging. He turned to Fred, "Just do what you have to, and no more. Keep tight control. I'll back you up. Now I'm going back to headquarters . . . Think it would be wise to move the rest of the Wealds closer to the city, Jordan?"

The D.C. said, "Not yet, general. I'll phone you in an hour and we can discuss the situation then."

The general nodded, said "Good luck," and strode out to his waiting horse and groom. Jordan said, "We'd better get moving, fast."

*   *   *   *

The Assistant Commissioner was a Muslim, a man in his sixties, grizzled in service and, as he at once told Fred, about to retire, here in

Hassanpore. He would obviously do anything he could to avoid reading the Riot Act, or letting it be thought in the city that he had caused the soldiers to open fire. He followed Fred from street to street as Fred visited his platoons, each of them split into two, one-half under the platoon commander, the other under the platoon sergeant; the halves could usually communicate, down transverse alleys, and so far, an hour after the message had come in, no crowd had approached. Several individuals had come, men and women, and the soldiers had let them pass. These few were obviously not going to assault the Hindus at the Raj Mandir. The heat was growing, the sun beating down into the narrow trenches of the streets, shimmering down the battered walls. The smells of the city grew with the heat, the piles of cow dung, pools of human, horse, donkey, and camel urine, offal, piled grain outside the food shops.

Then Fred heard it, a growing murmurous roar, as of a train in a distant tunnel, to the west . . . the direction of the mullah's tree, where the Muslims had been gathering. "Here they come, sir," C.S.M. Lodge said cheerfully. "About time, too."

The Assistant Commissioner wailed, "Oh, sahib . . . I . . . I am feeling not well . . ." He staggered back, his hands to his head.

Fred said, "Fix your bayonet, sarn't major, and if Mr Akbar Ali here tries to bunk, stick an inch or two into his arse. Mr Ali, sign the card and give it to me."

"Very good, sir." Lodge fixed his bayonet and said menacingly to the old Muslim, "You *baitho* here, got it? No *chalo* or I'll stick this up your *pichche*." Mr Ali signed the card with a shaky hand, and gave it to Fred, then groaned and leaned against the wall in the shade. The crowd roar increased. Fred said, "Stand your men to, Mr O'Connor." He stepped a pace or two forward and looked down the alley leading to the next street. Sergeant Bickers was there, waving back. Fred heard his shout, "All ready here, sir!"

Fred cupped his hands and shouted, "Remember, don't let them get closer than fifty feet."

The sergeant shouted, "Got it, sir!"

Then they came, round the corner 200 yards away, debouching into the street, a solid mass, filling the street from wall to wall, coming on like a bore up a river carrying debris before it, as the crowd carried a scum of weapons, old swords, clubs, fence stakes, pitchforks, pickaxes. There would be knives, too, plenty of them, but hidden for the moment.

Lieutenant O'Connor said, "Fall in! One round, standing, load! Apply your cutoffs! Corporal Waggoner, you will fire the first shot, on my order."

Fred said, "Bugler, blow a G."

The bugle blared and the crowd, now a hundred yards away, stopped, hesitant, falling silent. Fred said, "Mr Ali, tell them they can't come down here, or any other road this way. Tell them to disperse. Then read the Riot Act."

The Assistant Commissioner groaned and moaned. C.S.M. Lodge stuck a little of his bayonet into his skinny behind. The old man yelled, blood welling through his white pyjamas. He croaked in Hindustani, "The road is closed, by order of the Deputy Commissioner Sahib. Go back to your homes, or the soldiers will fire on you." Then he recited the few lines of the Riot Act, and suddenly disappeared.

The crowd may have heard every word, though Fred doubted it. But they understood the situation clearly enough. The road was closed and they had been warned to disperse. He said, "Mr O'Connor, when I say the word, have that man in the front shot, the one waving a big club . . . now he's turning to harangue the others . . ."

"Very good, sir. Have you got that, corporal?"

"Yes, sir."

The crowd advanced again, now shouting, "Death to the Hindus! Death to the infidels . . . death, death, death . . . !"

A hundred feet . . . eighty . . . Once more Fred ordered the bugle blown. Once more the crowd stopped. But only for a few seconds, then they came on again.

Fred said, "Kill that man."

"Corporal Waggoner, fire!"

The corporal fired. The tall man waving the club dropped as though all his muscles had been simultaneously cut, a bullet between the eyes. Another man behind him fell, grasping his face, which was spouting blood; the mangled bullet had gone through the first man's head and was now lodged in this second's, behind the cheek.

"Next, the man who's just drawn a big knife . . ."

"Private Jenner, got him?"

"Got him, sir."

The crowd was still coming on.

"Private Jenner, fire!"

The bullet rang loud in the echoing street and the man fell, shot through the heart. Now the crowd wavered, and the shouting of "Death to the Hindus" changed to a formless, aimless yelling. "They're panicking," C.S.M. Lodge muttered. "God knows what they'll do now."

Fred waited, his nerves taut. This was worse than going over the top, even though you knew you weren't going to get hurt.

"They're coming on, sir," O'Connor called. So they were . . . but

Fred stared . . . those men in front were trying to get back . . . the crowd behind was pushing them. That wouldn't make any difference, if they got close enough to grab the soldiers' rifles, and simply run over them, but . . .

O'Connor said, "Can we fire another two or three shots, sir? They're getting awfully close."

Fred thought, God, what should I do? If I fire, there'll be another Jallianwala Bagh. He cried, "Bugler, blow a G!" As the brazen notes died away between the houses Fred shouted to the C.S.M., "Tell them to turn round . . . Top of your voice . . . Now!"

Lodge stepped forward and roared in his parade-ground bellow, *"Pichche dekko! Pichche dekko . . . jaldi!"* O'Connor's platoon was lined up, ready to fire. O'Connor's hand was shaking.

The crowd turned slowly round, in twos and threes, singly and in whole groups. Fred said, "Now tell them to march, go!"

"Hut jao!" the C.S.M. bellowed. *"Chalo, chalo!"*

The crowd began to thin. Looking over their heads Fred saw that the people at the back were running now—so the people here at the front would soon be able to follow. They waited. O'Connor took off his helmet and mopped his forehead. In five minutes the street was empty, except for the two dead and one groaning wounded. Fred said, "Sarn't Major, take a runner, go to the Kotwali and tell Mr Jordan what's happened, and that we need something to take that man to the hospital."

He breathed out a long sigh and said, "Stand down three sections, Mr O'Connor. Tell them they did well. The stood-down sections can smoke, and rest, of course. I'm going to see what happened to the other platoons."

* * * *

They were at tiffin, and since it was a Thursday, which was a whole holiday in India, they were having curry and rice—today, egg curry. Beside Fred's plate there was a pewter tankard of Murree beer; Daphne was drinking nimbu soda. She was in the seventh month of her pregnancy. She emptied her glass and said, "Ashraf, *aur nimbu soda.*" The khitmatgar, wearing the embroidered regimental crest over his dark-green achkan, poured some more of the ready-squeezed lemon juice into the empty glass; then opened a bottle of soda in the corner, first covering the top with the leather shield which prevented injury if the bottle burst when the glass ball in the neck was pressed down.

Fred finished his beer and signaled Ashraf to bring him another bottle. Daphne said, "That's your third beer."

He said, "It's Thursday. I'm going to do some studying for the Staff College after tiffin."

"You should *really* study for the Staff College," she said. "You'll never get on if you don't go to the Staff College."

"Well, your dad didn't," he said. "And he seems to have enjoyed himself."

"It didn't matter in those days," she said, lifting her heavy body impatiently. "Besides, everything was much cheaper. We're going to need more money when the baby comes. If you were p.s.c. you'd be getting staff pay."

He said, "I'm not cut out for the staff, Daphne, and that's that. Saw too much of them in France . . . damn pansies with shiny boots and red tabs . . . didn't see them at all, though, when the Boches were close."

She said, "Well, you'll have to transfer to the Indian Army, then."

He said nothing. He knew that an Indian Army captain would be getting about fifty rupees a month more than he was; that came to fifty pounds a year—not to be sneezed at. But then he'd spend the rest of his service out here, and when the time finally came to retire, he'd have to settle down all over again in England.

As though she had been reading his thoughts, his wife said, "I don't want to go back to England . . . rain, cold, freezing houses . . ."

And no servants, Fred thought. That was what really worried her about the thought of going home. She'd been born out here; and though she'd returned to England for education, she had come back to India before she was eighteen, and her dependence on many servants and the memsahib's way of life had never been broken.

She said, "We could retire to Kashmir . . . a houseboat . . . the Dal Lake in winter, move to Nagim in summer . . . They're very cheap and it's so beautiful . . . dances at Nedou's . . . shopping on the Bund . . ."

"We must go there next time I can get a month's leave," Fred said. "I've heard so much about it from all the blokes . . . but retire there? Or anywhere in India? We might find our house burned down round our ears one day. I tell you, what I saw down in the bazaar made me see that things are a lot more dicky out here than they seem."

She said, "It would be all right if more people acted like General Dyer did at Amritsar. My father wrote that it's a pity you didn't give that crowd a real lesson. He read all about it in the *Civil & Military*, of course."

Fred said, "But I couldn't fire into the crowd when I saw that they were trying to get away. General Dyer fired 1,600 rounds. I fired two."

"Jordan's a weakling," she snapped. "Like most of the I.C.S. He cares more for the natives than he does for us. We'll be raped in our beds if they're not kept in their place. And it'll be worse with these Montagu-Chelmsford reforms . . . kowtowing to Gandhi, they are! Disgraceful!"

Fred gulped down some beer and returned to his curry, signalling for the khitmatgar to serve him more lemon pickle and mango chutney. He thought he wouldn't "study for the Staff College," i.e. sleep, after all, but go out for a walk along the canal bank, with Satan, the bull terrier. Satan liked to bite natives, but there wouldn't be many on the canal road. Perhaps he should have taken Satan with him into the city on Aid to the Civil. There'd been plenty of natives for him to bite there. Perhaps a dozen Satans would have done better than a company of British infantry, and not killed anybody.

*   *   *   *

Fred and Daphne arrived at Flagstaff House for the "cocktail" party by tonga, a two-wheeled pony-drawn cart where the driver usually perched on the swingletree, otherwise the weight of the two passengers in the transverse back seat would almost lift the underfed pony off the ground. It was not a dignified conveyance, and tonga ponies always farted excessively from the green grass that was their staple diet; but for the Strattons there was no other way to get about—they could not afford a car, and bicycling was unsuitable for the occasion.

The general's khitmatgar met them at the door as they climbed the steps under the porte cochère, and led them into the big high-ceilinged bungalow. Mrs Rowland came forward to greet them, both hands out—"Ah, Captain Stratton . . . Mrs Stratton . . . we are so glad you could come . . . Quentin's talking shop over there with Mr Jordan, I'm sure, but you can say hullo to him when you have been given a drink. We're serving sherry, *chhota pegs*, and Bronxes."

The drinks were set out on a side table. They contained no ice—no drink in India ever did, because the water from which the ice was made was certainly full of germs and bacteria. Bottles were nestled on ice, instead. Here, there were several sodas in a big bucket full of ice, with other bottles labeled BRONX. Daphne doubtfully poured some into a glass, while Fred helped himself to a *chhota peg*. Then Fiona said, "Now . . . you know Major and Mrs Ruthling, of the Punjabis . . . and this is Mr Trainor, who owns the big flour mills on the Jullundur road . . . and Mrs Trainor . . . and this is Mr Matra Singh. He's a painter, and a very good one . . ."

The painter was a tall young man with a curled and tied beard and a pale blue turban tied in the manner which Fred knew to be particular to the Sikhs. Daphne felt shocked; she had not expected to meet an Indian at Flagstaff House, of all places. She was sure General Rowland was not responsible for inviting him. His wife sometimes did and said the most extraordinary things: and Mrs Courtney had assured her that in their bedroom there was a large oil painting of Mrs Rowland playing golf in the nude—an obscene painting, hiding nothing. That was the kind of thing that made the natives think that memsahibs were no different from their own women.

The Sikh said, "Ah, Captain Stratton! You're the man responsible for seeing that the trouble in the city last week didn't cost more lives. Congratulations."

Fred said a little stiffly, "Thank you." He didn't know what to make of this Indian here, any more than Daphne did. And he didn't know how to discuss Aid to the Civil with an Indian. It was a contradiction in terms.

The Indian said, "I'd like to give you a painting, to show my appreciation. Would you care to come to my studio and choose one? It's in the Bazaar, just off Larkana, next to Ananda Ram's."

Daphne said, "We really don't have room for any more pictures in our house. My father gave us a large collection of water colours of Kashmir, done by his father."

"Thank you all the same," Fred put in. Daphne moved away and Fred followed. For a few moments they were standing isolated in the middle of the room, then the general glanced round, saw them, and beckoned. When they joined him, he said, "Jordan and I were talking about this fellow Gandhi and the Congress. He thinks that the civil disobedience movement will be very effective, in the long run."

Jordan blinked at Fred through his glasses—"I do. And we won't be able to handle it—or any other Indian politicial movement—unless we have a policy."

"Keep the peace," General Rowland said, his eyes very blue in his red face. "That's what we're here for, isn't it? Otherwise these fellows would be killing each other off like flies . . . as we saw the other day in the city, eh, Stratton? Or the Pathans would come down and there wouldn't be a rupee or a, ah, unravished woman between the Indus and the Jumna."

The Sikh painter had somehow appeared at the general's other side; and his eyes were gleaming. Fred thought, that fellow had a drink or two before he came here, and that's a pretty stiff *peg* in his hand now. The painter said, "We can defend ourselves and our women, general. We did it well enough under Ranjit Singh, before the British came."

The general said, "But there was always fighting between Hindu and Muslim and Sikh, rajahs and nawabs."

"And the British kept the spirit alive," the Sikh said. *"Divide et impera.* But Mr Jordan's right, things would be much better if there was a policy. The British Government declared a century ago that they were only here to make India fit to rule itself. When is that moment going to be? Who is going to decide it? More Indians are coming into the I.C.S every year . . . and now Indians can go to Sandhurst and get the King's Commission. But, the Montagu-Chelmsford reforms point one way, while Mr Justice Rowlatt's recommendations, and the Rowlatt laws, go exactly the other . . . So, what? And when?"

The Deputy Commissioner said, "I think the Home Government should make a statement about our exact aim, inside a stated time frame, so that we out here will know what we are committed to achieving. In the end they are the govern*ment,* we are the govern*ors,* which is a very different kettle of fish. They can censure and deplore General Dyer, but *we* have to remember that the European community out here has subscribed a huge sum for the general. *They* don't think he's a butcher."

"Say twenty years," the Sikh said energetically, waving his glass so that some whisky spilled on Daphne's dress. She drew back in disgust. The Sikh didn't notice—"Or, say, we'll hold elections in ten years, and the resulting Parliament can write a constitution . . . and when it's all agreed, you promise to abide by it . . . then either go, or perhaps stay under some sort of defence and commercial treaty, for a fixed number of years more."

Fred saw General Rowland's jaw set obstinately. Old Rowley wasn't going to march off just because a lot of natives told him to.

The Sikh said, "My dear general, the British Empire has seen its finest hour, in the war. Now it is about to break up, nibbled to death by people like Mahatma Gandhi . . . the Dominions will go first, becoming fully independent . . . then us . . . then Africa . . . then Oceania . . . It's inevitable. It won't be so bad. You'll see . . ."

*   *   *   *

Fred sat in the mess, drinking. It was midnight, and he was the only officer still here. Wednesdays were always guest nights; and as married officers had to dine in mess twice a month, they usually chose Wednesdays, though they didn't have to. His mess jacket and cummerbund felt tight and hot. Next week they'd be changing to cold-weather uniforms, including mess kit, but for now it was still the white drill jacket and trousers. The scarlet and blue would be hot as hell for a few weeks.

He pressed the bell for a waiter. A mess waiter came in and Fred said, "Another *chhota peg,* please, Thomson . . . no, make it a *bara.*"

"Very good, sir."

Have to make it a night soon, and toddle home to his bungalow, and bed. Daphne would hear from Gail Courtney that there hadn't been a big bash at the guest night and want to know why he hadn't come home sooner; but sufficient unto the day . . .

The whisky came and he drank, staring into the empty fireplace, ringed by the angled, padded bench. They were making a row in the city, and there must be a breeze coming this way, for he could hear the throbbing of drums . . . bloody Wogs.

He was an officer and a gentleman, at last. A sahib. Member of the upper classes. The baby, whatever it turned out to be, would be accepted as pukka, go to the right sort of school, and have a natural la-di-da accent. And it would be heir to the British Empire . . . which was disintegrating. Christ, how he'd worked for this . . . risked his life, lost his old friends, learned all the proper things to do, to say . . . shoot snipe, drink *chhota pegs,* wear tweeds . . . and now the whole bloody caboodle was slowly falling to pieces before his eyes.

"Waiter!" he called. "Another *bara peg!*"

*   *   *   *

Quentin Rowland lay in bed beside his wife Fiona, under the oil nude of her on the putting green, late summer light streaming impudently over her pale skin and the golden triangle at her loins, a half-smile on her parted lips. On the opposite wall there were two smaller oils, of men—himself to the right, Archie Campbell to the left; both in steel helmets, in dugout or trench, in cold weather, snow mantling the earth behind. All three paintings were Archie's, as were all the drawings and paintings in the drawing room and along the passages of the sprawling bungalow.

Fiona said, "Matra Singh wants to paint me. He is very talented."

"Not a nude!" Quentin said quickly. That would be too much.

"I don't think so, " Fiona said. "Though it wouldn't matter. He's very modern, and his style's rather like Modigliani's, only still more elongated. I don't think anyone would recognize me."

"Not a nude," Quentin repeated. He was secretly proud of the nude over the bed, and of Fiona, for not caring what anyone thought. But Archie had painted it: he didn't want any more, by any other hands.

She said, "What do you think of Guy's Foundation? The *C & M*'s had a lot about it."

He said, "I'm sorry that he's not going to stay in the R.A.F. There's no limit to how far he might have gone. But . . . it needed doing. Not by the Government, but by the people who came through whole, for those who didn't. We should be proud of him."

"I am," Fiona said. "And even of Virginia and her Sergeant Major, in a way. She did what *she* wanted to do, not what *we* wanted her to."

Nothing had worked out as he had expected, Quentin thought. Guy, he'd always thought, would design aircraft and play cricket for Kent, and probably England. Virginia would marry some nice subaltern in the Buffs, move to Canterbury, and live happily ever after. But Guy was the one-time Butcher of the air, a knight, a hero, and now a healer; and Virginia the fat, happy wife of a crippled Battery Sergeant Major, self-equipped with a Yorkshire accent to match his.

Fiona's hand crept out and moved down his chest and belly. Archie was watching, a weary half-smile on his haggard face, under the dull bowl of his steel helmet. Fiona knew he was watching . . . The two men over there on the wall were the other points of the triangle, anchored in the nude over the bed, legs a little spread. It was a firm triangle, full now of love and understanding. Quentin turned on his side and began to caress his wife's breast, leaning down to kiss her on her parted lips.

Daily Telegraph, Thursday, November 20, 1919

AMERICAN SENATE AND THE PEACE TREATY
MR LODGE OUTVOTED

New York, **Wednesday.**
The Lodge resolution for ratification with the reservations has been defeated, receiving only 55 votes for to 39 against. It thus lacked the necessary two-thirds majority. A resolution by Senator Reed to reconsider the motion was carried by 62 to 30, and another by Senator Hitchcock to ratify the Treaty without reservations was declared out of order by 50 to 43—Exchange Telegraph Company.

PRESIDENT'S LETTER

The letter of President Wilson to Senator Hitchcock, which was read this morning at a conference of Democratic Senators called to decide the Administration's final course of ratification, is expected to line up the Democratic Senators almost solidly against the Republican proposals for ratification. The letter advises the Senators to vote against the ratification of the Peace Treaty with the Foreign Relations Committee's reservations, and declares that the Committee's programme provides not for ratification but "rather for nul-

547

lification of the Treaty." The President said: "I understand the door will then probably be open for a genuine resolution of ratification. I trust all true friends of the Treaty will refuse to support Senator Lodge's resolution."

Cate looked up—"It looks as though the Peace Treaty is in trouble in the American Senate."

Isabel said, "It is. The Republicans are offering all sorts of reservations, but really they want to torpedo it altogether. No foreign entanglements, they say, and the League of Nations would put our finger in every pie, all over the world. Mr Wilson's not going to be able to get it passed . . . even if he was fit, and he's anything but . . . Do you realize that we'll be seeing Stella and John again inside a couple of months?"

"Yes," Cate said. "And I can hardly sleep wondering what she'll be like . . . whether John's hopes and plans for curing her have come to anything."

"We'll see for ourselves," she said. She turned to another page of her paper and after a moment said, "Guy must be working himself to death with that Foundation of his. There's something about it in the *Telegraph* nearly every day . . . and much more in the *Hedlington Courier,* of course. What can we do for him?" Isabel asked. "Thank you, Garrod, that's enough."

The maid went out. Cate said, "I wonder if any of them could work in the barns or fields . . . But if they could, the Foundation wouldn't take them. Guy can't help the fit as well as the sick."

She said, "I was thinking that perhaps we could give them a day in the country. Suppose you had a charabanc load down . . . it's very close, after all—one day a week during summer. Just let them walk or sit in the fields, hear the blackbirds."

"I'll talk to Guy about it," Cate said. "If he has a moment to spare."

England, Arizona: November, 1919

32   Stephen Merritt, sitting in the big bow window of the living room, looking out across the grey, choppy waters of Tappan Zee, wondered what had happened to fragment his family so violently. Before the war he had always envisaged John working in Fairfax, Gottlieb with him, marrying, buying a house on the river—over there in Tarrytown, perhaps . . . Betty marrying too, of course, some nice young fellow she'd meet here, and probably living in New York at first . . . Isabel would have remarried, perhaps Peter Van Dehofer down in Grandview, and they'd all be here, close but not too close, a family . . . But Betty had married an English poet, Johnny had gone off to the most desolate parts of Arizona, and Isabel, too, had married an Englishman.

He'd have to go over there himself to see what was happening at J.M.C. and H.A.C. The board had discussed the situation last week— they had a considerable investment in the two firms, which had done well so far; but matters could not be left as they were. It was hard to understand, from here, why some compromise could not be reached. So he'd have to go and see for himself; and while he was over there he'd see Betty and her husband and at least get a better picture than he had now of the kind of life they were living. In its way it was as hard to imagine as was John's and Stella's, out on the Navajo Reservation.

Tomorrow he'd send Betty a cable; right now he'd book his passage.

*   *   *   *

"My father's coming over," Betty said, putting down the cable form. "He'll be here on the 30th."

"Ah, but where will we be?" Fletcher said. "London? Paris? Edinburg? Dublin?"

"We're staying in Oxford till the 25th," she said. "Then we go back to Hedlington for a bit . . . Your hand's trembling, Fletcher, and your eyes are bloodshot."

Fletcher said, "I have a hangover, woman. What do you expect, if we sit up all night drinking brandy with the likes of Robert Graves and John Masefield and Edmund Blunden? Those folk have harder heads than you'd ever expect, hearing them talk . . . Let's go over to the Boar and have a hair of the dog."

"Let's go for a walk," she said. "And then to a pub at the end of town, not the Boar. It'll blow the cobwebs out of our heads."

He got up without a word and followed her down the stairs of the little hotel where they were living, and into the street. Betty loved Oxford. The Rowlands had all gone to Cambridge—she remembered talking to Naomi about it—but for herself she couldn't imagine anything better than Oxford. Who called it the City of Dreaming Spires? A bit over-romantic, especially now that it was bursting with young men back from the war, their faces etched with what they had seen; and though they were surprisingly gentle in voice and manner, they were not innocent, and never would be again.

Fletcher said, "Edmund said my poetry was stronger than his, because I'd been an Other Rank. He was an officer in the Royal Sussex . . . I think he's right. Good officers was in just as much danger as the men—more, mostly—and had it just as hard . . . but they weren't *of* us. Couldn't be, because they had to give the orders. That's why Rosenberg and me are the best. I'd like to have met Rosenberg . . . funny to think of a cockney Jew-boy writing great poetry about ordinary Englishmen at war."

She said, "Siegfried Sassoon was very flattering, again, when he came to tea."

Fletcher nodded—"Aye, he was."

"And you haven't written anything for three months, and that wasn't very good—you said so yourself."

"We've been traveling too much," he said. "And learning. Why, I've been seeing so much my head's crammed with it all . . . aero-engine factories, cotton mills, trawlers, banks, libraries, painters' studios, doctors' operating rooms . . . It's a wonder I've not gone dotty."

After a time, walking into the brisk cold wind, she said, "We've done enough of that. You've seen that there are other ways of life than yours, as it used to be . . . You've made some connection between the men you only knew as soldiers and their real lives. It's time we settled down and you started to write poetry. And it's time you heard some criticism, not all flattery."

"Why, woman," he protested, "what's wrong with having someone like my poems? It's better than having Mr Bridges and the rest of them say they're trash, only fit for the dustbin, isn't it, now?"

She said, "Yes, but you've been living on a diet of undiluted flattery ever since you came out of the army. It's a drug, just as strong as the heroin Stella was taking . . . I suppose she still is. Flattery's more subtle, that's all. After a time, you become dependent on it. You feel hurt—pain—if you don't get it. And your mind is affected, in that you lose your powers of judgment."

"Aiih, sounds terrible," he said. "Well, I'll be glad to settle down, and you'll give me all the hard words I need, won't you, love?"

"I will," she said. "Now, where are we going to live? Where are we going to put down our roots? A poet needs roots."

"I found that out these past months," Fletcher said. "Hey, look, there's Robert Graves. He can come and walk with us and . . ."

She said, "He hasn't seen us. Don't bother him . . . we have things to talk about between ourselves. Every time you meet another poet . . . or anyone who recognizes you . . . it becomes a party, drinking, congratulating each other on what jolly good fellows you are . . . We were asking, where shall we live? You were saying, you found out that you have to have roots."

Fletcher nodded, "Yes. While I was at the war I thought I was writing poetry about it, the war . . . but I wasn't. I was writing about my own people, and we had our roots right there, all of us did, in that mud and blood and dirt and mess. Then . . . it was good living in Granddad's cottage, but when he and his Woman had to move back, it was too bloody crowded in there, so we've been living in hotels, and trains, and more hotels, and more trains, and . . ."

"What about getting a house in Hedlington, and making that our home?" she interrupted.

He said, " 'Tis too much of a town, love. We'd meet people when we went out, 'stead of badgers or kestrels. We'd walk pavements instead of fields . . . and the Scarrow's too dirty to swim in, or fish in, in Hedlington."

She said, "We could probably get the Cottage, at Beighton. The people who bought it from John are not happy there, Aunt Susan told me. We'd have to modernize it."

"Why? We can manage with old-fashioned things, the way I always have."

She said, "No, Fletcher. You must concentrate on writing, not on mending the thatch, pumping water, carrying coal, cutting grass. And I may not be there all the time."

She let that sink in; but Fletcher did not seem to have been taken aback. He said, "Why not, love? Where are you going?"

"I want to go back to work at H.A.C.," she said. "I was very happy there. I was doing work that I was capable of, that I had the training for . . . and in the last two years I learned a great deal about aircraft design."

"I can fend for myself," Fletcher said.

"Oh darling, it's more than that," she cried. "I don't think you are really at ease, being looked after—having a woman at your personal beck and call. It's beginning to stifle you, and perhaps that's why you haven't written any poetry, rather than all the traveling and learning. I'll come home every evening, of course."

"I'll make your breakfast," he said. "I'll be up by then."

That was true, she knew; for he always got up early. It was old Probyn's teaching. To Fletcher the hours between four and dawn were the best of the day. That was why some of the parties in London and here in Oxford—indeed, wherever he had gone to learn, and to be lionized—had taken a severe toll of him; for he had still got up at four, after going to bed at three, or not at all.

She said, "I'll have to see if they'll take me back . . . The last I heard they're still on strike and I don't know whether they have my old job for me, or need me at all. But that's it—the Weald of Kent is your home and I will be happy to make it mine. Your work will be poetry, mine will be making aeroplanes . . . and we'll share love."

"When will we have babies?" Fletcher said.

She did not speak for a long time, then—"Here's the Green Man, Fletcher. It looks a nice little pub, and we've earned our beers now."

"That we have," he said, turning into the neat little pub beside the Isis. "But what about babies?"

"Oh," she said. "Give me a little more time, Fletcher. To know that I really want them . . . that I'm fit to be a mother, in this country, this century, this time."

"Fair enough," he said.

*　　*　　*　　*

John Merritt, perched on a stepladder arranging saddles and harness for sale on the side wall of the Trading Post, took the telegraph slip from the Navajo's hand and read it, holding the paper sideways to the light. It was from his father and read: *Sailing England Tuesday plan to return before end of year if possible hope to visit you January as must go San Francisco on bank business that month.*

John put the slip in his pocket and continued his work. It would be great if Dad could come and see them at home in the Trading Post. It was a far cry from River House in Nyack—farther still from Walstone Manor; but it *was* their home; and, for him, it felt like their first, and perhaps their last, for they had both settled in here in a way neither had experienced before. Stella was working on a loom at the end of the room now, with Mary Begay squatting beside her, occasionally moving the yarn for her. Her colours were well-chosen, though the lines were not straight and the patterns uninteresting. She was learning the craft, because it represented an important part of all Navajo women's lives, and nowadays, an important part of the total income of the Dinneh, the People, as the Navajo called themselves. A Navajo woman had to make saddle blankets for her husband's horse gear, other blankets to keep him warm, moccasins for his feet. She, and to some extent the whole family, were judged by the excellence of the work—and slowly the blankets or rugs with the traditional designs, Two Grey Hills, Crystal, Chinle, Rainbow Man, were becoming known to Eastern tourists. Stella, if she was to get a fair price for them, must know which were good and which were bad; the Navajo would not respect her if she did not, and she would find herself losing not only the tourists' custom, but the Navajos' willingness to sell through her.

Outside it was a dark day of clouds, cold in the wind. The snow would come soon, John thought. Then business would die down, for then the Indians could not come to the Trading Post except in emergency, or if there was a break in the weather and the snow was not lying too deep. Then they'd come out of boredom, Reinhart assured him, to drink coffee (at his expense if they could maneuver it), meet each other, finger the goods, recognizing the rings and turquoise brooches they themselves had made, now displayed under glass, and their wives' rugs, hanging on the wall . . . but buying nothing. And, of course, there would be no tourists.

He glanced down and saw that a Navajo was standing at the counter, alone, leaning on it. He might have been there ten minutes, but had said nothing. He was a fat man, fortyish, powerful, wearing a tall domed black hat with a beaded band, and a heavy concho belt. John called down, "Do you want me?"

"Perhaps," the man said, in Navajo.

John climbed down. He greeted the Indian ceremonially. The man returned the greeting. They discussed the weather—Yes, it might snow before the week was out. Last year it had snowed at this season, but not much. John thought the man was expecting to be offered a cup of coffee, but he would not do so. After a quarter of an hour the man said, "Benally Bekis—" (that meant Benally's Friend, the name by which he had been known ever since he came to the reservation, and the Dinneh had heard, all at once, without words, of his connection with Chee Shush) . . . "I want to pawn this belt."

John said, "Let me see it then, friend."

The man unbuckled the wide belt with the six great ovals of worked silver on it. It was good, John thought, very good, and the silver was studded with turquoise . . . it looked like high-grade Nevada turquoise, as Reinhart had taught him. He could send for Reinhart now, but damn it, he had to learn to make these decisions for himself. He thought, silver's about $1.35 an ounce now, and there must be a couple of pounds of it in the belt, plus the turquoise, and of course, the man's time and labour. He said, "A hundred and fifty dollars . . . for a year."

The man said, "Benally Bekis, look at it. A hundred and seventy-five."

"A hundred and fifty," John said. He smiled—"And a cup of coffee."

The Indian said, "It is done." They shook hands and John wrote out the pawn slip, calling, "Mary, bring coffee."

Half an hour later, the coffee drunk, the Navajo, whose name was Chischilly Nez, walked out, climbed onto his pony and rode away at a walk, into the north-west wind. A few minutes later Reinhart came in, rubbing his eyes, "Overslept a bit, John . . . What did Chischilly Nez want?"

"You know him?"

"Sure. He usually works the Grand Canyon, selling fakes to tourists at Williams as they get off the train . . . Ah, he pawned that?" He picked up the concho belt, lying on the countertop, and examined it carefully. His breath smelled sour, John thought, and his hands were shaking. Reinhart said, "This is not handmade . . . the silver's not pure, either. It was probably made in one of those factories in Phoenix or Fort Worth . . . Chischilly roughed it about a bit to make it look older, and handmade."

"What's it worth?"

"What you can sell it for," Reinhart said, grinning. "The tourists aren't going to know any better."

"They will, sooner or later," John said grimly. "Especially after we publish the book we are planning on Navajo arts and crafts. It's probably worth about sixty dollars then—the turquoise is good?"

Reinhart nodded—"That's about it. But sell it for what you can get, and before the pawn date. Every Navajo on the reservation will know in a day or two that you've been had, and will respect you for getting back at Chischilly."

John said, "Sorry, we're not going to do business that way. I'll hold it for the full year and then try to sell it for sixty dollars, and tell the buyer why he's getting it at that price." He looked directly at Reinhart, "And I think it's time you left. Thank you for all you've taught me, but . . . let's part friends."

Reinhart said, "Dropping the pilot, eh? . . . Well, it had to come sooner or later. I'll be moseying along."

"Goodbye." John watched him go. Now they were alone—he and Stella, and Peace: and the Navajos, their canyons, mesas and deserts, their impassive faces, their secret thoughts.

*　　*　　*　　*

The twenty or so hogans constituting Toh Natsi were not grouped together in a single settlement. The Navajo people did not like crowding, and they did like privacy; so the hogans were scattered over an area of three or four square miles along the banks of a sandy wash, which carried no water for most of the year. The people took their water—and the settlement its name—from a perpetual spring that trickled out from under the base of the red cliffs that bordered the wash on the south: Toh means water.

Stella Merritt, wearing a pleated Navajo skirt of deep blue taffeta, and a concho belt, a pink blouse, and a blanket thrown over her shoulders, reined in her pony and looked down from the top of the cliffs. Smoke rose from the nearest hogan . . . that was Hostin Yazzie's, Mary had said. She should go there, Mary said, though she would be given shelter at any hogan, as a stranger . . . even though they knew her. Hostin Yazzie had lost a son to the war, like the Benallys from Sanostee to the north; the Yazzie boy had not been killed: he had done worse—married an American girl from the East and settled in New York.

Peace was asleep in his blankets, looped and fastened in front of her. When they were at Fort Defiance in the Indian Service she had watched the Navajo women, herding the sheep, carrying their babies with them so, or in their arms, tied to cradle boards. The children were always calm and quiet, staring at her with big, round black eyes. And she had watched the white women, keeping their babies indoors from the sun, guarding them from the desert winds, the snakes and scorpions and unknowable germs; and in the same act, guarding from them the tremendous sunsets, the sense of height and space, the great sky, the sand, the wind. Now they were free, and she meant to go out among the people, all through the land, doing her husband's work, and she would take Peace with her, that he who had a birth of shame, and had no soil to call his own, might find it here. She carried no heroin, only three or four buttons of peyote; but she did not think she would need even them.

She stirred, and rode the pony down the steep trail from the mesa into Toh Natsi.

Outside the first hogan, by an unguarded loom, she reined in and waited. A woman came out and said, "They are away. They will be back by night."

Stella knew that the woman was speaking of the men of the hogan. She said, "I am Benally's Friend's Woman."

"We know. I am Nahilhabah Ashkey."

That was old man Yazzie's second wife. She was young, Mary had said; but that could mean anything. She was probably thirty-five, and looked fifty.

Stella swung carefully down from the pony's back and leading it a little distance off, hobbled it. The wind was blowing colder every day, but it would not snow tonight. The pony was a Navajo pony and would not freeze; Navajo ponies were never stabled.

She returned to the hogan and the woman said, "Come," and went in, stooping through the tunnel-like east-facing entrance.

There was another woman in there, much younger—one of the sons' wives, probably, stooped over the small fire, a pot on it. Like most hogans, the structure was hexagonal, about twenty feet in diameter, the walls of mud-chinked logs cantilevered in as they climbed higher to form a low domed roof, plastered with mud, leaving a hole in the centre as a chimney. The beaten earth of the floor was bare, except where sheep pelts and blankets had been laid along the outer wall, to sit on by day, to sleep in at night. Stella unfastened Peace and set him on the floor, noticing that the blankets along the wall were well-designed, well and carefully made. Mary was right; the Yazzie women were excellent weavers. Peace crawled away from her toward two other children, nearly naked, playing beyond the fire. For a moment Stella watched the baby, then remembered; she was in a Navajo house. If there was need, the babies would be tended to. Meantime, leave them alone.

She said, "Benally Bekis hopes you will bring in more rugs." She spoke in Navajo, not fluent, but it could be understood, unless she mismanaged the inflections that changed, say, "food" to "star."

The woman at the fire said, "He has taken over the Trading Post from Narrow Nose, they say. I have not seen it myself."

"It is true. We want the Dinneh to get more money for their goods. Benally Bekis's father is coming, in the Big Snow month, and we hope will come also one who writes . . . writes about such work as yours, in the big cities . . . that they might know how good it is, and pay more, for more we will then ask."

The senior woman said, "We can not make more, unless we make badly. We will not make badly."

Stella said, "We do not want to buy or sell bad work."

One of the children wailed. Stella thought Peace was chewing on something he had picked up off the dusty rug—perhaps a bone, or a crust of bread dipped in mutton fat. She said, "It is the same with the turquoise and silver"—she touched her concho belt and the heavy bracelet on one wrist—"The man who writes, will write that that work too is of value. Let the men, the *hastoi*, also know this."

"They will return before dark," the senior woman said. "You are not afraid to leave Benally Bekis alone with Mary Begay? She is young and pretty, and she has lived among Americans."

Stella smiled, "I am not afraid. Benally Bekis is my friend, as well as my husband. We have seen much together. We have seen pain together . . . That design has a name, sister?"

"Red Mountain Turtle, sister."

"I have not seen it at any trading post."

"It is not taken there. It is from the time of the Long Walk . . . It was made for a sing for deliverance from that place where the Americans took us . . . My father was taken, he saw the first carpet of this Red Mountain Turtle, made there by a woman of the Tshectalaini clan . . . We do not sell it, because it belongs to us, alone. No one who is not of the Dinneh could feel, seeing it, lying on it, what should be felt, and seen . . . and suffered."

Stella said nothing. It was proper. She would not try to persuade them to sell Red Mountain Turtle rugs, though they were very beautiful. She would not even mention the design to John. In time, he would learn about it, in his own way, and in the Dinneh's own time.

The hours passed; the women took the pot off the fire, and all ate out of it with their fingers. She, and the other women, found pieces of mutton and bread and beans and gave them to Peace. The men of the hogan came in, glanced at her, said nothing, ate, talked among themselves, curled up in their blankets, and went to sleep. Stella followed their example, lying beyond the fire, smelling the night, cold seeping down through the smokehole and gradually spreading across the floor as the ashes turned from red to pink to grey.

*   *   *   *

From Toh Natsi she rode to Lukachukai, and spent three days there, too; then to Dinnehuitso—three more days . . . then back to Merritt's,

Peace on her saddle bow. Now it was December, and Peace liked to sleep on the floor on a blanket, wrapped in another, not in his cot under sheets and blankets. He had spoken his first word—Toh: water.

This day, a week later, Stella awoke feeling that today she would come to some great decision, would make some great discovery; but she did not know what. Perhaps she would finally give up peyote in its turn, as the weed had supplanted heroin. Perhaps . . . she did not know. This feeling she had was not a Christian, or white, or "American" feeling, and certainly not English. It was Navajo; like the Navajo, she would wait for it to express itself, not necessarily in her or for her
. . .

Nothing happened, except that John seemed to be off his food, and by nightfall was wearing a drawn expression. At midnight, he tossing and turning, she asked him what was the matter; and at last he told her his stomach hurt. An hour later he was up in a hurry, and out into the cold wind and whirling dust. When he returned, he told her that he had vomited. There was no more vomiting and no diarrhoea, and in the morning he went to work in the Post, but looking more drawn than ever. Stella badgered him until he admitted that his belly was hurting more than ever, the pain centred in the right lower section. Mary, squatting in the corner of the room teaching Stella to weave, looked worried, and whispered that they had a famous "medicine man" in Toh Natsi who could perform a sing for Benally's Friend, which would cure him. Perhaps, Stella thought, but what could she do *now* to alleviate his pain? She found the first-aid book they had bought in New York, and studied the various disease symptoms . . . Influenza—this wasn't in the chest, so it wasn't the Spanish flu that was still sweeping the world, and which he had already had, in Beighton . . . Beighton, dear God, did it exist, did England exist? . . . Typhoid? The symptoms were not the same at all . . . Appendicitis—discomfort in the mid-abdomen gradually radiating to the right lower abdomen . . . pain increasing in severity . . . cramping and increasing tenderness . . . generally no fever or febrile symptoms . . . This was it.

She went to him, where he was leaning over the counter doubled up in pain, and said, "I think you have appendicitis, John. I'm going to take you to Fort Defiance and let Dr Owings look at you."

John muttered between clenched teeth—"Indian Service doctors are not allowed to treat anyone but Indians."

"Except in emergency!" she said. She turned to Mary Begay—"I am going to the Fort with Benally Bekis. Stay here with Peace. Sell what you can if anyone comes. The prices are marked. Do not buy or take pawn." Mary would have loved to haggle, the Navajos' chief pleasure in life; but she'd have to accept the boring routine of selling at the fixed price.

Together they dressed the patient in warm clothes, and helped him out to the Model T standing in front of the Trading Post. One of the men came out of the nearest hogan, watched for a few moments, and went back inside. They tucked John in the back, where he could lie curled up, and covered him with blankets. Then Mary wound the starting-handle crank, the engine fired, and Stella drove off carefully down the rutted track toward the main north-south cart trail from Shiprock to Gallup, near the eastern edge of the reservation. She should reach Fort Defiance in three or four hours.

It was then noon; an hour later, it began to snow. The snowflakes whirled in under the canvas roof of the tourer, covering the blankets under which her husband lay with snow. The windshield clotted so that she had to turn it down, and drive with the snow packing on her goggles: she always wore goggles driving in the reservation, if not against the dust, then the glare; and now, she was seeing her first real Navajo snowstorm. An hour later, going very slowly through the blinding storm, she missed the road, and the Ford dropped five feet off a culvert onto a big rock. It was a teeth-jarring crash, and she heard the sharp metallic crack at the front, and knew, before she climbed out into the snow, that the front axle was broken.

The snow was not very wet, and the temperature was dropping. It must be below freezing now; and would be near 10 degrees by night-fall. She had traveled this road half a dozen times, and thought there was a hogan or two somewhere close by. Through the whirl of the snow she made out the loom of the reddish cliffs to the right, the west . . . a notch, the hogans had been under there   . She bent over John and shouted, "Front axle's broken. I'm going for help. Don't move."

He moaned, through gritted teeth . . . "Don't . . . get lost . . ." She covered him again with the blankets, realizing in that act that suddenly, without warning, they were both facing death. This, then, was what her yesterday's "feeling" had portended. It has taken its time in revealing itself, but now it was here. No one might come on this track now for a week. Fort Defiance was fifteen miles away over the Chuskas, or twenty-five by the track round the southern end of them. Their fate depended on whether she could find the hogans she re-membered.

She set off, head bent against the snow, her blanket wrapped tight round her upper body, the deerskin Navajo moccasins sinking deep in the snow . . . four inches of it so far . . . She thrust on, snow crusting her goggles, stinging her cheeks, her hands biting cold . . . A corral

. . . a score of sheep, huddled in it, beside a lone juniper, gnarled and twisted, its grey branches beginning to bend down under the weight of the snow on them. The hogans would be very close—but in which direction?

She moved on carefully. The cliffs disappeared for a minute, appeared again, vanished once more. She saw the notch once, then not again. Suddenly she stopped . . . smoke! She had smelled smoke. She turned this way and that. The wind was from the north-west. She moved into it, staring . . . there, half-right, something straight-sided . . . a hogan. She struggled toward it and entered. It was crowded— three men, four women, five children, a fire burning, a pot on it.

She said, "Shenaali! I am Benally Bekis Be'tsan . . . he is in the car—sick . . . The car is broken."

The men rose, wrapped their blankets around them, and followed her out into the snowstorm. Twenty minutes later, following what she could of her footsteps, and walking with the wind over her left shoulder, as it had been on her right cheek coming out, she led them to the car. An inch of snow had drifted in over John by now. The Indians muttered among themselves, and at last two lifted John out and hoisted him onto the back of the third, a strong young man of about twenty-five. Thus loaded, they went slowly back to the hogan, and laid John down inside. The men stood over him, silent. One of the women said to Stella, "We have medicine for that."

Stella had been thinking, all the time they were coming back from the car. It was certainly appendicitis. She could not operate; and John's treatment could not wait. She said, "Benally Bekis has"—she said the word in English—"appendicitis." She pointed to her lower belly on the right side. She didn't know whether the men had understood or not; she continued—"He must go to the Fort Defiance medicine man—*now*."

The men said nothing for a while, then the elder said, "I am Peshlakai. It will take six, seven hours to the Fort. In the snow, perhaps longer. If it becomes colder, we may not reach there."

She knew he meant, we may die, of cold, of exhaustion, buried under snow, in a pass of the Chuskas. She said, "I know, Hostin Reshlakai . . . It must be done if it can be."

Peshlakai said, "It can be, if the gods help us." He turned and spoke rapidly. Stella did not understand much that was said, but saw that the women began to bustle, pulling meat out of the pot and wrapping it in corn leaves, bringing bread from a wooden box by the door. The men had all gone out into the snow. Stella waited.

The woman who had spoken before said, "Eat, sister. It may be many hours."

She ate what was given to her. John, lying beside her on the rugs, was pale as the ashes, his face contorting with pain, his forehead wet with sweat, his teeth bared, as he grated them to suppress his cries. An hour passed. Stella became more and more fidgety . . . but there was nothing else to do, that was proper, except wait.

Eventually the men returned. And Peshlakai said, "We are ready." Two of them came and wrapped John like a mummy in blankets, even to his head, wrapping the blankets round him, then two rugs, then tying them all firm with rawhide cords. Struggling outside with them, Stella saw that they had made a travois, and it was harnessed now to a pony. Two other ponies stood beside the first, heads down. The men lifted John's mummy-like shape onto the travois and tied it yet more firmly in place. Then Peshlakai pointed to the nearest pony, looking at Stella, and she swung up into the saddle. The older of the two other men followed suit on the second pony. One woman stood in the entrance to the hogan, watching. Without a word, Peshlakai struck the travois pony's flank with the flat of his hand, and it set off, one hoof after another plodding into the snow, now seven inches deep. The trailing poles of the travois made deep tracks in the snow as John's weight rode easily on them. The young Indian trotted briefly to get in front, to make trail. Stella followed in the rear. The snow continued to fall diagonally, the wind slowly shifting from north-west to north as the evening approached.

They had some light for the first two hours, then, for an hour, Stella could see nothing. She wondered how the pony could know where it was putting its hoofs. It was a Navajo pony, she thought; it knew not from the ordinary senses, but from a communion with nature that it shared with its brothers, the Dinneh. Death too, was part of the land, of this communion, and acknowledged as such.

After the first four hours the cold began to work through her blanket and the thick woolen clothes she was wearing . . . her shirt was wool, for she had known it would be cold in the Ford—but she had not expected this. One should always expect anything in this country. A Navajo did not assume that he was going to reach any place so many hours after he started out for it; he knew better . . . her toes were becoming numb . . . her hands . . . her nose . . . cheeks . . . Was she dreaming, or was the snow lessening? There was a foot of it on the ground now. What if the appendix burst . . . would John die on the spot? If they could reach Fort Defiance within, say, three hours after it had, could the doctors help him?

The travois stopped moving. Her horse almost ran over it, and then stopped so suddenly that Stella rocked forward over the saddle bow, grabbing hold of it to keep her balance. She had almost been asleep, then. She pulled out and rode up alongside Peshlakai. He said, "Dismount . . . walk . . ."

The other Indian swung down with her. The young man knelt before her, a shape in the glimmery white darkness, and began to take off her moccasins. "Sit," he said; and when she had, he rubbed snow on her feet, and then her hands . . . again on her feet, then on her cheeks. She felt the blood returning in painful, sharp stabs. Peshlakai said, "Eat!" He was eating, she could tell from the chomp of his jaws beside her; and she found the meat the woman had given her, and ate too.

Peshlakai grunted, "On." She struggled over to the travois and called through the mummy wrapping—"John? How are you? Are you cold?"

She heard his little groan—"No . . . belly hurts . . . like hell . . . Where are we?"

"I don't know . . . We're going on now." They mounted, moved on. How many hours gone? She had no idea. It was not necessary to know. Americans had to know the time; the Navajos lived without time, but in it. The question now was, not what time is it, but is it John's time to die? And who knew? How many miles gone, to go? She did not know that either. They were moving as fast as anyone could, through these mountains, in these conditions.

The moon was out, riding in a cold sky. There was no wind, and the snow had stopped. Her breath condensed inside her goggles and she had to keep taking them off and wiping them clear with her gloved hand.

An isolated rock, dim red in the moonglow, swam up out of the night ahead. A ponderosa pine perched on top of it, after growing horizontally for six feet, curved straight up toward the moon. Her heart leaped, for she knew that rock, that tree. They were close to the Fort. Close enough? Who knew? She wanted to urge the pony faster, to shout to Peshlakai, "Hurry, hurry!" . . . The ponies plodded on, the trails of the travois straight and deep in the untrodden snow. She saw the buildings of the Fort and again wanted to shout . . . a vagrant flurry of snow blotted them out, they no longer existed . . . was this the meaning of time, and place? They swam out once more, by a car parked beside the road—that was the Agent's Packard . . . here was the Agency . . . the store . . . the hospital.

They turned in through the open gate in the stone wall.

*　　*　　*　　*

John was sitting propped up in bed, his face brown against the pillows. In the three days since the operation he had recovered much of his colour, and a little of his strength, enough to hold out his hand to her and say "Thank you, Stella." He thought; I should say, you saved my life. But it wasn't appropriate; she knew she had, but their lives were one now. She had saved her own. She leaned forward in her chair beside the bed and kissed him on the cheek. Sitting back she said, "The day before you were sick, I had a feeling . . . a knowledge . . . that I was going to pass through some arch . . . in a cliff, or mountain. When you became ill, I thought, it is the bad spirit that was in me, passing into him. Then it seemed that the only way you could rid yourself of that spirit was by dying; so you would have died for me . . . first taking the spirit, and then dying so that it would die. But you were saved. The spirit has gone from both of us . . ." She held out her hands, bare, palms up—"I do not need heroin, or peyote . . . or even danger. I am whole."

He held her hands tight—"There's a long letter from Dad, on the chair there. He's going to lobby for the Navajo in Washington until . . . until I'm ready to take over, he says. But I'm never going to go back East. We . . . something's happened, recently, Stella. The Navajo have wholly accepted us. They trust us. We are of them . . ."

"I felt that some time ago," she said, "the night I delivered Hoskie Tsosi's baby."

"*This* is our home! These are our people. We'll never leave them."

She said slowly, "In spirit, no, John. But we can never lead them— they must lead themselves. And whenever their affairs, their fate, become centred off the reservation, they need guides. The time may come when the Dinneh will *send* us away, because the place where they then need our help is not here, but in Washington. You could never do as much for the Navajo and the Hopi here as you could if you were Commissioner of the Indian Service—or Secretary of the Interior."

After a time John said, "I can't believe it now, but my father thinks as you do, so it's possible, many years on. But it may never happen, and I'll be happier if it doesn't."

She said, smiling, "Me, too. But one thing that *will* happen, in about seven months, is that Peace will have a little brother. Or a little sister."

Daily Telegraph, Monday, December 1, 1919

AMERICAN INVASION

POST-WAR RECORD

From Our Own Correspondent, *New York*, Sunday. Nearly 7,000 passengers left New York yesterday for England by four liners, a record number of civilians leaving New York on any day since War was declared. They are a mere advance guard of the

tens of thousands who will follow in the spring and summer. London will have several months to prepare for invasion, and if London fails there will be a tremendous disappointment.

. . . Amongst the many notables on the White Star Liner *Adriatic* were Sir John Ferguson, Sir David Henderson, Lord and Lady Swaythling, Sir John and Lady Harrington, Sir Alfred Smithers, Sir Alexander and Lady McGuire, and Sir Thomas Lipton, who returns here again next April in an effort to win the America's Cup, and to take part in the tercentary celebration of the landing of the Pilgrim Fathers. Just as Sir Thomas Lipton sailed, a lady in deep mourning rushed aboard to thank him for his kindness to her late husband, an American surgeon who died in Serbia . . . The lady told reporters that Sir Thomas Lipton not only looked after the funeral arrangements, but what she valued most, himself provided the American flag to cover her husband's remains. "If all Britishers were like Sir Thomas Lipton," the lady said, "we would not need an Anglo-American alliance because we would have one already."

What a nice little vignette, Cate thought; though Sir Thomas's kindness had apparently been more to the surgeon's corpse than to his living person. And the bereaved lady's heartfelt expressions about an Anglo-American alliance made much warmer reading than the reports of the political in-fighting going on over there about the League of Nations.

Isabel said, "Have you read the piece about Mr Churchill and the League?"

Cate looked at the page he was reading and said, "Not yet, but I suppose it's here, under the headline U.S. SENATE AND TREATY— EFFORTS FOR COMPROMISE."

"Yes," she said. "Apparently he has written an article somewhere in which he declares that the League was conceived and pressed on the Peace Conference by America alone, and therefore America owes a duty to the world which she is quite sure to perform."

Cate said, "It doesn't look a bit sure to me. The Senate has already rejected the League once. Perhaps they don't agree with Mr Churchill's assessment of what their duty is."

Isabel sighed, "Oh dear . . . It all seemed so rosy, and clean, and right, when Mr Wilson was speaking . . . and was well."

Cate said, "I fear that eloquence won't count for much now that we're at grips with vital national interests . . . nor will Sir Thomas Lipton's generous treatment of the American surgeon's body."

England: December, 1919

33 David Toledano tossed and turned in the bed. He could not make himself comfortable, so that he could sleep, because his mind would not rest. Of course his father knew he was here, at High Staining; and that Helen was here, too, with little Boy. His father regularly employed spies in his business and it was natural that they should also report to him about his only son's private life. It was these same men who would have found out for his father about the character, lineage, wealth, and morals of the Jewish girls who had been put in his way ever since he came back from the war.

So, his father would know that he had been polite enough with the pretty, rich Jewish girls; but had seen more and more of Helen. Coming down to High Staining was, in his own mind at least, a declaration. If she would have him, he was going to marry her, and of course take Boy under his wing, too . . . bring him up as his real father would have wanted. But what would his own father think, say, do? Perhaps he would not care so much that Helen had had an illegitimate child; for he knew what the war had done, and in his youth, David knew, he had been a lover of many beautiful women, mostly Egyptians or Circassians, all kept in seclusion as though in a harem. His father was a very old-fashioned man . . . But it might kill him that his son was marrying a Gentile, then how could *he* face the great God, when his own time came?

It was four o'clock, the moon shining in through the window, hoarfrost on the panes, no wind, few clouds. He got up, dressed, and went silently out of the room and out of the house. The lane to

Walstone was a wall of moon shadow on one side, a ribbon of light on the other. The gravel crunched under his shoes as he swung along, cold gravel, frozen to the ground below. A hunting owl called over from the edge of the wood, but he did not see it. He walked faster, not knowing or caring where he was going.

From the shadow of the hedge, deep among the brambles and hazel bushes, Probyn Gorse, two pheasants in the tail of his coat, watched him approach. The Duke of Clarence crouched at heel, as silent as his master.

Probyn had heard the footsteps long before, and wondered whose they were . . . not Fulcher . . . surely not another poacher . . . Then he saw him, and recognized him—the big Jew staying the weekend at High Staining. He stepped out of the hedge a few yards ahead of David and said, "Morning, sir. Going to be a nice day."

David did not start. He knew Probyn slightly, and had heard much about him from Helen and, years ago, from Guy Rowland. It did not seem strange that he should rise out of the earth at half-past four and fall in to shamble along beside him. He said, "I couldn't sleep . . . because I want to marry Helen . . . Lady Helen . . . but I think my father would be very upset, because she's not Jewish . . ."

Probyn said nothing for a while, then—"No use asking if she'd want to become a Jew—she wouldn't . . . Well, I always tried to please my dad. Reckon us men always do, until we hit on something we've both got our minds set on, opposite ways, and we're both men and can't give way . . . then we go on our own ways, and four, five, ten years later, it's all blown over . . . but we never really grow up till it's happened . . . Marry her, sir. Won't find many better women than Her Ladyship, Jewesses or no . . ." He turned off into a footpath, instantly vanishing in the shadows, without another word.

*   *   *   *

David came back at eight, to find Helen alone at the breakfast table. Louise Rowland and the sole land girl now left at the farm were already out at work. Helen looked up from her kippers—"Good morning, David. Did you have a nice walk?"

"Yes," he said. "Twelve miles." He went to the sideboard, picked up a porridge plate, and ladled porridge into it. Behind him, Helen said, "I don't know how Mrs Rowland runs this place with no help but Frances and old Foden . . . Foden never was a very good farm labourer even before he went to France, and he certainly didn't learn anything out there . . ."

David turned and walked toward her. He said, "Will you marry me, Helen?" He stood, waiting, the plate of porridge growing hotter in his hand.

She looked up, lowering her knife and fork—"Are you sure you won't regret it later? I can not change my religion, you know."

"I know. And I'm sure."

"I will, then. I've always liked you. You've been so kind, generous . . . not with money, though that too, of course . . . just generous, with friendship."

"It was love."

She said, "I don't know about that with me yet, David. Perhaps it'll never be really love . . . but, everything else, yes, and perhaps . . . I can't promise."

"It doesn't matter," he said, and sat down opposite her. Louise Rowland came in, wearing outdoor farm clothes, with bedroom slippers. She had taken off her Wellingtons at the front door and left them on the mat just inside. She said cheerfully, "The milking's nearly done . . . and I need a cup of coffee."

David said, "Helen and I are engaged."

"Oh, my dear . . . how wonderful. Congratulations! Wait till I tell Frances . . . and Naomi, of course."

David sprinkled a little salt on his porridge—"Mrs Rowland," he said, "do you know if Naomi has any plans to live here . . . or run it as a farm?"

"Why, no," Louise said. "I'm sure she hasn't. We hoped that Boy . . . well, you know that."

David said, "I'd like to buy it for young Boy. And live here and work it as a farm until he's ready to take it over . . . if he wants to."

Helen was half on her feet, her hands to her face—"David! I've dreamed of . . . But are you sure you wouldn't mind, Mrs Rowland?"

Louise said, "It takes a great weight off my mind . . . and does what we always hoped for . . . gives High Staining to Boy's descendants. I can't run it any more. I've been dreaming of retiring, going to Torquay or Lyme Regis, to sit on a bench and look at the sea. I'll be happy to sell, and give some of the money to Naomi. She's going to stay in Hedlington, on top of her factory. This is the place for you."

"Now I have to tell my father," David said.

And Helen—"And I, mine."

*   *   *   *

Guy Rowland, sitting at the bare table in the great room, glanced at his wristwatch—nearly time to set out for Wokingham and his promised visit to his sister. He was beginning to make some more notes in the margin of the estimate he was studying, when the sound of footsteps made him look up. A man in his forties was coming toward him, his face gaunt, the hair slicked down with water . . . thin of body as well as face, weak but striving to keep his back straight and his head up . . . clothes ragged, boots falling to pieces . . . he was trying to put his feet down like a soldier, but not strong enough to do more than shuffle. He came to a stop by the table and stiffened to attention— "Wing Commander Sir Guy Rowland?"

Guy got up and put out his hand, "That's me." The other's hand was thin and bony and had no strength in it.

"Private Lucas, sir . . . 1st Battalion, Weald Light Infantry . . ." Guy felt the hand slipping out of his as the man slowly collapsed, falling at last to his knees as Guy grabbed him by the shoulders and eased him down.

He came round in a few moments, and Guy pulled him upright and sat him in his own chair, kneeling beside him—"Starved?" he asked.

Lucas nodded and Guy said, "I'll get you some hot milk in a minute, and something more substantial later . . . You served under my father?"

"Yes, sir," Lucas said. "Twenty-two years. Saw you once in the trenches, when you come up to visit him . . . on the Somme."

"But you're not still serving?"

"No, sir. I didn't want to go, but they demobbed me . . . couldn't get a job . . . all my people dead . . . had to spend my pension on doctors and medicines—piles, sir . . . stole some bread . . . went to gaol for a month . . . starved again . . . I want to work for you here, sir . . . for the other blokes . . . walked down from Brummagem . . ."

"God! Sleeping in hedges, at this time of year? How did you manage to keep shaved? And your boots clean?"

"I'm a soldier, sir."

"What can you do?"

Lucas hesitated, his head down—"Nothing, what will help you, I s'pose . . . I'd best get back to Brumm . . . I'm not taking any charity."

Guy said, "You're a real old sweat. You must be able to run a Crown & Anchor board."

Lucas looked up quickly, "That I can, sir . . . and all fair and aboveboard, too."

"Every soldier, sailor, and airman loves Crown & Anchor," Guy said. "But you can't do that eight hours a day."

Lucas said, "I can look after clothes and such, sir . . . make beds, keep a house regimental-like . . . clean floors, silver . . . iron trousers."

"And ladies' blouses?" Guy asked.

Lucas nodded; and Guy said, "Very well, you shall be my valet . . . and Florinda's lady's maid—up to a point—until she gets a real one, if she ever does . . . Now, sit tight, and I'll bring you that milk . . ."

*　　*　　*　　*

Harry Rowland lay dying in the high narrow bed in the cottage, his youngest son at his bedside. A wind blew down off Dartmoor and the trees in the wood behind the village thrashed against the cloudy sky, but it was not raining. That would come later, as the seagulls flew inland from the winter storm gathering in the Channel, and waddled up and down the furrows of the new-ploughed fields.

The telegrams had gone out, but so far only Tom had come. His father was propped up in the bed, his face ashen grey, breathing with difficulty, both hands lying limp, bony yellowish outside the coverlet. Tom reached out his hand, and took one of his father's, warming it with his own. Harry's eyes opened and he turned his head a fraction, looking at Tom as though seeing him for the first time. He said, "I should have gone years ago . . . before the war. I . . . we weren't the right people. We didn't understand . . . too much change . . . too much new . . ." His voice trailed away.

Tom said, "Don't talk, Daddy. Rest. I'll be here if you want me."

The old man continued obstinately, "We . . . like dodoes . . . relics from another time . . . our world gone, but we didn't notice . . . should have died in 1914 . . . better for everybody if . . . young generals, young ministers . . ."

"We couldn't have won without you," Tom said, seeing that his father's mind could not release the idea, "You represented　stood for . . . all that we were fighting for—ideals of decency . . . duty . . . the way an Englishman ought to live his life . . . treat people . . ."

The old man's eyes closed slowly. There had been an old lady, Tom thought; some old flame of the Governor's youth, whom he'd met again when he retired here. She'd been here earlier, but then she'd left.

The old man's eyes opened again—"Where are your wife and children, Tom? Downstairs?"

Tom said, "I have not married, Daddy." He braced himself—"I never will. I live with another man. I can not live with women . . . or love them, as a man should. I have tried, but I can not." An immense load seemed to rise from his chest and float, almost visible, out through the window rattling in its ancient frame.

His father said, "Are you happy, my boy?"

"Yes, sir. At last."

"Good . . ."

Tom heard footsteps on the stairs and turned his head. The door opened and his sister Alice limped in, her artificial leg creaking. He saw that she was pregnant, about five or six months. He was becoming quite expert, seeing so many of the Gavilan clients in that condition, coming to gaze hungrily at creations they would not be able to wear for some months. Behind Alice was his eldest brother Richard, looking drawn and tight-mouthed . . . worried about the strikes that were crippling his factories, of course . . . Quentin was in India; John dead of the influenza; Margaret killed in Ireland. The rest were here. He wondered if the Governor would notice Alice's condition, and ask how her husband was. But it was Richard kneeling beside the bed now; and his father's voice becoming feebler, a croak . . . They were all kneeling, Alice holding one hand, Tom on the other side, the other. An hour later Harry Rowland died, in the village where he had been born, a few days less than seventy-seven years before.

*   *   *   *

Ethel Fagioletti poured more tea for one of the four women sitting round the little front room of the sergeant's married quarters, and said, "The colonel wants to make Niccolo a C.S.M., but I told him, don't take it if you can help it."

"Why did you say that, Mrs Fagioletti?" one of the women asked. "It'll be more pay."

"We could all do with that," Ethel said. "But Niccolo's thirty-three, and if he gets C.S.M. now, he can't stay there for ever, can he? But he wouldn't succeed Mr Bolton as Regimental, because he'd be too junior. But when the *next* Regimental retires, then Niccolo would either have to take it, or go out himself. And he'd only be forty by then. That's no time for a man to put himself on the shelf . . . No, he ought to wait for four or five years before he takes C.S.M."

"I wish I could think clear, like you, Mrs Fagioletti," another woman said in a strong cockney accent. "You're a tower of strength to yer 'usband, we all knows that."

Ethel had never got over the surprise, and pleasure, of finding that other women looked up to her. Of course, it was partly due to the way their husbands looked up to Sergeant Fagioletti, M.M.; but some of it must be her own doing, and that thought gave her strength and wisdom to help them, if she could; and the more they came, the more she found that, digging within her own common sense and her experience, she could.

A woman with an Irish accent said, "They're asking my Paddy to go to Netheravon as an instructor. Do you think he should go?"

"Will there be quarters for you?"

"Oh aye, that there will, but . . . what'll happen when he comes back to the battalion? The officers will have forgotten him."

Ethel said, "He may not come back to the battalion, Mrs Geoghegan. It depends where there's a vacancy for a machine-gun sergeant. It might be the 2nd Battalion in India . . . And then you'd be out there, on the strength, for six years."

"Glory be! I never thought I'd see India, when Paddy enlisted in 1915, and us only a year married . . . You look a mite pale, Mrs Fagioletti. Shall we be leaving you to rest?"

Ethel blushed, looked down, and said in a small voice, "I think I'm pregnant."

"Glory be!" the Irishwoman cried. "Then your prayers to the Holy Virgin have been answered!"

Ethel nodded, saying, "Yes, and the doctor thinks it will be twins." She wondered whether it was the prayers that had at last succeeded; or Probyn's Woman's potions and strange instructions; or just Niccolo's powerful thing, plunging in and out of her. She blushed again at the thought—"More tea?" she asked.

"Why, thank you, Mrs Fagioletti, I don't mind if I do . . . My Frank's not good at figures. He says they'll never make him C.S.M., or even C.Q.M.S., unless he learns better arithmetic. But how can he do it?"

Ethel said, "There's courses you can apply for, that come by post. You can learn anything, really, if you want to. Niccolo's going to start two of them, next year, soon as Christmas is over . . . so's he can write better, and arithmetic. Because he knows enough for C.S.M. now, but not for Regimental . . . and after he's finished as Regimental . . . *if* he gets it"—she touched the tabletop religiously—"they may offer him Quartermaster, and then he'll have to have a lot more than he does now, especially with him being born an Eyetalian."

"Cor!" the cockney woman cried. "Niccolo, in the officers' mess!"

"I don't know why not," Ethel said a little stiffly. "It's just a matter of working hard, and making himself fit for it."

"Of course," the woman said hurriedly. "Of course, Mrs Fagioletti."

"And," Ethel said, "his brother-in-law *is* a lord."

*   *   *   *

Stephen Merritt, sitting across the desk from Richard Rowland, said, "I was sorry to read of your father's death, Richard."

Richard said briefly, "He was happy to go. He felt that England— the world—had changed too much for him to enjoy any more. And he was very tired." He waited. Stephen had not crossed the Atlantic and spent a week in London and in Hedlington just to commiserate with him about the Governor.

Stephen said, "I've been making inquiries about the situation here, Richard. Would you agree that we have two quite separate problems—first that there are bad relations between labour and management in both plants—and second, that it is very hard to sell big aeroplanes in the present state of world politics and economy. The truck business is doing better, but it is also facing rapidly increasing competition, and some nationalist hostility . . . strange, because H.A.C. uses American engines, too, but with the aeroplanes that doesn't seem to matter."

Richard said, "I agree. Those are the problems. And they're not connected."

"Well, let's take the second first. I have been told that there will be a market for aeroplanes designed to be flown off warships, special ships called aircraft carriers. The British Navy has to modernize. They're not going to get rid of battleships, but they must realize—they already have—the potential of aircraft carriers. I have checked this out . . ."

"That's Betty's idea," Richard said.

"She isn't the only one sharing it," Stephen said. "In any event I have checked it out as carefully as I can with the Admiralty, and with the Prime Minister. As you know, we have had relations with Mr Lloyd George dating back to before the war when he was Chancellor of the Exchequer. What would be your thought if I were to propose that we turn our attention purely to aircraft to co-operate with the navy? The British Navy—though I presume we would be able to sell our machines to Britain's allies, such as the French and Italians, and other nations . . . certainly if the British buy them others will be strongly tempted to do so, to keep up."

Richard waited, choosing his words. Betty had come to him with this idea, in a well-reasoned paper, the day after she rejoined the H.A.C. He had talked it over with Keble-Palmer, who had agreed that he could design such aircraft as well as anyone; but, there were the problems of any new design—draughting, re-tooling, testing, modifications. A lot of capital would be required, and at the end, perhaps failure to get any, or enough orders.

He said as much to Stephen Merritt. Stephen said, "All that you say is true. But we have not sold any more Buffaloes. And frankly, Handley Page has got the inside track in that field. I propose to recommend to the board that we convert as suggested at H.A.C., and drop all other projects." He went on without waiting for Richard to make any comment. Richard thought, too, that he detected a slight hardening of the voice, an augmentation of the flat Down East twang. "Now to labour relations . . . I have spoken to Mr Drummond, General Secretary of the Union of Skilled Engineers. He made it clear to me that the union has been and is ready to accept most of your conditions, if you would agree to the principle of a closed shop. They say they will go a very long way to save the jobs here."

"It's a matter of principle for me, too," Richard said stiffly. "Once we give an inch, they'll be telling us whom we must hire, whom we can't sack, even for absence, disobedience, insubordination . . . theft!"

Stephen said, "When I told him—Drummond—that we might be going to close the J.M.C., he became very agitated, and made still more concessions. We could have a closed shop at the H.A.C., with all the benefits of it, and almost none of the disadvantages. The union is willing to hamstring itself, to guarantee those H.A.C. jobs for its members."

"But . . ." Richard began, "you have not mentioned closing the J.M.C. before."

"No, but I have decided we must. It has made money. The shareholders of Fairfax, Gottlieb have done well from our investments in it. But now we ought to get a manager in, in Overfeld's place—but it's not worth it. We have looked at the graph curves of competition, marketability, available purchasing power . . . and now is the time to get out. I have contacted several people who are anxious to buy the plant as it stands. But I did not tell Drummond that . . . because of course the new owners will continue to employ as many, or more, union men as we would . . . I said at the beginning that we had two main problems, Richard. Actually, we feel we have three. The third is you. You have made this union problem a personal vendetta . . . Oh, I know about Bert Gorse and his past history with you, but you should never have let it become, and stay, personal . . . We have to end this strike. We have to get out of the motor truck business. We have to see that Hedlington Aircraft is not plagued by strikes in the future. To achieve these ends, we are removing you from your post as Managing Director of both companies."

Richard said at last, "The Governor was saying . . . his last words, nearly . . . that he was a leftover, didn't understand or like the world as it has become . . . I feel the same. I'm sorry I lost the fight."

"It was a fight that you couldn't win."

"Beaten by Bert Gorse!"

"Not him—changing climate. You've been like a man refusing to take off a heavy overcoat as the season changes . . . Things may come back your way, but not in our lifetimes . . . We propose to have Keble-Palmer manage the H.A.C. Betty will be made a director." He stood up—"May I use the telephone?"

Richard indicated it. Stephen picked it up and said, "Trunks," with a Museum number in London. After a time he said, "Mr Drummond? Merritt here. Mr Rowland has resigned . . . Good. Thank you." He turned to Richard—"The strike at H.A.C. will be over as soon as he can get through to Bert Gorse."

"What concessions did you get for my head?" Richard said bitterly.

"Enough," Stephen said shortly. "Richard, you are a business man. Millions of our bank's money is involved. What other decision was ever possible, in the circumstances?"

"You're right," Richard said at last. "Well, I'll clean out my desk and think what I am going to do next. Something I can do by myself, without any damned union looking over my shoulder, that's certain."

"Teach a course in business financing at some university," Stephen said. "That's been your forte, all along. Or get a job with one of the big banks, advising them on the same subject. David Toledano would welcome your advice, I'm sure. These companies here would have been in difficulties long ago if you weren't a genius in that field. Pass it on."

Deal with figures, Richard thought; but keep away from men, especially working men.

* * * *

It was almost dark when she came down the road, a shopping basket heavy on her left arm, a shawl over her head. Fletcher was waiting for her, ready, the lust urgent in his loins. She glanced back over her shoulder—the road was empty—and ducked through the gap in the hedge and into his arms. Her shopping bag was down, his overcoat spread, she was biting his ear, struggling to pull her skirt up, her drawers down, off, moaning. They'd met here long ago, in the first months of the war. Now she was married, to a farm labourer, and lived in the little cottage a mile up the road, toward Beighton.

He slid into her. She'd been thinking of this meeting too, for she was slippery and wet and eager. They coupled with frantic urgency, her buttocks lifting and banging against the ground and its carpet of dead leaves with his every fierce, powerful thrust. His tongue was half-way down her throat, the ecstasy coming . . . coming. She screamed, deep in her throat, the sound suffocated by his tongue, his mouth, his weight on her.

They lay still at last, her breathing coming in rasping groans, his gradually steadying. He rolled off her, staring up into the laced leaf-less boughs high above, against the clouds sailing over in the last of the steely light. She dressed, picked up her shopping basket, and leaned against him whispering, "Oh, Fletcher . . . Fletcher . . . when?"

He said, "Don't know . . . We've bought the Cottage in Beighton, and will move in in a couple of days . . . I could come down, though. 'Tain't far."

"Can't shop again till Thursday. No more money."

"Thursday then . . . same time?"

"Rain or shine. Fletcher, what's come over me? We used to do it, but it was never like this . . . I mean, I liked it then, I wanted it . . . but now, my drawers are soaked all day long, thinking of last time, or next time. What's become of me?"

Fletcher kissed her. No man could answer that question. She slipped back through the hedge and walked on the way she had been going, without looking back. They had been in the copse perhaps five minutes. Fletcher set off for his grandfather's cottage.

When he came in Probyn's Woman was over the stove. He thought, she must spend three-quarters of every waking hour there, in that position. She said, "Brush the leaves off your coat, afore she comes home, Fletcher."

Fletcher swore; and took off his coat and did as he was bid. He'd forgotten . . . always used to remember, as a young fellow, when it didn't matter; now it did, and he was getting careless.

His grandfather, sitting in a chair by the stove, looked up from a rabbit snare he was making, and said, "Who is it?"

"Molly Page," the Woman said. "Molly Fitch, that was . . . She's going to find out about it, you know."

Fletcher said nothing. Why didn't they mind their own fucking business? But then why had he started the affair again, three weeks ago, meeting Molly by chance on the road, in the dusk, and barely a word said, just falling into the wood, to fuck away like dogs in heat? He hadn't seen or thought of her in, what, three, four years before that. And he could always have Susan Makepeace, the *Honourable* Susan Makepeace, the rich London girl, whenever he wanted . . .

The Woman said, "She isn't enough for you?"

"Don't be daft, Woman," Probyn said. He understands, Fletcher thought; she doesn't, because she's a woman. The thing grabbed you by the balls and your prick ached, and the woman was looking at you, and you had to do it, like a bull had to when the cow came to him. That was what made him a bull.

He said, "I dunno, I wish . . . oh, fuck it!"

The Woman said, "How'd you like it if she did the same . . . with that tall fellow with the red head, who came down here sometimes."

"Ginger Keble-Palmer," Fletcher said. "He's been in love with her for years. Still is . . . Yes, she's having an affair. With aeroplanes. Making them. Designing them. She *has* to do it. Doesn't mean she don't love me. I could stop her, but I wouldn't have her then. She'd be something different . . . like other women. So I don't. Molly won't last long . . ."

"Then it'll be another one," the Woman said.

"Maybe. Probably. Like, she'll be falling for another aeroplane . . . but she comes back to me every night."

The door opened and his wife Betty came in, very smart in a simple woolen dress and half-length black coat and fur-trimmed hat. She went at once to Fletcher and kissed him. Then she kissed Probyn on the top of his head and smiled at the Woman, saying, "Anything I can do at the stove? It's a nice change after the draughting board."

The Woman said, "No. Dinner'll be in half an hour."

Betty stripped off her gloves slowly, and sat down at the deal table. She said, "I got a cable from John this afternoon. Stella's pregnant, and happy. He means, she's not taking drugs any more."

Fletcher said, "Good."

She said, "What have you been doing all day?"

"Sitting and thinking," he said. "Sometimes just sitting . . . and I finished the last of two poems for the third collection."

"Oh, wonderful!" She jumped up and flung her arms round his neck.

Holding her loosely, he said, "And I've decided what I'm going to do next—a long, long poem, about the new England . . . about what's happened to people here, through the war, both those who went over and those who stayed at home . . . about woman and children as well as men . . . all of us."

"A new Dynasts," she said thoughtfully. "Some of the critics are comparing you to Hardy . . . but with Shelley's lyricism instead of Hardy's pessimism . . . and Whitman's energy . . . Wonderful! So we'll live happily ever after in the Cottage, me creating aircraft that can land on seacraft . . . and you creating great poetry."

"And we'll both be ourselves, with it all," he said.

*   *   *   *

Guy Rowland said, "Frank Stratton was hoping to come over with us, but some disaster befell the plumbing at the Hall and he had to stay . . . We'll be ready for the first of our people before Christmas . . . the whole building won't be ready, of course—that'll take another six or eight months—but we felt it was important to get something started . . . to have something we can show prospective friends, and patrons . . ."

"What are you going to call the blokes you look after, and help?" Stan Robinson said, quaffing some stout from his heavy glass tankard, and setting it down again on the kitchen table.

Guy laughed—"We don't know yet. Inmates isn't the answer, is it? Clients? Patients? Foundationers might be right . . . because it can mean anything, and it doesn't have any pejorative or charitable connotation. Frank Stratton likes Foundationers . . ."

Two young women came in, one fairly tall and extremely beautiful, the other rather heavy, and pregnant, but with a pleasant smile and an obvious comfortable contentment in her manner. Florinda Rowland, the beautiful one, said, "Were you talking about Frank? Why does he have to keep that damned Victoria in the basement at the Hall?"

Robinson looked alarmed—"Victoria? He's got a lady . . .?"

"A racing motor cycle," Florinda said briefly. "He tunes it up in his spare time, and then untunes it . . . takes it to pieces, then puts it together again . . . goes vroom vroom at all hours of the day and night."

"It's his workshop," Guy said. "His tools and machines and gauges are there. And the Foundationers will love it. They'll want him to break the world speed record just as much as he does."

"When's he going to have a shot at it?"

"As soon as the weather warms up. The bike'll go faster in warm weather than cold, he says . . . And Brooklands will be open again."

Guy said, "Anne is pregnant, he told me."

Virginia said, "Thank heavens for that. That means they're really together again, everything forgiven and forgotten."

"It can't be forgotten," Stan said. "Not a thing like that, by a man like Frank Stratton. But if he says he has forgiven, he really has."

Florinda said, "Any stout for me, Stan?"

"Of course, madam . . . Florinda . . . I have to be so careful with the boys' parents that it slips out sometimes . . . sir, madam, my lord . . ."

He opened another bottle of milk stout and poured for Florinda. Virginia, standing in the doorway, wiping her hands absently on her apron, watched over them benignly. Her brother Guy said, "So—are you going to spend the rest of your life here, Stan?"

Robinson said, "We've been thinking, since you said you could find something for us at the Foundation."

"You have a lot to give," Guy said. "We wouldn't be just helping you out of charity."

Stan said, "I know. There's more in my head than gun drill on an 18-pounder . . . But we like it here. The people have been good to us. The pay's not great but with my pension and disability it's enough. If any of our kids have brains, they can get scholarships to good schools. And, you know what"—he leaned forward—"I've got my eye on the

Clerk of the Works' job. Mr Babcock has to retire in six years. Before then I'm going to learn his job inside out, and I'll ask for it. And I'll get it."

Guy nodded. The Clerk of the Works was in charge of all the maintenance of the school, repairs to buildings, plumbing, electricity, roads, gardens, playing fields. It was a good job for Stan. But it was also clear that Virginia did not want to move back into the upper-class society she had left in 1914. Some people had energetically moved upward in the turmoil of the war; Virginia had moved steadily and comfortably down; and she meant to stay where she was.

He said to her, "When's the baby due?"

"April . . . If it's the 23rd, your birthday, can we call it Guy?"

"Please, no. Too many Guys piling up. Call it George . . . It's St George's Day," Guy said. "Well, let's go for a walk on Caesar's Camp . . . all of us."

"Who's going to look after Katy?" Virginia cried.

"We'll take her with us . . . on our backs, in a pram, whatever . . . wake her up and dress her."

"But it looks as if it might snow!"

"All the more reason to get out. Come on!"

* * * *

The Countess of Swanwick, looking out of the window into Cornwall Gardens, thought, London's so *drab* these days. The little park was full of dead leaves because the house owners round the Gardens couldn't afford to pay a full-time gardener to keep the place in order. The road was lined with cars, standing against the kerb on both sides, cluttering up the neat Georgian line of the houses. Before the war there would have been nothing, for the carriages and the few cars would have been out of sight in the mews behind. But the mews were rapidly being converted into flats, or small houses; and everyone seemed to have a car, with no place to put it except in the street. The streets were made for vehicles to move through, she thought, not stand on . . . The pavements were usually dirty, with dogs doing their business where they shouldn't be allowed to . . . And the new owners or tenants of these once grand houses apparently could not afford to keep them up. Paint was peeling here, the plaster over there, a window broken somewhere else. The air was thick with beastly petrol fumes . . . which nowadays mixed with the smoke from the coal fires to make a London Particular even worse than it had been in the old days, and heaven knew it had been bad enough then. Why, she remembered coming home from a winter ball in '79, just before she married Roger, when the coachman had driven into the Serpentine, thinking he was still in Knightsbridge!

She sighed—it wasn't all bad. The poor were getting better food; young women didn't have to go into service and suffer as housemaids under tyrannical middle-class mistresses—they could be secretaries, factory workers, so many things. England was almost bankrupt, but people were still having babies, and those babies, when they grew up, would be English men and women. They'd deal with what they found . . . grow flowers, make gardens, sail the seas, fly the skies . . . Times had changed, and would change more. Change with them, or die. The diplodocus had had to learn that; and now, the aristocracy of the country.

The shot was from upstairs; she stiffened, but did not move. Roger would never learn, or change. After a time she turned and walked out of the room, up one flight of stairs and entered the earl's big study and library. He was crumpled over his desk, the service revolver on the carpet, a smell of cordite in the air. Blood and bone and brains spattered the books in front of him, but she had expected that . . . had been expecting it for months, she admitted to herself now. She looked down at him, whom she had loved, up to the end. She had married him for better or for worse; and remembered what he was when she became his wife, and countess.

She wondered what straw, exactly, led him to pull the trigger . . . Barbara's marrying the roughrider sergeant? Helen's illegitimate child by Boy Rowland? Having to sell Walstone Park to Hoggin? Seeing Hoggin become Lord Walstone, a peer of the United Kingdom? . . . Hoggin! The general state of the country—strikes, lockouts, unrest? 'God bless the squire and his relations, and keep us in our proper stations'. . . . no more of *that* now! Failing to make a go of it as Master of the North Weald Hounds? That was a severe blow. Helen, marrying David Toledano, next week? Probably that, she thought. Everything together, of course, but that, cutting the deepest.

She went out into the hall, and telephoned the police to tell them that the 9th Earl of Swanwick had committed suicide. No, he had not left any note.

Daily Telegraph, Saturday, December 20, 1919

ATTEMPT TO MURDER THE VICEROY OF IRELAND

BOMBS AND SHOTS

The long record of murder and outrage in Ireland culminated yesterday in an attempt to assassinate Viscount French, the Lord Lieutenant.

Mr Macpherson, the Chief Secretary, informed the House of

Commons of the leading facts concerning this dastardly crime. They are as follows:

At one o'clock, between Ashtown Station and the Ashtown Park gate of the Phoenix Park, four bombs or hand grenades were thrown from behind the hedge. The military guard fired upon the murderers, one of whom was on the road. He was shot dead . . . His Excellency escaped uninjured . . .

FUSILLADE FROM THICKET

From Our Own Correspondent, *Dublin,* Friday Night. Every loyal man in Ireland will offer his most hearty congratulations to Field-Marshal Viscount French on his escape from assassination at the hands of an armed band . . . The attempt . . . has aroused the utmost indignation amongst all loyal citizens . . . His worst enemy could not with truth impute to him unkindness or the slightest shade of harshness; he endeavoured to be firm, the country needed, nay, demanded, firmness, but he tempered firmness always with as much mercy as the spirit of sound justice might permit. All honest-minded Irishmen know well that the conspiracy of which today's attempt is but one evidence is too deep-rooted, too malign, to yield immediately to any treatment but one of stern repression . . .

"An outrage, indeed," Father Caffin said slowly. "And the perpetrator will be Michael Collins. He's a law unto himself, that man. He knows what he wants and how to get it, which gives him the strength of ten."

"But where will we go from here?" Guy said. "What is to happen to Ireland? More murders, counter-murders, counter-counter-murders?"

They were eating breakfast in the great dining room of Scarrow Hall, the three of them lost in its vastness, for the first Foundationers were arriving later this day.

The priest said, "Things have gone very far, but the outcome still depends, in the long run, on England . . . They say that Mr Lloyd George is going to make an important speech in the next day or two, about Ireland. If he can jerk himself out of the past . . . the mud of the past, that we are all mired in, English and Irish, Catholic and Protestant alike . . . then there is yet hope."

"I wish I could believe you," Florinda said. "But how can anyone deal with a man like you say Collins is?"

"By isolating him, my dear," Father Caffin said eagerly. "Do you not see that the Volunteers—Collins's men—are a minority? Do you not read the condemnations of the bishops, of the Cardinal himself, at every new assassination of a policeman, an official? And what is the invariable answer from Dublin Castle?" He paused while Lucas, wearing an incongruous blue suit, with a white shirt, stiff collar, and black bow tie, brought in a fresh pot of coffee and refilled all their cups. Then the priest continued, "Stern repression! Abolish the Dail Eireann. Abolish the Sinn Fein party . . . why, Mr Griffith said, that is to proclaim the Irish nation an illegal assembly! Instead, England must give . . . then Collins will not be able to make Irishmen believe that his way—of assassination and guerrilla war—is the only way to get what all Irishmen want."

"But Collins must realize that," Guy said. "So he will go on ordering murders, so that leniency, compromise . . . political advance, is made practically impossible for any British Government to grant."

"That's quite right," Father Caffin said. "And that's why David Lloyd George is the only man who can do it. He won the war. His power is still almost without limit. No one else could survive without the Carsons and F.E. Smiths . . . but he could. They could destroy another Prime Minister—but Lloyd George could destroy them, and save us from this impasse."

"Let's hope he does," Florinda said.

The priest said, "Let us *pray* that he does . . . But I confess to grave misgivings, indeed . . . The British Government is now calling for Englishmen to enlist in the Royal Irish Constabulary. The R.I.C. has always been a hundred percent Irish. Englishmen won't understand the people, or the land, or the background. And the people won't feel at all as badly about some English mercenary's being murdered as if it's an Irish Catholic neighbor with seven children . . . And it means two things—that a lot of police must be resigning from the Constabulary as a consequence of Collins's campaign of terror . . . and that the R.I.C. is also being expanded, and that can only be to enforce more repressive measures. Unless Lloyd George produces the miracle that only he can, I see a black time ahead . . . two, three years. I see civil war. There are strains inside the I.R.A., between those who want a Republic and nothing else—those who will be content with Dominion status . . . those who must have a unified Ireland, and those who believe it is impossible, or undesirable. Collins has enemies, and soon they'll be using the same methods against him that he's using against the British. Perhaps a new and better Ireland will be born of it, in the end, than could be created even by Lloyd George . . . but bloodstains take a long time to be washed out of one's soul, especially in Ireland."

Kent: Christmas, 1919

34 The little group waited in the doorway, watching. A long table ran down one side of the great room, under the tall windows, its surface littered with cardboard boxes, full of stiff red cloth, boxes of pins, scissors, pots of glue, small coils of thin wire, green tape. The people working at the table were all men. Some of them were seated on chairs in the normal way; others could not be, as they had no legs, and these were not in chairs but on padded boards set at the right height for them to work at the table. Several of the men could sit properly but worked with difficulty, for some had only one arm, and some were blind. They were making poppies, of cloth and wire, to be sold next Armistice Day for the benefit of the Foundation.

A blinded man had been appointed telephone exchange operator, for Willum Gorse had another job. He had a wheelchair now, and he had been practising making the artificial poppies for two weeks, and had showed such surprising aptitude that Guy and Florinda had appointed him head of that section. He had always been a little "simple," but that seemed to have vanished with his new authority. He wheeled himself rapidly up and down the table, commenting—"More tape round the wire there, Tomkins . . . 'Ere, them scissors, Johnson, you cut like this to make the petals, see? Not like this, what you've been doing . . . Put a piece of ordinary white cloth on the poppy, Ruttledge. If you can't see, you 'ave to make sure everything's just in the same place, reds here, whites here, wire here. Smithy, you see that it's all set out right for him, when you start for the day . . ."

From downstairs the roar of a motor-cycle engine, muffled by distance and the thickness of the floors, walls, and carpets, seemed to indicate that some chained beast was snarling out its fury at its captivity. On the floor above someone was playing a piano, and a male choir was singing with it, in harmony, stopping, starting again to the orders of a sharp, determined female voice. Outside the windows a light sleet was whistling across the lawns that swept down to the Scarrow and the boathouse, with its punts, canoes, and rowing boats.

In the doorway Sir Guy Rowland said, "This poppy making, and the accountancy class you've already seen, are mostly ways to pass the time for these fellows, until we find out, or ferret out, their more creative instincts. Some will never progress, probably, which is all right, too, as long as they're happy and feel they're doing something constructive, and not just being the objects of charity. You're going to be seeing and feeling a very different atmosphere here once everyone's found their feet . . . and perhaps their wings."

Lord Walstone, at his side, said, "Are these the worst blokes—the worst wounded, you'll be getting?"

Guy shook his head, " 'Fraid not. Some of the really bad casualties are still in hospitals . . . and some will never leave them. But we'll be getting men with no limbs at all . . . no faces . . . some purely mental, psychical wrecks . . . We don't really know yet whether we can manage them, at the same time as the physical wrecks, but we think the Governors and I—that they suffered together, and they'll recover together, if they can recover at all."

Lady Walstone said shyly, "So, really, it's the war that holds all these men together . . . even you."

Guy said simply, "Yes." He led forward and approached the table, stopping by the third man—"How's it going, Day?"

"My fingers is still like ruddy thumbs, sir," the man said. "Couldn't you get a girl to take over for me?"

Guy laughed and moved on, the others following. "All right, Clarke? Gaines, hey, you're cutting those petals too big." He turned to the Walstones—"Gaines lost his eyes at Jutland."

Ruth Walstone said, "When I had pink eye as a girl, Mr Gaines, I had some pattern cutting that I really wanted to get done. I measured the distances with the fingers of the other hand and cut along them . . ."

Gaines laughed ruefully, and said, "I was trying that, mum, and near cut my finger off." He held up a finger and they saw a bandage on it—"I'll learn in time. My P.O. always did say my head worked slower than frozen treacle . . ."

The party moved on. A man with one arm and a permanent frown, his teeth half-bared, was working ferociously at his task, at twice the speed of the men to his flanks, as though trying to do as quickly with one hand what they were achieving with two. Willum, hovering in his wheelchair by the group, said, "That's Meadows, sir. One of ours, he was. Wealds. Lost his arm at Passchendaele."

"I'm Lord Walstone," Walstone said, reaching out with his hand to shake Meadows' good left hand—"P'raps you know me better by my regular moniker, before His Majesty made me a peer . . . Bill Hoggin."

"Hoggin!" Meadows cried, dropping Walstone's hand as though he had found a scorpion in it. "Hoggin, of Hoggin's Plum and Apple Jam? Hoggin's Bully Beef? Hoggin's Meat and Potato Stew?"

"The same," Hoggin said proudly.

"Hoggin's Pig Swill!" Meadows said viciously, "except that the stuff you was sending us was 'ardly fit for even pigs to eat. I'd give my other arm to have 'ad you in the trenches with us, eating what you was making us eat."

Lord Walstone sputtered and turned red in the face. A few other men at the table were murmuring, "That's right! Hoggin's wasn't fit for pigs!"

Lady Walstone, née Ruth Stratton, cried, "Please . . . listen . . . I'm Lady Walstone, Bill's wife . . . Ruth Stratton that was. Any of you from round here will have known my dad, Bob, who was killed in the factory explosion in August '17 . . . When the war began, my husband was no more than a barrow boy, and he had me to feed and a baby on the way. He did some things he wouldn't do now, and he's sorry . . . he's come here now to tell you so . . . by helping to pay for this"—she waved her hand round the building—"by doing all he can to help Sir Guy and Lady Rowland help you. We all suffered in the war. We've got to forget all that, only remember that we were in it together, and we're going to stay together to help each other now."

Meadows, on his feet, his lips pursed, slowly relaxed. At length he said, "Sorry . . . Reckon if you hadn't made the money, somehow, I'd be playing a mouth organ in High Street." He stuck out his good hand. Walstone took it and shook heartily.

*　　*　　*　　*

They were sitting in chairs round the desk in Guy's office, which he shared with Florinda. Lord Walstone said ruefully, "That bloke really had his knife into me. I was only doing my best. If it hadn't been for me . . ."

His wife said, "We know, Bill. Everyone understands."

Rachel Cohen said, "You seem to be off to a good start, Guy. There's a good spirit, not too military . . . though I was wondering if it's a good idea, or necessary, to have the Foundationers use their military ranks, or call the people in authority, 'sir.' "

Her husband, Wilfred Bentley M.P. said, "I didn't hear much of that, Rachel . . . one fellow calling the man next to him 'sergeant' . . . everyone calling Guy, 'sir' . . . I think that's reasonable."

Guy said, "We thought we'd let them call each other, and us, whatever they feel like. We're only really concerned that they flourish and expand here, and that no one prevents anyone else doing it . . . which means acceptance of some discipline, some rules. From their point of view, it's a lot easier, and less formal than what they've known, either the discipline of a service, or the discipline of poverty."

Bentley said, "I agree. And I agree that we're off to a good start. I'll keep a stream of M.P.s coming down to you, which will help if you need money, either from the town, or from us . . . I myself will be down, but not very often. I feel that I must devote all my energy to seeing that there is never again any need for a Foundation such as this. That there shall be no more war."

Walstone said, "I thought we had a pretty good notion in that League of Nations . . . and then the Yanks went and pulled the plug on it. There's no 'ope of it working without them—they've got all the money already, and soon they'll have all the battleships and aeroplanes and guns and everything else."

Bentley said, "That was a great pity—the American Senate's rejection. I can't help feeling that a lot of the fault lies with Mr Wilson. He thought he could prevail by sheer superiority—of intellect, of moral righteousness. It didn't work with Clemenceau and Lloyd George, and finally it didn't work with his own people . . . But I don't agree that we are doomed without American help. The major danger spots are not in America, which apparently they intend to look after anyway, through the Monroe Doctrine . . . The biggest present danger is Russia."

Rachel said sharply, "The Russians see their revolution threatened by capitalist counter-revolutionaries inside their country and by foreign interference outside."

Lord Walstone said, "What are they marching into Poland for, eh?"

"You can't stand on the defensive if your enemies mean to destroy you," Rachel said. "They'll retreat inside their own borders as soon as they feel safe. Socialists are opposed to all war, and once the working class is in power everywhere, they will see that there is none."

"In a pig's eye, they will," Walstone muttered. "The Russians mean to shove their revolution down our throats, so the whole world will be singing the Red Flag."

Bentley said soothingly, "Europe is very unstable. Russia is certainly a threat until she settles down and until the outside world stops regarding her as a dangerous beast escaped from its cage. But there have been revolutions everywhere—Austro-Hungary—the kingdom of the Serbs, Croats, and Slovenes—Czecho-Slovakia . . . these new names still sound funny in my ears . . . Hungary, Poland . . . I personally think the biggest danger is Germany—humiliated, starving, its currency becoming worthless, saddled with impossible reparations. They were beaten, yes, beaten in the field, no doubt about that, but their men know they fought well, as well as anyone, better than most, against increasingly impossible odds. They have nothing to be ashamed of . . . Their pride will become a powder keg, waiting, growing more volatile, for years, decades perhaps . . . but if the right spark comes . . ." He shrugged, "The League of Nations will have to be very strong, and very wise, to contain that explosion . . . We must be going, Guy. I have a meeting with Keble-Palmer and Bert Gorse for lunch, about changes in Hedlington Aircraft . . . If there's anything I can do for you at Westminster, you know I will."

They all stood. Guy said. "And if there's anything I can do . . . about your problem—war—ask me. Between us, the Governors of this Foundation know a lot about the subject, and we are all well known in our own countries. If we speak together, with one voice, we will be heard."

*   *   *   *

"What am I to do about this?" Louise Rowland said, passing over the long, official-looking envelope, with the Government of India stamp and the notation ON HIS MAJESTY'S SERVICE. She found herself close to tears, and dabbed furtively at her eyes with her handkerchief. David Toledano took the envelope, and extracted the contents, which Louise had already read.

He said, "It's a demand for 64 rupees 14 annas 4 pies from the Indian Ordnance Depot in Lucknow, on account of two *pakhals* lost on maneuvers in 1914. It mentions a Court of Inquiry . . . so I suppose the Court found Boy responsible and said he had to pay."

"But he has . . . twice I think," Louise said. "He told me the last time he was here . . ." The tears were streaming down her face now. "Then Quentin made him pay again."

"That's true," Helen—now Lady Helen Toledano—said. "He told me, too, at the same time. He said the Indian Government was like an elephant, they never forget. But they were also like the Bourbons—they never remembered, either."

"This is too bad," David said. "But if he has paid . . . don't do anything. I know what the army's like. Some day the facts will trickle down to the right clerk   and you'll get back the overpayment that Boy made. In the middle of the next war, probably."

Louise dried her tears—"Don't talk about the next war," she said. "I know there's not going to be peace for ever, but I don't want to think about the next war." She looked across at Helen; she too had wept a little just now but her young face had recovered, and she looked serene, almost no trace of pink at her eye. She was wearing black, in mourning for her father. They were four at the lunch table; herself, David and Helen, and little Frances Enright, now foreman at the farm; Joan Pitman, Addie Fallon, and Carol Adams, the other Land Army girls, had gone, two to get married, one to look after aged parents. Two men had taken their places, both married and living in Walstone. Young Boy was upstairs, eating his lunch in the day nursery with the new Nanny.

Louise said, "I could leave tomorrow, you know, really."

Helen said, "Please, we'd be miserable if you weren't here to share Christmas with us."

"But, on your honeymoon . . ."

"It's the best honeymoon we could dream of," Helen said. "Being back at High Staining, knowing we're going to live the rest of our lives here—and bring up young Boy here, where he belongs . . . and which will belong to him. And with Frances . . . we went through a lot together in the war, didn't we? And we've never really had the time to, well, sort of have a communion over it. I wish Joan and Addie and Carol were here."

Frances mumbled something and looked down at her plate; but Louise knew she was deeply moved.

David said, "We're going to put lights all round the house, Aunt Louise . . . all round the eaves, over the roofs, everywhere . . . little oil lamps of clay, with wicks in them."

Louise looked puzzled. She said, "I remember Quentin telling us the Hindus did something like that, for some holy day, in India . . . I can't remember the name of it."

"Well, this is Chanukkah," David said. "The Feast of Light in the Jewish calendar . . . it ends tomorrow . . . we were married during Chanukkah, of course . . . very lucky, and very beautiful . . . It's nice when Christmas and Chanukkah come together." He stood up. "If you'll excuse me, I'm going up to talk with Young Boy. He ought to learn early that men, too, have a right to go into the nursery . . . and like to." He leaned over and kissed his wife on the top of the head. "By the way, have you entered him for school yet?" Helen shook her head. He said, "I'll do it then—Wellington, I suppose?"

"Of course. The Beresford, like his Uncle Guy . . . and his father. And his stepfather."

* * * *

Probyn's Woman stirred the big pot with a long twig. It had been peeled long ago so that the juices of the years, of chicken and mutton and carrot, barley and potatoes, tomatoes and onions, had steeped it, turning it from its original greeny white to a rich dark brown. The other woman in the cottage's front room was in her thirties, wearing lisle stockings, a large would-be fashionable hat, and a little make-up. Her accent was "refeened," that is, laboriously modified from its original Woman of Kent. She held a small package in her hand, a bundle of something wrapped in a twist of newspaper. She said, "Does it taste bitter? He has a very sweet tooth and will notice anything sharp."

"Try it before you give it to him," Probyn's Woman said. "It won't turn you into a man."

The other woman simpered—"And I am to give it to him near bedtime, in something he likes . . . like a little whisky and soda?"

"Or a cup of tea," the Woman said. "And mind you're wearing pretty drawers, 'cos he'll be on you like a bull."

The other blushed, muttering, "I keep wondering if it's another woman and he's, you know, spending himself on her."

"Don't you worry about no other women," the Woman said. "Just make yourself look nice, act nice, wear clothes what look like they're for whores, and give him that. That'll be two shillings."

The woman handed over a florin and went out, muttering her thanks. Five minutes later another woman knocked. The Woman said, "Come in." This woman was in her twenties, but dressed remarkably like the first, and speaking in a remarkably similar accent, or non-accent. She said, "I've come to see you . . . because . . . my friend said I should see you because . . . I don't know how to say it, but . . ."

"You're pregnant," the Woman said, "and you're not married."

"That's it," the other gasped with relief. "Five months."

"And the man won't marry you?"

"He's gone . . . three months ago. I don't know where. He hasn't written or anything. Men are such brutes, and . . ."

"Women are such ninnies," the Woman said. "I can't help you. You're too far gone." The younger woman began to weep silently, and the Woman's voice softened a little, "Look, there's lots of girls have babies with no husbands . . . war babies they was calling them till last year. A patriotic thing to do that was, then—make more soldiers to fight for England. Just have the baby and then tell your mum and dad. And get something to do . . . work."

The woman stood up, fumbling in her purse for money. She found the required florin and handed it over.

The Woman said gruffly, "Keep it. You'll need it. And next time, remember that florin'll keep you from getting in the family way again. Guaranteed."

"How will it do that?" the young woman said, astonished.

"Hold it between your knees whenever you're with a man," the Woman said.

Twenty minutes later another woman knocked. This one was in her forties, but once more remarkably similar to the first two in manner and dress. The Woman said, "You're Mrs Fagg, and you want to hurt Mrs Graveney."

The woman gasped, "But, how . . . ?"

The Woman said, "None of your business. Tell me what you think, what you know."

The client said, "She's having an affair with my husband. One day I seen him, down by the Scarrow, with her. They were doing, you know . . ."

"Fucking," the Woman said; the other winced, but nodded.

"He came home two hours later, and told me he had been on overtime . . . She's a . . . a bitch!" She spat out the word. "Trying to take my George away from me. He's weak, like all men, that's what he is, and she's . . ."

"Fifteen years younger than you," the Woman said. "And knows how to make a man look at her, and think of what's under her clothes."

The woman said, "What should I do? Just go and tell her that I know . . . that I'll   ?"

"That you'll scratch her eyes out if she don't stop it?"

"Oh, I couldn't do that," the other cried.

Too la-di-da, the Woman thought, and she only a small grocer's daughter from Headcorn. She said, "He'll get tired of her soon enough. Men do."

"But she ought to suffer," the client cried.

The Woman left the big pot, went to a corner, rummaged in a box. She pulled out a rag doll, about six inches high, naked, and obviously female from the pointed breasts sewn on above and the large slit sewn in below. She said, "Take this home and keep it in a safe place. Every day, as the church clock is striking twelve, say six curses on her, with this in your hand. And six more at five o'clock in the evening. And after each lot of curses, stick a hatpin into the doll where you'd like to hurt Mrs Graveney. Don't stick it into the heart, 'cos you might kill her, and then she'll haunt you till you die."

The woman took the doll, muttering, "And that will really hurt her?"

" 'Course," the Woman said. "Two bob and the cost of the doll, half a crown . . . four and six."

The woman paid, slipped the doll into her handbag, and hurried out.

Probyn came in shaking himself like a dog out of water. "Trying to snow out there," he said, ". . . smells like Irish stew."

"It is. I made six and six this afternoon. There it is."

Probyn whistled, pocketing the money—"Never thought you'd get these new folks coming to you, with their London ways. Think they know everything already, from books, I'd 'a said."

The Woman said, "They're no different from the rest. To look at, and listen to, they are . . . with their smart, cheap clothes and trying not to speak like country folk . . . but underneath, when it comes to real things, they're the same."

That's right, when you come to think of it, Probyn thought. It's the earth, and the water, and the air. Stood to reason they'd soon be the same as anyone else. This was Walstone earth, Kentish water, English air, and they were standing on it, drinking it, breathing it.

He sat down, and said, "I been teaching that young Rowland boy—Tim—how to cook a hedgehog. He's going to be a good man in the woods and fields, soon, day or night."

"And his sister, the girl, Sally?"

Probyn growled, "Her? She's going to be a whore, if you ask me. Like her mother, but more expensive, she having been brought up by the Rowlands."

*　　*　　*　　*

Richard Rowland, his wife Susan, and the three children, Sally, Tim, and little Dicky were decorating the Christmas tree in the back of the drawing room at Hill House. "Santy Claws come tonight," Dicky crowed excitedly.

Sally looked in a knowing manner at Richard and said "Yes, Dicky. Santa Claus will come tonight—down the chimney."

"Down chimney!" Dicky cried in delight. He gazed at the fireplace where a coal fire burned. His brow furrowed—"Santy Claws burn hisself?"

Susan said, "He likes fire and smoke, Dicky. They don't hurt him."

They finished the job and Nanny came to take Dicky to his supper and bed. Tim said, "Probyn showed me how to cook a hedgehog, in clay, this afternoon, Daddy . . . How soon can I have a gun? A .410?"

Richard said, "You love the country, don't you, Tim? Sit down . . .

listen. We meant to wait till after Christmas to tell you, but perhaps we'd better do it now . . . We're moving to London."

"To London!" Sally cried, jumping to her feet, her eyes shining. She was a big girl, well-developed for her age of twelve, breasts pushing out her woolen sweater, the curve of her buttocks already those of a grown woman.

"To London?" Tim cried, horror in his voice. "But . . . I can't shoot anything in London! There are no ferrets, no larks, no hares . . . nothing!"

Richard said, "You know I have left the factories here. But I'm only forty-nine and I can't just sit back and do nothing. David Toledano has offered me a job at his bank, to do with industrial financing . . . finding out what firms need money, how much, what for, and how best to get it to them, with safety for the bank, and benefit to them. I will be consulting with David and industrial experts all the time, and I can't do it from here . . . From London I can be in Birmingham in a couple of hours, and back the same afternoon. From here . . . four or five hours each way. So, we have to move."

"London," Tim muttered. "Fogs, people . . ."

"Harrods!" Sally said reverently. "Shall I be presented at Court, Mummy? What shall I wear? Shall I be a debutante?"

"All that's a few years off," Susan said. "I am sorry, Tim. I know how you feel . . . because I love it here too. I'm not really a town person, either. But we have to go."

"I'll steal the ducks' eggs off those lakes you showed us," Tim said. "And snare rabbits in Hyde Park, and . . ."

"I shall go to Uncle Tom's and become a mannequin," Sally said, sticking out her chest. "Men will crawl at my feet and I shall laugh at them, deep in my throat—ha, ha ha."

"You've been reading too much Elinor Glyn," Susan said. "Go and wash before supper."

*   *   *   *

Isabel Cate, standing in the window with her husband at her side, muttered, "Where is Mr Kirby? Doesn't he always come?"

"All my life, he has," Christopher said. "But perhaps he's not feeling up to it. He is seventy-nine after all. Rickman's here . . . and Miss Hightower, simpering at him, just as she always did at Mr Kirby."

Outside, it was still trying to snow, or sleet, and not quite succeeding. Twenty waits, led by the Reverend Gerald Rickman, B.D., curate of the parish of Walstone-cum-Taversham, were serenading the Manor with "Good King Wenceslas." Rickman was dark-haired, earnest, and had a Midland accent. It was understood that he would take over the parish as soon as Mr Kirby had the decency to die, or formally retire. The parish was in the Diocese of Rochester, and the Bishop had spent the thirteen months since the end of the war in vain hints. Mr Kirby apparently meant to die in his rectory; and the longer he could put off the succession of this fellow, who did not approve of blood sports, and spoke in an unctuous, condescending voice—the better.

"There are Betty and Fletcher," Isabel said, "singing away for dear life . . . I remember her writing, her first Christmas here, how much the waits had impressed her. That was the day she first met Fletcher."

The waits ended "Good King Wenceslas." In the pause before they began on their next carol, the Cates distinctly heard another choir, not far off, singing "O Come All Ye Faithful," the voices borne up to them on the wind from the south-west. The voices, male and female, were being accompanied by two cornets.

"What's that?" Isabel asked, as the waits outside started on "The First Noel," drowning out the more distant singing.

"Another party," Christopher said, "led by Captain Woodruff, to serenade the people in the new houses on Lower Bohun . . . He's organized a regular club, including the cornetists."

Isabel said, "Do you mind? It's like splitting the village into the old inhabitants and the newcomers . . . the past and the present."

He said, "It's inevitable. Walstone's going to be a melting pot, and soon the new people will think more as we do, and we'll think more as they do. I suppose Guy and Florinda are having carols at the Hall?"

She said, "She's arranged for some Hedlington waits to sing there, for those who can't move, but most of the Foundationers, led by Guy, are going in buses to Hedlington, to sing carols round town, at the Mayor's house, in front of a few pubs . . ."

"Wing Commander Sir Guy Rowland, V.C., K.B.E., D.S.O., M.C.," Cate murmured. "One of our greatest air aces and flying pioneers, and he never uses his rank, or his decorations, unless he has to. He's just Guy, or Sir Guy . . . while down there"—he pointed his chin toward the village growing awkwardly into a town below—"you can't take a step without running into the works of *Captain* Woodruff, wartime temporary officer."

"And gentleman?" she asked.

"No, that'll be permanent now. Rank is but riches, long-possessed—Burns . . . They're finishing. Signal them in for a glass of sherry, or a ginger wine . . . and Fletcher there will certainly have a whisky mac."

*   *   *   *

592

Seated comfortably on the big bay gelding, Guy Rowland surveyed with keen pleasure the animated scene on the sweep of graveled drive in front of the main entrance to Walstone Park. It was the Boxing Day meet of Lord Walstone's Hounds, once the North Weald Hunt, until its demise at the end of 1917 under its then Master, the late Earl of Swanwick. He remembered the New Year's Day meet of 1915, when he was not quite seventeen . . . things hadn't changed as much as you might have expected. Wilkinson was back from the Wiltshire Yeomanry as Huntsman, and Billing from the Royal Horse Artillery as one of the whippers-in. The other pre-war one, Snodgress, lay in a soldier's grave in Palestine, killed with his regiment of Hussars in the final advance on Jerusalem. His replacement was a young fellow . . . Guy didn't know his name . . . it was interesting to see that a young man would still make hunting his career.

Today it was the dog pack . . . a new terrier, of course; the old one had been given away, and was a farmer's dog in Beighton now, too old and fat to get his job back. Lord Walstone looked like a caricature of a war profiteer, fat-faced, fat-bellied, wearing the peaked velvet cap perched ridiculously on top of his balding head, sweating profusely even in the chill. The horses' hooves made deep impressions on the grass, for it was wet from the sleet that had fallen most of Christmas Day . . . There was Uncle Christopher and his new Aunt Isabel, he in pink, she in black, with top hat and veil . . . Wilkinson's whip was cracking out over hounds, as he yelled, "Garraway boick, Lancer, Driver, Baron, Chaser . . . boick, I say!" *Crack, crack,* and a sudden yelp from the too slow Chaser . . . He walked his horse over to the edge of the gravel, where Florinda was standing with Probyn, Fletcher and Betty Gorse, and five Foundationers from Scarrow Hall.

"A big field today," Florinda said.

"Old Eaves is capping them now," Guy said. "I didn't think too many of the new people would be interested, but they seem to be. And a good many have come down from Hedlington. Half a dozen from London, Eaves told me."

"They been told hunting's the right thing for a country gent," Probyn said, "and this is one of the closest packs to London."

Florinda said, "It'll become very fashionable if it provides reasonably good sport."

"With that fat old Hoggin as Master?" one of the Foundationers said. "Not bloody likely!"

Guy laughed—"Lord Walstone has never yet failed to get what he wants, Bright. If he wants to be known as Master of a great pack, he will be . . ." A servant approached, bearing a tray loaded with glasses of sloe gin and cherry brandy. Guy stooped, picked one off, said "Thanks," drank it in one gulp, and handed it back. "That's the stuff to give the troops! . . . They're moving off. Bye, darling!"

"Have a good time," Flo called up, blowing him a kiss. "And please don't break your neck. I *do* want a golden wedding binge . . . I'm going home now. These fellows are going to follow you."

Guy smiled down at the five Foundationers; one had only one leg, two only one arm, and the fourth was missing an arm and an eye; the fifth was ex-Private Snaky Lucas, almost fully recovered from near starvation. Somewhere, somehow, in the last few days he had acquired a bowler hat and a red-and-black striped waistcoat to go with his blue suit; the ensemble, he was certain, being the correct wear for a modern knight's valet.

Guy said to one of the one-armed men, "I thought you were against blood sports, Lindley."

The man who was missing an arm and an eye broke in, "He is, sir, but he's from Manchester. We told him, what the hell can he know about us country blokes if he doesn't know what we like. So we dragged him along. And we're ruddy well going to be in at the kill, too."

"By God, if you are," Guy said, "I'll see that the Master gives you the brush and the mask. Come hup, Hi say, you hugly beast!" He touched his spurs to the bay's flank and trotted off after the field, down the drive toward the East Gate and the Old Bridge.

*   *   *   *

Christopher was still dressed in hunting clothes, without his boots, wearing bedroom slippers instead, when the telephone rang in the hall. Garrod came in a moment later, saying, "It's for you, sir."

Christopher said, "Pour me another whisky, darling," went out, and picked up the receiver—"Cate here."

The tinny voice at the other end said, "I'm John Ross, Mr Cate, from the Chancellor of the Exchequer's office."

"Good evening, Sir John," Cate said. The caller was a well-known barrister and K.C., famous for his work in Admiralty courts during the war.

Ross said, "The Chancellor and the High Court judges wish to recommend you to His Majesty as High Sheriff of Kent. As you know, there has been no High Sheriff for the past six months . . . Are you willing to accept the post?"

Cate said slowly, "High Sheriff . . . It's really a figurehead post, isn't it, with everything actually done by the deputies, prison governors, and so on?"

"That's about it," Ross said. "He does have to make some ceremonial appearances, especially if His Majesty or the Lord Chancellor visit Kent officially . . . but otherwise, it's meant to be an honour. Well-deserved, from all we have heard in this six months of searching. Everyone we spoke to, who knew of you, said that you were the man who brought your area through the war with its spirit as intact as . . ."

"Not all its young men," Cate said.

"No."

Cate said at last, "Very well. I shall be honoured."

"Good. I am instructed to tell you that you may also have a Knight Bachelorhood, if you so wish."

Cate answered that more quickly, "Thank you, Sir John, but we've been plain Cates for thirteen or fourteen hundred years and it would be best if we stayed that way."

"I quite understand . . . Will you come up to London to see the Chancellor, early Monday? No. 11 Downing Street. He has to leave for Edinburgh at 10, so can you make it at 9 a.m.? It's early, I know, but . . ."

"I'll be there," Cate said briefly, and hung up. He returned to the drawing room, thinking, we'll take the late train up on Sunday night, and stay at the Cavendish. Rosa Lewis always made a stay interesting, and by now she should have recovered from losing Lord Ribblesdale.

He took the glass of whisky from the side table, where Isabel had put it, and said, "I'm to be High Sheriff of Kent . . . and we're going to London on Sunday night for a few days."

She jumped up and flung her arms round his neck—"Oh Christopher, darling! I thought no one would ever do or say anything to show appreciation for what you did here . . . what you're still doing. You've been the mortar holding it all together. You've held the people through the war, and now you're guiding them through the peace, toward the future." She kissed him long and lovingly on the forehead, holding his head in both hands.

He stood away. He said, "I wish I could have done as much . . . or anything . . . for my children . . . I think I will change and go and say some prayers at the War Memorial, Isabel."

"I'll come with you."

Daily Telegraph, Saturday, December 27, 1919

CHRISTMAS IN LONDON
PEACE AND PLENTY

This year, after an involuntary absence which had lasted since 1913, the Spirit of Christmas returned to London. It was the Spirit beloved of Dickens at the time he wrote the story of Marley's ghost; the Spirit of good cheer, of fun and laughter, the Spirit of the roaring hearth, with the reunited family circle around it . . . Since 1918 4,000,000 of "the boys" have returned, to compare their reminiscences of Christmastide in the Flanders mud, on the sands of Egypt and "Mespot," or amid the olive groves of Palestine, with the peace and the comfort and the plenty which have come to them this year as their reward . . .

The King, the Queen, the Prince of Wales, The Princess Mary and other members of the Royal family, with their customary forethought, sent to the various hospitals in London gifts of birds and other good things for the table, as well as toys to delight the hearts of the children. Soldiers who are under treatment in the various institutions were also remembered . . .

IN THE WORKHOUSES

The inmates in the workhouses and infirmaries were well catered for. Special dinners were provided, and in some instances pantomimes written by the staff were produced . . . A huge Christmas pudding, 300 lbs in weight, was the main centre of attraction at Kingston Workhouse. In its making there were used thirty pounds each of raisins, sultanas, currants, flour and sugar, ninety eggs, sixty pounds of suet, one and a half pounds of baking powder, fifteen pounds of peel, and seventy-five pounds of bread crumbs, all moistened with seven and a half gallons of milk, and flavoured with nine ounces of nutmeg, fifteen lemons, and eight ounces of spice . . .

CHARITABLE ORGANISATIONS

. . . On Christmas Eve Lady Stoll gave a party to the 205 disabled soldiers and sailors and their wives and children who live in the homes at Fulham provided by Sir Oswald Stoll . . . The children of the tenants, numbering over fifty, had their tea in the workshop, where Father Christmas . . . came down the chimney to the call of the chimney sweep, and proceeded to dismantle a heavily-laden Christmas tree. He handed toys to Fairy Greatheart (Lady Stoll) who presented them to the children . . .

"Fairy Greatheart!" Guy muttered. "Good God! Well, let it be a warning to us, not to think *we* are Fairy Greathearts, just because we are in a position to help a few of our fellow creatures." He looked at Florinda—"Our Christmas here went off pretty well, I thought."

She nodded, her mouth full of toast; when she had swallowed it, she said, "What's half a dozen drunks and disorderlies, and one broken arm, among so many? I thought that Meadows' recitation at the Christmas dinner table was the best part."

She stood and declaimed, in cockney—

" 'Twas Chrismus Die in the Work'us, that die of all the year,
When the paupers' 'earts is full of gladness, and their bellies full of beer.
Up spake the Work'us master, 'To all within these walls,
I wish a Merry Christmas,' and the paupers answered . . ."

"Dead silence!" Guy said, laughing. "Because there were ladies present. You don't count as a lady, but there were Mary Gorse and her girls, and Anne Stratton and hers, and Dorothy Norvell, and . . ."

She raised the coffeepot menacingly over his head, put it down, and said, "And then they gave us that marvellous wreath of poppies . . ."

He glanced at the wall beside him, where the red wreath hung, bedecked with green ribbons and a big illuminated scroll—TO SIR GUY AND LADY ROWLAND, OUR PALS, RESPECTFULLY, THE FOUNDATIONERS. He looked across at his wife and suddenly found his eyes blurring with tears. After a moment he said, "I can't believe it. The war's over . . . I don't want to kill anyone . . . And I've got you . . . you, whom I've loved more than half my life, and I'm only twenty-two."

She jumped up and came round the table to lean her breast against his head and, standing stooped over him, murmur, "You've got me, Guy. And I've got you . . . till death us do part."

It seemed ten minutes had passed when Padre Caffin came in, helped himself to a kipper, and said, "Fred Stratton's had a baby boy, out in India. Frank's had a cable."

"I expect his wife had the baby for him, padre," Florinda said, sitting down. "Sahibs don't do anything for themselves in India."

Caffin sat down, laughing, and Lucas poured out coffee for him. Caffin turned to Guy—"Guy, just before Christmas I had a letter from a young fellow I knew in Westport . . . a painter. He's starving out there, doing odd jobs to keep body and soul together. But he's a good painter, I'll swear he is. He didn't ask me for anything, but I've been thinking . . . could we bring him here and have him teach Foundationers how to paint and draw?"

Guy stared at the wall, the wreath, the scroll for a moment; then said, "Yes. One year at least. Minimum wage, and we buy his materials . . . Now, who can teach music?"

"Why, by Saint Patrick, I can," the priest said. "The piano, the fiddle, and the mouth organ!"

"We'll buy some mouth organs," Guy said, sitting back dreamily.

"We'll have a Foundation Band. It'll play at cricket matches at the County grounds, and . . ."

"That's something else I've been thinking about," the priest said. "You should get back to first-class cricket. You'll not be able to turn out every day, but . . . think of the publicity you'll be getting for the Foundation, Guy! And you must have some break from your work here."

Guy said, "I've thought of it. I might spend 1920 seeing if I can get back into form, then before 1921 tell the County they can have me, say, three matches a month, if they want me . . . Meanwhile, Florinda, why have we run out of red cloth for the poppies? And do you know that I've passed four other applications? So there'll be seventeen more Foundationers, not thirteen, arriving on the 2nd . . ."

*   *   *   *

The change ringers were beginning a long peal of Kent Bob Majors. Mr Rickman might not approve of fox hunting, but he was enthusiastic about most other folklore, and had eagerly joined the change ringers and learned their art as soon as he came to the parish. The sound of the bells came muffled by lightly falling snow through the darkness of early evening, to Walstone station, where Christopher and Isabel Cate waited for the 5.10 Hedlington train, with connections to London, Victoria. Beside them, where they stood near the west end of the platform, the up starting signal glowed red above them, a small pool of white light directly underneath it, from the unshielded opening in the bottom of the lamp. Their suitcases stood beside them, for Bertha, the stable girl, had taken the trap back to the Manor, on Christopher's orders.

A figure approached through the darkness, bustling along with the certainty of familiarity through the pools of yellow light from the platform lamps, past the big board inscribed WALSTONE . . . He peered at them—"Ah, Mr Cate . . . madam . . . Going up to London to see the King, sir?"

Cate laughed. "Just the Chancellor of the Exchequer, Mr Miller. I'll only see His Majesty if he makes a state visit to Kent."

"He will, sir, he will . . . But you'll still be living here, sir, in the Manor? You won't have to live in London?"

"Oh no. We'll be back on Wednesday . . . then we sail for America ten days later . . . then home to the same old life . . . paying bills . . . milking cows . . . mending hedges . . . hunting a few days . . . church on Sundays . . . trying to keep Probyn Gorse out of mischief . . ."

The stationmaster seemed reluctant to leave them and go on about his business, whatever it had been. He said, "It hasn't changed much, has it? Yet, everything's changed. Danged if I know how that can be, but it's so . . . isn't it, sir?"

"Yes," Cate said. "But I can't express or explain it, any better than you can."

"I wonder, sometimes," the stationmaster said hesitantly, "if we could 'a done any better—in the war, I mean. Might it be that if we'd all done better . . . *been* better, like . . . then we'd have our Charlie and Jerry here still, and you'd have Mr Laurence. I can't sleep at night, thinking, did we do all right? Was there any more we could have done? We won, but here *we* are, and everything's different, because Charlie and Jerry and Mr Laurence *aren't* . . . them and a million more, that ought to be."

Cate said, "We did all right, Mr Miller—your generation and mine. The young did better and we have to hand over to them now . . . to Sir Guy and Lady Rowland, to Captain Woodruff, Fletcher and Betty Gorse . . . I don't know what'll happen, but *they* . . . Charlie and Jerry and Laurence and the rest of them—they'll shape the future just as much by their deaths as by their lives. You and I will never forget them, because they were our sons. And England can never forget them, because they were its blood, and still are."

The signal wires running along the ground under the edge of the platform creaked and the signal dropped with a heavy clang, the light changing from red to green. The Hedlington train came chuffing up the slight gradient, its side rods clanking, a dim light cast forward from the single indicator lamp on its buffer beam.

"All stations to Hedlington!" Mr Miller cried. "Walstone! Walstone! All stations to Hedlington!"

The Cates climbed into an empty first-class compartment, and took facing corner seats. They looked at each other, serious, silent, loving, as the ancient engine determinedly chuffed and clanked through Felstead & Whitmore, Cantley, Scarrowford, to Hedlington, London, and the future, the Great War at last left behind, yet eternally with them, with the land on which the rails lay, and with the people in the surrounding darkness.